Jerusalem in Jeopardy

Mammoth hatch doors were lowering to create a mile-wide opening at the eye of the daisy design. A sparkling jade-green light spilled from the interior of the ship and washed over Jerusalem, illuminating the city as if it were some kind of magical kingdom. It was such a beautiful sight that, for a moment, it was possible to believe the aliens had benign intentions after all. But soon, the tip of a massive cone-shaped mechanism lowered through the opening.

"What in the world is that?" gasped Thomson.

Reg thought he knew. He clenched his teeth and fought against the impulse to abandon the novice pilots to make a run at the jewel-like cone. His fingers itched to unleash his Sidewinders at what he feared was some sort of weapon. But he remained on course, even as a tightly focused beam of white light stabbed downward from the tip of the cone and touched the golden cupola of the Dome of the Rock.

"Communications beam?" someone asked with withering hope.

Reg shook his head sadly. He did not say the words aloud, but mouthed them behind his oxygen mask: targeting laser. A moment later, to his horror, Reg saw that his instinct was right.

A blinding blast of light ripped out of the cone and smashed down on the golden-domed mosque, shattering the building into a billion pieces from the inside out. A dense pillar of fire began to build up over the blast site as the weapon continued to fire, adding more and more energy. Then, all at once, it exploded outward and began to rip through the city, a tidal wave of flame rolling across the ground, utterly destroying everything in its path. It only seemed to gather momentum as it moved. Spreading relentlessly from the epicenter, a fiery wall of destruction several hundred feet high moved beyond the walls of the city and into the surrounding hills and suburbs. With the speed and force of an atomic explosion, it scoured Jerusalem from the face of the Earth, vaporizing in a handful of seconds what it had taken humans two thousand years to build.

At length, the bright beam coming from the firing cone shut off. But still the explosion rolled outward. With a momentum of its own, the blast shot beyond the city limits, breaking apart the surrounding towns and villages. It threw automobiles, buildings, and bridges hundreds of feet into the air before burying them under a molten sea of flames.

Even after the flames themselves stopped moving outward, the residual heat continued for another mile, killing everything it touched. Where one of the most beloved cities of the world had stood scant seconds before, there was now only a twenty-mile circle of scarred, scorched earth. Half a million human lives had been extinguished.

None of the English pilots had spoken a word since the blast began. Reg broke the silence with a terse command. "You men continue south." Then he broke abruptly out of formation, turning to port for an attack run against the giant city destroyer.

INDEPENDENCE DAY:
War in the Desert

Other *Independence Day* titles from
HarperEntertainment

Independence Day
by Dean Devlin & Roland Emmerich
and Stephen Molstad

Independence Day: Silent Zone
created by Dean Devlin & Roland Emmerich
Novel by Stephen Molstad

INDEPENDENCE DAY: War in the Desert

Created by Dean Devlin & Roland Emmerich
Novel by Stephen Molstad

HarperEntertainment

A Divison of HarperCollinsPublishers

HarperEntertainment
A Division of HarperCollins*Publishers*
10 East 53rd Street, New York, N.Y. 10022-5299

This is a work of fiction. The characters, incidents, and dialogues
are products of the author's imagination and are not to be construed
as real. Any resemblance to actual events or persons,
living or dead, is entirely coincidental.

ISBN 0–06–105829–7

HarperCollins®, ®, and HarperEntertainment ™
are trademarks of HarperCollins Publishers, Inc.

Photo composit by Douglas Paul Design/Photograph
© 1999 UPI/Corbis Bettman

First printing: September 1999

Printed in the United States of America

Visit HarperEntertainment on the World Wide Web at
http://www.harpercollins.com

❖ 10 9 8 7 6 5 4 3 2 1

I'd like to thank Michael Hawley, Christopher Rowe, Paul Zahn, John Storey, Lisa DiSanto, Will Plyler, Dionne McNeff, and everyone who offered me help while I was writing this book. I apologize for taking so few of your excellent suggestions, but I'm a mule at heart. Finally, I need to thank John Douglas and my dear wife Elizabeth for putting up with me all the way to the end.

1

The Attack Begins

The original city on a hill, Jerusalem, was a symbol of all that was best and worst about human beings. It had stood for millennia above the Judean plane, protected by sturdy stone walls that had glinted gold in the sun since the time of Christ and, seven centuries later, the time of Mohammed. Those walls had held back large armies and entire nations of crusaders clamoring at its gates, desperate to enter, certain that being inside would bring them closer to the paradise of heaven. It had been conquered eighteen different times.

Over the years, the city's walls had borne witness to some of humanity's deepest and most uplifting meditations on the question of what it meant to be alive. But they'd also seen their share of needlessly spilled blood. There had been countless acts of pettiness, backstabbing and sadism— all committed in the name of a merciful God. A tenth century poet described Jerusalem as "a golden basin filled with scorpions." It was sacred ground to all three of the West's major religions: the place where King David's temple had housed the ark of the covenant, where Christ was crucified and resurrected, and where the prophet Mohammed stretched open his arms and ascended to heaven. It was said that you could choke to death in Jerusalem, the air was so thick with prayer.

Reg Cummins had first encountered the city as a grungy

twenty-year-old backpacker. He'd enlisted with the Royal Air Force but had three months until he was scheduled to report. In the meantime, he was determined to see some of the continent. From his home in Kew Gardens outside London, he traveled down through Italy and hopped a boat to Greece. After a month on the beach, he decided he was looking for something more, something further from his experience, something more exotic and challenging. So he went to Jerusalem. He slept where he could and spent his days exploring the covered markets, tunnels, and religious shrines. He drank tea and bargained in the souks, got himself invited to shabbat dinners then sang and danced with his hosts. He wandered the cobblestone streets, argued over the price of onions and the nature of sin, and spent a couple of nights camped out in a courtyard of African mud huts with the Ethiopian Coptic priests in their compound. Jerusalem had always made him feel vital and completely alive. That seemed like a very long time ago.

Now, several years later and hundreds of miles away, as he watched images of the city on television, Major Reginald M. Cummins, an instructor with the Queen's Flight and Training Group, Mideast section, felt dead inside. It was noon on July 3rd, and outside the sun burned hot white in the sky. He was in the Foreign Officers' lounge at the Khamis Moushalt Airfield in Saudi Arabia, along with every active-duty RAF soldier stationed in that country except the Commandant— all six of them—staring in grim disbelief at the CNN report unfolding on the screen.

An alien aircraft of staggering size had arrived the night before and parked itself directly over the ancient city. The hovering gray disk stretched out for miles in every direction, leaving only a ring of blue sky low on the horizon. When it arrived, the ground shook with its massive rumbling. It had moved at a constant speed and elevation, closing over the top of the city like the thick stone lid of a sarcophagus. The moment the ship stopped moving, everything had fallen deathly quiet.

The vessel looked like the very embodiment of evil. It was dark, hard and strictly utilitarian in design. It was gruesomely industrial and, at the same time, somehow alive. The whole dark mass looked biological, like an exoskeleton of some sort.

The sight of the gigantic airship triggered a wild, violent exodus. People gathered up whatever they could carry with them and ran. Over a million refugees were scrambling toward the hope of safety, some of them on the roads leading to Tel Aviv or Amman, others hurrying on foot through the hills. In most people's minds, it was the end of the world. For others, it was the armies of the Lord announcing the moment of redemption. By noon, the Jerusalem was empty except for military personnel, New Age types who had come to welcome the ETs, and stern religious zealots wielding bats and bricks, determined to protect their sacred buildings.

Variations of this scene were occurring all over the planet.

Less than twenty-four hours before, thirty-six of these enormous ships—soon to be known as city destroyers—had disengaged themselves from an even larger spacecraft, the "mother ship," which was one fourth the size of Earth's moon. Very quickly, they began their simultaneous, free-fall entry into Earth's atmosphere. They descended in huge billowing clouds of flame and smoke as the friction they generated combusted the oxygen around them. Upon reaching their target elevations, they came to a sudden and inexplicable halt. Completely unscathed, they drove out of the smoke clouds and moved into position over thirty-six of Earth's most populous and strategically important cities. None of them had made any discernible attempt to communicate.

Reg Cummins drew in a deep breath and turned away from the hypnotic images on the television set. Wanting to clear his mind, he walked to the bar at the far side of the room and poured himself the stiffest drink in the house: a glass of lukewarm soda water. The initial shock of the invasion was beginning to wear off and, in its place, a grim sense of helplessness was spreading around the globe. It was evident in the comments made by the CNN reporters, in the communiqués issued by the world's governments, and, as Reg could see with his own eyes, in the attitudes of his fellow pilots. Normally, they were an obnoxiously loud and boisterous group, always laughing, roughhousing and complaining bitterly about the hardships of life in this remote desert locale. Now they looked like a group of defeated men. They slumped in their chairs, as still as statues, and their heads hung in worry.

If the aliens decided to pick a fight, they wouldn't get much resistance from a group like this. Reg knew he had to do something to change the atmosphere. When his eyes fell on the billiards table in the center of the room, he knew what he had to do.

"All this alien nonsense is starting to bore me silly," he called across the room. "And you blokes are going to ruin your eyes watching that rot all day. Anyone interested in a game of pool?" Immediately, everyone's attention was sucked away from the news program. The men looked positively alarmed.

"Anyone interested?" Reg asked, nonchalantly selecting a stick from the rack on the wall.

"Impossible!" said one of the pilots.

"You? Play a game of pool?" said another in disbelief. "You're finally going to do something more than talk?"

"That is correct," Reg said, chalking the tip of his cue. "This time I'm really going to play. Anyone here think they're good enough to take me?"

The six pilots, wearing their flight suits in case they were ordered into the air on short notice, came toward the table. All of them had heard Reg talk about his days as a championship level player, but this was the first time any of them had seen him actually holding a cue.

"Who's the best player?" Reg asked, as if he didn't already know.

A tall, beefy man named Sinclair stepped up to the table chewing on the stub of a cigar. "That would be me, Teacher," he said. "You're serious, then? You want a game?"

"Oh, yes. I'm serious, quite serious."

Major Cummins (aka the Teacher, an affectionate nickname given to him by the Saudi pilots who were his students) was famous for three things: for being widely considered the best pilot in the Middle East; for having suffered a very painful and career-threatening lapse of judgment during the Gulf War; and for bragging about his days as a pool player before joining Her Majesty's Air Force.

"This is turning out to be a day full of surprises," said a man named Townsend. "First, a bunch of aliens arrive from outer space and now something truly shocking. I hope I'm dreaming."

"What's this all about?" Sinclair asked, snapping open the leather case that held his personal cue. "You trying to distract us from our troubles?" When Reg shrugged without answering, Sinclair invited him to lag for break.

Reg looked confused. He didn't appear to understand the question. "Why don't you go ahead and show me how it's done?"

"Gladly," Sinclair said with a smirk. He leaned over the table and stroked the cue ball to the far side of the table. It bounced off and rolled back to within an inch of the near rail. It was a nice shot, the onlookers agreed, one that would be nearly impossible to beat. Sinclair marked the position with a chalk cube, satisfied that he'd already won. "Your turn, Teacher."

Reg studied the table. "Now what's the idea here? I have to get the ball closer than yours without touching the wall, is that it?"

"That's it exactly." Sinclair grinned wickedly. "Best of luck to you."

Reg cleared his throat. "Well, here goes then," he said, lining up his shot. The awkward way he held the cue in his hands made it clear he didn't know what he was doing. He was on the verge of shooting when he suddenly backed away. "Wait, I just thought of something."

The men all moaned loudly, believing Reg was going to back out of it, but he surprised them again.

"We haven't made a bet. Shouldn't we make a wager of some kind?"

"What can you afford to lose?" someone laughed.

Reg looked at the man curiously. "Lose? What makes you think I'm going to lose?"

"Fifty quid then?" Sinclair asked, doubting Reg would want to risk that much.

"Make it hundred."

The men roared with laughter at his misguided bravado. Despite his obvious lack of skill, he actually seemed to believe he stood a chance against the mighty Sinclair. He leaned over the table again and quickly stroked his shot. The white ball sailed across the green felt.

"Too hard," Sinclair announced as soon as the ball rebounded off the far wall.

"I don't think so," said his challenger. "I'd say that's just about perfect." A moment later, the ball stopped rolling a mere fingernail short of the near rail. Reg looked Sinclair in the eyes. "Does this mean I get to break?"

The big man squinted back at him and nodded, beginning to realize that he'd been had.

Reg's break shot was a thing of beauty. The cue ball fired across the table with surprising power and scattered the colorful spheres in every direction. There were three soft thunks as two solids and a stripe fell into three separate pockets.

"Listen to the Teacher, friends," Reg said, circling the table like a jungle cat. "Today's lesson is about making assumptions and how much trouble that can get you into." He paused long enough to hammer the twelve ball into a side pocket and the nine into a corner. "I'm certain you've all seen that diagram about the word assume. You know, the one that says: when you assume, you make and ASS out of U and ME." He tapped the orange five ball in the corner. "Well, there's been too damn much assuming going on around here this morning and I'll give you an example. You all assumed that just because you'd never seen me play, that I couldn't find my way around a table." He glanced up at Sinclair and smiled. "Combination bank shot. Three ball in the far corner." A moment later, it fell in.

"The same thing is happening with these spaceships. Everybody's making assumptions." He sunk the two ball then broke into the exaggerated accent of a terrified Scotsman. "Oh, fer crackin' ice! These huge fookin saucers are parked all over the fookin warld. It can mean one thing and one thing only: total fookin annihilation fer the yewmin race." The men chuckled at his imitation, but they also got the message. In quick succession, Reg sank every ball left on the table then tossed his cue on the table. "The truth of the matter is, you just can't tell what sort of a player a bloke is until he makes a few shots. So let's wait to see what kind of players these aliens are before we quit and hang up our cues, okay?"

"And if they turn out to be sharks like you?" Sinclair asked with a laugh.

"In that case, we'll show them what kind of shooting good English lads can do, right?"

"Right!" the men answered in one voice. With the fire back in their eyes, the men began a raucous discussion of the punishment they would mete out if the aliens started any trouble. They were laughing and arguing when a blast of heat and bright light swept into the room.

The door of the darkened lounge had pulled open and Colonel Whitley, a man with the long neck and stooped posture of a vulture, stepped inside. He was the highest ranking RAF officer at Khamis Moushalt but had been in the Middle East only a few weeks. He carried a map of the region that he'd ripped from the wall of his office. He was sweating from his short walk across the base. It was already ninety-six degrees Fahrenheit outside and it was only going to get hotter.

"I'm going to need a volunteer," Whitley announced, knocking glasses and ashtrays off the bar so he could flatten out the map. "Here's the situation. Forty of our birds, Tornadoes, are trapped over the Mediterranean. They've been in a holding pattern for the last half-hour near Haifa. Somebody's got to go get them."

"Why?" asked one of the men. "What's the matter?"

Whitley grimaced in disgust. "Every nation in the region is closing down its airspace. Israel was the first. About an hour ago, they started chasing out all foreign planes, allies included. Five minutes later, Egypt and Syria started doing the same damn thing, so our boys can't just detour around. Besides, they're not fully trained pilots. They're just a bunch of warm bodies acting as chauffeurs. It's a hideous mess out there, hideous."

"What the hell is Israel's problem?" Sinclair asked. "Last night they agreed to allow foreign planes."

Reg took an educated guess. "There must have been a skirmish. If I know the Israelis, they've been shadowing every group of Arab planes that comes in for a look at that alien craft. Somebody started playing chicken—probably some Iraqis—and before they knew it, they were in a dogfight."

Whitley's dark eyes opened wide in surprise. He didn't know Reg well and, after reading his personnel file, regarded him with caution. "The major is correct," he told the men. "Two Iraqi planes were shot down. In retaliation, missiles were fired onto the road leading to Tel Aviv resulting in civilian casualties. Then, of course, all hell broke loose."

"Oh, that's bloody lovely," said one of the pilots in disgust, "that's just beautiful. The aliens must be laughing their little green arses off right now. They won't have to waste any ammunition in this part of the world. We'll kill ourselves off before the bastards have the chance to do it themselves."

"Enough talk," Whitley snapped. "Who's going?"

Six pilots loudly volunteered, but Reg quieted them with a look. "Sorry lads, winner breaks!" Then he turned to the Colonel. "I'm your man, sir. Where do those planes have to go?"

A bead of sweat rolled off the tip of Whitley's beak-like nose. "They're headed to Kuwait. But, look, Cummins," he said tensely, "maybe someone else would be better for this mission. It's not that I doubt your skills, but there are hundreds of warplanes out there from a dozen different nations. And as I say, these boys flying the Tornadoes don't know what they're doing. This is a live-fire situation and it's going to be, well, confusing."

The men fell into an awkward silence. They knew that the colonel's reluctance to give Reg the mission was based on something that had happened many years before, something none of them ever mentioned in front of the Teacher. Whitley, a newcomer to the base, didn't understand that his fears were groundless and that Reg was, by far, the best man for the job. He was the only one who had never flown alongside the Teacher and seen the impossible things he could do in a jet. Besides, Reg knew the region well enough to fly without navigation systems, and he understood the tactics of the Middle East's diverse air forces better than anyone.

Whitley's lack of confidence stung Reg like a hard punch to the heart, but he didn't let it show. "I'm your man, colonel," he repeated firmly. "I'll find those planes. I'll bring them to their destination safely."

Whitley shook his head. "I've read your file, Cummins. We can't afford any . . . lapses. Now, who else volunteers?"

The other pilots looked at the ceiling, at the television, anywhere but at the Colonel. It only took a second of being ignored for Whitley to realize that the decision had been made for him.

"So that's how it's going to be. Very well then, Major, the mission is yours. Good luck. Your take off has already been cleared with the tower."

"I'll see you gentlemen this afternoon," Reg said over his shoulder as he pushed open the door and headed away across the blistering hot tarmac. The others moved to the windows and watched him go.

Whitley crossed his long arms over his chest. "There goes a man looking for trouble."

"Not at all," said Sinclair. "There goes a man looking for redemption."

As his British Aerospace Hawk 200 thundered over the razor-wire perimeter fence of the Khamis Moushalt facility, Reg looked down at the base that had been his home for the last few years, a nine-square-mile patch of pavement in the middle of a desert. It was a horrible place to live and was considered the worst assignment an RAF man could draw. No one except Reg had ever volunteered to be there. Saudi Arabia could be a strange, hostile, and cruel place, ruled by restrictive Islamic social codes. But Reg had found the Saudis to be an honorable people and had made many genuine friends among them. He had trained many of the Royal Saudi Air Force's best pilots during his years in the country since Desert Storm.

There was plenty to think about during his flight north. His cockpit instrumentation was showing a contradictory jumble of digits and flashing zeroes. All satellite-dependent systems were unreliable. But he'd made the flight to Jerusalem many times and knew the way by heart. He tried to keep his mind clear, but couldn't help thinking about what Whitley had said about lapses. Could it be that the man had a point? After all, even though he'd engaged in hundreds of mock battles during the last several years, this was the first time he would be facing a live fire situation since his last, ill-fated sortie over Iraq.

As he flew past the ancient ruins of Petra, he got his first glimpse of the alien ship. It was only a gray blot on the horizon but Reg felt the hackles raise on the back of his neck. His warrior instincts told him to attack the thing at once, but as he came closer, it grew to an impossible, intimidating size and his passion cooled. Dominating the sky, it seemed to cover half of Israel. The astounding thing was that something so vast and heavy could float. It was an egregious violation of the laws of physics and the closer Reg flew to the city-sized airship, the more it dawned on him that he was in the presence of a powerful civilization far in advance of his own. He felt a sudden chill and began to grasp why not a single government around the world had decided to declare war on the uninvited guests.

At the same time, it produced a dark attraction. There was a certain sort of ominous, magnetic, unholy beauty to the craft. Its sleek gray dome, glinting in the midday sun, was made of an exotic material he'd never seen before. It was something out of a beautiful nightmare, like a medieval fortress from the twenty-fourth century built in the clouds.

Mesmerized, Reg flew closer until he became distracted by a stinging in his eyes. It took him a moment to realize that sweat was pouring down his face and blurring his vision. When he wiped his forehead clean, he noticed his hand was trembling. It had been so long since he'd felt anything resembling fear at the controls of a plane that he didn't recognize it for a moment. In a sudden rush of self-doubt, Whitley's words echoed through his head. Maybe he wasn't ready for the real thing.

Distracted, he didn't notice a pair of Syrian MiG Fulcrums moving up behind him at top speed. They passed above him by a scant few hundred feet, then deliberately cut across his path. When Reg hit the turbulence of their jet wash, his Hawk shook as though the wings would snap off. Regaining control, he rose a thousand feet in altitude and flipped his radio to the general frequency.

"Thank you, friends, for that warm welcome," he said to the Syrians, figuring that having had their fun, they would leave him alone. But his heads-up display showed them arcing around for another pass. Realizing he was under direct attack had a curious effect on Reg. His hands stopped shaking, his heart rate slowed and something like a smile crossed his lips. "If you boys want to dance," he said into his radio, "let's have a go."

Far below, he saw the brilliant blue of the Dead Sea on Israel's eastern border. He cut his speed to let the Syrian planes catch up. The Hawk's automated systems honked a warning alarm as the MiGs came within firing range behind him. When they were almost upon him, Reg snapped back hard on the controls and sent the Hawk into a sudden vertical climb. As he guessed, the faster, more maneuverable MiGs stayed on his tail, following him upward and closing the distance. He looped over backwards, pointed the nose of his plane to earth and plunged full-throttle toward the Dead Sea. The Syrians continued the pursuit.

The three planes plummeted toward the blue surface of the water at hypersonic speed. Reg gave no indication of pulling up. He increased his speed. In his earphones, he could hear his pursuers talking nervously in Arabic. Soon, they were screaming at one another to level off as their altimeter readings approached zero. They broke out of their dive, watching in amazement as the English plane continued to head straight down.

A big grin spread across Reg's face as he calmly brought his plane parallel to the water with plenty of room to spare. Just as he'd expected, the Syrians had pulled up in a panic, forgetting that zero on an altimeter indicated sea level. But the Dead Sea, the lowest point in Asia, was more than nine hundred meters below sea level.

With his confidence restored, Reg ignored the flashing lights on his display panel and crossed into Israeli airspace with an air-speed of 1,000 KPH and an altitude reading of minus 700 meters.

Outwardly at least, the gigantic alien ship over Jerusalem was an exact replica of the thirty-five others. The front of it was marked by a slender black tower, three-quarters of a mile tall, set into a crater-shaped depression in the dome. Soon after it had parked itself over the ancient capital, it began to spin slowly like a wheel, completing a revolution every seventy-two minutes.

Reg was approaching from the southeast but knew that the Tornadoes were on the opposite side, the northwest. He scanned the skies searching for the safest way around the fifteen-mile-wide obstacle, but everywhere he looked, Israeli jets were patrolling in clusters. Hundreds of other planes were prowling just beyond the border. Only the murky area directly below the alien megaship was deserted. Quickly deciding that would be the path of least resistance, he darted into the deep shadows cast by the floating behemoth.

The bottom of the ship was not the smooth surface it appeared to be on television. Instead, it was studded with endless rectangular structures the size of warehouses. They were arranged in precise rows and the spaces between them formed broad boulevards that ran to the center of the vessel. Subtle color differentiations on the surface created a pattern that looked like a vast daisy, the petals of which stretched several miles to the ship's perimeter. As he approached the eye of the flower, he glanced down at Jerusalem. The exact center of the giant ship was directly above the city's most distinctive landmark, the Al-Aksa mosque, the famous Dome of the Rock.

It occurred to Reg that the mazelike underbelly of the ship was a twisted mirror image of the beautiful city below. Jerusalem, one of the most revered cities on the planet, was staring up at a dark reflection of itself. He glanced down as he tore past the walled Old City.

Continuing on his way, he steered toward the horizon, a low, blue ribbon of open sky. When he emerged from beneath the ship, he flew unopposed to the Mediterranean coast and slipped out of Israeli airspace. It didn't take him long to locate the forty British planes. They were in a disorganized holding pattern, flying long slow loops about five miles from shore. He established radio contact with the group's commanding officer.

"Lost Sheep, Lost Sheep, this is Guide Dog. Do you read?"

A sputtering, panic-stricken voice roared back. "It's about bloody well time somebody showed up! Is that you in the Hawk, Guide Dog?"

"Affirmative. This is Major Reg Cummins out of Khamis Moushalt. I'm given to understand that you're in need of my services."

"This is Lieutenant Colonel Thomson. What we need is to get to a friendly airfield and land these planes!" the officer shouted. "We're not pilots, man. We've got no business flying these planes, especially in these circumstances. The blasted Israelis have been threatening to shoot us down. Now I'm ordering you to get us the hell out of here at once."

Although Reg had been warned that the men piloting these sophisticated warplanes were not the best pilots, he was surprised at the man's hysterical tone. "Colonel," Reg said calmly, "you and your men are in good hands. I intend to deliver all of you safely to our base in Kuwait. Now if you gentlemen will kindly follow me to the south along the coast . . ."

A new voice, much younger than Thomson's and speaking in a working-class London accent interrupted. "Pardon me, Major Cummins. No disrespect intended, but heading south takes us closer to that big ugly wanker sitting over Jerusalem. I, for one, would prefer to stay as far away from that monster as possible."

"That's quite enough, Airman Tye," Colonel Thomson said sternly. "Let the man lead."

"Airman? Did someone just say 'airman'?" Reg said incredulously. "What the hell is an airman doing flying a Tornado?" Like most militaries around the world, the RAF only gave wings to officers. "What's going on here, Thomson? You've got cadets flying these planes?"

Before Thomson could answer, Tye spoke up again. "It's worse than you think, Major Cummins. I'm not even a cadet. Just a lowly mechanic, but don't you worry about me. I've got it under control."

Reg had to admit that the kid had a point. It was hard to tell from a distance but Tye seemed to be handling his plane better than most of the others. Certainly much better than his commanding officer, Thomson. He wondered how it was that a mechanic had learned to fly one of Britain's newest and most lethal jet fighters, but decided not to ask.

"Hold on," demanded a new voice. "Why south? Last time I checked, Kuwait was east of here."

"Quite right. We could go that way," Reg said. "In fact, that's a brilliant plan if you chaps think you're ready to square off against the Israelis, the Syrians, the Jordanians, and the Iraqis. How does that sound?"

"Never mind," replied the voice. "I humbly withdraw the suggestion."

The young Londoner, Tye, spoke again. "Yes, when you put it that way, Major, heading south sounds lovely. Suddenly, I'd love to get a better look at that spaceship."

The group formed up behind Reg and flew along the coast keeping to an elevation only slightly lower than the edge of the alien ship. The closer they came, the larger grew the lump in Reg's throat. Guessing that the others must be feeling the same way, he choked down his fear and got on the radio playing the role of friendly tour guide.

"Coming up on your left, gentlemen, you might notice a very large, dark gray aircraft from outer space hovering just a few thousand feet above the ground. We ask that you kindly refrain from feeding the aliens and please remember to keep all arms and legs inside your cockpits at all times."

Nervous laughter came back over the radio and several men made jokes of their own. But just as they approached the nearest edge of the disk, shouting erupted. Movement was detected along the bottom of the craft. Reg immediately shed a thousand feet of altitude. When the Tornadoes followed him, they had a clear view of what was happening.

Mammoth hatch doors were lowering to create a mile-wide opening at the eye of the daisy design. A sparkling jade-green light spilled from the interior of the ship and washed over Jerusalem, illuminating the city as if it were some kind of magical kingdom. It was such a beautiful sight that, for a moment, it was possible to believe the aliens had benign intentions after all. But soon, the tip of a massive cone-shaped mechanism lowered through the opening.

"What in the world is that?" gasped Thomson.

Reg thought he knew. He clenched his teeth and fought against the impulse to abandon the novice pilots to make a run at the jewel-like cone. His fingers itched to unleash his Sidewinders at what he feared was some sort of weapon. But he remained on course, even as a tightly focused beam of white light stabbed downward from the tip of the cone and touched the golden cupola of the Dome of the Rock.

"Communications beam?" someone asked with withering hope.

Reg shook his head sadly. He did not say the words aloud, but mouthed them behind his oxygen mask: targeting laser. A moment later, to his horror, Reg saw that his instinct was right.

A blinding blast of light ripped out of the cone and smashed down on the golden domed mosque, shattering the building into a billion pieces from the inside out. A dense pillar of fire began to build up over the blast site as the weapon continued to fire, adding more and more energy. Then, all at once it exploded outward and began to rip through the city, a tidal wave of flame rolling across the ground, utterly destroying everything in its path. It only seemed to gather momentum as it moved. Spreading relentlessly from the epicenter, a fiery wall of destruction several hundred feet high moved beyond the walls of the city and into the surrounding hills and suburbs. With the speed and force of an atomic explosion, it scoured Jerusalem from the face of the Earth, vaporizing in a handful of seconds what it had taken humans two thousand years to build.

At length, the bright beam coming from the firing cone shut off. But still the explosion rolled outward. With a momentum of its own, the blast shot beyond the city limits, breaking apart the surrounding towns and villages. It threw automobiles, buildings and bridges hundreds of feet into the air before burying them under a molten sea of flames.

Even after the flames themselves stopped moving outward, the residual heat continued for another mile, killing everything it touched. Where one of the most beloved cities of the world had stood scant seconds before, there was now only a twenty-mile circle of scarred, scorched earth. Half a million human lives had been extinguished.

None of the English pilots had spoken a word since the blast began. Reg broke the silence with a terse command. "You men continue south." Then he broke abruptly out of formation, turning to port for an attack run against the giant city destroyer.

He was not alone. From every corner of the sky, pilots from every nation in the Middle East temporarily forgot their longstanding rivalries to attack their common enemy. Without a word passing between them, Reg joined a group of eight Iranian jets which adjusted their positions to make room for him in their formation. He had only a few missiles loaded aboard his Hawk, but when the Iranian flight leader shouted the signal, he fired two of them. His AIM–9 Sidewinders kicked forward and joined the barrage of Iranian weapons. They all exploded at the same time, a full quarter mile before reaching the polished surface of the alien craft.

"What the hell was that?"

As the missiles detonated, they produced an odd atmospheric disturbance. The air surrounding the city destroyer rippled visibly ike the surface of a pond disturbed by a handful of pebbles.

"Pull up!" Reg shouted to the Iranians. "They've got some kind of energy shield!"

The stunned pilots saw that he was right and yanked back hard on their yokes in a desperate bid to avoid the invisible barrier. For some, the warning came too late. Four of the eight splattered themselves against the shield and burst into flames without penetrating to the other side. As Reg and the others leveled off, they could see the same thing was happening all around them. Missiles and jets were exploding against the invisible wall protecting the dark ship.

In his headphones, Reg could hear Colonel Thomson screaming, cursing and demanding that he finish the job of escorting the squad out of the area. After studying the melee unfolding around him for another minute, Reg saw that there was little hope of damaging the ship. Reluctantly, he turned south to rejoin the Tornadoes.

Only a moment after he spotted the Tornadoes, the already-disastrous situation got worse, much worse. A fresh round of shouting erupted over the radio. Reg looked over his shoulder at the black tower that marked the prow of the city destroyer. Near the top of it, a portal had appeared. What had seemed like a solid surface only moments before now bore a wide opening from which hundreds of small craft were emerging. They ducked and turned with incredible aerodynamic agility, like an angry swarm of bees boiling out of a disturbed hive. They quickly split into packs and moved to confront the human jets.

"Finally," Reg said to himself, "someone our own size to pick on."

"What now?" Thomson shouted. "What do we do, Cummins?"

"There's only thing you can do in a situation like this, Colonel. Run like hell. Get out of here as fast as you can. I'll try to buy you some time."

Reg wheeled around to face the oncoming enemy and spotted a gang of ten or twelve of them headed his way. They were sleek, lethal-looking machines with large reflective windows and curved rods extending from their noses like sets of pincers. Instead of a stable formation, they darted over and under one another in a continuous shuffle. As they streaked closer, white-hot energy pulses formed between the pincers before firing through the air. They look like the scarabs in the Egyptian Museum of Cairo, thought Reg, but they fly like bats.

Before Reg came within range, the alien detachment came under attack. Arabs, Israelis, Turks, Greeks and Africans closed in on them and filled the air with missiles and large-caliber gunfire. Reg flew toward the melee, bobbing and weaving to avoid the stray blasts from the alien pulse weapons that were streaking through the air. A moment after he joined forces with a Sudanese pilot, the man's MiG burst into flames and disintegrated. The scarab that had fired the deadly shot buzzed over the top of Reg's Hawk. In a heartbeat, Reg banked hard and fell in behind him. The alien pilot seemed not to realize he was being followed. Or perhaps he didn't care. He swooped to attack another jet, an American F–15, but before he could fire another pulse blast, Reg locked on with his targeting system and sent a Sidewinder flashing through the air. It scored a solid hit, exploding with devastating power against the rear of the attacker.

"One confirmed kill!" he reported, keying his radio to the common band. But as the smoke cleared, he realized that he had spoken too soon. The attacker was still in one piece. It wobbled through the air for a moment, reeling from the force of the blast, before righting itself and moving on as if nothing had happened. "Bad news," he shouted. "These little buggers have shields, too! Break off the engagement."

That was easier said than done. The nimble alien attackers were destroying jets almost as fast as Reg could count them. It wasn't a dogfight, but a one-sided aerial slaughter. Reg turned south again and tried to find a way through the mayhem. More than one of the aliens sighted on him and came in firing pulse blasts, forcing him to use every trick in his considerable repertoire to avoid being shot down. Reg managed to stay alive, but the less-skillful pilots around him were not so lucky. Shaking off the last of his alien pursuers, he leveled out at five thousand feet, pushed his twin turbo fan engines to their maximum speed and tore south along the coastline. He saw no sign of Thomson or the others, and was thankful that they appeared to be safely out of the area. Then, a lone Tornado came roaring up behind him and stationed itself off his starboard wing.

"Who the hell is piloting that Tornado! You lot are supposed to be long gone!"

"It's Airman Tye, sir. I'm your new wingman."

A fast-moving pair of blips on Reg's radar screen told him danger was approaching. Two of the scarab attackers were giving chase and they were gaining fast. He might be able to save himself with clever maneuvering, at least for a while, but now he had to worry about the young fool of a mechanic who had come to help. Burning with anger, he looked to his right and leveled an icy stare at the man in the Tornado's cockpit.

Tye responded with an enthusiastic salute and a nod of the head.

"Listen to me," Reg called. "Do you know if that plane has had its avionics update yet?"

"Installed it myself, Major," Tye responded proudly a moment before a pulse blast sailed between their two planes.

"Major," the young man shouted, "we've got aliens right behind us!"

"I see them," said the Teacher as calmly as if he were conducting a routine training mission. "Now, here's what I'd like you to do. Come up about twenty meters and fire off the port chaff."

To Reg's surprise, Tye executed the order quickly and with great precision. As the enemy closed in behind them, a cloud of aluminum slivers exploded into the air. Designed to confuse the homing systems of enemy air-to-air missiles, the tiny magnetically-charged bits of metal adhered to the attackers. Blinded and confused, they broke off the pursuit.

"Excellent work, lad!" roared Reg. "Where did you learn to fly like that?" Then, before Tye could answer, Reg laughed and said, "Forget I asked. I'm sure I don't want to know."

"Cummins! Where are you? Cummins, is that you?" The desperate voice on the radio belonged to Colonel Thomson. "For the love of God, man, where are you? Help us."

"I'm here, Colonel. What is your position?"

"I don't know. I think we're . . . everyone's dead, everyone's been shot down. We tried to fight them off, but they have shields and they were everywhere. Everyone's gone."

Another Englishman shouted over the airwaves. "Guide Dog, this is Sutton. Colonel Thomson and I are circling just north of the Red Sea, over the town of Eilat."

Within minutes, Reg and Tye spotted their companions and flew to meet them. Of the thirty-eight Tornadoes that had gone ahead, only two remained. Thomson had calmed down considerably by the time they arrived.

"We're all that's left," he reported.

"What happened," Reg demanded. "You should've been out of the area long ago."

"We ran into the whole goddamn Egyptian Air Force," Sutton snarled. "They came roaring north, headed straight at us, and it was all we could do to get out of their way. We were in the process of regrouping when those little alien bastards came out of nowhere and chewed us to pieces."

"What do we do now?"

"I'm afraid escorting you to Kuwait is out of the question. Not enough fuel. Looks like I'll have to bring you boys home with me to Khamis Moushalt."

"Where the hell is that?" demanded Sutton.

"Just follow me," Reg answered. Continuing south from Eilat and hugging the edge of the Red Sea, the quartet soon crossed into Saudi Arabia. Partly out of habit and partly to restore a sense of purpose, Reg formed them into a staggered diamond formation. This lone sense of order in the aftermath of the devastating air battle attracted every lost pilot for miles around. One by one, they joined Reg's armada until they were nearly fifty strong.

Soon, the group was flying over the dramatically contrasting Asir mountain chain. The green western slopes ran down to the Red Sea and were lush with vegetation, while the eastern slopes were devoid of life and marked the edge of a vast, inhospitable desert.

A few of the pilots had come mentally unglued. Through his radio, Reg could hear them sobbing like small children and jabbering uncontrollably in languages he didn't understand. Trying to think, he blocked out the noise and almost missed the message coming from his home base. The voice was barely audible above the din. "Khamis Moushalt Airfield to southbound flight. Do you read?"

"Affirmative, Khamis Moushalt. This is RAF Major Cummins."

"Major," said the flight controller, "please instruct any RAF pilots in your group to switch to the private band. Over." Reg and the other Brits quickly complied.

"Hello, Major," Colonel Whitley said. "You're still alive!"

"Yes, a few of us survived. But only by the skin of our teeth. They destroyed Jerusalem. Wiped it off the map."

"Yes, I know. The attack was simultaneous and worldwide. All thirty-six of their ships fired at once. London, Paris, New York, Moscow, all of them. They're all gone."

"London," Tye repeated softly, expressing a huge amount of grief with a single word.

"Listen," Whitley went on, "I've been talking with the American commander. He's got thirty F–16s ready to escort you in. Add our six instructors, and you've got thirty-six. Will that be enough to hold off those aliens?"

"Don't bother," Reg shot back. "If the aliens come after us, more planes won't make any difference." He began explaining the shields they'd encountered on both the city destroyer and the scarab attack craft, but Whitley cut him off.

"What do you mean if they come after you?" Whitley asked. "You'd better have a look at your long-range radar."

Reg studied his screens and saw that they were clear. For a moment he hoped that the colonel was mistaken, but his heart sank into the pit of his stomach when he noticed a cluster of blips creeping into view at the top of the screen. It was a squadron of at least two dozen alien attackers.

"We are officially dead meat," Sutton groaned. "It's over."

"Our intel officer here in the tower has been monitoring your situation for several minutes. He's convinced the enemy is following you." Whitley paused to let the pilots draw their own conclusions. "Change your mind about that escort?"

"Negative!" Reg shouted. "I'm telling you that won't do any good."

"Then we've got a major problem," Whitley said, "because there's no way the Yanks can get all their planes off the ground before you get here. They've got over two hundred birds parked on the tarmac and if you bring—"

"I understand," Reg interrupted. "We'll turn to the east and lead them away from you."

"Very well," Whitley said after a brief pause. "Good luck, Cummins, and good luck to the rest of you men." Then he was gone.

Reg switched back to the common frequency and issued the new orders. "Turn away from the coast and proceed due east. We have a large force of alien attack craft closing to our rear. Turn east immediately." Most of the pilots were still too shocked and confused to oppose the order, despite the fact that there was nothing but empty desert in that direction. The entire group turned away from the water. All except for three planes. Reg's ordered them to rejoin the formation several times before deciding to chase after them. He called for Tye and Sutton, both of them decent pilots despite their lack of training, to form up on his wings.

Two of the renegade jets were Iraqis, the last people on Earth Reg wanted to shoot down. "Iraqi pilots, you are headed in the wrong direction. Our flight is heading east."

One of them shouted back that Reg could go to hell. He said that he and his partner were low on fuel and that there was nowhere to land in the desert.

Reg considered explaining the situation to them, hoping he could persuade them to cooperate. But there wasn't enough time so he adopted a more efficient approach. "British Tornadoes," he said, "you are red and clear. Lock on and fire at will."

"No! Wait!" cried the Iraqis. "We agree to follow you. We are turning!" Cursing energetically in Arabic, the two men reluctantly set off to the east. Reg sent Tye and Sutton with them to make sure they rejoined the rest of the group. Then he closed quickly on the last southbound plane, a twenty-year-old Chinese J–7 with Egyptian markings. The pilot was muttering unintelligibly into his radio mouthpiece and didn't respond to Reg's repeated warnings.

Hoping to snap the Egyptian out of his stupor, Reg flipped his Hawk over and moved up until he was right on top of the J–7. The canopies of the two planes were separated by only a few feet. The Egyptian looked up and saw the Englishman hanging upside down above him pointing to the east, but the strange sight failed to register in his grief-stricken mind. He continued along the same path, muttering the whole while.

Reg saw no harm in letting the man go his own. In his present condition, there was little chance of him leading the aliens to Khamis Moushalt or any other airfield. But Reg felt badly about leaving him, so he shot ahead and attempted to take the Egyptian "by the hand." He maneuvered himself directly in front of the other plane and began a gradual turn to port, hoping the disoriented pilot would unthinkingly follow him. But something went horribly wrong. A warning buzzer sounded, and when Reg twisted around, he saw an R.550 Magic missile streaking toward him, homing in on his heat exhaust. Reg screamed and jerked the controls hard to port, lifting as he went. The missile chased after him, quickly closing the distance.

"Damn it! Somebody finally caught me with my guard down." Although he'd been "fired" at hundreds of time in training exercises, he'd never been "killed." Then again, he'd never made himself into a sitting duck the way he had for this demented Egyptian.

Reg continued to turn as tightly as his Hawk would allow, the G force crushing him against the right-hand wall of the cockpit until he was headed back toward the J–7. Although he hadn't planned it, he realized that looping around had provided him with one last card to play, one last slim hope of avoiding being blown apart. He steered himself onto a collision course with the Egyptian, speeding toward him almost head-on, as the missile continued to hunt him down. He bore down on the plane until he was close enough to see the man's eyes looking back at him blankly. Then, at the last possible moment, he swerved and felt the concussion behind him as the Magic missile destroyed the plane that had fired it.

Without celebrating his narrow escape, without even glancing back at the falling debris, Reg sped east to catch up to the others. Of course, he was glad to have survived the encounter. But as he looked north and saw the squadron of alien attackers becoming visible in the distance, he realized that his being alive was probably only a very temporary state of affairs. Only a moment after struggling to save himself, he found himself hoping the aliens would chase him out into the desert and hunt him down.

But that didn't happen. The scarab planes resisted the temptation to snack on Reg's small band of refugee pilots and instead continued south toward the feast awaiting them at Khamis Moushalt. As he headed deeper into the desert, Reg switched over to the private frequency and heard the tower operator desperately calling out the alert. "Incoming! Incoming!"

2

Retreat

Leaving the Red Sea behind them, Reg and his motley crew of survivors headed out across one of the most inhospitable environments on the face of the Earth, the great sand desert of the Arabian peninsula. Stretching out to the horizon in all directions, it was an ocean of gently undulating sand dunes, some of them a hundred meters tall. Shaped by the wind, they looked like the cresting waves of the ocean that had once covered the land. The Arabs called it Rub al-Khali, the Empty Quarter. It was a place the fiercest Bedouin tribes feared to cross, even in the ubiquitous Toyota trucks that had long since replaced camels. The international borders running through the area had never been precisely defined. No war had ever been fought for its control. It was one of the only places on the face of the planet that no one wanted.

The shouting, arguing and whimpering that had filled the radio waves subsided as the pilots headed deeper into this awesome and pitiless landscape. Fuel levels were running dangerously low and the warning systems aboard the planes began to sound. It appeared as though they had eluded one enemy only to run headlong into the arms of another. Instead of a swift, explosive death from an alien energy pulse, they now faced a slow, painful one in the desert. Their only hope was to find one of the tiny oases that dotted the desert. But the Empty Quarter was roughly the size of Texas, which meant they were looking for a needle in a field full of haystacks.

Reg had visited a few oases. They were not grass green patches of land full of swaying palm trees that most Westerners imagined. Instead, they typically consisted of a few tiny buildings and an oil derrick or two. A few of the places were marked on Reg's onboard maps, but without satellite navigation systems the maps were useless. The Empty Quarter offered no permanent landmarks by which to navigate. It was a place that gave up no secrets.

One by one, the jets began to run out of fuel and fall from the sky. The first to go down was a Jordanian. Before he ditched his plane, the terrified pilot begged his countrymen to remember the coordinates and send rescuers for him as soon as they could. They promised they would, but everyone knew it wasn't going to happen. Moving deeper into the desert with each passing minute, the pilots scoured the landscape with their eyes and called for help over their radios. Four more pilots were lost to lack of fuel, and Reg began to feel the panic level rising in his chest like the waterline in a sinking ship. The red warning light on his own fuel meter began to blink. It was only a matter of time.

Just when all seemed lost, a Libyan pilot spotted what looked like a column of smoke rising on the horizon.

"That looks like an oil fire," said Tye.

As the group turned and raced in that direction, one of the Israelis, a man with a froggy voice, quoted from the Bible. "And the Lord went before them by day in a pillar of cloud." Then he asked, "Are you a believer, Major Cummins?"

"Let's just say I believe we're going to need all the help we can get," Reg replied.

The source of the smoke came into view. A crashed tanker plane was burning out of control. The jet fuel it had been carrying had spilled over a wide area and was belching a mushroom cloud of black smoke high into the hot, motionless air.

It took Reg a moment to recognize the place, though he'd flown past it with his students more than once. It was an oil-drilling station set atop a barren, rocky plateau. It was surrounded by a ring of stony hills that kept the ever-shifting dunes from burying the plateau in sand. Since Reg had seen it last, the site had been transformed. It was now a small military airfield. Over a hundred Saudi combat planes were parked alongside a freshly repaved landing strip.

"I don't believe my eyes!" Tye shouted. "We're saved."

"It must be a mirage," Sutton said. "What is this place?"

"My guess is that this must have been a designated fallback position for the Saudi military," Reg said. Then he added, "Would've been nice of them to let us know about it."

"Why haven't the bastards answered our distress calls?" Thomson fumed.

"I suggest we go down there and ask them."

None of the pilots bothered to request permission to land. Jostling for position, they lined up nearly nose cone to tail fin and descended toward the runway at the same time.

When Colonel Thomson saw the situation he was in, he shrieked and rolled out of formation. His fuel gauge had long since run to zero, but he decided it would be safer to risk another loop around. He hadn't flown a fighter jet for more than a decade and was more than a little rusty.

Earlier that morning, before dawn, he'd been in his office on the island of Cyprus, packing his personal effects neatly into cardboard boxes. The entire base was closing and he was preparing to be transferred to an aircraft carrier in the Mediterranean. Then the surprising news arrived that the colonel would instead be flying a Tornado jet fighter to Kuwait. He was given ten minutes to report. He poured himself a capful of whiskey and looked around the office, deciding what to bring. The first thing he picked up was the photograph of him standing between a pair of much taller men, President Whitmore and the Italian prime minister, but he quickly tossed it aside. He ended up taking just three things: a recent picture of his wife and three daughters, which he creased and slipped into his wallet; a red, dog-eared copy of *The Traveler's Guide to Handy Phrases in Arabic*; and a pearl-handled revolver his father had given him years before. He loaded the pistol, tucked it inside his jacket and left without closing the door behind him.

"Thomson, you were on a good approach," Reg said. "Why'd you pull up?"

"A man needs room to land a plane!" the colonel yelled back. "I'm not a damned stunt pilot!"

Resisting the urge to ask the colonel exactly what kind of pilot he *was,* Reg coached him into a passable landing. Tye and Sutton, on the other hand, handled themselves like seasoned veterans, landing their Tornadoes almost flawlessly.

When he lined up for his own landing, however, Reg's luck finally deserted him. His Hawk sputtered and flamed out as the final dregs of jet fuel were consumed. Quickly sizing up the situation, he saw there was no way to make an unpowered landing. Too many jets were still on approach and he was losing altitude fast. But there was an even more pressing problem. He was heading toward a row of gleaming Saudi F-15 Eagles parked near the foot of the runway and was going to demolish them if he didn't do something. Acting on instinct, Reg jammed his yoke all the way forward, tilting the nose of his plane straight down. The Hawk plummeted toward the ground like a heavy stone. A moment before he crashed into the plateau wall, he hugged his arms and legs close to his body and activated the explosive bolts of his ejection seat.

The clear canopy ripped away, and Reg hurtled out of the doomed jet fighter, flying *parallel* to the ground at a sickening rate of speed. The silk canopy attached to his harness acted as much as a drag chute as it did a parachute. As he shot through the air like a human cannonball, Reg caught a momentary glimpse of the dumbfounded expression on the face of a Syrian pilot who was flying in the same direction.

As his Hawk piled into the ground and exploded in a huge fire ball, Reg drifted down to the tarmac and hit the ground running, following the jets down the runway. Skidding to a halt, he hustled to flatten his chute and pull it to one side, where it wouldn't hamper the few planes left to land.

He marched down the runway until he noticed three British

pilots staring at him in disbelief. By the time he walked up to where they were standing in the shade of a freshly parked Tornado, he was drenched in sweat. It was well over 110 degrees Fahrenheit. One of the Brits was a gangly red-haired lad who was shaking his head in stupefied amazement. Reg didn't need to see a name tag to guess who he was.

"Better close your mouth there, Airman Tye. It's wicked dry out here in the desert."

Things in the camp did not get off to an auspicious beginning. The Saudis insisted on keeping the new arrivals away from their planes and tents. The contingent of international pilots was kept segregated on one side of the plateau, well away from the landing strip. The armed soldiers the Saudis posted along their *border* refused to answer questions, even from pilots who came from countries allied with Saudi Arabia.

To make matters worse, the pilots quickly balkanized themselves into national groupings and kept well away from their traditional enemies. Everyone in the international part of the camp, it seemed, was angry with the Saudis and deeply suspicious of one another. Even Reg Cummins was having trouble cracking the code of silence among the Saudi guards and wringing information from them. As he was trying, screaming erupted from the Israeli group.

The Israelis had been the first to isolate themselves from the others, most of whom were Arabs. There had been a great deal of shouting in Hebrew since they had withdrawn to the shade of their planes, but it seemed directed toward one of their own. After a shrill, piercing cry rang through the air, the man who seemed to be causing most of the disturbance broke free of the group and came sprinting wildly across the dusty earth toward Reg. Both Sutton and Tye, lounging in the nearby shade, stood to meet the challenge but Reg motioned them back.

"What are you?" demanded the crazed Israeli. He had a haunted, terrified look on his face and was dripping with sweat.

"Easy there, pilot," Reg said. "I'm an English officer. We're allies."

"English? What is English?" he screamed. Two of his countrymen ran up behind the man, whose name tag identified him as GREENBERG and took hold of his arms, but he continued to rage. "That means nothing now. I want to know if you are human? Are you a human or one of them?"

"Human," Reg assured him, "one hundred percent human."

The answer seemed to calm the man down, but only for a moment. With the strength that only the demented possess, he threw both the men restraining him to the ground and ran to the next group, the Iranians.

"What are you? Are you human?" he screamed at a muscular pilot who had stripped to the waist. The man didn't answer, but scoffed and turned away. When Greenberg took another step toward him, the Iranian threw a sudden, vicious elbow to the middle of the Israeli's face. A fountain of bright red blood flew through the air as Greenberg crumpled to the ground. One of the men chasing Greenberg started a shoving match with the Iranian and soon the entire Israeli contingent was converging on the site.

Reg groaned a little. "Let the games begin," he said, half in disgust before he, too, started hurrying toward the trouble. Before he got there, however, an unlikely figure appeared in the center of the impending storm, shouting for order in atrocious Arabic. The man waved a well-thumbed red phrase book in the air with imperious authority. Reg blinked. It was Thomson.

The gathering mob, which had been on the verge of embarking on a full-fledged rumble, came to a dead stop, startled by the force of the colonel's command, even though none of them had understood a word he had said. Thomson did not cut an impressive figure. He was an average-looking man, well under six feet tall, and a bit thick around the middle. He sported a pencil-thin mustache and, like many balding men, let what little hair was still left to him grow long enough to comb over the top of his shiny scalp. Curiously, despite being overweight, he hardly perspired at all.

"Now then," the little colonel roared, "what's all this nonsense about?" When the two sides recovered from their shock and again began to shout at one another, Thomson leapt between them, drawing their anger to himself like a lightning rod and diffusing it. As the dispute raged on, he continued to consult his phrase book and shout appropriate phrases over the noise of the assembly. In this manner, he staved off an all-out brawl long enough for Greenberg to be led away. The Israeli was covered in his own blood, and his nose was obviously broken.

Reg was feeling somewhat broken himself. He thought of Jerusalem, obliterated, and sympathized with the jabbering Israeli. After everything that had happened—the city leveled by an unfightable foe, the destruction of his home base, the loss of those pilots over the desert—Reg could understand why madness might be an attractive alternative. Giving in to fear and paranoia seemed, under the circumstances, perfectly natural. It relieved a man like Greenberg of the responsibility of figuring out what to do next.

Even as tensions between the Iranians and Israelis began to dissipate, Thomson continued to quote the scripture he found in his copy of *The Traveler's Guide to Handy Phrases in Arabic*. It wasn't clear whether he realized what an ass he was making of himself.

Finally, one of the Iranians who was laughing at him filled him in on a little secret. "Colonel, perhaps you are unaware of the fact that none of us standing here are speakers of Arabic, not native speakers at any rate."

Thomson, befuddled, looked at the man and then at his trusty handbook. "How do you mean?"

The Iranian laughed again. "We speak Farsi, and the Jews speak Hebrew. Actually, I have picked up a bit of Arabic, enough to know your accent is absolutely abominable!"

With tensions temporarily abated, the two groups returned to their respective enclaves. Reg, braving the heat, walked to the edge of the plateau and looked over the lip of the crumbling sandstone abutment. Below him, he watched a handful of Saudi soldiers trying to extinguish the still-burning remains of his Hawk and the crashed fuel tanker. The soldiers, wearing traditional red headdresses, and armed only with shovels and small fire extinguishers, did the best they could to suppress the flames. Great clouds of black smoke continued to billow into the windless blue sky. The smoke announced their location for many miles around, a beacon to wandering pilots. Indeed, more planes were arriving all the time, most of them straggling in from the north. But if human pilots could use the fires to find the camp, the aliens surely could as well.

When he rejoined the other pilots, Reg found a large number of them haranguing the guards. They were demanding to know the news from their home countries, if the aliens had landed, and whether or not their planes would be refueled. The more the guards refused to speak, the angrier and more insistent the pilots became. Reg noticed a couple of the Saudis slip away from the confrontation and hurry into the tent town they had erected among the planes on the far side of the runway. In addition to the tactical fighters, there were a number of transport and cargo planes. There was a fuel tanker identical to the one that had crashed and a score of private luxury jets, undoubtedly the property of wealthy families. Reg wasn't surprised to see the civilian aircraft because he was familiar with the way rich Saudis, especially members of the royal family, considered the armed forces almost as personal bodyguards.

Soon the two men who had slipped away returned, leading a small army of machine-gun-toting reinforcements. They fanned out and crouched along the runway as if they expected a battle.

Their commanding officer was a huge, powerfully built captain with severe eyes and a hooked nose. Like the other Saudis, he wore a *keffiyeh*, the checkered red-and-white headcloth held in place by black cords. Despite the oppressive heat, he was dressed in an olive drab uniform made of wool. All business, he marched toward the refugee pilots, shouting orders in Arabic. When he noticed the Israelis, however, he stopped in his tracks. For a moment, he seemed to be at a loss. Then he cleared his throat and made an announcement in English.

"Jews are not allowed in the Kingdom of Saudi Arabia. This is Islamic holy land."

Pilots from several nations were shouting, trying to get his attention, but all fell silent when the senior officer among the Israelis, who happened to be a woman, bulled her way to the front of the crowd. When he saw her, the Saudi captain backpedaled. He had just gotten used to the idea of dealing with Jews, but now a *female Jewish fighter pilot* who shared his rank? This seemed as impossible to comprehend to the Saudi as the sudden arrival of aliens from outer space.

"You don't want us here? We'd be happy to leave. Just give us enough fuel to get the hell out of here."

In rough English, the Saudi announced that the airfield was in a state of heightened alert until the fires burned themselves out. The pilots were to remain with their planes. Water and food would be brought to them, along with shovels so they could dig their own latrines. They were not, under any circumstances, allowed to leave the area that had been set aside for them until the commander of the base gave the go-ahead.

"And when might that be?" inquired Thomson.

"Commander Faisal is still studying the situation," came the reply.

"Well, what about an update on what's going on out there?" Everyone understood Thomson's vague wave to the north to mean the entire world.

"You must be patient, Colonel," said the hook-nosed man. With a last, hate-filled glare at the Israeli woman, he turned on his heels and walked away.

"Arrogant son of a bitch, isn't he?" asked Sutton. He was about Reg's age, somewhere in his mid-thirties, with a flattop haircut and a sharp cast to his features. He shook his head in disgust. "I don't know who's worse," he continued, "the aliens or these self-righteous bastards."

"The Saudis are all right," Reg said. "A bit high-handed sometimes, but they usually end up doing the right thing."

Sutton wasn't convinced. He lit a cigarette and squinted into the harsh afternoon sunlight. "We haven't been here an hour yet and already there have been a dozen arguments, one fistfight, and now we're being treated like bloody prisoners of war! I wouldn't say they're doing the right thing at all. No, things are not going well."

Reg didn't answer, just watched as the man inhaled deeply on his cigarette.

"Things are probably a bit more comfortable for whites up there in Kuwait," Sutton said. "Too bad you weren't able to follow your orders and get us through." With that, the lieutenant turned and walked back to the shade of his plane.

The blazing sun had one beneficial consequence. It made arguing while standing out in the open an impossibility. Soon, the pilots had retreated to their own mini-enclaves based on nation, still mistrustful of one another. They stretched out on the sand beneath their planes, fitfully trying to rest.

Reg saw soldiers of the Saudi army taking up positions all around the plateau. They were armed with "handheld" SAM launchers, bulky bazooka like weapons. He could see them on the high dunes in the distance. Ready to defend against incoming alien ships. *Futile*, he thought.

At one point, midway through the afternoon, a Jordanian pilot was called to the main camp. When he returned, word spread among the international pilots that the Saudis had asked him a few questions about the capabilities of the alien attack craft. The man had told them that others had been more involved in the fighting than he, particularly the British officer called Cummins, but they hadn't seemed interested. Sometime after that, the Saudis finally brought buckets of water and boxes of crackers and distributed them.

What news was passed among the pilots took a circuitous route. The Iraqis had made sure they were as far as possible from their sworn enemies, the Iranians. The Israelis stayed as far as possible from everyone.

It was Thomson more than anyone who facilitated communication. He spent most of the afternoon shuffling from one encampment to the next, bringing his own fussy brand of diplomacy to the situation. No one was convinced by anything he said,

but on the few occasions he stepped between arguing parties—
once there were even knives drawn—he gave the frustrated pilots
a way to back down without losing face.

Unwittingly, he also provided comic relief. Most of the pilots
were fluent in English, the international language of aviation, but
Thomson persisted in dragging out his phrase book and tripping
over elementary Arabic phrases at every opportunity. He would
deliver his mispronunciations with great authority, then move on
to the next group.

Eventually, he returned to the three British planes, where Tye
and Sutton lay sprawled in the sand. Reg was leaning against a
Tornado's landing gear, half-dozing.

"Keeping eyes open and ears alert, I see," Thomson said. He
was covered in dust from head to toe.

The two men on the ground just muttered and ignored the
colonel, but Reg asked, "Any news?"

Thomson looked over his shoulder at the various groups of
pilots. "It's shocking. Intellectually, I knew these people hated one
another, of course. It's all over the telly and the newspapers. But
to witness it up close like this, it's enough to turn your stomach."

Reg was no stranger to the strife of the Middle East, but this
was Thomson's first visit to the region. The colonel continued, "I
was talking to those blokes from Syria, for example. Educated
fellows, polite. Worried about their families, of course. But when
the subject of the Israelis came up it was like I'd thrown a switch
and turned them into demons or some such. They started going on
about how when night comes, they were going to sneak over there
with knives and sever a few heads. Quite disturbing really."
Thomson shivered in the heat. "Do you suppose we should go
over and warn them?"

Reg looked over at the large Israeli contingent and noticed
they'd posted guards of their own. "I wouldn't worry about them,
Colonel. They're used to being surrounded by unfriendly
nations."

Thomson studied the Israelis himself. "Humph," he said.
"Looks like somebody has already warned them. Still, if I was a

wagering man, I'd bet someone dies before the night is out."

Sutton stood, stretching. "I'd say chances are good that we'll *all* be dead before the night is out."

Thomson ignored the remark. The portly officer ran his fingers through his thinning hair before lying down on his back in the shade. He laced his fingers over the bulge of his stomach and fell instantly asleep. The roar of a Saudi jet lifting off did not drown out his snores.

Time passed, and the British pilots became lost in their own thoughts, speaking to one another very little. Reg scanned the airfield, hoping to catch sight of any of his former students, but saw no one he recognized. He was mystified by the behavior of their supposed Saudi allies, but was willing to wait at least a little while for more information.

The wait ended when the burly Saudi captain returned to "Embassy Row"—as Tye had taken to calling the international part of the airfield—and sent his soldiers to each contingent of pilots with a message. They asked each group to select a representative to meet with the camp's commander.

"I'll pass," Sutton said immediately. "There's no telling what mischief these blokes are up to."

"If they're serving food, sign me up," Tye chimed in. "I'm half-starved."

Sutton gestured toward the sleeping figure of Thomson. "Mr. Phrase Book over there is our ranking officer. Maybe we should wake him up."

Reg was a more logical choice to act as representative because of his years of working with the Saudi military. He was the only one of the Brits with the first clue about the political dynamics of the region, but he felt certain the Saudis weren't ready to hold a serious meeting so he leaned back against the landing gear. "I don't know what's worse," he said, "the colonel's snoring or the growls coming out of Tye's stomach. You go on ahead, lad, and if they're serving bangers and mash, bring us back a doggy bag."

Without waiting to hear Sutton's response, the gangly mechanic left to join the other representatives. Sutton turned away with a petulant shrug and returned to his spot in the shade. "Fine," he said.

Reg lay down on his back and closed his eyes. But before he could drift off to sleep, a harsh Saudi voice startled him. "Englishman, wake up." The burly captain was looming over him. "Is your name Cummins?"

After a glance down at his name tag, Reg smiled up at the soldier. "Yes, I suppose I am."

"You will come with me," he said impatiently, and when Reg didn't leap to his feet, he added, "Immediately!"

The two Brits exchanged a look. Sutton was alarmed. "I'm thinking it cannot be a good thing that he knows your name. I wouldn't go if I were you. Could be trouble."

As Reg stood and brushed the sand from his uniform, the Saudi repeated, "Immediately!"

Sutton scrambled to his feet. "You don't have to go anywhere with this damn towel-head, Major. He's got no authority over you."

Reg grimaced at his compatriot's ugly remark. "Sutton, don't worry. I'll go."

When the captain turned and began leading the way, Sutton caught Reg by the arm. "Take this," he said, showing him the pistol concealed in his waistband.

"Thanks just the same," Reg said with a glance toward the dozens of heavily armed Saudi soldiers around the airfield. "I doubt I'd have the chance to use it, even if I wanted to." With that, he moved off to join the representatives moving toward the Saudi camp.

As the group made its way between the white tents that served the base as barracks, Reg took special note of the civilians milling about, women and even a few children. The women were covered from head to toe in long skeins of black fabric, the *abayas* dictated by Muslim custom. Regardless of the temperature, Saudi women were bound by law to cover themselves like furniture in an abandoned house. It was a custom Reg found personally distasteful, but one he'd come to ignore.

The representatives were marched past an open-sided tent

crammed full of radio equipment. About a dozen technicians sat at their stations under a low roof of camouflage netting. They all turned and stared inquisitively at the foreign pilots.

A Jordanian pilot walking just ahead of Reg and Tye gestured toward the radio tent. "We should make friends with those men over there. Maybe they can tell us what's happening out in the world."

Tye took this immediately to heart. "Hello, gents," he called to radio operators with wave and a smile. "Any word from England?" The Saudis merely stared back at him. In the time-honored tradition of English speakers everywhere, Tye tried again, speaking slowly and in a louder voice. "WHAT . . . IS HAPPENING . . . IN ENGLAND?"

The only result of this was that the other dozen pilots walking with him began shouting questions of their own, mostly in Arabic. The Saudi captain barked an order, and the group moved on.

"That's *not* exactly what I had I mind," said the Jordanian.

"They weren't picking up anything, anyway," said Reg. "Otherwise, they would have been too busy to stare at us."

There were several small cargo planes scattered about the center of the camp, but by far the largest object in sight was an American-built C–230A cargo plane. It towered above the others, its great bulk providing shade for a dozen or so tents pitched beneath its one-hundred-foot height. The tail section had been raised on its hinges, allowing direct access to the belly of the plane. A squad of soldiers casually guarded the interior, sitting around the top of the landing ramp. They, too, stared at the bedraggled group of pilots, while tightening their grips on their AK–47s.

Finally the pilots came to a large tent at the very center of the Saudi camp. A noisy gas-driven generator provided power to the air-conditioning system cooling the tent's interior. A soldier stationed at the entrance seemed to have as his sole responsibility ensuring that the flap stayed closed. The tent had originally been white, but, like the others, was now coated with the tan brown dust of the surrounding desert. The hook-nosed captain roughly ordered the pilots to halt.

"That bloke's got a red-hot poker jammed up his rear, doesn't he?" asked Tye, eliciting a few chuckles. "Where exactly does he think we'd be wandering off to?"

"They are trying to show us how strong they are," answered the Jordanian, without emotion.

"Well, I wish he'd just lift something heavy above his head and have done with it," Tye replied. "It's too bloody hot to stand around in the sun. I feel like a slab of bacon that's been left in the skillet too long."

He looks it, too, thought Reg. The pale mechanic's skin was beginning to turn the same shade as his flaming red hair, and his shoulders were slouched. The sun was literally shrinking him.

Tye glanced around with half-closed eyes. The shade on the eastern side of the tent attracted his attention. "Why can't we wait over there?" he asked loudly.

Reg smiled. "I suppose you could try to walk over there and find out."

Tye considered the idea. "Say," he asked hesitantly, "don't they still stone people in this country? Cut off their hands and all that business?"

Reg shrugged. "It's a harsh place."

"Actually," said the Jordanian, eyeing the shade, "that's not a bad idea. Let's go and wait in the shade. We're all brothers here. No one is going to shoot us." He stepped out of line and began walking slowly toward the spot. The Saudi guards lowered their rifles at him, ordering him back. But he continued moving, hands in the air, speaking in a friendly tone. "The sun is making us ill," he explained.

They tried to block his path and push him back toward the others, but the Jordanian bulled ahead, eventually pushing his way past the last guard and sitting down in the shade. The other pilots followed his example, ignoring the threats and warnings from the soldiers. Once they had all seated themselves along the side of the tent, the corporal who had been left in charge of the situation tried to save face by yelling, "No more moving! I order you to sit down and stay where you are!"

The pilots looked up and down the line at one another and, for the first time, shared a smile. It was a small victory, but it was something. Tye stretched out his long, tired legs and turned to the Jordanian. "This is much better. Cheers!"

"Yeah, that was a pretty good move," said the Israeli representative, adjusting his thick eyeglasses. "Now ask them to bring us some Cokes, and maybe some sandwiches."

The Jordanian and the Israeli introduced themselves to the Brits. The Israeli's name was Yossi. His voice sounded like gravel and he had a shock of short black hair. The black-plastic frames of his glasses dominated his face. He seemed about Tye's age and Reg thought he looked more like a math student than a fighter pilot. Although Yossi had a friendly demeanor and even cracked a few jokes, he never smiled.

The Jordanian, Edward, was closer to Reg in both age and height. He, too, was friendly with the Brits who sat between him and the Israeli pilot. Except for Yossi's initial comment, the two of them studiously avoided speaking to one another.

Tye pointed to the small green, white, and yellow patch sewn on to Edward's flight suit below the Jordanian flag. "What's that insignia?" he asked.

Edward glanced over at Yossi. "Ask your Jewish friend over there," he said. "He knows what it is."

Yossi looked at the patch. "It means he's a Palestinian. Half the Arabs in Jordan are Palestinians and the king lets a few of them join the armed forces so the others can feel better about themselves."

Tye, always more interested in machines than politics, turned to Reg for clarification. "Palestinians and Israelis don't get on very well, do they?"

Yossi answered instead of Reg. "Arabs are like Gentiles," he said. "You've got bad ones and you've got good ones."

Edward snorted. "And the only good Arabs are the dead ones, right?"

"Hey, look, I got no problem with you," Yossi shot back, pointing a finger. "Israel, Jordan, whatever. We don't even know if they exist anymore, but if you want to carry on old fights, I'm ready."

Edward laughed again. "Take a look around you. You're not in Tel Aviv, my friend. You should watch your tongue out here." He gestured broadly at their surroundings. "These Bedouins have a saying: *A night in the desert is long and full of scorpions for the man who does not belong there.*" He flashed Yossi a smile that managed to be simultaneously cheerful and threatening.

The large Saudi captain emerged from the tent with someone Reg guessed must be Faisal. He was a dark-skinned man in his late forties and had flecks of gray running through his carefully trimmed beard. The long, cream-colored robe he wore loosely over his military uniform made him look like a sheik. He seemed completely relaxed, even jovial, as he strolled away from his tent, speaking in a low voice to the captain, but Reg sensed that he could be a dangerous man.

The two men ambled to an open spot in the sand where they were met by a soldier who handed them a pair of rolled up mats. At the same time, one of the radiomen approached from the communications tent carrying a portable Sony stereo.

A different soldier threw a bundle of mats toward the pilots, and several of the men casually stood up to take one. "What's going on?" Tye wondered aloud.

On all sides, men began to spread the mats on the ground. The soldiers guarding the pilots laid their weapons aside and knelt in the sand. The radioman pushed a button on the stereo and the musical voice of a prayer leader, a *muezzin*, filled the air. All of the Saudis and most of the international pilots prostrated themselves on their mats, bowing their heads to the north.

"Oh, now I remember," whispered Tye, "Islamic people have to pray five or six times a day, don't they? And they all face that same city, what's the name of that place? Mazatlan! That's it, they all pray towards Mazatlan."

"Mecca," Reg corrected him. "They face Mecca, the Holy City."

The muezzin's song, rich and clear, rang through the camp

and echoed off the surrounding hills. All of the Muslims in the camp, soldiers and civilians, prayed together, and a feeling of tranquility fell across the plateau, stilling the most warlike of hearts.

Tye rocked back and forth as he listened to the singing, then leaned toward Edward. "That's actually quite beautiful," he said before narrowing his eyes and giving the Palestinian the once-over. "Hey, why aren't you praying with them?"

"Because I'm a Christian," Edward replied. "Why aren't you?"

When the prayers were over, the hook-nosed captain and the man in the cream-colored robes stood and continued speaking quietly to one another. From their gestures and glances, it was clear they were discussing what to do with their unexpected guests. They appeared to take special note of Reg and the Israeli representative, Yossi. After a few moments, they walked toward the strip of shade where the pilots had planted themselves. Reg and the others labored to their feet and dusted themselves off in preparation for the meeting.

"Welcome!" shouted the burly captain sternly. "Our most respected leader, Commander Ghalil Faisal, welcomes you. But he warns you that this place is a military facility of the Kingdom of Saudi Arabia, governed by the laws of the Holy Koran." As the captain spoke, Reg and Faisal stared at one another, sizing each other up. "The Saudi people are famous for their generosity," barked the captain. "Our supplies will be shared with all of you. Our bread will be your bread. You will receive tents, food, and water."

"All of us?" asked Yossi in his raspy voice.

The captain gritted his teeth and looked away from the Jewish pilot, offended by his very presence. He glanced toward Faisal, who returned a barely perceptible nod.

"Our commander has declared that the old battles are over. The hospitality we show to our Muslim brothers and our friends from the West will also be offered to the Zionists during their temporary stay in our country."

Faisal then offered the pilots a perfunctory salute and withdrew to the air-conditioned comfort of his tent, adjourning the meeting without having spoken a single word.

"You will follow me to the supplies," shouted the captain, turning on his heels and marching away. The pilots looked at one another in confusion before following. *Was that it?* Between them, they had a thousand urgent questions about the situation in the rest of the world and what the Saudis planned to do. The captain heard their grumbling. When they returned to the C–230 cargo plane, he paused at the foot of the access ramp. "There will be another meeting tonight. You may discuss your questions with Faisal at that time."

The huge plane was the supply depot for the camp. The crates and storage tanks stacked inside held enough provisions to sustain the troops for several weeks. Tye was the first one inside the plane. Rubbing his hands together eagerly, he faced a gray-haired supply officer across a small table.

"I'd like a big juicy cheeseburger, please, no pickles. And a side of chips."

The supply officer blinked in confusion before handing Tye a large bundle that included a four-man tent, a plastic water bucket, blankets, a first-aid kit, and a copy of the Koran. Heading back down the ramp, Tye thumbed through the book, disappointed. "This is all in Arabic," he complained to Reg, "and there's no pictures."

Reg looked around and noticed a group of soldiers lounging in the shade beneath the cargo plane. One of them stood up and came trotting into the sunlight.

"Teacher!" he shouted. "I can't believe it. Major Cummins, how are you? How did you find us here?"

"We were in the neighborhood and thought we'd stop by to say hello." Reg smiled.

The Saudi officer was in his late twenties, light on his feet, and wore a flashy gold chain around his neck. His striking green eyes and dashing good looks gave him the appearance of a young movie star. His lips curled into a mischievous grin below his light mustache. The two men shook hands then kissed on each cheek, in the Arab style.

"Well, I'll be damned," Reg said, shaking his head in disbelief. "Khalid Yamani is here." Of all the Saudi pilots Reg Cummins had trained, of course it would be this one who found him here. "I see you're loafing in the shade, as usual."

"No, no, Teacher," Yamani protested good-naturedly. "As always, I am working very hard. I wanted to keep working but these men," he said, gesturing to his friends, "they are soft. They begged me to give them a short break because they could not keep up with me. What could I do?"

The other soldiers heard him lying and shouted a few comments of their own. Khalid waved them off and flashed Reg a disarming, high-wattage smile.

Khalid Yamani was probably the worst student Reg had ever tried to teach, but also one of his favorites. He was an easily distracted, sometimes reckless pilot and at first Reg had been mystified over why he had been promoted to the advanced tactical fighter school. Only when he tried to have the young man sent down—for his own safety—did he learn that Khalid's father was one of the richest and most influential men in Saudi society, an oil baron with vast, worldwide holdings who kept close personal counsel with the king.

Reg was a respected and well-liked teacher but he was also very demanding. He had absolutely no tolerance for sloppiness and lack of concentration. At first, his students didn't understand the ferocious anger he turned on them when they made lazy errors, but eventually someone would tell them, explaining in whispers or waiting until Reg wasn't around to hear.

Khalid had driven him crazy on several occasions, but the young man had such a charming, good-natured way about him that Reg could never stay angry for very long. Khalid's love of life was so infectious that he'd occasionally managed to drag Reg with him to off-base parties, swanky, secretive affairs held in private homes where upper-class Saudis dressed in Western-style clothing and sipped alcohol. The parties were an open secret and were rarely disturbed by the religious police, as long as they remained behind closed doors. Khalid, a handsome fighter pilot and eligible bachelor from a wealthy family, was invited to many such gatherings and never missed the opportunity to attend. He reveled in Western habits, being largely westernized himself. He'd spent his high school years in Houston, Texas, while his father bought and reorganized an oil company there.

"As a matter of fact, Teacher, I've been expecting to see you. The men have been talking about a trick someone used against the aliens—using chaff to blind them. I said to myself, 'Self, that sounds like Reg Cummins.'"

"You heard about that?" Tye asked, impressed.

"It wasn't me," Reg said quickly. "It was this beanpole of a mechanic here. He flew a very respectable flight." He introduced the two men, who shook hands warmly.

"The major is just being modest," Tye said. "I fired off the chaff, but he was the one who came up with the idea. I was too busy wetting myself to come up with anything that clever."

The three of them continued talking until all of the representatives had received their supply packages. As they started back, Khalid took Reg by the arm and led him in a different direction. "Stay a while, Teacher, there's someone I'd like you to meet. But first I have a question: *Can we win?*"

"That's the question of the hour isn't it?" Reg thought for a minute before answering. "I'd say we've got a snowball's chance in hell."

"Ah," grinned Khalid, "excellent! Then there *is* a chance." He gestured toward a row of private jets. "Teacher, my father is here. He is not well, and I know it would ease his pain to meet you. Would you mind?"

It wasn't an offer Reg could very well refuse. "I'd be honored."

The two of them moved along the perimeter of the Saudi tent town, maintaining a low profile, until they reached a luxury Learjet tied down near the lip of the plateau. The sun was low on the horizon and the heat was lifting. Reg noticed a large tent standing by itself quite some distance from the rest of the camp.

"What's going on out there?" he asked.

Khalid shook his head sadly. "They are calling it the Tent of the Fearful. Since the demons began to arrive, many people are losing their minds. Last night, they screamed and screamed. No one could sleep."

"I don't hear anything now."

"Morphine," Khalid explained before climbing a set of steps. The Yamani family crest was painted prominently on the exterior of the plane. Khalid paused on the top step and turned to Reg. "When I told you my father was not well . . ." He didn't finish the thought, but gestured meaningfully toward the Tent of the Fearful before heading inside.

The interior of the plane was a different world. It was a soothing, air-conditioned place with art on the walls and plush carpeting. There was a kitchenette/dining area with marble countertops and leather upholstery.

Khalid stepped through an interior doorway into his father's room and turned down the volume on a wall-mounted television set. Karmal Yamani was a frightened, unshaven, elderly man with bloodshot eyes. He lay on a narrow bed, his head propped up by a spray of golden pillows. While vice minister of petroleum exports, he and his brother had been the chief architects of the 1973 oil embargo, an exercise in economic brinksmanship that had quadrupled his nation's wealth almost overnight. He was known as one of the most shrewd and powerful men in the Middle East, but none of that was evident at the moment.

"Father! I have excellent news," Khalid said very loudly. "Here is a great friend of mine, Major Reg Cummins. He was over Jerusalem when the attack began. He tells me that the aliens are very strong, but he is confident that we can beat them. He believes we can win the war!"

The old man pushed himself up into a sitting position and a looked at Reg hopefully. "How? How can we defeat them?"

Reg silently cursed Khalid for putting him on the spot. He didn't want to lie, but telling the truth threatened to crush the old man's fragile spirit.

He hesitated, choosing his words carefully. "Well, for one thing, we've discovered we can blind them temporarily. We're studying how to use that to our advantage," Reg said. "Besides, sir, human beings are a tough lot. We always seem to find a way."

"Blind them, you say?" The elder Yamani's self-control was returning. He straightened his clothes and apologized for his appearance. "It is embarrassing for me to receive you like this, major, but since the spaceships arrived I have not been a well man."

"We're all in a state of shock," Reg said. "It's very understandable."

"Yes, my condition is not uncommon during wartime"— Yamani nodded—"but it is a very dangerous one. Great fear can be contagious, spreading from man to man until an entire army can no longer fight. We must quarantine those whose knees have turned to water, as mine have. This is the same advice I gave to Ghalil Faisal. Are there any such men among the foreign pilots?"

"One or two," Reg answered.

"You must isolate them immediately! Move them to the tent in the desert with the others! Khalid, arrange this with Faisal."

Each time Khalid heard his father mention Faisal's name, he made a sour face and pretended to spit on the floor. "The man is a swine," he said with a vehemence Reg didn't understand.

Just then, a jet fighter screamed overhead and Mr. Yamani's composure collapsed completely. He rolled away from the window near his bed, shielding himself with the blanket. Khalid went to his side and tried to comfort him as Reg stood by awkwardly. Although the old man could diagnosis his condition, he was obviously helpless to control it. Eventually, Khalid led Reg out of the room and back to the kitchen area.

"Thank you, Teacher," he said, pulling bottles of French mineral water from a refrigerator and sliding into one of the seats at the table. "He is more at ease now." Reg took a couple of dates from a bowl and popped them in his mouth as Khalid poured. "Now, tell me what happened over Jerusalem, Teacher, every detail. Together we will discover a weakness, a way to fight them."

Reg swirled the water in his glass. "I could use something stronger if you've got it," he said.

Khalid started to get up, but quickly changed his mind. "It would be unwise of me to offer you alcohol on my father's plane, but I will try to send a package to your tent this evening." He pointed forward and aft, indicating there were others aboard the jet.

After much prodding, Reg began to recount the one-sided battle he'd fought that day. Up to that moment, he'd been doing his best to keep the memory of it buried, but now he let the scene flood back to him. He talked about the enormous firing cone and the circular wall of destruction it had unleashed. He described the missiles exploding against the giant ship's shields, the ill-fated dogfight with the scarab attack ships. In a very real sense, the memory of the massacre was more devastating than the event itself. Several times during the retelling, Reg had to stop and gather himself before going on. And each time he did so, he would glance out the portal and see the Tent of the Fearful in the deepening twilight.

During one of these pauses, a door opened and a beautiful young woman in her early twenties stepped into the dining area. Tall and slender, she wore her lustrous mane of coal black hair pulled back into a thick ponytail. She was dressed in blue jeans and a T-shirt bearing the logo of Stanford University. Reg's eyes couldn't help lingering over the curves of her body. It had been a long time since he'd seen a Saudi woman in anything except a black shroud, and longer still since he'd seen a woman as beautiful as the one that stood before him. One look into her bright green eyes told him she had to be Khalid's sister.

Khalid was not happy to see her. The moment she showed herself, he began shouting in Arabic and waving her out of the room. She studiously ignored him, casually moving to a set of cabinets above the sink. When she stood on her toes and reached for the handles on the high doors, the T-shirt climbed her torso revealing the clear dark skin on her stomach and the small of her back. Reg reached nervously for his water glass without looking away, without even blinking.

Khalid sprang to his feet, showering her in curses and demanding that she return to her quarters. He pounded his fist on the table, spilling his water. This finally cracked the young woman's cool demeanor. She turned away from the cabinets and shouted back venomously at her brother before approaching the table.

"This must be the English pilot you've spoken of so often," she said to her brother in a flawless American accent. "You never mentioned that he was so handsome." If the comment was designed to get under Khalid's skin, it worked. He erupted into a fresh round of shouting. She ignored him and locked eyes with Reg. "Forgive my brother's idiotic behavior. He pretends to be progressive but he's a very typical Saudi male chauvinist pig." With that, she left the room leaving the two men in silence.

"Well, that was interesting," Reg said, pouring Khalid a fresh glass of water. "I've never seen you react like that to a Saudi woman in Western clothes."

"My sister!" Khalid said, scowling at the closed door. "She has always been defiant, but now it is worse, much worse. Since she returned from America, she does nothing but make trouble. I apologize that you had to see her like that."

Reg hadn't exactly minded. In fact, he thought of asking Khalid to invite her back in, but decided to say nothing.

"We are seeing this problem more and more in Saudi Arabia," Khalid told him.

"What problem is that?"

"These girls," he said with a dismissive wave. "They return from university in Europe or America with the idea of challenging the man's authority. They rebel against everything, mindlessly. It lasts until they marry and begin to bear children."

Reg bit into another date. From an Englishman's perspective, the way Saudi women were treated amounted to legalized slavery. They were kept virtual prisoners in their own homes and had few legal rights to protect them from the whims of their husbands, fathers and brothers. Some years earlier, the entire English military presence had withdrawn from the country in protest when a

Saudi father legally executed one of his daughters by drowning her in the family swimming pool after finding her alone with an unmarried man. The man was not charged.

Khalid sat down and sipped his water, then whispered across the table. "Fadeela is an especially unhappy and willful girl. I am sad to say that the blame for this must rest largely with my father. He has allowed her to develop unrealistic expectations about her future."

"Such as?"

"It is not important," Khalid said with a sudden, broad smile. "But I pity the man who takes her one day to be his wife. He will be buying himself a lifetime of headaches. But enough! We have more important matters to discuss."

Still convinced he could discover a chink in the alien armor by listening to Reg's account, Khalid began quizzing him on every aspect of their technology. But they were soon interrupted again, this time by a knock on the outer hatch. A soldier had arrived with an important message. Khalid excused himself and spoke to the man outside.

Reg hungrily filled his mouth with dates and studied the richly appointed interior of the jet. He was still chewing when a door opened and Fadeela returned. He watched her reach into the cabinet above the sink and retrieve a bottle of brandy then slide into the seat across from him. She poured drinks into a pair of fresh glasses and leaned toward him intensely.

"I've been listening to you talk to my fool brother. Before he comes back, I want you to tell me your plan for defeating the invaders."

Reg's eyes opened wide. *Plan? He didn't have so much as a single solid idea, much less anything that could be called a plan.* But his mouth was too full of sweet, sticky fruit to say any of this to the woman staring at him across the table. He held up a finger and chewed rapidly. Hoping to clear his mouth, he took a swig of the drink she'd poured him. While it was an excellent brandy, it was also the first alcohol to pass his lips for many months. He shuddered and coughed as it crashed through his system. It was some moments before he was able to speak.

"Here's the thing, Miss Yamani, I don't have a plan. I don't think anyone does. We've never seen anything like this before, and at the moment, my only plan is to stay alive long enough to make a plan."

"Unacceptable," she said, shaking her head in disappointment. "We cannot simply wait here, huddled in the desert, while the world goes up in flames. They're moving, you know. They're moving toward a fresh set of targets. While you sit here chattering with Khalid and eating dates, we're being systematically exterminated."

Systematically exterminated. The ugly phrase put a knot in Reg's stomach and he reached for the bottle. "What about you?" he asked, pouring. "Do you have any ideas?"

For the first time, Fadeela's expression softened. She seemed surprised to be asked for her opinion. "Of course I have ideas. But this is Saudi Arabia and none of the men in charge is interested in what a woman might have to say."

"I'm listening," Reg said evenly.

"We need to find a way to penetrate their shields. How can we circumvent them? Are they vulnerable to electricity? To chemicals? Maybe to something as simple as water? We must try everything. What about nuclear weapons? We should be laying plans to attack their mother ship which is out in space. Perhaps that one does not have shields. There are still a thousand options."

Reg nodded seriously, as if he were considering her ideas despite their obvious impracticality. It didn't take Fadeela long to realize what he was doing.

"Don't patronize me, Major Cummins," she hissed. "It is true that I have no military training, but at least I realize the need to find a solution as quickly as possible. And the first thing I would change is that you foreigners should not be kept in isolation. We should all be talking to one another, searching for a strategy. We need more communication, not less. But that idiot Faisal does everything he can to keep you divided. It is easier to control you that way."

"In all fairness, Miss Yamani, the foreign pilots were divided long before we arrived here."

"Stop calling me Miss Yamani. My name is Fadeela," she said. "The point is that we can no longer afford to act like Saudis, or Iraqis, or Egyptians, or whoever. We must begin to think and act together, as humans!" She paused long enough to take a sip of her drink.

"I notice you and your brother have at least one thing in common. You both seem to dislike this Faisal character."

Fadeela's lips curled when she heard the name. "Ghalil Faisal makes all of his decisions based on his own interests. He is a snake."

"I'll keep that in mind."

There was an awkward silence during which Fadeela continued to stare across the table as if she were waiting for him to say something brilliant, something that would lead to the swift and sure destruction of the invaders. Reg tried to avoid making eye contact. Each time he looked at her, he felt thrown off-balance by her disconcerting green eyes and the beauty of her face—inappropriate thoughts during a military strategy session. He glanced out the window and saw that Khalid was still talking to the soldier.

"Major, I must ask you another question."

"Stop calling me 'Major,'" he said, imitating her. "My name is Reg."

She didn't react. "I am wondering, Reg, what is it that you fight for?"

The question took him by surprise. "I'm not sure what you mean. Are you asking what *cause* I'm fighting for?"

"Precisely. Do you fight for the love of your country?"

"I *serve* my country," he told her, "but I'm not one of these rah-rah, Rule-Brittania types."

"For a wife and children then?"

"Haven't got any of those. Why are you asking?"

Fadeela studied him sadly. "Because I don't see the man my brother has described to me."

"I'm afraid Khalid has a tendency—"

"His tendency," she interrupted, "has been to describe you as an intelligent and resourceful warrior. But you don't look that way to me."

Reg's anger flared suddenly to the surface. "Look here, princess, I'm awfully sorry I can't whip up a quick fix to your pesky alien problem, but I've trained half the men in your bloody air force. I'm a pilot and a teacher, and a damned good one. I don't need to apologize to you for not being something else!"

Fadeela leaned toward him, matching his anger. "The time for teaching is past us. Now is the time for action, for warriors. But you have nothing to fight for."

They stared murderously at one another until Reg sniffed and turned away. "It's been a long, hot day and I'm completely knackered. Maybe—"

"And don't call me princess," she interrupted again. "I hate that. I am *not* a princess." She stuffed the cork back into the bottle, put it back in its place then headed toward her room. She stopped and turned, wanting to say something before she left. All the harshness left her face as she struggled to find the words she wanted, but after a moment of trying, she gave up and closed the door.

3

Meetings

By the time Reg made his way back to the international side of the runway, darkness had fallen. He found that a small forest of tents had sprouted beneath the wings of the jet fighters. Reg had thought that the tents, a goodwill gesture from Faisal, might have fostered a spirit of cooperation among the different groups of pilots. Instead, they had only encouraged the contingents to move farther apart. The Iraqi tents were pitched as far as possible from the Iranians, Reg noted, and the Israelis appeared to have negotiated with the Jordanians so that Edward and his friends formed a buffer zone between Muslim and Jewish camps. A diagram of the camp would have nicely illustrated the geopolitics of the region.

Reg made his way toward the British tents, pitched directly beneath the wings of the Tornadoes. As he passed behind the one enclave, laughter rang out. Looking over, he saw that Thomson was sitting cross-legged among a group of Syrian pilots. As he thumbed through his phrase book, straining to read in the dim light cast by the small dung fire, one of the pilots threw some dried branches across the flames. The smell of sandalwood floated through the chill night air.

It's good he survived, thought Reg of the lieutenant colonel. *He may be setting himself up as a laughingstock, but he's doing a good job as ambassador-at-large, too.*

There was no movement at the British camp. A neat stack of dung briquettes sat next to a basket of scented kindling, but neither had been disturbed. Reg assumed the other two Brits were talking with some of the internationals. He'd not been lying to Fadeela when he told her he was tired, so he chose a tent at random and lifted the flap, intending to crawl inside and go to sleep.

There was a sudden movement inside the tent, followed immediately by the unmistakable metallic click of a pistol being cocked. Reg stumbled backward as Sutton emerged from the tent, looking around wildly, obviously just awakened.

Seeing Reg sprawled on the ground, Sutton put the gun on safety, and growled, "Damn it, Cummins! What the hell are you doing sneaking about?"

Sitting up and dusting sand off of his flight suit, Reg said, "Tad jumpy, aren't we?"

Tye crawled out of another of the tents, as Sutton replied, "You scared the piss out of me. In case you haven't noticed, there's an alien invasion going on. Call your name out next time." Sutton reached back into the tent for his boots, pulling out a pack of cigarettes as he did so.

Tye said, "So, Major, I guess you're pretty tight with the Saudis."

"What are you going on about now, Tye?" asked Reg.

"Well," said the young man, "that big captain knew your name. So did that Saudi pilot at the supply plane. Then you went off to the private planes while the rest of sat out here freezing our arses off. What kind of crazy place is this, anyway? Hot as the devil during the day, then cold as a Shetland Islands winter at night."

"That's the desert for you," said Reg. "As to being 'in tight,' that's probably an exaggeration. I have a few friends in the Saudi military establishment. Quite a few of these fellows went through the Flight and Training program at Khamis Moushayt."

"One of the Saudis at the supply plane told Yossi and me that you're a top gun, that you kicked some serious butt in Desert Storm."

"You heard wrong," said Reg a little too harshly. He didn't

want to discuss his performance during the conflict with Iraq.

Sutton had his cigarette lit and was looking doubtfully at the fuel they'd been provided for a campfire. "This grease monkey is convinced you're going to save us." He picked up a briquette and sniffed it. "What is this shit, some kind of charcoal?"

"You've got it backward. It's charcoal made out of shit," said Reg. "That's dried camel dung, Sutton." As the lieutenant cursed and began scouring his hands with sand, Reg turned to Tye.

"Look, lad," he said, "I can fly a plane, sure. But no amount of fancy flying is going to do us any good against these aliens. You saw their shields. You saw the maneuverability those fighters of theirs possess. If we're going to beat these bastards, it's not going to be through head-to-head aerial combat."

"Especially since there probably aren't that many combat aircraft left to send against them," said Sutton. "Rumors are going around, pretty much confirming what we heard from Khamis Moushayt before they went off the air. Thirty-six cities destroyed, and now the blighters have moved on to have a go at another thirty-six. A radio message came in from some Druse militiamen holed up in the mountains of Lebanon. They reported that the Jerusalem ship was moving into Jordan."

"What about the one over Turkey?" asked Reg, worried that they might have two ships to worry about in their neighborhood instead of just one.

"We've not heard anything at all from farther north," said Tye. "Which is just as well, I suppose, given what these Saudis are planning."

"And what's that?" asked Reg.

"That tall Ethiopian, Remi, told us that the Israelis told him the Saudis had been talking to the Egyptians. Apparently, they plan to go in with guns blazing if the local ship moves toward Mecca. They told the Egyptians the only way to get their planes refueled was to help defend the city."

Reg nodded meditatively. "Makes sense," he said. "From a Muslim's point of view at any rate."

"It doesn't make any kind of sense at all!" Sutton said.

"This Faisal is apparently some kind of religious fanatic!"

"Oh, come off it, Sutton," Reg said. "Mecca is one of the high holy sites of Islam. They've already seen Jerusalem destroyed, and the bulk of Saudi Arabia's domestic military doctrine is built around defense of Mecca. A lot of these pilots would consider it their sacred duty." Reg paused. "I hadn't thought of it; Jerusalem, Rome. I wonder if the aliens are intentionally targeting religious sites."

Tye pursed his lips. "Wasn't there one over Los Angeles?"

"Good point," conceded Reg. "It was just a theory."

Sutton angrily flicked his cigarette butt into the sand. "Don't give me that rot about 'sacred duty,'" he said. "These foreign pilots will take the Saudis' fuel and *say* they'll defend the city, all right. And then as soon as they're in the air they'll head off in whatever direction they please."

Tye chimed in, "That's what Lieutenant Sutton says we should do, too."

Sutton crouched in the sand between Reg and Tye. He handed his lighter to Tye and indicated that he should hold it to light the map he sketched in the sand.

"Look here," he said. "If these holy warriors will top off the tanks in our Tornadoes, we might be able to make it to Diego Garcia." He sketched a long line to the British possession in the Indian Ocean, site of a major British air base.

Reg shook his head. "We don't even know if the facilities there still exist. The aliens could have been there by now."

"That's a risk I'm willing to take," replied Sutton. "At least there's a chance we could be back among our own kind."

Reg sighed and crawled into one of the tents. "You're even less bright than I'd thought, Sutton," he called through the canvas. "Think about it. If we hadn't spotted the smoke from that crashed tanker today, we'd be dying of thirst in the deep desert, assuming we survived bailing out of our planes. And now you want to fly over open ocean with no satellite navigation aids and intermittent radio communications, hoping that you'll find the island before your fuel gives out."

"I'd risk it to get out of here," came Sutton's reply. "Look, Cummins, I think it's great that you're having a love-in with your Arab pals, but we've got to launch a counterattack against these damned aliens before it's too late. Sitting out here in the desert is a waste of everybody's time. We should *all* get back to our own armies. That's the only way we have a chance of making a difference; it's the only way to make sure we have a planet left to fight for."

Reg lay on his back in his tent. He had to admit that Sutton did have a point. There were too many factions in the desert camp, all working at cross-purposes. It would be impossible to plan an effective assault on the aliens.

He closed his eyes. It had been a terribly long day, the longest day of his life, and he desperately needed rest. But as he lay there, he couldn't stop his mind from churning. Sutton's last remark had been too close to the question Fadeela had asked him: What do you have worth fighting for?

When the moon had climbed above the dunes towering on the horizon, the representatives from each country present were again called to Faisal's tent. The British decided to try to get away with sending three representatives. Reg, Thomson, and Tye left Sutton to hold down the fort.

As they approached the runway, they were met by a pair of Israelis: the thin, bespectacled Yossi and his female commander. From the moment the Brits saw her, they could tell the Israeli pilot was wound tight. She had a trapped look. The name on her flight suit was Marx, but she introduced herself simply as Miriyam. She was short, solid, and strong. The dark circles under her eyes were visible even by moonlight, and her mass of coiled auburn hair bounced with an anxiety of its own.

"I can't believe that they've kept us out here all day," she said. "We need just two things from these Arabs: jet fuel and access to their radios. We have to insist on this, as a group. If they won't give us what we need, we'll have to take it."

Reg looked at Yossi, who merely shrugged. Neither the two of them nor Tye wanted to attempt calming Miriyam down. But then Thomson stepped into the breach.

"Captain, you might want to exercise some restraint in this meeting, as a woman. These Arab men are extremely old-fashioned, you know, not exactly a bunch of women's libbers."

Miriyam stepped up and grabbed Thomson by the lapels. The two of them were approximately the same height, but Thomson easily outweighed her. She took no notice of that as she lifted the colonel off his feet and spoke through clenched teeth. "I can handle myself."

As she eased Thomson to the ground, however, some of the anger seemed to go out of her. "I apologize," she said. "Of course you are right. I will try."

As they approached the command tent, they could see that it was already crowded. The flaps had been tied back, and several Saudi soldiers stood guard. The five of them stepped up to the entrance and peered inside. The tent was crowded with forty or fifty people, a mixture of Saudi officers and foreign pilots. They stood in small groups, speaking in hushed tones. Low-ranking officers moved through this edgy crowd, offering steaming tea in plastic cups. It had the appearance of a grim cocktail party.

As the five new arrivals hesitated at the entrance, a handsome Saudi officer made his way through the crowd, opening his arms to greet them.

"*Salaam alechem*, my brothers. I am Ghalil Rumallah Ibn-Faisal. It is the will of God that we meet here this evening. He has brought you here to support us in our fight against this most terrible enemy."

Reg hadn't recognized the camp's commander without his robes, but he saw now that this was the man who had spoken with the Saudi captain at the prayer session earlier in the day. Now he was dressed in a sharply tailored khaki dress uniform. Numerous military decorations were plastered across his chest.

Thomson greeted the man warmly. *The man's only been in Saudi Arabia for a day*, thought Reg, *but he already knows that flattery is the grease that turns the wheel here.*

"You Saudi chaps deserve three cheers from all of us," said

Thomson. "It took crack judgment and foresight to organize this camp as quickly as you've done. Without this base we'd all be lost, completely lost."

That's true enough, thought Reg, as a big smile spread across Faisal's face.

"How did your lot pull this all together so quickly?" Thomson asked.

Faisal joined them outside the tent and spoke. "I tell you, when I first saw the fires in the sky I trembled like a woman, but then I sank to my knees and prayed for direction. And Allah, in his wisdom, showed me what I should do. He told me to build an army in the farthest desert, where my people could gather themselves until the chosen moment. From this place, it was revealed to me, we will join the battle and win a glorious victory."

Reg kept his features schooled in a neutral expression, as did all of the others except for Miriyam, who scowled. And Thomson, of course, who nodded and grinned broadly.

"Sounds marvelous," said the colonel. "If this vision of yours is correct, it sounds like we can't lose."

Miriyam suddenly let out a sharp cry of disgust. "This is not a time for children's stories," she hissed. "God did not bring me here to fight under Arabs! We demand that you give us fuel at once so that we can return to Israel."

Yossi put his hand on her shoulder in an effort to calm her outburst. That only succeeded in making her angrier and louder. She pushed his hand away and stepped closer to Faisal.

"You can all stay out here in the middle of nowhere and talk to one another as long as you please!" she shouted. "Just give us our fuel!" The sound of her voice made several people in the tent turn to see what was happening.

Faisal's reaction surprised Reg. He expected the commander to react to Miriyam much as Khalid had to Fadeelah that afternoon. Instead, Faisal only seemed amused. In a voice loud enough to be heard throughout the tent, he addressed Yossi.

"Mr. Israeli," he said, "your superior officer, he is acting like a woman." Then, pretending to see her for the first time, he gasped, and said, "Allah be praised! He *is* a woman!" A wave of nervous laughter swept through the tent, but Faisal's smile melted as he took in the group of Brits and Israelis. He spoke again, this time much lower, and in a menacing tone.

"I am bound by a very old Bedouin custom," he told them. "I must welcome all who reach my tent. Even if he is my worst enemy, even if he is a jackal who murdered my only son, I must welcome him for a period of three days."

"What happens after three days?" asked Tye.

"The wise guest," answered Faisal, "doesn't stay to find out." He motioned for a pair of guards, who stepped between the Israelis and the entrance of the tent. Then he turned and looked directly at Reg.

"I think it would be best if these people waited outside. Englishmen are well-known for their fondness for Jews, so we will trust you to represent their interests at our planning conference." With that, he clapped a friendly hand against the back of Tye's neck, causing the sunburned mechanic to wince, and led the British pilots into the tent.

Thomson worked fast, attempting to smooth over the incident at the entrance. He introduced himself and his comrades. "We're beginning to add up to quite a force," he said to Faisal.

"Yes, Colonel," came the reply, "and we expect more pilots to join us soon. Small groups of planes have hidden themselves throughout the Empty Quarter. We are finding more of them with each passing hour through our radios."

Reg spoke for the first time. "There's a difference between gathering firepower and building an army, Commander. Without a common purpose, this is just a collection of men and machines." Thinking of Fadeelah, he continued, "There are some who might say that you've been hampering any chance for unity."

Again, Faisal looked amused. "Quite the opposite," he said. "In fact, I am confident that this meeting tonight will bring us together." With that, he walked away.

When he'd reached the lectern set up at one end of the tent, the Saudi commander addressed the crowd. "Take your seats, gentlemen," he called. The men arranged themselves on the carpets in a rough circle, with Faisal at the head. A dozen or so Saudi pilots, including, Reg noted, Khalid Yamani, sat in a row behind Faisal. Reg noticed for the first time that the coffee and tea services along one wall were being attended by a group of Saudi women, a flock of crows in their veils. Reg searched for a sign that Fadeela might be among them, but there was no way to penetrate the disguising *abayas*.

"This morning," Faisal began, "thirty-six of the planet Earth's largest cities were reduced to ash by the alien devils. The large ships, those of you who fought at Jerusalem called them city destroyers, then proceeded toward a second round of cities. Flights of the smaller ships have destroyed many secondary targets along the way, concentrating on military bases." There was an easy murmur in the crowd.

"Some of the second-wave cities have already been destroyed," Faisal continued. "Others face certain destruction within a short time. The situation is dire. But I do not believe that it is hopeless!" The commander pounded on his podium to emphasize this last point.

"The question before us now," Faisal said, "is a simple one. What course of action shall we follow? I seek your counsel. Who among you will speak first?"

The leader of the Iranians sprang to his feet. "We must attack them immediately!" he shouted. "Every pilot we have should be in the air." A handful of the men and even a few of the women shouted their approval, but one of the Syrians quickly rose to his feet, quieting the crowd.

"I agree with my Iranian brother that we must strike back as soon as possible," he said. "But we have seen their power. They are demons, yes, but demons possessed of incredible strength. Our normal tactics are useless against this enemy."

Another Syrian rose and picked up where the first had left off. "Therefore," he said, "we have developed a plan. A way to use the enemy's own tactics against them."

"Rather than attacking from many directions," continued the

first, "we will fly in a single column as we saw them do in the attack at Khamis Moushayt." Reg was startled at this revelation. He hadn't been aware that any intelligence on the Khamis Moushayt attack had been gathered.

"Using such a maneuver," the Syrian went on, "we can combine all of our firepower, bringing it to bear on a single concentrated point."

Anticipating the obvious argument, the second man spoke again. "This will, of course, leave our flanks exposed. We will surely lose many planes. But we believe that, in this way, we can break through the unseen shell that protects them."

Conversations erupted all over the room, points and counterpoints relative to the Syrian proposal being argued with ferocity. Just as Faisal was about to bring the group back to order, the voice of the Jordanian delegate, Edward, rang across the tent.

"These are the most powerful enemies humanity has ever known," he said. "We must use the most powerful weapons humanity has ever developed against them."

The room quieted instantly. Edward continued to speak into the stillness. "The Jews have nuclear weapons. But where are the Jews?" He looked around the room. "For the first time in my life, I want to see Jewish people, and now they have all disappeared."

Faisal spoke. "In fact," he said, "the Zionists are delaying the use of nuclear force only at the request of the United States. The American president has convinced the international community to delay their use until we can be sure that the aliens are vulnerable to them. They are preparing to launch a nuclear strike against the city destroyer approaching their city of Houston even as we speak."

A cocky young Iraqi pilot stood. "Chemical weapons, then. They might eat through those shields." The room exploded into debate once more, with the Iranians hurling invective against the oblivious young Iraqi. The Iranians well remembered the hundred thousand of their countrymen who had died when Iraq violated international law and used poison gases and biological agents in the Iran–Iraq conflict.

Faisal quickly brought their debate to a close, however. "This is not an option," he said flatly. "The Kingdom of Saudi Arabia does not own these ghastly weapons, and we will not permit their use within our borders."

With weapons of mass destruction at least temporarily ruled out, more and more of the pilots began speaking in favor of the Syrian plan. The feeling that some sort of immediate action was called for ran high in the tent.

Thomson, surprisingly, had remained quiet throughout the discussions, choosing instead to watch the interactions with great care. At length, he leaned over and spoke to Reg and Tye. "Look at these international pilots, will you? I don't believe they give a flying fig what we decide to do here. I suspect that as soon as they're fueled up and in the air, they'll be heading for home."

"I'm sure Faisal has given that possibility some consideration," Reg said dryly, still looking at the gallery of women. If Fadeela was among them, she made no sign.

"Major!" hissed Tye, drawing his attention back to the front of the tent. Faisal was pointing directly at him.

"For those of you who do not him," said the Saudi commander, "this is Major Reginald Cummins. He has lived among us for a long while, teaching our most advanced pilots. They tell me that he is the finest pilot in the Middle East." Reg saw Khalid nodding enthusiastically behind Faisal.

"Teacher," said Faisal, in an almost imploring tone, "tell us what we must do to defeat this enemy."

Placed firmly on the spot, Reg had no choice but to stand and address the crowd. He was sure they did not want to hear what he had to tell them.

"I know many of you were not involved in the fighting this morning," he said. "And I can understand your impulse to attack. But I know that many of you *were* there"—Reg glared at the Syrians as he said this— "and I can't believe that you're proposing a direct assault.

Some of the pilots who had remained silent until now nodded agreement. Reg continued, "The aliens are capable of putting five hundred of those attacker craft into the air within a matter of seconds. And when we fought them toe-to-toe this morning they went through us like we weren't even there. Even if we assume that a combined arms attack against the city destroyer's shield will bring it down—and I have my doubts about that—we'd be sitting ducks for half a thousand screaming fighters that carry their own shields! They'd take out every plane in your 'column' in a heartbeat. Why start a fight if we don't have the slightest chance of winning it?"

Pilots from more than one country shouted to be heard at once. The gist of what they were saying was that every hour of delay meant more devastation.

"Until something changes," Reg continued over the protests, "it would be suicide to confront them. As long as those shields are in place, there's nothing we can do."

"I think," said Faisal, "I think that our friend would not be so ready to make sacrifices if we were discussing English cities."

"At least one English city *has* been destroyed, Commander," Reg said. "As a matter of fact, except for the Israelis, we're the only people here who have lost a city to these attackers."

Thomson stood, joining Reg. He said, "We're looking at the bigger picture. This battle can't be about individual cities or countries. Not Birmingham or Cairo or Timbuktu. We are discussing how we can save the *world*."

Edward spoke again, tears in his eyes. "As we speak, one of the city destroyers is approaching my capital. That is my home. It is where I left my family. I don't know if my children are safe." He made no move to wipe away the moisture from his cheeks. "Amman will be destroyed in fire, and there is nothing I can do to prevent it. But I agree with these Englishmen. We must hold back and wait for the right moment to strike.

"It is logical that if they have come here to invade the Earth," Edward went on, "eventually their ships will land. Perhaps when they do, their shields will come down. And when that happens, we will be there to destroy them. But only if we are still alive. For the time being, we should wait."

Once more, discussions broke out around the room. As he

seated himself again, Reg felt a hand on his shoulder. Tye leaned over and whispered to him, "Have you forgotten about Lieutenant Sutton's plan, sir? We're supposed to convince them to get up into the air so we can head away."

Hearing him, Thomson leaned over to answer. "Odds are, that's what half the people in this tent are discussing right now."

Faisal allowed the debates to simmer for a few moments before he called for order.

"There are two plans before us," he said. "Some of you believe that we should strike immediately with all of our forces. Others counsel patience, advising that we wait for a surer opportunity for victory. I believe that the correct path lies between these two options. The orders I was given state that I am to continue standing Saudi policy and protect all parts of the kingdom. But after hearing your wisdom, I realize that these dark times call for compromise.

"For now, we will follow this good Jordanian's advice and bend our efforts to learning more about these villains. However, on one thing we must remain firm. If the aliens should send a ship against Mecca, the Holy City of our Prophet, then we shall attack no matter the cost. No matter the cost."

Tye whispered to Reg, "I told you that's what we heard."

"Because of the constraints on our supplies, I can only offer Saudi jet fuel to those pilots who will join us in this glorious task."

Exasperated, Thomson stood again. "We just went over this. Whether it's Mecca or any other city, the fact remains that a premature attack would be suicide. If we learn that a city destroyer is moving south, then we should, of course, evacuate the city, but there's no reason to send good men to their deaths."

Faisal spread his arms, holding palms upward. "All things are in the hands of Allah," he said. "A man who martyrs himself in the defense of Islam we call a *shaheed*, a witness. Those who join Faisal's *jihad* to defend Mecca will all bear this most honorable title."

Reg remembered what Fadeela had told him about Faisal's

thirst for glory. *And now he's running his own private* jihad, he thought.

Thomson was flustered. "Wouldn't it please Allah all the more for you to show patience and wait for a real chance to beat these monsters?" he asked.

"Allah rewards no one more richly than the *shaheeds*," Faisal countered. "A man who dies in the name of God while defending Islam ensures a place for himself and his family in Paradise, where he will be rewarded with seventy-two virgins."

"Virgins? What have virgins got to do with this?" asked Thomson, incredulous.

"Sounds lovely to me," said Tye.

Reg took advantage of the rough laughter that followed Tye's wistful comment to whisper to Thomson, "Don't try to argue the Koran with a Muslim, Colonel."

"Colonel Thomson," Faisal said, "perhaps it is impossible for you, a Christian man, to appreciate how important Mecca is to Muslims. We face it five times each day during our prayers. It is never far from our thoughts. It is literally the center of our world. It would be a form of suicide for us *not* to defend the city." He looked around the room. "How many of you Muslim soldiers are prepared to do nothing while Mecca is destroyed by fire?"

Faisal's gaze slowly swept the room his expression stern. Naturally, no one raised his hand. The commonality of purpose that appeared to pervade the room seemed, for the moment, quite genuine. But Reg's gut told him that the enthusiasm for Faisal's plan was manufactured, a smoke screen designed to give the pilots the opportunity to fuel up their jets and return to their home countries. Reg sighed, and stood once more.

"It's a bad plan, and I won't participate in it," he said. "Until the situation changes, it doesn't matter what city we're defending. And as to the holy purpose of this mission," Reg paused, not at all relishing what he was about to do, "as to the holy purpose, well, I hope none of you have it in the back of your minds to take advantage of Faisal's plan to fuel up and return to your homelands. It would be a simple matter, after all, for Faisal to keep a couple of chase squadron planes in flanking positions with orders to shoot down any deserters."

Many in the tent stared at Reg in angry silence, stunned that he was ruining their plan for escape. Faisal broke the silence.

"Major Cummins, your points are well made, and you are quite correct. I have anticipated that there might be some small number of false hearts and anticipated as well the necessity and the *means* to punish traitors and deserters."

His point to the other pilots made, Faisal turned a venomous grin on Reg. "I am not surprised that you cannot feel sympathy for a Muslim cause despite the friendship and admiration your Saudi students feel for you. I understand that you shot down a young Egyptian pilot this morning." He paused to let the accusation linger in the air for a moment. "Shot him down like a dog, though you had no authority over him, because he refused to obey your orders."

"That's a bloody lie, and you know it, Faisal!" shouted Tye, leaping to his feet for the first time.

Reg gestured for the mechanic to be seated, taking the opportunity to calm his own seething anger. "I didn't fire on the Egyptian, Faisal. I did what I had to do to save myself, and I did so in an attempt to lead the aliens away from Khamis Moushayt."

"And Khamis Moushayt is now in ruins, yes? And so the Egyptian boy is dead for no reason, as dead as all of the British and American pilots whom you failed to save when you fled into the desert."

Many of the Saudis and those international pilots who had not been part of Reg's group were now whispering to one another in angry tones, gesturing at him with thinly veiled contempt.

"Major Cummins," Faisal continued, "if you choose not to fight, so be it. May Allah forgive you." He turned to address the entire group. "And may Allah forgive all of you who will not join me in pledging to defend Mecca.

"Those of you who do not wish to join the *shaheeds* may leave us now. Your input is no longer needed."

During the first tense moments before anyone stood to leave,

Reg tried unsuccessfully to make eye contact with Khalid, but the usually cheerful young man was staring somberly at his feet. Edward was the first to stand and leave. Much to everyone's surprise, all three Syrians followed immediately behind the Jordanian. Then Remi, the lone Ethiopian, left. With a disappointed sigh, Tye stood, his head reaching almost to the roof of the tent.

"Well, I'd say that was a smashing failure. We might as well get out of here." One by one, exactly half of the international pilots filtered out of the tent. Reg was among the last to leave.

Before he turned, Faisal smiled at him once more, and said, "Who's standing in the way of unity now?"

That bastard planned every bit of this meeting, start to finish, thought Reg.

Outside, Thomson and Tye stood waiting for him.

"You didn't win us any friends with your last speech, Major," Thomson said.

"I'm not running for Most Popular Fighter Pilot, Colonel," Reg said, voice clipped. "Believe it or not, I'm trying to keep us all together."

Tye wasn't convinced. "Lieutenant Sutton's going to go ballistic," he said. "Now there's no chance for Diego Garcia." He glanced back into the tent. "No chance for virgins either, I'll warrant."

The Saudi guards posted outside the meeting didn't order the pilots back across the runway, so they stayed, waiting for the meeting to break up. None of the international pilots would even glance in Reg's direction.

The various factions whispered ominously to one another, glancing over their shoulders to make sure none of the Saudis was within earshot. It was a novel sight to see Miriyam, the Israeli firebrand, in hushed conversations with pilots from Iraq, Iran, and even Syria. Reg was certain they were hatching some scheme for seizing control of the fuel tanker; but as he was being shut out, it was only a guess.

Thirty minutes later, the meeting inside the tent was over, and the participants began to stream out into the cool midnight air.

They seemed to be in high spirits, confident that they would either turn back the invasion or earn Paradise trying.

Reg kept an eye out for Khalid. He wanted to speak to the young pilot and his father. It was Reg's hope that the elder Yamani held enough influence—and still had enough of his wits about him—to steer Faisal away from his plan. But when his former student emerged from the tent, Faisal himself his escort, arm draped over the younger man as if the two were long-lost brothers, Reg could only watch as they wandered away between the tents, locked in discussion.

"The meeting is now finished. You will return to your encampments!" It was the burly Saudi captain again, looking menacingly strong as he herded the international pilots across the runway.

Reg hung back in the shadow of an F-15 and managed to escape the notice of the Saudi guards. Once he was sure he was unobserved, he trotted quietly through the camp, making his way to the line of Learjets. Moving surreptitiously from plane to plane, he eventually came to the Yamani jet, light streaming from its portals. With a last glance around, he climbed the stairs and raised his hand to knock on the hatch.

"There is no one inside who wishes to speak to you, Major Cummins," came a soft voice from beneath the plane's fuselage.

Reg was startled, but he maintained an even demeanor as he leaned over and peered into the darkness beneath the jet. In her black *abaya*, Fadeela Yamani was an invisible specter. Only when her green eyes caught a flash of light from across the camp could Reg make out her location.

"I need to speak to your father and brother, Miss Yamani," Reg said formally. "Your Commander Faisal is determined to kill every man in this camp in his quest for personal glory."

"I am sure that is true, Major Cummins," she replied, stepping out of the shadows and motioning for him to join her on the ground. "But Ghalil ibn-Faisal is in that plane right now with my brother, seeking my father's blessing."

Reg glanced up at the portal nearest to him. Sure enough, just then Faisal's bulk passed the window as he paced, arms waving, obviously exhorting the Yamani men to throw their support to him.

"Guess I'll have to talk to them some other time," Reg said. He considered his best route back to the British tents, but then decided he wasn't quite ready to face Sutton's inevitable tirade. There was a break in the plateau lip near the Yamani jet, a draw filled with sand forming a rampway out into the dune sea.

"Think I'll just take a walk then, if you'll excuse me. Good evening, Miss Yamani."

He turned to go, but she caught his arm. "Major, wait. I'll join you."

Reg guessed that Fadeela was waiting outside of the plane on the orders of her father or brother, so that she would not disturb their meeting. He knew that her suggestion that she join him could land her in quite a bit of hot water if they were caught.

"Miss Yamani, the risk—"

"The risk, Major Cummins," she interrupted, "is mine to take." With that, she took his arm, and they walked quietly out into the dunes.

Once they were away from the camp and hidden from view in a depression between dunes, they sat on the slip face of one of the hills of sand and looked up at the stars.

"I'm surprised that you have any desire to be around me after our last conversation," Reg said.

"I was at the meeting tonight," she said. "And yes, I could tell you were trying to pick me out. I can play the anonymous role Islam demands of me when it suits my purposes, Reg."

Noting that they were on a first-name basis again, Reg asked, "What about the meeting made you decide that I was worth a stroll in the desert?"

Fadeela reached up and took off her headdress, shaking her hair loose and breathing the night air. "I decided that I was wrong about you, somewhat," she said.

"Somewhat?"

"Yes. You are a sensible man to oppose Faisal's plan, but you do not dismiss him or the others as fanatics as some among the Christians and Jews surely have."

"I've been knocking around the Islamic world for a long time, Fadeela. I know what Mecca means to you."

"No," she said. "Not to me. I am not Muslim, Reg, not in a way that the *imams* would acknowledge. I believe in a motivating force in the universe, but I do not believe that its only aspect is the God of the Prophet. There is much wisdom in the Holy Koran, and I pray dutifully. But when I open my heart in prayer, the God I feel is a nurturing force, feminine . . . and empowering."

Reg considered this. "I think you're right about the *imams*, there, Fadeela. Sounds a bit California."

"I asked you before what you had to fight for, Reg. You couldn't answer. In the meeting, though, I saw a spark of something in you. Maybe I should rephrase the question. Tell me, Reg, what do you believe in?"

"Well," Reg answered, "my mum raised me as a devout Apathetic, but as the years have passed I've found I just don't care that much about it anymore."

She chuckled, but didn't let him off the hook. "Always the glib comment," she said. "At least when you're not facing down enemy fighters."

"No," said Reg, "I'm at my glibbest in those situations."

"Warrior and clown, then," she said. "And neither mask is enough to hide the pain beneath."

Reg sat stock-still. How could she know?

"Do you know what I want, Reg Cummins?" she asked. "I want to drive a car. Isn't that funny? With all of the restrictions placed on women in Saudi Arabia, these clothes, our subservience to our husbands, with everything else, what I miss most about Stanford is driving. I suppose if I ever want to drive again, I'll have to go back there."

Relieved that she seemed to be changing topics, Reg replied, "Khalid said that your father was comparatively liberal with your upbringing."

"He was," she said. "He gave me enough freedom to want

more. That's another reason I can't say I'm really Muslim any longer. My cousins and aunts, they're all capable and intelligent women. Many of them chafe against the system, sure, but eventually they capitulate. Well, that's my word. They would probably say they grow up."

"It's a harsh system," Reg said.

She indicated the desert with a graceful sweep of her arm. "It was designed for a harsh people, Reg, a harsh people living in a harsh place. I can't live in it and be true to myself, but I can't condemn it outright either. Oh, I fight with Khalid to be sure. He really is a pig. But I don't want to cause him pain, any more than I want to cause my beloved father pain. But for me, pain is something to be healed"—she raised the scarf in her hand—"not hidden."

Hook, line and sinker, thought Reg, realizing that she'd caught him. *And I can't believe this, but I think I'm glad she did.*

Reg brought his hands together and thought, trying to find words. Finally, he said, "I flew bombers before I switched to fighters, in the war, I mean."

Before he could go on, a shout rang across the desert. "Miss Yamani? Are you out there?" It was Faisal.

"Damn the man!" she hissed. "He finished meeting with my father and brother earlier than I expected."

Other voices called her name, the sounds drifting across the dunes.

"You have to hide, Reg," she told him. "I will let them find me, but it is death for you if they find us together! Faisal will have you shot on sight!"

With that, she stood and headed back for camp. "Fadeela, wait!" Reg called softly, but just as she reached the crest of the dune, a flashlight beam played across her, illuminating her face as she hastily knotted the head scarf into place.

A gravelly voice shouted in Arabic, and Reg could hear more men converging on the opposite side of the dune. He crawled stealthily to the lip and looked down to see Faisal confronting Fadeela. A half dozen soldiers stood around him and a small, wrinkled man with a full turban and a long gray beard. Reg recognized the man as a *mutawa*, sort of a religious policeman.

The man was soundly berating Fadeelah, raising a hand as if to strike her, but instead stripping her hastily tied scarf from her head. Several of the soldiers laughed coarsely.

Eventually, Faisal stepped in front of the religious man and waved him off. He stepped closer to Fadeela and spoke to her gently. To Reg's shock, he reached out and gently stroked her face with the back of his hand. This sort of thing was expressly forbidden, Reg knew, but the *mutawa* just stood by, grinning. *Must be in Faisal's pocket,* thought Reg.

Fadeela stood her ground, straight as an arrow. Only when Faisal leaned in and made as if to kiss her did she break away, running for the ramp of sand that led to her father's plane. A pair of the soldiers moved to intercept her, but Faisal called them off. He said something to the *mutawa,* and they both laughed.

When the Saudis had gone, Reg crept away, making for the British tents.

4

A Much Too Crazy Plan

The second day of the end of the world began in silence. There were no sobs from those who had cracked under pressure. The foreign pilots who were unable to maintain at least a veneer of self-control, such as the Israeli Greenberg, had been removed in the night to the Tent of the Fearful, where they were injected with morphine.

Reg lay in his tent as the sun began to climb. The sounds of the camp slowly coming to life around him drifted through the canvas, but having made enemies of almost everyone in the camp the previous evening, Reg felt no great need to venture forth just yet.

Even as the morning wore on, the level of activity did not begin to approach the breakneck pace of the day before. It was as if everyone in the camp had taken time to ponder the tremendous gravity of the situation before them. Millions of people all around the world were dead, and more were no doubt dying with each passing moment, victims of a merciless enemy of seemingly limitless power. An enemy that Ghalil ibn-Faisal would soon be leading many of them against, no matter the odds.

Reg had no doubt that Faisal would lead his men against whatever city destroyer was nearest, whether it was actually headed toward Mecca or not. It was clear to him that Faisal intended to turn the desperate situation to his own advantage, no matter who suffered in the process. He would gladly pervert his pilots' genuine religious fervor to his own ends and force the less devout among them along by whatever means he had at his disposal.

The presence of the foreign pilots had no doubt complicated Faisal's plans considerably, but the man had proven to be a fast thinker, rapidly turning any situation to his own advantage. Reg thought of all of these things, and of Fadeela, until the heat of the day eventually forced him to leave the tent.

It was around ten in the morning and the sun had only just begun its daily assault, already pushing the mercury past a hundred degrees Fahrenheit. The other British pilots were just returning to their area, pink-faced and soaked with sweat. Thomson had brought Reg some breakfast, a paper cup filled with cold yellow beans in a spicy red sauce. Tye contributed some broken crackers from one of his many pockets to round out the meal.

None of the three had done much more than mutter a greeting before Reg dipped his cup in the communal water bucket and sat back on his haunches in the fractionally cooler shade of a Tornado.

Thomson, looking as if he were finally running out of hope, spoke to Reg. "Guess you haven't heard about Houston, then," he said.

Reg remembered Faisal's news of the Americans' planned nuclear assault from the night before. A single glance at the faces of the other three RAF men was enough to tell him that the attack had met with failure.

"We're screwed backwards and sideways," said Sutton. "What else can we throw at those bastards?"

"Edward talked to one of the radiomen. They said the Americans reported that the destroyer didn't even move when the bomb went off. Those shields must be impenetrable."

Reg took a drink of water. "I wonder if this changes Faisal's thinking at all," he said.

"I hope not," muttered Sutton darkly.

Reg looked around at the other three men, noticed how none of them would meet his eye.

He sighed, and chose Tye. "Okay, what is it?" he asked the tall youth.

"What's what?" Tye asked in turn.

"What is it you're not telling me?"

"I don't know what you're talking about," Tye answered. Reg hadn't thought it possible for the mechanic to turn any redder, but as he lied, Tye's face glowed a fraction more crimson.

Thomson shifted uncomfortably, then threw his hands up in the air. "It's vile," he said, "but we can't just sit out here forever."

"Did we not agree just five minutes ago not to tell him until after the Saudis took off?" snarled Sutton.

Reg held up his hand. "No, no," he said to Thomson. "Don't go against the plan. What if I'm captured, and Faisal turns his knife boys loose on me to find out what I know, eh?"

He stood and stretched, looking around at the other international contingents. He saw that the Israelis had removed the access panels from their fighters and were tinkering in the electronics compartments.

"As long as I don't know what you lot are up to, I can't give away the plan," he said, turning back to the others. He walked over and crouched next to Sutton.

"As it is, I'll have to tell them something to save my own skin, of course. Just make up something nonsensical. What should I tell them?"

The surly lieutenant scooted away from Reg. "I don't care what you tell the buggers," he said.

"How about this, then?" Reg asked. "How about I tell them that we've estimated that the Saudis have about two hundred men in this camp all told, and that we figure they've got about a hundred and twenty operational planes." Tye looked up at Reg, eyes wide.

"Once they fly off to bring everlasting glory to Ghalil ibn-Faisal," Reg continued, "that leaves just eighty or so soldiers guarding the camp—and the fuel dump. And, of course, the fifty or so international pilots who haven't signed on with Faisal's *jihad,* I suppose they'll still be here. Playing cards, probably."

Thomson looked vaguely embarrassed, but said nothing. "Next," said Reg, "I'll get really creative. I'll tell them that the Israelis almost always stockpile small arms and the odd submachine gun on their planes in case they go down in hostile territory. These Arabs will believe any crazy thing about the Jews, won't they, Sutton?"

"Who told you?" the lieutenant muttered under his breath.

But Reg wasn't finished. "Now, by that point, Faisal's men will probably be really angry with me. They'll ask me what kind of fools I take them for. *'The foreign pilots conspiring to take over the camp once the bulk of our forces are away?'* they'll say. *'That crazy Miriyam distributing guns?'*"

"You've made your point, Major," said Sutton.

"*'Do you think we're children, Englishman?'* I hope there's no kicking. I can't bear to be kicked. *'What makes you think we'd believe the foreigners would come up with such a STUPID, BLOODY OBVIOUS PLAN?'*"

"Sutton here was pretty sure it would work," said Tye.

"Shut up, Tye," said Sutton.

Reg turned to the colonel. "You realize there are civilians over there," he said.

"I told you he'd be a problem," Sutton fumed to the others. "Look here, Cummins, that Miriyam has got it all figured out. You can sit here and take shit from Faisal all you want, but the rest of us have better things to do. The only thing we need from you is that you keep your mouth shut, understood?"

"Lieutenant Sutton," said Reg, "if I didn't know any better, I'd think that you just addressed a superior officer in a disrespectful tone. Shame, shame, Sutton. Shame, shame."

Before the lieutenant could reply, there was a commotion on the opposite side of the runway. One of the radiomen, still wearing his headphones, was trotting toward the British planes. He was clutching a piece of paper in his hand and shouting in Arabic. One of the guards along the perimeter of the foreign enclave waved him through.

The man stood before them, then, still shouting, obviously repeating himself and stumbling over words in his haste.

"What the devil is he saying?" asked Thomson, frantically thumbing the pages of his phrase book once more.

Reg had been listening to the man closely. Finally, he raised his hands, indicating that radio operator should calm down. "*Feh hemt, feh hemt*," said Reg. *I understand, I understand.*

The radio operator nodded, then ran to the next encampment, where he spoke just as swiftly to the Egyptians.

Reg spoke to his companions. "He says they're picking up some kind of message in English, along with some Morse code. They can't understand all of it. Let's go have a look."

"Wait," Sutton said. "That doesn't make any sense. They've got plenty of men over there who speak English. They don't need us. Sounds like an ambush."

Reg looked at Sutton gravely and nodded. "You may be right. They'd obviously want us to be standing next to *their* airplanes instead of *our* airplanes when they open fire. I'll give you a detailed report if I make it back alive."

When Reg began running toward the radio tent, he found that Thomson was right on his heels.

"Slow down, Cummins," puffed the colonel. "I'm coming along."

"What about Sutton's ambush?" Reg asked.

"To hell with Sutton." The portly colonel waved his arms. "I'm going to ambush *him* if I have to stay around him much longer."

Members of almost all of the other international contingents were converging on the radio tent. Reg was startled to see that many of them were now openly carrying weapons. Sensing one such armed man beside him, Reg turned to see Yossi, trotting along and carrying an Uzi.

When he saw Reg looking at him incredulously, Yossi shrugged, and said, "Miriyam said I should invite myself along. I thought I'd stick close to you Englishmen, since 'your fondness for Jews is well-known.'" His imitation of Faisal was surprisingly good, but Reg doubted that it would come in handy if any of the Arabs were unhappy with a gun-toting Israeli showing up at the radio tent.

There was a crowd around the radios. The shaded area beneath the open-sided camouflage tent looked like an electronics bazaar. Much of the equipment Faisal's team had gathered up was surplus, some of it older than the soldiers themselves. The tent resembled an Arab market, with fifty different conversations going on at once. But the noise and activity quickly melted away as the foreign visitors stepped beneath the canopy inside. As Reg had feared, the Arabs interpreted Yossi's presence as a taunt.

Khalid hurried toward Reg and pulled him to one side. "They have destroyed Amman, and now they are moving south. I spoke with Faisal and tried to convince him we should follow your advice, but he is committed. Unless the ship changes course, he will order an attack within the next two hours."

As Reg listened, he watched over Khalid's shoulder, keeping an eye on the other Saudis. Some of them were demanding that Yossi state his business, meaningfully grasping the handles of their pistols. Finally, one of them thumped the Israeli in the chest, and shouted, "*Imshi!*" *Scram!*

Reg interrupted Khalid. "How do you say 'lawyer' in Arabic?"

Khalid blinked, confused by the question. But he answered. "*Advocat.* Why?"

"Going to use some Thomson school diplomacy," Reg said before he joined the knot of Saudis surrounding Yossi. Once among them, he shook his finger at the largest man, loudly proclaiming something in halting Arabic. There was a brief silence, then all of the Arab speakers in the area began laughing.

Remarkably, Thomson had left his phrase book at the camp. "What did you say?" he asked.

"I said not to worry about Yossi. He's our lawyer."

One of the radio operators pointed at the machine gun the Israeli soldier held and cracked a joke of his own, which Khalid translated: "*Yes, and I see he remembered to bring his fountain pen!*" When the men had had their laugh, they began turning back to their workstations.

"Now," Reg asked, "where's this Morse code?"

Khalid led the way to the center of the tent, where the camp's best radio was being monitored by a trio of technicians. They were all listening intently, scratching out notes on pads of paper. By their expressions, Reg could tell they were frustrated. One of them slipped off his headphones and handed them over to Reg.

He put them on, expecting to hear a sequence of dots and dashes. Instead, there was a roar of static. It seemed to be nothing but a storm of interference noise, but then he heard it: a faint voice shouting through the blizzard. Reg closed his eyes and tried to make out what the voice was saying. . . . *States government has captured . . . shield we will . . . alien mother ship outside . . . do not engage . . . forces happy . . .* The voice belonged to an American man who was speaking in an urgent but controlled tone. It seemed impossible to piece together the fragments of what he was saying.

If this broadcast is coming from America, thought Reg, *there's no telling how many times it's been relayed, boosted, and amplified before it reached the Empty Quarter*. "Can't make it out," Reg said to the operator sitting next to him. "It's just so much sonic mush." He began to remove his headphones, but the Saudi motioned for him to keep listening.

"Wait," said the man. "You will hear."

He was right. A few seconds after the voice transmission was finished, a Morse sequence began. This, too, was faint, frequently interrupted, and barely audible. Reg quickly realized the spoken message was being repeated in this different form. He grabbed a pad and pencil and began writing, decoding as he went. The brief message was continuously recycling itself, and, after ten minutes, Reg had as much of it as he thought he could gather.

Everyone in the tent waited anxiously as Reg compared his own notes to those taken by the other men. Like a person solving a crossword puzzle, he fit the pieces together fragment by fragment. When he was finished, he read it over a couple of times and couldn't help but smile. When he stood up from the table, every pilot in the immediate vicinity rushed up to hear the news.

"It's from the Americans," he announced. "They want to organize a counteroffensive." A guarded cheer went through the crowd.

"It's about bloody time," Thomson harrumphed. "What's their plan?"

"It's . . . well, it's damn creative."

"Read it!" several men demanded. Soldiers and civilians were streaming in from all directions.

Reg cleared his throat. "It says: 'To any and all remaining armies of the world. The U.S. military has captured one of the alien attack ships, has learned to circumvent and disable its protective shield. We will attempt to disable all shields worldwide. Preparing now to infiltrate alien mother ship outside Earth's atmosphere and use computer interface to temporarily disable source of shields. If successful, we anticipate only a small window of opportunity. Please commit all possible military resources to worldwide synchronized attack to begin at approximately 03:15 GMT. We will announce success or failure of our mission at that time. Conserve your weaponry. Do not engage enemy. Accept civilian losses. This action authorized by U.S. President Thomas Whitmore. Continue to monitor this frequency. Relay message to other forces in your area. Happy Independence Day.'"

As one of the radio operators repeated the message in Arabic, the tent and surrounding area filled with murmured discussions. Reg looked down at the paper in his own hand. The word *harebrained* went through his head, followed closely by *impossible*.

But then again, at least it's a plan, he thought. *And who knows? The Americans have surprised me before.*

After the initial flush of enthusiasm, questions and reservations about the plan started to crop up. How were the Americans going to get into the mother ship? How were our computers going to interface with the alien technology? How would anyone know when the shields were down, assuming they ever came down at all? "No, no!" protested one of Khalid's men. "This is a bad plan, too much crazy."

But this man was in the minority. More and more of the pilots, both Saudi and international, began discussing how the group might work together to fulfill their role in it.

Then, from the edge of the tent, a booming voice interrupted the gathering. "We Arabs are a proud people until our foreign masters tug on the leash," said Commander Faisal, striding to the center of the group. "Then we forget our own obligations in an instant." He was obviously displeased with the way some of his men were embracing the new plan. He shook an admonishing finger at them. "As soon as the Americans, the *infidel* Americans, speak, you turn into lapdogs! A few words over a radio, and you forget the Holy City!"

Reg felt the energy and enthusiasm begin to drain from the group. The influence that Faisal had over his men could not be underestimated. He was a charismatic man, capable of rousing hearts and raising morale with a few well-chosen words.

Somebody needs to choose the right words to turn this thing around, Reg thought. *This American plan is madness, but it's the only chance we've got.* Reg looked at Thomson, considering whether the colonel would be able to turn the tide of opinion against Faisal.

"I think someone's trying to get your attention, Major," Thomson said. Reg looked to where the colonel was pointing and saw a handful of Saudi woman. Piercing green eyes stared at him from behind the shrouding *abaya* of the tallest. It could only be Fadeela.

Knowing that there was no way, in this public forum, that she would be able to speak to him, Reg watched as she slowly raised her arm and pointed directly at him.

She's thinking the same thing I am, Reg thought, *and she wants me to talk to these men. But they despise me after last night!*

Fadeela lowered her arm, but continued to hold him in her gaze. He could see the questions in her eyes. *What do you have worth fighting for? What do you believe in?*

Reg considered then that Fadeela Yamani might be the bravest person he had ever known. She lived her life as if walking a treacherous path, fraught with danger. Holding to the strictures of her society on the outside, internally she longed for a life of independence, of freedom of a sort no one in her position should ever hope to obtain. But she did not give up hope; she did not give up the fight.

It's her, Reg thought, simply. *She's worth fighting for. I believe in her.*

Reg saw a half-full water barrel immediately behind the spot where Faisal still stood, haranguing his men. He walked over to it and did something guaranteed to draw the rapt attention of every one of these desert-bred men. He turned it over.

Faisal cursed and leapt away, narrowly avoiding muddying his highly polished boots. When he turned, Reg had already overturned the barrel and climbed atop it.

Reg clutched the American message in his hand and held it above his head. "This plan," he said in a loud voice, "may be the most foolhardy damned plan I've ever heard of. There's no logic to it! It depends on a thousand variables and perfect timing among hundreds of units spread across the globe." One of the Saudi soldiers started to approach, but Reg saw Faisal wave him off. *He thinks I'm going to argue for doing nothing*, thought Reg. *Good.*

Reg caught the eye of the pilot who had disparaged the plan earlier. "'Too much crazy,' right? Risking all on a one-in-a-million chance that the Americans will accomplish what? That they'll shut down the shields for a few moments at best! Their President Whitmore must think we're crazy!" A few of the Saudis were nodding, but Reg saw that more of them were disappointed that he wasn't arguing *for* the plan. *I don't want to be a disappointment*, he thought, and continued speaking.

"Or maybe I should say that Whitmore must *hope* we're crazy. The Americans must *hope* that we'll join them. That is, after all, what they're offering us. Hope. The first glimmer of hope we've had since the aliens destroyed Jerusalem."

"Hear, hear!" shouted Thomson. Several of the other pilots joined him in shouting encouragement.

"We're from different countries," Reg continued. "We speak different languages. Two days ago some of our countries were openly hostile to one another. Do you remember? Do you remember two days ago? It seems like ten years, doesn't it? Those old conflicts, those hostilities, they're meaningless now. What's important is what we have in common. What we have in common is the greatest enemy mankind has ever known. And now we have hope!" More of the men shouted approval, and Reg kept on.

"We have hope that we can knock the invaders from the skies! We have hope that we can take back what is ours! We have hope, a *real* hope, of fighting a battle we can win!" They were his now, Reg saw. Every pilot within earshot was clapping and shouting, banging their hands against barrels like impromptu percussionists or simply jumping up and down. Every pilot except one.

It's one thing to convince them, thought Reg, staring at the grim visage of Ghalil ibn-Faisal, *but another thing altogether to convince the man with the power.* Again, Reg remembered what Fadeela had told him, that here was a man motivated solely by personal glory.

"Or maybe," Reg said, holding his hands up for silence, "maybe we should act prematurely. Maybe we should throw ourselves against the aliens *before* their shields are knocked down, *guaranteeing* that they will destroy us, and survive us. Maybe we should make a futile gesture instead of a genuine attack, and *ensure* the destruction of Mecca. And Riyadh. And Baghdad, and Addis Ababa, and every other place any of us hold dear.

"Maybe it won't come to that, though. Maybe some pilots from somewhere else in the world will be able to take out our assigned city destroyer after they've saved their own people. After all, just because we don't fulfill our part of the bargain doesn't mean that the other thirty-five ships won't go down. Just the ship in the Middle East left. And why? Because when it finally counted the most, the people of the region couldn't act together for the common good. When it finally mattered the most, the chance at the glory of victory wasn't enough to make them see something bigger than their own problems."

"No!" shouted a voice from the crowd, and Reg saw that it was Yossi.

"We *can* work together," said another voice, a Syrian.

"Can you?" asked Reg. "Can Muslims and Christians and Jews fight side by side?" The crowd roared, *"Yes!"*

"Can Persians and Arabs and Europeans and Africans unite to rid the world of this horrible scourge?" And again they roared, *"Yes!"*

Then Reg threw his own arms into the air, and shouted, "Victory!"

The cheer spread through the whole camp in a heartbeat. *"Victory! Victory! Victory!"* The desert rang with the international chorus.

Climbing down from his makeshift pulpit, Reg caught sight of Fadeela once again. Was it possible to notice a grin from behind an *abaya*? He thought so.

"You are quite a speech maker, Major Cummins," someone behind him said. It was Faisal, of course. "I can raise no objection to the American plan now. But it will have to be incorporated into my own, of course." The Saudi commander held up a dispatch.

"The alien ship has turned south, toward Mecca. We will fly to defend the Holy City, as planned. If the Americans have brought the shields down by the time we arrive, so much the better." Faisal wadded up the paper and threw it in the sand at Reg's feet.

"In *either* case," he continued, "once they pass the city of Usfan we will attack."

5

Counterattack

The main battle in the camp that afternoon was between dehilitat-ing heat and the determination of the pilots to prepare their planes for the showdown. The work required them to spend long stretches of time exposed to the punishing sun. They stripped parts off of the damaged jets in order to repair others, replenished their fuel tanks one bucket at a time, and jury-rigged missile firing systems to accommodate unfamiliar weaponry. There was little time to dis-cuss strategy and tactics. As the sun leaned to the west and the men in the radio tent continued to track the city destroyer's progress toward Mecca, the pilots went through their final checklists.

At five-thirty the planes were lined up on the runway, ready to go. Nearly two hundred pilots climbed into their cockpits and fired up their engines. But Reg was still on the ground inspecting the Tornado that had been Thomson's plane and stealing occa-sional glances toward the Saudi camp. Since Thomson was the least accomplished pilot among the Brits, he had volunteered to sit with the Saudi radio technicians to help decode the next mes-sage from the Americans. Sutton and Tye, already strapped in, were watching Reg, wondering what was taking him so long. A moment later they had their answer. From between the Saudi tents, a veiled woman emerged and marched purposefully onto the runway. Her black, ankle-length *abaya* moved in time with her long, athletic stride, and she carried something in her hand.

Reg knew who it was. Like a smitten teenager, he'd delayed getting into his plane for as long as he could, hoping that she would find some way to see him off. He'd hoped that she would wave to him from between the tents, or send word through a messenger. But Fadeela was bolder than that. She walked directly up to him, ignoring the hundreds of people who were watching, and handed him a photograph. Reg caught a quick glimpse of her bright green eyes before she turned on her heels and walked away without a word.

He looked down at the photograph. It showed a young girl—too young to wear a veil—riding a camel toward the finish line of a race. Her green eyes were turned toward the camera, and she was laughing triumphantly. He turned it over and read the words written on the back: "A kiss for luck."

A smile spread across Reg's face as he tucked the photograph into his breast pocket. *It's almost as if she can read my mind,* he said to himself as he climbed into the jet. *It's exactly what I needed. Something to remind me what I'm fighting for.*

They flew west, nearly two hundred strong, to the edge of the desert before turning due north. Eighty of the Saudi planes took the lead, flying in crisply formed wedges. They were followed by the international pilots, seventy-three of them, straggling along in ragtag fashion. Another Saudi squadron brought up the rear, prepared to hunt down any pilot who tried to run. They followed the Asir mountain chain up the country's west coast. The terrain on the two sides of the mountains was starkly different. To the left, the hills were covered with trees all the way down to the lush coast of the Red Sea. To the right, rocky cliffs and canyons ran down to the lifeless floor of the Empty Quarter's great sand desert. There was no sign of the enemy, but for the first time in years, Reg felt nervous being up in the air.

As they approached Mecca, they looked down at an awesome spectacle. From all directions, the Islamic faithful were converging on the Holy City. For mile after mile, the highways were choked with traffic. Brightly painted buses, private cars, and rivers of people on foot were all surging toward the famous mosque.

"Major Cummins," Faisal's voice came over the radio, "ahead you can see our Holy City. I think you are very fortunate to see this sight. Under normal circumstances, of course, only believers are allowed here. So today, I declare you and the others to be honorary Muslim pilgrims—*hajjis*."

"*Allah inshallah*, old bean," Reg said, smiling.

As they caught sight of Mecca's great mosque, they saw that there was a sea of believers crushed into the immense courtyard. They were moving in slow circles around the cube-shaped Kaaba, the shrine that stood at the center of the open space. According to Muslim belief, this stone structure was originally build by the first man, Adam. As the planes roared past, many of the Arab and African pilots broke into the same ritual prayers being chanted by the faithful below: Lord God, from such a distant land I have come unto Thee . . . grant me shelter under Thy throne.

Several minutes north of Mecca, Faisal's voice returned to the airwaves and called everyone's attention to a small city nestled in the hills. It was Usfan, the place he had chosen as his line in the sand, the point beyond which he would not allow the aliens to pass.

Directly ahead, the monstrous bulk of the city destroyer hovered like an airborne cancer between the blue sky and the dun brown earth. The radios erupted with nervous chatter as the pilots called out the sighting. A moment later, Thomson's voice came from the radio tent back in the Empty Quarter.

"Sounds as if you've made visual contact. Is that right?"

He was answered simultaneously in half a dozen languages. Everyone monitoring the frequency confirmed that the destroyer was in sight, then began asking the colonel for information on its airspeed, elevation, and distance.

"Pilots, pilots," Thomson broke in, "these transmissions are being recorded. Please try to speak one at a time, and identify yourselves when you do."

"What the hell is the point?" asked Sutton, his voice dripping with disgust.

"The point, Lieutenant Sutton, is that you never know. If you chaps pull off a miracle and beat these sons of bitches, it'll be one for the history books. This audiotape we're making might show up on the BBC someday, and you'll be famous."

Sutton scoffed. "Thomson, I wish you were up here to see this thing we're facing. Then you wouldn't sound so damn chipper. In a day or two, there's going to be no one left to read any history books. But go ahead and make your tape. Maybe the aliens will find it someday and get a good laugh out of it."

Tye came on the radio. After stating his name as the colonel had asked, he said, "The thing I would like to add to the historical record is that I wish Sutton would keep his bleeding pie hole closed until he has something useful to say for himself."

Several other pilots laughed and seconded Tye's motion.

At a distance of fifty miles, the dome-shaped saucer began to dominate the skyline. It was plowing inexorably forward at approximately two hundred miles an hour, the embodiment of certain doom.

Faisal continued to lead them straight toward the obsidian tower that marked the prow of the destroyer until, at a distance of twenty-five miles, he banked away to the right. Group by group, the rest of the jets followed suit.

"Ten more minutes, Teacher," Khalid radioed to Reg. "In ten minutes we find out if the Americans were successful. I don't think the alien ship will reach Usfan before then."

"I agree," Reg said, "but that's not going to leave us much of a cushion."

"Not to worry," Miriyam said. "I already did the math. We have twenty minutes until they get to Usfan."

"Which means we have a little more than ten minutes to bring down the destroyer before it reaches Mecca," Reg pointed out. He studied the massive alien ship before adding another thought. "Even with their shields down, our missiles might not be enough."

"Luckily we are not the only ones here," said Remi, the Ethiopian pilot they'd met the previous afternoon. "More and more jets are coming every minute." It was true. There were at least a dozen groups of fighters in the area, but they looked pathetically small compared to the advancing city destroyer.

"There is no reason to worry," Edward said, trying without success to mask the fear in his voice. "Today will be like the story of David and Goliath. We'll find a way to knock down this giant with our small weapons."

Yossi couldn't let the opportunity to needle Edward slip past. "David was a Jewish hero, you realize."

Edward laughed. "Yes, I know. But he's like the Palestinians. We used to fight your Israeli armored jeeps with only bricks and stones."

"And look how successful you were," said one of the Iraqis. "You had to run away and live in Jordan."

After a long pause, Edward spoke again. "You're right. But today will be different. Today, the little guys are going to win."

Pondering Edward's prediction, the pilots maintained a tense radio silence for the next few minutes, hoping to hear from the Americans. At exactly 6.15, the moment the message was scheduled to arrive, the radio erupted with shouting. It was not the Americans; it was Faisal. He began issuing a long string of orders, speaking only in Arabic. The Saudi jets that had been flying at the rear of the formation accelerated past the international contingent to join the rest of their countrymen.

"Would someone care to translate?" Tye asked. "What's going on?"

"It's obvious, isn't it?" Sutton grumbled. "They're preparing to attack."

Reg could see that Sutton was right. Faisal wasn't going to allow the Americans any extra time, even though the destroyer was still miles from Usfan. As the Saudi F–15s positioned themselves, Faisal monopolized the airwaves, calling to his men in an urgent but controlled voice.

Reg thought a premature strike would be disastrous on two counts. Not only would it be a waste of scarce firepower; it might also draw the scarablike attacker ships into the air. If their shields were still operational, they would make short work of the few hundred jets that had massed for the counterattack. He shouted into his radio, trying to get the Saudi commander's attention and urging him not to jeopardize this last, slim hope of bringing down the enemy ship.

Faisal ignored the warning and continued speaking to his men in the rhythmic, hypnotizing voice of a fire-and-brimstone preacher. Although Reg couldn't understand the individual words, he knew Faisal was exhorting his pilots to bravery and self-sacrifice, preparing them for martyrdom.

"I'd just like to point out," Sutton said quietly, "that now would be an excellent time for us to get the hell out of here." Ever since the Saudi watchdog planes had moved forward to join the attack formation, members of the international squadron had been quietly peeling away and flying toward their home countries. Nearly a third of them were gone. "Anyone out there interested in heading for Kuwait?"

No one answered. Everyone who was going to run had already done so. As Faisal's speech built in intensity, Reg and the others kept their ears open, hoping to receive word from the Americans before the Saudis launched their attack.

"Khalid Yamani, can you hear me?" Reg called. "You've got to convince him to wait. Tell Faisal to give it five more minutes."

There was no reply.

As Faisal's speech reached a crescendo, he shouted a question to his men, and they responded with a roaring war cry. Then the entire squadron turned as one and broke into an attack run. They dived at a steep angle, picking up speed as they streaked toward the their target, the destroyer's obsidian tower. To Reg, it was a horrible, incomprehensible sight. He sensed that a hundred men were about to give up their lives in exchange for nothing.

"Khalid, if you can hear me, break off," Reg said desperately. "Get out of there before they launch their attack ships. Save yourself for the real battle." To Reg's surprise, Khalid answered.

"Too late, Teacher," he said in a calm but tremulous voice. "Together, we will either shoot these infidels down, or we will die in glory. All things are in the hands of Allah."

"The words of a doomed man," said Miriyam.

Reluctantly, Reg admitted to himself that she was right. There was nothing more he could do for Khalid. "Let's start climbing," he told the others as he pulled back on his controls. "As soon as they launch, we're going to have company up here."

"Alien fighters?" Edward asked.

"And plenty of them."

As Reg turned, he couldn't resist taking one last glance back at the diving squadron. When he did, he noticed something out of place. One of the Saudi jets lagged behind the others before turning sharply in a new direction. Reg thought he could guess who was piloting the rogue jet.

"Commander Faisal," he said, "it looks as if you have broken formation. Where are you headed?"

There was no answer. The squadron continued to plunge toward the mammoth alien airship.

Reg shouted, "I repeat: Saudi commander, you have broken formation. You are currently running in the wrong direction."

This time Faisal answered. "Do not interfere!" he screamed. A moment later, he had gathered himself and continued in a calm voice. "I'm afraid you are mistaken, major. You must be watching the wrong plane."

Reg stared down at the tiny shape of the wayward F–15 and decided to bluff. "Negative, Faisal. I'm directly above you. Close enough to read your wing markings. You are running away from the engagement."

After a moment of hesitation, Faisal answered. "Stay out of this, Cummins! I am not running. I am . . . I am positioning myself to observe the attack."

"Admit it, Faisal!" Reg shouted. "You're saving yourself because you know what's going to happen to those men. Order them to it break off."

"Damn you, Cummins, stay quiet! Cooperate with me and you will be rewarded."

"And if I don't?"

"Then I will personally shoot you out of the sky."

Reg, boiling with anger, resisted the impulse to swoop down on Faisal and unload every piece of ammunition he had aboard his aircraft. Instead, he sucked in a deep breath then growled into his headset. "I wouldn't advise it. You'd only be wasting another one of your king's planes."

Faisal scoffed. "King Ibrahim is no longer a factor. The Saudi Air Force is now completely under my command and it is my will that—"

Reg cut him off and switched back to the previous frequency. "Khalid, look around. Faisal's gone. He knows you're doomed and he's saving himself. Get out of there now!"

Khalid and several of his fellow pilots began speaking to one another and quickly realized that Reg was right—Faisal had deserted them. Khalid swung into a turn, shouting instructions in Arabic.

"What's he saying?" Reg demanded.

Edward translated. "He's calling on the other pilots to follow him."

Only twenty of them did. They wheeled out of the attack formation and began looping around to rejoin Reg's squadron just as the Saudis fired on the destroyer. They unloosed a huge barrage of Sidewinders and Sparrows, which sliced through the late-afternoon sky, all headed for the same target area. Taken together, the missiles carried enough explosive charge to flatten a medium-sized city, but when they came to within a quarter mile of the destroyer, they all detonated harmlessly in midair. The protective shield was still in place. It became visible momentarily as it rippled gently under the impact. Shouting and cursing, the Saudi pilots fought to turn their planes in time to avoid crashing into it.

A moment later, Reg's fear became an ugly reality. A large portal suddenly appeared near the top of the gleaming black tower. Where a moment before there had been only a smooth, polished surface, there was now a gaping orifice leading onto a wide tunnel. Within seconds, hundreds of alien attacker ships darted into the open air like hornets spewing from a disturbed nest. They scattered in every direction, but the main force shot down the face of the tower to engage the Saudi squadron. In the dogfight at the base of the tower, the Saudi jets were outnumbered five to one by their shielded enemies. The slaughter was under way.

"Where are those damned Americans?" Reg growled as he watched the scarab fighters annihilate the Saudi forces.

Khalid and his small band of renegades were racing toward the international pilots' position. A group of perhaps fifty aliens fell in behind them, knitting through the air fluidly in their distinctive over-and-under formation.

"Should've headed for Kuwait when I had the chance," Sutton said when he saw them coming.

"Let's get the hell out of here," Reg shouted. "Head west, directly into the sun. Now!"

"What about Khalid? Shouldn't we help them?"

"No. There's nothing we can do. Follow me!"

The sun was just above the horizon but still blindingly bright. As Reg flew toward it, a strange clicking disturbance sounded in his earphones. Fearing that it was the sound of alien homing devices, he ordered his fellow pilots to shed altitude and pick up speed. Then, like a trumpet blast, Thomson's voice burst onto the airwaves.

"They're down!" he bellowed. "The shields are down! The Americans are telling everyone to attack immediately, before they go back up!" All at once, Reg recognized that the clicking sounds were Morse code.

"Thomson, are you sure the message is accurate?"

"Yes, yes! We're getting reports of damage to the alien destroyers. It's not just the Americans. Everybody's hitting them."

A lethal smile crossed Reg's lips, and his fear evaporated. His hands, which had been shaking, steadied themselves. He knew that the absence of the shields was no guarantee of victory, but he relished the idea of meeting the aliens in a fair fight. A moment before he whipped his Tornado into a sharp turn, he spoke calmly to the others. "You heard the man, ladies and gentlemen. It's party time."

As the international pilots hurried to defend Khalid and his besieged cohort, there was a flash of green light in the distance and cheering on the airwaves. One of the jets had scored the first kill against an alien attacker.

"Bloody amazing!" said Tye. Hearing that the shields were down was one thing, but actually seeing one of the invincible aliens bite the dust was quite another. Suddenly the pilots were like a pack of wolves with the taste of blood in their mouths. They jammed their controls forward and rocketed toward the conflict.

"They're on our tails," Khalid yelled. "Help us!"

"Fly directly into the sun!" Reg shouted. "We're headed straight toward you."

"Where are you? I can't see you!"

"That's the point, Khalid. You can't see us, and, hopefully, neither can they. When I give the order, I want you and your boys to break into a vertical climb. Straight up, you got that?"

The F–15 Eagle flying just behind Khalid's was vaporized by one of the alien pulse blasts. "Yes, yes, I understand. But hurry!" Khalid's group continued to fly blind, weaving and jigging, as the alien contingent behind picked off one after another of them.

"Almost . . . almost," Reg repeated calmly. Then, when the nose of his plane was less than a mile from Khalid's, he gave the order.

"STRAIGHT UP! NOW!"

Dogged pursuers, the alien ships followed the Saudis upward, losing speed and exposing their undersides as they did so. Without realizing it, they'd lined themselves up like ducks at a shooting gallery. They never saw the international pilots coming. In a matter of seconds, more than half of the alien column was destroyed. A flash of jade green light accompanied each kill.

"Go in groups," Miriyam shouted. "Hunt them down."

It was good advice, but Reg knew he was good enough to be a group of one. After assigning Tye and Sutton to chase down one of the nearest alien craft, he set his sights on another. He quickly tucked himself behind the targeted ship and began angling for a proper shot. The alien pilot ignored him, turning to attack a pair of Iraqis. It was obvious to Reg that whoever—or whatever—was flying the attacker, no adjustments in tactics were being made to compensate for the loss of the shields.

"Not much of a thinker, I see," said Reg, launching a Skyflash missile. It struck the alien ship squarely, blowing it to jade-green smithereens. It was the precise shade of green that Reg had seen cast on Jerusalem moments before the city was destroyed. Must have something to do with their energy source, he noted.

All around him, other pilots were bringing down alien ships. He heard the Ethiopian, Remi, shout, "Now go back to hell where you came from," a second before he destroyed the alien he was chasing. When Miriyam and Yossi fired simultaneously at the ships they were following, two more green flashes lit up the sky.

"And Israel scores two!" Yossi shouted like the announcer at a soccer game.

"Saudi pilot," Edward warned, "you have an enemy to port."

Reg looked above him and saw that Khalid was in trouble again. He responded at once, climbing to put himself in position. But before he arrived, Khalid had executed a wing-over roll, doubled back on his enemy, and destroyed him.

In his steady, workhorse way, Sutton was destroying alien ships and keeping Tye out of harm's way. There was nothing spectacular or daring in the way he operated his plane, but his pursuits were patient and relentless. Rather than use up his supply of missiles, he was doing all his damage with the Tornado's 27mm cannons. He didn't call out his kills as many of the others were doing, choosing instead to go quietly about his business.

Tye, on the other hand, a mechanic who had never fired a missile before, began celebrating loudly after one of his missiles connected with an enemy target. It didn't matter to him that he'd used up nearly all his ammunition, or that the attacker he'd destroyed wasn't the one he'd been aiming at. Just killing one of the bastards was enough. He went on whooping and cheering until Reg reminded him that the battle was only beginning.

In Hebrew, Farsi, Turkish, English, Amharic, Yoruba, and several dialects of Arabic, the pilots cursed and taunted their non-human enemies. As the last few alien ships were being hunted down, Reg took a moment to watch the other pilots at work. One of the Iraqi pilots, he noticed, was especially effective, gunning down one attacker after another.

"This one is the bread!" the Iraqi yelled as he dropped his MiG–29 behind his next target.

"I think you mean toast," Tye corrected him.

"Yes, the toast!" the boyish-sounding Iraqi agreed as he unleashed a volley of armor-piercing shells. "This one is the TOAST!" The large-caliber bullets ate away at the attacker's shell until it exploded into a messy green blur of debris.

Once the last attacker had been shot down, the group turned its attention back to the city destroyer, which was moving inexorably forward, undeterred by the loss of its shields. It had already swallowed Usfan in its shadow and was closing in on Mecca. If the ship could not be shot down, or driven away from the city very quickly, hundreds of thousands of lives would be lost, and one of the earth's most important cities would be obliterated.

As Reg led the way toward the front end of the city-sized craft, he watched the bombing attacks already under way. A group of MiGs was circling the crown of the destroyer's domed roof completely unopposed, strafing and bombing at will. Their missiles gouged deep craters into the armored surface, but it was not nearly enough. The ship was so large that the damage was inconsequential.

As Reg studied the problem, some of the pilots in his group raced ahead and fired a salvo of missiles. They struck squarely and caused spectacular explosions, but the problem was the same. The exterior shell was not penetrated, and the destroyer continued to move calmly forward as placidly as a bull moves through a swarm of flies. It only decelerated when its prow approached the northern outskirts of Mecca and began to seal off the sky over the crowded city.

"It's impossible," Sutton announced with characteristic pessimism. "We just don't have the firepower."

"He's right. At this rate, it'll take us a week to knock this thing down."

"Only a few minutes until it fires on the city. We've got to do something quickly."

"Let's use everything we've got, then go and find some more weapons."

"Where are we going to find them?" Miriyam asked. "All the bases are destroyed. I've only got two Sidewinders and a Python left."

Remi, the Ethiopian pilot, suggested using the last of their armaments against the skyscraper-like tower. "It looks like a control tower," he pointed out. "If we can damage it, they won't be able to steer. Even if they fire on Mecca, maybe they won't be able to go on to the next city."

Behind Reg, the team raced toward the leading edge of the megasaucer and watched its seventeen-mile-wide shadow darken the city below. There was bad news waiting for them when they arrived. Remi's idea, although logical, wasn't working. A group of Egyptian and Sudanese jets were skirmishing with a swarm of the scarablike attackers, and firing on the tower without effect. The structure, anchored into a wide dimple in the ship's surface, was made of a material that absorbed the missiles' impact without breaking apart.

"Scratch that bright idea off the list," Sutton droned. "Now what are we supposed to do?"

No one answered. The group seemed to be at a loss.

But Reg had an idea, one that had been brewing ever since the battle above Jerusalem. He craned his neck back and studied the polished face of the jet-black tower. He noted that the large portal that allowed the alien attackers to pass in and out of the ship was still open. *What would happen*, he wondered, *if I ducked inside?* Since his Tornado obeyed a different set of aerodynamic principles than the attackers, which could come to a dead stop and still remain airborne, he could guess the most likely outcome: He would merely splatter himself against an internal wall or other immovable object. But the destroyer was now completely covering the city below, and unless something was done quickly to disrupt the alien attack, hundreds of thousands of lives would be lost.

As the other pilots in his group discussed their next move, Reg tuned them out and kept his eyes on the portal, wondering if he should take the risk of flying into the alien ship. The question wasn't whether he would survive—that seemed unlikely—but whether he'd accomplish anything. In a way, it was the same question he'd been asking himself ever since the Gulf War. He'd spent the last several years in Saudi Arabia trying to work off the insurmountable debt he owed to the people of the area. Was the kamikaze mission he was contemplating a way of settling the score?

Shouting from the other pilots snapped him back into the present. The clicking noise had returned to the radio.

"We're getting another message from the Americans," Thomson told them. "It's brief. Hold on a moment while we decode it." Thirty seconds later, Thomson came back onto the airwaves. By that time, the destroyer had come to a dead stop above the city, centered over the Great Mosque. "Good news, excellent news. Finally, we have—"

"WHAT DOES IT SAY?"

"Right. Sorry about that. It says: Small missile strike against firing cone at center bottom causes chain-reaction explosion. Guarantees total kill."

"A total kill, you say?"

"That's what it says here," Thomson assured them. "'Guarantees total kill.'"

Yossi cracked a joke. "And we get our money back if we're not one-hundred-percent completely satisfied, right?"

After a last glance at the open portal, Reg pointed the nose of his jet at the ground. "Follow me," he called to the others. "Let's go find that firing cone."

As the group shed altitude and took a look at the underside of the destroyer, they realized that reaching the center would be no easy task. More than a hundred of the surviving alien fighters had massed themselves in the deep shadows and were flying in agitated circles, firing their pulse cannons down at the city. At the same time, the people of Mecca had no intention of going down without a fight. They'd installed dozens of surface-to-air missile stations and were using them with impunity. Their rockets flew straight up and smashed into the ship's hard underbelly.

As they patrolled the perimeter of the gigantic ship and surveyed the scene, a set of enormous doors at the center of the ship began to retract. Soon, all of Mecca was bathed in the resplendent green light that spilled out of the destroyer's interior.

"Listen up," Reg said. "We've going to play follow the leader, and we've only got one chance to do it right. We'll go in single file, fast and tight, nose to tail. I'll take the point and keep the path clear until I'm out of ammunition. After that, Miriyam moves to the front. When she's empty, you back there in the second Iraqi plane, what's your name?"

"Mohammed."

"I've been watching you. Nice shooting back there. Do you have any missiles left?"

"Yes, of course. I hate to waste them."

"Excellent. You're up third. The rest of you save your missiles for the target."

"And then?" someone asked.

"If we're not dead by then, we'll think of something. Now fall in behind me," he called, before leading them under the edge of the destroyer.

Even though the sun was beginning to set, the sudden transition from the light of the open sky to the oppressive gloom below the ship meant the pilots had to fly blind until their eyes adjusted. Maintaining his speed, Reg focused on the lowering hatch doors and the green light that showed between them. Entering the airspace under the destroyer was like flying into an enormous round room with no walls to hold up the ceiling. Reg stayed as high as he dared, only two hundred feet below the underside of the ship, which was studded with rectangular structures that looked like hanging storage containers. These large, boxlike structures were arranged in precise rows, and the gaps between them created a dizzying optical illusion of slow-motion movement as the jets raced past. Adding to the disorientation was the fact that the main source of light was the reflected green glare coming from the city below. This created the sensation of flying upside down over a dark industrial landscape.

Fighting through his own confusion, Reg steered his group gently away from oncoming bands of attackers, doing his best to conserve his weaponry. After destroying a handful of the attackers, he shouted, "I'm out! Miriyam, take over."

The Israeli captain took a different approach. Instead of avoiding confrontations with the enemy planes, she steamrollered straight ahead and blasted everything that stood in her path. Very soon, the last of her missiles was spent, and she called for Mohammed to take over.

Just then, a surface-to-air missile streaked upward and demolished the Iraqi MiG carrying the last of Mohammed's fellow countrymen. The young pilot took over the point position, but was clearly unnerved. He began veering off course, leading the team off course.

"Follow the street!" Reg coached, and it was obvious to everyone what he meant. The wide paths between the outcropping buildings above them formed wide, straight "boulevards" that ran from the edges of the ship to its center. Although the firing cone and the hanging doors were still miles away, the "street" was directly above and provided a clearly marked path to their destination.

Just as Mohammed regained his bearings, trouble came streaking toward him in the form of an alien attack squadron. A tightly clustered group of at least forty fighters was headed directly toward them. Mohammed hesitated for a moment, stricken with indecision. By the time he activated his missiles and sent them flying, he knew it was too late for the pilots behind him to fan out and try to slip past the onrushing enemy squadron. All nine of the missiles he'd fired connected with their targets, but the rest of the alien force continued toward him, firing their pulse cannons as they came. The balls of condensed energy sliced wildly through the air, narrowly missing Mohammed's MiG. Acting on instinct, the young Iraqi shouted out an order to the rest of the crew.

"UP! UP! Pull up!"

Since they were already skimming the underside of the city destroyer, the other pilots couldn't believe what they were hearing.

"There's no more room," yelled Sutton, who was flying in the second slot. "We're up as far as we can go."

But when Mohammed lifted away, giving him a clear look at the aliens bearing down on them, Sutton jerked back on his controls and followed the Iraqi pilot upward. One by one, the rest of the team quickly followed suit.

Besieged by a hailstorm of pulse blasts, and moving at close to Mach speed, Mohammed led them higher and higher until they were flying down the center of one of the so-called streets, which was barely wide enough to accommodate their wingspans. The hanging buildings on either side of them rushed past in a blur, the ceiling was only a few feet from the tops of their cockpit canopies, and more than one pilot was screaming at the top of his lungs. With a razor-thin margin of error, they held their collective breath and concentrated on steering straight down the narrow pathway until the attackers shot past them below.

When they ducked back into the open air, the alien squadron was well out of range, and they appeared to have an unobstructed path to the center of the ship. As the pilots cursed and panted and wiped the sweat from their brows, Reg congratulated Mohammed. "That was a nifty bit of work, lad."

"Nifty?" Tye asked, incredulous. "It was like flying through a shoe box. Remind me never to get into a coach with either one of you two maniacs."

Mohammed stayed in the lead position, steering toward the gap between two of the giant hatch doors. The firing cone, visible beyond them, was now fully extended. In a matter of moments, its destructive power would pulverize Mecca.

"More bad news," Sutton reported. "We've got a bogey ahead and to the left."

Reg peered down and saw that, indeed, an aircraft was streaking upward at a steep angle into their path. But it wasn't an alien attacker. It was a Saudi F-15.

Reg keyed his radio. "Commander Faisal, I thought you'd be halfway to Riyadh by now. Decided to come back and join us?"

"I have come to save my people!" he shouted back.

Unfortunately, Faisal wasn't traveling alone. He had picked up one of the alien attackers, and it was closing behind him.

"You've got company," Reg told him. "There's an attacker below and behind. Don't bring him up here, we're in position."

"There is no time!" Faisal screamed back. An intense beam of white light was shooting from the tip of the firing cone, fixing itself on one of the tall minarets of the Great Mosque. "They are going to fire!"

Faisal continued on his course, oblivious to both the alien behind him and the fact that his trajectory conflicted with Reg's squadron's. When the other pilots recognized the danger he was putting them into, they shouted at him to lead the attacker away. Faisal jigged and juked as the attacker began to fire its pulse weapon, but maintained his bearing.

"He wants the first shot," Khalid said. "He's going to cut us off."

"I'll take care of this," Reg said, diving out of line. He jammed the controls forward, milking every kilonewton of power from his twin turbofans. When he leveled off, he was right behind Faisal. "Turn off, Faisal!" Reg threatened.

"Shoot him down," one of the pilots urged.

Reg was sorely tempted. He wasn't actually out of missiles. He was still holding a Skyflash under his left wing, just in case. He sighted on Faisal's F-15 and wrapped his hand tight around the grip trigger. But instead of downing the treacherous Saudi commander, he abruptly cut the fuel supply to his engines. Then he accelerated again as the alien fighter moved ahead of him. In a few seconds, he had positioned himself, locked on, and fired. The alien ship blew apart in a bright green flash.

Faisal jostled his way to the front of the line. To avoid a collision, Mohammed was forced to swing away only seconds before reaching the giant hatch doors. In order to shoot the gap and save himself, Mohammed swerved back toward the group, forcing everyone to decelerate. By the time they came into the clearing around the firing cone, Faisal's missiles were already streaking away.

"Fire! Fire everything!" Reg yelled.

Scores of missiles shot toward the glittering weapon. Faisal's AMRAAMs got there first and blew two large holes into the massive green structure. Debris rained into the sky. A moment later, when the other missiles struck, a chain reaction began to travel up the firing cone and into the body of the destroyer, just as the American communiqué had promised.

Reg looked up into the glowing recess of the ship. A massive open chamber surrounded the dangling gun tower. And through the blaze of the explosions, he caught a momentary glimpse of the destroyer's interior: The central chamber was a single room approximately three miles across, with towering vertical walls. Hundreds more of the attacker ships were moored in clusters around the periphery. It looked like the inside of a high-tech beehive.

"It's starting to blow; let's get out of here!"

The quick series of muffled explosions that traveled up the pylon-shaped firing cone were giving way to stronger and stronger blasts. Shrapnel and smoke filled the air.

As the pilots turned and raced to get out from under the destroyer, there was a brief, dizzying moment when their planes appeared to lose speed and come to a dead stop. But it was only another optical illusion, caused when the destroyer above them began to move. With astonishing power, the megaship accelerated to high speed in only a matter of seconds. It quickly outpaced the jets, leaving them behind as it streaked away to the southeast. Just as it began to lift away, a massive explosion ripped through the top of the dome like a shotgun blast blowing through the top of a skull. It hobbled forward at reduced speed until an even larger explosion tore away its entire left side. Still moving, it began to list and sink toward the desert floor.

Cheering and screaming, the surviving pilots chased it out over the desert, emptying their guns and using the last of their missiles against the dying giant. Exploding from within, it lost momentum and finally plunged toward the earth. It bellied out on a rocky plateau, bounced once into the air, then slid for several miles before coming to rest in a huge cloud of dust.

Through it all, Reg maintained his calm, professional demeanor. As a wild celebration broke out in the air around him, he climbed to a higher altitude and scanned the darkening horizon. He checked his gauges and flipped through the various radio frequencies as if he were just finishing up another day at the office. He couldn't help taking a dim view of the disorderly air show going on below him. It went against every habit he had developed during his years as a teacher. Every channel was filled with deafening, whooping cries of victory. Ecstatic pilots flew barrel rolls and loop-the-loops over the burning wreckage, firing their guns recklessly as they went. Clenched fists pounded out their excitement on the walls and canopies of a hundred cockpits.

Reg tried to ignore them. He tried to remain calm. He fought against the urge to join the celebration for as long as he possibly could. But the revelry was infectious, and soon he was grinning from ear to ear. Then he found himself pumping his fist in the air.

"We did it!" he shouted. "I can't believe it. We beat the bloody bastards!"

The giddy realization that they'd done the impossible, that they'd saved the planet from these seemingly invincible foes, surged through him all at once, and he found himself shouting and laughing along with the others. He got on the radio and added his voice to the sea of noise. He roared and laughed. He shouted until his throat was hoarse and his eyes were filled with tears, ecstatic that he was victorious and alive.

Order began to restore itself when Faisal began calling out a message in an enthusiastic tone of voice. He shouted happily back and forth in Arabic with some of the other pilots. Reg could tell he was delivering instructions of some sort, but the only thing he could understand was the name of a city—At-Ta'if. By the time he found Khalid on the radio, Faisal was long gone.

"He says he's already spoken to the king," Khalid translated over the noise of the celebration. "We're directed to land at At-Ta'if because the king wants to congratulate all of us personally. There's going to be a party."

"I should bloody well hope so," said someone with a Londoner's accent.

"Is that you, Tye?" Reg asked. "I thought you'd be in Paradise with those seventy virgins by now."

"Seventy-two, actually. No, not yet, Major. Maybe I've got nine lives. What say we get out of here and go see about this party with the king?"

"You go ahead. I'm going to wait for the smoke to clear so I can take another look at the ship, just to make sure. Did Sutton make it?"

"Hate to disappoint you, Major, but yes, I did," Sutton said.

"Glad to hear it. You two follow the others to At-Ta'if and warm things up for me."

They pulled away, and Reg patrolled the sky, waiting for the evening winds to clear the dust and smoke away from the downed destroyer. He wasn't alone. Twenty or thirty other pilots were also biding their time, flying laps around the crash site until they could inspect the kill. Khalid was one of them. He sounded hesitant and distracted over the radio, not like he'd just helped win a stunning victory.

"Khalid," Reg said, "I thought you'd be off meeting the king by now. What's the matter?"

"I'm worried about Faisal," he explained. He reminded Reg that an hour before he'd disobeyed orders and deserted his squad during an attack. Even though it proved to be the right move, he didn't know how Faisal would react.

"If Faisal's as shrewd as I think he is," Reg said, "he won't want an investigation. He wasted the lives of a whole squadron. Besides, he got what he wanted. Mecca wasn't destroyed, and now he'll probably run around telling everyone that he's personally responsible for saving it." Reg chuckled at the idea. Khalid, who knew Faisal better, didn't.

Reg thought about it for a minute and came up with an idea. He radioed Thomson, still at the tent in the Empty Quarter. Earlier, the colonel had mentioned that he was tape-recording their transmissions. "Thomson, do you think you can get me a copy of that tape?"

"I'm not sure," he answered. "The tape doesn't belong to me, and the equipment out here isn't exactly state-of-the-art, but I can try. Any particular part of it?"

"The whole thing. And, Colonel, it's important. See what you can do."

"No promises, Cummins. I'll see you at At-Ta'if in a couple of hours. Word is that the Saudis have some planes coming to pick us up. We're all a bunch of bloody heroes, mate."

"Roger. See you there."

The air over the destroyer began to clear. The sun had already extinguished itself in the Red Sea, but in the last lingering light of day, Reg and the others saw what was left of the ship. To their dismay, they noticed that roughly a quarter of it was still intact. When it hit the ground, the whole vehicle had splintered, cracked into millions of pieces the same way a car's windshield breaks during a collision. Like tempered glass, it sagged in places but still retained some structural integrity.

Yossi was among the circling pilots. "Hey, I might want my money back on that guarantee," he said in his thick accent. "Does that look like a total kill to you?"

"It looks fairly dead from my angle," Reg countered, "and it looks like it's burning inside. I wouldn't worry about it. The impact of the crash probably killed anything that wasn't nailed to the walls."

"Probably you're right."

Both of them were thinking the same thing: Probably wasn't good enough. They made a couple of additional passes, scanning for signs of movement, until it was too dark to see much of anything. Then they flew off to join the rest of the pilots at At-Ta'if.

Inside the ship, large doors were rolling closed to contain the spread of what the aliens hated most: fire.

6

Victory Party

The airfield at At-Ta'if served both civilian and military purposes. The swarm of alien attack planes that had pounded the place with bursts from their energy cannons didn't discriminate between the two. Nearly every building at the facility had been destroyed. In the absence of electrical power, ground crews had lined the only undamaged runway with pots of kerosene and set them ablaze to guide the victorious pilots to the ground.

Reg, Yossi, and Khalid were among the last to land. When they taxied up to the damaged main hangars, there was a cheering crowd waiting to greet them. Their nationality made no difference to these people. The only thing that mattered was that the pilots had saved them from the horrible, ghastly invaders. The civilians rushed in to surround the planes, cheering and shaking their fists in victory. A contingent of Saudi soldiers pushed their way through the crowd and led the pilots to a fleet of waiting limousines.

"Welcome to being heroes, gents." Tye was standing in one of the limos, his head and torso poking through the sunroof. He towered above the roof of the car like a sunburned giraffe. "There's a party in our honor at the royal family's compound. Hop in."

They left the airfield and sped east through one of the finest suburbs of At-Ta'if, Tye still hanging out the sunroof. But the trip wasn't all cheering and smiles. Parts of the city had been hit hard by pulse blasts. They drove past working-class Saudis who were retrieving their possessions from smoldering buildings. In one spot, bodies were laid out on a sidewalk, surrounded by mourners. When the drivers slowed to steer around the pedestrians, Reg looked out his window and made eye contact with an older, unveiled woman. She was cradling a dead boy in her arms and wailing with grief. But as the limousine passed, she did a remarkable thing: She pumped her fist in the air and let out a ululating war cry in honor of the victorious pilots. Beneath the surface of their new riches and creature comforts, Reg realized that Fadeela had been right: The Saudis were still a fierce, desert people.

A short time later, they arrived at their destination, the royal family's summer palace, and entered a world of nearly unimaginable opulence. Behind the heavily guarded gates, a broad swath of manicured lawn rolled up a gentle slope toward a magnificent white mansion. It was an architectural fantasy, part storybook European castle, part Arabian palace. A pair of domed minarets stood on either side of the ornately tiled building. The winding driveway led them beneath canopies of palm trees and ferns. All the doors and windows of the great house had been thrown open, revealing that a lavish party was under way inside. Guests spilled out onto the tiled verandas and balconies overlooking the gardens.

Their limousine driver steered away from the main house and took the sweaty pilots to the compound's Olympic-sized swimming pool. They showered in the cabanas and changed into the Arab-style clothing provided for them. The ankle-length shirts, called *thobes*, fit Yossi and Reg comfortably, but Tye's was a full six inches too short. They marched up the hill to join the gathering.

"I feel like I'm wearing a dress," Reg complained.

"How do you think I feel," Tye said, his hairy, freckled shins poking out below his hemline.

"Don't worry. Both of you look very beautiful and sexy," Yossi joked without smiling. Then, looking around him, he said, "To have a garden like this is every Arab's dream."

The grounds were lush beyond reason. There was a greenhouse full of orchids. Pomegranate and citrus trees grew beside birds-of-paradise, date palms, and many other exotic plants. There were peacock blue tiles lining a circular fountain and actual peacocks wandering the lawn. Mercedes-Benzes and Rolls-Royces were parked along the driveway, and a group of well-heeled Saudis stood admiring an elaborate, man-made waterfall. Off in the distance was another building that looked like a French château. As the three men began climbing the steps to the party, waiters rushed toward them to offer golden caviar and sweet tea.

"I can't believe this place," Reg remarked, as they crossed the patio.

"What's the good of owning a country if you don't have a nice house or two," deadpanned Yossi.

The elaborate main doors of the house opened onto a ballroom. Well-dressed men, and Saudi women with sheer veils concealing their diamond necklaces mixed with soldiers and pilots in loud conversation. There were more than two hundred people inside, but the room was large enough to accommodate twice that number.

When they saw Reg enter, many of the pilots broke off their conversations and came over to greet him. They were all heroes to the world, and Reg was a hero to them. One by one, they embraced him, some of them with tears in their eyes. Khalid was among them.

With a big grin on his face, Reg put an arm around his old friend.

"We made it. We actually did it."

"It was a piece of pie. I mean *cake*. It was a piece of cake."

The two of them laughed. Khalid stepped back and admired his friend's new wardrobe. "You look good in Saudi fashion, Teacher. It suits you. But on you," he said, turning to Tye, "it looks like a dress."

A hyperkinetic American woman, wearing a wireless headset, introduced herself to Reg as Mrs. Roeder. Blinking rapidly, she explained that she and her husband were "event coordinators for the House of Saud." She pointed out Mr. Roeder, a man in a suit and tie, who was standing halfway up a staircase on the far side of the room. He nodded back. She took Reg by the arm and began leading him across the room. "The scuttlebutt is that you sort of took charge of the non-Saudi forces during the air battle today and helped Commander Faisal out," she said.

"Helped him out?" Reg asked with an incredulous glance. "I suppose that's one way of putting it."

"Well, the king heard about it, and he's very anxious to meet you." She glanced up at the balcony overlooking the party. A grinning elderly man in a white robe leaned over the balustrade and beckoned them upstairs. Reg recognized him immediately, having seen his photograph hundreds of times. It was Ibrahim al-Saud, the king of Saudi Arabia. Faisal was standing right behind him.

As Mrs. Roeder led them up the stairs, Khalid put a hand on Reg's shoulder.

"Have you heard from Thomson? Did he get the tape recording?"

"He'll be here soon," Reg assured him, as Mrs. Roeder tugged at his arm. "Nothing to worry about."

"I suppose I should say thank you," the American woman said, speaking a mile a minute. "We all should. You guys were incredibly brave up there today."

"All in a day's work," Reg joked.

"I mean, what do you say to a bunch of guys who just saved your life? Thanks, right?" Just as quickly, she was on to another subject. "Let me tell you something. It wasn't easy pulling this party together. Everything is such a mess out there. It's absolutely crazy. *You* try getting fresh lettuce in the middle of an alien attack. But the king really wanted to express his appreciation so we're doing the best we can." She was distracted by a message coming through her earpiece and stopped to listen.

"This one?" she asked, pointing toward Khalid. "Got it." With a professionally ingratiating smile, she put her hand on Khalid's shoulder.

"Sir, they're asking that you not come upstairs. They'll talk to you later. Would you mind?"

It looked like Faisal might make trouble for Khalid after all.

Maybe for Reg as well, since he'd loudly urged Khalid to disobey the orders to attack. The two men exchanged a tense look before Reg continued up the stairs.

"I'll put in a good word for you," he said.

Once he was above the crowd, Reg scanned the partygoers, looking for Thomson. The colonel's diplomatic skills would've come in very handy right about then, but he was nowhere to be seen. Instead, Reg's eyes fell on a tall, veiled woman standing near the doors. Despite her coverings, he knew instantly that it was Fadeela. Standing with a group of women, she raised her glass ever so slightly in a clandestine toast. Reg smiled conspiratorially as he reached the top of the stairs.

"Your Majesty, may I present Major Cummins of the British Royal Air Force."

Reg had never met a king before and didn't know what he was supposed to do. After running his fingers through his hair, he did the same thing he would have done upon meeting the queen of England. He knelt down and bowed his head.

The king's broad grin erupted into a belly laugh. When Reg looked up, everyone around him was laughing, too. Mrs. Roeder joined Reg at floor level and blinked.

"There's really no need for that, Major. In this country, people consider the king their equal. A simple handshake would be appropriate."

Chagrined, Reg got to his feet. Obviously there was no harm done because the king put his arm around Reg like he was part of the family and introduced him to eight or ten of his brothers, nephews, and advisors. The patriarch of the al-Saud clan was well into his seventies, a tall thin man who was a little unsteady on his feet but mentally very sharp. He offered Reg a chair.

"Commander Faisal informs me," the king began with a twinkle in his eye, "that you were a great hero today. That you rallied the foreign forces on our soil and led them capably in the battle."

"I did what I could," Reg replied, shooting a glance at Faisal.

"No, no. It is not a time for false modesty. If Faisal tells me it is so, it is so. And he tells me that without you, our Holy City would have come to ruin. For this we can never thank you properly. We al-Sauds are the custodians of Mecca, and it is a responsibility we take very seriously. You have given us a very great gift in helping to save Mecca from these godless invaders, and it is my plan to reward you handsomely."

Reg's ears perked up. When the king of Saudi Arabia, one of the wealthiest men in the world, used the words "reward you handsomely," he wasn't talking about a gold watch and a weekend in Bahrain.

"There is no need to decide now. Think about it for a day or two and decide what you would like to have. If it is within our power, it shall be done."

Reg surprised himself by immediately glancing toward Fadeela.

"That's very generous. I'll give it some thought," he said. "Can I ask why you didn't want to see Khalid Yamani? He deserves as much thanks as I do."

The expression on the old man's face instantly soured.

"Karnak Yamani has long been a valuable and beloved servant of ours. He has done much to enrich the people of our country, but his son, Khalid, has brought him nothing but shame and grief. Faisal has told me Khalid was a student of yours."

"That's right," Reg said. "He's also a friend."

"I see," said King Ibrahim, with obvious displeasure. But my offer to you is still good. You will be rewarded for your bravery just as Khalid Yamani will be punished for his cowardice."

"Cowardice?" Without meaning to, Reg scoffed at the king's words. "Without Khalid we might not have succeeded today. He should get as much credit as anyone. He showed more courage than some of your other pilots." Again, Reg glanced pointedly at Faisal.

The king's eyebrows arched, and his face iced over. He exchanged a few words with Faisal before turning back to Reg, explaining a little history to him in a chilly tone.

"I am told you were a pilot during the Gulf War and that you made a rather serious and costly mistake, is this right?"

"Yes, sir," Reg admitted, suddenly quieter. Every high-ranking Saudi knew about Reg's "mistake."

"In that same war, your friend Khalid Yamani also made a very grave mistake. Yours was an error of judgment made under the stress of battle. And I understand your superiors have forgiven you." That was partially true. "But Lieutenant Yamani's error was made in calmness. His heart, I am afraid, is corrupted with the poison of"—he turned to one of his assistants for a translation—"poisoned with malice and jealousy."

Faisal leaned forward and explained. "He accused me of lying and of cowardice. He said I was not the one who repulsed the attack of the Iraqi national guard. It was a serious matter to do so," he said in a threatening way that implied Reg would be wise not to make the same mistake. "But, because of the great standing and reputation of his father, he was spared from the punishment he deserved. Today he ran from the battle and disobeyed my orders. This time there can be no mercy."

"Mercy? Mercy?" Reg asked, getting visibly angry. "Why should he need your mercy?" Mrs. Roeder quickly put a firm hand on Reg's shoulder to remind him where he was, but it didn't do much good. He yelled past the king at Faisal. "You ordered those men to their deaths when you could have waited. Khalid was right to disobey that order. I would have done the same thing."

Faisal turned to the king. "You see, even the foreign pilots clearly understood my orders."

Without meaning to, Reg had further incriminated Khalid.

The king stood up to show that the interview was over.

"Tonight is a time for celebrating. We are here to rejoice in our victory. We will handle this unpleasant business at a future time. I am sorry to have detained you for such a long while, I'm certain you have friends and comrades you wish to greet more than a tiresome old man. Mr. and Mrs. Roeder, please invite Major Cummins to the events tomorrow and make sure he has everything he needs." He smiled warmly and clasped Reg's hands in his own. "Once again, we thank you most humbly."

Reg stood up, but wasn't quite ready for this royal audience to end. He already knew what he wanted as his handsome reward:

He wanted Khalid to be fully exonerated. But the Roeders each took one of his elbows and firmly guided him toward the stairs.

"Take a tip?" Mr. Roeder asked. "Don't raise your voice to anyone in the royal family. Doesn't usually work out in your favor."

"Major, if you don't have any plans for tomorrow, please come out to the spaceship with us," Mrs. Roeder said in one ear.

"The king is heading out there in the morning with a huge entourage," her husband said in the other.

Reg looked surprised. "The spaceship? Aren't you worried about survivors?"

"We're *hoping* for survivors." Mrs. Roeder blinked. "The king wants his picture taken with some of them. You know, standing there with his boot on their necks and his sword raised in the air. Something to boost morale while the country's getting back on its feet."

"But more importantly," Mr. Roeder went on, "how are we going to learn about them if there aren't any survivors. We've got to make these suckers talk. Find out where they came from and why they did this to us."

"Exactly. The king has already called some translation experts in from Switzerland."

"They're mathematicians and biologists mainly," Mr. Roeder said, glancing at his watch. "People who might be able to figure out how to communicate with the aliens."

"Not that the Saudis don't know how to interrogate a prisoner, you understand, but this is a unique situation. They're arriving tonight."

"I hope you'll come tomorrow. There's going to be film crews, foreign ambassadors, and lots of the royals. It should be interesting. A real historic-moment type of situation."

"Also, that would be the perfect time to ask for your reward from the king, so we could get pictures of the whole thing. It'd save us from having to set up a separate ceremony."

"Well, it was sure nice to meet you. All you pilots are being housed in the guest quarters on the far side of the pool. Looks like a French château, you can't miss it. Very luxurious. You'll love it." Then they hurried away to take care of other business.

Reg searched the party, looking for Khalid and Thomson. If the colonel had the tape, it would be enough to make Faisal back off. It contained the proof of his cowardice during the dogfight.

Reg found Tye instead and enlisted his help. The two of them searched the extensive grounds of the royal compound. As they hunted through the gardens, checking the various gazebos and greenhouses, they passed a large gaggle of strolling Saudi women.

"Babe alert," Tye said out of the side of his mouth. "Check out those sexy veils!" But as they passed by, it was the women who did the checking out. The black-gowned figures surrounded the men, sizing them up, and offering opinions on their manly attributes.

"How handsome this one is."

"I like the other one. Cute, la?"

"Not enough muscle. I think he will blow away in a strong breeze."

One of them stepped forward and, although it was dark, Reg knew who it was beneath the dark headcloth. She complimented him.

"He is handsome, brave, and unafraid of women. Why don't we have more Saudi men like this one?"

When Reg took her by the arm and pulled her aside, the other women gasped at his forwardness.

"Major Cummins," Fadeela protested, "every garden has a thousand eyes. This is not a safe place for us to talk."

"Listen, Fadeela, I've got something important to tell you." He paused to consider how he should break the news. It was just long enough to give her the wrong idea.

"There is a rumor," she said, "that the king will reward you with whatever your heart desires. If you are going to ask my advice about choosing a Saudi bride, I can recommend a very lovely and talented young woman."

"That's not it," he broke in. "Khalid's in trouble. Serious trouble, I think."

"What has he done now?" she asked, suddenly serious.

"Today, in the air, Faisal ordered his men to attack the destroyer before the shields came down. It was a stupid order, and all the men who obeyed it are dead now. Your brother broke away with a few others. I think it was common sense, but the king is calling it treason. He also mentioned that Khalid did something like this before, that he crossed Faisal during the Gulf War."

"Where is my brother now?"

"We've looked everywhere for him. I think he might have run off somewhere."

"Faisal will be the ruin of my family yet! He is more treacherous than the aliens who tried to destroy us!" She sat down on a garden bench and put her head in her hands.

"What happened before?"

"According to my brother, Faisal ordered an attack on a few Iraqi jets flying inside their own borders. They shot the planes down and then flew home, where Faisal created an elaborate story about facing down a large group of bombers. It was all designed to turn him into a hero. When Khalid went to his superiors, he was told to keep his mouth shut so he wouldn't embarrass the Saudi army. It was my brother's word against Faisal's and that of his henchmen. I must go and find my father. He will be forced to bargain with this evil man for my brother's amnesty."

"I may be able to help," Reg said.

"This is a Saudi matter now," Fadeela said. "No outsiders will be allowed to speak at the trial."

"I won't need to speak. I can give Khalid something to use against Faisal." Then he told her about the recording.

"Not only is he handsome and brave and unafraid of women, he is very clever as well."

Just then, a messenger arrived. He was one of Fadeela's nephews, who spoke to her urgently in Arabic.

"They've arrested Khalid at the airport," she told Reg. "He was trying to escape in his plane. They're bringing him back to stand trial tonight. The king is very angry." As she and her friends hurried away toward the palace, she turned and called back to

Reg. "Please bring us the recording. My brother's life may depend on it."

"Did you see that?" Tye asked when the women had gone. "I was only about sixty-five virgins short of paradise."

"Let's go."

"Go where?"

"Back to the airfield. We've got to find Thomson."

Standing at the edge of the runway, they watched as the two C–130s landed, then kept careful eyes on the gangplanks as the passengers disembarked to the cheers of the crowd. It was past midnight, and the crowds were thinning, but there were still a lot of people out there. Thomson was nowhere to be seen. Reg approached a man with a familiar face, the burly Saudi captain who had treated them so roughly the day before. Reg was a little apprehensive about talking to him again, and was surprised when the big man turned to him with a smile and lifted him off the ground in a bear hug. When asked if he'd seen Thomson, the captain looked around him, surprised that the British lieutenant colonel wasn't among the disembarking passengers.

"Everyone wants to find this little man," he said.

"Who else?" Reg asked.

"I don't know. Some soldiers who arrived with the transport planes," he said. "They were looking everywhere for him."

"Some of Faisal's men?"

The captain didn't know.

"Are you thinking what I'm thinking?" Tye asked. "That Faisal's covering his trail?" Reg didn't answer, but it certainly looked that way.

By the time they drove back to the palace, Khalid's trial was almost over. It was being held in the king's quarters on the second floor of the palace. Guards had been posted at the bottom of the main stairway to ensure privacy. Nevertheless, a steady stream of soldiers and members of the royal family passed back and forth through the cordon, delivering news to those waiting on the main floor. Most of the guests, including the pilots, had gone off to bed or to more private parties. A somber mood had settled over the fifty or so people who were still there.

One of the Saudi royal princes approached Tye and Reg, eager to share what he knew.

"That fool Khalid Yamani told them everything. He should have remained humble and silent and begged for mercy. But instead he became angry and accused Faisal of stupidity and cowardice. Now they will be harder on him."

"How hard?"

"Usually these things are settled with money, and the Yamanis are rich," the prince said, "but they were lenient with Khalid the last time. This time the penalty will almost certainly be death."

Reg tried to persuade the guards at the base of the stairs that he had important evidence to present at the trial, but they wouldn't allow him to pass. Frustrated with his helplessness, he spotted Mrs. Roeder pacing the balcony, talking into her headset. He caught her attention, and she signaled she'd be right there. In the meantime, Fadeela arrived, escorted by her nephew and a few of her veiled friends.

"Major Cummins, you are just in time, thanks be to Allah. Where is the tape?"

"The man who made the tape wasn't on the plane back from the Empty Quarter. I'm still looking for him. I'm sorry."

Fadeela made a sound as if she'd been wounded.

"What can I do for you, Major?" asked Mrs. Roeder, coming down the stairs.

He asked her to speak with the king and try to persuade him to delay the sentencing until Thomson could be found. She blinked back at him.

"I'll see what I can do," she said in that breezy, American way that meant he was asking for the impossible.

Fadeela walked past Reg and took hold of Mrs. Roeder's arm, pulling her closer and whispering something to her. Then she removed one of the ruby rings from her finger and pressed it into the American woman's palm. Mrs. Roeder hurried up the stairs into the room where the trial was being held.

"If only we could find Thomson," Reg said to Fadeela with a worried look. "I'm afraid something might have happened to him. Faisal has every reason to want that tape as badly as we do."

One of the guards barked a warning, reminding them it was forbidden for them to speak to one another. Reg fixed him with a stare, daring him to enforce the rule. The soldier backed off.

"Major Cummins," Fadeela began quietly, "you have been of great service to my family, and I appreciate everything you have done. I believe you tried your best, and I wish things had turned out differently. Good-bye, and thank you again."

She turned away from him and surrounded herself with her friends. Reg didn't know what she was talking about, but it didn't take long for him to find out. Faisal came striding out of the king's quarters and hurried down the stairs. In spite of their previous encounter, he greeted Reg warmly. He looked relaxed and, as usual, supremely confident.

"What do you know about Thomson?" Reg said in a not-so-friendly tone. "He wasn't on either one of the planes coming back from the camp, and he was seen talking to some of your men before he disappeared."

A look of concern spread across Faisal's face. "Yes, I learned a few moments ago that he was not aboard the evacuation flight. I have been waiting to see him myself. I believe he made an audio record of today's battle, which I would like very much to play for the king. It confirms Khalid Yamani's guilt. I hope nothing has happened to Colonel Thomson. He is an excellent man."

"You know as well as I do that tape would ruin you. How convenient that it didn't show up."

"I'm confident that it will, eventually."

Fadeela came to the stairs and spoke to Faisal in Arabic. Whatever she said put a smile on his face. They said a few things back and forth, none of which Reg could understand, before she lifted her veil away from her face. This shocked the people around them but delighted Faisal, who laughed in recognition. For the second time in as many days, he had seen this beautiful woman's naked face. An elderly man standing nearby was not amused. When he saw the maiden exposing herself in the company of men, he used his walking stick to strike her hard across the back of her legs and yelled at her. Reg grabbed the old man and pulled him roughly away from Fadeela.

"It looks to me like you care too much about this girl, Major," Faisal said.

"I'm a friend of the family," Reg said.

"And soon, a friend of her husband as well," he laughed. "We've just now made an interesting arrangement. If her father agrees, which I believe he will, Fadeela and I will be married tomorrow." Faisal headed back up the stairs, chuckling to himself.

"*Married?* What did you say to him?" Reg demanded.

Fadeela didn't answer him. Instead, she and her friends hurried away.

Down the slope from the royal mansion, past the swimming pool, was a large château, a gaudy replica of a famous French castle in the Dordogne Valley. The sounds of laughter, conversation, and music drifted out its windows and into the warm night air as Reg and Tye came walking somberly down the hill. The news that Fadeela was going to marry Faisal had hit Reg hard, and he was in a mild state of shock.

"That poor girl," Tye said, "trading herself away to save her brother. She must love him. I don't know if my sister would do the same for me."

Reg was hardly listening. In the short time he'd known Fadeela, he'd come to admire her spirit, the way she refused to be dominated. She was tough, beautiful, and ruthlessly honest. The more he learned about her, the more he felt himself drawn to her. It was for her sake that he had found the courage to stand atop a water barrel and convince a hostile group of soldiers they should support the American plan to defeat the city destroyer. But now, only a few hours after deciding that Fadeela's freedom was something worth fighting and dying for, it had been ransomed away.

When they entered through the arched stone doorway of the

château, they were greeted by a butler, who returned their military uniforms, laundered and ironed. The man led them down the richly appointed hallways, carrying a lantern to light the way since the electricity was not working. Reg would have been happy to call it a night, but Tye came into his room after getting changed.

"Time to join the party, sir. Throw that uniform on and let's go."

"Not tonight," Reg said. "Too much on my mind. Besides, I feel like I could sleep for a month."

Tye did not find that answer acceptable. "Listen to yourself. A few hours after you save planet Earth from certain doom, and you're ready to mope around your room and turn in early." Reg looked at his watch. It was past midnight, but Tye wasn't finished. "I know you're unhappy about this business with Fadeela, but that's exactly why I'm not going to let you sit in here by yourself. Let's go. You can sleep when you're dead."

Two minutes later, they were walking down the hallway with candles, poking their heads through open doorways to inspect the parties going on inside the rooms. Behind one of the closed doors, they heard Miriyam's voice. It sounded like there was a party going on inside, so they knocked.

"We are nobody inside of here," laughed a man with an Arab accent.

"Go away," yelled another. "We gave at the office."

"Only pilots allowed inside!"

Tye banged hard on the door. "It's the police. What are you doing in there?" A moment later the door opened a crack and Yossi's face, framed by his thick glasses, poked outside. When he saw who it was, he pulled the door open wide and offered a crisp salute.

"Major Cummins, nice to see you. Come in."

A dozen people were crowded into the candlelit room, laughing and talking. It was a scene that would have been impossible before the invasion. Miriyam, an Israeli, sat on a sofa squashed between Edward, the Palestinian from Jordan, and a gray-haired Syrian pilot with his arm in a sling. Yossi, the Ethiopian Remi, and one of the Iranian pilots crowded around Reg, welcoming him to the party. Everyone was relaxed and in high spirits.

They laughed and talked about what it had been like facing the aliens that afternoon until there was another knock at the door. It was Sutton, returning with a case of warm beer. He was followed inside by Mohammed, the crack Iraqi pilot who had flown so brilliantly. He looked different than Reg expected him to. He was in his early twenties, with a gap-toothed smile and a peach-fuzz mustache.

"Good flying out there today," Reg said when they were introduced. "Where'd you learn to handle a plane like that?"

"Naturally I am a very great pilot," he announced with a big grin. "I am an Iraqi." The other pilots moaned when they heard him bragging and pelted him with pillows from all directions. Mohammed ducked and moved for cover.

"I heard a nasty rumor down in the service kitchen," Sutton said, offering Reg a beer. "Khalid's sister is going to marry that bloody Faisal. If she doesn't, he's going to have Khalid's head lopped off. It's all anyone's talking about. And get this: They're going to have the ceremony out at the crash site tomorrow while the king's having his photo taken with a bunch of dead aliens."

"Let's *hope* they're dead."

"Of course they are. Nothing could have survived that crash."

"It's disgusting," said Miriyam. "The way they treat the women in this country is disgusting. The men take many wives and keep them like prisoners and slaves."

"That is the old way," a Saudi pilot said from across the room. "We young Saudi guys, we only have one wife. It's better than it was." He was trying to be conciliatory, but it didn't stop an argument from starting to boil. Miriyam, the only woman in the room, tried to show the Arab men in the room that they were all sexist pigs. Predictably, they took offense, and the shouting match was on. It was still raging ten minutes later when Reg slipped out the door and returned to his room.

He lay in bed for a while listening to the sounds of the celebration before drifting off into unconsciousness. Less than two hours later, he woke out of nightmare and sat bolt upright in bed. Realizing he wouldn't be able to get back to sleep, he put on his freshly laundered uniform and went downstairs.

The royal servants were busy preparing a lavish breakfast for the pilots in the châtcau's lobby. Buffet tables were piled high with food, but the only thing Reg wanted was black coffee. While he was drinking it, two more pilots came downstairs and joined him: Mohammed—the young Iraqi—and the captain of the Israeli pilots, Miriyam. The three of them sat down on plush couches beneath an original oil painting Reg recognized as the work of the French post-impressionist Bonnard. While the other two chatted groggily, Reg stared out the darkened windows trying to answer a question: The night before, he'd helped win the most important battle humanity had ever fought. So why did he feel so dead inside the next morning?

He stood up, and said, "I'm not waiting any longer. I'm heading out to the ship."

Miriyam and Mohammed looked at one another in surprise, then followed him out the door.

7

"Into the Ship"

Reg, Miriyam, and Mohammed were taken to the At-Ta'if airfield by one of the army of limousine drivers who would transport the royal entourage out to the crash site later that morning. The first people they met upon arriving there were a squad of United Nations Peacekeepers. They were Frenchmen who had come from Somalia to help the Saudis in their "mop-up operation." Their commanding officer, a man named Guillaume, was frustrated with the Saudi ground crews. They said the earliest the Frenchmen could be airlifted out to the downed alien ship would be that afternoon.

"You have many helicopters empty," Guillaume shouted angrily, pointing to a group of H–110s sitting idle near a ruined hangar.

"It cannot be helped," one of the Saudis told him, glancing toward the heavens.

Reg received a very different reception. A handful of the Saudis knew him from Khamis Moushayt, while many others recognized him as one of the pilots who had saved Mecca. They crowded around him, Miriyam, and Mohammed, smiling and shaking hands. There would be no problem arranging a trip out to the ship. Arrangements were made immediately.

When Guillaume and the other Peacekeepers saw what was happening, they were incensed. "You can find a way to bring these tourists, but not for us?"

Reg pulled Guillaume aside and offered him a deal. In exchange for the privilege of flying out to the ship aboard "Reg's" helicopter, the Frenchmen promised to allow Reg and his two partners to accompany them on their trip inside the ruined city destroyer. Guillaume was a stocky, rough-looking character with a bushy blond mustache and piercing blue eyes that matched the blue U.N. beret he wore on his head. His face was full of small scars that looked like the results of a grenade explosion. He didn't like having to strike deals in order to do his job, but he accepted, and within a few minutes, his squad of eighteen lifted off in one of the H–110 helicopters.

A pink glow, the first light of the new day, filtered through the smoke and grit hanging over the eastern horizon. What was left of the ruined alien ship was still smoldering. It had come to rest in a hard, stony part of the desert, seventy-five miles southeast of At-Ta'if. In the murky light, it looked like a strange, archaeological wonder, a ruined city from some long-lost civilization. The desert was alive with hundreds of trucks and tanks stationed around the perimeter of the felled giant. They looked pathetically small, like Lilliputians surrounding a sleeping Gulliver. The greater part of the destroyer had been flattened or torn away completely by the chain-reaction explosions. What remained was nothing more than a steaming jungle of carbon black debris.

Reg ordered the pilot of his chopper toward the front of the destroyer, the only part that was still largely intact. This wedge-shaped remnant towered above the rest. There was a four-mile curve at the nose of the destroyer, and it was two miles deep. The roof over this fragment maintained its convex shape, but in some places had lost its structural integrity and hung like a heavy sheet of shattered glass on the supporting structures hidden beneath it. The whole thing looked unstable. Although it was only a fraction of what it had been, it was terrifyingly large.

There are going to be survivors, Reg thought.

"Fly inside," he told the pilot. He pointed toward one of the large breaks in the dome. The pilot thought he was kidding. He wasn't. The hole in the roof was the size of a small lake. After hovering over it uncertainly for a moment, and looking nervously again at Reg, the pilot let his craft sink into the opening. They dropped fifty feet and noticed something climbing the walls around them. The soldiers nearest the open door switched on the flashlights attached to the barrels of their assault rifles and took aim. They were surrounded by vines as thick around as a man's waist, which was extremely thin given their incredible length. They appeared to be made of stone.

The shaft they had flown into was seemingly without bottom. Even under the glare of the flashlights, they couldn't see the floor of the room. Since the roof had been blown out, it seemed that a powerful explosion must have traveled upward through the shaft. There was no way to tell whether the vines showed signs of damage. A hundred feet separated them from the nearest wall, but the sense of claustrophobia was strong. Guillaume yelled at the pilot to take them back toward the open air. The pilot glanced at Reg, who nodded his agreement.

It was hard to say whether the vine-structures were grown or manufactured. There was a regularity to the way they snaked up the walls that didn't look quite natural. Reg hardly thought about it. He sat in the copilot's chair feeling numb and heartbroken. The only thing he was anxious to do was verify that there were no survivors. When that was done, he would leave Saudi Arabia the fastest way he could.

Outside, they followed the slope of the ship down to the main concentration of Saudi forces. Their path brought them to within a mile of the huge black pillar that stood like a monumental skyscraper at the nose of the destroyer. It was leaning now, held up by a section of the dome that had deep fissures running through it. But the gleaming structure itself showed no signs of damage.

"That's where we're going to find them," Guillaume said, sitting next to Reg. "It's probably their control tower."

"Looks like the tower is about to tip over backwards. I'd hate to be inside when that happens."

"I hope they are still alive," Mohammed said, hungry for a

fight. Instead of answering him, everyone turned away to look at the impossibly large scale of the craft.

As the sky brightened, Reg could see the terrain surrounding the ship more clearly. They were far from the nearest village, and farther still from At-Ta'if. The terrain was uneven. Acacia and other scrub brush clung to the walls of the wadis, shallow canyons formed by rainwater. The rest was low rocky hills all the way to the horizon.

Ground troops had already penetrated into the ship. A spectacular triangular breach had opened at the edge of the craft, a mile from the base of the black tower. Trucks were driving up into the gap and disappearing into the darkness of the interior.

Before the helicopters touched down, a jeep came speeding toward them from a headquarters tent. The man in the passenger seat was an older, rail-thin Saudi who stood straight up and held on to the windshield for balance as the vehicle swayed and jolted beneath him. He didn't look like a soldier. He was unarmed and wore an ankle-length *thobe*. But his businesslike demeanor made it clear that he was an officer with a lot of work to get done. Before the jeep had come to a complete stop, he jumped into the sand and marched closer to the helicopter, keeping one hand on his *keffiyeh* to keep it from blowing off his head. Guillaume and Reg met him under the whirling blades, where the three of them shouted to one another over the noise until the Frenchman waved his troops onto the ground.

When the helicopter lifted away, the Saudi addressed the soldiers in fluent French. He identified himself as Lieutenant Rahim, briefed them on the situation inside the destroyer, and said that he would personally lead them inside for a look around. He made it clear that the Peacekeepers would be asked to leave once they had determined there were no survivors, because the king had declared the crash site a national military facility. When he was finished speaking, he turned to Reg and asked, in English, if there were any questions. Reg shook his head no.

"What did he say?" Miriyam asked one of the Peacekeepers.

"He said the aliens are all dead."

A troop truck lumbered forward, and the men piled in, taking positions on facing benches. There were no seats left by the time Reg and Miriyam followed Mohammed up the steps, so they decided to stand. They quickly thought better of it once the big truck began lurching over the bumpy earth. They immediately sat down on the floor of the truck and ended up clutching the legs of the soldiers to keep from being thrown around. Lieutenant Rahim was a man in a hurry to overcome some serious obstacles, at least that's how he drove. He smashed into potholes and ran down the banks of ten-foot-deep wadis while turned halfway around in his seat briefing the soldiers on the situation. The U.N. squad held on tightly and listened to him yell over the grind of the engine, their powder blue jumpsuits matching the early sky lightening above them. They were a seasoned group of professional soldiers who worked so well together they hardly had to speak. Reg felt like they would be able to take care of business if it came to that.

When the truck arrived on flatter ground, the baby-faced soldier whose leg Reg was holding, bent forward and asked a question. "Does this mean we are in love?" His comrades all burst out laughing. His name was Richaud, the joker of the squad. Reg sat back, a little embarrassed. Another man nudged him with a boot, the squad's medical officer. He looked down at Reg and shook his head.

"Your skin is very red, too much sun. Put your hand out." He uncapped a tube of ointment and squeezed some out. Reg thanked him and put it on. "You three look pretty funny down there. How did you come together?"

"It's a long story."

The man's name was LeBlanc. He had a stray eye, said he was a medical doctor, and had the curiosity of a ferret. He kept glancing ahead, anxious for the encounter to begin.

As they approached the giant triangular break in the wall of the destroyer, the huge bulk of it hung over them, hundreds of times the size of Saudi Arabia's largest supertanker. The way up into the ship was via a steep, uneven pile of rubble. Debris had spilled out of the opening, creating a natural ramp. A man directing traffic at the foot of the slope raised a red flag and brought Rahim's wild ride to a temporary halt. The path up the ramp could only accommodate one-way traffic, and a convoy was coming down at that moment. Two pickup trucks and a jeep were moving slowly and carefully along the treacherous path. As they sat there idling, Reg was sure Rahim wasn't going to be as cautious. As the vehicles got to the end of the ramp, Rahim released the emergency brake and lurched forward. But when he saw what was tied to the front of the jeep, he hit the brakes again.

The next moment, everyone was craning their necks to see. The men in the jeep had a carcass tied across the hood, like deer hunters returning home successful. It was a gray bulky mass that looked like a giant crustacean shell, except that it had a stump of a face. Long bony arms and legs mingled with the ropes, as well as a profusion of thick tentacles, some of which had worked their way free and were dragging along behind the wheels. The body seemed too thin to support the heavy, scalloped shell of its head and thorax, but the limbs looked strong. They were muscular and covered by an exoskeleton. Stretched over the engine of the jeep, the alien's body was nearly ten feet long and the color of a freshly unearthed grub. Guillaume yelled at his troops to stay where they were as he and Rahim jumped out to have a look. After a moment, the jeep took off to the north. Reg could see that it was headed toward the area a couple of miles away that was being prepared for the royal photo op. It didn't surprise him when Guillaume returned and explained that since the corpse was in good shape compared to most the Saudis were finding, it was going to be used in the ceremony.

Instead of driving up the ramp and into the ship, Rahim ground his engine into gear and turned south, following the two trucks. A few hundred yards later, they came to the place where the Saudi army was dumping the alien bodies. It was a quarantine area, and a stench like ammonia was thick in the air. Everyone got out of the truck and walked up to a roadblock that was guarded by a pair of Pakistani men in turbans.

The two trucks they had followed stopped next to a long pile of slick gray body parts and immediately began to unload more of the same. The flatbeds were piled high with the wreckage of alien bodies. Arms and legs and skull fragments were dragged off the trucks and tossed onto the five-foot-high pile that was already forty feet long. Reg and Guillaume said they wanted a closer look, so Rahim led them past the armed guards. Guillaume stopped and called back to LeBlanc, the medical officer, waving him forward. The biting, acrid smell in the air became stronger the closer they got to the meat pile.

"This is a very bad job to have," LeBlanc said to Reg as they watched the men off-loading the stinking cargo. The dead bodies were a potential biohazard, and no self-respecting Saudi was going to sully himself with that sort of work. Instead it was done by Filipino and Indian men who wore only gardening gloves. In lieu of gas masks, they'd tied shirts around their heads to cover their noses. At least there wasn't a lot of blood. In fact, there wasn't any. LeBlanc pulled on a pair of surgical gloves and moved up to the small mountain of carnage. He yanked a section of tentacle away from the pile. Reg looked over the man's shoulder as he examined it.

"Is this air safe to breathe?" he asked the doctor. "Aren't foreign microbes a danger? Things we have no immunities to?"

LeBlanc sniffed at the air. "It's nothing. A little ammonia, it keeps you awake." He lifted the severed end of the thick tentacle to his nose with both hands and smelled it carefully. "This is not the source of the odor. It makes no smell. It is strange," he said, examining the eight-inch-thick tube of flesh. "No bones, no shell, no blood vessels."

He used a pocketknife to scrape away the sand clinging to the moisture and dig out a square of white flesh. After sniffing at it and running it between his fingers, he shrugged and tossed it aside. "Like a lobster," he said, looking up at Reg with his wandering eye. He was a strange man.

The tentacle was covered with a tough, gray skin that had striated markings like those found on the body of an earthworm. At its tip was a tough, two-fingered pincer claw. When each half closed, they formed a spearhead. After playing with it for a moment or two longer, LeBlanc returned to the pile and retrieved a three-foot-long slab of shell and carried it back to Reg. The inside was covered in some kind of sticky gelatin or fat. LeBlanc gathered up a glob of it, then watched it slowly plop off the end of his knife blade.

"This is the substance that is making the smell," he announced, his eyes watering slightly from the fumes. When he flipped the twenty-pound fragment over, the left half of a bony face was staring back up at him. A smooth, rounded forehead bulged above a deep black eye socket. There was no eye. The lower half of the face, where the mouth would be on a human, was a confused mass of cartilage tissue full of crisscrossing channels, as if it had been hacked at with a machete. It was part of the creature's exoskeleton.

"That's the ugliest damn thing I've ever seen," Reg said.

LeBlanc seemed surprised. "I was just now thinking how much they look like us." He ran his fingers over the seam at the center of the face. It made a clean vertical break from the middle of the forehead down to the middle of the amorphous chin. LeBlanc said it must be like the shell of an oyster or a giant clam. "But it's strange," he said, rolling it over once more. "If it's like a shell of the clam, where is the clam?"

He walked back to the pile and picked up a soft torso with one thin arm attached to it. He carried it back to Reg and tossed it on the ground. With a deft incision, he split the chest open and pulled back the dermal walls.

"You see? It's *très* bizarre. There are two different species." He used his knife to poke at the innards of his latest find. "These small animals, they have the internal organs. But the big ones, *pffft*, they are shells, they are empty."

Rahim and Guillaume had walked to the far end of the quarantine area, keeping well away from the alien corpses. Both of them were anxious to leave when they returned to where Reg was standing.

"The smell is horrible. I have seen enough," said the Frenchman.

"Yes, everything is under control," said the Saudi lieutenant. "Let us continue."

Reg nodded that he, too, was ready to leave this area and enter the ship. The penetrating ammonia vapors were heavy in the air, causing his eyes to water. If the air was contaminated with foreign pathogens, it was too late to do anything about it. Hundreds of men would have already been infected. But as the three of them started back to the truck, LeBlanc whistled sharply through his teeth and waved them over to where he was kneeling. He'd found something in the sand.

It was a greenish thing about an inch long and was squirming like a bristled caterpillar. LeBlanc said he thought it was some form of plant life. In the few minutes since he'd discovered it, he said, the wriggling, wormlike organism had nearly doubled in size.

"Regardez," he said. "Look at this." He extended one of his gloved fingers and held it half an inch above the ground. The tiny creature lifted straight up, straining to reach the finger. When LeBlanc moved his hand slightly to the left, the tiny form bent in that direction.

"It senses your body heat," Reg said, "or maybe it smells you."

"Maybe," allowed the doctor. "I believe it wants something else. I think it feels the moisture." The doctor pulled his hand away, then watched as the small green shape turned and began wriggling toward the nearest source of moisture—the alien cadavers. When it had traveled a couple of inches, LeBlanc unscrewed the cap of his canteen and poured a small amount of water into the sand. The organism turned and immediately began burrowing into the wet spot, sucking the moisture out of the sand. As it did so, its body grew visibly, doubling in length.

"Interesting," said Guillaume, looking slightly queasy. "Where did you find it?"

"Here," LeBlanc said, "in the pile."

"Maybe there's more," Reg suggested. "There's plenty of moisture in these bodies." Thinking that Reg was probably right, LeBlanc began removing body pieces from the top of the heap and tossing them aside. He didn't have to dig very deeply before he found proof that Reg was right. The plants were growing at an exponential rate just below the surface of the heap. Thousands of slender, translucent tendrils many feet long had grown in thick bunches throughout the pile of biowreckage. They were glass-clear and writhed in protest to being exposed to the morning sun. Within moments, they changed color and began to turn green.

"This plant, it is very dangerous," LeBlanc said. "If it finds a lake or an ocean, maybe we cannot stop the growth. It must be contained here before it spreads."

"It might be a source of food for the aliens," Reg surmised. There was no way of knowing how many months or years or centuries they had been traveling through space. A fast-growing plant like this one would create an abundant source of nourishment. "The doctor's right," Reg said. "If this plant spreads, we could have an ecological nightmare on our hands."

Rahim immediately issued orders that no more bodies be brought out of the ship until the problem was better understood. Then he went to inspect one of the trucks that had been carrying the bodies to the quarantine site. First he checked the tires, then popped open the hood and looked into the engine compartment. Cursing in Arabic, he reached down and pulled away a handful of the vines. They had already overgrown the truck's radiator. Immediately, he regretted having touched them. He threw them aside and wiped his hand vigorously on the material of his robe. "Burn them," he shouted to the men off-loading the bodies, "burn everything, including the trucks."

After meeting with the officers in charge of the quarantine area and making sure they understood the danger LeBlanc had found, the men returned to their own vehicle. After inspecting it for signs of the aggressive plant, the Peacekeepers piled in.

Rahim drove back toward the triangular breach in the wall of the destroyer and headed up the uneven ramp of debris. Although the path to the opening was treacherous and bumpy, Rahim drove fast. The soldiers riding in back were tossed around roughly, but they were eager to get inside and begin the work they had come to do. It was an ironic mission for a U.N. peacekeeping force: locate survivors of the battle and kill them.

They came to the top of the ramp and drove onto the smooth floor of the city destroyer's main deck. The gray walls that closed in around them were the color of graphite. They towered above the truck, smooth in some places and intricately worked in others, like large sections of circuit board. The ceilings of the first rooms they entered were low, but as they penetrated deeper, the domed roof climbed higher. Rahim was forced to slow the truck to a few miles per hour as he steered through the obstacle course of shattered walls and missing sections of floor. The first few hundred feet of the ship were a warren of collapsed passageways and work spaces extending both horizontally and vertically. Shafts of sunlight leaked in where the roof had torn away, but it was soon dark enough that Rahim switched on his headlights. Even though all of the internal walls were badly fractured, most of them appeared to be sturdy; others were teetering on the brink of collapse. It was like driving through a darkened house of cards that threatened to fall apart at any moment.

As he approached a narrow gap between two towering walls that had fallen against one another, Rahim honked his horn and flashed his headlights to alert oncoming drivers to his presence. Then he drove through the opening.

On the other side, they entered a curved hallway of monumental proportions. It was several hundred feet across and long enough that it disappeared around the bend of the ship in either direction. It was completely empty and reminded Reg of an underground flood channel he and his friends had played in when they were children, only this place was a thousand times larger. The truck suddenly felt like a small toy moving across the smooth floor of the chamber. A trail of burning flares marked the path to the far side of the space. Rahim hit the gas and sped into the darkness. He didn't slow down when they came to a soft spot in the road, a place where the floor hung limply into whatever open chamber lay below. It felt like driving across a swaying trampoline until they climbed up the other side and found solid footing once more.

As they approached the opposite wall, Reg looked up into the gloomy light and saw that there was a series of large rectangular openings, each one a doorway to a new level of the ship. On either side of the portals were massive, swollen structures that looked like the roots of some enormous tree. They were grayish white and stood out against the rest of the dark wall.

Rahim stopped the truck near the portal on the ground floor and everyone climbed out. The Peacekeepers switched on their flashlights and inspected the rootlike structures. It quickly became apparent that they were hollow inside and formed a natural staircase to the portal doors above.

"They are growing a lot of plants in here," Miriyam observed.

Reg nodded as he studied the way the hollow structure twisted its way up the wall, but it looked as much like a thick vein as it did a root. He was quickly coming to realize that the ship was composed largely—if not completely—of organic materials. He and Miriyam walked past a group of Saudi soldiers who were standing near their trucks and smoking cigarettes, until they came to the place where the towering wall joined the floor. Reg knelt down and inspected the corner.

"What do you see?" Miriyam asked him.

"Look at the way the cracks run through the floor and travel up the walls."

"What about it?"

"It means they're built from one piece of material. This whole room," he said, gesturing toward the massive hallway, "was cut from a single block. Unless . . ."

"Unless what?"

"Unless it was grown."

"If it was grown," Miriyam said, "it means we are inside a large animal. That the whole ship was living at some time."

"Not a very comforting thought, is it?" Reg moved his hand over the wall. Despite the hairline fractures running in all directions, the surface was smooth and hard. The texture was closer to leather than metal. It gave like soft wood when he drove his thumbnail into it and left a mark.

Some of the Peacekeepers had climbed up the hollow rootlike

structures and were beginning to investigate what lay behind the portal doors. Rahim yelled up at them that those areas had already been searched. They were identical in every detail to the room on the ground floor, the next stop on the tour he was giving them. As the Frenchmen began to climb down, Rahim led the way through the floor-level portal into an area he called the room of the barrels.

Inside, under a low ceiling, was another huge room. Battery-powered work lights were switched on to reveal a series of low walls that reached halfway to the ceiling and formed a kind of open maze. Rahim led the way to a hexagonal tank that was four feet deep and twelve feet across. The soldiers peered over the edge and saw themselves reflected in a shallow pool of silver liquid. Half-submerged in the shiny solution was a large pale body, an alien exoskeleton. It had long, powerfully built arms and legs. Instead of feet, it had a pair of hooked toes that curled forward like a ram's horns. The hands were similar to human hands. Each one had three bony fingers that reached lengths of up to twelve inches. But the part of the body that drew the most attention was the giant clamshell that composed the head and thorax region of the animal. It was split open along the seam running from the pointed crest of down to its abdomen. As LeBlanc had noted earlier, there were no internal organs. The interior walls of the shell were pinkish gray muscle. At the bottom of the tank, there was a piece of machinery that looked like a harness or mold. When the ship crashed, the body had torn free of the harness, and most of the fluid had sloshed out of the vat.

"This one, it is more smaller than the ones we found outside," LeBlanc pointed out. The body was about six feet long.

"Yes, yes," Rahim agreed. "It is still young, still growing. We believe this entire area is a farm to grow these creatures. They tell me this liquid is a growth culture. A preliminary chemical analysis shows a balanced pH and many hormones and nutrients."

"They're growing these bodies the same way our scientists culture cells?" Reg asked.

"Exactly," LeBlanc said, "but the level is very sophisticated, far beyond our ability."

"Is it alive?" Mohammed asked, peering down at the alien.

"No," Rahim answered definitively. "All of them are dead. We are certain of this." To prove his point, he took out a pistol and shot into the tank. The large body remained as lifeless as it had before.

"Remarkable," LeBlanc gasped. He shook his head in awe of the alien scientific accomplishments. "They have done what we cannot do: pluripotent cell differentiation. This is something we humans cannot do. Maybe in one hundred years."

Miriyam was puzzled. "I don't understand how a species of animals can exist if they have to be grown like this. Don't they have sex?"

LeBlanc looked at her with his stray eye from the opposite side of the tank. "You have to understand that this one is not the real alien who drives the ship and fires the weapons. This one, it is only an armor, an empty body for the real aliens. They sit inside the shell like a little . . . how do you say? . . . the little man who rides the horse."

"Jockey?"

"Exactly. The real alien sits inside this empty body like a jockey. Without the little one inside, this one is without the life. *C'est brillant, n'est-ce pas?*"

"Yeah," Miriyam replied sarcastically. "They're real geniuses."

Guillaume glanced curiously around the mazelike room of the barrels. "All of these pools have bodies in them?"

"Yes," Rahim said. "And the same on the floors above. There are thousands of these barrels."

As they talked, the long fingers of an exoskeletal hand lifted over the side of the tank and reached into the air. An "alien" voice called out, *"Aidez-moi! Je suis mort!"* It was Richaud, the same baby-faced soldier who had joked with Reg in the truck. He had found a severed arm lying nearby and was using it to put on a show for the others. No one found his impromptu puppet show particularly amusing. After a sharp word from Guillaume, Richaud tossed the arm away.

Rahim led the group through the labyrinth of half-wall partitions until they arrived at an open pit. It was as big around as a manhole leading down to a sewer. Turning to LeBlanc, he gestured toward the hole in the floor. "The plant you found outside is also here." When flashlights were pointed into the opening, they saw what he meant. The same glassy vines were clinging to the walls of the round shaft, writhing and wriggling in slow motion.

"Maybe there's water down there," Reg said, "or some other source of moisture."

"Perhaps," said the doctor, leaning over the opening with a flashlight and trying to measure the depth of the shaft. "Or perhaps there are more bodies."

"It's nice and dark down there," Miriyam said. "It's a place survivors would hide."

"We've got to find a way down to the lower levels," Reg said to Guillaume.

"I already thought of that." The Frenchman grunted. "My scouts have found an opening. Follow me."

Not far from the large door they'd stepped through to enter the room of the barrels, there was a long rip in the floor just wide enough for a large man to slip through. The floor of the next level was visible about twenty feet below. The Peacekeepers broke open their backpacks and began unpacking the gear they would need.

Lieutenant Rahim thought Reg and Guillaume were crazy for wanting to go belowdecks with such a small force, but he could see he wasn't going to be able to stop them. Reluctantly, he decided to join them.

Using ropes, the Peacekeepers were lowered through the opening two at a time. Guillaume ordered two of them to stay behind and keep an ear to the radio. Reg, Mohammed, and Miriyam were the last ones down. When they assembled on the lower level, they found themselves in a wide, rectangular passageway. The first thing Guillaume did was to order thermal and sonic scans, both of which came back negative. The weak light filtering down through the shaft cast a dim glow on the floor. Otherwise, they had only their flashlights. The floor felt spongy under their feet. Both it and the walls appeared to be made of muscle or some other living tissue. Thick bundles of the sinuous, fleshy material were coiled around one another, the color of granite and as flat as a brick wall. The material looked as if it had been pressed and compacted. But as LeBlanc pointed out, the walls had probably been grown that way, through the use of molds. As the group set off, Reg had the uneasy feeling he was moving through the bowels of some enormous living creature.

"I think you were right," he said quietly to Miriam, who was walking beside him.

"About what?"

"If there's anything still alive in this ship, this is where we'll find it."

"I felt much braver about all of this ten minutes ago," she said.

"Too late to turn back now. Where's the kid?"

"Leading the way, I think."

Moving in a loose line behind Guillaume and his two advance men, they walked fifty yards before they came to an opening in the wall. It looked like a sphincter muscle and stood three times as tall as a man. A thick lip of tissue lined the opening, floor to ceiling. The advance men went forward to inspect it, moving the last few feet on their stomachs and peering over the bottom of the lip. After a moment, they stood up and went into the chamber beyond. When they waved the others forward, they found a large, roughly oval chamber. The walls were made of the same material as in the passageway, with one conspicuous difference: They were full of small, rough-hewn caves that looked as if they'd been chopped, or eaten, out of the walls. Some were twenty feet long and had two doorways. Others were shallow depressions in the face of the wall. The soldiers found matting and shreds of dried vegetation in the deeper caves, which led them to conclude they had discovered sleeping quarters. But there were no bodies, no physical trace of the aliens they were hunting, so they moved on.

Farther down the passageway, they found a similar chamber, and then another. Their progress was slow because Guillaume insisted that each chamber be approached and examined with caution. Mohammed and Rahim both grew impatient. Mohammed because he was eager to find something that was still alive, and Rahim because he wasn't. He was anxious to get back to his own work, and pointed out the obvious: The passageway gave onto only one sort of room. Since there were no signs of survivors, he suggested they return to the surface.

"No. They are here," Mohammed said. "We must find them." He turned and led a hurried march toward the next opening. Along the way, they found a place where the wall had torn away from the floor, opening a gap to the next floor down. Reg had a claustrophobic moment when he saw that the gap was wide enough to slip through. He knew they were going to descend to the next level.

"Are there any signs of life?" Guillaume asked the first man through the crack. When he replied in the negative, the leader of the Peacekeepers looked at Reg. "Maybe we have gone far enough."

The last thing Reg wanted to do was wriggle into the hole and descend yet another level, but he shook his head. "We have to keep going," he said. "King Ibrahim and several hundred civilians are heading out here from At-Ta'if. We've got to make sure there won't be any surprises."

"And quickly," Rahim added. "There are many preparations still to be made before the king's arrival."

"Let's go then." Guillaume ordered two of his men to stay behind and maintain radio contact with the outside. Within minutes, the others had squeezed through the opening to the floor below. The new passageway was not straight and square like the one above. The walls were rough and curved like a mine tunnel and left only enough room for two people to walk abreast. The tunnel showed signs of use. The lower half of it, including the floor, had been worn smooth, and there were grooves and dents running continuously about three feet above the ground. The crack they had lowered themselves through was on the ceiling now, and it narrowed as they followed it a short distance to a door that blocked their path. It was a heavy, rounded shell that closed against a bulkhead partition. At the center of the door was a battered, copper-colored medallion about the size of a dinner plate. At one time, there must have been a flowerlike design etched into the metallic substance, but only traces of it remained around the edges.

"Open it," Guillaume said to one of his scouts.

The man reached out and touched the medallion with one finger. The door flew open and slammed against the wall. Flashlights explored the next part of the tunnel until the door slowly began to move closed again. When Guillaume touched the medallion, it shot open again. He stepped across the threshold and waved the others to follow him.

"Wait," Reg said. "Does that door open from the other side?" Guillaume, Mohammed, and the others who had stepped through turned and examined the door for a moment before it sealed behind them.

"That is a very good question," Guillaume called back. His voice came through the crack in the ceiling that extended a few feet into the far part of the tunnel before ending. "Don't touch the door. I will examine it." A moment later, he shouted through the crack that there was no way to open it from the other side.

After warning Guillaume to step away, Reg reached up and put his hand on the medallion. He felt a small electrical shock as the door swung open and smashed against the wall again.

"This is a one-way street," Miriyam observed.

"We'll need to leave someone here to open it," Reg said.

Guillaume posted two more guards and continued into the darkness of the next segment of the tunnel. Soon, they found a differently shaped door built into the sidewall of the tunnel. It was wider than the first one and slightly lower, but had the same copper medallion set outside it. Mohammed reached it first, but when he touched it, nothing happened. Others tried with the same result. They tried to force it open, but soon realized it was futile and continued to advance. They found several more of the side doors, none of which would open, before they arrived at another bulkhead. After posting another pair of guards to keep the door open, the remaining fourteen people stepped through.

Part of the ceiling had collapsed in the next segment of the tunnel. Without opening to the upper level, it drooped into their path. Two of the Peacekeepers ducked their heads and moved under it. They called out that one of the side doors had been forced ajar.

"See what is behind it," Guillaume ordered.

"A side tunnel," they reported.

"Check the first fifty meters."

After a tense moment of waiting, the two men came out from under the sagging ceiling and said the tunnel led to a cavelike room. There were no signs of survivors.

"We are going very slowly," Mohammed complained. "We have to find them fast and kill them."

Guillaume snapped at him to shut up and keep out of the way. Mohammed was in no mood to back down. He took a menacing step toward the rough-looking Frenchman, but Reg caught him by his skinny arm before he could do anything foolish. He pulled the young Iraqi past Guillaume, ducked under the low part of the roof, and entered the side tunnel.

After only a few steps, the walls opened around them, and they were standing in a cave. It was more like an underground cavern, full of stalactites and stalagmites. There was a forest of them, hanging from the ceiling and rising out of the floor at regularly spaced intervals. The columns looked as if they had been built little by little, by accretion, the way coral grows or the way wax builds up at the bottom of a candlestick. But the precise distances between them made it obvious that they were not naturally occurring. Scattered around on the floor were small objects that appeared to be hand tools, and larger ones that looked like water troughs. The space felt more like a factory than a cave, and there were a million places to hide.

When thermal and sonic scans came back negative, LeBlanc broke away from the others and rushed up to examine the nearest column. It was a stalagmite about four feet tall, jade green, and composed of a crystalline substance. It showed signs of having been scraped, chiseled, and hacked at.

"Look at this," the doctor said eagerly. He had his flashlight pointed at the top of the tapering stump. "Growth rings, the same that you have inside a tree." He looked up at Reg with his stray eye and nodded admiringly. "They were good farmers, these aliens."

"I recognize that color," Miriyam said.

"So do I," Reg nodded. "The color of the light surrounding the firing cone."

"Maybe they use this crystal as a power source."

"Yes," said LeBlanc. He took out a knife and used it to scrape off a layer of the material, then raked it into a sample bag. The others began to wander deeper into the chamber, finding various tools on the floor: rasps, chisels, machete-like blades—all of them smaller than human tools. The large objects that looked like water troughs were filled with small sacks made of a hard, flexible skin. When LeBlanc opened one of them up with his knife, he found it was filled with powder of the same jade green color. The doctor was convinced that the crystalline residue provided the aliens with a renewable, self-sustaining fuel that could be converted into enormous amounts of power. He pointed out that the sides of the trough matched the groove marks worn into the walls in the passageway outside. "So if we follow the marks on the walls, eventually . . ."

"Eventually, we'll get to the engine room," Reg finished the thought.

"We can learn how they converted this stuff"—he pointed to his sample of powder—"into such a great explosive. Maybe we will learn something good from them."

One of the Peacekeepers shouted and dropped his rifle, batting at something in front of his face. Instantly, a dozen rifles were pointed in his direction. It was the baby-faced soldier, Richaud. He spit on the floor and turned to the others, explaining that he'd run into something that felt like a spiderweb. He cracked a joke in French that brought a nervous chuckle from a few of the Peacekeepers, but Guillaume was not amused.

"Stay quiet and watch what you're doing," he told the soldier, then motioned for the doctor to go and have a look at him. But

before LeBlanc could get to him, Richaud made a noise, and his
body tensed up like a bird dog. He pointed toward a section of the
room near the entrance where the ceiling had sagged almost to the
floor.

"What is it?" Guillaume demanded.

"Can't you hear that?" Richaud asked. No one breathed as
they listened for whatever it was that had spooked the Frenchman. "It's alive," he said.

"What is?"

"No," Richaud said, "no, no, NO!" He reached up and clutched
the sides of his head and screamed. The others ran to Richaud's
aid. He fell to the floor in the grip of a painful seizure and began
to convulse. Reg and some others helped pin the soldier's flailing
body to the floor so that LeBlanc could have a look at him, but
there was nothing the doctor could do. Blood began to stream out
of Richaud's nostrils and ears. His eyes, wide with terror, went
pink, and then bright red. He continued to struggle and shout
incoherently until his body went limp.

"He's dead," LeBlanc said in amazement.

"He said he ran into a spiderweb. Maybe it's poison,"
Miriyam suggested.

Every flashlight in the room turned toward the ceiling, but
there was no sign of anything that looked like a spiderweb, only
the carefully arranged rows of stalactites. As Reg scanned the
chamber, a strange feeling came over him. At first he thought it
was a powerful sense of déjà vu. But he quickly realized it was
more than that. He was thinking in a way he didn't recognize at
all. It was another presence inside of him, a mind thinking inside
his own.

Miriyam noticed that Reg had gone still and silent. "What's
the matter?"

He turned and looked at her, but couldn't answer. As his
mouth moved, struggling to form words, a sharp pain gripped his
neck and spiked upward into his brain. He screamed and grabbed
his head as Richaud had done. As he collapsed to the floor, he felt
a tremendous weight crushing down on his skull and tried franti-

cally to push it away with his hands. He forced his eyes open and looked at the ceiling above him. At the same time, he saw himself lying on the floor, surrounded by people trying to help him. This second point of view, which overlapped his normal vision, came from low on ground, from the area below the collapsed ceiling, the same place Richaud had pointed to a moment before. Whatever the thing was that had invaded his brain, Reg realized it was there, nearby on the floor. The already-unbearable pain ratcheted upward in intensity, and he felt himself beginning to black out. His assailant, whatever it was, was reaching across the room with its mind, infiltrating his nervous system and working him like a puppet. With the last of his strength, he struggled to turn and lash out at his attacker, but there wasn't much he could do. His body went limp. But Reg didn't lose consciousness completely, and the pain did not leave him. He understood that there was only one way to relieve his suffering: He had to answer a question.

The question was not put to him in words, but in the form of images and an urgent sensation of need. He found himself standing in a huge, dark, cathedral space hiding from a band of filthy, vile creatures that had him surrounded. He knew somehow that these creatures were an enemy army, and he could feel the intense hatred and loathing they had for him. He sensed the presence of others, his own kind, hiding in the darkness.

Reg realized that he was inside a group mind—hundreds of individuals thinking together as if all tuned to the same radio frequency and able to communicate instantaneously by means of shorthand image/thought/impulses. Two overpowering sensations coursed through this group mind: a burning physical hunger and an intense loathing for the army of humans. Then the interrogation began. There was a great gash in the wall of the cathedral, a towering triangular opening. Beyond it, a bright sun beat down on the sands of a hostile alien planet. Outside, in the distance, a caravan of enemy vehicles was approaching across a barren plateau. The mind ordered him to divulge everything he knew about this approaching force. Reg recognized that they were limousines and armored military vehicles, being seen through the eyes of the aliens. To his horror, he was being asked to act as a spy for the aliens, to help them prepare an attack. But such was his fear and confusion that he complied without the slightest hesitation. In a rapid-fire sequence of half thoughts, he communicated everything he knew about the group and their plans, then begged for the excruciating pain to end. But the response from the mind was an order to die instead. It reached into him and forced his heart to stop beating, his lungs to stop breathing.

As Reg slipped toward death, he realized that he could resist, that the power of the group mind was not absolute. In some way he couldn't fully understand, he realized that the aliens couldn't control him without his consent. For a moment, his will struggled against the Will that was controlling him. He felt himself regaining some control, but when the pain intensified, he lay back and obeyed the command to die. Darkness.

There was a series of quick explosions, and then someone was speaking to him in a language he didn't understand. Reg's eyes shot open without being able to focus, and he gasped for air. An indistinct figure hovered over him, preparing to inject him with a hypodermic needle. In a daze, Reg swatted his hand at the needle and knocked it away. Slowly, he realized the strange language was French and the figure leaning over him was LeBlanc.

"You are not dead," the doctor said with surprise.

"Over there," Reg groaned, pointing in the direction of his attacker. "An alien. It's alive." He turned his head in that direction and saw Miriyam inspecting something under the collapsed ceiling with a machine gun in her hands.

"It's not alive anymore," she told him. "I killed it."

"How? How did you know?" Reg asked.

"You told us," said the doctor with the stray eye. "Don't you remember? We had no idea, but then you pointed to where it was hiding."

"It must have been trapped there when the ceiling fell on it," surmised Guillaume. "Are you okay? Can you walk?"

"We have to get out of here, have to run." Reg pulled himself into a sitting position and tried to shake the cobwebs out of his head. The attack had left him disoriented and slightly dizzy. "They're coming."

A shock of fear ran through everyone in the room. "Who's coming?"

"The others, the aliens. They know where we are," Reg said, struggling to find his feet. "We have to get outside and warn them."

LeBlanc prevented Reg from standing up. "What are you talking about? Tell us what happened."

"It used its mind. Some kind of telepathy," Reg explained, sorting through the experience, trying to make sense of it. "They were asking me things, torturing me."

"They? How many?"

Reg shook his head. He didn't know. "Many."

Guillaume knelt down beside him and spoke in an urgent whisper. "We found only one of them. Where are the others? How do you know they are coming?"

"Oh, my God," Reg gasped when he realized he'd given the aliens information they could use to attack the people in the royal entourage. "Let me up. They're going to attack. We've got to warn them."

Guillaume grabbed him by the collar, shook him roughly, and held him in place. "You're talking nonsense. Tell us what happened!" The Frenchman's scarred face was close to his, illuminated in the glow of the flashlights.

"This one," Reg began, pointing to the creature Miriyam had shot, "invaded my mind, attacked me with its mind. But there were others, other minds. They communicate . . . I don't know how to describe it . . . they think together, as a single mind. When this one reached inside of me, I was also inside of it. There was a melding, and I saw through its eyes, but I also saw through the eyes of the others. I saw what they were seeing. They're at the entrance to the ship, looking out of the same opening we drove through when we came in. Right now, the king and his people are arriving outside. The aliens are going to ambush them. They're going to kill the king."

Guillaume was alarmed, but remained skeptical. Reg had been through a traumatic experience and was badly shaken. The pain could have caused him to hallucinate. He had one more question. "How do the aliens know it is the king?"

"Because I told them," Reg answered. He shook free of Guillaume's grip, stood up, and began moving unsteadily toward the exit. Mohammed took Reg by the arm and assisted him.

"I think he is right," Rahim said, checking his watch. "King Ibrahim is scheduled to arrive exactly now. We must warn him at once."

The Peacekeepers followed Reg, Mohammed, and Miriyam through the side tunnel and into the main passageway. They turned and hurried toward the first bulkhead door. The Peacekeepers radioed to the men on the far side of the door to open it but received no reply.

Guillaume had given them orders to keep it open at all times.

Reg took the machine gun Miriyam was carrying and smashed the butt of it against the door, signaling to the men on the other side. When there was no response he threw down the gun and wedged his fingertips into the thin gap between the door and the bulkhead. "Help me!" he yelled over his shoulder. First Miriyam and then a few of the Peacekeepers stepped forward to try and pry the door open, but they did so reluctantly. If the men on the other side touched the copper medallion, the door would fly open and crush them against the wall. The bayonets the Peacekeepers had on their rifles provided them with the leverage they needed, but it took the full strength of six men and one woman to pull the door open twelve inches.

"Movement behind us. Something is coming," one of the soldiers standing farther back yelled to Guillaume.

"Pull harder!" Guillaume shouted.

When Rahim came forward to lend his strength to the effort, Miriyam turned and grunted at him. "You are skinny. Reach through. Touch the medallion."

"But the door will open too fast."

"Do it!"

The rail-thin Saudi lieutenant pushed his way past the soldiers straining against the strength of the door and reached his arm into the next chamber. "I will count to three," he told them. But he never got the chance to start counting. Something grabbed his arm and pulled hard enough to break his neck when it slammed against the side of the door. The others backed away, startled, and let the door smash closed on his limp body. A moment later, a tentacle the size of a python slid through the opening and began slashing through the air, searching for another victim.

The group retreated from the door and started in the other direction, but soon realized they were surrounded. The collapsed section of the ceiling that sagged into the passageway was moving. Although it weighed several tons, something was walking below it, lifting it out of the way as easily as if it were a bedsheet hanging on a clothesline. One of the soldiers moved closer and lay on his stomach, peering ahead with his flashlight.

"Two pairs of feet," he called back to the others.

As they braced themselves for the attack, there was an explosion in the passageway behind them. The door had been opened. They wheeled around to see a gruesome and terrifying sight: a ghost gray stump of a face jutting toward them from the center of a wide, flaring shell. The creature was an eight-foot-tall exoskeleton, one of the biomechanical suits of armor they'd discovered lying in the vats of liquid two floors above. It filled the doorway. The multiple pairs of tentacles on its back waved through the air like the hypnotic, ophidian locks of Medusa's hair, and the sight of the creature turned the humans momentarily to stone.

All except Mohammed. He was carrying the machine gun Miriyam had tossed to the floor. As soon as the hissing, many-armed beast revealed itself, Mohammed lowered the gun and charged ahead, firing and screaming as he went. His bullets bounced off the hard shell, but their collective impact began to crack it apart. When he was almost to the bulkhead, the pointed tip of the skeletal head shattered completely and broke away. It made no difference. With alarming agility and speed, the hideous creature darted through the bulkhead and speared the young Saudi in the chest with a tentacle, spraying blood everywhere. As

Mohammed's body dropped to the floor, the Peacekeepers opened fire and hit the monster with hundreds of rounds of ammunition, knocking it a few steps backwards. Each bullet chipped away another piece of bone, but only little by little. It took several seconds of sustained firing until the thing died.

"Go! Go! Back to the entrance!"

The team broke into a sprint down the hallway, stepping over and around the fallen alien. When they were through the bulkhead, they stumbled on the bodies of the Peacekeepers who had been guarding the door. A moment later, the first of the two aliens behind them stepped clear of the fallen ceiling. The soldier bringing up the rear of the retreat didn't notice until it was too late. The big creature raced down the tunnel twice as fast as the humans and quickly caught them. One by one, the men running at the end of the line realized they were lost and turned to make their last stands. Each one blasted the alien with as many shells as he could before being trampled, killed, and tossed aside. Reg was running just behind Miriyam and Guillaume. Like the others, he was terrified out of his mind and desperate to climb out of the tunnel. But when he realized what was happening behind him, he stopped running and wrested the machine gun away from the Peacekeeper who had taken it from the dead Mohammed.

"Keep going," Reg told the man, then pressed himself against the side of the tunnel and watched the flashlights of the last two men running toward him. He had decided to help them slow the aliens down in order to give Miriyam and the others time to escape. But the men didn't see him waiting and when he pushed away from the wall and began running alongside of them, he startled them so badly that they tripped over one another and went down in a heap. Reg fell with them and watched the flashlights break free and go rolling across the floor. As the men scrambled to collect their guns, the sound of rushing feet came toward them. They turned and fired into the darkness. They fired until their ammunition was nearly spent.

When they picked up their flashlights and looked behind them, fragments of an exoskeleton were spread across the floor of the tunnel, the bulk of it lying only a few paces away. Despite having been torn to pieces, the body was struggling slowly forward, determined to complete the hunt. Reg and the two men turned away from it and ran as fast as they could. Far ahead, they saw the bobbing flashlights of the main group. Then they heard gunfire and screaming.

"Stop," one of the Peacekeepers beside Reg said. "Back the other way."

"No, keep going." But the man had already turned and headed back in the other direction. Reg and the remaining soldier continued to run, but they slowed their pace because everything had gone silent and still ahead of them. A pair of rifles lay on the ground, the flashlights attached to them creating a dim pool of light on the floor.

"Maybe we *should* go the other way," the Frenchman said.

"No, there's another one back there."

"Yes, but only one. How many are up ahead?"

"Switch off your light. Let's keep going." The two men walked at a fast march through the pitch-darkness, feeling their way along the curving, uneven walls and keeping their fingers tight against the triggers of their guns. They walked for a long time before they heard a sound.

"Psst. Over here." The voice belonged to Guillaume. He told them not to turn on their lights, but he turned on his, keeping the palm of his hand closed over the bulb. Reg felt his way along the wall until he reached the spot. He could feel people huddled low against the wall, but couldn't immediately tell how many. Clumsily, he made his way close to Guillaume.

"Another one just ahead, twenty meters," he told Reg.

LeBlanc's voice whispered out of the inky blackness. "Put all your bullets to the face of the shell. We must kill the little one inside."

There was another report of gunfire, this time far down the narrow passageway. The man who had turned back had obviously found something. When the firing ceased abruptly, everyone could imagine what had happened. "We've got to do something," Reg said. "We're going to have company in a minute."

Miriyam said, "Better to take them one at a time."

And a moment later they heard the scraping of footsteps ahead. Guillaume switched on his flashlight, and the group opened fire. But the skeletal warrior quickly retreated behind the first curve in the tunnel.

Reg knew immediately that the creature was stalling, waiting for the one that was coming from behind so they could work together. Reg snapped a fresh cartridge of shells into the machine gun. "We can't wait any longer," he said, and started forward.

"Remember to aim for the head," Miriyam said, joining him.

The creature retreated no farther. When the team came around the bend in the tunnel and began blasting away, it charged forward. The head-thorax shell dipped forward slightly, as if the alien wanted to gore them with the blunt tip of the pointed head. The team's decision to concentrate their firepower on the face led to mixed results. The hard material quickly fractured and then broke apart, but before the alien inside the suit could be killed, the exoskeleton turned away from the gunfire, scampering backward toward them, tentacles first. Guillaume fired until his ammunition was spent, then moved forward to use the tip of his gun as a spike. Before he could do so, one of the flailing tentacle arms connected and sent him sprawling against the wall. Guillaume was down but not out. As the exoskeleton stepped past him, he sprang to his feet and attacked it with his hands. He reached through the shattered face of the shell and grabbed hold of the squirming alien within. When he did so, the biomechanical suit of armor lost its coordination. The tentacles went limp, and the knees buckled. As the suit clattered to the ground, Guillaume was left holding a slender gray body about three and a half feet tall. It thrashed violently, trying to escape, but the Frenchman had his powerful hand wrapped tight around its tiny throat. Guillaume screamed out in pain when the alien attacked him mentally. He reached up to his own throat as if he were being strangled by an invisible hand. Reg and the others ran forward to give help, but before they reached him, Guillaume had smashed the creature's head open against the floor. Behind a set of delicate, almost-human facial features, the alien's brain was a swollen disk extending off the back of the skull. A thin membrane was all that protected the brain, and it split open easily under the force of Guillaume's strength. The small gray body was slathered in a layer of clear gelatin and smelled powerfully of ammonia.

Miriyam stepped over the fallen body armor and led the way down the tunnel to the final door. They shouted at the top of their lungs to the men on the far side, but received no reply. On the ceiling, a small part of the crack the team had descended through extended past the door. It was no more than eight inches wide, too small to fit through.

"Open the door!" Miriyam screamed toward the opening. Although she assumed the two men stationed in the tunnel were dead, she hoped the men on the floor above would hear. Reg brushed past her and wedged the bayonet on a rifle he took from one of the soldiers into the crevice between the door and the bulkhead. The blade bent out of shape.

"He is coming. He is behind us," LeBlanc warned.

Reg took a flashlight from the soldier whose rifle he had and used it to examine the door. There was a thick band of ligament running down one side of it, acting as a hinge. With the bayonet, he stabbed into the tough, sinewy material and sliced away a small piece. But there wasn't time to cut through it by hand.

"Stand back!" he warned the others, then sent a spray of carefully aimed bullets into the hinge. When Miriyam saw what he was doing, she picked up the machine gun and joined in, the two of them firing until their ammunition was gone.

Behind them, the rest of the team opened fire on the armored warrior stalking them through the tunnel. While the others held the creature at bay, Reg and Miriyam attacked the remaining part of the hinge, and the door soon gave way. There was barely time to get clear of its path before it crashed to the ground. Without looking back, the two of them stepped over the door and raced into the next segment of the tunnel.

"Ladies first," Miriyam said, when they reached the tear in the ceiling. Reg obliged by lacing his fingers together and boosting her up to the opening. As she wriggled through the gap, the others arrived where Reg was standing, and he began lifting them toward the opening one by one. After the second soldier escaped, Miriyam dropped a pair of fresh assault rifles, taken from the Peacekeepers above, into the opening. They arrived just in time. LeBlanc and Guillaume picked them up and sent a volley of shells flying at the skeletal attacker, momentarily arresting its progress.

"Doctor, you're next," Reg said, waiting to boost the man up.

"No," Guillaume shouted, "you go." He positioned himself so that Reg could climb his body like a ladder and grab the hands reaching down through the hole. The men above quickly lifted Reg out to safety. Then he turned to do the same for LeBlanc.

A rope was tossed down to Guillaume, who grabbed it with one hand and fired with the other. As Guillaume wriggled through the hole and rolled away, a tentacle shot through the gap, trying to catch him. It wound around LeBlanc's leg instead and yanked him roughly toward the opening. Reg reacted quickly and caught the terrified doctor under the arms, helping to resist the strength of the tentacle. Before the others could help, another snakelike appendage darted out and grabbed Reg by the ankle. Screaming in pain, LeBlanc was torn from Reg's grasp and disappeared into the hole. Reg would have gone in behind him if Miriyam hadn't opened fire and severed the tentacle.

They heard the doctor screaming in pain on the floor below as more tentacles reached up and searched for more victims. When Reg hesitated, unwilling to leave LeBlanc behind, Miriyam pulled him away from the opening.

"We can't help him," she said. "Let's go."

The handful of survivors took off running down the rectangular passageway until they found the first opening, the one that led to the main deck of the alien ship.

8

A Good Old-Fashioned Turkey Shoot

"Allah preserve us, it looks a lot bigger than it did on TV."

King Ibrahim stepped from the back of his limousine at about nine in the morning and gaped at the staggering size of the wrecked fragment of alien airship. The rest of the royal motorcade, a mile-long line of limousines, rocket-launching vehicles, and M1A1 tanks, rolled past him and parked in no particular order near the collection of tents and the scaffolded stage set up near the edge of a bluff. The king's advance team had selected this site, a mere three hundred yards from the edge of the ship, primarily for the backdrop it offered: a view of the triangular opening half a mile away and, beyond that, the mysterious obsidian tower leaning above the curve of the dome. It had all the makings of a surreal media event: The small stage was dressed in the Saudi national colors of green, black, and white. Sprays of flowers lay in the sand around it. Waiters poured out of the kitchen tent as the king's entourage continued to arrive, circulating among the cars with drink trays. Workmen were putting the finishing touches on the bright pink bridal tent, where the wedding ceremony would be held. There was a Sikh bartender, dressed in turban and tuxedo, offering nonalcoholic champagne to the guests. Musicians had been hired, and red carpets had been rolled out.

Mr. Roeder jogged up to the king's limousine to begin briefing him on the preparations, but King Ibrahim had only one question on his mind. "Did you find me an alien or not?"

The American pointed to a jeep parked a safe distance away and the gray skeletal carcass tied across its hood. Patiently, he explained the details of the predatory green plant and the high risk of infection involved in using a corpse for the photo session. He urged the king to stay away from it.

"I came here to kill an alien. Couldn't you find me one that was still alive? Half-alive?"

"I'm afraid they're all dead, Your Majesty."

Frustrated, the king grabbed a pistol and took off down the hill, chased by a flock of camera crews. While he was gone, the crew of pilot heroes was ushered up onto the platform for group pictures. In addition to the foreign and Saudi pilots who had flown with Faisal from his camp in the desert, there were dozens of others who had answered to America's call to attack. In all, there were more than a hundred men representing nineteen different countries. Conspicuously absent were English major Reginald Cummins and the lone female pilot, Israeli captain Miriyam Marx. The pilots were in high spirits, but it took them quite a while to work out the question of who would stand next to whom. Victory had warmed them to one another personally, but the photographs would be lasting documents, and no one wanted to look like he was cozying up to the enemy.

"Say cheese!" the photographer yelled.

He took a series of shots—looking serious, looking happy, shaking their fists angrily—or, in Tye's case, flipping the bird at the wreckage that dominated the skyline behind them. The whole group beamed with pride. They had accomplished a hugely heroic deed, and their faces showed it. When they stepped off the podium, each pilot was handed a yellow rose and an envelope full of cash by one of the royal grandchildren. They were mingling with high-ranking Saudis when a shot rang out. In the distance, the king had fired a single bullet at the dead alien.

He rode back up the hill in a jeep, and, when he arrived, unsettling news awaited him. An assistant pulled him aside and handed him a phone. One of his field generals was on the line. He said a Frenchman had stormed into the headquarters tent only moments before, claiming to have been attacked inside the ship. According to the man's story, he'd ventured down into the bowels of the city destroyer with eighteen men and lost most of them to a handful of aliens.

"How many of these stories have you heard?" the king asked.

"This is the first one."

"Do you believe him?"

"Yes, sir, yes."

After inspecting the extraterrestrial cadaver, the king had lost his appetite for confrontations with any living members of the species. The size and strength of the body he'd seen were alarming. He wondered if the ammonia fumes he'd breathed might be poisonous. The idea of coming out here was beginning to feel like a huge mistake. "General, send search parties inside to check this man's story. Call me the moment you have news." The patriarch scanned the curved dome of the ship for a moment before making an announcement. "This isn't what I was expecting! It isn't right. We are going back to At-Ta'if."

"What about the wedding?" asked an advisor.

Ibrahim growled. He'd forgotten about that. He marched off in a new direction, this time to find Faisal.

The groom-to-be had slipped a gold-trimmed robe over his uniform and was surrounded by a group of fawning well-wishers, who parted for the king when he approached.

"*Faisal*," the old man said, "I have changed my mind. Let's return to the palace and hold the ceremony in my gardens."

Faisal was mortified at the idea. A ceremony in the desert was the final brilliant element of the story he was constructing for himself. When future generations recounted his heroic deeds, he wanted it to end with the storybook flourish of a battlefield wedding. . . . *Then, after laying low the enemies of God, the warrior knelt before the site of his victory and took as his reward the most beautiful bride in all the land. The king himself performed the marriage, whereupon Faisal, in his wisdom and mercy, freed the bride's brother after lecturing him sternly before the people.* . . . Thinking fast, Faisal proposed the compromise of dispensing with the formal ceremony. All that was necessary was for the king to stand over the couple and declare them man and wife.

King Ibrahim wasn't happy with the proposal, but he agreed. "Bring that Yamani girl up here," he shouted, "so we can finish this business and go home."

When the bride's chauffeur opened the door, the shrouded figure that stepped out wasn't Fadeela. It was Faisal's wife, Hajami. She was five years older than her husband and, under normal circumstances, a timid personality. She had been rich when she married the ambitious young Saudi Air Force lieutenant from a penniless family who had promised her that she would always be his only wife. She had given him her fortune and three male children. The night before, when she learned of Fadeela's marriage proposal, she had argued savagely with her husband. Then, after Fadeela's friends decided to boycott the wedding, Faisal added insult to Hajami's injury by commanding her, under threat of divorce, to help prepare the body of his new bride. This was intimate work that required hours to accomplish: All of Fadeela's hair, except head hair and eyebrows, had to be removed; she was bathed, powdered, and perfumed, before intricate designs were painted on her hands and feet with henna dye. The whole time the two women worked together, Hajami maintained an icy silence.

Drums began to beat when the bride showed herself. She stepped out of the car wearing a simple white dress and flowers woven into the long braid that trailed down her back. Her face was uncovered and her feet were bare. If she was embarrassed about being seen this way, or distraught about marrying Faisal, she didn't show it. She moved in a businesslike manner past the gawking soldiers, grinning princes, and admiring foreigners. As she passed a gray Mercedes sedan, she paused long enough to tap her fingertips against the tinted glass of the rear window. A pair of manacled hands pressed against the inside of the pane. They belonged to Khalid. Faisal had promised Fadeela that her brother would be released immediately following the ceremony.

A few more strides brought her to her father's car, a blue Rolls-Royce. Mr. Yamani was indignant about being forced to trade his daughter for his son and made no attempt to disguise his newfound disgust with Faisal, a man he had counted among his friends. At the same time, he was choking with fear. Despite constant reassurances that there were no alien survivors, the sight of the destroyer awakened the sense of doom that had nearly driven him insane during the previous days. When Fadeela came within reach, he clutched the sides of her face tenderly and put his forehead against hers, apologizing with tears in his eyes for failing her. Reluctantly, he began to lead her to the place where Faisal and the king were waiting.

They had only gone a few steps when shouting erupted among the soldiers. A battered truck was climbing onto the bluff and speeding directly toward them. Warning shots failed to slow it down. Just as the soldiers took deadly aim, the driver slammed on the brakes and jumped out. It was Reg. His uniform spattered with blood, he came running toward the entourage, shouting like a wild man. Miriyam was right behind him. They'd dropped Guillaume at the Saudi army's headquarters tent on their way past. The pilots who recognized them ran forward to hear their news. Reg shouldered his way past the men, screaming at everyone to run for their lives.

"You've got to get out of here! Turn around and go!" In his fury to make them understand, he manhandled a prince or two, physically pushing them toward their vehicles. "Where's the king? Let me talk to the king!"

Instead of the king, he was confronted by half a dozen muscular Saudis, who blocked his path. Reg knocked two of them over and kept going. But a moment later he was tackled from behind and subdued by many pairs of hands. With both arms twisted to the breaking point behind his back, Reg was led through the murmuring crowd and then roughly thrown facefirst to the ground.

"Major Cummins, I've been expecting you." Faisal was grinning down at him, as unruffled and smugly confident as ever.

"Listen to me," Reg snarled, his heart still pounding, "I've been inside the ship. They're alive, many of them, hundreds, maybe thousands. They're going to attack." He pointed toward the breach. "They're going to ambush us."

Faisal wasn't buying it. He figured Reg had ulterior motives for disrupting the marriage. "They must be very friendly, these aliens of yours. How nice of them to explain all their terrible plans to you." His easy smile changed to an expression of disgust, and he ordered his men to take Reg away. Before they could, the king intervened.

"Major, what happened to you?" he asked.

Faisal yelled. "It is a trick. He only wants to interrupt our celebration."

"Silence! Let him answer."

Reg shook free of the guards and began telling his story. The bloodstains on his uniform were still moist, and there was a wild urgency in his voice. It didn't take long for him to convince the king he was telling the truth. Before he had told everything, the king had ordered his assistants to begin turning the caravan around.

"One more thing, Your Majesty," Reg said. "They know you are here. When they attack, they'll look for you first."

Faisal snorted at Reg's melodramatics. "He's making this up! How can he possibly know these things?"

But King Ibrahim was already on the move. He hurried back to his limousine, got in, and screamed at the driver to take him away at once. Faisal walked over to Reg and leaned in, menacingly close. "You're a dead man, Major,"

"And you're a lying coward, Commander."

Shots rang out in the distance. Screams spread through the entourage as everyone turned to face the destroyer. The first alien had come out of the ship.

The lumbering, top-heavy beast pushed through a narrow opening near the triangular breach, moved a few strides out into the sand, and stopped. Ignoring the machine-gun fire, it made a 360-degree scan of the area. The flaring shell of its upper body rose to a pointed tip, and its heavily muscled arms reached almost to the ground. The bullets nicked away pieces of the exoskeleton until the shell cracked and caved in. A moment later, the whole wretched mass toppled over facefirst.

Soldiers and civilians stopped in place and looked on in stunned silence. As the king's limousine sped away, they watched foot soldiers move toward the fallen alien, guns at the ready.

While they were examining it, a second creature emerged. This one never hesitated. It hit the ground running and sprinted across the sand. Hugging the curve of the ship, its path took it directly in front of the royal entourage. It moved awkwardly across the sand and rocks, having evolved in some very different environment. The feet were hooked forward in such a way that the creature moved along standing atop its toe knuckles. The effect was something like a circus bear mincing forward on its hind legs. Still, the beast scurried along at surprising speed, twice as fast as a man.

A cheer went up when the machine-gun fire snapped the creature in half. Its waist was nothing but an exposed spinal column. When it broke, the torso went flying in one direction while the legs went in another. But the thing didn't die. The alien riding inside this suit of armor commanded the arms and tentacles to dig. Within seconds, it built itself a shallow foxhole.

New aliens began appearing every few seconds. Some ran zigzag patterns through the open desert until they were gunned down and killed, but most of them sprinted between the entourage and the massive outer wall of the destroyer, like ducks in a shooting gallery, trying to reach the foxhole. Almost none of them made it. The soldiers at the edge of the bluff began firing larger weapons, and the crowd cheered each time one of the skeletal bodies exploded. Some of the limousines began leaving. Many more were pinned in by parked cars and couldn't move. Drivers leaned on their horns, adding to the noise of the gunfire.

As the alien death toll climbed, the sense of panic abated. They had seemed invincible in the air but appeared helpless on the ground. It looked like the tables had turned. Some people climbed atop their vehicles to watch as others wandered closer to the action. Everyone wanted to see the monsters pay for the atrocities they had committed against humanity.

Faisal smelled another opportunity. Although he was an Air

Force officer, he used his status as the man who had saved the Arab world to seize control of the ground army. He called forward a division of tanks and ordered his soldiers to follow them to the front of the conflict. He would join them as soon as he could find a camera crew. They moved off, leaving Reg to his own devices.

He retreated through the tangle of parked cars and found Mrs. Roeder. She was standing on the hood of limousine, talking into her headset radio. Reg jumped up onto the car and urged her to help evacuate the area. The American woman blinked at him in confusion. "Major, I admit you were right about there being survivors, but look around. This thing is shaping up into a good old-fashioned turkey shoot."

Indeed, the aliens were being killed almost as soon as they showed themselves. Most of them, at least. The handful that survived the sprint past the entourage joined their legless companion in the foxhole. It was now a long deep trench, and growing by the moment.

Not far from where Reg was standing, Tye checked his watch, then announced dryly, "I'd say it's time to run like hell."

Remi couldn't have agreed more. "But our driver is stuck. We need transportation." Like the other pilots, he trusted Reg and Miriyam's assessment of the danger. He called a huddle with some of the other pilots and quickly formed a plan. They would escape in the old truck Reg had commandeered earlier. Miriyam had thought to take the keys. Yossi slipped in behind the wheel and turned over the engine. Edward and Sutton were next to him in the cab.

"What are you waiting for? Let's go."

"What about Cummins?" Yossi asked. "We can't leave him."

Sutton wasn't sure Reg was worth the trouble, but volunteered to go get him. He dashed off, leaving Edward and Yossi, Palestinian and Israeli, together in the cab of the truck. There was an uncomfortable, dangerous silence between them. Looking for an excuse to step outside, Edward studied the mayhem surrounding them and noticed a nearby truck with dozens of rifles lying in the back. He hurried over and grabbed an armful of them along with several boxes of ammunition. He jogged back to the truck and was loading them into the cab when a face appeared at the driver's side window. It was the burly Saudi captain from the camp. He grinned at Yossi and popped open a switchblade.

"*Get lost, you talking donkey,*" Edward said in Arabic. "*This is our truck now.*"

"*Shut your mouth, filthy Palestinian dog, or I'll cut your Jewish boyfriend's throat.*" Pleased with himself for foiling the Zionist plot, the muscular captain opened the door and prepared to pull Yossi outside. Before he could do so, he felt the barrel of a gun pressing against the small of his back. A quick hand reached around and lifted his pistol from its holster.

"Drop the knife," came a voice from behind him. It was Miriyam. "If you cooperate, you live. If you make a noise, you die."

The Saudi knew she meant business. What was more, she'd probably get away with it. The sea of noise surrounding them would easily mask the sound of a bullet. His options, it seemed, were limited. Miriyam hustled him to the back of the truck, which was covered by a canvas roof, and made him climb inside. She told him to lie on his stomach, then sat on his back with her pistol pressed to his skull. The truck ground into low gear and started to move.

A few yards away, Sutton spotted Reg. "Cummins, let's get out of here," he yelled. "A group of us are taking that truck of yours and leaving." Reg hesitated. Mrs. Roeder was picking up the first reports of trouble coming from inside the ship, and Reg wanted to know what was happening. Sutton didn't wait. As soon as he'd delivered the message, he turned and left.

Saudi jets were gathering in the sky, and a pair of helicopters thwacked at the air overhead, moving toward the alien foxhole to finish off the survivors. Through the mayhem, Reg spotted Fadeela. Her father had spirited her away from the shooting and was shouting instructions to the driver of the car in which Khalid was being held prisoner. When she glanced in his direction, Reg waved his

arms in the air and caught her attention. Their eyes met for a
moment before Mr. Yamani dragged her by the wrist toward his
own blue Rolls-Royce limousine. They piled inside and took off
across the open desert at the head of a four-car caravan. It took
Reg a while to realize that Sutton had gone. He was already
climbing into the rear of the truck, which was turning around,
preparing to leave.

The next ten seconds changed everything. Pulses of white
light, energy bursts like the ones they'd faced during the dog-
fights, flew out of the triangular breach and struck the helicopters,
destroying them instantly. Until that moment, the aliens had
shown no signs of being armed. More pulse blasts sailed upward
and began picking off the Saudi jets high above. Others whizzed
toward the tents and the tangle of cars parked on the plateau. A
limousine not far from Reg took one of the sizzling, fist-sized
projectiles. The front end was turned into shrapnel and the entire
vehicle tossed sideways. A separate flurry of shots came from the
foxhole. Screaming and panic erupted on the plateau as the
entourage was caught in the cross fire.

And their troubles were only beginning. Seconds after the
shooting began, the alien ground army started pouring out of the
destroyer. Hundreds of aliens, clad in their eight-foot-tall exoskeleton suits of armor, raced down the ramp of debris, firing as
they came. Marching out behind them were scores of strange-
looking chariots. These vehicles looked like oversize dark brown
toboggans that had sprouted short sticklike legs. Each chariot carried a pair of aliens sitting side by side. The chariots looked too
flimsy to handle the weight of their bulky passengers, but they
raced down the sloping ramp with ease and, when they reached
the desert floor, fanned out in several directions to surround the
humans. It was the same type of blitzkrieg strategy their attacker
planes had used the day before. Within seconds, the chariots had
outpaced the alien foot soldiers. While some of the chariots trotted onto the plateau, others raced around the perimeter and began
chasing down the cars that were trying to escape.

Reg turned and broke into a dead run, trying to catch up to his friends in the battered truck. Everything was chaos around him. Cars and people were smashing into one another, desperate to get away in time. The truck was just gathering speed when Reg raced up alongside it. Edward threw open his door and helped Reg pull himself inside.

With bullets and enemy pulse blasts flying through the air, Yossi stomped on the accelerator pedal and flew down a steep embankment, nearly rolling the truck. "Which way? Which way do I go?"

"That way," Reg said without hesitation, pointing east. In the distance, he could see the line of cars carrying the Yamani family. One of the alien chariots was following them. Unaware that they were being pursued, the Yamani caravan was bumping along slowly through a shallow valley. Yossi floored it and made up some ground, but they were still far behind when the aliens fired their first shot.

The car at the rear of the caravan exploded and flipped in the air. Once the other limousine drivers realized the danger behind them, they gunned their engines and tried to get away. They stayed together and raced along the bottom of a wide, shallow wadi. In his haste, the lead driver failed to notice the walls of the gully slowly closing in around him. Instead of steering toward the open, high ground, he drove into a shallow canyon, following its twists and turns. The wadi walls were only four feet tall in some places, but they were too steep for the limousines to climb. The many-legged chariot chased after them, closing in.

Reg and Edward told Yossi to follow the cars into the wadi, but he swerved away and climbed a small embankment instead. It turned out to be the right decision. Keeping to higher ground, he raced along the top edge of the wadi, catching occasional glimpses of the aliens ahead. The difference in terrain allowed them to close the gap until they came within firing range.

Edward passed the rifles he'd taken to the soldiers riding in back. Miriyam had let the Saudi captain up, but she continued to keep an eye on him.

"What about him?" Remi shouted to her. "Give him a gun?"

The Israeli woman and the Saudi man stared one another down. It was a long, steely stare, during which neither of them blinked. Remi watched them until he began to laugh. "You guys are too tough! You're scaring me."

Miriyam blinked first. She took a rifle from the African, then called across the truck to the Arab. "What's your name," she asked him.

"Ali Hassan."

"Ali, my name is Miriyam." She tossed him the rifle. "From now on, we fight together."

Ali couldn't help but grin. Needless to say, he'd never met a woman quite like this Jewish warrior. "Okay, sounds good to me."

Tye and Sutton were already in position. They had cut away the canvas tarp covering on the left side of the truck and were waiting for a clear shot at the alien chariot, but they were only getting occasional glimpses. Each time they sighted on the aliens, the aliens' pointed skeleton heads disappeared again behind the banks of the wadi.

"Faster, man, let's go," Edward screamed at Yossi. "You drive like my grandmother."

Behind the wheel, Yossi was driving as close to the soft edge of the wadi as he dared. "Who are these people we're chasing?" he wanted to know.

"Friends of mine," Reg said.

"Your Arab girl?"

Before Reg could answer, they drove downslope and saw the alien chariot right beside them, not twenty feet from the driver's door, speeding along a parallel course. The oversize aliens were crouched forward behind the chariot's front wall as the skinny legs of the sledlike vehicle pumped furiously in the sand. No steering controls or instrumentation of any kind was visible. The chariot seemed to guide itself around the obstacles in its path. A moment after gunfire started raining down on them, the big shell head of the creature closest to them turned to look up at the truck. Then it raised its arm and pointed one of its elongated bone fingers at Yossi. A pulse blast shot toward them and tore through the roof of the cab, inches above the driver's head.

Cursing in Hebrew, Yossi turned away and slowed down.

"What are you doing? Chase them!" Reg yelled.

"What are you, crazy? I'm not killing myself to save a bunch of rich Arabs."

That was the wrong thing to say. Edward took out a pistol and pointed it at the driver's head. "Drive, asshole, or I'll kill you and follow them myself." When Yossi hesitated, Edward squeezed the trigger until the hammer cocked into position.

"Okay, hold on tight." He slammed the gas pedal down and headed after them. Before they could catch up, a pulse blast toasted the third vehicle, and shots were whizzing past the gray Mercedes carrying Khalid.

Remi shouted forward to the men riding in the cab. "We need more ammunition."

"Make it count," Edward told him, handing him a few twenty-four-round magazines. "This is the last we have."

An explosion flashed up out of the wadi, and, a second later, they caught sight of the car in which Khalid was being held a prisoner. It was turned upside down and burning. The soldiers in the back quickly used up their remaining bullets.

The chauffeur of the last car, the blue Rolls-Royce, slid open the glass partition and called back to his passengers. "Around the next turn, I'm going to stop. When I do, get out fast. I'm going to back up and ram them." The earthen walls were closing in on them, leaving only a few feet of clearance on either side, and the alien chariot was gaining on them. This was their last hope. "Hold on!"

After crashing through a barrier of acacia bushes and fishtailing around a bend, the driver slammed on the brakes. Fadeela threw open her door and pulled her elderly father into the sand. When they were clear of the door, the tires spun, and the Rolls started moving in reverse. The aliens' chariot came speeding around the corner right on cue, moving too fast to swerve out of the way. But as the chauffeur bore down on them, the thin insectile legs of the chariot sprang into the air and clattered over the roof of the Rolls as it passed underneath. The chariot settled smoothly to the ground and rushed past Fadeela and her father before it could slow down and stop. Then it turned in place and began marching back for the kill.

Fadeela heard a rumbling sound in the air as the chariot trotted closer, and one of the aliens leisurely raised a pointed finger in her direction. But both the creatures turned their heads in a new direction when a large shape came flying over the edge of the embankment. The battered Saudi army truck soared through the air and landed on top of the aliens and their chariot with a loud, splintering crack.

The people inside the truck were thrown forward like a collection of rag dolls. But none was seriously injured, and they came staggering outside to inspect the damage. The aliens, their exoskeleton armor, and their transport had all been mashed into an indistinguishable pulp. A few of the chariot's stick legs continued to twitch weakly as the smell of ammonia wafted into the air.

Reg jogged down the wadi to where Fadeela was holding her badly shaken father. When he got there, she stood up and threw her arms around him and squeezed him tightly, burying her face in his chest. When Mr. Yamani saw this, he snapped out of his teary-eyed stupor, stood up, and moved toward them. Reg assumed the old man was angry, when he was only grateful. He threw his arms around the both of them and held them while he cried.

As the others inspected the bodies under the truck, Miriyam warned everyone that the aliens could attack without touching, but that didn't stop Tye from climbing halfway under the truck when he noticed something moving. He was, after all, a mechanic. "Somebody come and have a look at this," he yelled. When the others came around to where he was, all they could see were his long legs lying in the sand. "Down here, look at this!" They squatted and saw him only inches away from an undamaged bony hand. There were four spiky gray fingers opening and closing very slowly.

"Don't touch it," Miriyam screamed at him. "It's still alive."

"Do I look insane? Of course I'm not going to touch it. But look at this gizmo on the hand. It's some kind of light display." He pointed to an amber-colored circular disk set into the back of the hand. It was blinking out a message or a picture—he couldn't tell which—composed of tiny diamond shapes.

Miriyam wasn't much concerned with his discovery. She understood the danger he was in, so she ducked underneath the foul-smelling truck and pumped a few slugs into the broken chest of the armor, making sure the little one inside was dead.

"Okay I think you killed it," Tye called. "The blinking stopped." He pried the disk out of the bone with a pocketknife and brought it out into the sunlight wrapped in a handkerchief. The top of it was like a thin sheet of amber-colored glass. It wasn't glass, though, because there were veins running through it. When he flipped it over, Miriyam recognized the coppery material lining the bottom—it was the same substance she'd seen on the doors in the bowels of the destroyer. She suggested showing it to Reg.

Yossi lit a cigarette and blew the smoke at Edward as he walked past. "You still think I drive like your grandmother?"

"No, you proved me wrong. You're a very fine driver," said the Palestinian as he reached into the breast pocket of Yossi's shirt, took the last cigarette out of the pack and lit it. "Probably you could have done even better if it was Jews inside the cars, instead of a worthless bunch of Arabs." He wadded up the empty package and tossed it at Yossi's feet.

No one was quite sure which direction they should go from there, but everyone agreed it should be *away* from the downed alien destroyer. The Yamanis' driver knew the area well and said there was an oasis town not far away. The truck was damaged but still operable. They found a place where it could be driven out of the wadi, then towed the limousine out as well. As they were preparing to drive away, a pair of men came walking toward them: Khalid, still in his handcuffs, and his jailer. They'd climbed out of their burning Mercedes seconds before it exploded. Mr. Yamani howled with joy at the sight of his son still alive. Fadeela ran forward to greet him. When they came closer, Reg told the jailer to unlock Khalid's handcuffs, but he refused.

"The instructions of Commander Faisal were clear," he announced in an official tone of voice. "Khalid Yamani will be freed only when the wedding has been completed."

The pilots exchanged glances with one another and without a word being spoken, they fanned out to surround the man. They might have been enemies in the past, but they were slowly forging themselves into a coherent unit. The jailer became visibly nervous when he realized what he was up against.

"Listen to me, little man." Miriyam started toward him, ready to settle the matter in her less-than-delicate way when a big hand fell on her shoulder and arrested her progress. It was Ali.

"Let me." He walked up to the guard and stood over him menacingly. "Do you know who I am?"

"You are Ali Hassan."

"That's right." He snatched away the jailer's keys and unshackled Khalid's hands. "I am Ali Hassan, and from now on I will fight with these people."

9

An Oasis Town

About noon, the freshly dented Rolls-Royce and the equally battered old truck came to the oasis town of Qal'at Buqum. It was no more than a cluster of swaying green palm trees in the middle of an arid valley baking in the sun. From a distance, it looked an all-too-perfect mirage, except for the twenty-story-tall steel radio tower that rose from the center of town. Under normal circumstances, it was a dusty village with two hundred permanent residents. That day, there were almost a thousand people within its limits, down from the three thousand that had slept there the night before. You could walk from one end to the other in ten minutes. Brightly painted shops and houses with crumbling mud-plaster walls lined the road, standing shoulder to shoulder with the prefab commercial buildings built since the oil boom. On the eastern horizon stood the Asir mountains, the great barrier between Qal'at Buqum and the sea.

The town's central square was an asphalt parking lot overgrown with weeds around the edges. The Saudi military had established a command post there, retreating into the shade of the nearest building, the post office, to escape the intense midday heat. Some of the soldiers had been on the plateau with the royal family and their guests when the ambush took place.

As Reg and his crew were piling out of their truck, they were surrounded by children trying to sell them things. Yossi pushed them aside as he moved past on his way to the Saudi headquarters. The others did the same. The last ones out of the truck were Tye and Sutton.

Sutton hesitated before wading into the mob of dirty children. He looked back and saw that Tye had taken out the amber medallion and was examining it for the umpteenth time.

"Will you quit fiddling with that blasted thing and let's go?" He jumped to the ground, and the children immediately swarmed around him, showing him wristwatches and sunglasses for sale. They tugged on his clothing, shouting, "This very good, this very cheap." Sutton roared angrily at them to get away, and they shrank from him in fear.

"For Pete's sake, man, they're just kids." Tye hopped out of the truck and waved hello. In a flash, the little salesmen were on him, pushing and shouting and shoving their wares into his face.

"My name Mohammed," said the tallest boy. He had dark eyes and the wispy beginnings of a mustache. His skin was as dark as Remi's. He slid an arm around Tye's waist. "I am your friend. You come with me the shop my cousin. Very good merchandise, very good price."

"I've got a friend named Mohammed. Did anyhow. Sorry, boys," he announced. "I'm broke. *Me no money.*" Of course, that wasn't quite true. He had a thick wad of Saudi riyals, the equivalent of five thousand American dollars, stuffed into his undershorts.

Even though the kids were pushy, Tye couldn't help feeling sorry for them. They were scrawny and dirty and looked like they didn't live anywhere in particular. One boy caught the tall Englishman's attention. All he had to sell were some old magazines. He opened one of them for Tye's inspection and held it toward his face. Just when they were letting Tye go his way, Sutton bolted back toward them and grabbed one of the oldest boys by the scruff of the neck, then shook him. "Sutton, what are you doing?"

"You little sneak," Sutton yelled at the kid, walking him roughly over to Tye. "Give it back to him." The boy, Mohammed, was terrified, crying and pleading with Sutton in Arabic.

"You're scaring the hell out him, man. Let him go."

"He's faking it," Sutton said. He shook the boy again and told him to quit crying or he'd call the Saudi soldiers over. "Thief get hand chop chop." Realizing Sutton wasn't going to fall for his act, Mohammed snapped out of it and straightened up.

"I no t'ief. You drop this one." He opened his hand and showed Tye the amber medallion he'd taken from Tye's pocket.

"Well that's interesting," Tye said, bending over to study the disk. "It's working again. Can I have my handkerchief, please."

"I no take—" When he began to protest, Sutton twisted the collar tighter around his throat. Mohammed pulled out the handkerchief and handed it over. Tye lifted the disk away from the boy's palm and it went blank again. He put it back down, and it lit up again.

"Isn't that queer?" Deciding it probably wasn't dangerous, he set it in his own palm. It worked again. He looked up at the pickpocket and smiled. "Thanks. I think you figured it out." Sutton turned him loose, but only after planting a hard kick in the seat of his pants. The boys all cursed them as they walked away to join the others pilots.

They found the rest of the squad standing around the village's post office, directly under the radio tower. Lookouts had climbed to the top of the twenty-story structure to keep a watch for any unwanted visitors. The soldiers who had escaped from the ill-fated photo session at the crash site had a grim tale to tell. Nearly everyone had been killed. The aliens took a number of additional casualties, but the battle had been a one-sided rout. After surrounding them, the chariots had moved in and systematically hunted the humans down. There had been several cases of "brain torture," an interrogation technique. Reg knew exactly what they were talking about, having suffered through it himself. The tanks had done almost no damage because the alien pulse blasts shorted out their electrical systems, and the Saudi Air Force couldn't get close enough to give effective air support. It was, in short, a slaughter.

Ali and Khalid were given assault rifles, but the soldiers refused to issue weapons or ammunition to any non-Saudis. They did, however, introduce Khalid to the town's leading merchant, an old woman in a traditional Bedouin dress and a black cloth wrapped around her leathery brown face. When Khalid asked if she had any ammunition, she squinted at his weapon.

"What is that?" she asked. "A Kalashnikov? I think I can help you. Do you have any money?"

Remi took out the envelope he'd been handed during the ceremony and tossed it to Khalid. "Buy the store," he said.

Khalid Yamani was used to handing out large sums of cash, not receiving them. He chuckled and said he'd bring Remi plenty of change, then started following the old woman toward her store.

"Always go in groups," Miriyam said. She pointed at Sutton and told him to go with Khalid.

Sutton didn't appreciate her tone of voice. "Yes, sir!" he said, and gave her a sarcastic salute before leaving.

"Why did you bring that guy?" Yossi asked when Sutton was gone. "He is a pain in the ass."

"You noticed that, too, eh?"

After a while, the heat drove them toward the shade of the oasis's palm grove, where the temperature was twenty degrees cooler. As in many oasis towns, the actual springs at Qal'at Buqum were buried under concrete and surrounded by barbed wire. The pools of dark water babbling beneath the trees were all man-made and supplied by underground pipe. There were picnic benches, trash cans, and brick ovens for family barbecues. Scores of refugees from the cities had taken up residence in this shady park, living mostly out of the backs of their cars. Some of them wandered over to speak with the multinational squad of pilots when the sound of automatic gunfire came from overhead. The men perched in the radio tower were firing at something and shouting to the soldiers standing in the square below. The white flashes of an alien pulse weapon tore through the air and smashed into the radio tower, sending the lookouts plummeting to their deaths. The civilians hit the deck as Reg and his crew ran back toward the square. The destructive pulse bursts were coming from inside a walled compound just across the town's only road.

Reg found the ranking Saudi officer hiding in the bushes beside the post office. He and his men had already devised a plan to surround the compound. Before Reg could talk to them, they took off, running in crouches.

"Don't these bastards have anything better to do than follow us around?" Sutton asked, gesturing toward the alien hiding place. He and Khalid were back from their shopping spree and started passing out magazines full of cartridges.

"We should follow them," Khalid said, watching the soldiers advance. They had reached the edge of the road without incident. Making it across was going to be another matter.

When Miriyam stood up to survey the situation, a pulse blast tore into the front wall of the post office, only inches from her head. It didn't seem to bother her much. She squatted and conferred with Reg. "It looks like there's only two of them over there."

"They like to start small," Reg said, "then rush in and hit you from all sides."

She turned around and looked into the parklike oasis, thinking the same thing Reg was thinking. "If they get into these trees," she said, "they'll be able to drive us out into the open."

"We've got to split up and defend the perimeter."

"You're right. Three groups of three." She pointed at Tye and Ali. "You and you, follow me." Then she turned and hurried along the wall, leading the group toward the rear of the post-office building. From there, they headed off in different directions.

Reg, Remi, and Khalid ended up together. They jogged through the trees, keeping alert for signs of danger. As they passed campsites, Khalid shouted to the people in Arabic, warning them of the possible danger. Reg stopped and took a long look around.

"If you were an alien," he asked, "which way would you come?"

"Wherever there's no people to shoot at me," Remi answered.

Khalid disagreed. "They are hunters. They will go where they can kill."

Through the trees they spotted the shell of a long, narrow, abandoned building. The doors, roof, and windows were all missing. It had become a temporary home to several families of refugees. There was laundry hanging on the bushes nearby and the smoke of a cooking fire, but otherwise no signs of life.

"That's it," said Reg, and the three of them ran to reach the spot, splashing through a knee-deep pond that stood in their path. They could feel the presence of the enemy before they heard the moaning that came from inside the walls of the structure.

"Look over there in the bushes," Remi said. Two bodies, a man and a woman, lay flat on their backs with blood coming from their ears, eyes, and noses. Their eyes were wide-open, as if the last thing they'd seen had surprised them.

Reg heard a gasping, shuddering noise that sounded like someone being electrocuted. He led the way to the building, put his back against the wall, and edged toward an open window. Reg grabbed Khalid's arm and gave him a piece of advice. "Let's don't do anything crazy here. We've got to stay alive if we're going to kill them." He knew his friend sometimes couldn't distinguish between bravery and recklessness. But the warning fell on deaf ears. Khalid went straight to the window and looked inside. What he saw made him recoil in horror.

One of the aliens was kneeling in a doorway with the tentacles of his biomechanical suit holding three separate victims pinned to the floor. There were two children and a woman, their bodies convulsing in pain as the alien interrogated them mentally. Khalid screamed at the thing and opened fire. He sent a sustained volley of gunfire in through the window. The creature reacted by shuffling backwards into the next room, dragging one of the children with it. Khalid leapt inside and ran to the doorway. A pulse blast sliced through it and exploded against the far wall, nearly taking Khalid's handsome face with it.

The inside of the structure was a labyrinth of decayed walls and leaning doorways. By the time Reg and Remi climbed inside,

Value Village

The Ultimate Treasure Hunt

3405 - 34th Street N.E.
Calgary, Alberta
GST #824583512

01-24-2014 FRI #201902

BOOKS	1.99T
SUBTL	1.99
GST	0.10
TOTAL	2.09
CATEND	5.10
CHANGE	3.01

ITEM   1
SUPERVISOR   7010 11:38TM

7 Day Exchng. Exclusions Apply.
No Refunds.

the creature had retreated deeper into the building, dragging the child with it. Khalid bolted through the doorway into the next room and was immediately surrounded by pulse blasts. Despite the danger, Reg and Remi followed him in.

Dodging the explosions, they followed the sounds of the alien through two more doorways. Khalid was about to step through the third when Remi held him back. They listened. The sound of sporadic gunfire was coming from several places in the oasis. During the spaces of silence, they could hear the child's labored breathing on the other side of the nearest wall. Remi pointed into the next room. It was waiting for them.

When Khalid peeked around the corner, there was a loud crunch, then something flew out of the doorway. It was the child's body, a girl about nine years old. She slid down a wall and landed in a broken heap. Reg thought Khalid would rush into the room, looking for revenge. Instead, he kept his cool. "There's a window behind him. You keep him busy, and I'll surprise him from outside." The men nodded as Khalid hurried back the way they'd come.

Reg and Remi kept their weapons trained on the doorway as the harsh sun beat down on them through the open roof. Then Reg pulled Remi closer to the wall and pointed up. He could give the murderous invader something else to think about by firing a few shells over the top. But as Remi was boosting him up, Reg lost his sense of balance. A strange sensation moved through him, a sensation he recognized as the presence of an alien mind.

As his Ethiopian comrade looked on in confusion, Reg sank to the floor, grimacing in anguish. The creature was reaching through the wall to infiltrate Reg's mind. A cramping pain shot through him, as if his body was a pincushion pierced by freezing cold needles. As quickly as it began, Reg knew there was only one way to make it stop. He had to tell everything he knew, had to open his memory to the intelligent presence inside him. And he did. At the alien's command, he conjured up the mental image of the post office and the Saudi soldiers trying to get across the road, then he "remembered" something he'd never seen before:

a view from inside the compound, looking out at the post office and the radio tower, and as fast as he could think it, he was identifying the directions the soldiers would come from, then he was huddled in the bushes listening to Miriyam say, "three groups of three," and running toward the back of the building and splitting up. The pain and the rapid series of images running through his mind confused him, made him feel the need to show the alien everything it wanted to see. And then he was showing himself, sending an image of him and Remi huddled at the base of the wall. *And the third one, where is the third one?* It wanted to know about Khalid, and, for the first time, Reg resisted the thing's power, tried to deny it, but the memory-images were coming out of him in an unstoppable stream. He pictured Khalid running back through the tangle of walls toward the empty window frame. He tried to stop thinking, tried to take back control of his mind, desperate not to betray his friend, but found himself imagining Khalid running along the outside wall toward the alien's hiding place. Then he found a way to resist. With all the concentration he could muster, he steered his image of Khalid away from the wall and toward trees of the oasis. It was like guiding a dream while he was having it. To sustain his concentration, he made the image of Khalid start doing the first crazy things that came to mind. Khalid began to skip, then jumped into the air, grabbed the branch of a tree, and flipped himself impossibly high in the air like a gymnast.

The alien mind flared with anger inside his own, realizing Reg wasn't cooperating. The painful seizure intensified, and the wordless question rang through him: *Where is the third one?* But Reg was learning quickly. In his imagination, Khalid was suddenly dressed in top hat and tails, dancing through the oasis like Fred Astaire in the old movie Reg had seen a week earlier. The pain began to subside as Reg began to understand how he could control the confrontation with the invisible presence. The idea occurred to him that he might even be able to turn the tables and attack his attacker. At that point, the alien presence quickly withdrew.

A second later, the real Khalid leaned in a window and blasted away at the bioarmor until it collapsed, and the alien was torn to shreds.

In another part of the oasis, Tye had injured himself twice before his team had spotted any of the invaders. First he cut his hand tripping over a garbage can, then twisted an ankle trying to run backwards. For his own safety, Miriyam assigned him to stay where he was and "guard" the center of the oasis. Then she and Ali disappeared into a thicket of tall ferns and densely clustered palms.

The twigs and dried leaves on the ground crunched under their boots as they prowled forward, glancing at one another through the vegetation. The pair of them were about as different as two people could possibly be, but they shared soldiering skills in common and were able to move ahead efficiently and quietly, coordinating their movements with subtle gestures and facial expressions. Miriyam froze in mid-stride when she heard Ali tap his finger against the side of his assault rifle. He had seen something. She followed his gaze until she saw it, too. Far ahead, one of the tentacled gray giants was coming toward them. It was following a trickling stream of runoff water into the oasis.

Speaking only with his hands, Ali suggested they put themselves in the predator's path and lie in wait. Miriyam agreed and followed him toward a little clearing where the water ran close to a set of picnic tables. After selecting their hiding places, they settled in to wait. Between occasional bursts of gunfire coming from the battle near the post office, they could hear it rustling closer. Ali couldn't see it from where he was, so he relied on Miriyam to monitor the thing's progress. She was hiding behind a tree and peeked around it every so often, then nodded in his direction. Then she looked around the oasis as if she were just realizing where she was. She shook her head and smiled at the absurdity of the situation. Ali smiled back at her, agreeing wholeheartedly. Silently, she asked if he was scared. He looked back at her with an expression that said of course not. But a moment later, he changed his mind and nodded that yes, he was. Terrified, in fact. They both smiled again until Miriyam realized the rustling had stopped.

She peeked out and saw something repulsive. The creature had stopped and lowered itself into a squatting position over the water. The large skull-thorax opened slowly, like the halves of a clamshell, to reveal the smaller body tucked inside under a layer of clear gelatin. It was an indistinct mass of tissue except for the bulging eyes. They stood out like a pair of polished-silver goose eggs. Ali snapped his fingers to get Miriyam's attention, but she waved him off without looking away from the gruesome sight. The alien lifted itself partially out of the body cavity and reached down to the water with its two-fingered hands. Although it made no attempt to scoop the water up or lower its mouthless face to the surface, it appeared to be drinking, absorbing the water through its skin.

Miriyam put her fingers to her lips, slid away from her tree, and began snaking silently closer. To get the shot she needed, she had to get down into the streambed away from intervening obstacles. She would be vulnerable, away from cover, but she wanted to pick the enemy off with one shot rather than risk a prolonged firefight. She crawled forward on her stomach until there was nothing between her and her target. Before she could kill it, the sound of an automatic weapon erupted in another part of the oasis. The alien darted back into its burrow and the bioarmor snapped closed. It started marching forward, fast. Miriyam had nowhere to run.

Ali reacted quickly when he saw she was trapped. "Here I am!" he cried. He stood up and showed himself in the clearing, waving his arms. He taunted the creature with choice Arab-style insults. "Come get me, you son of a jackal; come close so I can spit in your mouth."

A twelve-inch-long finger pointed at him, and a pulse blast sizzled between the trees, exploding into the picnic table beside Ali, tearing it to pieces. Running in a crouch, he got out of the clearing and into the trees, where he figured he was safe. "You missed me, you scab on a monkey's ass."

Miriyam bolted out of the streambed and ran for the nearest cover. She ducked behind a thick palm just as a white flash ripped into the other side of the trunk and broke the tree in half. It crashed down, pinning her to the ground. Ali made it over to her and tried to lift the tree away.

"Get me out of here!" She winced.

"I will," he said. Then he slipped out of view.

"Ali, don't leave me here, you bastard."

The exoskeleton's head was in sight, bobbing above the vegetation as it moved steadily forward. Miriyam didn't have a clear line, but she took aim the best she could and began to blast away. Ali hurried back with a thick plank of wood from the ruined picnic table and wedged it under the fallen trunk for leverage. The powerfully built soldier lifted the tree away as Miriyam continued to fire. The alien was almost on top of them. Its shell was cracking under the barrage of Miriyam's bullets, but not giving way. It was too late to run. The creature stepped out of the streambed and pointed its curving spike of a finger down at Miriyam.

Before it could fire, a series of gun blasts came from a new direction and hit the side of the shell. This distracted the creature just long enough for Ali to swing the wooden plank. With a loud cracking noise, the alien's hand broke off and hit the ground. Squealing in pain, the alien sent a tentacle forward to impale Ali, but he dodged it and jabbed the end of the plank into the thing's face. The shell wall collapsed, and when he pulled the wood away, Miriyam pumped bullets into the opening he had created.

The eight-foot-tall body wilted into a heap on the ground.

Miriyam and Ali breathed a sigh of relief, then looked to see where the mysterious salvo of shots had come from. Tye jogged up to them and looked down at the dead alien. "There's got to be a better way of killing these things," he said.

In another area of the oasis town, Yossi, Sutton, and Edward were about to discover a better way. The three of them were pinned down behind a low stone wall, with bullets whizzing over their heads in one direction and alien pulse blasts going in the other.

The land was higher at one end of the oasis, ending in a set of hills. The slope had been graded into a series of terraces, three-foot-tall walls made of stone. A large group of Saudi civilians, members of the same clan, had been living there since the invasion started. When they heard the shooting begin, they grabbed their weapons and rushed out to the stone walls, using them as barricades. They opened fire when a pair of tentacled killers came marching down the slope. When the Brit, the Palestinian, and the Israeli rushed up the slope to help them, a second pair of aliens appeared at the top of the hill and began blasting away. After slaughtering the defenders near the top, the aliens began picking off humans one at a time with their pulse weapons. The members of the clan hid themselves at the base of the slope, doing their best to keep the alien invaders at bay.

But their numbers were dwindling quickly. The day before, in the air, the pulse blasts coming from the alien attack planes had been only marginally accurate, connecting with their targets about ten percent of the time. But in their bioarmor, the aliens were much more lethal. Every thirty seconds, it seemed, the humans sustained another casualty, especially those trapped on the terraced hillside. The pulses couldn't reach them behind the walls, but almost everyone who broke into the open and dashed for the bottom of the hill was picked off.

Edward was desperate to get off the hill. "We've got to create a diversion and get down into the trees."

"Go ahead," Yossi sneered. "You'll never make it. We've got to wait for them to come to us."

"We're dead. We're definitely dead," Sutton moaned.

A couple of kids bolted into the open, running together. While everyone else was trying to get *off* the slope, these two came out of the trees and started advancing up the hill. The sound of clanking bottles came from the cardboard box they carried between them. They crouched a little as they ran, but otherwise failed to appreciate the danger they were in.

"I don't believe it," Sutton said. "Those are two of the little punks who pickpocketed Tye."

"What are they doing?"

"Sounds like they've got bottles," the Englishman said. "Maybe they're going to try selling us some sodas."

The men cringed as they watched the boys zigzag their way up the hill, waiting for the inevitable flash of the alien weapons that would tear their bodies apart. But somehow, miraculously, they made it all the way up and joined the others behind the wall.

"What the hell are you doing?"

"We kill dem," said the younger boy.

"We have many bombs we make," announced Mohammed. He tipped the box and showed them what was inside: bottles filled with gasoline. Rags had been stuffed into the openings to act as wicks. Mohammed pulled out an engraved silver lighter and pretended to light the gas-soaked rag, then pantomimed throwing the bottle at his young friend, who summed up their strategy in three words.

"I am boom."

"Yes, we know. Molotov cocktails," Sutton said, shaking his head sadly. "The problem is that these creatures are wearing armor. They're protected. We need bazookas, not these rinky-dink little bottle bombs." The boys didn't understand a word he'd said.

"I am boom," repeated the younger boy.

"How much?" Sutton asked sardonically, assuming the boys were there to make a sale.

"Very good merchandise, very good price," Mohammed said with a grin. "For you, my friend, price is free." He offered one of the homemade weapons to Sutton, who refused it.

"I'll stick to bullets, thank you."

"They're coming," Yossi announced. The others peeked over the top of the wall and saw the four exoskeletons moving closer, one terrace at a time, peppering the area with pulse blasts as they came. When they noticed the human heads peeking over the top of the wall, they changed direction, moving in for a quick kill before continuing down into the trees.

The younger boy lit a bottle, stood up, and threw it as hard as he could. Rather than duck back down, he watched its flight through the air. Before it hit anything, he was dead. A pulse blast hit him square in the solar plexus and knocked him twenty paces down the slope. The alien energy bursts caused different kinds of damage depending on the material they interacted with. They twisted the heavy steel girders of the radio tower out of shape, but didn't explode human flesh. The boy's body was smashed, blackened, and bloody, but still in one piece. Mohammed's first reaction was to run to his friend, but Sutton pulled him back and pinned him against the wall, holding him there until he stopped struggling. An angry roar of gunshots came out of the trees, but the aliens continued to advance.

Yossi lit one of the gasoline-soaked wicks, sneaked a quick look over the wall, then threw as best he could, grenade-style, protecting himself from the counterfire. The bottle landed without exploding.

"That was terrible," Edward said. "You throw like my grandmother."

"You think you can do better?" He handed over a lit Molotov cocktail. "Show me." Edward measured the weight of the bottle in his hand before setting it aside and picking up a heavy stone.

"I know you Palestinians like to throw rocks," Yossi said, "but these guys aren't Jewish soldiers with rubber bullets."

"Just watch," Edward said. He lobbed the heavy stone high into the air in the direction of the aliens. As it reached the top of its arc, he stood up and tomahawked the bottle thirty-five feet on a straight line. As he hoped, the aliens were distracted by stone falling toward them. The bottle shattered against the blunt bone face of the closest creature and spread fire over the surface of the bioarmor. Edward ducked behind the wall again before a single pulse blast was fired.

Behind the wall, the men heard squealing and thrashing. They peeked over the edge and saw the creature staggering around, swatting at the flames with its tentacles. The walls of the big skull-thorax shell opened, and the fragile, skinny creature riding inside jumped out of the suit. Before it could scramble into the nearest bushes, a barrage of bullets came from the trees at the base of the slope and ripped it to shreds.

"Incredible! It worked!" Sutton shouted. He patted Mohammed on the shoulder. "He went boom!"

"Don't be too happy," Edward cautioned. "There are three more, and they're coming this way."

Sutton stole a glance over the wall and realized he was right. "Don't these things learn?"

"Let's hope not," Edward said. Then he turned to Yossi, who was staring at him, impressed, and explained his skill with Molotov cocktails. "I got some practice during the Intifada."

The Israeli lit a couple more of the wicks. "This time, I won't throw like your grandmother. I'll pretend I'm throwing at Yasir Arafat."

The attack continued. The aliens followed their strategy of trying to surround the soldiers, but it wasn't enough. The men spread out and torched the creatures wherever they tried to cross the wall.

Half an hour later, all the aliens in Qal'at Buqum were dead.

Those who had defended the oasis gathered near the post office, comparing notes and carrying the wounded to an infirmary at the end of town. Despite their victory and the fact that they'd found a reliable way of killing the invaders, there was only a guarded optimism. The officer in charge of the Saudi forces, fearing another sneak attack, sent dozens of men to stand sentry duty around the perimeter of the oasis.

In the strategy session that ensued, much of the discussion centered on acquiring the right weapons—flamethrowers. The Saudis had them, of course, but not many. None of the men milling around the center of town had ever trained with one. Locating them and getting them to where they were needed was going to take time.

Reg went to the Rolls-Royce and found Mr. Yamani exactly where he'd been since they arrived in Qal'at Buqum an hour before. He was curled up on the backseat with his arms wrapped around his head. Reg ducked inside to try and reassure the old man that he was safe, at least for the time being, but couldn't get a response out of him. He was trembling and mumbling to himself in Arabic. Khalid came up behind Reg and was angry that Fadeela had left her father in such a state.

Someone told them she had gone to the infirmary, and Reg volunteered to go and look for her. He walked down the road to the edge of town until he found the building. It was a dilapidated doctor's office that was ill equipped to handle the dozens of injuries sustained during the battle. He found the doctor in charge, a man who wore slacks and a silk shirt instead of the more traditional Saudi garments. He spoke English with a Scottish accent.

"She said her father was uncontrollably nervous and wanted something to calm him down. I kicked her out and told her not to come back until she was decently covered." Then he looked Reg over disapprovingly. "Why do you want to find her?" Reg didn't answer the man, just turned and left. As soon as he was on the street again, he saw the old truck coming in his direction. Miriyam and Remi were riding up front with Ali, who was driving.

"Hurry up and get in," Miriyam said. "We're going to a place where we can get some weapons."

"What's the big hurry?" Reg asked, glancing toward the center of town. A large convoy of military vehicles had begun to arrive.

"It's Faisal. He has taken Khalid prisoner again, and he's looking for you. Get in."

There didn't seem to be much choice, so Reg jumped in the rear compartment and watched the oasis town slowly recede from view. When he finally sat down, he noticed there was a man he didn't recognize riding along with them. It was a Saudi soldier with his *keffiyeh* pushed down to cover his face. There was something oddly fragile about the soldier, and when "he" finally looked up and smiled, Reg saw that it wasn't a man after all. It was Fadeela.

10

Ugly Weapons

As they motored east along a lonely stretch of highway, the only traffic they encountered was a convoy of military jeeps heading in the opposite direction and a Saudi army helicopter that buzzed up behind them before shooting ahead. It was about three in the afternoon, and the sun was at its most punishing. In the back of the truck, the breeze kept skin temperatures down, but the metal floor and walls were hot to the touch.

Tye hardly noticed. He had spread some rags on the floor near the tailgate and was busy examining his growing collection of alien biohardware. In the aftermath of the battle, he'd dislodged two more medallions from the backs of alien hands. But his concentration was centered on the examination of something that looked like a slightly warped piece of half-inch pipe. It was one of the pulse weapons.

Using a heavy stone, he'd broken open an exoskeleton forearm and dug the thing out. It lay just below the shell, nestled in the ropy white meat. Although it was the color and consistency of tooth enamel, the tube had soft flanges attached to its sides. He had found them wrapped around the muscles in the arm, and they had to be peeled away one by one before the weapon could be lifted out of its resting place. These flanges were about three inches long and one inch wide. They were flat and resembled the rubbery leaves of seaweed, but were the color of copper and composed of the same material found on the backs of the medallions. The pulse weapon looked more like a skinny prehistoric fish than any kind of gun he'd ever seen. It was hollow and open at the end where the ball of condensed energy was expelled. The other end was swollen and green—the same shade of green he'd seen flying along the underside of the city destroyer. The same green, Reg told him, as the crystalline pillars growing in the bowels of the ship.

"That thing is disgusting," Sutton told him. "Don't touch it. It's probably full of germs."

"I wiped it off," Tye said. "It's not like it's rotting meat or anything. It's some kind of machine." The other passengers had a hard time buying that. It didn't look like a machine.

"I don't like it," Edward said. "Remember when the Americans brought back rocks from Mars? The newspapers talked about the danger of germs or bacteria that we can't defend against. And that was only rocks; this thing came out of a body."

For once Yossi agreed with something Edward had to say. "I think we should get rid of it. It could be poison. Why take the risk?"

"If it's true," Fadeela said, "that the aliens have some strange diseases, it's already too late. Thousands of people throughout the country must have already been exposed to them. And we don't even know about the rest of the world."

The debate ended when Tye reached down and picked the thing up with his bare hand. The coppery flanges came to life and wrapped themselves around his arm, strapping the machine to his forearm. Startled by the rapid movement, the others recoiled, but Tye was more fascinated than afraid. He lifted his forearm close to his face and examined it closely before turning to the others. "I think it likes me."

"See if you can make it fire," Reg said.

Since there was nothing that looked like a trigger, Tye did as he'd seen the aliens do. He pointed his arm out the back of the truck and extended his finger. Nothing happened. He picked up one of the medallions and touched the coppery side to various parts of the device. He peeled it off and allowed it to reattach to his other arm. He flexed his muscles and shouted, "Fire!" but couldn't get the weapon to work. He turned to the others and shrugged. "Maybe you have to be eight feet tall and really, really ugly for it to work."

"If that's the case," Sutton joked, "you're our best candidate."

"Let me try it," Reg said, moving closer and reaching for the device.

Tye pulled away, not ready to relinquish control of the object. "This one's mine. You'll have to go out and find your own." He was only half kidding.

Reg explained his theory that the way to trigger the firing mechanism might involve some sort of telepathy or mental suggestion. "I've been thinking about these suits of armor they wear. How do they control them? It can't be that the suits are imitating the movements of the little guy operating them. For one thing, there's no room to move inside those chest cavities. And besides, the aliens don't have tentacles, but their suits do. It might be a simple matter of willing it to work. Let me see it for a minute."

Again, Tye pulled it away from Reg. "I've got plenty of mental control. I'll try it." He raised his arm and pointed his finger, this time with more ceremony. Speaking like a medium conducting a séance, he said, "I command you to fire a pulse blast. I am visualizing a pulse blast firing out of you. I command you to fire!" He was perfectly sincere, but some of the others began laughing at him.

"Oh ferchrissake, man, give me that thing."

Fadeela spoke on Reg's behalf. "Michael, let Reg try it. He has been inside their minds twice already. Perhaps he can make it work."

Sutton was enjoying the show. "Do you have any idea how ridiculous you people look? May I remind you that this thing is from another galaxy, designed by an intelligence we don't understand?"

"Oh, go ahead," Tye said, holding his arm out so Reg could peel the rubbery flippers away from his skin. The instant Reg's fingertips came into contact with the device, there was a blinding flash. An energy pulse sailed into the sky for a mile or so before dissipating.

"Okay, you win." Tye peeled the tube off his arm, set it on the floor of the truck, and pushed it toward Reg. "Whatever you got from those aliens, it works."

Reg held the thing over his arm and allowed it to cling to him. His sweat quickly collected in pools under the flippers, which clung to his arm like clammy leaves. He willed the device to fire again, but had no more luck than Tye.

He continued fiddling with the strange device until Fadeela finally solved the riddle. She moved down to the end of the truck and told Reg to point the gun down at the shoulder of the road rushing away behind them. Then she touched the tip of her finger to one of the coppery flippers and, a second later, a pulse ripped out of the gun and exploded in the dirt.

"Now aim over there, at those rocks," she said. And again the gun went off a second after she touched it. The pulse flew in the direction of the rock formation he'd pointed at, but didn't connect. After some experimentation, the operating principles of the weapon became clear to them. Getting the weapon to fire required two or more people making contact with it and mentally commanding it to send out a pulse. Aiming it was just as easy. If both shooters agreed where they wanted the pulse to go, it went there.

It was an awesome weapon: lightweight, powerful, accurate, and didn't seem to need reloading. By force of will alone, it could be made to deliver one pulse per second. The team began to have fun with it, imagining they were blasting away at tentacled exoskeletons. They passed it around, and everyone learned to use it. Everyone except Sutton. He was waiting to be asked, but the invitation never came. Eventually, he moved toward the cab of the truck and pretended to take a nap.

"It makes sense," Reg said. "They think together, as one mind. But we're all separate. This little gizmo seems to need the go-ahead from more that one mind before it will fire. They must have built that function in, designed it that way."

"If we could build guns that worked the same way, it would solve a lot of our problems in the world," Edward mused. "If it always took more than one person to squeeze a trigger, we'd have less violence, especially killings. There would be no more lone gunmen going on killing sprees."

"Can you describe what it's like?" Yossi asked Reg. "What is this telepathic interrogation they do?"

"You mean the mind-lock?" Reg asked.

"Yeah, what does it feel like?"

"And how did you know there was more than one mind?"

Reg wasn't sure he could describe the sensation. He tried. At first he fumbled for the words, but then started talking more freely. He was still telling them about it when the truck pulled off the road and approached the gates of an isolated military facility.

Ali got out of the truck and talked to the soldiers in the guardhouse for several minutes before he convinced them to roll the gates open and allow the truck to pass.

They drove into what looked at first to be an ordinary Saudi military base: jeeps, trucks, Quonset hut military barracks, and a few hangars alongside a poorly maintained landing strip.

Almost at once, the international crew realized something was amiss. The base was large enough to require several hundred personnel. But even in the middle of the afternoon, there was not a single person outside. The tires on the jeeps and trucks were flat, as if they hadn't been moved for a long time. The curtains and blinds were all drawn. None of the buildings seemed to have any air-conditioning units. Obviously, the entire base was some sort of decoy. They asked Ali about it, but he waved them off, telling them he didn't know anything about the place.

Farther on, they came into a well-tended part of the facility and were surprised to see a series of greenhouses surrounding a large one-story building. A sign in front identified it as the Al-Sayyid Agricultural Research Facility. The helicopter that had passed them earlier was parked on a patch of lawn between the greenhouses and the main building. The pilot of the craft saluted them as they drove past.

"Don't you think that's a little odd?" Reg asked. "There's not a farm within a hundred miles of here." No one knew quite what to make of the place, but they all had other issues on their minds.

"Maybe they want to make their desert bloom," Yossi suggested, and they left it at that.

Ali drove past the last set of buildings to the end of the paved road and headed out onto a dusty, rutted trail that took them into a field of weeds and tall bushes. When they'd driven half a mile, he stopped the truck and turned off the engine.

"This is it," he announced to his bewildered passengers. He left the trail and walked toward a dense clump of thorny bushes, which he kicked aside to clear a path. At the center of the weed patch, they found themselves standing on a slab of concrete. Ali stomped on the ground with his boot until he heard a hollow sound. He then brushed away a layer of sand and dirt to reveal an iron door. Further searching led him to an electric switch box. He flipped it open and entered a sequence of numbers on the keypad hidden inside. There was a sharp click when the door unlocked automatically.

"I thought you didn't know anything about this place," Reg said.

Ali shrugged. "I lied." He lifted the door and led the way down a set of stairs.

The bunker was roughly the size of a basement for a house that was never built above. Its concrete walls were lined with steel shelving stocked with cardboard and metal boxes. Everything was coated in a layer of fine dust. When they wiped away the dust and read the packing labels, Edward and Ali were disappointed with what they saw.

"What does it say?" Miriyam asked.

"Gas masks," Edward told her. "Nothing but gas masks."

There were also rubber suits, medical supplies, and oxygen canisters—things you'd need in the event of chemical warfare. Ali was unfazed. He said they should keep looking, that there were flamethrowers down there somewhere.

Eventually, he found what he was looking for. A pair of

antique flamethrowers that looked like thick-barreled field guns from World War I. He carried them out into the light and laid them on the ground.

"We came all the way out here for these?" Tye asked. "I'll be surprised if they still work."

"They work," Ali assured him, lifting several canisters of fuel out of the bunker. The Cyrillic lettering stenciled onto the tanks indicated that they had come from the former Soviet Union. Ali also found a pair of rotting leather harnesses that allowed the tanks to be strapped to the back of the soldiers using the weapons.

Edward volunteered to act as the guinea pig and test them. After connecting a tank to a flamethrower, he strapped the equipment on and lit the small pilot light at the tip of the gun. Then he pointed it out into the sand and squeezed the trigger. A roaring gush of flame spewed out and shot more than a hundred feet through the air. Alarmed, Edward quickly released the trigger, but the flame continued to flare out of the gun until the canister was empty. When it was finished, there was a trail of fire burning on the desert floor.

"It still works," Edward observed.

A few minutes later, as they were loading their supplies into the truck, they heard the sound of gunfire in the distance. It came from the agricultural facility. The team quickly piled into the truck and raced toward the greenhouses to see what was going on. They were still a mile away when they saw the helicopter parked on the lawn explode under the impact of an alien pulse weapon.

"Whoa! Stop the truck!"

Ali had the accelerator jammed down on the floor. The engine screamed in second gear before he shifted into third and raced forward. He gave every indication that he was going to drive right up to the front doors, whether the aliens were there or not. The passengers yelled at him to slow down, that he was going to get them all killed. Through the dingy glass of the greenhouses that surrounded the research building, they could see the movement of large shapes, aliens in their biomechanical armor. The only person the driver would listen to was Miriyam. She directed him to steer a course between two of the greenhouses and then to stop along a blank wall on the main building. Everyone grabbed weapons and jumped out of the truck, taking cover behind it.

Miriyam whispered some orders to Yossi in Hebrew. He took off running, following the wall until he got to the corner of the building, and peered around it.

"What the hell are we doing?" Sutton asked nervously. "This place looks like a plant nursery. Let them take it." Yossi looked back and flashed a signal to Miriyam.

"He sees them," she told the others. "Stay close behind me. We're going in."

"Like hell we are." The other soldiers glanced behind them at Sutton. "I'm staying right here. It's stupid chasing them inside. Better to burn the place down and kill them as they come out." His idea would have carried more weight if not for the sound of gunshots coming from the interior of the building. Someone was in there defending the place, and, from the sound of things, needed help fast.

Miriyam didn't stay to argue. She pointed a finger at Tye. "You. You stay here with him." Then she hurried forward, scanning the area with her assault rifle, to join Yossi.

Reg told Fadeela to stay behind and keep an eye on his mates, but she ignored him. Gripping her rifle clumsily, she chased after the others. By the time she and Reg reached the corner, both Israelis were advancing along the wall of one of the greenhouses. They stopped and waved the others forward. When the group assembled, they were near the ruined helicopter. Miriyam signaled for silence, then pointed through the smudged glass of the greenhouse at an armored alien standing on the other side, its tentacles waving idly in the air as it kept watch over the building's entrance. Two of the many-legged chariots stood beside him.

"I'll take care of this one," Edward said, prowling forward with the flamethrower. Once he reached the corner of the greenhouse, he would be able to torch the alien in the back. Ali grabbed him by the arm and said not to use the flamethrower, that they couldn't risk setting fire to the building.

"Why?" Edward asked. "What's inside the building?"

The muscular Saudi captain declined to say, but obviously had his reasons. He led Edward back around the greenhouse to a safer angle. The alien sentry noticed them too late. Another roaring jet of fire spit from the barrel of the antique weapon, overwhelming the creature and one of the chariots. Within seconds, the exoskeleton toppled over and split open. The goo-slathered creature inside climbed out and tried to run. Remi killed it with a single shot.

"Let's move." Miriyam waved the others toward the building, and they darted for the open doors.

The team ran up the steps and hustled inside. Edward and Ali, coming from a different angle, were a few steps behind the others. As they reached the bottom step, gun blasts sounded from inside, and the team came scrambling back through the entrance with an alien warrior right behind them. As they scattered in all directions the skeletal figure lifted its powerful arm and took aim with its bony finger.

Edward, standing only ten feet away, closed his eyes and squeezed down on the handgrip of his flamethrower. When the canister was empty, the huge gray skeleton came crashing out of the fire and tumbled down the stairs. When the sides of the great shell head retracted and the delicately built creature within fell squirming and screeching to the ground, Yossi put a bullet into its head.

"We must go inside," Ali yelled. "There are . . . we cannot let what is inside burn. It is very dangerous." Edward's flamethrower had set the building on fire.

"Tell us what is inside," Miriyam demanded.

The captain hesitated, but finally blurted out the truth. "Biological weapons, chemical weapons. I don't know. But they are very dangerous, very dangerous. We must not let them escape into the air."

"Biological weapons?" Miriyam yelled. "Why do you have such filthy things? It is illegal!"

"There is no time to argue," Ali told her. "We must not let these weapons be captured."

Afraid of what might happen if he waited a moment longer, Ali rushed up the stairs and plunged through the fire-engulfed entrance room. The others followed him in. Stumbling and groping their way through the flames, they broke though into an adjoining hallway. With Ali and Miriyam in the lead, they began moving through the building, throwing open the first few doors they found. Behind the doors were private offices crowded with bookshelves and tables full of blueprints.

"Let's go! We've got to hurry," Miriyam yelled. She turned a corner in the hallway without checking first and took a pulse blast in the face. She flew backwards, slamming against the opposite wall. A second later, two aliens came screeching around the corner. The one in front was squeezing off pulse blasts to clear the way while the one behind him carried a silver box in his arms.

Reg opened one of the office doors and pulled Fadeela inside. Those who couldn't get out of the hallway rolled into the corners. They fired their weapons as the huge creatures trotted past them, but the aliens, seeing the fire ahead, ignored them. Afraid of the fire, the lead alien lowered its shoulder and crashed through one of the office doors. The other one followed him inside, and, a second later, there was a crash of breaking glass. They had escaped through one of the windows.

"They're getting away," Edward yelled, chasing into the office after them. When he reached the window frame, he took aim at the fleeing figures and prepared to blast them with liquid fire. Ali rushed in, grabbed the barrel of the flamethrower, and pointed it at the ceiling.

"Don't do it," he said in Arabic. "You'll kill all of us." In one motion, the creatures threw themselves into their chariot and began to race away. There was no possibility of catching them. "Come," Ali said, "we have to hurry." He pulled Edward back into the hallway, and they moved to where Fadeela and Remi were examining Miriyam. The pulse blast had turned her head into a blackened gourd with a few ringlet curls still hanging off the back.

"She's dead," Ali said sadly, "but we have to keep moving." He led the way down the twisting hallway, staying a few steps ahead of the others. They came to a set of glass security doors that required an electronic key. They'd been rammed open just wide enough to allow an eight-foot-tall body with a flaring head shell to slip between them. Ali raced through and into the next room, which was a laboratory full of sophisticated equipment arranged into several workstations. The bright white walls were splattered with blood. Four mangled bodies, men in lab coats, lay sprawled on the floor. Ali stepped over them and went to a steel door that looked like a walk-in safe. He got into position, then gave Yossi the nod to tear the door open. When he did, smoky wisps of chilled air floated out. The door led to another room, a refrigerated laboratory. Overturned tables and broken glass were strewn on the floor. Ali inched through the doorway. Yossi, close on his heels, scanned the frosty interior with the barrel of his assault rifle and halted when he saw something move. Ali stopped short when he felt Yossi's hand on his back. Without a word, Yossi reached past him and pointed toward the danger. Hiding in the corner, behind a set of rolling shelves, something twitched about three feet above the floor. To Ali it looked like the end of a tentacle. But as he moved closer and leveled his weapon, he saw that it was a human hand.

A man in a white lab coat was cowering in the corner, arms wrapped around his head. He was shaking with fear and with cold. He screamed when he heard the footsteps, and tried to burrow deeper into the corner. When they lifted him to his feet, there were trickles of blood coming from both nostrils, and the whites of his eyes had gone bright red. Ali picked him up and dragged him out of the cold room into the main laboratory.

"Where are the chemicals? We have to get them out of here."

The man looked at Ali blankly, then turned and stared around him at the bloodstained walls and the bodies on the floor. He didn't seem to recognize where he was, but his eyes focused when he noticed Edward's uniform. He snapped out of his daze and smiled weakly at the man with the flamethrower.

"*You're Jordanian? Me too,*" he said in Arabic, then immediately burst into tears.

"Where are the weapons?" Ali insisted. "Where are the chemicals?"

The man ignored the question, sinking to his knees and apologizing desperately to Edward in Arabic. Ali reached down and shook him. "The building is on fire," he shouted. "Where are the chemicals?"

The man continued to whimper as if he were begging for forgiveness. Reg got to his knees so he could talk to the man face-to-face. "It was inside you, wasn't it? Inside your head, hurting you and demanding to know things. And you told it everything it wanted to know so the pain would go away." The man's eyes opened wide in a new kind of terror, but Reg quickly moved to put him at ease. "They did the same thing to me. They're doing it to a lot of people. There's no reason to be ashamed. But right now the building is on fire, and you have chemical weapons in here. Where are they?"

"Not chemical," the man said softly. "Biological. We culture biological weapons, and they're gone. They took everything. We were evacuating and had packed everything we didn't destroy. There is a helicopter waiting outside."

"So there's nothing left?"

"Nothing," the man said. "The alien monsters took everything that was still here.

When Reg was convinced the building was clear of bioweapons, he picked the man up. "Is there another way out of here?"

The scientist was unsteady on his feet but walked under his own power to a side exit and led them outside. He sat down against one of the greenhouses while Ali went back inside to retrieve Miriyam's body. He carried her out on his shoulder and looked around for the best place to leave her. He decided on the greenhouse and carried her inside. Yossi found a shovel and dug a grave while the others talked to the scientist.

Reg didn't know much about biological weapons; none of them did. He knew they were meant to take advantage of human susceptibility to disease, that they were universally despised and widely manufactured. He knew that they were unstable weapons, difficult to control once they had been deployed.

"What were you making in there?"

"Too much." The scientist sobbed. "I told the Saudis we were producing too much, that it was dangerous." He looked up at the pilots, hoping for sympathy, but found only stern, impatient expressions. As he realized that they would force him to reveal the lab's secrets, his tone swung from apologetic to defensive. "I want to say, first of all, that most of our work here does not involve biological warfare."

"I hear you," Reg said evenly. "Go on."

He said that the lab's *research* required the production of many infectious cultures including smallpox, encephalitis, cholera, typhoid, and influenza. But the two agents they harvested in the greatest quantities were the bacterium anthrax and ebola, a virus. While insisting that the lab served only "experimental purposes," the scientist explained how the two agents were mixed to weapons-grade strength and stored inside glass tubes. If released into the environment, the two substances would create a highly lethal one-two punch. Anthrax, he said, strikes quickly, manifests as bloody lesions on the skin, and is lethal in fifty percent of cases. Ebola, the scientist explained, takes slightly longer, but kills ninety percent of the time. Within days, it would bring on high fever and internal hemorrhaging. In the final stages of death, the carrier would thrash about, spilling contaminated blood. The infection had the potential of spreading widely before symptoms could arise.

"And you created these things?" Fadeela asked. The scientist didn't answer.

Edward spit in the dirt where the man was sitting.

"Can the aliens use them?" Reg asked. "Aren't they hard to deploy?"

"I'm sorry. They know to use them; I told them several different ways. They forced me to tell them."

"What's the most efficient way to use them?" Tye asked. "Assuming, of course, that you're bent on world domination and want to kill as many humans as you possibly can."

The man was sure of his answer. "In aerosol form, during the early morning, so they can create droplets and spread along the ground, and best if sprayed from a high elevation over a population center."

"This stuff the aliens took, how many people could it kill?"

The scientist shrugged and said the question was impossible to answer.

"How many?" Fadeela insisted.

"Theoretically, several times the population of Earth. But realistically, only a few million."

When she heard those words come out of his mouth, Fadeela raised her rifle and almost shot him. "Don't say *only* a few million."

"They were never meant to be used!"

"How did they take the stuff?" Reg asked. "Did they just come in and raid the refrigerators?"

"As I told you, we were preparing to leave," the scientist said. "We had orders to relocate to the national facility in Riyadh. We had all the toxins packed for transport."

"Packed how?"

"Padded containers, this big," he said, miming a one-foot-square box with his hands, "with a handle."

"How many?"

"Two. The other one went out this morning."

"So all they took was one container?"

"Yes."

"Was it silver?" Reg asked, remembering seeing it in the alien's arms.

The scientist nodded and broke down in tears when they were finished questioning him. They left him sitting there and went inside the greenhouse, where they stood around in silence for a while, looking at the ground where they'd buried Miriyam. Everyone in the room realized how serious the situation had become. Even though a mere fraction of the alien population had survived the downing of their ship, it was beginning to look as if they were still strong enough and smart enough to win the war on the ground. Not only had the aliens carefully researched the Earth's ability to defend itself before arriving, they were also capable of gathering sensitive information at will. Tye walked outside and studied the workings of the amber medallion until the others were ready to leave. Obviously, they had celebrated their victory prematurely.

11

A Roadside Encounter

The drive back toward the oasis was silent and slow. Despite the urgency of their errand—warning the Saudi Air Force not to bomb the alien ship for fear of dispersing the biological weapons—they traveled along at only thirty miles an hour. The truck's engine was threatening to mutiny. The needle on the temperature gauge was in the red. The oil light was flashing, and they were low on fuel. But there was another reason for their slow progress. Miriyam's death had stunned all of them, made them feel that their efforts at resistance were doomed to failure. No one felt the loss more acutely than Ali. The first time he'd met her, they had almost punched each other's lights out, but since then, he'd learned to admire and rely on her.

It was late afternoon, and the sun was a bright orange ball hanging over the Asir mountains, directly ahead of them. Ali squinted as he drove, doing his best to steer wide of the places where tongues of sand had licked up onto the highway. For miles around, the terrain was a flat wasteland of sand and stony hillocks, with a few patches of withered scrub brush.

Twenty miles from Qal'at Buqum, they spotted a metallic glimmer in the distance. It was coming from the solar panels mounted on the roof of an isolated gas station they'd passed on the way out. The main building was a modern box of glass and steel that looked like it had fallen off the back of a truck headed for a more civilized part of the world. Ali pulled in to the station, planning to stop just long enough to fill the tank and let the engine cool.

The station was open for business and attended by two older Saudi men who sat outside leaning against the wall of the convenience store. They were listening to loud, whining Arabic music and smoking tobacco from a *hookah*, a water pipe. Neither of the men gave any indication that the extraordinary events of the last three days had changed their lives in any way. When Ali skidded to a halt at the pumps, one of them went inside to tend the store, while the other slipped his shoes on and sauntered over to pump the gas. Fadeela was the first one out of the truck. She asked the attendant whether the station had a phone or a radio. Of course he had a phone, he answered, but it required a satellite uplink and hadn't been working since the trouble began.

"We have information for the army at Qal'at Buqum," she said, "an important message."

The man shrugged and pointed down the road. The only way to contact the army would be to go there in person. He didn't seem at all surprised to be conversing with a beautiful Saudi woman dressed in combat fatigues. Nor did he bat an eyelash when her traveling companions turned out to be three Brits, an Ethiopian, a Jordanian, an Israeli, and a powerfully built Saudi who was content to stay behind the wheel, looking crumpled and lost in contemplation. As he'd done ten thousand times before, the old man lifted the nozzle out of its cradle and began filling the gas tank while the passersby stretched their legs and wandered inside the store.

There wasn't much of anything on the shelves, and some of what there was looked as if it had been there for years. The pilots picked up everything that looked edible and as much bottled water as they could carry. Sutton was at the counter negotiating the price of dried dates. He picked up the entire display and set it down in front of the shopkeeper.

"How much?"

The man, who spoke not a word of English, calmly picked up

a pencil and wrote the price on a slip of paper. When he pushed it across the counter, Sutton realized the Saudis didn't use Arabic numbers. Realizing he'd need help, he called Edward over, and a price was quickly established.

"We must look pretty strange to you," Edward said to the old man in his own language. "I bet you don't get many groups like us." The man flicked his hand lazily through the air as if batting the question away.

"You'd be surprised," he said. "If you stay in one spot long enough, eventually you see everything. Believe it or not, the whole world comes down this road, little by little." He gave the impression that nothing could surprise him, but his world-weary eyes widened slightly when the pilots began pulling huge amounts of cash from their envelopes to pay for their purchases.

Yossi bought two packs of cigarettes and tossed one at Edward before heading outside and walking across the asphalt toward the bathrooms, which were in a separate building, closer to the road. A moment after the convenience store's door closed behind Yossi, it swung open again. Tye rushed inside, agitated and out of breath.

"Look at this," he yelled, pushing his way up to the cash register. "I think I've found something." He had one of the amber medallions resting on the palm of his hand and put the other two on the counter.

"Will you stop playing with those things," Sutton said. "Has it ever occurred to you that you might be giving away our position every time you start fiddling with them?"

"That's exactly what I want to show you. Take a look." As he had shown them before, when the device came into contact with skin, hundreds of tiny diamond shapes appeared, seeming to float just below the transparent surface. Although they assumed the slowly pulsating shapes formed an intelligible pattern, they were unable to determine what it was.

"Help me," Edward said. "I can't read alien."

Tye grabbed for the first stray hand he could find. It turned out to be Fadeela's. He held it down on the counter and dropped the medallion into her palm. Using a pencil he found on the counter, he pointed at one of the tiny shapes near the periphery of the display surface. "Keep your eyes on this dot," he said. Then he put a second medallion in the shopkeeper's hand. When he did, the diamond shape in question doubled. When he picked up the third medallion in his own hand, it tripled.

"That's us," Reg said, figuring it out. "We're on their screens."

"I knew it. You're showing them where we are," Sutton said.

"Pretty interesting, don't you think?" Tye asked.

"Maybe too interesting," Fadeela said. She took the pencil from Tye and pointed to a double diamond moving slowly across the screen. "It looks like this one is coming in our direction." After watching for a moment, the others could see she was right.

"It looks like they're coming from the north," Reg said. "Try moving your hand to a new angle." Fadeela did, and the diamonds on the screen adjusted to her new position. "It works like a compass."

"More like a global positioning device."

"Well, whatever it is, let's go out and have a look."

They hurried out of the store and ran around the back side of the building. Far to the north, something was moving across the open desert fast enough to kick twin trails of dust high into the air.

"Are all of you dense?" Sutton demanded. He slapped the medallion out of Tye's hand and sent it skittering across the asphalt with a kick. "You're leading them straight to us. We've got to make ourselves scarce. I'll get Yossi. The rest of you get the truck started."

"Hold on there," Reg said, still staring across the sand. "I've got another idea."

Five minutes later, a pair of alien chariots trotted out of the desert and parked themselves on opposite sides of the restroom building. Their passengers dismounted and took a long look around. After a moment, the two that had stopped closer to the store turned and marched toward the men's bathroom. Except for their hideous, otherworldly appearance, they could have been just two more motorists who had stopped to use the facilities before continuing on their journey. Most of the pilots were hiding inside the store, along with the two men who ran the station.

"Okay. *Now* I have seen everything," one of the old men said in Arabic.

A heartbeat after the first alien walked through the bathroom door, he was blown back outside by the jet of fire shooting from Edward's flamethrower. His startled companion backed away, but didn't get too far before Remi stepped outside and unleashed a second torrent of flames. Both skeletal bodies staggered through the flames, slapping at themselves with hands and tentacles until the walls of their suits opened and the creatures inside squirmed out and tried to run. One of them collapsed in the fire. Edward polished the other one off with a single shot from his pistol.

Even before they saw the flare of the flamethrowers, the other two aliens knew there was trouble. One of them came sprinting around the corner, moving too fast to maintain its balance. The knuckles of its curved toes slid out from under it, and it spilled sideways to the ground. As it fell, it fired a series of quick shots that sent Edward and Remi scrambling back into the men's room for cover. The creature used its tentacles to lift itself to its feet, then began marching deliberately toward the rest room, firing one pulse blast after another. The blasts tore into the wall, tearing it down a few bricks at a time. The remaining alien brought the chariot around to offer backup. Maintaining a cautious distance from the building, the alien brought it to a stop in the middle of the highway. Its comrade continued to pulverize the front wall of the restroom building, moving closer each time it fired.

"They're in trouble," Yossi said. "Let's help them."

"Where's that alien gun?" Reg asked Tye. "Time to give it a test." The men rushed toward the exit doors, leaving Fadeela with the dumbstruck shopkeepers. She was about to follow them outside when she had an idea. She picked up one of the amber medallions and pressed the coppery side against the back of her hand. As soon as she did so, the alien firing the pulse blasts froze for a moment and swiveled its magnificent shell head around to look in her direction. Then it pointed its finger straight toward her.

"Get down!" she yelled. The old men hit the deck a split second before a white flash shattered the window and tore into the store.

This momentary distraction was all the opportunity Remi needed. He popped out of the men's room and discharged another spike of liquefied fire. It splattered against the alien's back. As the creature screeched and fell to the ground, the other soldiers opened fire on the alien sitting in his chariot. Before their bullets could do more than ding against his armor, the creature ducked behind the protective front wall of the vehicle. Under a hailstorm of bullets, the sled broke into a backwards sprint, moving just as smoothly as it did when running forward.

"Come back here, you bloody wanker," Sutton shouted after the retreating vehicle.

"That's the first time we've chased one off," Tye observed.

"We've got him outnumbered and outgunned," Reg said. "He's the first one to show any sense."

But the creature's retreat was only temporary. After stopping a safe distance out in the desert to survey the scene, it charged to the attack once more. The alien kept low behind the superhard material of the chariot's front wall and fired blindly as it came.

Tye was amazed. "It's like a pit bull with a bone in its mouth. It just doesn't know when to give up." A moment later, a pulse zinged past him and ripped into the front wall of the station house.

"Keep him pinned down," Reg yelled to Sutton and Yossi. "We'll move up and get the angle on him." Then he and Tye hustled forward to the edge of the road and took cover behind a stack of discarded tires. Tye unwrapped the pulse weapon and let it climb onto his arm. Then he stole a glance over the tires and was alarmed to see the chariot heading directly toward them. He was nervous and breathing hard.

"What if it doesn't work this time?" he asked, looking down at the thing on his arm. Reg patted him on the shoulder and tried to reassure him.

"Remember: It's all mental. If we both tell it to fire, it'll fire. All we have to do is concentrate. Aim right at the head, and we'll be okay."

While bullets and pulse blasts ripped by in opposite directions overhead, Reg and Tye hunkered down and waited. The next time they peeked out, the front wall of the chariot was nearly on top of them. It was about to pass well within a tentacle's reach.

"One shot," Reg said. "Make it count."

Tye extended his arm like a rifle, and Reg gripped the copper-colored flippers. When the front end of the chariot brushed past, they came face-to-face with the crouching exoskeleton. The eight-foot-tall beast recoiled when it saw the humans. Reg mentally willed the gun to fire, but nothing happened. The sight of the hideous beast so close to them had distracted Tye from his purpose. With a screech, the startled alien lifted a tentacle to lash at the men.

"Fire!" Reg yelled, visualizing the pulse leaving the end of the weapon. It worked. The shell face blew apart just as the tentacle came across the side of Tye's head; it connected with the force of a heavyweight's punch and sent Tye flying. Reg pulled out a pistol and stood over the still-quivering body. A pair of reflective eyes stared up at him through the jagged opening in the armor. He pointed the pistol and prepared to kill it, but hesitated. *Would it be possible*, he wondered, *to take the thing prisoner? Could I interrogate it the same way they did to me?* He could feel it trying to attack telepathically, but its mental energy was very weak. Reg knew it was dying. He was still standing there thinking when Sutton ran up and pumped twenty shells into the opening, turning the alien's head into a lumpy liquid paste. Sutton could have gone on firing, but Reg stopped him.

"First the Israeli woman, and now Tye." Sutton was trembling with anger. "He wasn't much of a soldier, but one hell of a nice kid."

"I'm not quite dead yet," came a voice from behind them, "just resting."

Blood was streaming down the side of Tye's head. He'd lost a chunk of his left ear, but was otherwise uninjured. With help from the others, he got to his feet and slowly regained his balance. "I'm fine," he said. "I've taken harder hits during rugby matches."

Once he saw that Tye was going to pull through, Sutton regretted sounding like a mollycoddler and changed his tune. "It's your own fault, you know. You ever hear of a thing called ducking?" Then he took one of his friend's arms and led him back toward the damaged service station.

Yossi had gone to check on Edward and Remi. They came out of the destroyed rest room and extinguished their flamethrowers. The three men walked over to the alien chariot and took their first unhurried look at the inside of the vehicle. Like the other alien technologies they'd seen, it looked like the shell of a living thing. The riding area was shaped like a shallow bowl coated with a thick slathering of the same clear jelly lining the inside of the bioarmor cavities. Sand, dust, and twigs covered this sticky substance everywhere except where the aliens had recently been kneeling. There were no steering controls, knobs, or dials. There wasn't even anything to hold on to.

"Should we burn it?" Edward asked.

"No," Yossi told him. "Maybe we can use it." He whistled Reg over to take a look, then used a pocketknife to scrape away the layer of gelatin until he reached the layer of tough gray meat lining the inside of the shell. "Watch out, it might jump," he warned the others before stabbing down at the meat with his knife. Nothing happened. Although the surface of the flesh gave when he touched it with his blade, he couldn't tear it open.

"He wants to steal their car," Edward said when Reg walked up.

"Maybe it works the same way as the pulse weapon," Yossi said. "I think we should try it."

Reg looked down at the sand-soaked goop lining the inside of the chariot. "It'd be nice if we could run it through a car wash and clean it up first." But he agreed that they should experiment. He used Yossi's knife to clear the gunk away from a second area, then pressed a finger down onto the shell's spongy lining. Nothing happened until Yossi did the same thing. With both of them touching it simultaneously, the joints in the stick-figure legs flexed and bristled. "Make it walk," Reg said.

Yossi looked at him uncertainly. "How?"

"Just imagine it. Try to picture in your—"

"Agh!" Yossi yanked his hand away when he felt the thing begin to step forward. The legs quit walking the moment he broke the contact. He looked at Reg. "It is very disgusting."

"I agree. Let's try it again."

Within a few minutes the two men were walking the chariot around the grounds of the filling station like a clumsy, obedient dog. Using nothing more than their fingertips, they learned to make it stand in place, turn in a slow circle, and move in any direction they ordered. It was easy once they got the hang of it, simply a matter of will. But they couldn't get it to move as gracefully as the aliens had. The legs became confused whenever the men gave it conflicting mental signals. They also learned that the gelatin material was an essential part of the operating system. When they cleaned it completely from an area, the vehicle didn't register their skin contact.

It was Fadecla who stopped them. "It's time to go," she said, reminding everyone they had an important message to deliver to the army at the oasis.

"I think we should take this thing with us," Yossi said. "It could be useful."

"It's too big," Fadeela told him. "There isn't room in the truck."

But Reg knew what he had in mind. He grimaced down at the chariot's bed of slime and then up at his Israeli ally. "All right. But it's going to be a long, sticky ride."

A few minutes later, after saying good-bye to the elderly gas-station keepers, the truck rolled out onto the road and turned in the direction of Qal'at Buqum. A few car lengths behind, Reg and Yossi sat cross-legged in the alien chariot, their rear ends sunk into the layer of extraterrestrial ooze. They looked like characters in a futuristic version of *A Thousand and One Nights*, riding a strange-looking magic carpet across the desert.

12

Back to the Oasis

The sky was black, except for a streak of violet hanging over the western horizon when the old truck grumbled to the top of a rise in the road overlooking what still remained of Qal'at Buqum. The only lights in the oasis came from the scattered fires burning the last of its buildings. Ali pulled onto the shoulder and steered toward a cluster of civilians who had gathered on a bluff above the ruined village.

When they saw the alien chariot skulking through the darkness behind the truck, the civilians panicked. Shots rang out. Fortunately, neither Reg nor Yossi was hit. Word of the captured vehicle spread fast, and soon there were a hundred people crowded around the sled-shaped craft. The human charioteers brought it around to the front of the truck and parked in the one remaining headlight to give everyone a chance to examine it. Some of them used the opportunity to throw stones and kick at the sticklike legs. When Reg made no move to stop them, neither did the others. These people had every right to be angry. Angry not only with the armor-clad alien warriors who had decimated their town, but with Faisal's army, which had allowed it to happen.

Soon after Reg's group had stolen away to the east, Faisal and his advisors had concocted a plan which they quickly put into motion. After dumping poison into the outdoor pools and burying a few land mines, they withdrew their forces toward the mountains and established a camp. The townspeople were left to their own devices. As the old woman who had sold them ammunition earlier that day put it, they were left as bait. Most residents had loaded their possessions into their cars and driven into the mountains, taking the road toward Dawqah on the coast. Others, the people standing around them, had retreated a few thousand yards into the desert, onto the bluff. A handful of desperate men, with only a few weapons among them, had stayed behind to defend the oasis.

Late in the afternoon, the people on the bluff had watched the chariots come across the desert and spread out around the oasis before entering en masse. The men and boys who had stayed behind were counting on Molotov cocktails as much as on guns to repel the attack. Apparently, it didn't work very well because the aliens used very few pulse blasts to subdue the human defenders. One group of survivors made it to the edge of the oasis, but when they tried to run across the open desert, a chariot followed them out and caught them one by one. As it began to get dark, the fires started, and the oasis village was burned to the ground. Some of the chariots had left again in the direction of their crashed airship, but no one could agree on how many.

Reg stared down the hill as the last of Qal'at Buqum's fires burned down. A pair of headlights came over the distant horizon, headed along the road that would take them through the center of the village. Everyone on the bluff watched quietly as the headlights entered the town, paused for a few moments near the central post office, then continued up the hill in their direction. Reg and the others ran out into the road to meet whoever was coming up the hill, which turned out to be a pair of Saudi soldiers in a jeep. The civilians surrounded their car, asking questions about their village. The soldiers said they'd seen nothing but a few dead humans and burning buildings. They said they were on an important errand and couldn't answer any more questions. The driver put the jeep in gear and began plowing slowly through the crowd until Ali Hassan stepped into their headlights. When they saw him, the soldiers killed the engine and got out of the car. Ali told the crowd to stay back, then held a short conference with the pair. The three of them talked for a few minutes before returning to the jeep. Ali sat in the driver's seat and spoke on the radio, shouting angrily into the handset. When he was finished, he began arguing with the soldiers, who drove away only after Ali threatened them at gunpoint.

"What was that all about?" Reg asked, when Ali came striding toward him a moment later.

"We need to talk," the Saudi captain said, clapping one of his powerful hands onto Reg's shoulders and escorting him toward the truck. When they were inside, he told Reg to roll up his window, then looked around to make sure no one was lurking nearby.

"What the hell is going on?" Reg asked. He didn't know what Ali had learned from the passing soldiers, but clearly it wasn't good news.

"It's Faisal. He's moved his army into the mountains. They are about six miles up the road that leads to the town of Dawqah, I know the place. It is easy to defend. If the aliens attack him there, he will make them pay."

"Then let's hope they do attack. But not until *after* we've convinced Faisal not to bomb the destroyer." Reg stayed quiet for a moment or two, waiting to hear the reason for the private conference. But Ali only stared straight ahead, gripping the steering wheel as if he meant to strangle it.

Eventually, Reg broke the silence. "How long will it take to reach Faisal's camp?"

"There is a problem."

"Yes, I was beginning to suspect as much."

After glancing around once more, Ali explained. "Faisal has given an order. The order is to kill Reg Cummins. There is a reward for the man who does it."

"I see. Well, I'm sure it's a large reward," Reg said, pretending to be flattered by the attention.

Ali looked him in the eyes and nodded seriously. "Very large."

"Interesting," Reg said calmly, as he began to think about the fastest way out of the truck. "Obviously, you learned about this from those soldiers in the jeep."

Ali shook his head. "I spoke to Faisal on the radio. He told me that if I didn't kill you myself, I can never come back."

"And you'd like to go back?"

"Naturally."

Reg casually slid his hand close to the door handle, preparing to escape if Ali reached for his pistol. "That puts you in a bit of a predicament. Have you decided what you're going to do?"

Ali smiled. "Yes, I have. I told Faisal something I learned from American movies. I said, '*go screw yourself!*'" Ali laughed, and Reg joined in, uneasily. "And then I said something else, something stupid maybe."

"What was that?"

"I told him to call off the order. I said that I'm going to kill him if anything happens to you."

Reg stared at him for a minute without blinking. "You really said that?"

Ali sighed and nodded, indicating that the decision hadn't been an easy one.

Reg was impressed. The first words he could remember coming from Ali's mouth were a chauvinistic warning to the Israeli pilots that no Jews were allowed in Saudi Arabia. But now he'd made an irreversible decision to join a group that included a Jew, an ill-behaved Saudi woman, a Palestinian, and three Westerners—one of whom had a price on his head. Reg knew it was one thing for him, a foreigner, to cast his lot with this ragtag, international group, but was quite another for a Saudi officer to do the same thing, especially on his home soil. It took real guts. Or insanity. Or both.

"Did you tell Faisal about the biological weapons?"

"He already knew about them," Ali said. "He said there is a plan to attack the ship by air and land. I told him that we believe the germ canisters are inside the ship. Will that stop him from going ahead with his plan? I don't know."

"Well, after your conversation, I don't think you should be the one to go up there and try to talk him out of it."

"I don't think Faisal would be happy to see either one of us."

"Still, we ought to send someone up there to try to convince him." Neither one of them said it, but they knew that Fadeela would be the most logical candidate for the job. She had bargaining chips at her disposal that no man could possess.

"Good," Ali agreed, and opened his door. "But first we have to get out of this area. These people will soon hear of the reward on your head. Probably, they will not try to harm you. But they have lost their homes and everything else. They are desperate. We should find another place." He stepped out of the truck to begin collecting the rest of the team.

"One more thing," Reg said. "Just in case I don't get a chance to say this later: Thanks."

Ali smiled. "No problem."

A few minutes later, they were on the road again. The civilians of Qal'at Buqum, emboldened by what they'd heard from the soldiers in the jeep, started marching down the hill in a group to see what remained of their homes and shops. Reg and the team decided to escort them in case they ran into any trouble. If the town was clear, they would proceed with the task of stopping Faisal from bombing the downed destroyer.

Only one of the truck's headlights had survived when Yossi had driven it over the embankment that morning and smashed down on the alien chariot. Like a growling cyclops, the battered vehicle rolled down the middle of Qal'at Buqum's only road at five miles per hour. Walking alongside and behind it were a group of Saudis, some of them carrying guns, some of them armed only with sticks and stones. Edward and Remi protected the truck's flanks with their flamethrowers. Reg and Yossi knelt in the alien chariot, one hundred feet behind, resting the barrels of their assault rifles on the curving front wall. Tye and Fadeela were ready with the pulse weapon.

Lying in the road were the remains of several of the men who had tried to fend off the alien attack. Some of the corpses were blackened by pulse blasts, others showed signs of having succumbed to the pain of mental interrogation. It wasn't until they were approaching the post office at the center of town that they realized why the place felt so empty: The trees were gone. The two thousand palms and tamarind trees that had provided a lush canopy of green on either side of the road were missing. When they turned the headlight of the truck into the park, they saw what remained: felled and twisted trees, many of them broken off at the roots, others left standing but stripped of their foliage. The floor of the oasis had been swept clean of the ferns and ground-cover plants that had been there only hours before. Even the bark had been peeled away from the tree trunks.

The trees had been damaged in two ways: Some had been broken, probably by the strength of the biomechanical armor. On other trees, the bark and leaves had been stripped away in furrows, almost as if they'd been cleaned with a large potato peeler. The furrows were continuous, traveling in spirals up the length of the trunks. It looked as if they'd been eaten, but there was no evidence that either teeth or blades had been used.

Yossi returned from a quick foray deeper into the oasis and said he'd found an undamaged glade of trees surrounding one of the larger artificial ponds. The team decided to investigate, and Ali ran the truck over a curb and entered the park. The moon, the truck's remaining headlight, and the small flames licking from the barrels of the flamethrowers all combined to cast eerie, crisscrossing shadows through the broken, denuded trees.

When they came to the glade Yossi had described, it didn't take long to discover that the aliens had left something behind. Dozens of white globules glistened in the glare of the headlight. Roughly the size of basketballs, some of them sat on the ground lining the banks of the pool, others drooped from the tree trunks.

"What the hell?" Sutton asked, leading the rest of the team close to one of them. It clung to the yellowish base of a tamarind tree, dangling about a foot above the ground.

"It looks like a ball of phlegm," remarked Tye.

"Or a cocoon," Fadeela said.

"I'm going to see what's inside," Reg said, pulling out a pocketknife. "Do me a favor, will you? If anything jumps out at me, kill it before it can do anything nasty."

Then he reached out and sliced through the membrane. It was hollow inside, like a pouch. When the incision was long enough, the membrane tore open and a lump of flesh spilled onto the ground: an alien embryo. It was alive.

"Get out of the light," Reg said, leaning down for a closer look at the thing. Its tiny platelike head was translucent and fully formed. There was no skull, so Reg could see the brain working like a muscle just below the skin. Its pulpy limbs were still incipient little stubs that writhed through the air like the antennae on a garden snail.

"It wants to be cuddled," Tye joked grimly. "He thinks you're his daddy."

"Well, let's see if baby's hungry," Reg said. He reached up and pulled off a handful of the tamarind's red-and-yellow-striped flowers and sprinkled them onto the young alien's body. Within seconds, they began to break down and dissolve.

"It's digesting them."

"I'm officially disgusted now," Sutton remarked.

"That explains the damage to the other trees," Fadeela said. "The spiral markings. If they feed by dissolving their food and absorbing it through their skins, they could have crawled up the trees, eating as they moved. There doesn't seem to be any mouth." The fetus's eyelids opened a crack, and the fetus looked up at the humans. Its silvery eyes reflected like mirrors in the light. Reg looked up suddenly and scanned the area as if he'd heard something.

"What is it? What's the matter?"

"I'm not sure," he said, "but I don't think we're alone. Let's fan out and see what we can find."

"What do we do about Junior?" Tye asked.

"Leave it," Reg said. "We'll have to burn the glade before we leave."

Suddenly, there was a rush of movement in the bushes on the other side of the lake. The group hurried toward the source of the noise, letting the flamethrowers lead the way. By the time they arrived, whatever had made the noise was gone.

"Look at this," Yossi said. There was a fresh splash of water on the ground near some bushes. "Something was hiding here, watching us."

"Found a footprint," Sutton announced. "Only two toes on it. Headed that direction." The team moved where he'd pointed, toward an area thick with ground cover. They fanned out and beat the bushes as they advanced. They'd traveled less than fifty paces when Fadeela stopped.

"There it is," she whispered. "There it is." The others didn't know where she was pointing them. Then she muttered something in Arabic, buckled at the knees, and fell to the ground. When the others reached her, she was clutching the sides of her head and moaning in pain.

"It's close by," Reg shouted. "Find it before it kills her." The others scattered in all directions, kicking the bushes and checking behind every tree. Reg got down on his knees and forced Fadeela into a sitting position. "Where is it?" he asked, shaking her. "Show me where it is! Point to it!"

Desperate to help her, he picked her up in his arms and began to carry her out of the area. Only then did she extend her arm and point toward her attacker. She pointed straight up into the trees. Reg looked up and saw a pair of silver eyes amid the fronds of a palm. He reached for his pistol, took aim, and squeezed off several rounds. A moment later, the alien body came plunging through the air and hit the ground.

Fadeela's body, which had been rigid and trembling, relaxed into Reg's arms. A moment later, she opened her eyes and looked up at him. When she realized what had happened, she tried to smile but ended up crying. Sutton was the first one to reach them.

"You need to get her out of here," he said. "We'll destroy the rest of these egg sacs and meet you out on the road."

Reg nodded gratefully and carried Fadeela out of the trees.

After carrying her out to the trees, Reg had set Fadeela down near the edge of the road and rocked her in his arms while she cried. The encounter with the alien hadn't done her any lasting physical damage, but she was badly shaken. Between sobs, she tried to explain the fierce, overwhelming malice she'd felt from the alien mind.

"I never imagined there could be such a hatred," she said. "They only want one thing. They want us dead and out of their way." Her eyes had widened as she came to the dread realization of how focused the aliens were on annihilating the human race. When a fresh tear had run down her cheek, he reached out to catch it on his finger. He had only been attempting to comfort her when he leaned down and whispered to her, "I know, I know," he'd said, "but you're going to be all right now. I'll see to that."

As soon as those words had left his mouth, Fadeela changed. Her body began to stiffen, and she pulled away from him. "I can take care of myself. Take your hands off of me and get away."

It had been nearly an hour since then, and they hadn't spoken a word to each other since. They rode in the back of the truck along with Sutton, Remi, and Tye. All five of them sat facing in separate directions, lost in their private ruminations. They had managed to avoid being killed thus far, but they were beginning to think it was only temporary. Although they tried not to, they couldn't help sniffing at the air every now and again, wondering if they'd be able to tell when the deadly pathogens would surround them, let loose from the vials the aliens had stolen.

Eventually, Ali slowed the truck, pulled off the road, and parked behind a stand of tall brush that would hide them from any passing vehicles. They had come within a mile of the turnoff to Dawqah, the road that led to Faisal's hiding place in the mountains. Dried twigs and branches were strewn around on the ground, and everyone wanted to build a fire, but it was too dangerous. The flames might be spotted by a roving band of alien chariots. Or they might attract soldiers with orders to kill Reg.

A brief meeting was held at the tailgate of the truck, during which two goals were agreed upon. First, someone had to go to

Faisal's camp and make sure he understood that attacking the downed destroyer meant exposing the entire country to anthrax and ebola contagion. Second, Reg and Ali had to leave the country as soon as possible. The team would have to split up, something none of them wanted.

"I'll go up there and speak to Faisal. I'm the logical choice," Edward said. Remi and Yossi volunteered to go with him.

"He'll be surprised to see me again," Yossi said. "We'll be able to convince him."

Ali endorsed the plan and began working out some of the particulars, when Fadeela broke her silence and made an announcement.

"No," Fadeela said. "I am the one who must go to speak with Faisal. The rest of you will put yourselves in grave danger by showing your faces there. You probably wouldn't be able to get close to him. But I am certain I can convince him. I will make him listen."

"The woman is right," Ali said. "Edward can drive her. Is everyone agreed?"

"I will go alone," Fadeela said. "You can drive me to the turnoff, and we will find someone who is driving to the camp. I will go with them while the rest of you escape."

Reg was about to raise an objection when Fadeela shot him a determined look. Obviously, she had made up her mind to go.

"No, no objections," he said.

"Fine," Ali announced. "We will rest for half an hour and then set out."

Reg wandered away from the others and found a place to sit where he could watch the highway. Every few minutes, a lone truck or a fleet of jeeps would rumble past. After a few minutes, Fadeela walked over and stood near him. She looked at Reg in the dim light of the moon and smiled.

"I'm glad to see you're feeling better," he told her.

"Actually, I'm worse, but thank you. I came to say good-bye, and to apologize for the way I spoke to you before."

"Totally unnecessary," he said, hanging his head. When

Fadeela laughed out loud, Reg looked up, wondering why.

"You're acting like a wounded puppy. I don't think you understand why I was upset, and before I leave I wanted you to know why."

"I'm all ears, princess," Reg said, looking at her expectantly. The moment the nickname princess had come out of his mouth, he regretted using it. He called her that only because he was feeling betrayed by her decision to go to Faisal's camp. It made sense that she should be the one to go, but he couldn't help feeling that she was somehow choosing Faisal over him.

"My wish is to be attacked by another alien," she said.

"Huh?"

"Yes. I hope it happens again, because the next time, I will be stronger. I am going to control it, just as you did in the oasis. I think I understand now what you meant about being able to resist them."

Reg scowled at this ludicrous idea. "I, for one, hope you don't run across any more of them. I hope none of us do."

"You don't think I'll be able to resist? You think I'm too weak?"

"Not at all."

"Yes, you do. You said it just now. You called me princess again."

"Look, I don't really think you're a princess. I was just . . . I'm sorry I said that. You've been fighting like a banshee all day, and you deserve some credit."

"What is a banshee?"

"A jinn. You've been fighting like a jinn. You saved Edward and Remi's lives at that petrol station this afternoon. That whole wall would have collapsed if you hadn't worked that trick with the medallion. You bought them the time they needed to stay alive."

"But as you point out, it was only a trick. Now that I understand what the enemy is, I know that tricks are not enough. I want to be taken seriously. I don't want to be treated like a helpless little girl." She imitated the way Reg had spoken to her earlier:

"'*It's going to be all right. I'll take care of you. Don't worry.*' I want to be like that Jewish woman. What was her name?"

"Miriyam."

"Yes, Miriyam. She was *useful*. She was a real soldier. Let me ask you something about her. Did you like her?"

"Yes, I did. She was a brave woman."

"As I suspected. And what about me, do you like me?"

Reg looked up at her, surprised by the question. "Yes," he said after a moment. "I like you very much."

"Why?"

"Why do I like you?"

"Yes, why?"

"There are lots of reasons," he said vaguely. But after thinking it over for a moment, he decided on an answer. "I like that you hate being called a princess. I like your bravery and the fact that you want to be braver still. Most of all, I like that you haven't given up."

Fadeela smiled broadly. "An excellent answer," she said, "a very correct answer. I have not given up. In fact, I have an idea to discuss with you. It's a plan that may strike you as too bold, but I've been thinking about—"

"Whoa! Hold on." Reg held up his hands. "Turnabout is fair play. What about me?

"What about you?"

"I think you're attracted to me. I think you like me," Reg said, going out on a limb. "Am I right?"

Fadeela grimaced and looked impatient. "Of course I'm attracted to you. You're handsome, brave, intelligent, moderately well educated, young, strong, and a good listener. I've practically been throwing myself at you since the moment we met, but right now I have something more important to discuss with you. May I go on?"

"Please do."

"I've come up with a plan, and I want you to tell me what you think of it. What time is it now?"

He checked his watch. "Quarter to one."

"That leaves only a few hours until morning. If the aliens are planning to use the germ weapons they took today, won't they do so early in the morning?"

"I don't know. That scientist we met seemed to think that would be the best time. The most lethal time."

"After the hate I felt coming from the alien that attacked me, I would expect them to try and maximize the killing power. We have to go to their ship and find those weapons before they can be used."

Reg thought she was joking, but quickly realized she was completely serious. "That's madness. We can't waltz in there, grab the stuff, and run."

"Why not?"

"Well, there must be a thousand reasons, but the main one is that they'd kill us before we got inside. Secondly, if we did manage to make it inside, they'd kill us there. And don't forget, we don't *know* the canisters are inside the ship. That's nothing but a hunch. But let's say they *are* inside. You must have noticed that the ship is a rather large place. We could wander around in there for weeks without finding what we were looking for. Furthermore, if we show up and start shooting, what's to prevent them from using the weapons immediately? I could go on and on, but I hope that gives you the idea."

"We have to try," she said, then began to address his concerns one by one. "We have proven we can fight against them. If we move quickly, we can break past them and get inside. The germ canisters must be inside the ship, since they have nowhere else to go. We will find them in the black tower because these are important weapons and they would be taken to the control center of the ship. Since we are a small group, we will rely on stealth more than on our guns. If we move quietly and strike quickly, we can find the weapons before they are used. I think it's worth a try."

"You left out something important. Once we've rushed in there and gathered up enough poison to wipe out the entire planet, how do we get out again without releasing it into the atmosphere?"

"I leave that part to you. A chance to prove yourself." She smiled.

"Utter madness. As bad as the American plan to bring down the shields," he said, shaking his head. But Fadeela could see that he was thinking it over, walking through it step by step. And the longer he thought about it, the more he became convinced that it had a chance—an infinitesimally tiny chance—of actually working.

"It would take an incredible amount of good luck, and we wouldn't be able to do it alone. But I admit that in theory, at least, it could work if we had help from someone with an army at his personal disposal. Someone like Faisal. Without him, there's no way." As far as Reg was concerned, the question was closed. Fadeela took an oblique approach to opening it again.

"Reg," she said quietly. "Your pain is showing again. Your fear. If there is ever to be a future for us, you must tell me. What happened to you during the Gulf War?"

He felt the doors to his heart start to slam closed inside his chest, but managed to keep them ajar long enough to ask, "Your brother never told you?"

"I know there was an accident. But I want *you* to tell me. Please. I think it is relevant."

He didn't see how it could be, but trusted her enough to go on. Once he started talking, he realized that despite having thought about it every single day, he hadn't talked about it out loud for a long time. "Not much to tell really. I was flying a bombing run out of Dhahran. It was the second day of the war. We'd been out the day before and had some good success. Hit most of our targets without losing anyone, so we were all feeling good. Confident. Especially my group. We were more than confident. We were so damned cocky we were getting reprimanded right and left by our superiors. I remember that before we went up that morning, there was a briefing session where they showed us photographs with the latest target information. You know, hit this building, don't hit that one, watch out for anti-aircraft positions at points X, Y, and Z. And I'm sorry to say that I hardly paid any attention. I was just so anxious to get on with it.

"When we came in over Baghdad, their guns started pumping more flak into the air than I thought possible. It was an incredible fireworks show. I was certain our group leader was going to turn back, but he didn't. He set us loose, and we flew right into the middle of the firestorm. This might sound childish, but once I was over the city, I felt like I was playing a video game. I was dodging shells like mad and hunting down my targets at the same time. I didn't care how dangerous it was. Back in those days, I thought I was immortal, and nothing could scare me. I was having fun. And getting the job done. I hit a warehouse next to some railroad tracks, then an electrical station. Then, as I was making a turn, I saw a building I recognized from the briefing session. It wasn't on my list, but there it was right in front of me, so I said why not and dropped one of my smart bombs. I can still see it as if it were yesterday. It was a reddish brown round building and my bomb hit the bull's-eye. Went through the roof exactly in the center. I was pretty proud of that shot, especially since I hadn't even taken any time to line it up.

"I didn't realize there was a problem until I landed. The reason they'd showed us the picture of the round building was to tell us *not* to hit it. That previous intelligence had been updated. It was a college gymnasium that was being used to house the people who'd been bombed out of their houses. And I'd had a merry old time killing and injuring them. The final toll was somewhere around a hundred and eighty people.

"A few years later I came back to teach air combat to young Arab hotshots like your brother. You can believe I make sure they learn to do things carefully. I'm the RAF's poster boy in the fight against carelessness." He looked over a Fadeela. Her expression hadn't changed at all. "Does that answer your question?"

She spoke quietly. "You feel guilty, and you've come back to our country to redeem yourself."

Reg shrugged.

"Then, Reg, this is your chance. When you were over Baghdad, you were playing a game, and you killed a hundred and eighty nameless, faceless Arabs. I think you're different now. You understand that we Arabs aren't merely pieces moving across your game board. You can never bring those Iraqi people back to life, but you can save others. Millions of others."

He knew she was right. The plan she'd outlined was dangerous to the point of absurdity, but he had to give it a try. He owed the families of his Iraqi victims at least that much. And even if he'd never made that horrible mistake, he would have gone through with the plan for the sake of the woman sitting next to him. Remembering something important, he suddenly sprang to his feet.

"What is it?" Fadeela asked.

"The other day Faisal said something to Yossi and Miriyam. He said that even though they were Jewish, and he didn't like them, they had the right to stay with him for three days. Was he just making that up?"

"Not at all. It is a very old tradition of ours. If a stranger enters your camp, you must offer him comfort for three days."

"You think Faisal would honor the custom if he saw me?"

Fadeela thought for a minute. "If there are others around him, witnesses, then he would have no choice." Reg stood up and looked around. He spotted Ali standing near the truck and started walking toward him.

"Where are you going?" Fadeela asked him.

"I'm going to pay your fiancé a visit. But I'll need that uniform you're wearing before I go."

13

To the Camp

"He's a dead man," Sutton droned, as Reg and Fadeela climbed into the rear area of the battered truck.

Yossi reluctantly agreed. "Faisal's going to kill him the minute he shows his face."

"If he gets that far," Tye chimed in.

When Reg had explained that he was going to disguise himself and sneak into the army's camp in the hills, they had tried to talk him out of it. But Reg wanted to do more than merely warn against bombarding the ship while there were bioweapons inside. He also wanted to enlist Faisal's help. Without it, they would have no chance of pulling off Fadeela's plan.

"I'll see you all in a couple of hours," Reg said, as Ali slipped behind the wheel and started the engine. "Then we'll have some real fun."

"We'll be here waiting for you. Be careful," the others called back, waving and smiling as if they were optimistic about his chances. Faisal seemed to get whatever he wanted from his troops, and at that point he wanted Reg Cummins's head. Under those circumstances, visiting his camp armed with nothing more substantial to protect himself than some ancient Bedouin custom seemed, at best, recklessly dangerous.

"See you soon," Sutton called, as the truck drove away. "In the next life, that is."

Driving with the headlights off, Ali prowled up the highway and reached the Dawqah turnoff without incident. After parking the truck at the isolated crossroads, he came around the back to discover that Reg and Fadeela had switched uniforms along the way. She was now dressed as a British flight instructor and he as a Saudi infantryman.

"How do I look?" Reg asked

Ali wanted to answer that he looked like an English pilot wearing a Saudi uniform. The olive green fatigues, which had been baggy on Fadeela, fit Reg snugly. His wrists and ankles protruded awkwardly beyond the cuffs, and the shirt would barely button closed over his chest. Three days of exposure to the sun had darkened his skin to the point where he might be able to pass, in the darkness of night, as an Arab, but his whiskers had bleached blond.

"You look fine," Ali lied without hesitation, "but take this." He took off his *keffiyeh* and set it on Reg's head, pulling it down until it covered his eyes. "That's better."

"Someone is coming." Fadeela said, looking down the highway.

The three of them waited tensely as the headlights came toward them through the warm night, then turned up the mountain road. It was a convoy of sand-stained Toyota trucks carrying steel water drums. Ali stood in the road and waved them to a stop. After a brief conversation with the driver of each vehicle, he came to where Reg and Fadeela had hidden themselves.

"You can ride with these men," Ali told Reg. "They are delivering water to the camp."

Reg tilted his head back so he could see the line of trucks. "Good enough," he said, staring toward the road. "I'll ride in back with the barrels."

"Wait!" Fadeela stopped him.

"What is it?"

She looked him over, worried about his appearance. She made a quick adjustment to his uniform. "Let me hear what you are going to say when someone asks you a question."

Reg grunted inarticulately.

"Perfect." She smiled.

"Guess I should go," Reg said without moving. He lifted the edge of his *keffiyeh* so he could see Fadeela's face.

She looked up at him, concerned. "And remember: Get yourself as close to Faisal as you can before you speak to him, preferably when there are many people around him. If you can put a hand on him—"

"I know. I know." They'd already gone over the best way to approach Faisal several times. "But before I go . . ."

"Yes?"

"Don't you wish to wish me good luck? In England, it would be appropriate to give me a kiss right about now. It's sort of a tradition." Although it was dark, he saw that his words had startled her. Nevertheless, her lips parted slowly into a warm smile.

"I'm always interested in trying new things," she said softly. She moved toward him until her lips were only inches from his. "If and when you make it back alive, we should discuss this subject at length." Then she stepped back and offered him a military salute.

Reg let his *keffiyeh* fall again to the bridge of his nose. "I'll definitely take you up on that," he said, then began shuffling his way toward the idling Toyotas. As he wandered half-blind into the headlights, the men in the trucks all noticed his strange behavior and the fact that his uniform was too small. Reg groped the air until his hands found the tailgate. With Ali's help, he climbed on and perched atop the stack of steel water drums.

"How long should we wait for you?" Ali whispered.

"Not long. If I'm not back in a couple of hours, move on to Plan B without me."

Ali was confused. "Plan B? What is that?"

"You'll think of something."

Ali grinned and stepped away, motioning the convoy to continue. But the driver of the lead vehicle waved him over for a word. He was concerned.

"Who is this lunatic you're putting on my truck?" the man asked. "What's the matter with him?"

Ali leaned in close and stared menacingly at the driver. "Can you keep a secret?"

Intimidated by Ali's size and strength, the man nodded vigorously that he could.

"He's royal. One of the king's favorite nephews. He went crazy under all the pressure, so I'd stay out of his way if I were you. Don't even talk to him."

"Yes, yes, I understand," the man stammered. "Thank you, sir." Then he shifted into gear and started up the twisting mountain road. The higher the road climbed, the more treacherous the turns became. Steep canyon walls rose on either side, and Reg quickly understood why Faisal had chosen to retreat to this place: It was safe and easy to defend. Dirt service roads ran along the clifftops, allowing troops and weapons to be moved into place. In the moonlight, Reg could see the silhouettes of field cannons, mortars, and rocket launchers overlooking the road. If the aliens tried to force their way through the pass, it would be like shooting fish in a barrel. The obvious difference, of course, would be that the fish would be shooting back.

When they'd traveled four or five miles, the first trees began to appear, and soon they reached the army's main staging area: a large, level field on the south side of the road. Hundreds of soldiers, their weapons, equipment, and vehicles were located in the dried grass. The noise of gasoline-powered generators jackhammered the air, and high-intensity lamps flooded the field with a glaring light. The water trucks turned off the road and, moving slowly, followed the tire tracks that led to the center of the camp. Just as Reg was about to slip over the side and make his way to the nearest shadows, the convoy was stopped for an inspection.

Reg pushed the *keffiyeh* even lower over his eyes and slouched against the water drums. One of the soldiers walked around behind the truck. When the man spoke, Reg shrugged his shoulders and grunted noncommittally. Apparently, this answer was not satisfactory because the guard repeated the question, testily this time. Reg knew he'd have to try something else. After hesitating for a moment, he imitated something he'd seen his student-pilots do a thousand times: He waved a hand at the heavens, and said, *"Insha'allah!"* It was an all-purpose phrase meaning; *Who knows?* Or *It's in God's hands.* It was the thing people said when they didn't know what else to say. Luckily, it seemed to amuse the soldier. He chuckled and waved the trucks forward.

As they moved deeper into the camp, Reg waited for an opportune moment to slip away. Despite the late hour, everyone was wide-awake and buzzing with energy. Groups of soldiers were everywhere: Most of them were moving from place to place, preparing for the next confrontation. They drove past a cluster of utility vans that had been outfitted to act as mobile field-communications centers and on toward the loudest, brightest, noisiest part of the camp: the mess tent. Reg jumped to the ground, walked alongside the truck for a few paces, then turned away as if he knew exactly where he was headed. Some soldiers spoke to him, but he kept his head down and brushed past them without drawing much attention. Or so he hoped. As he moved away from the lights, he began to breathe easier until someone came up from behind and grabbed his arm.

"You are the Englishman, the Teacher. I know you."

Reg wheeled around to find himself face-to-face with a tall man in a well-tailored blue suit caked with dust. He looked like a commercial airline pilot. He had wavy hair combed straight back, a small goatee, and bright teeth that he displayed in an ear-to-ear smile. Reg recognized him as the Yamanis' chauffeur.

"My name is Abdul. What happened to your uniform?"

"Happy to see you again," Reg whispered. He clamped a friendly arm around Abdul's shoulders, then forced him to walk. "Listen, I'm looking for someone, and I want you to help me find him." Abdul nodded. He was a little confused about where Reg was leading him, but he agreed to help.

Not far away, a tent flap pushed open, and a clutch of Saudi officers stepped out of the command tent. When Faisal ducked outside and strode past them, they hurried to keep pace. He was on his way to the radio vans with a message he wanted relayed to his advance troops, the men stationed closest to the fallen destroyer. It was important enough that he wanted to explain it himself. When they saw him coming, the communications technicians snapped to attention and saluted. Faisal ordered them to ease and asked for the latest reports. It was evident from their faces that his soldiers regarded Faisal with a type of respect akin to awe. He had already defeated the aliens once, and they believed he could do it a second time. They would have followed any order he gave them.

"The message shall say exactly this: King Ibrahim is hiding here in the mountain pass to Dawqah with an army of less than one hundred men to protect him."

"But, sir, we just monitored one of the king's communiqués. He is in At-Ta'if."

"Can our advance troops hear those same broadcasts?"

"No, sir."

"Then deliver the message as I gave it to you. Say that if the king is killed, the army will surrender. Tell them to remain in their positions but intercept any enemy forces that advance in this direction."

"He is setting a trap, a very intelligent trap," one of the radiomen told the others enthusiastically. They quickly joined him in loud praise of the strategy. By that point, all of them knew the aliens were interrogating the humans they caught, and the information they gleaned gave them a powerful advantage, By planting the false information in the minds of his men, Faisal was trusting that it would eventually make its way into the alien consciousness. It might have been the first interspecies disinformation campaign. After basking in the adulation of his troops, Faisal and his officers turned to go, but a strange-looking soldier stepped into their path and lifted his *keffiyeh*.

"Good evening, Commander," Reg said with a level stare. When Faisal saw who it was, he nearly tripped over his own feet trying to back up. He glared at Reg and reached for his pistol. Very loudly, Reg invoked the Bedouin custom of hospitality. "I ask to be accepted as a guest in your camp!" he shouted.

There was a moment of tense silence. From the murderous

looks he was getting, Reg thought every man in the camp must know about the price Faisal had put on his head. But the next moment, the commander regained his composure and relaxed. He even forced himself to chuckle. The others followed his lead.

"Major Cummins, you startled me."

"I am asking to be accepted as your guest," Reg said again, just as loudly.

"Gentlemen," Faisal said, turning to the others, "this is one of the pilots who assisted me in destroying the enemy over Mecca. Everyone will treat him as a brother while he remains here with us." He spoke to them with a broad smile that disappeared the moment he turned back to face Reg. "What do you want?"

"I was at your base in Al-Sayyid today when your stockpile of biological agents was taken by the aliens."

Before he could go on, Faisal interrupted him, saying that Reg was mistaken. "Saudi Arabia has no biological-weapons program." Then he sent his radio operators back to work and led Reg several paces away so they could speak without being overheard. His officers followed. "There is no need for my men to know about the weapons you are talking about," he said angrily.

"I disagree. We're all in danger of being exposed to some very lethal diseases. If the aliens can figure out a way to deploy those poisons, everyone from here to Sweden is in danger."

"Yes, I know," Faisal shot back. "But I don't think you came here to criticize us for having developed these weapons."

"You're right. I came here because I've got a plan to get them back. Actually, it's Fadeela's plan." When they heard her name mentioned, Faisal's officers tensed up and looked as if they might come at Reg all at once. On the day that should have been his coronation as a major hero, Faisal had suffered the pain of having his bride-to-be "kidnapped" by a band of foreigners. The men surrounding him seemed anxious to avenge their hero's suffering.

"Where is Fadeela now?" Faisal asked.

"Safe," was all Reg would say.

"Women are so unpredictable, so full of surprises, don't you agree, Major?"

Reg didn't return the smile he was offered. "Fadeela's no ordinary woman."

Faisal only shrugged, then ordered his officers to leave them. Reg wasn't happy to see the men leave. Although they were hostile, they were also witnesses that would make it difficult for Faisal to go back on his promise of hospitality. Faisal walked to the front of the command tent and invited Reg inside. He smiled that smug smile of his when Reg thought twice before heading into the tent.

"Major, you would not have come here unless you needed my help with your plan. I think you have no choice but to trust me."

Realizing he was right, Reg went inside, and the two antagonists talked for the next half hour. Outside, a dozen men held their ears close to the tent, trying to eavesdrop on the conversation. They heard Faisal laugh when Reg explained what he wanted to do. "It would be suicide," the commander said loudly. But Reg doggedly continued to explain how the plan could work in a voice that was too low for the men outside to hear. They argued about the dangers of the biological weapons, air support, and the equipment Reg and his team would need for their raid. The men listening knew Faisal was seriously considering lending his help when he poked his head outside and asked for one of his lieutenants, a man who had climbed the first few stories of the tower at the front of the alien ship.

When the two men finally emerged from the tent, they synchronized their watches, looking somber but optimistic. Faisal carried a handwritten list which he turned over to one of his supply sergeants. "Major Cummins will be traveling to Dawqah with a fragile cargo," he announced, gesturing past the hilltops toward the Red Sea. "Give him one of our best trucks and all the supplies on this list. Make sure it is organized and ready for him in ten minutes." Then he leaned in close to Reg, and whispered. "Your plan is dangerous, but I believe it can work. I expect to see you and your people back here within a few hours. With Fadeela Yamani, of course," he added.

"If we're lucky, *and* we get the air support we need," Reg said, "you'll see her."

"Good luck," he said, smiling. The two men shook hands

before Faisal turned away to attend to other business. Despite his encouraging tone, he was certain he would never see Reg Cummins again. Or Fadeela Yamani. They would both be killed before they ever set a foot inside the ruined city destroyer. He was resigned to the fact that the legend he was creating for himself would take on a bittersweet twist at the end: *But before they could be wed, his lovely bride was carried into the desert and slain by the savage infidels.* It wasn't the ending he'd imagined, but it was one he could live with.

When Faisal was gone, the Yamanis' chauffeur, Abdul, approached Reg enthusiastically. "Dawqah? Why are you going there? Mr. Yamani and I will go with you."

"Abdul, where is Khalid? I have to talk to him."

"Impossible," Abdul said, pointing to the surrounding hilltops. "He is somewhere up there, a prisoner. No one may speak to him, only his father."

"Well, let's talk to his father, then." They went to the Yamanis' Rolls-Royce and, when they opened the back door of the limousine, found Mr. Yamani disheveled, sitting bolt upright, yelling into a cellular phone. He appeared to be midway through an argumentative strategy session with the Saudi king. Although he seemed in better spirits than the last time Reg had seen him, there was a manic quality to the way he spoke into the receiver and slashed his free hand through the air. Abdul, like an orderly in a psychiatric ward, reached into the car and took the phone away from the old man, gently but firmly.

"I told you, sir, the telephone is not working. But look who is here. You have a visitor. Do you remember Major Cummins? He is going to Dawqah."

Yamani looked up, confused. He stared at Reg for a moment without recognizing him. Then his expression changed.

"The Teacher! Come in, come in." Warmly, he waved Reg inside and offered him the seat facing his own. He seemed all at once to regain control of himself. "Do you have any news about my daughter? They tell me she was killed today, but I don't believe them."

Reg assured him that Fadeela was alive and well. Then, looking into the old man's eyes, he asked a series of questions in order to determine the man's mental state. Yamani recognized the patronizing tone in his voice.

"I have not completely lost my mind, Major Cummins, and I will thank you not to speak to me as if I have. The telephone, it is simply a game. A way of thinking out loud while I sit here with nothing to do. Now, tell me, what is this about going to Dawqah?"

We're not actually going to Dawqah," Reg explained. "That's just the cover story."

"I don't want to hear a story. I want to hear the truth."

As quickly as he could, Reg outlined the plan, leaving out one important detail. He didn't say that Fadeela would be joining the raiding party. There wasn't any point in adding to the man's burden. Mr. Yamani appeared to follow Reg's explanation, nodding and grunting at the appropriate moments. But when he was finished, Yamani seemed lost again.

"Dawqah is a nasty little town," he said. "The beaches are polluted with oil, and there is absolutely nothing to do there. I suggest we rendezvous in Jeddah instead. Have you ever been to Jeddah?" Reg could see he was wasting valuable time.

"Take care of yourself, sir. It's time for me to go." He started out of the car, but Yamani grabbed his sleeve and held fast. He seemed to be having another painful moment of clarity, but it was impossible to be sure. Tears welled up and poured down his cheeks.

"I am grateful, very grateful to you. Tell Fadeela that her old father is joining the war, that he is going to fight from now on."

"I'll tell her," Reg promised. But the once-great man didn't hear him. His mind had darted off in a new direction, and he began shouting angrily at his chauffeur.

"Abdul, coffee! Where are you? Bring me some coffee. Don't you realize we are at war? You know I can't fight without my coffee!"

It looked like the last war Mr. Yamani would ever fight was

the one for control of his mind. Reg figured the chances of him winning were somewhere between slim and none. Then again, he reminded himself, the old man had a better chance of making a full recovery than he and his ragtag unit had of living past sunrise.

He didn't check to see if the supply sergeant had given him all the items on the list. He got in the truck and drove away at once, wondering if he could trust Faisal. A couple of miles down the road, he pulled off the road after a blind curve to make sure he wasn't being followed, then continued down the hill.

1 4

The Raid

When Reg pulled an armored Mercedes truck off the road and drove toward the stand of scrub brush, everyone's mood changed dramatically. The fact that he was back made it seem like anything was possible. Sutton and Yossi ran out to meet the truck and jumped on the running boards.

"Cummins," said Sutton, "you're the luckiest son of a bitch I've ever met. I'm beginning to think I ought to stick close to you. Maybe some of that luck will rub off."

"Luck?" Reg asked with a cockeyed grin. "Maybe. But also a lot of skill."

"More like a lot of chutzpah." Yossi laughed.

Once Reg pulled the truck to a stop, the others bombarded him with questions about what Faisal's reaction had been, the size of the army in the hills, and the dangers he had faced.

"Faisal's got over a thousand men up there. I asked him to give me half of them for an assault on the spaceship's tower."

"What'd he say?"

"After he stopped laughing, he said no. He wasn't taking me seriously at all until I played my trump card." He broke off and looked at Fadeela. "I told him who came up with the idea of raiding the ship. And I told him we were going ahead with it whether he helped us or not. That got his attention. Suddenly, he couldn't help me enough. He started pulling out maps, ordering supplies, calling soldiers into his tent to give us scouting reports. And he promised we'd have air cover. A group of Saudi jets will be waiting for us when we get to the city destroyer."

"But no troops?" Fadeela asked.

"No troops," Reg said.

"In other words, he refused to help us."

Reg shrugged. "He gave us these supplies," he said, gesturing to the cargo bed of the truck, "and he didn't kill me. Didn't even send anyone to follow me."

"What do you make of it?" Edward asked.

"He wants us to go to the tower," Ali said. "He doesn't think we'll survive."

"Exactly," Reg said. "The only reason he gave me these weapons and let me go was so we'd all go into the destroyer." He shot another look at Fadeela for her reaction before asking, "Who knows what time it is?"

"Two A.M.," Yossi said, "which leaves only about three hours until dawn."

"Then we've got to hurry," Reg said. "Everyone pull these supplies off the truck and pick out a weapon or two. The more the merrier. We can discuss the rest along the way."

But before Reg could contemplate loading himself down with firearms, there was a pressing piece of business. He grabbed Fadeela and pulled her to the front of the truck. "Take off those clothes," he said. "This uniform is too tight. It's killing me." He leaned against the battering ram that extended off the front of the chassis, pulled off his shoes, then began unbuttoning his shirt.

"What else did Faisal say?" she asked, beginning to unlace her own boots.

"He had a message for you."

"What was it?"

"He said for you to be careful. Isn't that a classic? After I explained what we're proposing to do, he turns to me with a perfectly serious expression on his face and says, '*Tell her to be careful.*'"

"We are going to be married soon. Naturally, he is concerned," she said facetiously, trying to laugh it off. *But not concerned enough to try to stop me*, she thought. As much as she despised Faisal, the fact that he hadn't tried to keep her away from the spacecraft hurt her. By giving Reg the weapons, he was actually encouraging her to go and probably get killed.

"Hurry up with those pants," Reg said, slipping out of the ones she had lent him. "Faisal also said he wouldn't have given me any help at all if it hadn't been your plan. He said you were a brave woman, and he's looking forward to seeing you again soon. Or something along those lines. I don't think he meant a word of it." Waiting for Fadeela to get undressed, Reg stood there in nothing but his jockey shorts and a pair of dirty white socks as easily and unself-consciously as if he were in a preflight locker room talking with a fellow pilot. Earlier, when he and Fadeela had exchanged uniforms in the back of the moving truck, they'd modestly turned their backs to one another. But now he stood in plain view of her, too focused on the details of the plan and the danger that lay ahead to feel the slightest twinge of embarrassment.

Fadeela hesitated. "Please turn around."

He did, and changed the subject. "I spoke to your father. He seems fine, in better spirits. That chauffeur of yours, Abdul, is taking good care of him. Your father had a message for you, too: 'Tell my daughter I've joined the fight.'"

"What about Khalid?"

"I wasn't able to talk to him, but I think he's fine. Faisal's got him posted to a gunnery battalion on the canyon cliffs. Ah, that's a thousand times better," Reg said as he zipped himself into his own trousers again. "I don't know where you found that uniform, but it rides awfully high in the crotch."

"I plan on having it altered as soon as I can make an appointment with my family's tailor," she shot back.

"Smart aleck." Reg grinned. "Let's go pick you out a weapon. Maybe a rolling pin." He led the way to the back of the truck, where the others were outfitting themselves. Ali had found a five-foot-long field gun that fired rounds the size of Cuban cigars. It was designed as a stationary weapon, but the broad-chested soldier took his *kef-*

fiyeh back from Reg and tied it around the gun to create a shoulder sling. Edward strapped a flamethrower harness onto his back. A far cry from the antique weapon he had used the previous afternoon, this new flamethrower featured a lightweight ceramic canister that carried double the fuel, had adjustable settings, and didn't require a constantly burning pilot—a major asset during a sneak attack. Remi, who along with Sutton was going to stay outside and guard the entrance while the others entered the ship, had chosen a bazooka-style, shoulder-mounted rocket launcher. Reg picked up a fully automatic machine gun and offered it to Fadeela. "Think you can handle one of these, or would you rather help Tye operate the alien pulse gun?"

She accepted the machine gun, but then muscled past Reg and picked up the only remaining flamethrower. "I'll take this one, too. Fire is what they hate the most. Fire is what I'm going to give them." She slipped her arms into the harness assembly, then moved off to discuss the weapon with Edward.

"I don't like it," Ali whispered to Reg. "She's not a soldier; she's a woman, and she doesn't know what she's doing."

Reg glanced over his shoulder. "I'd be careful about saying that to her face," he told Ali. "She's liable to barbecue you."

Fadeela must have heard them talking. "Is there a problem?" she asked, moving closer and holding the nozzle of her weapon menacingly in Reg and Ali's direction.

Ali glared at her for a minute before backing down. "No, there is no problem."

"Good." She turned around and fired a test shot at a set of nearby rocks. Night turned to bright day as the powerful jet of fire shot fifty feet and splattered against the stones. Because the fuel was laced with generous amounts of napalm, the fire continued to burn long after it hit the ground.

Ali's anger flared as hotly as the flames. "What are you doing, stupid woman? You're showing the aliens where we are."

Fadeela mocked him. "Why are you so afraid? Don't worry. If the big bad aliens come, I'll protect you." Edward laughed at her joke, but Ali was far from amused.

As the napalm-enhanced fire burned and dripped down the rocks, Reg called everyone together for a final strategy session. "Listen up. Even with Faisal's help, this isn't going to be easy. Everything within ten miles of the ship is heavily patrolled. The aliens move in pairs on their chariots. Hopefully, we'll see them before they see us. But according to Faisal, they've got another trick: They bury themselves in the sand like land mines and pop up when humans come too close. Keep your eyes open. Faisal will be sending jets to bomb the northern edge of the ship. We'll approach from the south and slip into the tower during the distraction."

"If we can get past the patrols," said Ali.

"Right. We won't know if we can do that until we're out there. We may have to turn back."

"No turning back," Fadeela said matter-of-factly.

"She's right," Yossi said. "If they release those weapons into the air at dawn, we're dead just the same. Better to go down fighting."

Reg squatted and drew a picture of the tower in the dirt. "I've been told there's no way to enter the tower directly from the outside, so we'll have to enter here, where the right side of the tower meets the front of the ship. The Saudi army was exploring this opening when the aliens began their attack."

"What did they find out?" Remi asked.

Reg shrugged. "There weren't any survivors." He looked at the anxious faces around him. "Hopefully, we'll have better luck."

"Let's climb to the top of those rocks so we can have a look around."

Tye and Yossi, who were riding next to Reg in the chariot, looked at the almost vertical stone cliff in front of them, then at one another, then finally at Reg. It would have been safer to dismount and climb up the slope under their own power, but neither of them objected. Instead they concentrated on moving toward the top of the stone wall and, through the magic of alien bioengineering, the chariot began to pick its way up the craggy cliff. The angle was so steep that they would have slid off the back of the chariot if it hadn't been for the ingenious harness Tye had made by fastening several lengths of nylon rope around the body of the sled-shaped alien construct to keep them in.

"Don't try to steer," Reg insisted. "Don't tell it which way to go; just focus on getting to the top. It's like a horse—it knows the best way."

When the chariot stopped at the top of the rocks, Reg lifted himself out of the layer of foul-smelling ooze that coated the seating area and surveyed the valley ahead through a pair of binoculars. He looked nothing like the unassuming man who had entered Faisal's camp earlier that night. Now he was heavily armed with an automatic machine gun on his back, a belt of grenades slung over his shoulder, and a holster on each hip. One holster held a .357 Magnum loaded with armor-piercing shells. In the other was a flare gun.

Only a couple of miles ahead, the mountain-sized remains of the alien city destroyer loomed in the darkness. The light of the moon glimmered across what remained of the domed roof, and there was just enough light for them to see their objective: the tower rising from the front of the ruined spacecraft. Far to his right, Reg looked out on the plateau that was to have been the site of Faisal's wedding. It was littered with destroyed and abandoned vehicles. The flags and bunting decorating the photo platform fluttered in a warm breeze blowing across the desert from the south. Everything was perfectly quiet except for the idling engines of the two trucks nearby.

"Something is very wrong with this picture," Reg said as he searched for signs of alien activity through the binoculars. At the base of the tower, he spotted the large opening Faisal's men had told him about. It was big enough to drive a truck through. "We should have run into some resistance by now. We should have seen them at least."

"Don't sound so disappointed," Yossi said. "After all, we're trying to avoid them, remember?"

The agreement Reg had made with Faisal was simple enough. It called for the team to elude as many of the alien patrols as possible until they were within ten miles of the fallen ship. At that point, they would send up flares to signal the Saudi Air Force to begin bombing the far side of the ship as a diversionary tactic. Despite the high loss rates the Saudis had sustained each time they had tried to make bombing runs on the remains of the destroyer, Faisal had assured Reg that air cover would be waiting for him by the time he arrived at the ten-mile perimeter. Since the aliens were mysteriously absent, it didn't appear they needed any help to make it inside. But what about on the way out, assuming they lived that long? If they managed to find and recapture the case of biological pathogens, the aliens weren't likely to let them escape without sending chariots to chase them. In that scenario, a few well-placed bombs dropped in the path of their pursuers would make a world of difference.

"You think those Saudi jets will show up?"

Reg shrugged and came back to the chariot. When he sat down, the conductive goop accepted him with a slurping noise. "Faisal promised they would, but obviously that's no guarantee. If we're going in, we have to assume there won't be any help."

Yossi nodded and thought the situation over. "Who needs them? The aliens have gone away and left the front door wide-open. Maybe we can sneak in and out before they come back."

Tye couldn't believe it was going to be that easy. "Maybe they're *not* gone," he said. "Maybe they're hiding just inside that opening waiting to zap us when we step through. Or maybe they're sleeping and when they hear us—"

Reg interrupted him. "That's the risk we have to take."

"And we better do it soon," Yossi said. "Only a couple of hours until dawn."

Tye unwrapped a couple of the amber-colored medallions and laid them on his forearm. He fiddled with them for a moment, but could find none of the black diamonds that signaled alien proximity. "The coast is clear," he said. "In fact, it's empty."

"Let's get back to the trucks," Reg said.

The chariot obeyed immediately and bolted down the steep, uneven slope. The skinny, bone white legs took them bouncing, bucking, and stumbling forward until they reached the desert floor once again, then whisked them smoothly up to the driver's side window of the lead truck, where Sutton was behind the wheel. Edward sat next to him in the cab, monitoring the reports coming over the radio in Arabic. Remi and Fadeela were in the cargo area, keeping their eyes peeled for the enemy, while Ali drove the other, older truck.

"You smell that?" Sutton asked, sniffing the air with ferretlike intensity. "Something smells funny, like mildew or something." Like the rest of them, he was hyperalert to signs that the biological weapons had already been released. In addition to noticing odd smells in the air, they'd imagined burning sensations in their noses and lungs and spotted ominous-looking clouds on the horizon, only to have them turn out to be bushes or stands of rock.

"Smells like you're imagining something," Remi called down to the driver.

Reg said, "It doesn't look like Faisal's boys are going to show. But we don't need them. Actually, it's better this way; gives us the element of surprise."

"Yeah, but on the way out?"

"That's a lifetime from now," Fadeela said.

Reg grinned at her choice of words.

Then Sutton surprised them all by yelling, "If we meet any damned resistance on the way out, we'll blow their bloody heads off! Let's go. Let's rock and roll."

"Wait a second. Listen to this." Edward, who had been listening to radio reports, leaned past Sutton so he could make eye contact with Reg, sitting in the alien chariot outside. "I think I found out where our spacemen are. They've sent an army to At-Ta'if. Right now, they're attacking the southern outskirts of the city."

Sutton asked, "So they're gone?"

"If they are," Reg said, grinning, "that would make it a whole lot easier to sneak in, wouldn't it? Turn toward the ship," he said aloud. When he, Yossi, and Tye simultaneously willed it to happen, it did. The chariot turned sharply and began trotting forward, awkwardly at first, until the men mentally agreed on the speed they wanted. With a clear set of mental commands steering it, the chariot moved across the sand smoothly and gracefully.

"It's like a magic carpet," Tye said, as they picked up speed. The pace they settled on was fast—as fast as the bioengineered dune buggy would carry them, which turned out to be forty miles per hour. They slowed down only once, as they came to the last earthen barrier and looked across the wide-open no-man's-land in front of them. Ali parked the battered old truck there, leaving it as an emergency backup, then jumped into the back of the Mercedes. Now the only obstacles standing between them and the unbelievably large mass of the city destroyer were the destroyed vehicles left behind by the Saudi army. Once they were out in the open terrain, the Mercedes quickly outpaced the chariot. Sutton kept the pedal to the metal and shot ahead, literally leaving Reg and his fellow drivers in the dust.

As they raced closer, the staggeringly large tower seemed poised to topple over and crush them like fleas, its great height creating the optical illusion that it was about to fall forward. The three men crouched behind the front wall of the chariot expected pulse blasts to begin raining down at them at any moment. Sensing their fear, the chariot veered sharply away from the tower and started across the open desert.

Reg choked down the fear that was rising in his chest and sounded an order. "Concentrate on following the truck!" And a moment later, the vehicle did exactly that. But it wasn't the last misstep. Each time one of the men glanced up at the darkened, blank face of the tower, the chariot responded to his terror and tried to steer away. Then, to add to their problems, they noticed something new and truly alarming. There was a massive tubular form crawling down the front face of the tower, like a ten-foot-diameter snake, something that definitely hadn't been there during the daylight hours. The chariot balked under the confusion of conflicting mental signals it received from its drivers, then came to a dead halt.

"What the hell is that?"

Switching on their flashlights, they saw what appeared to be an enormous root or section of pipe. Growing up the wall of the tower, it rose beyond the limits of their vision and appeared to be growing right before their eyes, causing the tower to undulate and move.

"I don't like the looks of that," Tye said, his voice full of jitters. "They've planted their magic beans, and this is the beanstalk we're supposed to climb up, right?" But as they watched the slow movements, they realized that it wasn't growing out of the ground. It was growing *down*, burrowing deeper by the moment.

"Better to take our chances on the inside," Yossi said, and the chariot moved off. They turned the corner of the tower and raced to where the others were preparing to enter the break in the destroyer's wall. Ali had already broken open several flares and tossed them inside the ground-level opening, determining that the first few yards at least were safe. He and Fadeela stood at the ragged opening, impatient to slip inside.

"Did you see that thing climbing up the tower?" Edward asked in a harsh whisper, bringing a pair of lightweight thermal blankets to the chariot.

"It's not climbing," Tye answered him. "It's digging itself into the ground."

Edward spread the blankets under the rope harness at the back of the chariot to create a "passenger area." Most of the gelatin coating had already been scraped away. The blankets were to prevent any further contact with the goop. Getting three people to cooperate in the driving was tough enough. They didn't need six people steering.

"Hop on," Reg told Edward. He did, and the chariot jogged forward to where Ali was standing guard over the opening. Sutton ran up behind them before they went inside. "Tye," he whisper-shouted, "leave us one of those disk things of yours. And don't you people be in there forever. Remi and I can't sit around picking our noses out here past sunup." Tye tossed him one of the medallions. "And one more thing," Sutton called. "Good luck."

Ali and Fadeela stepped through the opening, made a quick inspection, and waved for the chariot to follow them.

Inside, the team found themselves facing a tangle of collapsed walls. What had once been a series of rooms and passageways was now utterly smashed to pieces. They quickly found a path through the charred, broken debris and arrived at the sidewall of the tower, which extended deep into the body of the ship. This wall was made of a different material and had sustained no visible damage.

"Wait here," Ali told the men in the chariot as he moved to inspect the wall. "You too," he told Fadeela when she followed him. She ignored him and accompanied him into the long, partially collapsed corridor that ran along the edge of the wall.

"It's thin," Ali said, rapping his knuckles against the wall.

Fadeela pushed against it. It didn't give. It felt like a razor-thin sheet of rough-cut glass. She told Ali to shoot his way through it, and both of them backed away. Ali fired a single shot and, when the wall held, went to inspect the damage. Not even a nick. He and Fadeela waded a few paces into the darkness of the corridor, trying to find the end of it with their flashlights, but it was too long. They ran back to the chariot, jumped on the back, and took hold of the harness ropes like bull riders at a rodeo.

"Straight ahead," Reg commanded, and the chariot bolted forward, carrying the six heavily armed humans with ease. They set out at a cautious trot, but soon increased their speed by urging the chariot to move faster. The trip over the uneven floor felt like riding a rickety roller coaster. They were tossed one way, then the other, straining the whole while to spot signs of danger. They sped forward for a long time until they reached the end of the tower and turned the corner.

"Stop!"

The chariot legs went stiff and stopped short. Ahead, dim round lights glowed out of the jet blackness, weakly illuminating the floor and walls.

"Back up," someone hissed. The chariot shuddered but stayed put.

"No, don't," Reg countered. "They're not moving."

"What is it?" Tye whispered, extending his arm over the front rail of the chariot so Yossi could help him fire the alien pulse weapon if need be.

"They're not moving," Reg said again. "Let's go for a look." After a moment of hesitation, the stick legs began moving forward again, but slowly and reluctantly now. As they came closer, it became apparent that they were not the first humans to enter the tower. The lights were coming from a cluster of Saudi jeeps that must have been parked there since the alien ambush almost twenty-four hours earlier. There must have been fresh batteries to keep the headlights lit up for all that time. A ghostly rustle of static came from the radio of the closest vehicle. There was no trace of any soldiers, but they could see where the last man had been and what he'd been doing. His rifle was leaning against the inside of the open door and his water bottle was balanced on the narrow dashboard. He'd been talking on the radio and writing something down when the trouble began, probably very suddenly. His clipboard lay nearby on the ground. Edward picked it up and began studying it. There were no signs of the physical struggle everyone knew must have taken place.

The jeeps were parked outside the opening to the tower. Where once there had been a great, towering wall, there was now only a confusion of bent structural bars and shreds of fire-blackened sheeting. The first several stories of the tower were exposed to view where the wall had torn away. They were ruined completely, blasted to pieces by explosions and the crash. The rear cargo areas of the jeeps were loaded with recovered artifacts, most of them tagged and labeled. Mostly, they were pieces of shattered machinery, and all were composed of organic matter.

"You still think we're going to find that silver case?" Reg asked Fadeela.

"Or die trying," she said, lifting her gaze and flashlight up to explore the massive, shredded wall of the tower. "If it's here, that's where we'll find it."

Edward found something that helped confirm her suspicions.

"This is not good news." He came toward them, reading from the clipboard. "The men in these jeeps were climbing the tower and searching for survivors. Then, on the level thirteen, something happened."

Reg and Fadeela spoke at the same time. "What does it say?"

Edward shook his head. "That something grabbed them. Then it says control room."

Reg arched an eyebrow. "Control room? On the thirteenth floor?"

Edward took the report off the clipboard and stuffed it in his pocket. "That's what it says."

"Well, what are we waiting for? Let's go have a look around." Reg had already estimated that the height of each of the exposed floors was sixty feet. Getting to the thirteenth floor would be the equivalent of climbing a fifty-story building.

"Check this out," Tye called softly. He'd found a platter-sized object in one of the jeeps. "It's the granddaddy of all medallions." It was the color of liquid amber and had the same hair-thin veins running through it as the disks he'd been carrying with him. "Watch. It lights up when you touch it." Tye rested his palm on it and a fuzzy, fast-moving image formed on the surface. The image was too indistinct to recognize, but it seemed to be shifting and changing at a chaotic speed.

Reg leaned in for a better look. "What's it doing?"

"Beats me," Tye said, "but it looks like a broadcast, doesn't it?"

"Check your medallions. See if we're still alone in here."

When Tye pulled them out of his pocket, he got two surprises. First, the complex, shifting pattern of diamonds was gone and in its place was a flower design that covered the entire face of the disk. It was the same rigidly symmetrical "daisy" pattern found on the bottom of the city destroyer. Second, he could feel the small medallion drawn to the larger slab like a magnet. It gave him an idea. "These two pieces are attracting one another," he told Reg. "That must be the basis of their tracking system."

"That's fascinating," Reg said impatiently. "Are there any aliens around?"

"That I can't tell you," Tye admitted. "But if I see any, you'll be the first to know."

Reg whistled through his teeth and waved everyone toward the tower. Seeing that the lower floors had been decimated beyond use, he moved directly to one of the X-shaped structural beams and began to climb. Each girder was as tall as he was, and there were about ten of them between floors. They were made of bone, or something very similar to it, and were encrusted with a brittle moss that flaked apart under their hands. As they climbed the first several stories of the mile-high tower, they saw that the floors were made of the same razor-thin material as the exterior walls. The loose edges fluttered like pieces of tissue paper in the breeze Reg made as he climbed past. Despite its seeming fragility, the material was strong enough to withstand the powerful explosions that had obliterated most of the ship.

They continued to climb up the girders until they were dripping with sweat, and their arms began to tire. Young, lanky, and unencumbered by heavy weaponry, Tye scaled the support beams more easily than the others. Still, he was the first to suggest looking for a different way up. "This is taking too long," he called down to the others. "There must be a better way to the top."

"Keep moving," Ali grunted from below, and the team continued to climb, painfully, floor by floor, up the stack of X-shaped girders. Eventually, they reached a place where the damage was less severe. A ceiling of the ultrathin material prevented them from climbing higher. They left the girders and moved deeper into the tower.

With Reg in the lead, they moved at a fast march through the piles of twisted debris. The enormous room had been turned into an empty box by the force of the explosions. They walked uphill through the leaning skyscraper, then broke into a jog until the front wall of the tower came into view. The destruction was less complete here, and it was possible to imagine what the interior must have looked like before the crash.

Sections of transparent wall still stood in places, or hung from the ceiling like ragged sheets of ice. They had once divided the floor into smaller rooms, workstations of some kind. When Ali rapped on one of the walls with his knuckles, the vibrations caused it to make a humming noise.

"Look at this," Tye called from the far side of the glassy barrier. He'd found a room that was only slightly damaged. It was the size of a small auditorium, and there were low black benches arranged in rows. Hanging on the forward wall was a flat, squared-off sheet of material that looked like a modified tortoiseshell. "Looks like a really uncomfortable movie theater," he mused, sitting down on one of the benches. The seat of his pants was still wet with the thick gel that lined the floor of the chariot. It made a rude noise as he sat down. "Aaagh!" Tye jumped up immediately when the bench moved beneath him. "What in the—"

He reached down and touched it again, with his hand this time. The surface of the bench was as hard and as smooth as polished marble. But when activated by the galvanic charge coursing through his fingertips, it bubbled to life, its surface rising into a series of inch-tall welts. Struggling against the impulse to tear his hand away, Tye held it in place and watched in horrified fascination as the transformation of the stonelike material continued. Tiny lines of light appeared in the surface, first as a dull glow, but then brightening to form a complex grid. Within moments, the entire length of the bench lit up with a visual display, showing an unintelligible, highly complicated blueprint: half anatomical drawing and half engineering schematic. They realized it wasn't a bench but a table designed to be used by a creature half his size.

Reg had forged ahead to the front wall of the tower. When the others followed him, they saw bands of blotchy light leaking through a network of narrow "windows." A series of thin geometric lines ran the entire height and length of the huge wall, each one emitting an uneven greenish glow. Reg stared up at the strange green lines, trying to understand the significance of the pattern they made. When he brought his face close to one of them, he saw that the large plates covering the outside of the tower were connected to one another by some sort of dense, stringy ligament.

In some places, all that stood between Reg and the outside world was the same ultrathin material that was used in the construction of the rest of the tower. This time it was more than semitransparent. Reg could see through it to the desert outside, which was brightly lit in a sickly, green-tinted glare.

"What is it?" Fadeela asked.

"They're windows," Reg said. "They seem to be amplifying the light outside. Take a look." The others pressed close to the spy holes and stared through them.

"Fantastic!" Tye said.

"It's like looking through night-vision goggles," Edward said. "And a magnifying glass."

The scene was almost too bright for their eyes. The rocky hills and wadis of the desert floor were illuminated in a harsh glare, as if enclosed in a giant copying machine. At the same time that it amplified the light, the material acted as a telescope. When Edward spotted a shape moving across a dune top far in the distance, the image quickly focused and enlarged until he could see that it was a lone alien soldier out on patrol in a chariot. The magnification continued until he could make out the individual tentacles on the armored creature's shoulder blades and the glowing three-inch medallion on the back of his bony hand. He stepped back, blinked his eyes, and his vision returned to normal.

"Very strange," he said. "Someday I'm going to build a house with windows like this."

"I can see Sutton and Remi," Yossi said, pressing his forehead against the surface and looking straight down. "They look nervous."

"Now we understand why we are losing so many planes when we try to attack them here," Ali said, pondering the windows. "They can see us coming from a great distance."

"Which means," said Edward, pointing out the obvious, "that if there are any survivors in this tower, they probably watched us drive up."

"Doesn't matter now," Reg said, checking his watch under the beam of his flashlight. "We're not climbing fast enough. We've been inside almost an hour and we're just past halfway up. We've got to find a faster route."

"Yeah, but where?" They scanned the ruined monumental space with their flashlights but saw nothing that looked remotely like a staircase. In the distance, near the center of the tower, rubble was piled high around a set of columns that reached to the ceiling. They headed in that direction.

Along the way, they passed an overturned set of the black worktables. When they came close to them, Yossi stopped short, froze in his tracks, and swung his machine gun into position. Holding his flashlight steady, he stared straight ahead with all the concentration of a bird dog, while the others fanned out to surround the spot. When he gave the signal, they began closing in from all sides, aware that if it was an alien they'd cornered, a telepathic attack was imminent.

Everyone held their breath and stepped closer, their weapons trained where Yossi was pointing. There was a rustling sound and then a flash of movement as a small gray body leapt from its hiding place and darted in one direction, then another, looking for a way past the humans.

Ali and Yossi both shot at the thing, but missed. Their bullets ricocheted into the distance. With surprising speed and agility, the creature bolted forward and would have gotten away if Reg hadn't pounced and knocked it to the floor. He grabbed it around the neck and felt his fingers sink into the spongy flesh.

When the shock wave of pain tore through his body, Reg was ready. He lifted the creature off the ground and slammed it against one of the touch-activated tabletops.

The pain's not real, he told himself. *You can resist it.*

Once more, Reg lifted the homuncular body with his half-paralyzed arm and brought it crashing down against the stone-solid surface of the table, sending a telepathic message of his own: *Obey or die.* But the alien continued to resist. Reg continued to pound it against the tabletop until its body went as limp as a rag doll and it fell into a stunned submission. Then he leaned over it and saw himself reflected in the surface of the alien's silvery eyes. Reg had been waiting for a moment like this: He tried to read the alien's mind. He conjured up the image of the silver box from his memory and attempted to "send" the image to the alien.

"Where is it?" he demanded loudly. "Where's the box?"

When he received no answer, Reg fed the creature another mouthful of tabletop.

"It's dead," Edward told him.

"No," Reg said. He could feel the thing's consciousness. It was monitoring him, playing possum. But he didn't know how to access its thoughts. Telepathy was, after all, an alien skill, not a human one.

"What should we do with it?" Fadeela asked.

"Kill it," Reg said, searching the bulging silvery eyes for signs of fear. The only thing he felt in return was a hateful defiance. Ali stepped up to the table, lifted the butt end of his heavy, five-foot-long gun, and held it over the alien's enlarged brainpan.

"Should I?"

Last chance, Reg warned the creature. Its eyes closed calmly a moment before Ali slammed his weapon down and split open its skull. Reg felt the life slip out of the little body in his grip. He backed away, wiping his hands clean on his uniform and breathing hard.

"I really hate those little bastards," he said.

The team regrouped and continued the search, marching quickly through the monumental darkness. They had only gone a short distance when they saw the flash of an alien pulse weapon and heard a startled scream that sounded like Tye. The others hit the deck and prepared to fire in the direction of the noise, assuming the bioarmored aliens had finally shown up to defend the tower.

"Sorry!" Tye called through the darkness. "That was only us." He and Yossi had gone ahead of the others and found something that had startled them.

"Come this way," Yossi called, signaling with his flashlight. "We found something." The others raced forward and saw the two men investigating a deep recess in the wall.

"What is it? What did you find?"

Tye was down on his knees leaning into an opening, shining his light straight down. "It's a shaft of some kind."

"Ugh! What are those things on the walls?" Fadeela asked, disgusted by what she saw. The inside of the shaft was lined with sickly-looking white strands.

"I don't know, but I just lost my appetite," Ali said. The vertical tube seemed to travel the entire height of the tower, and its walls were overgrown with slender white tendrils that hung limply in tangled masses. Reg thought the tendrils looked like relatives of the vines he'd seen growing in other parts of the ship.

"There's that horrible smell again," Edward said, backing away. "Ammonia."

Tye turned to face the group. "That smell could be a good thing. Think about it. The pulse gun, the chariot, their bioarmor."

Reg understood instantly. "Of course. This is another one of their machines. But what?"

"I think it's a lift," Tye said. "It's got to be." He cautiously leaned over the edge and peered once more into the bottomless pit. "All of their technology is basically ripped off from other species or cultures. They must be zipping around the universe, conquering one planet after another and adapting the technologies and life-forms they find to serve their own purposes. You know what I think this shaft must have been?"

The others didn't have a clue.

"A giant esophagus," he announced with a dramatic expression. "The aliens probably found some poor brontosaurus-sized slob, cut his throat out, put it in one of those liquid growing vats of theirs and—voilà!—instant elevator. These stringy white things hanging down the sides are cilia, just like you find in the human windpipe. I'll wager ten quid that if we touch them, they'll do something." He glanced around at the others. "Any takers?"

"Maybe they have stairs," Yossi offered.

When no one volunteered, Tye took matters into his own hands, literally. He reached out and grabbed one of the gooey white strands. Instantly, the entire shaft erupted to life. Tens of thousands of white tendrils began to whip around the interior of the shaft in a writhing frenzy. Pleased with himself, Tye smiled an I-told-you-so smile, not noticing that the strands were crawling up his arm. By the time he realized what was happening, the stringy tendrils had wound themselves around his shoulder and pulled him inside.

The group had just enough time to recoil in horror and level their guns at the man-eating tendrils before Tye came flying out and landed, ass over teakettle, in a heap ten feet away. The tentacles all dropped limp, and the shaft went quiet again.

"Michael, are you all right?" Fadeela asked.

Tye sat up and spit out an oily piece of tendril. "It wasn't exactly a Riviera holiday, but yeah, I'm okay." He was covered head to foot in a fine layer of the foul-smelling slime.

"There goes your elevator theory," Yossi smirked.

"Not at all," he said, getting to his feet. "I got a little nervous is all. Once I was inside, the only thing I was thinking about was *getting out*, not *going up*. It did what I asked. Maybe I'll have one more go. I don't think it's dangerous." Before the others could dissuade him, he marched back and jumped inside. The long strands flared to life again, whipping back and forth like overcaffeinated sea snakes, and caught him. He screamed suddenly and was carried off. A moment later, the movement stopped suddenly, and the tendrils all fell dormant.

Carefully, Reg leaned a few inches into the shaft and looked up, then down. "Tye! Can you hear me?" He backed away from the opening when he heard something coming toward him from above. Tye's helmet flew past, falling to the bottom. "Tye!" Reg shouted again, then, straining to hear a response. He was about to give up when the millions of thin white strands whipped into a frenzy of movement once more. Reg leapt back from the opening and, a second later, Tye came flying out of the shaft and landed once more in a heap.

"Gotta work on the landing, but I think I'm getting the hang of it," he said.

"We thought this thing ate you for breakfast," Reg said. "Where'd you go?"

"Up. How far up, I'm not exactly sure." He looked at Yossi through the darkness. "I told you it was a lift," he said. "And guess what it turns out to be?"

"A lift?"

"Precisely. This time, when I went inside, I thought about moving upward. Just like with the chariot. Next thing I knew, *whoosh*, I was going up."

"See any shiny metallic cases up there?" Reg asked, glancing at his watch.

"I didn't stay long enough to look around," Tye answered.

"Wait a second," Edward said. "The report on that clipboard, it said something grabbed them, remember? Then it said control room. The case is up there, it has to be."

"That's what I've been saying all along," Fadeela pointed out. "Let's ride this thing to the top."

Tye lectured the group. "Don't be distracted once you get inside. Think about traveling up, concentrate on getting to the top." He reached his arm inside and brought the stringy white cilia to life once more. They wrapped themselves around his lanky frame and dragged him inside. "Can you see me in here?" Tye called through the storm of movement.

He was fully engulfed, but the others caught occasional glimpses of him—a kneecap here, an elbow there. They watched Tye think himself up a few feet then back down again until he was hovering in front of them again. Without leaving the shaft, he called through the rustling cilia, "Everybody clear on the concept?" Then, without waiting for an answer, "Good. See you at the top."

Yossi was the first to follow. He took a deep breath and stepped bravely to the threshold of the shaft, but lost his resolve and hesitated, staring into the grasping tendrils, overwhelmed by the strangeness of what he was about to do.

"This is *not* why I joined the Air Force," he moaned, closing his eyes tight and leaning forward until he felt the moist strands begin to lash softly across his face and chest. The next thing he knew, they had wrapped themselves around him and dragged him inside. It was an odd, terrifying sensation. He suddenly found himself floating in a zero-gravity environment. The moist white strands came at him from every angle and buoyed him up, each one lifting a tiny fraction of his weight. When he opened his mouth to yell, the strands darted into his mouth. He batted at them with his arms and kicked with his legs, but felt no resistance. It was like fighting against the air. Individually, the tendrils had very little strength, but they were wickedly quick and adjusted to changes in his position as fast as he could make them. It took a second or two for Yossi to realize that although he was floating inside the shaft, he wasn't moving. *I need to move up*, he remembered. The mere thought wasn't enough, it had to be a positive act of will. *Up, up, I want to move up!* Sensing his desire through the conductive medium of the gelatin, the tendrils obeyed. Yossi shot upward, tumbling end over end. Once he stopped struggling, the ride was surprisingly comfortable. Then it came to an abrupt end. He was spit out of the shaft and crashed to the floor. When he looked up, Tye was looking down at him.

"Weird, isn't it? Come on, get out of the way before the next person comes through." Still slightly disoriented from the experience, Yossi allowed Tye to drag him to one side a moment before Edward came crashing out of the esophageal bioelevator. One by one, the others followed until the group had reassembled on the new, higher stage of the tower.

"That was disgusting." Fadeela winced, wiping the film of clear gelatin off her face. "Are we at the top?"

"Doesn't look like it," Reg said with a sinking feeling. He moved a few strides into the cavernous space. It was a virtual replica of the floors below, full of the same shattered walls and pieces of broken equipment. In the distance, the false daylight filtered through the gaps between the exterior plates. "It looks like there's at least one more floor above."

Through the semitransparent ceiling, they could see what appeared to be an open chamber above. It looked completely empty. The team marched toward the front of the tower, keeping their eyes open for a way up to the next story.

"I just realized something" Reg announced. "This floor above us, it has to be the exit bay for their attacker planes."

"Yeah, I think you're right," Tye said, nodding. He was the only one who had been with Reg during the first attack over Jerusalem, when hundreds of the disk-shaped attackers had come swarming out of an opening about three-quarters of the way up the face of the tower. "This is the tunnel they flew out of. It's as wide as the tower itself."

Ali cursed in Arabic, then said, "There's got to be a way around it."

"Maybe along the sides," Fadeela suggested, and started to walk in that direction.

"Sounds logical," Ali grudgingly agreed, and began to follow.

Just then the walls began to quake violently, followed by a booming explosion. The floor shifted sideways beneath their feet, powerfully enough to knock all of them to the ground. With a shudder, the tower leaned another degree off center. The entire structure teetered back and forth as the support beams on the lower levels decided whether to give way and collapse. When it seemed as if they would hold for a while longer, Fadeela was the first to break the silence. "And what exactly was that?"

"I think your fiancé's planes have decided to show up after all."

"Just when we need them least," Edward observed. "They're going to knock the tower over before we can get outside."

"It's getting close to sunup," Reg announced. "We've got to find these bioweapons."

"No, seriously," Edward said, "they're going to knock the tower over. Isn't it time to get out of here?"

"Plenty of time left." Reg smiled. His expression changed suddenly as an idea occurred to him. He broke into a jog, searching the ceiling with his flashlight.

"What is it?"

"This way." The others followed, weaving through the obstacle course of ruined workstations and collapsed walls. A hundred yards before they reached the sidewall of the tower, Reg stopped and pointed his flashlight up at the ceiling. "There it is."

Lying massively on the floor above was the titanic taproot they'd seen as they entered the ship. It looked like an oil pipeline stretching away toward the front of the ship. If it were still growing and burrowing into the earth, there were no signs of it. The thing lay motionless.

Ali stared up at the giant organic tube, stunned by a horrible epiphany. "They're not going to put the biological weapons into the air. They're going to put them into the ground."

Tye was confused. "Uh, wouldn't that be a good thing? To bury the poisons?"

"Into the water, the groundwater," Ali explained. "This is the desert, but there is water. An underground river, one of the largest in the world. It supplies the cities in the north with their water." He shook his head thinking how many people would be infected if the water supply were contaminated, and how quickly the carriers would infect others.

"Look up there," Yossi said, pointing his flashlight at the ceiling. Dimly visible through the ceiling were the bottoms of alien feet. Three sets of them came padding alongside the taproot until they were directly overhead. Yossi followed them with his flashlight.

"Turn that thing off, you jackass," Edward hissed. "You're showing them where we are."

But the aliens already knew where the humans were. They lingered for a moment, looking down through the semitransparent material before heading off in a new direction. Fadeela raised her flamethrower to take a shot, but Reg stopped her.

"Let's follow them."

He bolted into the darkness, blazing a trail over and around the piles of debris lying in his path. He used the flashlight attached to his machine gun to keep track of the alien feet, unconcerned that he was giving away his own position. He chased them a couple of hundred yards until they disappeared. The others followed as best they could. By the time they caught up to him, Reg was climbing a sort of trellis composed of thick diagonal bars. He was already halfway to the top and didn't look back to see if the others were following.

Out of breath by the time he climbed to the top, he found himself in the long, low corridor of the attacker exit bay. He took a few strides into the empty space and strained to hear the sound of the retreating aliens over the pounding of his own heart. But the only noise came from the rest of the team struggling up the trellis. As they stepped away from the trellis, he switched on his flashlight briefly and scanned the new room. In the distance, there was the ten foot-tall taproot running past a set of columns, but otherwise the space was vacant. It was just tall enough to accommodate one of the sixty-foot-long attacker ships. The floor and ceiling were covered with skid marks where the wobbling airships had brushed against them.

There was no sign of the aliens.

"Did you see which way they went?" Yossi asked. He and Tye had their forearms locked together, ready to fire the alien pulse gun.

"No," Reg answered. "But I've got a feeling they're still nearby."

"Listen," Fadeela said. "Outside. You can hear the bombers." The tunnel was open at one end. The sound of the distant jet engines echoed down the corridor, and there was a slight breeze.

"First things first," Ali said. "We've got to destroy that root before they can use it to poison the water supply." The taproot was more than a hundred yards away.

"You're right," Reg said uneasily. He had the sense that the team was being watched. "Let's head in that direction, but not in a bunch. We're making ourselves an easy target. Edward, you and I will go first. The rest of you follow in pairs."

Reg took off, running in a crouch, but stopped suddenly after only a few steps.

"What is it?" Edward asked.

ZAP! A fist-sized ball of light sliced through the darkness. As Edward twisted and ducked out of the way, he raised his free hand instinctively to shield himself. The green pulse streaked past his hand, removing four of his fingers and leaving a burn mark across his forehead as it went. He screamed in pain and hit the floor as a second blast sailed over his head.

Reg and Ali opened up with their guns, blasting away in the direction of the attack. Tye and Yossi sent a pulse blast of their own skittering away into the darkness. But it was Fadeela who put the aliens on the defensive. She charged toward the source of the enemy fire, squeezing out a long arc of flame as she ran. The fire lit up the gloomy corridor and exposed their attackers.

There were three aliens—two of them in exoskeletal armor. The warriors were marching inexorably forward with their fingers extended in the firing position until the fire overwhelmed them. They recoiled from the flames and, in their panic, tripped over their biomechanical legs and crashed to the ground.

"Hold your fire," Reg screamed. Fadeela was in the way, charging forward without a thought for her own safety. Before the lumbering giants could regain their feet and escape, she sprayed them with a heavy dose of thick liquid fire. By the time their thorax shells popped open and the creatures within wriggled into the open, Reg and Ali had come forward and were in position to finish them off.

"There's one more," Ali shouted as he ran past the smoldering bodies, "this way." They chased the fleeing alien into the shadows of the exit bay, moving toward the open front of the tower and leaving the light of the flames behind them.

"More fire," Reg yelled when it seemed the alien would escape.

Fadeela raised her flamethrower and was about to send out another plume of fire when she realized there was no need. She knew exactly where the alien was standing. It was to her right, not far away, cowering against the tower's sidewall. Without a word being exchanged, all of the humans turned in the same direction and slowly raised their weapons toward the spot. They knew what they were going to see: a tall, unarmed alien with opalescent white skin. And when they aimed their flashlights in that direction, that is exactly what they saw. The alien moved very slowly away from the wall, its huge eyes squinting into the glare of the flashlights, and raised its hands above its head.

It told them it wanted to surrender.

15

A Very Close Encounter

Another bomb rocked into the downed spacecraft. The tower absorbed the shock wave without tilting any farther off center, but as it swayed and shook beneath their feet, Reg and the others were reminded that time was running short. Dawn was quickly approaching and the Saudi jets outside were threatening to fell the tower like a tall tree.

The alien stood perfectly still, its goose-egg eyes reflecting the beams of the flashlights. The only movements it made occurred inside its body. Beneath the translucent membrane of its skin, knots of tissue clutched and released in peristaltic motion. This creature was not like the others the team had encountered. It stood a full head taller, and its skin glistened a nacreous white. Its emaciated limbs looked long and graceful in comparison to its smaller, grayer brethren, but, like them, its face was nothing more than a blunt spot on the front of its neck. Its large brain hung off the back of the skull like a meaty, pie-sized tumor.

The frail captive had ample reason not to move. It had a large-caliber field gun, two flamethrowers, two fully automatic machine guns, a pistol, and an alien pulse weapon pointed its way. The humans who held these weapons were waiting for the creature to make the slightest of false moves, anything that would give them the excuse they wanted to blow it to bits. They were nervous, frightened, and thirsty for revenge, but something told them it would be a mistake to squeeze their triggers. The alien lifted its white, two-fingered hands in the air as a sign of its surrender and "spoke" to Reg.

In a single, sustained, telepathic thought, it communicated several ideas at once. It told Reg: that there were no more bio-armored soldiers nearby; that it was personally incapable of violence; that it would cooperate fully if the humans gave it a chance; and that killing a potentially useful prisoner would be a grave tactical error.

It took a long, confusing moment for Reg to sort out the multilayered mental message the alien was sending. It came to him as a *feeling* rather than in the symbolic language he was accustomed to using. The communication was both a physical sensation that tingled through his nervous system and a recognizable emotion. There were no words, no need for interpretation, no possibility of misunderstanding. But the ideas were piled on top of one another, strung together in a way that took some getting used to. Once he began to understand the telepathy, the ideas resonated with a strange familiarity through some long-unused section of his brain. And there was a rationality to the communication that caught Reg off guard. All the aliens he'd faced previously had sprung at him mentally with the same ferocious energy they used in their physical attacks. This "Tall One," on the other hand, was serene, intelligent and—more importantly—afraid to die.

Without lifting his eyes away from his prisoner, Reg began to explain to the others what the alien had told him. There was no need. The rest of the team could also *hear* the alien thinking.

"It's reading our minds," Ali said nervously. "We should kill it."

"No. *We* are reading *its* mind," Tye said. "Aren't we?"

"Don't kill it!" Edward demanded. "There's no need. It's not going to hurt us, and we need its help."

"Not going to hurt us?" Yossi asked. "What about your hand?"

Edward had his mangled left hand tucked under his right arm to staunch the bleeding, but kept his flamethrower in the ready position. He and the alien answered Yossi's question simultaneously, one silently, the other aloud. "It's the others ones who shot me," Edward insisted, "the ones in the suits of armor. This one is different. Can't you feel what it's telling us?"

"I think he's right," Tye said. "Maybe it knows where the biological weapons are."

Reg tightened his grip on his .357 Magnum, walked forward until he was standing within an arm's length of the five-foot-tall ghostlike figure, and pointed the gun at its forehead. The alien didn't flinch, but everyone sensed its panic level rising. As calmly as he could manage, Reg spoke to it. "I'm going to put a big, messy hole through your ugly face unless you help us. Understand?"

It understood.

"We're looking for a silver case. It's full of little glass test tubes, and we want you to . . ." Reg didn't need to finish putting the idea into words. The alien was already answering. It pointed one of its hands, a set of banana-sized pincers, toward the horizon of the ceiling, then "spoke" once more. In one mental stroke, it told them, in no particular order: that the silver case would be found on the floor immediately above; that it would gladly lead them to the spot; and that the biological poisons were still safely inside their sealed tubes. There was no question about what the alien wanted. It was trying to exchange cooperation for survival.

"I don't like it," Ali grumbled after *listening* to the alien. He turned and swept the darkened exit bay with his flashlight. "I've got a bad feeling. He wants to trap us. Why are the weapons upstairs? Why aren't they over there?" He pointed the flashlight in the direction of the distant taproot. "It doesn't make sense."

"Why don't we ask him," Fadeela said. She walked angrily to where Reg was standing, gave the alien a sharp thump on the chest with the warm tip of her flamethrower, and spoke to it in heated Arabic. She wanted to know what the taproot was for.

The Tall One was remarkably forthcoming in its reply. Without words or images, it answered Fadeela's question in surprising detail: The massive root, nearly two miles long from end to end, customarily served as a food source for the aliens and had been grown from a tiny seed; the one growing down the side of the tower had been altered to grow in such a way that it would serve as a powerful pump; the tip of the plant had already penetrated to the level of the groundwater; the test tubes were to have been snugged into a specially designed insertion, a cartridge chamber, and then forced downward under explosive pressure; the first anthrax deaths in the northern population centers would have occurred within seventy-two hours. The alien understood, and began to explain, the geometric progression of infection among the human population. The lethal efficiency of the plan seemed to please the creature.

"That's enough!" Fadeela shouted. She felt like punching the balloon-headed creature right between its bulging chrome-colored eyes. Before she could, Reg made a decision.

"This is our best bet," he announced. "We'll follow our little friend upstairs. If he leads us to the silver case, we'll let him live. If not, he's vapor, and we'll come down here and destroy that big root." He started the alien marching with a shove.

He knew Ali was probably right. Chances were good that it was leading them into an ambush. There was no way to know for sure. Even though the individual they'd captured seemed to be cooperating, Reg knew the aliens worked together as seamlessly as bees from the same hive and that they had descended on Earth intent on exterminating humanity. They were colonizers, and cold-blooded killers. It made sense that there would be a trap waiting for them on the floor above, and that's exactly what Reg was hoping for. If the silver case was the bait, there was always a chance of getting away with it before the trap was sprung.

As they walked, Yossi tore off his shirt and used it to make bandages and a tourniquet for Edward's wound. "Listen, I know you don't like to take advice from Jews," he told Edward, "but next time, don't try to *catch* the bullet. *Try getting out of the way.*"

Tye took off his belt, looped it, and slipped it over the alien's head to create a choker leash, which he promptly handed to Reg. The alien's head bobbed heavily atop its thin neck as it shuffled across the floor. Its movements were stiff and wobbly at the same time, somewhat like an old man's.

Very quickly, they came to a trellis of diagonal bars like the one they'd found earlier. Reg kept the alien tightly tethered with the belt leash as they began to climb. Ali and Yossi helped Edward up the bars. Fadeela shot ahead and reached the new level first. By the time the others caught up to her, she had already wandered beyond the short entrance hall and out into the open, exposing herself to the danger of being picked off by a sniper's pulse blast.

She was standing in a room that was as wide as a prairie and of incredible height. It had once been full of tall crystalline spires, towers within towers, most of which were now reduced to a jagged rubble. The architecture was stark and utilitarian. In many places, the spires were still connected to one another by horizontal footbridges. There were plenty of places left to hide; enough to hold a small army. But it would only take a sniper or two to finish the team off. They stopped at the end of the low hallway and crouched at the threshold.

"Woman," Ali hissed at her quietly, "come back here before you get all of us killed."

"Quiet, dog breath," Fadeela answered at normal volume. She was staring straight up, lost in contemplation of the vast ceiling, which was composed of thousands of diamond-shaped panes of the light-amplifying, telescoping glass. Light from the outside world poured in through the panes as if it were midday, but only through a few at a time. Circular clusters of them lit up to create a moving pattern across the ceiling, like a half dozen spotlights sliding across the skies over a destroyed city. Reg leaned out of the hallway far enough to follow Fadeela's gaze. He looked up at the hazy blob of light she seemed to be following as it traveled, a few panes at a time, across the ceiling. The moment he focused his eyes on it, it began to change. Suddenly, the windows showed him a fighter jet streaking silently through the predawn sky at a high altitude. A moment later, the image magnified and refocused until he could see that it was an American-built F-15. The image magnified again, and he could read the serial numbers stenciled onto the undersides of the plane's wings. He blinked and looked away, slightly disoriented.

Tye stared out into the open space ahead with a combination of awe and dread. "What drives such small creatures," he asked, "to build on such a gigantic scale?" As if the proportions of the room were too grand to contemplate, he turned his attention to something small. The floor was covered with pieces of debris, some of which looked like tools or machine pieces. Tye stretched one of his long arms through the doorway and picked one of them up. It looked like an ordinary ball bearing, but stung his fingertips when he squeezed it. An inspection under his flashlight showed him that it was covered with bristles, a stiff metallic fuzz. He put it in his pocket and was about to back away from the opening when the alien *spoke* again.

This time, no one could feel the thoughts except Tye. It "suggested" that he pick up one more, and it forcibly steered his attention to something that looked like a half-melted black pen. The alien told him it was a medical tool that could be used to treat Edward's wounds. When Tye retrieved it, the alien communicated to the rest of the group what the wand could do: stem Edward's bleeding; repair the shattered bone; clear and cauterize the wound; and accelerate the regrowth of the skin.

"It could be a weapon," Tye pointed out, looking down at the lightweight object. One end of it flattened out into a dull blade.

"Give it to him. Let him try," Edward said urgently. The bandages Yossi had made for him were already saturated and dripping with blood. If the bleeding didn't stop soon, he wouldn't be able to keep pace with the others.

After a nod from Reg, Tye held the instrument out and let the alien's thick awkward fingers take it from him. The creature fumbled with the tool for only a moment, then tossed it aside before Edward could finish unbandaging his mutilated hand. By the time he did, the bleeding had already stopped. A moment later, he realized the pain was gone, too.

"That's a good start," he said. "But can you grow my fingers back?" The alien no longer seemed interested. It turned away and began walking toward the open room. It stopped when it came to the end of the leash and felt the belt tug at his throat. After a moment of hesitation, Reg followed the alien out of the hallway.

The dimly lit space around them was quadruple the size of the largest domed sports arena on Earth and was filled with softly pulsating light. In addition to the spotlights of false daylight coming from the ceiling, there was a strobing, flashing light coming off the floor. As they walked farther into the room, they discovered the source of this strange light.

Huge slabs of the same amber-colored substance had been set into the sloping, bowl-shaped floor in the shape of a flower. Each petal was the size of a soccer field and was glowing a warm orange color through the darkness. A few strides brought them to the end of the nearest petal. It was cracked and broken. In places, large chunks were missing after being damaged during the ship's crash. There was evidence that something or someone had been collecting the missing sections and setting them back into place like the pieces of a mammoth jigsaw puzzle. As with the plate of the same material Tye had found in the back of the jeeps, the glassy "petals" were emitting a shifting pattern of light. Blurred, fast-moving images streaked across the surface, but were unintelligible to the humans. A long walk from where they were standing, down at the eye of the flower, there was an amber lump that stood on a pedestal several inches above the floor.

"Okay, we're here," Reg told the alien. "Where's the box?"

Still eager to help, the creature communicated another cluster of associated ideas. The box, it told them, lay open on top of a worktable in one of the laboratory rooms at the far side of the tower; it gave them the exact location and showed them the best path to take. The instructions were so clear that any one of the humans could have drawn a map. The alien began to shuffle its feet, prepared to lead them to the spot.

"We don't need that thing anymore," Ali said, gesturing toward their alien guide with his weapon. He was more convinced than ever that they were being led into a trap. Telepathic assurances aside, the crumbling spires that rose on both sides of the path they would take offered the perfect hiding places for snipers. "We know where we're headed. We can go by ourselves. Edward and Yossi, you come with me. The rest of you wait here for us. We'll be back soon. I hope."

The three men jogged off without any further discussion and quickly began to fade from view behind the screen of eerily pulsating light. Reg pulled the Tall One back toward the shelter of the entrance hall and maintained a watchful attitude, while Tye and Fadeela moved deeper into the room and explored the erratically flashing light of the flower.

"It's the mother of all medallions," Tye said, "the heart of their tracking system." He pulled one of the small medallions out of his pocket and felt it drawn toward the floor, like iron to a magnet. When the small disk touched his skin and activated, the pattern it showed was a representation of the huge flower-shape that lay stretched out below him. "Hmmm. I wonder what happened to all those little diamond shapes."

"I think I know," Fadeela told him, pointing toward the amber blob at the center of the flower. "There they are."

Cautiously, the two of them walked down toward the spot where the petals came together and examined the glowing lump set on the pedestal. It seemed to be made of the same material as the broken amber slabs around them, but it was definitely alive. It was a foot-tall mass of semiliquid biomatter contained within thin membrane walls. Its body produced a phosphorescent light from within, except on one side, where the skin was black.

"Looks like an octopus," Fadeela said, her lip curling in disgust.

"Looks like a big brain to me."

"A brain with legs?"

A series of thin arms grew from the bottom of the transparent blob and reached out to connect with each of the eight gigantic petals. Where they attached to the blob, these arms looked as moist and frail as a snail's body, but solidified as they fused with the surface of the amber material. Beads of an oily liquid ran down the organism's sides like sap leaking from a tree.

"There are your diamonds," Fadeela said, pointing toward the black spot on the blob's flank.

Tye squatted for a closer look and realized she was right. Except for a very few strays, all of the tiny diamonds had clustered in one spot on the side of the bloblike body. He thought it over for a minute before asking a question. "At-Ta'if is to the north, isn't it?"

"The northwest. Why?"

Tye glanced around the interior of the tower to get his bearings. "So northwest is that direction," he said, pointing. Fadeela understood what he was getting at. The dark diamonds had all clustered on the northwest wall of the gelatinous body.

"So, this octopus is keeping track of where all the aliens are. And Edward was right about the radio reports. They're attacking At-Ta'if." They noticed that the petal extending in the direction of the battle was flashing and pulsing much more rapidly than the others.

"That must be how it works," Tye said. "Now, if each of these petals functions like a giant medallion, they won't work unless they're being touched by some living thing. We could royally screw the alien army by killing this brain-thing. Their whole tracking and guidance system would shut down." Tye pulled a knife from the leg pocket of his uniform and was about to plunge it into the soft body when the alien "spoke" urgently from the distance, offering some insights into the flower-shaped apparatus.

This time, the interconnected telepathic ideas were embedded in a background sensation of painful loss. Although it was not a human emotion, both Tye and Fadeela winced with sadness the moment they felt it. It was a deep feeling of separation and the aching wish to be reunited. They quickly realized that these feelings were coming from the lump of biomatter that sat sweating on the pedestal. Somehow, the alien was making it possible for them to feel what the simple organism was feeling: an intense chronic sadness, the same traumatic sense of loss a mother feels for her stolen children.

The emotion suddenly vanished and the Tall One *explained* to them: that every piece of the amber material, down to the tiniest sliver, *knew* where all the other pieces were; that the magnetic attraction between the fragments was a result of a desire to be rejoined; and that the amber-oozing creature at the center of the device was, in many respects, like a human—filthy with excrement, semi-intelligent, and wallowing in base emotions.

When the explanation was over, Tye backed away from the blob remorsefully. "I can't do it," he said, reaching into his pocket and pulling out his last two medallions. "Go on, be free," he said to the disks, as he tossed them toward their parent. "Go keep Big Mama company."

"Michael, you were right!" Fadeela said. "We have to kill this thing. Their whole navigation system will crash."

Tye knew she was right, but hesitated and stared down at his shoes. The Tall One had left him with a deep sympathy for the tortured creature, which the aliens had been holding as a prisoner for who-knew-how-long. He turned the knife over and over in his hand, trying to gather the strength to murder the poor animal, when he noticed something moving between his feet. Something was on the story below, on the floor of the exit bay.

He dropped to his knees, pressed his face close to the semi-transparent flooring material, and cupped his hands around his eyes to block out the strobing light. He saw what looked like a trio of small manta rays swimming through murky water, but quickly realized they were three alien skulls seen from above. They were making their way toward the taproot, and one of them was holding a square silver object in its arms.

"What are you doing, praying?" Fadeela asked. When Tye didn't answer, she turned away to deal with the blob animal herself.

As carefully and quietly as possible, Tye stood up and began to walk back toward the spot where Reg was standing guard over the captive alien. He realized that the Tall One had deceived them. Instead of luring them into a trap, it had led them up here on a wild-goose chase in order to give the others time to complete their plan of poisoning the region's water supply.

"Where are you going now?" Fadeela demanded.

"Back in a minute," he answered as casually as he could manage. He thought he could hide his thoughts from the alien. "Just need to talk to Reg for a moment." To distract himself from what he'd learned, he began to whistle as he walked. But he was too nervous to carry a tune. The closer he came to Reg, the stronger became his desire to turn around and walk the other way. He didn't realize what was happening at first and pushed himself forward. His pace grew slower and slower, as a paralysis fell over his limbs. Then he stopped moving altogether. Only then did he realize that the Tall One, standing beside Reg like a docile house pet, was exerting a form of telepathic control over him. He opened his mouth to shout out a warning, but found he couldn't speak. He tried to turn around, but his feet were rooted to the floor. Trapped inside his uncooperative body, he waited in the darkness for Reg or Fadeela to notice that something was wrong. Then a strange idea infiltrated his consciousness: *The way to solve this problem is to kill myself.* He looked down and realized he was still holding the knife. The blade slowly tilted upward. Tye, knowing what was about to happen, struggled desperately to regain control of his arm, but couldn't. The knife jerked upward and stabbed into his left shoulder, where it lodged deep in the muscle and ligament. As if in a dream, he worked the blade free, then immediately plunged it into the softer tissue of his stomach. Although stupefied by what he was doing to himself, he felt no pain and was unable to make any sound. He pulled the knife free once more and prepared to stab into his heart when a shot rang out.

Tye collapsed to the floor and howled in pain. The next thing he knew, Reg was kneeling beside him, checking his wounds.

"Am I dead?" Tye asked.

"No. But our little helper is. He made you do this, didn't he?"

Tye nodded. "Listen, they're down there, right below us. And they've got the case." He quickly explained what he'd seen through the floor, then lifted his head and looked at his wounds. "I'm not going to die or anything like that, am I?"

"Wait here for the others," Reg said, then turned and sprinted away just as Fadeela ran up to the spot.

"Reg, wait," she called. "Where are you going?"

He didn't answer. He tore into the dark hallway and flew down the trellis ladder. A few seconds later, he was running headlong through the darkness of the exit bay with his machine gun gripped tightly between his hands. He didn't switch on his flashlight for fear of showing the aliens where he was. Instead, he took his best guess about where the taproot was and plunged blindly ahead. To his right, the first violet-blue light of morning showed the outline of the rectangular opening at the front of the tower. In a few minutes, there would be enough light to see where he was headed. But he didn't have a few minutes to spare. He continued moving forward, all of his senses on alert, searching for the aliens Tye had seen. When he heard a noise in the distance, he stopped running and stood stock-still. Above the sound of his labored breathing and furiously pounding heart, he heard it again. It was the sound of the clasps being opened on the silver case. He aimed his machine gun at the sound, then switched on his flashlight.

A pair of bulging silver eyes looked back at him from beside the taproot, only a few strides away. It was another Tall One, awkwardly manipulating the metallic suitcase that Reg had been chasing ever since he first saw it at Al-Sayyid. One of the three clasps was still fastened. He'd arrived just in time.

"Back away, handsome," Reg growled at the alien, trying hard to sound cool, composed, and in control, when the truth was that he was terrified. When the alien didn't obey, Reg gathered himself and started moving forward, ready to blast through the alien's scrawny chest if it made a sudden movement. There were two more Tall Ones standing nearby, but they seemed unconcerned with Reg's presence. They turned their backs to him and resumed the tasks they'd been performing before he'd interrupted them. Although Reg didn't look in their direction, he found that he knew precisely what they were doing: going ahead with the deployment of the biological weapons. They were breaking open the membrane that covered the fourteen slotted cartridges that would accommodate the test tubes.

Just give me the box and I won't hurt any of you, Reg told them without a sound escaping his lips, but he was also thinking, *As soon as I have it I'll kill all three of you.* He edged forward until, face-to-face with the nearest Tall One, he extended a shaking hand and grabbed the handle of the silver case. When at last he had the thing safely in his grasp, a nervous smile crossed his lips. He breathed a huge sigh of relief and wiped the sweat from his eyes with the sleeve of his uniform. Now that he was holding all the cards, he could relax. *Three quick bullets*, he thought, *one for each of these ghouls, and then I can leave.* But before he could finish the job, the machine gun began to feel heavy in his right hand, and he let it rest on his hip. *Three quick shots,* he told himself.

Then again, he thought, there was no real need to kill them. The Tall Ones didn't seem to be violent like the smaller aliens. They were, in fact, a rather admirable species. Reg began more and more to see the situation from their perspective and had soon developed second thoughts about taking the biological weapons away from them. After all, they were only doing what was necessary. Their invasion of the Earth was a matter of their own survival, not some random act of cruelty. Compared to humans, they were kinder, cleaner, better organized, more peaceful, and, ultimately, wiser. They were, in short, the far superior species and deserved to inherit the Earth, even if they planned to stay only a short while.

It was a horrible idea, but it continued to unfold in his mind with an undeniable logic, like the blossoming of a sweet, poisonous flower. He suddenly saw humanity through the eyes of the aliens: a race of filthy and sadistic animals, the equivalent of cockroaches with guns. Suddenly, he regretted having killed the Tall One who had led him upstairs. The gentle creature had only been trying to help, keeping the humans out of the way while the final preparations were made to inject the microbes deep into the earth. Instead of being thankful, Reg had blown its brains out, murdered it execution-style.

The hatred and contempt the Tall Ones felt for him awakened all of his own self-hatred and brought him crashing back to the event that had shattered his life several years before: his ill-fated bombing run during the Gulf War. He remembered walking into that postflight debriefing room feeling like he was the king of the world, then the next moment wanting to curl up and die when they told him what he'd done. The whole gruesome scene replayed itself as if it were happening again for the first time. He remembered standing in front of a television watching rescue workers pull the dead, the maimed, and the burned out of the rubble of the gymnasium his missile had destroyed, and he wanted nothing more than to end his own miserable life.

He set the silver case on the floor and backed away, lost in the miasma of his guilt and self-loathing. Then he swung his machine gun over his shoulder and began to walk toward the opening at the end of the exit bay. Reg knew what he had to do: throw himself into the air and fly down to the desert floor.

As these thoughts dominated his mind and controlled his actions, another part of Reg was kicking and screaming with the desperation of a drowning man. Trapped inside his own mind and disconnected from his body, he struggled to regain control and shake off the effects of the telepathic haze the Tall Ones had cast over him. But thrash and struggle as he might, he continued to march toward the precipice. In his anxiety, his mind flashed back to the question he'd asked himself after surviving that first catastrophic encounter with the alien attackers: *Had he lived to fight again or only saved himself for a more horrible death later on?*

Now he knew. He was doomed as certainly as a man in a canoe speeding toward a waterfall without a paddle. And he told himself he'd been right all along: The people of Earth were too divided among themselves to answer the challenge of the highly disciplined alien forces. They'd come close with their too crazy plan, they'd shot the city destroyers out of the air. But that was cold comfort for a man marching toward his own unwilling suicide. He thought again of what he'd told the pilots gathered around the radio tent in the desert: that the only sane thing was to try something crazy.

In the sky beyond the exit-bay door, Reg heard a familiar

sound: the screaming turbines of a jet as it dropped into a bombing run. He watched the plane rocket toward him out of the distance, hoping it would destroy the tower before the biological
poisons could be released. But long before it came within firing
range, it disintegrated in the green flash of a pulse burst.

"Reg! Reg!" He heard Fadeela's voice over his shoulder. Part
of him wanted to turn around, if only to see her one last time
before he died, but the other part thought she'd try to stop him
from doing what needed to be done. He broke into a jog.

DO SOMETHING! Reg screamed inwardly, but the nightmare
continued to sweep him toward the opening. The southeastern
horizon appeared before him like a pastel landscape painting,
framed by the monumental rectangle of the exit bay. Only a few
seconds before he would have stepped off the edge, he remembered how he'd tricked the alien behind the wall in the oasis, how
he'd used his imagination to make Khalid, like a character in a
dream, begin doing all sorts of improbable things: turning somer-
saults and flipping himself through the trees like a gymnast.

DO SOMETHING! DO SOMETHING CRAZY! Instead of trying to resist his forward momentum, Reg willed himself to run
even faster. To his surprise, it worked. Then he imagined himself
skipping like a carefree schoolboy, and his body responded again.
He pictured himself moving side to side, sliding his feet like an
ice-skater. Soon his body responded, but he was still moving forward. He needed something crazier and needed it fast. So he did
the first thing that came into his head: He danced. He broke into a
very bad imitation of the dancing he knew from old musicals, a
sliding athletic dance like Gene Kelly used to do. Even though his
feet wanted to carry him straight ahead, he steered them into a
sidestep shuffle. He was almost at the edge of the precipice. *Keep
dancing!* he told himself. It took all his energy to maintain his
concentration. He tried everything he could think of: spinning,
leaping, tumbling, stomping his feet. Each of these strange gyra-
tions worked for only a few seconds until the impulse to jump
reasserted itself and carried him another step forward. Desperate
to save himself, Reg started shucking and jiving, jitterbugging

and hoofing, flailing around spastically, doing whatever odd movement came to mind. He kept it up until Fadeela's voice broke the spell.

"Reg! What are you doing?!" she yelled as she came running toward him down the immense corridor.

He backed away from the opening and, horrified at what he had been about to do, turned around to see her emerging from the shadows. "Over here," he yelled to her. "I'm all right now. I almost jumped."

She ran toward him without slowing down. "Come on, we've got to hurry. Let's jump together." She grabbed him by the arm and tried to tug him into the open air. When he resisted, she was angry and confused. "What are you doing?" she demanded. "We've got to jump. They're waiting!"

Reg wrapped his arms around her waist and lifted her off the ground. "Sorry, princess, you're coming with me." She thrashed from side to side and kicked savagely as Reg turned and started back into the exit bay. Less than halfway back to the spot where the aliens were readying the biological poisons, Ali, Edward, and Yossi came jogging up from the opposite direction.

"Help me!" Fadeela shrieked. "He's gone insane. Help!"

The three men stopped running and looked on in bewilderment as Reg explained the situation. "She's trying to jump out of the tower," Reg told them. "The aliens, they're controlling her. Help me hold her."

"Why are you doing this?" Ali asked. "You understand what we have to do." He gestured Yossi and Edward to move in from the sides, while he moved cautiously forward, speaking in a soothing voice as he prepared to spring at Reg. "Let her go, Reg. Put her on the ground."

Reg tightened his grip around Fadeela's waist and whispered into her ear. "Princess, I know you're in there. I know you can hear me. I want you to pretend you're riding a bicycle. Start kicking your legs."

She replied by butting the back of her skull against the bridge of his nose. Just as Yossi and Edward closed in from either side and prepared to grab him, Reg tried one last time. "Kick, Princess." Then he lifted her even higher off the ground and charged at Ali.

"I am not a princess!" she screamed. And her legs began churning in front of her like the blades on a threshing machine. Ali was standing in the way as Fadeela, legs pumping, came flying toward him. Reg threw her on top of the Saudi captain and, as the two of them crashed to the floor, he lowered his head and bulled his way past them, narrowly escaping the grasping hands of the other two men.

Running as fast as he could, Reg raised his machine gun in one hand and his pistol in the other and began blasting. As he came closer to the place where the aliens were working, he felt a numbness spread through his limbs and his pace slow to a trot. As the paralysis continued to spread, Reg gritted his teeth and pushed himself forward. He could feel the Tall Ones watching him from the darkness, trying to force their way back into his mind. Struggling with all his might against the invisible power, he dragged himself as close to the aliens as he could. Then he stopped and went perfectly still. His left hand went slack, and the pistol dropped to the floor. He appeared to be dead on his feet. He closed his eyes and felt/listened to the telepathic bombardment coming at him from three separate directions. Something like a smile flickered faintly across Reg's lips when he realized that he knew exactly where each alien was standing. *Three quick bullets*. Reg snapped his machine gun into position and fired three shots into the darkness.

There was a crash as the silver case hit the ground and glass test tubes bounced on the floor. The silent screaming in his head went quiet, and the strength returned to his arms. He was sure the Tall Ones were dead. He moved forward a few steps until he felt the hardness of a test tube under his boot and stopped short. He backed up and squatted down, feeling for the vial with his hand, hoping it wasn't broken. If it was, he would be dead in a matter of days, perhaps hours. Luckily, it seemed to be in one piece, and he slipped it into his shirt pocket. He set the gun aside and moved around the floor on his hands and knees, groping for test tubes as he listened to the shouts of Fadeela and Ali as they ran toward him.

"Over here!" he called to them. "But watch your step. There are test tubes all over the floor."

By the time Reg killed the aliens, the four of them had run to the edge of the tower and were about to throw themselves off the side. Their flashlights lit up the area. Everything was riddled with bullet holes: the bodies of the three Tall Ones, the side of the taproot, and even the silver case.

"Oh, no. If any of the tubes are broken . . ." Edward began.

". . . we might as well go back and jump," Yossi finished the thought. They began searching the floor and quickly found half of the fourteen test tubes, all of them with their seals in place. Five more were discovered inside the taproot, already loaded into the slots that had been grown for them. The meat of the root was wet and orange, like the flesh of a ripe mango. Ali reached inside and gingerly worked them free one at a time, then handed them to Edward, who used his good hand to place them, ever so carefully, back into the battered case.

"I've got another one right here," Reg said. "Give me some light." He reached into his shirt pocket and pulled out the tube he'd stepped on with his boot. It was cracked from top to bottom, but not all the way through. The structural integrity of the tube hadn't been violated. The honey-colored liquid inside looked harmless enough, like a sample of clean motor oil. Reg gazed nervously at the deadly nectar, which was enough, in theory, to send the entire human species into extinction. "Hey, Edward," he said with a slight quiver in his voice, "I think you'd better get over here with that case before I drop this thing." His fingers were trembling and continued to do so until the fragile beaker was resting peacefully in its foam channel.

"We need one more," Edward announced. "Be careful where you step."

As the team searched the floor on hands and knees, a pair of explosions shook the tower. A handful of Saudi jets were still in the sky, intent on toppling the tower. The massive structure groaned loudly and tipped even farther. All the equipment the Tall Ones had left scattered on the floor began sliding. Shouting filled the exit bay.

"Time to get out!"

"Let's go! Back down to the shaft!"

"Not yet!" Reg yelled. "Listen!" Cutting through the rest of the noise was the high-pitched tinkle of rolling glass. The final test tube was skittering downslope with the rest of the debris.

"Hurry! Before it breaks."

They chased the sound of the tube through the darkness.

"I've got it!" Yossi shouted. He carried it to Edward, using both hands. When it was finally locked inside the damaged case, he took off his glasses and wiped the sweat from his forehead.

"Now can we please get the hell out of here?"

They ran to the trellis and began to climb down, Edward hugging the case to his chest. They were almost to the floor of the lower story when Fadeela stopped and looked around.

"We're missing someone. Where's Michael?" she asked. In all the confusion, they'd left him behind.

"I'm right behind you!" came a voice from above. They turned their flashlight upward and saw him climbing down the bars. His uniform was soaked in blood from his wounds, and it looked like his stomach was severely distended. When he caught up to the rest of the team, Yossi turned a flashlight on his swollen belly.

"What, did they make you pregnant up there?"

"Oh, that?" Tye asked, patting the front of his uniform. "I decided to bring Big Mama along with me. She's practically human."

"No!" Fadeela said. "You've got to leave it here. If you bring it, they'll know where we are. We can't let them get the bioweapons back."

"We'll talk about it outside," Reg said. He knew Tye had saved the strange creature for "humanitarian" reasons, but he suddenly realized it might serve another purpose. The six of them rushed across the floor, threw themselves into the esophageal elevator, then climbed down the several flights of X-shaped girders. Bomb blasts continued to rock the tower. As quickly as their feet would carry them, the team was on ground level once more. They hurried out of the tower, looking for the chariot they'd left near the abandoned jeeps.

Tye lagged behind the others. He had made the first part of the trip down without any assistance, but his stab wounds began to take their toll as he climbed down the last few stories. He couldn't use his left arm, and his stomach was cramping. Reg and Ali stayed behind the others to help him. As they brought him down, the entire tower groaned and leaned, threatening to collapse at any moment. When they came running out of the tower and into the area where the jeeps were parked, they learned that the chariot was gone. Yossi, Edward, and Fadeela were laboring to push-start one of the jeeps.

"Get in," Yossi yelled, as soon as the engine kicked to life. Ali and Reg tossed Tye into the passenger seat and jumped aboard a second before Yossi slammed his foot down on the pedal and went careening around the corner. He took them bumping and swerving along the side of the tower until they saw daylight filtering in through the gash in the exterior wall. There was no way to make the jeep climb over the debris that the chariot had crossed on the way inside, so they left it behind and exited the city destroyer on foot.

It was murky dawn outside. There was a roar of jets in the air and the screeching death throes of the tower behind them. Reg loaded the flare gun he'd been carrying and shot one flare after another into the air as they ran into the desert, trying to put as much distance as possible between themselves and the ship.

"Where's Sutton?" Edward yelled, carrying the case with great care. Despite all the mayhem surrounding him, he kept his attention focused on making certain the case wasn't jostled or dropped. As they hurried away from the tower, Fadeela ran up alongside Reg.

"Okay, that was my part of the plan," she told him. "I got us into the ship and outside with the silver box. The rest is up to you."

Right on cue, a growling noise came rumbling toward them, and soon they saw the headlights of the Mercedes truck. Sutton pulled up and skidded to a stop.

"We're being bombed!" he screamed. "Whose idea was this?"

Reg helped Tye climb into the front seat, then jumped in himself. Remi helped the others pile into the back. When they were all aboard, they shouted in one voice at the driver: "Go!"

Sutton was spitting mad. "This is Faisal's doing, isn't it? If I get my hands on that bastard, I'll tear him apart. Here we are trying to save his damnable country, and he starts bombing us. Remi and I were nearly blown to bits out here while you lot were lollygagging inside. And what happened to you?" he asked Tye. "What's that under your shirt?"

"Trouble ahead!" Reg called, pointing out the front window.

Straight in front of them, standing atop a sand dune, was a fully armored alien warrior. It raised its arm into the firing position and pointed its finger at the truck. Everyone ducked, but there was no blast of light. The creature merely stood there watching the truck come closer. After a moment of hesitation, it lowered its head and charged the Mercedes. Remi, riding on top of the cab, fired his rocket launcher, and the warrior's bioarmor blew apart a half second before Sutton smashed into it with the truck's battering ram. The tires trampled over the body. Turning an alien into roadkill did wonders for Sutton's mood.

"Take that, you ugly piece of crap," he bellowed. He turned to his passengers with an exhilarated smile on his face. "That felt rather good."

"I'm glad you think so because here comes another one!" Tye said. As before, one of the exoskeletal beasts had them dead to rights. It pointed its long finger at the grille of the speeding truck, but did nothing.

"They're not firing at us," Reg noticed. "They must be afraid of hitting this." He patted the lump under Tye's shirt. Ali opened up with his field gun as Remi launched another bazooka shell. The creature was torn to pieces. Sutton steered around it.

"You're right," Tye realized. "That's exactly it. They're afraid to hit Big Mama. And they all know where she is. They can feel her."

"What the hell are you talking about? Who is Big Mama?" Sutton asked. Tye tore open his shirt and introduced them. When he saw the gelatinous lump of biomatter throbbing and glowing phosphorescent against Tye's bleeding stomach, Sutton nearly jumped out of the moving vehicle.

"Oh my God, what is that thing?"

"Big Mama is sort of like a brain. She directs traffic for the aliens, lets them know where they're at."

Sutton was disgusted. "It's a *brain*? You *took* a brain? Get rid of it!"

"Watch out!" Another alien stepped into the truck's path. It didn't hesitate as the others had done, but charged immediately toward the Mercedes's headlights.

"Bring it on, bug boy!" Sutton yelled. Instead of trying to steer around the creature, he veered directly toward it, spoiling for another head-on collision. He was expecting Remi to use his rocket launcher again, but there hadn't been time to reload. The creature lowered its head like a bull, and there was a thunderous crack when it collided with the steel bar of the truck's battering ram. Fragments of the head-thorax shell flew high into the air, but they didn't feel the creature's body under their tires.

"It's hanging on," Remi shouted from his perch. The big Ethiopian scooted himself to the driver's side of the cab to get a clear shot at the thing. Before he could, the front left tire exploded and the truck lurched to the side. A second later, the first tentacle threw itself over the hood and stabbed through the sheet metal. Sutton kept the accelerator pedal crushed against the floorboard as a second tentacle reached up and wound itself around the side mirror.

"Steer," he told Tye. He took out a pistol and started to open the door, ready to polish the creature off with a bullet or two. But the third tentacle was deadly. It broke through the windshield and smashed Sutton's head against the back wall. Another long arm snaked in through the open door and wrapped itself around the driver's body. Remi fired at last, and all the tentacles fell limp at the same time. The alien fell to the sand, dragging Sutton outside with it.

Reg slid past Tye, took the wheel, and accelerated. "Check your medallion," he said. "See if there are more of them ahead of us."

Tye's mind was blank, still processing what had just happened. "Sutton's dead," he said meekly.

"The medallion. Check it," Reg yelled.

Absently, Tye searched through his pockets until he remembered he'd left his last medallion in the tower. But the one he'd given Sutton was sitting on the dashboard, folded into a paper napkin. He unwrapped it and put it against his skin.

"Not working," he told Reg. "Still getting the flower design."

"What about that thing?" Reg pointed to the brainlike blob resting on Tye's lap. "Does it show where the aliens are?"

Tye studied the warm lump's transparent skin and the mass of diamond shapes that were all gathered on one side of the body. He experimented with it for a moment before figuring it out.

"What does it say?" Reg asked.

"It looks like we've got several hundred aliens moving in this direction." He looked up at Reg. "They're leaving At-Ta'if, and I think they're coming after us."

"Perfect," Reg said. "How far away are they?"

"How should I know? I guess we're just going to leave him back there?" he said, glancing into the side mirror and watching Sutton's body recede from view.

Reg kept his eyes focused on the rough terrain ahead of him, driving as fast as he could. It was a long way back to Faisal's camp.

16

Into the Hills

The fifth day of the invasion began in worse fashion than any of the others. Reg found the road a mile before the Dawqah turnoff. He stayed off the asphalt, driving along the rough shoulder at forty-five miles per hour in order to keep the flat tire on the rim as long as possible. When they reached the isolated crossroads, the sun was lifting in the east. Several miles behind them, a massive dust cloud indicated pursuit by the alien army. The flat tire made the truck difficult to steer. Reg muscled it onto the pavement and pulled hard to make the turn into the hills.

"Can't we go any faster?" Tye asked, glancing behind them nervously. "They're definitely catching up."

"Only a few more miles," Reg said. "Faisal's got enough fire-power up on those cliffs ahead of us to sink a battleship. We're almost home." Reg started up the winding incline at an average speed of thirty miles per hour. But a mile up the road, there was a sharp left-hand turn that pulled the tire off the rim and nearly sent the truck and its lethal cargo sailing over the embankment.

After that, Reg drove in a shower of sparks. The unprotected rim scraped against the road, wearing away by the moment and leaving a continuous scar in the surface of the road. There was no choice except to keep going. The rocky canyon walls rose up to enclose them, and Tye scoured them with his eyes, desperate for some sign of the well-equipped army Reg had described.

"Where are they? There's no one here."

"They're here. Just a little farther." The mountain pass looked like a completely different universe now that it was daylight, but Reg began to suspect that Tye was right. They should have seen some of the larger guns by now. The rim continued to grind away on the roadway, and each turn was more difficult than the last. Ali climbed along the outside of the truck and slipped in behind the wheel to relieve Reg when he had exhausted the strength in his arms. They were six miles up the road, and the rim was nearly down to the brake shoes.

"There they are!" Tye shouted. "We made it."

Standing in the middle of the road ahead of them were a handful of Saudi soldiers manning a roadblock. To the left, Reg recognized the field that had been occupied by Faisal's army only hours before. It was empty. On the cliffs to the right were some jeeps with turret guns, but no heavy artillery.

"That stinking bastard!" Reg shouted. He assumed Faisal had double-crossed him, that he'd evacuated the canyon and left him to die as a twisted form of revenge. But when the soldiers came forward, they explained what had happened.

"The aliens left their ship and marched against At-Ta'if. The king ordered our commander to defend the city." They claimed not to know anything about Reg or biological weapons or a raid on the ship. Faisal was so sure that Reg, Fadeela, and the others would be killed, he hadn't even bothered to tell his men about it.

"Where are your vehicles?" Ali asked.

The man said they'd been left with two jeeps, both of which were up on the cliffs keeping a lookout. When Ali had explained about the biological weapons they were carrying and that the alien army was chasing them, the leader got on his radio and called the jeeps down. Ali held a brief strategy session with the soldiers while the jeeps came bumping down the dirt trail along the face of the cliffs above them. When they'd agreed on a plan of action, Ali found Reg.

"There is a road that follows the crest of the mountains," he explained, pointing uphill. "It is about one mile from here. They have two jeeps. One will carry the weapons down to Dawqah. I will take the other jeep and lead them along the mountains. I will need the thing Tye took from the ship. They will follow it."

"Good idea," Reg said, "but I'm the one who should lead them into the hills. You know the area. You've got to—"

Before he could finish his sentence, a streak of light ripped across the sky and smashed into one of the jeeps moving along the trail, demolishing it. It rolled off the trail and tumbled down the hillside, breaking apart on road. The soldiers in the other jeep stopped and took cover behind their vehicle. A moment later, they suffered the same fate. A pulse blast tore into the side of the vehicle and flipped it over. A few hundred yards downhill, a pair of aliens had climbed one of the cliffs with their chariot and were firing into the clearing.

Edward and Reg raced back to the truck. Reg climbed in the back, grabbed the silver box, and tossed it out to Edward, whose heart almost stopped beating when he saw the deadly microbes flying through the air. He caught it as gently as he could, then took off running uphill. Reg strapped on a flamethrower and came around to the passenger door. The translucent amber creature was lying on the front seat. Reg unfastened a couple of shirt buttons, pressed the organism to his stomach, then buttoned back up. A few seconds after he left the truck, it was destroyed when one of the alien projectiles smashed into it. Edward was already a hundred yards closer to the crest of the hill, running as fast as he could and not turning back.

"Ali," Reg yelled, "you follow Edward; make sure he gets away." He patted the lump under his shirt. "I'll lead them up onto those rocks to buy you some time."

Ali nodded and started to run. Reg crossed the road and headed across the field that had been Faisal's headquarters. Above the far end of it was a steep outcropping of rocky hills. It would be difficult for the aliens to follow there. The Saudis on the hilltops began firing into the canyon. They were answered by flurries of pulse blasts. Halfway across the field, Reg heard someone calling his name. He looked back at the road. Fadeela was waving good-bye, half a step ahead of Ali, who was urging her forward. Reg gave her a farewell smile and a crisp salute before continuing on his way.

The rocky ground was treacherous and steep. Reg ran blindly, letting the topography dictate the path he took. Weaving around boulders and leaping over ditches, he ran until he found himself hemmed in by sheer walls of crumbling rock. He tried to climb, but with one hand holding the flamethrower, he could only make it halfway up the wall. He turned to check behind him and saw an alien chariot coming over the rocks in the distance. He slid his arms out of the harness and tossed the flamethrower, canisters and all, onto the shelf of rock above him. Even with both hands free, it was a difficult to reach the top. The rocks crumbled to gravel when he tried to pull himself up. When he finally squirmed over the side, he found himself stranded on an isolated stone shelf, a flat rock fifty feet across. If he was going to continue moving, Reg had only two choices: Go back the way he'd come, or scale another crumbling rock face.

He glanced around the shelf and judged it as good a place as any to die. He still had two canisters of fuel for the flamethrower, enough to buy Edward a few more minutes of time. He pulled the brain-shaped amber lump out of his shirt and set it in the sun, then retreated behind a boulder to wait. He could hear the aliens moving closer, stumbling over the rocks in their cumbersome biomechanical suits of armor. It sounded like there were hundreds of them. The waiting seemed eternal. He fought back the urge to spring out into the open and blast a few of them with fire, knowing that every second he could stall them increased the chances of Fadeela and the others being able to escape. He imagined they must already be past the summit and starting down the other side of the mountain. As he pictured them running, he suddenly realized he couldn't let the aliens take him alive. If so, they would learn where the biological weapons were. He checked his pistol and found he had two bullets left, which was one more than he needed.

The aliens arrived and surrounded the shelf. Reg listened to their tentacles scraping at the rock walls as they tried to climb. Then the first one lifted its enormous shell head over the lip of the rock. Reg swung his flamethrower around, waiting for it to show itself fully before he fired.

Machine-gun fire came from the cliffs above. The bullets chipped away at the alien's exoskeletal armor and knocked it back over the side. Reg looked up and saw a white barrier fence, the type that lines the curves of mountain roads to keep careless motorists from driving off the sides. He could see people shouting and running. They looked like civilians. One of them stood at the edge, a man who took off his *keffiyeh* and waved it through the air as he shouted down the hill. Reg signaled for the guy to stop making a target of himself before he was picked off by a pulse weapon. Before he could make the man understand, a dozen blasts of light flew up the canyon and exploded where the man had been standing. When the dust began to clear, the man was gone, and Reg thought he must be dead. A moment later, however, he was standing there waving and shouting again. He was shouting in English and seemed to know Reg's name. More pulse blasts ripped into the cliffs on which he stood. At the same time, two of the aliens came over the edge of Reg's shelf and started toward the amber homing device.

"Over here, boys." The shell heads swiveled on their thin waists to face Reg, who blasted them with a burst of his flamethrower. The burning skeletons staggered off the edge of the shelf and fell onto the rocks. That left Reg with one canister of fuel. He decided he would let them get to the organism next time and give them a chance to pick it up before he toasted them.

Once again, the man on the cliffs was yelling down to Reg. *Who is this fool?* Reg wondered. And then he recognized the voice. It was Thomson!

Reg darted into the open, picked up the organism, then returned to the edge of the stone shelf and looked over the side. Dozens of aliens were massed just below him. They were climbing over one another to reach the top. They looked up at Reg, who held the organism out in front of him.

"Looking for this?" he asked before spraying them with the final burst of his flamethrower. As they writhed, he looked up and saw that there were several hundred aliens swarming toward him through the canyon. Arms lifted toward him from every direction, but none of them fired. Either they'd been trained not to risk damage to the brainlike creature, or it disabled their weapons, Reg couldn't tell which. He ran to the base of the next cliff, stuffed the organism back into his shirt, and began climbing. Before he'd gone very far, there were aliens climbing after him. They would have caught him easily except for the bullets coming from above. Each time one of them got close to Reg, it was knocked off the rock by a hail of small-arms fire.

Arab voices cheered him on from the road above, urging him to keep climbing. A strong hand reached over the last ledge and pulled Reg up to safety. It belonged to a wrinkled, elderly woman who looked old enough to be Reg's grandmother. But she was large and strong, and it hurt when she slapped Reg on the back to welcome him. He rolled away from the edge and surveyed the situation. The defenders of the clifftop were a motley group indeed. Half of them were women and many of them were elderly. By the way they were dressed, he recognized them as Yemenis. The women wore a distinctive, beaked sort of veil, and the men all had broad daggers, *djambiyas*, tucked into their belts. Crouching behind their barricades, they looked more like a crowd rioting for better retirement benefits than an army capable of repulsing the brunt of the alien attack. Thomson ran forward in a crouch.

"I'm beginning to wonder about you, Cummins. You pissed off everyone out in the desert, and now you've done something to make the aliens mad. They seem to be following you."

Reg was incredulous. "What are you doing here?"

The colonel rolled his eyes. "I could write a book. Come on, follow me." He led the way to the opposite side of the road, where they would be out of the line of fire. Parked along the shoulder was the Yemeni caravan's transportation: horses, camels, bicycles, motorcycles, and a few passenger cars.

Thomson explained that after the city destroyer was shot down, some rough-looking customers showed up in the desert asking about Reg. He'd hidden himself in the dunes until they flew away, then accepted a ride in a helicopter to Khamis Moushayt. From there, he'd gone to the town of Abha in Yemen, where he'd enlisted in this civilian army that was coming to join the war in the desert.

"We've been traveling since yesterday noon, and just when we got to our turnoff road, I recognized that Ethiopian chap from the camp. He told me you'd gone this way."

As Thomson spoke, Reg looked down the other side of the mountain. As he'd seen many times from the air, one side was a collection of desolate stone canyons leading down to the inhospitable desert, while the other was moist, green, and overgrown with trees. The verdant western slope was steep. It plunged dramatically down to a narrow coastal plane. Beyond that was the Red Sea. The smokestacks of the oil refinery at Dawqah glinted back at him in the sun, as if trying to catch his attention. Reg remembered what Mr. Yamani had said about Dawqah being a "nasty little town." But from where he stood, it sparkled like the promised land. He interrupted what the colonel was saying.

"Thomson, I need a car. I have to get to the coast." He lifted the amber-colored organism out of his shirt and showed it to him. "They're chasing me because of this."

"Oh, Lord," Thomson said, recoiling from the pulsating mass. "What is it?"

"No time to explain. But they can sense where it is. I want to lead them down the coast. If I stay here, all these people will be slaughtered."

"Come with me."

They jogged down the road until Thomson found someone he recognized, a young man in tight slacks and a silk dress shirt. He looked like he was dressed for an evening of disco dancing except for the *djambiya* tucked into his wide leather belt. Whipping out his trusty phrase book, Thomson said a few words to him in pidgin Arabic.

"*Mish mumkin*," the man said. *Impossible*. His car keys made a visible lump in the tight fabric of his pants pocket.

"Show him," Thomson said. Reg obliged. When the man saw the brainlike blob he took out his keys without another word and tossed them to Reg. Thomson led him to a battered Ford sedan. Reg jumped in and started the engine.

"You coming?" he asked Thomson.

"I'll take my chances here."

"Get these people out of the way if you can. They're not going to make much difference."

"Good luck."

"See you around." Reg had shifted into drive and put his foot on the gas, when Thomson remembered something and called to him.

"I almost forgot. Here's that tape recording you wanted." From his breast pocket, he pulled out a cassette tape and handed it through the window. "I wouldn't play it in front of Faisal if I were you. He comes off smelling pretty rotten."

"You're a good man, Colonel."

"Tally-ho and all that rot," he shot back, as Reg hit the gas and sped away.

When he came to the road leading down to the coast, he saw Remi among the men firing at the advancing aliens. He honked the horn until the big Ethiopian turned around and ran to the car. He jumped in and they took off down the hill, driving slowly and honking their horn. Reg thought the rest of the team might be moving through the trees and wanted to draw their attention. It worked. About two miles from the turnoff, they encountered a beanpole of a man with bright red hair standing in the middle of the road with his legs spread wide and a rifle pointed at them. It was Tye.

When Reg rolled to a stop, the others came running out of the trees and crammed themselves and their weapons into the two-door sedan. Edward was the last one standing outside.

"Too many big people and too many guns," he said. Reg, Ali, and Tye were already crowded into the front seat, with Ali's field gun stretching from one door to the other. Edward handed the silver case delicately to a pair of hands in the backseat before climbing inside to join Fadeela, Remi, and Yossi. Before the doors were closed, Reg put his foot through the floor and sent them hurtling down the road.

"Where are we going?" Ali asked, then quickly changed his mind. "Don't tell me. I probably don't want to know." After a couple of miles, the team convinced Reg to slow down. They had a large start on the aliens, and as long as they kept the pace above fifty miles per hour, the chariots couldn't gain on them.

As the others watched out the rear window for signs of danger, Fadeela was developing another plan. "When we reach the coastal road, there is an airport a few miles north of Dawqah. We can take a plane from there to Jeddah, where someone will know how to dispose of these horrible weapons.

Reg kept his eyes on the road and said that was a good idea. When they came out of the trees and saw the coast road in front of them, everyone breathed a sigh of relief. They were almost home free. They turned north onto the highway and increased their speed. There was traffic on the highway, but not much. Many of the cars they passed were loaded down with families and as many personal possessions as they could carry. The faces behind the windows looked tired and frightened. Hardly anyone gave Reg or the overcrowded Ford a second glance. For a few moments, it felt almost like an ordinary day. The other drivers were observing the speed limit and the rules of the road. Some of them flashed dirty looks at Reg as he sped past them, not suspecting the car with the Yemeni license plates contained enough weapons-grade poison to kill everyone in the Middle East. Even though it was still a few miles ahead of them, Reg could smell the gaseous stench of the refinery.

"I don't believe it," Yossi said from the backseat.

"What's that?" Tye asked.

"They're coming through the trees. All of them." They all turned to see what he was talking about and could hardly believe their eyes. It looked like an avalanche moving diagonally down the mountainside, shaking the trees as it came. The alien army had left the winding road to take a more efficient angle of pursuit

They crashed down the slope at a phenomenal rate of speed, weaving around some trees, knocking the others to the ground.

A blaring horn brought Reg's attention back to his driving. He swerved back into his lane a second before colliding head-on with a semi. Ali had already figured out what Reg had in mind and pointed him toward the exit he wanted. Then he turned around and told the others what he thought the crazed Englishman behind the wheel had in mind. When he was finished Reg looked at him, impressed.

"I thought the only mind readers around here were the ones from outer space."

They sped toward the front gates of the refinery and the guards who stepped out of their kiosk to question them. The car crashed through a fence and charged into the facility. They followed the road between a pair of gigantic storage tanks, then past the separating station with its open construction and vertical spires rising like stainless-steel minarets. Soon they came to a round, heavily fortified building that looked like it must be the refinery's control room. When the Ford skidded to a halt, a half dozen men who had been standing around drinking coffee and talking scattered in all directions, thinking they were under attack by terrorists.

Ali caught one of them and dragged him back to the car, explaining, as politely as he could under the circumstances, that they needed access to the refinery's computer system. When the man asked why, Ali told him.

"We need to spill all the oil on the ground and set the place on fire."

"Are you crazy?"

"That has nothing to do with it! Show us the computers!"

The man scoffed and refused to cooperate. The team did what they could to convince him. Fadeela told him that several hundred, perhaps thousands, of aliens would be arriving at the refinery within the next few minutes, and Reg showed him the amber-colored organism. Still the man refused. But he changed his mind when Yossi shot him in the forearm, then pushed the man's nose with the hot end of his pistol.

"I'll count to three," said the Israeli. "One, two—"

"Don't shoot!" shouted the injured man. "I will take you inside!"

He led them up a set of steel stairs and entered a numerical code into the keypad next to the door. It opened, and Ali shoved the man through the doorway. Tye, Fadeela, and Remi followed him.

"What about the case?" Edward asked. "We have to get these biological weapons out of the area."

"We'll burn them," Reg said, "along with everything else."

"That's too dangerous. There's still time to get them out of here."

Reg tossed the keys to Yossi. "Go with him." And after wishing both men luck, he entered the control room.

At first, the technicians inside resisted. They said it was impossible to spill the oil intentionally, that the computers weren't designed to do such things. The only way to accomplish what the team was asking would be to physically destroy the pipelines one by one. The whole time they talked, Tye leaned over the main routing screen, studying it. When Reg came to look over his shoulder, he saw a complicated diagram showing a tangle of lines and a confusing galaxy of blinking lights. The display was no more comprehensible to him than the designs he'd seen on the tops of the black tables inside the tower.

"It looks simple enough," Tye said. "This board controls the movement of oil through the entire refinery. It allows them to pump it out of one tank and into another. See how the pipelines are all numbered to correspond with the switches here at the bottom. Then you've got your pressure gauges and automatic shut-offs at intervals along each pipe." He pointed to various spots on the schematic, assuming Reg was following along.

"So how do we spill the oil?"

"Easy. We close down all the lines and start all the pumps at the same time. Then we sit back and wait for the pipes to burst under the pressure." He started throwing switches with both hands, activating some and deactivating others, while Reg looked on skeptically. It couldn't be that easy, could it? For a minute, it seemed to work. Red lights started flashing and warning buzzers sounded. But then everything returned to normal. Tye scratched his chin, thinking. "The system senses the pressure buildup and shuts down the pumps."

"How do we circumvent the shutoff system?" he asked the technicians.

"*Mish mumkin*," one of them said. "We cannot override the fail-safe. It's all automatic."

"Yossi and Edward are coming back. And they've got company," Fadeela announced, looking out a window. Reg knew what she was talking about and dragged one of the technicians across the room to show him. The man looked outside and couldn't believe his eyes. Less than a hundred yards from him, a pair of ugly gray creatures with heads that looked rather like overgrown oyster shells were riding a walking sled and firing blasts of white light out of their fingertips. He stared at this startling scene for a moment or two, then ran to the switchboard and began pulling wires from the underside of the console. He shouted to his colleagues, who joined him at the control boards. Within seconds, the red lights and warning buzzers came back to life. The muffled sound of explosions came through the walls. All around the refinery, pipes began splitting open. Oil sprayed high into the air in some places and flowed out in dark rivers in others.

"We have done what you asked," said the man who had torn out the wires. "Now let us leave. We have helicopters. You can go with us."

"Wait. We're not finished. How can we light the oil? We have to set it on fire."

The man tossed Reg a book of matches and turned for the door. Almost as soon as it sealed behind him, something slammed against the outside wall on the opposite side of the room. Four armored aliens, sensing the presence of the amber organism, were trying to break in to retrieve it.

"Everybody outside!" Leaving the brain inside, the team raced out the door and made sure it was sealed behind them. They ran

to take cover behind the next building and saw the Ford parked
there. Ali found his field gun in the backseat and strapped it over
his shoulder. A moment later, Edward came around the corner
carrying the silver case. Yossi was right behind him.

"What happened?"

"We couldn't find our way back to the front gates until it was
too late. They're all crossing the highway," Yossi said. "More
than a thousand of them."

"We should have destroyed the weapons before," Edward
said. "I'm going to do it now."

"How?"

"Give me those matches and I'll climb up there." He pointed
to the ladder rising up the side of one of the ten-story-tall storage
tanks. "When I'm inside, I'll set the whole thing on fire."

"My God," Tye said, impressed with the man's conviction.

"I'll go with you," Yossi said, "I've got a lighter. And besides,
you can't trust a Palestinian with a big job." It was Yossi's idea of
a joke. For the first time since they'd known him, he smiled.

Edward shook his head and appealed to the others. "Now do
you see why we can't stand the Jews?" But he returned Yossi's
grin, and said, "Come on, madman, let's go." The two men ran
toward the nearest storage tank and began climbing the vertical
steel ladder as fast as they could, bickering as they went.

Remi tipped over a trash can and found a discarded newspaper
to use as kindling. "Let's get started," he said, and led the way
toward the nearest lake of freshly spilled oil. They lit the newspaper and dropped it onto the oil, expecting it to erupt immediately
into flames. Instead, the oil soaked into the paper until the fire
went out. They tried again, this time using more paper to make a
hotter fire.

"It's supposed to burn," Reg said.

A car came speeding around a corner not far away and turned
toward the main gate. Before it got very far, a pulse blast ripped
into its side. The vehicle flipped over and burst into flame. When
they saw this, the team turned toward Tye.

"One step ahead of you," he said, pulling out the alien weapon and unfolding the cloth he used to carry it. He let the flipperlike protrusions wind themselves around his forearm, then invited Reg to help him. "What do we hit?"

"Anything that will blow up."

But the pulse weapon proved no more useful than the burning newspapers. They used it to blow open the side of an oil tank, to tear a gaping hole in the side of a building, and to dig craters in the ground where the oil was pooling. But they couldn't start a fire.

They did, however, attract the attention of a squad of aliens, who came away from the control room to investigate. Ali knocked them backwards with a few blasts from his field gun while Reg and Tye picked them off one by one with the pulse gun. But more of them started coming around the corner. They came by the dozens, fearless behind their armor, and advanced on the four troublesome earthlings.

"We have to fall back," Ali said.

But Reg disagreed. He pointed to Edward and Yossi, who were only halfway to the top of the ladder. They were shielded from view of the aliens by the curve of the tank. "We've got to hold them here until those two are inside. Then we'll fall back."

"By then it will be too late," Fadeela said. "They're surrounding us."

There was no choice but to stay and defend their position. The best they could hope for was a fiery death, that once the two men were inside the tank, they would be successful in blowing it up and that the fire would spread. If not, all they would have accomplished was leading the aliens out of the desert and into the more densely populated coastal plain. And there was still a chance of the anthrax spores and ebola virus being spread.

When Edward reached the top, he handed the case to Yossi, lifted the cap door at the side of the roof, and lowered himself inside. After taking the case back, he started down the ladder that ran along the inside of the tank. Then, as Yossi was climbing in after him, a series of loud explosions came from the far end of the refinery.

"Sounds like bombs," Remi remarked.

"Yes, and helicopters," Ali added.

"It must be the men from the control room," Fadeela said. "They said they had helicopters."

But a moment later, they saw a squadron of Apache helicopters rising over the oil field, firing missiles down at the alien army and starting a massive fire in the oil, a fire which quickly began rolling toward them. When pulse blasts began zipping toward the helicopters, they ducked behind the outlying buildings. Then another group of the fearsome gunships appeared on the opposite horizon and fired another volley of shells down onto the oil-soaked grounds.

"They're starting fires around the perimeter," Reg observed. "Smart boys."

As soon as the aliens turned to fire on the second group of helicopters, the Apaches lowered out of view, and a third group lifted from the direction of the highway. When their shells slammed into the ground, a wall of fire cut off the team's only means of escape. They were boxed in.

Reg looked around and nodded approvingly, thinking, *Now that's the way you run an aerial assault.* He didn't know if any of the men piloting the helicopters had been his students, but that didn't stop him from feeling proud of the way they were conducting the operation. They were achieving their objectives without taking unnecessary risks and were displaying extraordinary teamwork.

"Where in the hell did these guys come from?" Tye wondered.

"They must be Faisal's men," Reg said.

The aliens panicked when they found themselves surrounded by fire. They ran in crazed circles, firing their weapons into the flames. Some of them opened their shells and jumped out. The ones who had been firing at the team forgot about them and rushed off to join the mayhem.

Yossi climbed back to the opening in the top of the tank. Reg noticed him because he was waving his arms and shouting, but he wasn't shouting to Reg or the others. A helicopter came from th direction of the highway, broke through the wall of flame, and hovered over the tower long enough to allow Yossi and Edward to climb in. It wasn't one of the Apaches, but a civilian helicopter.

"Hey, what about us?" Tye shouted. He and Remi ran to the nearest ladder and began to climb. Ali slung his gun over his back and followed them. Reg and Fadeela found another ladder, and they, too, began to climb. The helicopter disappeared only moments after they started up the ladders, but they all continued climbing. The steel rungs were hard on their hands, especially Fadeela's. The harsh metal rubbed through the skin on her palms, and she was bleeding before they were halfway up. At the three-quarters mark, her arms were so tired they began to shake.

"I know you're going to think I'm a princess, but I don't know if I can make it to the top. Let me stay here and rest. You can go around me."

"I'll help you."

"No. Let me do it myself. I just need to rest for a while."

Reg stared up at her, watching to make sure she didn't lose her grip when he noticed something strange. Although neither of them was moving, he could feel movement in the ladder. He looked down and saw an armored alien climbing up behind them. It was moving fast, taking the rungs two at a time and using all twelve of its limbs to pull itself upward.

"I hope you're ready for this," Reg said. He climbed another step and shocked Fadeela by wedging his head between her legs and lifting her backside onto his shoulders. Before she could protest, he started climbing as fast as he could. There was no need to look down to see if the alien was getting closer. Reg could feel it gaining on them through the vibrations in the ladder. When they got to the top, Reg fired his last bullet at their pursuer, then he and Fadeela ran onto the curving roof of the tank. From their new vantage point, they could see the Apache helicopters surrounding the refinery. They were keeping low to the ground, well away from the fires they'd started. The civilian helicopter they'd seen pick up their comrades was coming in for another pass, but the alien was already at the top of the ladder. It stepped onto the roof and let the humans regard it in all its horrible glory. The tentacles sprouting from its back waved in the air like a gruesome peacock spreading its tail feathers. As the helicopter came closer, the creature ignored it and marched toward Reg and Fadeela. As it stepped onto the crest of the roof, a pulse blast whizzed past Reg's ear and struck the exoskeleton square in the face, shattering the armor and knocking it over the side of the tank. When Reg spun around, he saw Tye and Remi waving to him, the alien tube gun sandwiched between their arms.

"I don't believe it," Fadeela muttered when she saw the royal crest painted on the door of the helicopter. "It's the king's private helicopter." But that surprise was nothing compared to the one she got a moment later when a disheveled old man leaned his head out of the cargo door and waved them inside. It was her father, Karmal Yamani.

Fadeela allowed Reg to help lift her over the landing bars, then reached back to help pull him inside. She sprang into her father's arms as the chopper began to lift away. The old man winked at Reg over his daughter's shoulder.

"I told you I had joined the fight."

"You did this? I thought it must be Faisal."

King Ibrahim turned around to face them from the copilot's seat. "Faisal is still driving in circles in the desert wondering where the aliens went."

As the pilot lifted the chopper away from the roof of the storage tank and turned to head away, the ship listed violently toward the copilot's side. Something heavy had grabbed onto the landing gear, and everyone inside knew immediately what it had to be. Before anyone had a chance to reach for a gun, a tentacle reached into the rear passenger area and began to slash through the air. Reg, closest to the door, picked up the first heavy object he could lay his hands on, a fire extinguisher. Ignoring the tentacle, he rushed toward the open door and leaned outside. The mangled exoskeleton was only a few feet below him. Its huge head-thorax shell had been shattered, but its many limbs were wrapped tightly around the landing bars. Reg used the extinguisher to deliver

hard blow to the center of the cracked shell, knocking a large section of it away. The alien hidden below the shell was now
exposed to view, but before Reg could deliver a second blow, the
tentacle clipped him hard on the back of the head. He felt himself
go light-headed, then collapse. The fleshy arm wound itself around
his neck and began pulling him outside. Fadeela caught him by
the feet and struggled for a moment against the more powerful
alien. Her resistance bought just enough time for the king to open
the copilot's door and peer down into the hideous confusion of
limbs and broken shell. Staring up at him were a pair of bulging,
reflective eyes. He drew a pistol from the folds of his robes and
put a single bullet into the alien's head. As it died, all the life went
out of the biomechanical suit of armor. The tentacles, including
the one around Reg's neck, went limp, and the creature plunged
to the ground.

"*Allah-u akbar*," cried the king, shaking a fist at the alien as it
fell away. "You see? Finally, I got my wish to kill one of them! I
did it! I killed him." The aging monarch continued to celebrate as
his pilot swooped to the next storage tanker and set down long
enough for Ali, Remi, and Tye to climb aboard. Reg was beginning to recover his senses by the time they all stepped inside.
"Did you see?" King Ibrahim asked the new passengers. "I killed
one of them!"

As the helicopter lifted away from the refinery, there was a
series of powerful explosions that sent fire roaring high into the
air. The intense heat began exploding the holding tanks, feeding
the already-raging fire with ton after ton of additional fuel. Soon,
every square inch of the refinery was fully engulfed. The helicopter gunships patrolled the perimeter of the blaze in case any of
the aliens escaped, but none did.

The king ordered the helicopter to hover nearby as the inferno
consumed the enemy forces, then told his pilot to take them to
Jeddah.

Ali leaned forward and spoke bluntly to the king. "We cannot
leave without our friends, the two men who were picked up first."

King Ibrahim turned around in his chair and arched an eyebrow. "One of them is a Palestinian masquerading as a Jordanian, and the other is a Jew. You call these men your friends?"

"Yes," Ali answered without hesitation. "Good friends."

Mr. Yamani assured the muscular captain there was no reason to worry about Yossi and Edward. "They are in good hands. My son, Khalid, is with them. He will escort them back to At-Ta'if, where the biological weapons will be destroyed."

"Khalid has been released?" Fadeela asked her father. She was on the floor of the helicopter, sitting next to the still-woozy Reg.

"Yes, Faisal let him go this morning before he retreated from the mountains. I think he expected your brother to die at the hands of the aliens."

"Speaking of Ghalil Faisal," said the king, unbuckling himself from his chair and moving aft to join the others, "I spoke to him by radio earlier today. He had many interesting things to say about you, Major Cummins. Not very positive things, I am afraid."

"That doesn't really surprise me," Reg said. "Faisal and I haven't really hit it off during the past few days."

"In fact," the king continued, "he would like to see you arrested. According to him, you have committed several criminal acts since the invasion began." Fadeela sat bolt upright, ready to defend Reg against Faisal's accusations. Before she could say a word, both her father and the king spoke to her sternly, telling her to let Reg answer for himself.

The king outlined the most serious of Faisal's allegations: that Reg had shot down an Egyptian pilot over whom he had no authority because the man had refused to obey his orders; that he had urged Saudi pilots to disobey their orders during an engagement with the enemy; that he had kidnapped a Saudi woman, Fadeela, on what should have been her wedding day; that he had trespassed on the grounds of the Saudi military facility at Al-Sayyid; and that he had stolen weapons and ammunition from that same facility. Considering that all these acts had been committed within a span of less than four days, it was quite an impressive list. When the king was finished, he asked Reg to answer the charges.

"They're all true," Reg said without batting an eyelid. "And if

I had to do it all again, I'd make the exactly the same decisions."

It wasn't the answer the king had been expecting.

"I was never kidnapped," Fadeela couldn't help interjecting. "It was my choice to go with these people." The king ignored her and stared intently at Reg, waiting for him to go on.

First, Reg explained the circumstances under which he had "shot down" the Egyptian pilot who refused to turn away from Khamis Moushayt. King Ibrahim listened carefully, running his fingers through his beard until Reg was finished.

"If what you say is true, and I believe that it is, you must be quite a fine pilot."

"He's the best," Tye interjected.

King Ibrahim nodded. "So I have been told. But do you also admit that you urged our pilots to disobey Faisal's orders over Mecca?"

Tye, Remi, Ali, and Fadeela all broke into the conversation at once, insisting that Reg had acted with good cause. Reg quieted them with a gesture and continued speaking to the king.

"I did what I thought was right," he said. "I knew Faisal was making a horrible mistake, that he was sending those men to their deaths."

"*Knew* or *believed?*" the king asked.

Reg hesitated for a moment before answering. "I believed so."

"In other words, your assessment of the situation differed from Commander Faisal's?" In only a few moments, the king had cut to the quick of the matter.

"Yes, it was my assessment against his. But before you have me arrested, there's something I think you should listen to." He pulled out of his pocket the audiocassette Thomson had given him. "Have you got a tape deck in this copter?"

The question stung the monarch. "Major Cummins, this is the royal helicopter. Of course there is a cassette player." He took the tape from Reg and plugged it in. A moment later, the sounds of the air battle over Mecca filled the helicopter's passenger compartment. King Ibrahim turned the volume up loud, and for the rest of the flight to Jeddah, hardly a word was spoken.

When they arrived at King Abdul Aziz International Airport at about four in the afternoon, the helicopter swept past the large tent-shaped *hajj* terminal built especially to accommodate pilgrims en route to Mecca. The pilot landed the craft on a helipad outside the terminal reserved for the exclusive use of the royal family. There was a large contingent of soldiers and servants waiting there to greet them. One of the faces in the crowd was familiar. It was Faisal. He stood about a hundred feet from the helicopter, his olive green uniform encrusted with the sweat and dust accumulated during a long day of chasing the alien army across the desert. He smiled menacingly at Reg when the two of them made eye contact, then sent some of his soldiers to surround the king's chopper, just in case Reg tried to make a run for it.

But Reg had no intention of running. When he saw Faisal, he jumped out of the helicopter and marched directly toward him. Fadeela and the others followed him outside, leaving the king still listening to the recording. "Where the hell were you?" Reg demanded loudly as he marched threateningly toward Faisal.

The Saudi commander retained his customary poise, refusing to return Reg's hostile tone. As his soldiers stepped into Reg's path, he smiled easily and shook his head in disbelief. "I was absolutely correct, wasn't I? You are a difficult man to kill."

"Where were you?" Reg repeated fiercely. "We agreed we would work together."

"So we did," Faisal said, moving closer. "I ordered the air strike against the alien ship, just as we planned. But my pilots told me you never came outside."

"That's a lie. I fired a dozen flares into the air when we came out. Those jets were supposed to follow us to your camp in the hills. They didn't. But we made it into the hills without them, only to find you gone."

"A matter of priorities, Major. The city of At-Ta'if came under attack during the night. I was forced to relocate my forces before you returned. In doing so, praise be to Allah, I saved thousands, perhaps hundreds of thousands of lives." Faisal and the men around him realized that this was a lie. By the time his forces arrived at At-Ta'if, the aliens had already left to chase Reg and his team across the desert. But he was accustomed to taking credit for more than he actually accomplished. "In any case," he went on, "we were successful in removing the biological agents from the alien ship before my planes destroyed it completely. You have been very helpful. And what is more, you have brought Fadeela back to me without a scratch on her pretty face."

Before Faisal could protect himself, Reg swung at him and connected. The blow landed squarely on the tip of Faisal's chin and sent him sprawling to the ground. A pair of soldiers grabbed Reg and pinned his arms behind his back while others leveled their guns at Remi, Ali, and Tye.

Faisal picked himself off the ground, rubbing his jaw, and gave Reg a deadly stare. He paused for a moment deciding how best to hurt him before issuing a command to his men. "Take the girl inside and wait for me." A pair of soldiers each grabbed one of Fadeela's arms and forced her toward the terminal building. Held at gunpoint, Ali and the others were powerless to stop them.

Faisal moved uncomfortably close to Reg, until they were practically nose to nose. "When my pilots first told me you'd come out of the ship alive," he hissed, "I was disappointed. But now I see that this way is better. Not only will I be able to enjoy the sweet fruit of this woman, but I will also have the pleasure of attending your public execution." Reg struggled to free his arms for another swing, but the soldiers held them fast. Instead, Faisal delivered a crushing punch that connected with Reg's rib cage. He was preparing to hit him again when the loudspeakers mounted to the exterior of the terminal building came to life and began blaring out a recorded conversation.

REG: "I repeat: Saudi commander, you have broken formation. You are currently running in the wrong direction."

FAISAL: "Do not interfere! . . . I'm afraid you are mistaken, major. You must be watching the wrong plane."

REG: "Negative, Faisal. I'm directly above you. Close enough to read your wing markings. You are running away from the engagement."

FAISAL: "Stay out of this, Cummins! I am not running. I am . . . I am positioning myself to observe the attack."

REG: "Admit it, Faisal, you're saving yourself because you know what's going to happen to those men. Order them to it break off."

FAISAL: "Damn you, Cummins, stay quiet! Cooperate with me and you will be rewarded."

REG: "And if I don't?"

FAISAL: "Then I will personally shoot you out of the sky."

REG: "I wouldn't advise it. You'd only be wasting another one of your king's planes."

FAISAL: "King Ibrahim is no longer a factor. The Saudi Air Force is now completely under my command and it is my will that—"

As Faisal listened, horrified, he forgot completely about punishing Reg and looked around desperately for the source of the embarrassing transmission. He soon spotted King Ibrahim staring at him sternly from the shadowy recesses of the royal helicopter. Brushing past Reg, Faisal ran to the helipad. "Stop this recording at once!" he shouted.

"Why should I?" the king asked.

Faisal stammered out an answer. "Because this is not . . . this was . . . you are exposing military secrets. You are . . . people may misunderstand."

"I don't understand," said the king, feigning confusion. "You said before the tape would prove Khalid Yamani's guilt and establish your bravery in the battle. This tape doesn't match the story you told everyone after the battle. In fact, it sounds as if you turned and ran."

Faisal glanced around helplessly at the loudspeakers, which continued to broadcast the sounds of the battle to the entire airport. "There is no need to continue playing the tape. I will explain everything," he told the king. "After all, you need me."

"How so?"

"I am the Saudi hero who saved Mecca!" he shouted. "Do you want to give the credit to a bunch of Western infidels and Jews? I can be very useful to you and your family. Without me, you will appear weak. As if you needed help from outside to protect the Holy City."

"I'm not so sure," said King Ibrahim, stroking his beard. "It seems to me Khalid Yamani acted quite bravely during the battle. Perhaps he will be accepted as our country's hero during the battle. But as I say, I'm not certain. That is why I am broadcasting the tape right now over several military frequencies to all parts of the country. This time, we can let the people decide who they consider their hero."

When Faisal learned that the entire nation was listening to the recording, he realized at once that he was finished. There would be no way to explain why he had flown away from that first bombing run, or why he had muscled the others out of the way to get the first shot for himself. It was all there on the tape, and he knew it. He backed away from the helicopter, then turned and ran toward a jeep that had been left unattended.

King Ibrahim made no move to stop him. Instead, he watched as Faisal jumped into the vehicle and drove away, burning with humiliation. A moment later, he picked up the handset on his radio and spoke to someone inside the terminal building. He ordered that Fadeela Yamani be found and brought outside again as soon as she was decently covered. Then he called to Reg.

"Major Cummins, come here please. We have not finished all of our business together. There is still the matter of your reward."

"Don't forget about your friends," Tye joked, as Reg began moving back to the royal helicopter.

Reg seemed in a great hurry to speak to the king. He hurried along for a few paces, then broke into a full run. It wasn't that he was eager to collect his reward; he was concerned about Fadeela. He informed the king that their chat would have to wait until he was positive Fadeela was safe. The old man laughed at his earnest concern and assured him he had already taken care of the matter. Then he invited Reg inside the helicopter, where the two men sat face-to-face for the next several minutes, negotiating. After some time, Mr. Yamani was called in to join them. The three of them were still talking when Fadeela reemerged from the terminal, escorted by a different set of soldiers. Somewhere, they had found a spare *abaya* and given it to her so she could cover herself. Reg happened to glance up from his conversation long enough to take in the strange sight of her: a battle-tested woman warrior wearing dusty combat fatigues beneath a long skein of black fabric that reached nearly to her ankles. Her boots, stained with oil and blood, protruded from below the cloth. She came striding out of the terminal in an unladylike fashion and joined Tye, Remi, and Ali. The three men pointed toward the helicopter, explaining the situation to her. When she learned what Reg and her father were discussing with the king, she put her hands on her hips and shook her veiled head back and forth to express her displeasure.

A few moments later, the three men stepped out of the helicopter and moved to join the others. Reg trailed along behind the two older men, who chatted amiably with each other as they doddered slowly across the landing pad, ignoring the last hour of the day's punishing heat. They smiled broadly, as if they were both pleased with the arrangement that had been hammered out. Reg's expression, on the other hand, gave no indication of how the negotiations had gone. When at last they reached the place where Fadeela and the others were waiting, the king's mood suddenly changed.

"I do not understand these Englishmen," he began loudly. "For his role in protecting our nation, I promised to give Major Cummins anything it was within my power to grant him. I offered him millions of dollars, my properties in Hawaii, one of my personal jets. But he insisted on asking for something else," he said, glancing toward Fadeela, "something that is not mine to give. The most I was able to do was to speak on his behalf to my old friend Karmal Yamani. Perhaps to save me from appearing ungenerous, Mr. Yamani has consented to the major's request." Then he turned to face the shrouded figure of Fadeela. "You must be quite an extraordinary young woman. The only thing he asks for is for you."

Fadeela's anger boiled over. "And you, the ruler of Saudi Arabia, custodian of the holy cities of Mecca and Medina, appear quite willing to oblige him. You give a Saudi woman to a Western man like you were handing over a cow." The king took a step backward, startled by the woman's outburst. He was trying to deliver the good news that she was going to get what she wanted, and was unprepared to face her wrath.

"I think you don't understand," King Ibrahim said.

"I understand that you men believe you can control me like a piece of property, trade me to one another like an old car. And in this case, you can't claim it is the will of Allah because he's not even a Muslim." Although her face was covered, Reg could feel Fadeela's green eyes staring at him like a pair of burning X-ray beams.

"She thinks I've asked to marry her," Reg said, explaining Fadeela's reaction.

"Haven't you?" she asked in a smaller voice.

Reg shook his head no.

"The very opposite," the king told her. "He has asked that you be given the power to choose your own husband. Accordingly, your engagement to Ghalil Faisal is officially canceled. Of course, if you still wish to marry Faisal, you may. Or anyone else for that matter."

"Is it true?" Fadeela asked her father.

He nodded that it was. "And if you wish to continue your education, either here or abroad, you are free to do so. I am not sure how many universities are left standing, but this time I will not interfere with your studies. It is up to you to decide."

"So, if I want to marry this man," Fadeela said, taking Remi by the arm, "I may do so without asking anyone's permission?" The king and her father nodded, but Remi warned her that his wife probably wouldn't like the idea. Fadeela, enjoying the idea of her new freedom, moved to Ali and took him by the arm. "Or this man?" Again, the answer was yes. Nodding, she turned, and as she began moving toward Reg, Tye couldn't resist clearing his throat ostentatiously.

"Aren't you forgetting someone?" he asked, pretending to be hurt.

"Forgive me." Fadeela laughed. She took hold of Tye's arm as she had with the other men, and asked, "Or this one?"

King Ibrahim and Mr. Yamani both made the same joke. "No, not that one!"

When Tye had recovered from his momentary heartbreak, Fadeela walked over and stood in front of Reg. "Thank you. This is a wonderful gift."

"It's the least I could do. After all, you gave me what I needed most: something worth fighting for."

"I'm smiling."

"I'm glad."

"But I hope you don't expect me to act like a foolish girl and ask you to marry me."

"That thought never crossed my mind, princess."

"Liar. But tell me, is it true you turned down all the riches King Ibrahim offered you?" When Reg said it was, Fadeela shook her head in disappointment. "You could have made the rest of your life relatively comfortable. Isn't that the goal of all Westerners? But now, I'm afraid you've made things difficult for yourself." Again, she shook her head sadly.

"I'd appreciate any advice you could give me on the subject," Reg said.

"Actually, I've already come up with a few ideas. Shall we walk?"

The two of them strolled away from the others, past the helicopter, and out into the late-afternoon sun. They walked up and down the apron of the nearest runway for a long while, making decisions about the future.

About the Author

This is STEPHEN MOLSTAD's sixth book for Centropolis Entertainment, where he heads the newly-formed Publishing Division. In addition to collaborating on the Hugo-nominated novelization of *StarGate*, he wrote the novelization of *Independence Day*, and a well-received prequel novel, *ID4: Silent Zone.* Since graduating from the University of California, Santa Cruz, he has spent his time traveling, playing pick-up basketball, and teaching English and drama. He invites your comments at molstad@centropolis.com.

STEVE ALTEN

MEG

APELLES PUBLISHING

Copyright ©2008 Steve Alten

ISBN: 978-1-59955-169-2

Library of Congress Control Number: 2005903669

Published in the United States by Apelles Publishing, an imprint of
Cedar Fort, Inc., 2373 W. 700 S., Springville, Utah 84663
Distributed by Cedar Fort, Inc., www.cedarfort.com

Submit all requests for reprinting to: Cedar Fort, Inc.,
2373 W. 700 S., Springville, Utah 84663, 1-800-SKYBOOK

Cover Design by Erik Hollander: www.erikART.com
Composition by Greenleaf Book Group LP

To personally contact the author or learn more about his novels,
go to www.SteveAlten.com

For more information on Adopt-an-Author, go to
www.AdoptAnAuthor.com

Printed in Canada

10 9 8 7 6

ACKNOWLEDGMENTS

I owe a lot to *MEG*, for it was this, my first novel, that began my career as a writer.

With this imprint, *MEG* has now been with three publishers and two Hollywood studios, a third (and final?) looming on the horizon. It's been a roller coaster ride, but I am grateful for the privilege of the journey.

First and foremost, my appreciation to my friend and producer, Belle Avery, president of Apelles Publishing, for optioning *MEG* as a book and movie, and for putting together the *MEG* production team. To Lloyd Levin, Larry Gordon, Shane Salerno, Jeff Katz, Ken Atchity, Jan De Bont, and especially my friend and fellow scribe Nick Nunziata . . . thank you. A special thanks to producers Mark Johnson and Roy Lee for their valued advice, and to Joel Corenman for his support.

Thanks to the Apelles team: Lyle Mortimer, Lee Nelson, Bryce Mortimer, Doug Johnston, and Heather Holm, and John Jesse at Jesse and Read. Good publicists are hard to find, and I have a great one in Lissy Peace at Blanco and Peace, as well as a terrific literary agent in Danny Baror at Baror International. To Joel McKuin at Colden, McKuin & Frankel, Rob Parker at Sianna, Carr, and O'Conner, and Matthew Snyder at CAA, thanks for being in my corner.

A very special thanks to my viral publicity guru, Trish Stevens, and her staff at Ascot Media Group (www.AscotMedia.com).

MEG is the cornerstone of the Adopt-An-Author program, a non-profit organization that encourages teens to read. To my friend and valued assistant, Leisa Coffman, and to the tireless Barbara Becker . . . I could not do it without you. And to the brilliant Erik Hollander, your covers continue to amaze me.

Finally, to my parents for all they have done and continue to do; to my wife, Kim, and to my children . . . you are my light. And to all the loyal MEGheads out there . . . keep the faith!

—Steve Alten, Ed.D.
March 4, 2008

To personally contact the author, send an email to
Meg82159@aol.com

To receive free monthly newsletters, go to www.
SteveAlten.com and click on "FREE UPDATES."

To learn more about the Adopt-An-Author program, go to www.AdoptAnAuthor.com.

This novel is dedicated to my father,

Lawrence Alten

Thanks, Dad . . .

NOVELS BY STEVE ALTEN

MEG Series
MEG: A Novel of Deep Terror (Tsunami Books)
The TRENCH (Pinnacle)
MEG: Primal Waters (Tor/Forge)
      coming in May 2009
MEG: Hell's Aquarium (Apelles Publishing)

DOMAIN Trilogy
DOMAIN (Tor/Forge)
RESURRECTION (Tor/Forge)
      coming soon . . .
PHOBOS (Apelles Publishing)

GOLIATH (Tor/Forge)
      coming soon . . .
SORCERESS

The LOCH (Apelles Publishing)

The SHELL GAME (Sweetwater Books)

For more information, or to receive monthly
newsletters go to www.SteveAlten.com

MEGALODON

Late Jurassic—Early Cretaceous Period
The Coast of the Asiamerica-Northern Landmass
(Pacific Ocean)

From the moment the early morning fog had begun to lift, they sensed they were being watched. The herd of Shantungosaurus had been grazing along the misty shoreline all morning. Measuring more than forty feet from their duck-billed heads to the end of their tails, these reptiles, the largest of the hadrosaurs, gorged themselves on the abundant supply of kelp and seaweed that continued to wash up along the shoreline with the incoming tide. Every few moments, the hadrosaurs raised their heads like a herd of nervous deer, listening to the noises of the nearby forest. They watched the dark trees and thick vegetation for movement, ready to run at the first sign of approach.

Across the beach, hidden among the tall trees and thick undergrowth, a pair of red reptilian eyes followed the herd. The Tyrannosaurus rex, largest and most lethal of all terrestrial carnivores, towered twenty-two feet above the forest floor. Saliva oozed from the big male's mouth; its muscles quivered with adrenaline as it focused on two duckbills venturing out into the shallows, isolating themselves from the herd.

With a blood-curdling roar, the killer crashed from the trees, its eight tons pounding the sand and shaking the earth with every step. The duckbills momentarily

froze, then rose on their hind legs and scattered in both directions along the beach.

The two hadrosaurs grazing in the surf saw the carnivore closing in on them, its jaws wide, fangs bared, its bone-chilling trumpet drowning the crash of the surf. Trapped, the pair turned and plunged into deeper water to escape. They strained their long necks forward and began to swim, their legs churning to keep their heads above water.

Driven by hunger, T. rex crashed through the surf after them. Far from buoyant, the killer waded into deeper waters, snapping its jaws, straining to shorten the distance. But as it neared its prey, the T. rex's clawed feet sank deep into the muddy sea floor, its weight driving it into the mire.

The hadrosaurs paddled in thirty feet of water, safe for the moment. But having escaped one predator, they now faced another.

The six-foot gray dorsal fin rose slowly from the sea, its unseen girth gliding silently across their path. If the T. rex was the most terrifying creature ever to walk the earth, then *Carcharodon megalodon* was easily lord and master of the sea. Sixty feet from its conical snout to the tip of its half-moon-shaped caudal fin, the shark moved effortlessly through its liquid domain, circling its outmatched prey. It could feel the racing heartbeats of the hadrosaurs and the heavier thumpa, thumpa of the T. rex, its ampullae of Lorenzini tuned in to the electrical impulses generated by the pounding organs. A line of neuro-senses along its flank registered each

unique vibration in the water, while its directional nostrils tasted the scent of sweat and urine excreted from its floundering meal-to-be.

The pair of hadrosaurs were paralyzed in fear, their eyes following the unseen creature's sheer moving mass, which circled closer, creating a current of water that lifted and dragged the two reptiles into deeper waters. The sudden change panicked the duckbills, who quickly reversed direction, heading back toward the beach. They would take their chances with the Tyrannosaurus.

Thrashing and paddling frantically, they moved back into the shallows, feeling the mud swirling beneath their feet. T. rex, waiting in water up to its burly chest, let out a thundering growl, but could not advance, the predator struggling to keep from sinking farther into the soft sea floor.

The duckbills neared the reptile's snapping jaws, then suddenly broke formation, swimming in separate directions and passing within a few harrowing feet of the frustrated hunter. The T. rex lunged, snapping its terrible jaws, howling in rage at its fleeing prey. The duckbills never stopped, bounding through the smaller waves until they staggered onto the beach and collapsed on the warm sand, too exhausted to move.

Still sinking, the Tyrannosaurus had to struggle to keep its huge head only a few feet above water. Insane with rage, it lashed its tail wildly in an attempt to free one of its hind legs. Then, all at once, it stopped struggling and stared out to sea.

From the dark waters, a great dorsal fin was approaching, slicing through the fog.

The T. rex cocked its head and stood perfectly still, instincts telling it that it had wandered into the domain of a superior hunter. For the first and last time in its life, the Tyrannosaurus registered the acidic taste of fear.

The Tyrannosaurus felt the tug of current caused by thirty tons of circling mass. Its red eyes followed the gray dorsal fin until it finally disappeared beneath the murky waters.

T. rex growled quietly, searching through the haze. Leaning forward, it managed to free one of its thickly-muscled hind legs, then quickly freed the other.

On the beach, the hadrosaurs took notice and backed away—

—as the towering dorsal fin rose again from the mist, this time racing directly for the T. rex!

The reptile roared, accepting the challenge, its jaws snapping in anger.

The wake kept coming, the dorsal fin rising higher . . . higher, while underwater, the unseen assailant's head rotated slightly, its jaws hyperextending seconds before it slammed into the T. rex's soft midsection like a freight train striking a disabled SUV.

T. rex slammed backward through the ocean, its breath blasting out of its crushed lungs, an eruption of blood spewing from its open mouth seconds before its head disappeared beneath the waves. A moment later the dinosaur surfaced again, drowning in its own blood

as its rib cage crumbled within the powerful jaws of its still-unseen killer, its gushing innards blocking its esophagus, strangling it to death.

Seconds later, the once-mighty land dweller vanished beneath a swirling pool of scarlet sea.

The hadrosaurs had watched the scene unfold, and were now whimpering and waiting, their bladders releasing in fear. Long moments passed, the sea remaining silent. The spell of the attack broken, the duckbills abandoned the beach, lumbering toward the trees to rejoin their herd.

An explosion of ocean sent their heads turning as the sixty-foot shark burst from the water, its enormous head and muscular upper torso quivering as it fought to remain suspended above the waves, the broken remains of its prey grasped within its terrible jaws. Then, in an incredible display of raw power, the Meg shook the reptile from side to side, allowing its massive rows of seven-inch serrated teeth ripped through gristle and bone, the action spraying pink froths and gouts of gore in every direction.

Finally *Carcharodon megalodon* crashed back into the sea, sending a great swell of water high into the morning air.

No other scavengers approached the Meg as it fed in the shallows. The predatory fish had no mate to share its kill with, no young to feed. A rogue hunter, territorial by nature, the Meg mated out of instinct and killed its young when it could, for the only challenge to its reign came from its own kind. An evolutionary marvel that

had evolved over hundreds of millions of years, it would adapt and survive the natural catastrophes and climatic changes that caused the mass extinctions of the giant reptiles and countless prehistoric mammals. And while Megalodon's own numbers would eventually dwindle, some members of its species would manage to survive, isolated from the world of man in the perpetual darkness of the unexplored ocean depths . . .

THE PROFESSOR

"It was the ancient predecessor of our modern-day great white shark, only it was fifty to seventy-five feet in length, weighing close to seventy thousand pounds. Can you visualize that?"

Professor Jonas Taylor looked at his audience of just more than six hundred and paused for effect. "I find it hard to imagine myself sometimes, but we know for a fact this incredible monster did exist. Its head alone was probably as large as a Dodge Ram pickup. Its jaws could have engulfed and swallowed a dozen grown men whole. And I haven't even mentioned the teeth: razor-sharp, seven to eight inches long, each possessing the serrated edges of a stainless-steel steak knife."

The thirty-nine-year-old paleontologist knew he had his audience's attention, despite the fact that it had been years since his last public speaking engagement. Lecturing in front of a nearly sold-out crowd was not something Jonas had anticipated. He knew his theories were controversial, that there were as many critics in the audience as there were supporters. Still . . . just to be heard, to feel important again . . .

He loosened his collar and took a slow, deep breath, forcing himself to relax.

"Next slide, please. Ah, here we have an artist's rendition of a six-foot diver as compared with a sixteen-foot great white and our sixty-foot Megalodon. I think this gives you a fairly good idea why scientists refer to the species as the king of all predators."

Jonas reached for his bottle of water on the wooden podium, took a sip. "Fossilized Megalodon teeth found around the world tell us the species dominated the oceans for tens of millions of years, perhaps even longer. Who knows how old unfound Meg teeth buried in the depths might be? The big question is—why did the species die off at all. We know sharks survived the cataclysmic events that occurred about sixty-five and forty-five million years ago, events that wiped out most land animals and prehistoric species of fish. We know Megalodon's major food source—whales—was still quite abundant. In fact, we have Megalodon teeth that date back only a hundred thousand years. From a geological perspective, that's a tick of the clock, one that indicates our two species no doubt shared the planet at the same time, Homo sapiens dominating the land, Megalodon the sea. So, what happened?"

Jonas paused for effect, casually shuffling his cheat sheets on the wooden podium. "There it is, people, one of the great mysteries of the paleo-world. Of course, theories abound. Some so-called experts believe the staple of Megalodon's diet had once been large, slow-moving fish, and that the sharks couldn't adapt to the smaller, swifter species that exist today. Another theory is that falling ocean temperatures contributed to the creatures' demise."

An elderly man raised his hand emphatically from his seat in the first row, obviously wanting to be heard. Jonas recognized him, a former colleague at Scripps. A former critic.

"Professor Taylor, I think we'd like to hear your theory as to the disappearance of *Carcharodon megalodon*."

Murmurs of approval followed. Jonas loosened his collar a bit more. He rarely wore suits, and this eighteen-year-old wool itched like hell.

"Those of you who know me or follow my work are aware of how my opinions often differ from those of most paleobiologists. Many in my field spend a great deal of time theorizing why a particular species no longer exists. I prefer to focus my energies on how a seemingly extinct species might still exist."

The elderly professor stood, readying his verbal assault. "Sir, are you saying you think *Carcharodon megalodon* may still be roaming the oceans?"

Jonas waited for quiet. "Not necessarily, Professor, I'm simply pointing out that, as scientists, we tend to take a rather short-sighted 'if we haven't seen it, it doesn't exist anymore' approach when it comes to declaring certain marine animals extinct. For instance, it wasn't long ago that scientists believed the coelacanth, a species of lobe-finned fish that thrived three hundred million years ago, had gone extinct over the last seventy million years. That so-called fact held up until 1938, when a fisherman hauled a living coelacanth out of the deep ocean waters off South Africa. Now scientists routinely observe these 'living fossils' in their natural habitat."

The elderly professor stood up again amid murmurs from the crowd.

"Professor Taylor, we're all familiar with the discovery of the coelacanth, but there's a big difference between a five-foot bottom-feeder and a sixty-foot predator!"

Jonas checked his watch, realizing he was running behind schedule. "Yes, I agree. My point was simply that I prefer to investigate the possibilities of a species' survival rather than add to the unproven conjecture regarding extinction among marine dwellers. Somehow, the scientific world has taken an 'it's dead until it shows itself' approach, and that simply doesn't work when it comes to fish."

"Then, again, sir, I ask for your opinion regarding Megalodon."

More murmurs.

Jonas wiped his brow; Maggie was going to kill him. "Okay, here it is: First, I disagree entirely with the theory regarding Megalodon being unable to catch quicker prey. We've learned the conical tail fin of the great white, the modern-day cousin of the Megalodon, is the most efficient design for propelling a body through water. As I've already stated, we know Megs existed as recently as a hundred thousand years ago. Then, as now, the predator would have had an abundant supply of slower-moving whales to feed upon.

"I do, however, agree that diminishing ocean temperatures would have affected these creatures, specifically their young, which would be more vulnerable to colder water. May I have the next slide, please? Sorry, one more."

A slide showing a series of maps of the changing planet over a three-hundred-million-year period appeared on the screen above his head. "As we can see, Earth's continental masses have shifted considerably over time." Jonas pointed to the center diagram. "This is how our planet looked about forty million years ago, during the Eocene. As we can see, the landmass that would become Antarctica separated from South America at about this time and drifted over the South Pole. When the continents shifted, they disrupted the transport of poleward oceanic heat, essentially replacing the heat-retaining water with heat-losing land. As the cooling progressed, the land accumulated snow and ice, which further lowered global temperatures and sea levels. As many of you know, the most important factor controlling the geographical distribution of a marine species is ocean temperature.

"Now, as the water temperatures dropped, the warmer tropical currents became top-heavy with salt and began running much deeper. Unlike air, salinity determines which currents run deeper, not temperature. In this example, the ocean temperatures were cooler along the shallower surface waters, with a tropical current, laden heavy with salt, running much deeper.

"Based on the locations of fossilized Megalodon teeth found in the rivers of South Carolina and other locations around the world, we know the sharks frequented shorelines, a fact most likely due to pregnant whales' preference for birthing their young in shallow-water lagoons. That's not to say the Megs

didn't hunt in the open oceans. It simply means we have a tendency to draw conclusions based on the monsters behavior in the shallows.

"Now, about two million years ago, our planet's inhabitants had to deal with the effects of Earth's last major ice age. As you can see from this diagram, the deeper tropical currents that had provided a refuge for many marine species were suddenly cut off. As a result, a host of prehistoric fish, including generations of Megalodon young, died off in great numbers, unable to adapt to the extreme drops in oceanic temperatures."

The elderly professor called out from his seat. "So then, Taylor, you do believe that Megalodon became extinct as a result of climatic changes." The older man smiled, satisfied with himself.

"A decimated population doesn't necessarily equate to extinction. Remember, I said I prefer to theorize on how a species might still exist. About fifteen years ago, I was part of a scientific team that first studied deep-sea trenches. Deep-sea trenches form the hadal zone, an area of the Pacific Ocean about which scientists know virtually nothing. Deep-sea trenches form along the boundaries of two oceanic plates, where one plate melts back or subducts into the earth. Prior to 1977, scientists believed the abyss was actually barren; after all, how could life exist without light, or photosynthesis? When we actually bothered to take a look, we discovered hydrothermal vents—miniature volcanoes of life-giving chemicals—spewing mineral-rich waters at temperatures that often exceeded seven

hundred degrees Fahrenheit. At some point, these minerals level off about a half-mile or so above the sea floor, creating a layer of insulation that keeps in the heat, forming what we now call a hydrothermal plume. In essence, you have an anomaly of nature, a tropical current of water—an oasis of life, if you will—running along the very bottom of the ocean in complete darkness. And these hydrothermal vents don't just spew hot water and minerals, they support life forms never before imagined . . . life forms whose food chain relies on chemosynthesis—chemicals in the water."

A middle-aged woman stood and asked excitedly, "Did you discover a Megalodon down there?"

Jonas forced a smile while he waited for the crowd's laughter to subside. "No, ma'am. But I'll show you something that was discovered in the abyss more than one hundred years ago that might be of interest." Jonas pulled out a glass case, roughly twice the size of a shoe box, from a shelf beneath the podium. "This is a fossilized tooth of *Carcharodon megalodon*. Scuba divers and beachcombers have turned up fossilized teeth like this by the thousands. Some are tens of millions of years old. This particular specimen is special because it's not very old. It was recovered in 1873 by the world's first true oceanic exploration vessel, the British HMS *Challenger*. Can you see these manganese nodules?" Jonas pointed to the black encrustations on the tooth. "Recent analysis of these manganese layers indicated the tooth's owner had been alive during the late Pleistocene or early Holocene period. In other

words, this tooth is a mere ten thousand years old, and it was dredged from the deepest point on our planet, the Mariana Trench's Challenger Deep."

The crowd erupted.

"Professor! Professor Taylor!" All eyes turned to an Asian-American woman standing in the back of the auditorium. Jonas stared at her, caught off guard by her beauty. Somehow she looked familiar.

"Yes, go ahead," said Jonas, motioning for the audience to be quiet.

"Professor, are you saying that Megalodon may still exist in the depths of the Mariana Trench?" Silence took the room. It was the question the audience wanted answered.

"Theoretically, if members of the Megalodon species inhabited the waters of the Mariana Trench two million years ago, waters that maintain deep tropical plumes created and nourished by hydrothermal vents, then it's not beyond the realm of possibility that a branch of the species might have survived. The existence of this ten-thousand-year-old fossil certainly justifies the possibilities."

"What nonsense!" Mike "the Turk" Turzman, a popular local radio talk show host specializing in cryptozoology stood in the aisle, shaking his head. "There are no hydrothermal vents in the Mariana Trench. None!"

Jonas shook his head. He had heard excerpts of the Turk's recent interview with Richard Ellis, a painter and self-proclaimed expert on all things nautical who

had lambasted Taylor's research. "Just for the record, Mr. Turzman, recently the Ocean Exploration Ring of Fire Expedition surveyed more than fifty volcanoes along the Mariana Arc. Ten of these volcanoes had active hydrothermal systems. A follow-up expedition a year later found these hydrothermal systems were quite different from those found along the mid-Atlantic Ocean ridges, harboring all sorts of exotic life forms. So maybe the next time one of your guests decides to publicly critique my research over the airwaves, you'll do some fact checking of your own!"

A smattering of applause escorted "the Turk" back to his seat.

"Professor!" A middle-aged man with a young son sitting next to him raised his hand. "If these monsters still exist today, why haven't we seen them?"

"A good question," Jonas said, pausing as a beautiful blonde woman, tan and in her early thirties, strutted down the center aisle. Her classic topaz evening gown hugged a flawless figure, exposing athletic legs. Her male escort, also in his thirties, trailed behind, his long, dark hair slicked back into a tight ponytail, which contrasted with his conservative tuxedo. The pair took the two empty seats reserved in the front row.

Jonas composed himself, waiting for his wife and friend to be seated.

"Sorry. You asked why we haven't actually seen a Megalodon, assuming members of the species still exist. First, sharks that inhabit the midwaters and deepest realms of the ocean have no physical need to surface

and flash us a telltale dorsal fin. Second, assuming a population of Megalodon did inhabit the waters of the Mariana Trench, it would have to be hard pressed to abandon that tropical bottom layer and its only known food source. The Challenger Deep is seven miles down. The water temperature above the warm layer is near freezing. The Meg might venture into that cold layer, ascending a mile or so at the most, but at some point, it would head back down to the warm layer again.

"Last, sharks are the one species that don't cooperate when it comes to leaving behind evidence they existed, especially those inhabiting the abyss. Unlike mammals, sharks do not float to the surface when they die, as their bodies are inherently heavier than seawater and contain no air sacs. Their skeletons are composed entirely of cartilage, so unlike dinosaurs and many species of bony fishes, there are no Megalodon bones to leave behind, only their gruesome, fossilized teeth."

Jonas caught Maggie's eye, her expression burning into his skull. "One . . . uh, other thing about the Mariana Trench. Man has only ventured down to the bottom twice, both expeditions occurring in 1960 and both times in bathyscaphes, essentially steel balls, hardly useful for exploration. In other words, we simply went straight down and back up again. The reality is, we've never come close to exploring the trench. In fact, we know more about distant galaxies than we do, a 1,550-mile-long, 40-mile-wide isolated section of the Pacific Ocean, seven miles down."

Jonas looked at Maggie and shrugged. She stood, pointing to her watch.

"You'll have to excuse me, ladies and gentlemen. This lecture has lasted a bit longer than expected and I'm due—"

"Excuse me, Taylor, one important question." It was the Asian-American woman again. She seemed perturbed. "Before you began studying these Megalodons, your career was focused entirely on piloting deep-sea submersibles. I'd like to know why, at the peak of your career, you suddenly quit."

Jonas was taken aback by the directness of the question. "First, I didn't quit, I retired. Second, my reasons are my own. Next question?" He searched the audience for another raised hand.

"Pretty young to retire, weren't you?" She was standing now, approaching from the center aisle. "Or maybe it was something else? You haven't been in a submersible for what? Seven years? Did you lose your nerve, Professor? Inquiring minds want to know."

The audience chuckled. No one was leaving—this was getting good.

Jonas felt trickles of sweat drip from his armpits. "What's your name, miss?"

"Tanaka. Terry Tanaka. I believe you know my father, Masao, CEO of the Tanaka Oceanographic Institute."

"Tanaka, of course. In fact, I think you and I met several years ago on a lecture circuit."

"That's right."

"Well, Terry Tanaka, since your inquiring mind insists on violating my privacy, let's just say, after a dozen years with the navy, I felt it was time to stop risking my life piloting deep-sea submersibles and join the academic circuit, researching prehistoric species like the Megalodon." Jonas collected his notes. "Now, if there are no other questions . . ."

"Dr. Taylor!" A balding man in his fifties, with tiny wire-rimmed glasses stood in the third row. He had bushy Andy Rooney-like elfin eyebrows and a tight, nervous grin. "Please, sir, one last question, if I may. As you mentioned, the two manned expeditions to the Mariana Trench occurred in 1960. But, Professor, isn't it true that there have been more recent descents into the Challenger Deep?"

Jonas stared at the man, red warning flags fluttering in his head. "I'm sorry?"

"Come now, Professor, you made several dives there yourself."

Jonas was silent. The audience began to murmur.

The man's bushy eyebrows raised, lifting his glasses. "Back in 1989, Professor. While you were still doing work for the navy?"

"I'm . . . not sure I understand." Jonas glanced at his wife like a condemned man.

Maggie looked away.

"You are Professor Jonas Taylor, aren't you?" The man smiled smugly as the audience broke into light laughter.

"Look, pal, I think you have your facts wrong, and I'm really running late. Drop me an e-mail or something. Oh . . . uh, thank you all for attending."

A smattering of applause trickled out amid murmurs from the crowd as Jonas Taylor stepped down from the podium. He was quickly approached by students with questions, scientists with theories of their own, and old colleagues desperate to say hello before he left. Jonas shook as many hands as he could, signed a few books, then apologized again for having to run.

The ponytailed man in the tuxedo squeezed his head through the swarming crowd. "Hey, J.T., the car's parked outside. Maggie says we need to leave now, bro."

Jonas nodded, finished signing a book for an admiring student, then hurried to the exit at the back of the auditorium where his wife was tapping her freshly pedicured toes, waiting impatiently.

As he reached the door, Jonas caught a glimpse of Terry Tanaka, looking at him from behind a sea of people. Her almond eyes seemed to burn into his as she mouthed the words, "We need to talk."

Jonas held up his watch and shrugged. He'd had enough of the verbal assaults for one night.

As if in response, his wife yelled through the exit door, "Jonas, let's go! Now!"

GOLDEN EAGLE

The limousine raced along the Coronado peninsula. Bud Harris was in back with Maggie, concluding a business transaction on his cell phone. Jonas sat across the aisle from Maggie, his back to the driver. He watched Bud absentmindedly finger his ponytail like a schoolgirl, then glanced over at Maggie. His wife of ten years looked very much at home on the wide leather seat, her slender legs crossed, a glass of champagne balanced in her fingertips. *She's grown used to his money*, Jonas thought. He allowed his mind to wander, imagining her in a bikini, tanning herself on Bud's yacht.

"You used to be afraid of the sun," he tossed out.

"What?"

"Your tan. You used to say you were afraid of skin cancer."

She stared at him. "I never said that. And it looks good on camera."

"What about your sister's melanoma—"

"Don't start with me, Jonas. I'm not in the mood. This is probably the biggest night of my career, and I had to practically drag you out of that lecture hall. You've known about this dinner for a month, and look at you—why the hell are you wearing that piece-of-shit suit? I should have tossed that in the Goodwill bin years ago."

"Hey, lighten up. This was my first time back on the lecture circuit in over two years, and you come prancing down the aisle like Madonna—"

"Whoa, guys, time-out!" Bud closed the cell phone. "Everybody take a breath and let's all just calm down. Maggie, this was a big night for Jonas too, maybe we should have just waited in the limo."

"A big night? Are you serious? Bud, do you know how long I've waited for this opportunity, how hard I had to work while I watched my husband flush his career down the toilet? Do you know how many times we've had to refinance the house, live off credit cards, all because Professor Jonas here insisted on studying dead animals for a living? Now it's my turn, and if he doesn't want to be here, that's fine by me. Let *him* wait in the limo. You'll escort me tonight."

"Oh, no, keep me out of this," said Bud.

Maggie frowned and looked out the window, the tension hanging in the air. After a few long minutes, Bud broke the silence. "Hey, uh, I spoke with Henderson. He thinks you're a shoo-in for the award. This really could be the turning point in your career, Maggie, assuming you win."

Maggie turned to face him, managing to avoid looking at her husband.

"I'll win," she said defiantly. "I know I'll win. Now pour me another drink."

Bud grinned, filled Maggie's glass, then offered the bottle to Jonas.

Jonas shook his head and sat back in his seat, staring absently out the window at the passing scenery, wondering who the blonde stranger was seated across from him.

Jonas Taylor had met Maggie Cobbs eleven years earlier in Massachusetts during his deep-sea pilot training at the Woods Hole Oceanographic Institute. Maggie had been in her senior year at Boston University, majoring in journalism. The petite blonde had at one time vigorously pursued a modeling career, but lacked the required height. Upon entering college, she had reset her sights on making it as a broadcast journalist.

Maggie had read about Jonas Taylor and his adventures aboard the *Alvin* submersible. She knew the former college football star was a celebrity in his own right and found him physically attractive. Under the guise of doing an article for the university press, she approached the naval commander for an exclusive interview.

Jonas Taylor was amazed that anyone like Maggie would be interested in deep-sea diving, or his own interests. His career had left him little time for a social life, and when the beautiful blonde showed signs of flirting, Jonas asked her out on a date. They hit it off almost immediately, and Jonas invited Maggie to the Galapagos Islands on spring break. She accompanied him on his last dive in the *Alvin* into the Galapagos Trench, and took up scuba at his urging.

Maggie was impressed by the influence Jonas wielded among his navy peers, and loved the excitement and adventure associated with ocean exploration. Ten months later they married and moved to California, where Jonas was preparing for a top-secret naval mission in the western Pacific.

For the small-town girl from New Jersey, California was the land of opportunity. She had always chased fame and the celebrity life, and quickly hired an agent to full-court press her pursuit of a career in the media. With Jonas's help, she was hired as a weekend correspondent at an ABC flagship station in San Diego.

And then disaster struck. For six months Jonas had been training to pilot a new deep-sea submersible. The target—the Mariana Trench. On his third dive in thirty-five thousand feet of water, the veteran pilot had panicked, surfacing the sub too quickly. Pipes had burst, causing pressurization problems that led to the deaths of the two naval scientists onboard. Jonas had survived—barely—only to learn his commanding officer blamed him for the incident. The official report called it "aberrations of the deep," and the event destroyed Jonas's career in the navy. Worse, it permanently scarred his psyche.

Maggie watched, helpless, as her husband floundered with bouts of depression. Months of psychiatric sessions followed—sessions that eventually refocused the once goal-oriented naval officer on another field—paleobiology. Jonas would earn his doctorate at

Scripps, while penning several books on the subject of extinction among deep-water species.

Without Jonas's naval income, Maggie's lifestyle quickly changed. The San Diego position turned out to be a dead-end job, and her life was suddenly thrust into that of the mundane.

Then, by chance, Jonas ran into Bud Harris, his former teammate at Penn State University. Harris, thirty at the time, had recently inherited his father's shipping business in San Diego. He and Jonas took in a few football games, but the paleobiologist was constantly doing research, leaving Maggie to entertain her husband's new best friend.

Bud used his father's connections to get Maggie part-time work as a writer for the *San Diego Register*. In turn, Maggie convinced her editor that Bud's shipping business would make an interesting article for the Sunday magazine. It was the excuse she needed to follow Bud around the harbor, with trips to his dock facilities in Long Beach, San Francisco, and Honolulu. She interviewed him on his yacht, sat in on board meetings, took a ride on his hovercraft, even spent afternoons learning how to sail.

The article she wrote became the *Register*'s cover story and made a local celebrity of the wild and woolly millionaire; his charter business boomed. Not one to forget a favor, Bud helped Maggie secure a weekend anchor spot with a local television station. Fred Henderson, the station manager, was a yachting partner of Bud's. Maggie started by doing two-minute

fillers for the ten o'clock news, but it wasn't long before she maneuvered herself into a staff position, producing weekly features on California and the West Coast. While Jonas floundered as an author, Maggie Taylor was becoming a local celebrity.

Bud climbed out of the limo, extending a hand to Maggie. "Maybe I ought to get an award. Whaddya think, Maggie? Executive producer?"

"Not on your life," Maggie replied, handing her glass to the chauffeur. The alcohol had settled her down a bit. She smiled at Bud as they ascended the stairs of the Hotel del Coronado, Jonas lagging behind. "If they start giving you awards, there won't be any left for me."

They passed through the main entrance beneath a gold banner welcoming "The 15th Annual San Diego MEDIA Awards." Three enormous crystal chandeliers hung from the vaulted wooden ceiling of the Silver Strand Ballroom. A band played softly in the corner while well-heeled guests picked at hors d'oeuvres and sipped drinks, wandering among tables draped with white-and-gold tablecloths. Dinner would soon be served.

Jonas suddenly felt underdressed. Maggie had told him of the affair a month ago but had never mentioned it was black tie.

He recognized a few television people in the crowd, provincial stars from the local news. Harold Ray, the fifty-four-year-old co-anchor of Channel 9 Action News at Ten, smiled broadly as he said hello to Maggie.

Ray had helped secure network funding for Maggie's special about the effects of offshore oil drilling on whale migrations along the California coast, and now the piece was one of three competing for top honors in the "Environmental Issues Documentary" category.

"You just may take home the Eagle tonight, Maggs, Ray said, his eyes wandering toward her tantalizing cleavage.

"What makes you so sure?" she cooed back.

"For one thing, I'm married to one of the judges!" Harold said, laughing. Eyeing Bud's ponytail, he asked, "And this must be Jonas. Harold Ray—"

"Bud Harris, friend of the family," Bud replied, shaking his hand.

"Bud's my . . . executive producer," Maggie said, smiling. She glanced at Jonas. "This is Jonas."

"Sorry, big guy, honest mistake. Say, didn't we do a piece on you a couple years ago? Something about dinosaur bones in the Salton Sea?"

"You may have. There were a lot of newspeople out there. It was an unusual find—"

"Excuse me, Jonas," Maggie interrupted, "I'm just dying for a drink. Would you mind?"

Bud pointed a finger in the air. "Gin and tonic for me, J.T."

Jonas looked at Harold Ray.

"Nothing for me, Doc, I'm a presenter tonight. One more drink and I'll start making the news instead of reporting it."

Jonas forced a polite smile, then made his escape to the bar. The air was humid in the windowless ballroom, and Jonas's wool jacket felt prickly and hot. He asked for a beer, a glass of champagne, and a gin and tonic. The bartender pulled a bottle of Carta Blanca out of the ice. Jonas cooled his forehead with it and took a long draft.

He looked back at Maggie, who was still laughing with Bud and Harold.

"Another beer, sir?" The drinks were ready. Jonas looked at his bottle, suddenly realizing he had emptied it. "Give me one of those," he said, pointing at the gin.

"Me too," a voice said behind him. "With a lime."

Jonas turned. It was the balding man with the bushy eyebrows. He looked at Jonas, peering over his wire-rimmed bifocals with the same tight grin on his face. "Funny coincidence, meeting you here, Doc."

Jonas regarded him suspiciously. "Did you follow me here?"

"Hell no," the man replied, scooping up a handful of almonds from the bar. He gestured vaguely at the room. "I'm in the media."

The bartender handed Jonas his drink. "You here for an award?" Jonas asked skeptically.

"No, just an observer." He put out his hand. "David Adashek. *Science Journal*."

Jonas shook his hand.

"I enjoyed your lecture tremendously. Fascinating stuff, about the Mega . . . What did you call it?"

Jonas sipped his drink, eyeing the reporter. "What is it you want?"

The man finished a mouthful of almonds, washing it down with a swig of his drink. "My sources tell me you made a series of dives for the navy in the Mariana Trench."

"Your sources tell you it was top secret?"

"So I heard. I also heard the navy was looking for a site to bury radioactive waste. That's a story I think my editors would have a great deal of interest in."

"Then you should pursue it, but not with me."

"Oh, I already have a source, a good one, too. Former navy guy, just like you." Adashek slipped another almond into his mouth, chewing it noisily like a stick of gum. "Funny thing, though. I interviewed the fellow about it four years ago. Couldn't get a word out of him. Then last week he calls out of the blue, says if I want to know what happened I ought to talk to you . . . Did I say something wrong, Doc?"

Jonas's brown eyes blazed at the shorter man. "Enjoy your dinner." He turned, walking back toward his table.

Adashek bit his lip, eyeing Jonas narrowly.

"Another drink, sir?" the bartender asked.

"Make it a double," Adashek said sharply, scooping up a handful of nuts.

From the other side of the room, a pair of dark almond eyes followed Jonas Taylor as he made his way across the ballroom, watching as he took a seat next to the blonde.

Four hours and a half-dozen drinks later, Jonas stared at the Golden Eagle now perched on the white tablecloth, a TV camera clutched in its claws. Maggie's whale film had beat out a Discovery Channel project on the Farallon Islands and a Greenpeace documentary on the Japanese whaling industry. His wife's acceptance speech had been largely a passionate "save the whales" plea. Her concern for the cetaceans' fate had inspired her to make the film, so she said. Jonas had wondered if he was the only one in the room who didn't believe a word she was saying.

Bud had passed out cigars. Harold Ray made a toast. Fred Henderson stopped by to offer his congratulations and say if he wasn't careful Maggie would get snapped up by a major station in Los Angeles. Maggie feigned disinterest. Jonas knew she'd heard the rumors . . . she had started many of them herself.

They were all dancing now. Maggie had taken Bud's hand and led him onto the floor, knowing Jonas wouldn't object. How could he? He didn't like to dance.

Jonas sat alone at the table, chewing the ice from his glass and trying to remember how many gins he'd downed in the last few hours. He felt tired, had a slight headache, and all signs pointed to a long evening still ahead. He got up and walked to the bar.

Harold Ray was there, picking up a bottle of wine and a pair of glasses.

"So how was Baja, Professor?"

Jonas wondered if the man was drunk. "Baja?"

"The cruise."

"What cruise?" He handed his glass to the bartender, nodded for a refill.

Ray laughed. "I warned her three days was no vacation. Look at you, you've already forgotten."

"Baja? You mean . . . last week." Then it hit him. The trip to San Francisco. The tan. *Bud Harris.*

"Too many margaritas, Professor?"

Jonas stared for a long moment at the glass in his hand, then scanned the dance floor for his wife. The band was playing "Crazy," the lights dimmed low, the couples dancing close. He located Maggie and Bud, clinging together like a pair of drunks. Bud's hands were caressing her back, working their way down. Jonas watched as Maggie absentmindedly repositioned his hands to her buttocks.

Blood rushed into Jonas's face, the veins in his neck throbbing. He slammed his drink down, then made his way awkwardly across the dance floor.

Oblivious, Maggie and Bud continued to grind their groins against one another, lost to the world.

Jonas tapped Bud on the shoulder. "Excuse me, pal, but I think that's my wife's ass in your hand."

Maggie and Bud stopped dancing, a look of apprehension coming over the millionaire's face. "Easy big guy, I was only—"

The right cross was a glancing blow, but still had enough force to send Bud crashing into another couple, then sprawling to the dance floor.

The band stopped playing.

The lights came up.

Maggie looked at Jonas, aghast. "Are you crazy?"

Jonas rubbed his sore knuckles. "Do me a favor, Maggie. Next time you take a cruise to Baja, don't come back." He turned and left the dance floor, the alcohol spinning the room as he strode toward the exit.

Jonas stepped out the front entrance and ripped off his tie. A uniformed bellboy asked him for his parking stub.

"I don't have a car."

"Would you like a taxi, then?"

"He doesn't need one. I'm his ride." Terry Tanaka stepped out the door behind him.

"Man, when it rains it pours. What is it you want, Tracy?"

"It's Terry, and we need to talk."

"You talk, I need to puke." He staggered down the block, searching for a trashcan, settling for the back of a dumpster.

Terry turned her back as he heaved his dinner. She searched her purse, then tossed him a pack of gum when he finished. "Now can we talk?"

"Look, Trixie . . ."

"Terry!"

Jonas sat on the curb and combed his fingers through his hair. His head was throbbing. "What is it you want?"

"Me following you here, it wasn't my idea. My father sent me."

Jonas glanced back at her. "Masao's an old friend. Find me on Monday, we'll talk. This isn't exactly a good time . . ."

"Ever hear of UNIS?"

"UNIS? Yeah, it's some kind of deep ROV, isn't it?"

"Unmanned Nautical Informational Submersible. UNIS. Our institute holds the patents. They're made for deep-water assignments, their hulls able to withstand 23,000 pounds per square inch of pressure."

"I'm happy for you. Now I need to find a cab and a bottle of aspirin."

She removed a manila envelope from her purse and shoved it in his face. "Look at this."

He opened the envelope and removed a black-and-white photograph taken underwater. The image was of a UNIS, lying on its side, its hull crushed almost beyond recognition.

Jonas looked back at the woman. "What the hell did this?"

UNIS

The Dodge Caravan sped along the rain-slick streets of San Diego, Terry at the wheel, challenging every yellow traffic light. Jonas laid back in the passenger seat, the window open, the cool breeze soothing his headache and sore knuckles. His eyes remained open and on the road—the woman's driving was making him nervous—but he kept studying the photograph in his mind.

Taken 35,000 feet beneath the surface of the western Pacific, the black-and-white photograph showed a spherical remote-sensing device resting near a dark canyon wall. Jonas was somewhat familiar with these remarkable robotic devices, having followed their development in science journals. He knew JAMSTEC, the Japan Marine Science and Technology Center, was involved with the Tanaka Institute in a joint project.

"My father agreed to deploy twenty-five UNIS robots into the Challenger Deep in exchange for financing for our whale lagoon in Monterey," Terry told him as they reached the freeway. "The UNIS array was designed to monitor tremors along a 125-mile stretch of the underwater canyon. Within days of the system's deployment, our surface ship, the *Kiku*, began receiving a steady stream of data, and seismologists on both sides of the Pacific were studying the information eagerly.

"Then something went wrong. Three weeks after the launch, one of the robots stopped transmitting data. A week later, two more units shut down. When another

one stopped a few days after that, JAMSTEC cut off our funding, forcing my father to do something."

Terry looked at Jonas. "He sent my brother, D.J., down in the *Abyss Glider*."

"Alone?"

"D.J.'s the most experienced pilot we have, but I agree with you. In fact, I told Dad I should have gone with him in the second glider."

"You?"

Terry glared at him. "You have a problem with that? I happen to be a damn good pilot."

"I'm sure you are, but at thirty-five thousand feet? What's the deepest you've ever soloed?"

"I've hit sixteen thousand twice, no problem."

"Not bad," Jonas admitted.

"Not bad for a woman, you mean?"

"Easy, Gloria Steinem, I meant not bad for anyone. Very few humans have been down that deep."

She forced a smile. "Sorry. It gets frustrating, you know. Dad's strictly old-fashioned Japanese; his grandmother was a geisha. Woman are to be seen and not heard. It drives me crazy."

"Finish the story. What happened with D.J.? I assume he took this photo?"

"Yes. The photo came from his sub's video."

Jonas glanced again at the photograph. The titanium sphere had been cracked open, its tripod legs were mangled, a bolted bracket torn off. The hull itself looked battered beyond recognition.

Jonas studied the image. "Where's the sonar plate?"

"D.J. found it forty yards down-current. He hauled it up—it's at the Institute back in Monterey. That's why I tracked you down. My father needs you to take a look at it."

Jonas stared at her skeptically. "Why me?"

"He didn't say. You can fly up with me in the morning and ask him. I'm taking the Institute's plane back at eight."

Lost in thought, Jonas almost missed his driveway. "There—on the left."

She turned down the long, leaf-littered driveway, then parked in front of a handsome Spanish Colonial buried in foliage.

Terry switched off the engine. Jonas turned to her and narrowed his eyes. "Masao sent you all this way, just so I could render an opinion on scrap metal?"

"My father needs advice about redeploying along the Challenger Deep."

"You want my advice? Stay the hell out of the Mariana Trench. It's far too dangerous to be exploring, especially in a one-man submersible."

"Everything's dangerous to a man who's lost his nerve. D.J. and I are good pilots, we can handle this. What the hell happened to you anyway? I was only seventeen when we first met, but you were different. I still remember you turning me on with your piss-and-vinegar attitude."

Jonas blushed. "Shit happens when you grow old."

"You're not that old, but you're afraid. What are you so afraid of? A sixty-foot great white shark?"

"Maybe I'm afraid of Asian women with bad attitudes."

She smirked. "Let me tell you something. The data we collected during those first two weeks the UNIS array was functioning was invaluable. If the earthquake detection system works, it'll save thousands of lives. No one's asking you to dive the Challenger Deep, we simply want your opinion on why the UNIS was damaged. Is your schedule so damn busy that you can't take a day to fly up to the Institute? My father's asking for your help. Examine the sonar plate and review the video that my brother took and you'll be home to your darling wife by tomorrow night. We'll pay you for your time, and I'm sure Dad will even arrange a personal tour of our new whale lagoon."

Jonas took a breath. He considered Masao Tanaka a friend, a commodity he seemed to be running short of lately. "When would we leave?" he asked.

"Meet me tomorrow morning at the commuter airport, seven-thirty sharp."

"The commuter . . . we're taking one of those puddle jumpers?" Jonas swallowed hard.

"Relax. I know the pilot. See you in the morning."

Jonas exited the car and watched her drive away. "What the hell are you doing, J.T.?"

Jonas shut the door behind him and switched on the light, feeling for a moment like a stranger in his own home. The house was dead quiet. A trace of Maggie's perfume lingered in the air. *She won't be home until late,*

he thought. *Ah, who are you kidding, she won't be home at all.*

He went into the kitchen, pulled a bottle of vodka from the cabinet, then changed his mind and turned on the coffeemaker. He replaced the filter and added some coffee, then filled the slot with water. He ran the faucet, sucked cold water from the spigot, and rinsed out his mouth.

For a long moment he stood at the sink, staring out the back window while the coffee brewed. It was dark out, all he could see was his reflection in the glass, all he could think of was a song from his navy days, the Talking Heads . . .

And you may tell yourself, this is not my beautiful house, and you may tell yourself, this is not my beautiful wife! Same as it ever was . . . Same as it ever was . . . Same as it ever was . . .

When the coffee was done, he grabbed a mug and the pot of coffee and went into his study.

Sanctuary. The one room in the house that was truly his own. The walls were covered with contour maps of the ocean's continental margins, mountain ranges, abyssal plains, and deep-sea trenches. Fossilized Megalodon teeth cluttered the shelves of a glass bookcase, sitting upright in their plastic support holders like small, lead-gray stalagmites. A framed photo of a great white shark hung above his desk, sent to him by Andrew Fox, son of Rodney, the famous Australian photographer who had nearly been bitten in two by a great white many years ago. Now the entire

Fox family made a living taking pictures of the very animal that had scarred Rodney for life . . . and had given him life.

Jonas set the coffee mug down beside his computer, then positioned himself at the keyboard. A set of jaws from a twelve-foot great white gaped at him from high above his monitor. He punched a few keys to access the Internet, then typed in the Web address of the Tanaka Oceanographic Institute.

Titanium. Even Jonas found it hard to believe.

NIGHT OWLS

Jonas gulped the hot coffee and waited for the Web site to upload. He typed in the word "UNIS."

UNIS
Unmanned Nautical Informational Submersible

Originally designed and developed in 1989 by Masao Tanaka, CEO of the Tanaka Oceanographic Institute, to study whale populations in the wild. Reconfigured in 1996 in conjunction with the Japan Marine Science and Technology Center (JAMSTEC) to record and track seismic disturbances along the deep-sea trenches.

Each UNIS system is composed of a three-inch-thick titanium outer shell. The unit is supported by three retractable legs and weighs 2,600 pounds. Each UNIS robot is designed to withstand pressures of 23,000 pounds per square inch. UNIS communicates information back to a surface ship by way of fiber-optic cable.

UNIS INSTRUMENTATION:
Electrical Fields
Mineral Deposits
Salinity
Seismic Equipment
Topography
Water Temperature

Jonas reviewed the engineering reports of the UNIS systems, impressed by the simplicity of the design. Positioned along a seismic fault line, their tripod legs burrowing deep into the ocean floor, the UNIS remotes could detect the telltale signs of an impending earthquake, providing, as Terry had said, an invaluable early warning system.

Southern Japan has the misfortune of being geographically located within a convergence zone of three major tectonic plates. Periodically, these plates grind against each other, generating about one-tenth of the world's annual earthquakes. One devastating Japanese quake in 1923 had killed more than 140,000 people.

In 1994, Masao Tanaka had been desperately seeking funds to complete his dream project, a monstrous man-made cetacean lagoon, or whale sanctuary. JAMSTEC had agreed to fund the entire project if the Tanaka Institute would complete the UNIS project. Now the system's breakdown was pushing the Tanaka Institute toward bankruptcy. Masao Tanaka was desperate; he needed Jonas's help.

Jonas took a long swig of coffee. *The Challenger Deep*, he thought to himself. Submarine experts referred to it as "hell's antechamber."

Jonas just called it "hell."

* * *

Twenty miles away, Terry Tanaka, freshly showered and wrapped in a hotel bath towel, sat on the edge of her queen-size bed at the Holiday Inn, her blood

pressure still elevated. Jonas Taylor had really irked her. The man was obstinate, with strong chauvinistic ideas. Why her father had insisted their team seek his input was beyond her. Pulling out her briefcase, she decided to review the personnel file on Professor Jonas Taylor.

She knew the basics by heart. Educated at Penn State, advanced degrees from the University of California, San Diego, Scripps Institute of Oceanography, trained at the Woods Hole Oceanographic Institute. Author of three books on paleobiology. At one time, Jonas Taylor had been considered one of the most experienced submersible argonauts in the world. He had piloted the *Alvin* submersible seventeen times, leading multiple explorations to four different deep-sea trenches in the 1980s. And then, seven years ago, for some unknown reason, he had simply given it all up.

"Doesn't make sense," Terry said aloud. Thinking back to the lecture earlier that evening, she remembered the bushy-eyebrowed man who had practically accused Jonas of piloting an expedition into the Mariana Trench. Yet nothing in his personnel file indicated any trip to the western Pacific, let alone the Challenger Deep.

Terry put the file aside and powered up her laptop. She entered her personal code, then accessed the Institute's computers.

She punched in "Mariana Trench."

FILE NAME: MARIANA TRENCH

LOCATION:
Western Pacific Ocean, east of Philippines, close to island of Guam.

FACTS:
Deepest known depression on Earth. Measures 35,827 feet deep (10,920 m), over 1,550 miles long (2,500 km), averages 40 miles in width, making the trench the deepest abyss on the planet and the second longest. The deepest area of the Mariana Trench is called the Challenger Deep, named after the Challenger II expedition that discovered it in 1951. Note: A 1 kg weight dropped into the sea above the trench would require more than an hour of descent time just to reach bottom.

EXPLORATION (MANNED):
On January 23, 1960, the U.S. Navy bathyscaphe *Trieste* descended 35,800 feet (10,911 m), nearly touching the bottom of the Challenger Deep. On board were U.S. Navy Lt. Donald Walsh and Swiss oceanographer Jacques Piccard. In the same year, the French bathyscaphe *Archimede* completed a similar dive. In each case, the bathyscaphes simply descended and returned to the surface ship.

EXPLORATION (UNMANNED):
In 1993, the Japanese launched *Kaiko*, an unmanned robotic craft, which descended to 35,798 feet before

breaking down. In 1997, 25 UNIS robotic submersibles were successfully deployed by the Tanaka Oceanographic Institute along the Challenger Deep's seafloor.

Terry skimmed through the file. Nothing about Jonas Taylor here. She keyed in "Naval Exploration."

NAVAL EXPLORATION: (see) *TRIESTE*, **1960.** *SEACLIFF*, **1990.**

Seacliff? Why hadn't the name appeared in the data above? She probed further.

SEACLIFF: **ACCESS DENIED.** **AUTHORIZED U.S. NAVAL PERSONNEL ONLY.**

For several minutes, Terry attempted to gain access to the file, but it was hopeless. She signed off and closed the laptop, thinking back to the lecture. Her first meeting with Jonas Taylor had been ten years ago at a symposium held at her father's institute. Jonas had been invited to speak about his deep-sea dives aboard the *Alvin* submersible. At the time, Terry was fresh out of high school. She had worked closely with her father, organizing the symposium, coordinating travel and hotel arrangements for more than seventy scientists from around the world. She had booked Jonas's ticket and met him at the airport herself. She recalled developing a schoolgirl crush on the deep-sea pilot with the athletic build.

Terry looked at his picture again in her file. Tonight, Taylor had clearly lacked the confidence of their earlier meeting. He was still a physical specimen, possessing a handsome face, bearing a few more stress lines around the eyes. The dark brown hair was turning gray near the temples. Six foot one, she guessed, about 195. But something was missing on the inside.

What had happened to the man? And why had her father insisted on locating him? As far as Terry was concerned, Jonas Taylor's involvement was the last thing the UNIS project needed.

*   *   *

Jonas woke up on his office sofa, his wool suit jacket serving as his blanket. A dog was barking somewhere in the neighborhood. He squinted at the clock: 6:00 a.m. Computer printouts from the overflowing catch tray were scattered around him. He sat up slowly, his aching head pounding, his foot knocking over the half-empty coffeepot, staining the beige carpet brown. He rubbed his bloodshot eyes, then glanced at the computer. His screen saver was on. He tapped the mouse, revealing a diagram of the UNIS remote, glowing on screen. His memory came flooding back.

The dog stopped barking. The house seemed unusually quiet. Jonas got up, went into the hallway, and walked down to the master bedroom.

Maggie wasn't there. Their bed hadn't been touched.

MONTEREY

Terry spotted Jonas as he crossed the airport tarmac from the parking lot. She jogged out to meet him.

"Good morning, Professor" she said, just a little bit too loud. "How's your head?"

"Don't ask." He shifted his duffel bag to his other shoulder. "Talk softer, and stop calling me Professor. It's Jonas, or Taylor. Professor makes me feel old." He eyed the waiting plane. "Kind of small, isn't it?"

"Not for a Beechcraft."

The plane was a twin-turbo, with a whale logo and "TOI" painted on the fuselage. Jonas climbed aboard, tossed his bag behind him, then looked around. "Okay, where's the pilot?"

She gave him a mock salute.

"You? No way—"

"Hey, let's not start that shit again. I'm licensed and qualified, and if it makes you feel any better, I've been flying for six years."

Jonas nodded uneasily. It didn't make him feel better. It just made him feel old.

"Are you all right?" she asked as he fumbled with his seat belt. "You look a little pale."

Jonas nodded. "Low blood sugar."

"In back's a refrigerator, might be some apples. If you'd rather sit in back there's plenty of room to stretch out. Barf bags are in the side pocket." She smiled innocently.

"You're enjoying this."

"In all honesty, I never imagined an experienced deep-sea pilot like you would be so squeamish."

"Just fly the damn plane," he said, his eyes compulsively scanning the dials and meters on the control panel. The cockpit was a little tight, the copilot seat felt jammed up against the windshield.

"That's as far back as it goes," Terry told him as he searched for a lever to adjust the seat.

He swallowed dryly. "I need a glass of water."

She noticed his trembling hands. "In back."

Jonas got up and struggled into the rear compartment.

"There's beer in the fridge," she called out.

Jonas unzipped his duffel bag, found his dop kit, and took out an amber medicine bottle filled with small yellow pills.

Claustrophobia. His doctor had diagnosed the problem after the accident, a psychosomatic reaction to the stress he had endured. A deep-sea pilot with claustrophobia was as useless as a high diver with vertigo. The two just didn't mix.

Jonas chased down two of the pills with water from a paper cup. He stared at his trembling hand, crumpling the cup in his fist. He closed his eyes for a moment, then took a long, deep breath. When he slowly opened them and looked at the crinkled cup in the palm of his hand, he was no longer shaking.

"You okay?" Terry asked through the door of the cockpit.

Jonas looked up at her. "I told you, I'm fine."

*   *   *

The flight to Monterey lasted two and a half hours. The pills eventually took effect, allowing Jonas to relax. They were following the coastline north, flying over Big Sur, one of the most dramatic landscapes on the planet. For seventy-two miles violent Pacific waves crashed against the foot of the Santa Lucia Mountains, all bordered by California's scenic Highway 1, a mountainous roadway with harsh grades, twin bridges, and blind turns.

Terry spotted a pod of whales migrating south along the shore. "Grays," she said.

"Cruising to Baja," he mumbled, thinking of Maggie.

"Jonas, listen . . . about the lecture. I didn't mean to come off so harshly. It's just that Dad insisted I find you, and frankly, I didn't see the purpose of wasting your time. I mean, it's not like we need another submersible pilot."

"Good, because I wouldn't be interested."

"Good, because we don't need you!" She felt her blood beginning to boil again. "Maybe you could convince my father to allow me to follow D.J. down in the second *Abyss Glider*?"

"Pass." He gazed out his window.

"Why not?"

Jonas looked at the girl. "First, I've never seen you pilot a sub—"

"I'm piloting this plane!"

"It's totally different. You're dealing with harsh currents, water pressure—"

"Pressure? You want pressure? Hold on!" Terry pulled back on the wheel.

Jonas grabbed the dash in front of him as the Beechcraft rolled into a series of tight 360s, then dropped into a nauseating near-vertical nosedive.

The plane righted itself at 1,500 feet, as Jonas puked across the dashboard.

THE REPORTER

David Adashek adjusted his wire-rimmed bifocals, then knocked on the double doors of Suite 810. No reply. He knocked again, this time louder.

The door opened, revealing a groggy Maggie Taylor, wearing nothing but a white robe. It was untied, exposing one of her tan breasts.

"David? Christ, what time is it?"

"Almost noon. Rough night?"

She smiled, still half asleep. "Not as rough as my soon-to-be ex-husband's. Come in before someone sees you."

Adashek entered. She pointed to a pair of white sofas that faced a big-screen TV in the living area. "Sit."

"Where's Bud?"

Maggie curled up on the far sofa opposite Adashek. "He left about two hours ago. You did a nice job of harassing Jonas at the lecture."

"Is all this really necessary, Maggie? He seems like a decent enough guy—"

"So you marry him. After ten years, I've had enough."

"Why not just divorce him and get it over with?"

"It's not that simple. Now that I'm in the media's eye, my agent says we have to be very careful about the public's perception. Jonas still has a lot of friends in this town. He has to come off as a lunatic. People have to believe that his actions brought this divorce on. Last night was a good start."

"Okay, so what's next?"

"Where's Jonas now?"

Adashek pulled out his notes. "He went home with the Tanaka woman—"

"Jonas? With another woman?" Maggie laughed hysterically.

"It was innocent. Just a ride home from the awards. I followed him to the commuter airport earlier this morning. They're headed to Monterey. My guess is to that new whale lagoon the Tanaka Oceanographic Institute is constructing along the coast."

"Stay with him, and keep me informed. By the end of next week, I want you to go public with the navy story, emphasizing the fact that two of his crew were killed. Once the story hits, you'll do a follow-up interview with me, then I'll push for the divorce, public humiliation and all."

"You're the boss. Listen, if I'm going to be following Jonas, I'll need some more cash."

Maggie pulled a thick envelope out of her robe pocket. "Bud says to save the receipts."

Yeah, thought Adashek, *I'm sure he needs the write-off.*

LAGOON

"There it is." Terry pointed to the shoreline as they descended toward the sparkling Monterey Bay.

Jonas sipped the warm soda, his stomach still jumpy from Terry's little air show. His head pounded, and he had already made up his mind to leave immediately after meeting with Masao. As far as he was concerned, Terry Tanaka was the last pilot he'd ever recommend to descend to the bottom of the Challenger Deep.

Jonas looked down and to his right. An empty man-made lagoon stretched out like a giant bathtub on a ten-mile-square parcel of shoreline just south of Moss Landing. From the air it looked like an empty oval-shaped swimming pool. Lying parallel to the ocean, the structure was just over three-quarters of a mile in length and a quarter mile wide. It was eighty feet deep at its center, with walls two stories high and enormous acrylic windows along its southern border. A concrete canal at the far end of the lagoon ran west, connecting the man-made tank with the deep waters of the Pacific.

The lagoon held no water yet, only scaffolding. If and when it was ever finished, the massive steel doors located at the canal entrance would open and the lagoon would fill with seawater. It would be the largest man-made aquarium in the world.

"Impressive. If I hadn't seen it with my own eyes, I wouldn't have believed it," Jonas said as they prepared to land.

Terry nodded. "My father's dream. He designed it to be a living laboratory, a natural yet protective environment for its future inhabitants. Each winter tens of thousands of whales migrate along California's coastal waters to breed in the shallow lagoons around Baja."

Jonas rolled his eyes at the mention of Baja.

"Dad's thinking of ways we can coax a few females inside."

"Toss 'em some money, that should do it."

*   *   *

Twenty minutes later, Jonas found himself looking into the smiling eyes of the lagoon's owner.

"Taylor-san!" Masao Tanaka hustled over from his jeep to shake Jonas's hand. Tanaka had grayed since the last time Jonas had seen him, his goatee practically white, but the almond eyes were still full of life. "Let me look at you. Ah, you look like shit. Smell like it too! Hah. What's the matter? You don't like flying with my daughter?"

"No, as a matter of fact, I don't." Jonas gave the girl a look to kill.

Masao glanced at his daughter. "Terry?"

"His fault, Dad. It's not my problem if he can't handle the pressure. I'll be in the projection room." She walked off the tarmac, heading toward the three-story building at the end of the lagoon.

"My apologies, Taylor-san. Terry is very headstrong, she is somewhat of a free spirit. Is that the term? It is difficult raising a daughter without a female role model."

"Forget it. I really came up to see you and your whale lagoon. Looks amazing from up there."

"I'll give you a tour later. Come, we'll get you a fresh shirt. Then I want you to meet my chief engineer, Alphonse DeMarco. He is reviewing the video D.J. took in the trench. Jonas, I really need your input."

Jonas tossed his duffle bag in the back of the jeep and the two men climbed in.

*   *   *

A short while later, Jonas was cleaned up, wearing a new shirt, and seated in a projection room, the underwater video playing on a large screen. The image showed a spotlight cutting a beam through the clear, dark water. The wreckage of the UNIS loomed into view. It was lying on its side at the bottom of a canyon wall, wedged in between boulders and mud.

Alphonse DeMarco, a squat man carrying a wrestler's physique, stared at the monitor in the video-editing suite. "There it is. D.J. found it half-buried a hundred yards south of its original position."

Jonas rose from his seat and approached the screen. "What do you think happened?"

DeMarco watched the image change, the spotlight roaming over the scarred metal surface of the crushed submersible. "The simplest explanation's always the best. The robot got caught in a landslide."

"A landslide?"

"They're a frequent occurrence in the trench. Just look at all of those rocks."

Jonas walked to the table behind them. The retrieved half-shell of the sonar plate lay there like a severed piece of abstract sculpture. Jonas touched the torn edge of the metal dish. "The titanium casing's more than three-inches thick. I've seen the stress-test data—"

"The shell may have developed a crack on impact. The currents are incredibly strong."

"Is there any evidence—?"

"The UNIS recorded an increase in turbulence almost two minutes before we lost contact."

Jonas paused, then looked back at DeMarco. "What about the other damaged robots?"

"Both recorded similar changes in turbulence. If a landslide got this one, we can probably assume the same thing happened to the others."

Jonas turned toward the monitor. "You've lost four units," he said. "Isn't it pushing the limits of probability to say they've all been destroyed in landslides?"

DeMarco removed his glasses and rubbed his eyes. He'd had this argument with Masao more than once. "We knew the trenches were seismically active. Phone cables that cross other canyons are broken by landslides all the time. All this means is that the Mariana Trench is even more unstable than we expected."

"Changes in deep-sea currents often precede landslide activity," chimed in Terry.

"Jonas," said Masao, "this entire project depends on our ability to determine what happened to these robots and correct the situation immediately. We've located the last UNIS, the only one of the four not

located directly along the canyon wall. I've decided we must retrieve this robot. My son . . . he cannot do the job alone. The job requires two subs working together: one to clear the debris and steady the UNIS while the second sub attaches the cable."

"I'm going, Dad," said Terry. "I've trained for this, I can get it done."

Masao was about to reply when Jonas yelled, "Stop the tape!" He pointed to the screen. "Go back," he called out to the projectionist. The image rewound. "Good, that's good. Let it play again from there."

They stared at the shifting image on the screen. The spotlight circled to the opposite side of the UNIS sphere, partially submerged in rocks and mud. The light shone into the debris near its base.

"There!" Jonas said. The projectionist froze the frame. Jonas pointed to a tiny white fragment wedged under the submersible. "Can you blow that up?"

The man punched some buttons and a square outline appeared on screen. Moving a joystick, he positioned the square around the object, then pulled it out so that it filled the entire screen.

The object appeared triangular and white, but fuzzy and unclear. Jonas stared at the screen. "It's a tooth," he stated.

DeMarco moved closer, scrutinizing the image. "A tooth? You're nuts."

"Al," commanded Masao. "Show the proper respect to our guest."

"Sorry, Mas, but what our professor here's saying is impossible. You see that?" He pointed to a bolt dangling from a steel strut. "That's a bolt holding one of the UNIS legs. It's three inches long." He pointed to the fuzzy white object below it. "That would mean that . . . thing . . . whatever it is, is at least seven, eight inches long."

He looked at Masao. "There's no creature on earth with teeth that big."

* * *

Masao held a photograph of the blown-up video frame in his hand as he, Jonas, and Terry followed the main interior corridor leading into the giant bowl-shaped arena that surrounded the Tanaka lagoon.

"Taylor-san, with all due respect, I don't see how this can be a tooth. It's too narrow—"

"The Meg's bottom teeth are narrow, they're used to puncture their prey to allow the top teeth to rip apart the meat."

"It's also white. There are no white Megalodon teeth."

"Mas, white indicates it's not a fossil, that the creature who owned it may still be alive. It's the reason we have to retrieve that tooth. It proves my theories."

Terry shook her head. "The Megalodon man here's letting his mind play games with his head, he's seeing only what he wants to see. There are no giant great white sharks in the trench. And even if there were, since when do sharks eat titanium robots?"

"They don't," Jonas snapped, "unless the titanium robots happen to be transmitting electrical signals, like your UNIS. Years ago, I was hired by AT&T to investigate problems they were having with a fiber-optic cable system they had just installed along the ocean floor, stretching from the eastern seaboard to the Canary Islands. The cable was laid in six thousand feet of water and was armored with stainless-steel mesh, yet the sharks still attacked it, tearing it up, costing the company millions of dollars in repairs. The sharks' ampullae of Lorenzini were attracted to the electronic booster signals originating in the fiber-optic bundles."

"Ampullae of who?"

"Lorenzini," Jonas shot back. "It's a cluster of sensory cells located along the underside of the shark's snout." Jonas stopped Masao. "Mas, I need D.J. to recover that tooth; it's very important to me."

"What about you, Jonas? Would you accompany my son in the second glider?"

Terry's almond eyes blazed. "No way! If anyone's going down with D.J., it'll be me!"

"Enough!" Masao looked at his daughter, the old man's eyes fierce. "I am here to show our guest the whale lagoon, this other matter shall be discussed at the proper time."

Terry waited for her father to move on, then glared back at Jonas. "This discussion isn't over."

They reached a ramp leading into the arena, following it into daylight.

The man-made lagoon was enormous, spread out before them like God's bathtub. Massive drains were set every forty feet, allowing circulation pumps to filter seawater. Fake rock formations situated along the bottom concealed acrylic windows accessible beneath the lagoon's basin. Thick two-story windows along the southern wall of the tank reminded Jonas of stadium skyboxes. The arena's bowl provided bench-style seating for 10,000, yet still allowed patrons to view the Pacific Ocean, sparkling just above the facility's western wall.

Jonas was awestruck by its immensity. "God, to see a pod of gray whales in here . . . you could watch them for days on end and not be bored."

Masao Tanaka stood in front of them proudly, a tight smile etched across his face. "We do nice work, eh, my friend?"

Jonas could only nod in agreement.

"This lagoon has been my dream since I was six years old. Forty million dollars, almost seven years of planning, four years of construction, Jonas. I did all I could, gave it everything I had."

He turned and faced them again, tears in his eyes. "It's too bad she is never gonna open."

MASAO

Jonas sat in the bamboo chair and gazed at the setting sun as it kissed the Pacific horizon. Masao Tanaka's home had been built into the Santa Lucia Mountains in California's Big Sur Valley. The cool ocean breeze and magnificent view were intoxicating, relaxing Jonas for the first time in as long as he could remember.

Despite his daughter's objections, Masao had invited Jonas to spend the night. Terry was in the kitchen at her father's request, preparing a plate of jumbo shrimp for the barbecue.

Masao emerged from the house, checked on the gas grill, then walked around the pool and took a seat next to Jonas.

"Terry says dinner will be ready soon. I hope you're hungry, Jonas. My daughter is a very good cook." He smiled.

Jonas looked at his friend. "I'm sure she is. I just might need a food taster to make sure she didn't drop arsenic into my serving."

Masao smiled, then shut his eyes and breathed deeply. "Jonas, you smell that ocean air? Makes you appreciate nature, eh?"

"Yes."

"My father . . . he was a fisherman. Back in Japan, he would take me out almost every morning. My mother, Kiku Tanaka, she died when I was only four. There was no one else to take care of me. Just my father.

"When I was six, we moved to America to live with relatives in San Francisco. Four months later, the Japanese attacked Pearl Harbor. All Asians were locked in detention camps. My father . . . he was a very proud man. He could never accept the fact that he was in a prison, unable to fish, unable to live his life. One morning, my father just decided to die. Left me all alone, locked in a prison in a foreign land, unable to speak or understand a word of English."

"I'm sorry. You must've been pretty scared."

Masao smiled. "Very scared. Then I saw my first whale. From the prison gates, I could see them leap. The humpbacks, they sang to me, kept me company at night, occupied my mind. My only friends." He closed his eyes for a moment, lost in the memory.

"You know, Taylor-san, Americans are funny people. One minute, you feel hated by them, the next loved. After eighteen months, I was released and adopted by an American couple, Jeffrey and Gay Gordon. I was very lucky. The Gordon family loved me, supported me, put me through school. But when I felt depressed, it was always my whales that kept me going."

"Now I understand why this project means so much to you."

"Hai. Learning about whales is very important. In many ways they are superior to man. But capturing and imprisoning them in small tanks, forcing them to perform stupid tricks so they can receive their rations of food, this is very cruel. This lagoon, it will allow me to study the whales in a natural setting. The lagoon

will remain open so the whales can enter and exit of their own free will. No more small tanks. Having been locked up myself, I could never do that. Never."

"The lagoon will open, Masao. JAMSTEC won't hold the money back forever."

Masao shook his head. "Unless we can get the array working again, it is cancelled."

"What about finding another funding source?"

"I tried, but my net worth is too leveraged. No bank will support my dreams. Only JAMSTEC. But they don't care about building lagoons, they just want the UNIS array to monitor earthquakes. The Japanese government will not back down, there are careers at stake. We either fix the array or declare bankruptcy."

"You'll finish the lagoon, Masao. We'll figure out what happened."

"What do you think happened?" Masao's eyes blazed into Taylor's, searching for answers. "You really think it was a big shark?'

"Honestly, Masao, I don't know. DeMarco may be right. The UNIS robots could have anchored themselves too close to the canyon wall. But I can't imagine a boulder being able to crush titanium like that."

"Jonas, you and I are friends. I tell you my story, now you tell your old friend Tanaka the truth. What happened to you in the Mariana Trench?"

"What makes you think—"

Masao smiled knowingly. "We've known each other . . . what? Fifteen years? You lectured at my institute at

least a dozen times. Now you underestimate me? I have contacts in the navy too, you know. I know what the navy says happened. Now I want to hear your side."

Jonas rubbed his eyes. "Okay, Masao, for some reason it seems the story's being leaked anyway. There were three of us who trained aboard the *Seacliff*, the navy's prototype for a new deepwater submersible. I was the pilot, the other two crewmen were scientists. We were measuring deep-sea currents in the trench to determine if plutonium rods from nuclear power plants could be safely buried within the Challenger Deep. At least that's what I was told."

Jonas closed his eyes. "I guess we were hovering about four thousand feet off the bottom, just above the warm layer's ceiling. It was my third descent in eight days, too much really, but I was the only qualified pilot. The scientists were busy conducting tests, they had just lowered a vacuum hose to the sea floor, collecting rock samples. I was looking out the porthole, staring down at this ceiling of swirling soot, when I thought I saw something circling just below the layer."

"What can you see in darkness?"

"I'm not sure, but it appeared to be glowing white, and it seemed very big. At first I thought it could be a whale, but I knew that was impossible. Then it just disappeared. I figured I had to be hallucinating."

"What happened next?"

"I . . . to tell you the truth, Masao, I'm not sure. I was so tired, could barely keep my eyes open . . . but suddenly I opened my eyes as this huge triangular

head emerged out of the hydrothermal ceiling. It was monstrous, as big as a truck, its jaws filled with huge teeth. I don't remember much after that. They say I panicked, dropped every weight plate the sub had and rocketed toward the surface. We ascended way too fast, and something went wrong with the compression system. The two scientists died. I woke up in a hospital three days later . . . never knew what happened."

"And you think it was a Megalodon?"

"Mas, before this accident happened, I didn't even know what a Megalodon was. It was only after . . . it was after I saw a psychiatrist that I started piecing things together."

"But the monster . . . it never pursued you to the surface?"

"I don't know, apparently not. Like I said, I blacked out, but it could have overtaken us at any time. My guess is it wasn't interested in being in that cold layer, where the water temperature's barely above freezing."

"Two men died on your watch. Knowing the kind of man you are, that karma must have been hard to live with."

"Still is. Not a day goes by I don't think about it. I spent three weeks recovering in a naval hospital, then went through months of psychoanalysis. Not a fun time." Jonas looked to the horizon. "The truth is, it's been so long, I've begun to doubt my own memories of the event."

Masao sat back in his chair. "Jonas, I believe you saw something, but I don't think it was a monster. You

know, D.J. tells me there are giant patches of tubeworms located all along the bottom. D.J. says these worms reflect light, glowing in the dark. You never did make it to the very bottom of the trench, did you?"

"No."

"D.J. made it. That boy loves deep-sea exploration, says it's like being in outer space. Jonas, I think what you saw was a patch of tubeworms. I think the currents pushed them in and out of your sight line, your submersible's exterior light catching their glow. That's why they seemed to disappear. Remember, you were exhausted, staring into the darkness. The navy worked you too hard, three dives in eight days is not safe. And now you've spent seven years of your life hypothesizing how these monsters may still be alive."

Jonas sat in silence and listened.

Masao placed his hand on Jonas's shoulder. "My friend, I need your help. And I think maybe it's time to face your fears. I want you to return to the Mariana Trench with D.J., but this time you'll make it all the way to the bottom. You'll see these patches of giant tubeworms for yourself. You were once a great pilot, and I know in my heart you still are. You can't live in fear your whole life."

"What about Terry? She wants to make the dive—"

"She's not ready. Too headstrong. No, I need you. And you need to do this, so that you can get on with your life."

Tears formed in Jonas's eyes. "Okay . . . I'll go back." He choked back a laugh. "Boy, your daughter is going to be pissed at me."

Masao smiled grimly. "My daughter will get her opportunities on other dives, but not in this hellhole."

"Agreed."

"Good. And when all of this is over, you will come work with me at the lagoon, okay?"

Jonas nodded. "We'll see."

THE *KIKU*

The American Airlines jumbo jet soared 36,000 feet above the blue carpet of the Pacific Ocean, five hours out of San Francisco.

Terry rose from her aisle seat and headed back toward the plane's restroom. Alphonse DeMarco, seated in the middle seat next to her, took advantage of her leave to stretch. In the window seat next to him sat Jonas Taylor, a briefcase-sized *Abyss Glider II* flight simulator on his lap.

Jonas had been at it for hours, maneuvering the two joysticks, trying to coordinate yaw and pitch with speed and stabilization. The AG II was a one-man, deep-sea submersible, the same model that had carried D.J. to the bottom of the Mariana Trench. Jonas would accompany him in a second sub to retrieve the damaged UNIS. He was already familiar with the basic design, having piloted the AG I, the sub's shallow-water predecessor, several years earlier. Now all he needed was to familiarize himself with the new deep-sea design. There'd be plenty of time for that. It was a twelve-hour flight across the Pacific to Guam, not counting a stopover in Honolulu for refueling.

Terry's attitude toward Jonas had gone from cold to ice. She was visibly hurt that her father had ignored her qualifications to back up D.J., and felt Jonas had lied to her about not being interested in piloting the sub in the Mariana Trench. She even refused to help train Jonas on the simulator.

The *Abyss Glider II* simulator used two computer joysticks to "steer" the submersible by simulating adjustment of its midwing and tail fins. Because most of the trip to the bottom was in complete darkness, the pilot had to learn to "fly blind and disoriented," navigating the craft to the bottom using readouts alone. For this reason, piloting with the simulator was very much like piloting the real thing. So similar, in fact, that Jonas had to stop working, close his eyes, and try to relax.

Staring out the window, he thought about his conversation with Masao Tanaka. It had never occurred to him that he could have been focused on tubeworms.

Riftia. Jonas had seen smaller varieties of the species growing in clusters around every hydrothermal vent he had ever explored. The tubeworms were a luminescent white, possessing neither mouths nor digestive organs. They relied on thick colonies of bacteria living inside their bodies. The worms supplied hydrogen sulfide, which they extracted from the sulfur-rich waters of the trench. The bacteria inside the worms used the hydrogen sulfide to make food for themselves and their host.

Prior to 1977, man believed life could not exist in the absence of light. Since humans need sunlight to exist, the assumption was that all lifeforms had to have it. It was the kind of logic that Jonas despised—logic brought about only by assumption, not actual research. Since no light could penetrate the deepest trenches of

the sea, then photosynthesis could not exist, and life could never get a foothold in the abyss.

And then the *Alvin* submersible went down to the seafloor, and all the old textbooks were thrown out the window.

Jonas had seen it for himself. Colonies of hydrothermal vents supported a unique food chain by spewing searing-hot water and vast amounts of chemicals and mineral deposits out of cracks in the seabed. The high sulfur content, poisonous to most species, became food for a variety of deep-sea bacteria. The bacteria, in turn, were living inside worms and mollusks, breaking down other chemicals into usable food. The massive clumps of tubeworms also consumed the bacteria, and a variety of undiscovered species of fish ate the tubeworms.

The process was called chemosynthesis: bacteria receiving energy from chemicals rather than energy from the sun. Despite man's common beliefs, life flourished in the darkest, seemingly most uninhabitable location on the planet.

Now, twenty years after the discovery, scientists were theorizing that all life on our planet originated from these deep-sea vents.

D.J. had told Masao that the tubeworm clusters in the Challenger Deep often covered vast expanses along the bottom. It was possible, thought Jonas, that he had been staring at a worm cluster through the swirling debris of minerals, fallen asleep, then dreamed the triangular head.

The thought made Jonas ill. Two men had died for his mistake, two families shattered. At least the Megalodon defense had served to lessen his guilt. Coming to grips with this new evidence that he might have imagined the whole incident was not sitting well with his psyche.

One way or another, Jonas knew Masao was right; he had to face his fears and return to the trench. If a white Megalodon tooth could be found, it would justify seven years of research. If not, so be it. One way or the other, it was time to get on with his life.

*   *   *

Fifteen rows behind Jonas and DeMarco, David Adashek closed the hardback *Extinct Species of the Abyss* by Dr. Jonas Taylor. He removed his bifocals, positioned his pillow against the window, and fell asleep.

*   *   *

The navy helicopter flew low above the waves. The pilot glanced over his shoulder at Jonas and DeMarco. "She's just up ahead."

"About time," DeMarco said, turning to wake Terry. She'd been sleeping since they'd left the naval station in Guam.

Jonas trained his eyes on the horizon, a faint line separating the gray ocean from the gray sky. He couldn't see anything. *Maybe I should have slept*, he thought, rubbing his eyes. He was certainly tired enough. They'd been traveling for more than fifteen hours. Moments later he saw the ship, a flat speck quickly growing larger.

The *Kiku* was a decommissioned Oliver Hazard Perry–class guided missile frigate, disarmed and reconfigured for ocean research. The Tanaka Institute had purchased the 445-foot-long steel ship from the navy three years ago, rechristening it the *Kiku*, in honor of Masao's mother.

The frigate was perfect for deep-sea research. Removing the SAM missile launcher from her bow gave the crew plenty of deck space on which to work. Situated in the stern was a reinforced-steel winch and A-frame, designed to lift even the heaviest submersible into and out of the sea. Behind the winch was a massive spool containing more than seven miles of steel cable.

Forty feet of deck separated the winch from two hangars located in the stern. One held the twin pair of *Abyss Gliders*, the one-man submersibles that D.J. and Jonas would descend in; the other stored the ship's helicopter. Steel tracks embedded within the deck allowed the crafts to be rolled in and out of their respective hangars.

A pilothouse overlooked the bow from the second deck and contained the navigator's console board, which drove the two GE LM 2500 gas-turbine engines. A short corridor connected the pilothouse to the command information center (CIC). This once-secured room was always kept cool and dark, illuminated only by the soft blue overhead lights and the colorful computer console screens situated along the interior walls. The weapons stations, which had once controlled the frigate's SAM and harpoon missiles,

antisub torpedoes, and a variety of other guns and countermeasures had been replaced with computers that now monitored the deployed UNIS systems, retrieving data from the robots implanted along the Challenger Deep seven miles below the ship.

The *Kiku*'s CIC also contained the hull-mounted Raytheon SQS-56 sonar and Raytheon SPS-49 radar systems, the exterior dishes of which could be seen rotating on two towers rising twenty-five feet above the upper deck. All of these systems were linked to a computer integration program that displayed the information across a dozen computer consoles.

Below the control deck were the galley and the crew quarters. The triple-stacked coffinlike bunks of the navy had been torn out, the interior reconfigured to accommodate more private quarters for the crew of thirty-two. Below this deck was the engine room and the main machinery that drove the twin-shaft propellers. As large as she was, the *Kiku* was a fast ship, capable of speeds up to twenty-nine knots.

As the helicopter approached the aft deck, Terry pressed her face to her window. She could see a young man in his early twenties standing on the main deck, waving. His body was lean and taut with muscles, his skin a deep Asian tan. Terry waved back excitedly. "D.J.," she said with a grin.

Terry's brother grabbed her bags the moment she stepped off the chopper.

He received his older sister's hug, then turned to Jonas. With their black hair, dark eyes, and bright smiles they almost looked like twins.

"D.J., this is Jonas Taylor," she said. "Don't call him Professor, it makes him feel old."

D.J. dropped the bags and shook Jonas's hand. "My sister's a pistol, huh?"

"A real delight."

"So," D.J. said, "I hear you're going to be descending with me into the Challenger Deep. Sure you're up to it?"

"I'll be fine," said Jonas, sensing D.J.'s competitive nature.

D.J. turned to Terry. "Does the doc here know Frank Heller's on board?"

Terry smiled coyly. "Gee, I don't know. Jonas, did Dad happen to mention that to you yesterday?"

Jonas felt the breath squeeze out of his chest. "Frank Heller's part of this expedition? No, your father definitely didn't mention that to me."

"I take it you two have a history?" asked D.J.

Jonas regained his composure. "Frank Heller was the physician in charge of a series of dives I piloted for the navy seven years ago."

"My guess is you two haven't kept in touch," Terry said, the sarcasm dripping.

"No. And if Masao had told me Heller was part of this mission, I doubt I would have come."

"Guess that's why Dad didn't mention it," chuckled D.J.

"If I had known, I would have told you myself," said Terry. "It's not too late to recall the chopper."

Jonas stared at Terry, his patience wearing thin. "I'm here. If Frank Heller has a problem with that, I guess he'll have to deal with it."

D.J. turned to DeMarco. "How'd he do with the simulator?"

"Not bad. Of course, the program lacks controls for the mechanical arm and escape pod."

"Plan on at least one practice run before we descend then," said D.J. "We'll give you a few hours to get your sea legs."

Jonas shrugged. "Whenever you're ready. Why don't you show me the *Gliders*."

As they approached the glider hangar, a large dark-skinned man in a red knit cap appeared on deck, accompanied by two Filipino crew members.

"Professor Taylor," D.J. said, "Leon Barre, the *Kiku*'s captain."

Jonas shook the French-Polynesian's hand, the man's calloused grip revealing the strength of an ox. A tiny silver cross dangled from his neck. "Welcome aboard," he said, his baritone voice booming. Barre tipped his hat to Terry. "Madam," he said reverently.

DeMarco slapped the big man's shoulder. "You putting on a little weight, Leon?"

Leon's face darkened. "The Thai woman, she fattens me like a pig."

DeMarco laughed, turning to Jonas. "The captain's wife's a hell of a cook. We could all use a little of that, Leon. We're starving."

The captain grunted an order to the Filipino sailor at his side. The sailor bowed, then rushed off toward the *Kiku*'s infrastructure. "We eat in an hour," the captain announced, then turned and left.

Jonas, D.J., DeMarco, and Terry walked across the wide deck to where the two *Abyss Glider* submersibles were perched on dry mounts.

D.J. beamed proudly. "So? What do you think?"

"Smaller than I remember."

"Like glass coffins," chimed in Terry.

Jonas ignored her. "I piloted the AG I in shallow waters. The AG II was still on the drawing board back then."

"Come on, Taylor," said DeMarco. "I'll give you the nickel tour."

The subs were ten feet long by four feet wide and resembled fat torpedoes with wings. They were one-man vessels, the pilot entering an internal Lexan-glass pod through a hatch in the tail section. Lying prone, the pilot used dual joysticks to "fly" the vessel. The clear nose cone allowed for 360 degrees of visibility.

"Lexan," said DeMarco, slapping his palm across one of the glider's nose cones. "This plastic's so strong, it's used as bulletproof glass in presidential limousines. The entire escape pod's made of the stuff. The AG I's were refitted with it several years ago."

Jonas inspected the plastic cone. "I don't remember escape pods being in the original design."

"They weren't," said D.J. "We added them after we realized they could make the craft neutrally buoyant.

The entire chamber's technically the escape pod. If the *Glider* gets into trouble, simply pull the lever located in a metal gear box along your right and the interior chamber will separate from the heavier tail and wing sections. It's like being in a buoyant bubble. You'll rise right to the top."

DeMarco frowned. "I'll give the tour, kid. After all, I did design the damn things."

D.J. smiled at the engineer. "Sorry."

DeMarco took center stage, obviously in his element. "The biggest challenge in deep-water exploration was to design and build a hull that's both buoyant and strong enough to withstand tremendous pressures. The other problem we had to deal with in getting to the bottom of the Challenger Deep was the length of time it takes for a submersible to travel seven miles straight down. The *Alvin*, the *French Nautile*, and the *Russian Mir I* and *II* are all bulky vessels that can only descend at a rate of fifty to one hundred feet per minute. At those speeds, it would take us well over five hours just to enter the trench."

"And," added D.J., "those subs can't even descend beyond twenty thousand feet."

"What about JAMSTEC's *Shinkai 6500*?" asked Jonas. "I thought she was designed to reach the bottom."

"The *Shinkai* was designed for a maximum depth of twenty-one thousand feet," corrected DeMarco. "You're thinking of JAMSTEC's latest unmanned sub, the *Kaiko*. Until D.J. piloted the AG II last week, the

Kaiko was the only vessel, manned or unmanned, to reenter the Challenger Deep since the *Trieste* in '60. She spent just over a half hour at a depth of 35,798 feet, two feet shy of the record, before suffering mechanical problems."

"Now the record's mine," said D.J. "Guess I'll be sharing it with you soon, Doc."

"Should've been me," mumbled Terry.

DeMarco ignored the siblings' comments. "Those other subs I mentioned have hulls made of a titanium alloy, similar to our UNIS systems. Half your power source is exhausted in just piloting the heavily weighted sub along the bottom, all so you can drop the weighted plates later to surface. The *Abyss Gliders* are made from a reinforced, positively buoyant ceramic capable of withstanding forces greater then twenty thousand pounds per square inch. With her maneuverable wings, she'll fly to the bottom at a rate of six hundred feet per minute and float back to the surface without the use of weights. Saves a ton of battery power."

Jonas nodded. "How will we bring the damaged UNIS to the surface?"

"Look beneath the belly of the sub," instructed D.J. "There's a retractable mechanical arm with a claw. The arm has a limited extension of about six feet directly in front of the nose cone. The claw was designed to gather specimens. When we make our descent, you'll take the lead. I'll follow in my sub, which will have a steel cable attached to my mechanical claw. The damaged UNIS has several eye bolts located along its

outer casing. Once you clear the debris away from the UNIS, I'll attach the cable and the *Kiku*'s winch will haul the unit back to the surface."

"Doesn't sound too bad."

"It's a walk in the park, but it's still a two-man job," said D.J. "I tried to attach the cable on my first descent, but there was too much debris covering the UNIS. I couldn't maintain the claw's grip on the steel cable and clear the rocks away. The currents are just too strong for one glider."

"Maybe you were nervous," added Terry.

"Bullshit," responded her brother.

"Come on, D.J.," Terry said, directing her comments at Jonas. "You told me it's kind of scary down there. It's not even the constant darkness. It's the claustrophobia, knowing that you're seven miles down, surrounded by thousands of pounds of pressure. One mistake, one crack in the hull, and your brains implode from the change in pressure." Terry glanced at Jonas, looking for a reaction.

"Ah, you're just jealous," said D.J. He looked to Jonas, his face full of animation. "Truth is, I loved it down there! What a rush, I can't wait to go back. I thought bungee jumping and parachuting were cool, but this beats the shit out of them."

Jonas stared at the young man, recognizing traits from his own youth. "You consider yourself an adrenaline junkie?"

D.J. calmed himself. "Me? No . . . I mean, yeah, I'm an adrenaline junkie, sure, but this is different. The

Challenger Deep . . . it's like being the first person to explore another planet. There are these huge black smokers everywhere, and the weirdest fish you ever saw. But why am I telling you? You've been on dozens of trench dives before."

Jonas tugged on one of the red vinyl flags with the Tanaka logo attached to the back of each sub. "I've piloted more than my share of dives into deep-sea trenches, but the Mariana Trench is a whole different ball game. I suggest leaving the cowboy stuff behind."

He looked back toward the *Kiku*'s infrastructure. "Where can I find Dr. Heller?"

D.J. threw a glance at his sister. "He's in the CIC, I think."

"Good. See you at dinner." Jonas turned and walked away.

HELLER

Jonas followed a main corridor to a door labeled "Operations." He entered the dark chamber humming with computers, video monitors, and radar and sonar equipment.

A gaunt man with short-clipped gray hair and heavy, black-framed glasses was bent over a control panel, pecking at computer keys with his long fingers. He looked up at Jonas, his moist gray eyes swollen behind the thick lenses, then turned back to his computer, studying his monitor. "Another fishing expedition, Taylor?"

Jonas paused a moment before he answered. "That's not why I'm here, Frank."

"Why are you here?"

"Masao asked for my help."

"The Japanese have no sense of irony."

"Like it or not, we're going to have to work together, Frank. The only way to find out what's going on down there is to haul up the damaged UNIS. D.J. can't do it alone—"

"I know that!" Heller rose quickly and crossed the room to refill his coffee. "What I don't understand is why you should be the one to go with him."

"Because nobody else has been down there in the last thirty years."

"Oh yes they have," Heller said bitterly. "Only they died making the trip."

Jonas broke eye contact. "I want to talk to you about that. I . . ." Jonas searched for the right words. "Look, there hasn't been a day that's gone by in the last seven years that I haven't thought about the *Seacliff*. To be honest, I'm still not sure what happened. All I know is that I believed I saw something rise up from the bottom to attack our sub, and I reacted."

"Reacted? You panicked like an ensign on his first day at boot camp." Heller moved to Jonas, standing nose to nose. His eyes burned with hatred. "Maybe your little confession makes everything all right in your book, but it changes nothing with me. You were daydreaming, Taylor. You hallucinated, and instead of reasoning, you panicked. You killed two of our team. Mike Shaffer was my friend, I'm godfather to his kid. I live with your mistake every day."

"I'm sorry."

"Do you know what really ticks me off? You've spent the last seven years making a career of justifying the existence of this Megala-shark, substantiating your fabricated excuse so you wouldn't look so bad." Heller was shaking with emotion. He took a step back and leaned against his desk. "You make me ill, Taylor. Those men didn't deserve to die. Now here we are, seven years later, and you still can't face up to the truth."

"I don't know what the truth is, Frank. Maybe I dreamt it, maybe I was looking at a cluster of tubeworms. All I know is that I screwed up. Don't forget, I almost died down there myself. Now I've got to deal with this thing for the rest of my life."

"I'm not your priest, Taylor. I'm not here to take your confession or hear about your feelings of guilt."

"And what about your contribution to the accident?" Jonas yelled back. "You were the physician of record. You assured Danielson that I was medically fit to make a third dive. Three descents within eight days! Do you think that decision may have had anything to do with my ability to function?"

"Don't blame me for following orders!"

"Orders?" Jonas paced, his blood pressure simmering. "You said it yourself, wrote it on the official report: 'psychosis of the deep.' You and Danielson forced me to pilot those dives without sufficient rest, and then the two of you railroaded me, set me up to be the navy's fall guy . . . to cover your own asses."

"It was your fault!"

"Yes," whispered Jonas, "it was my piloting error, but I never would have been placed in that position without your involvement or Danielson's. Now I've decided to go back down, to finally face my fears, to figure out for myself what happened. Maybe it's time you faced up to your own responsibilities."

Jonas headed toward the door.

"Hold it, Taylor. Look, maybe you shouldn't have been in the trench on that third dive. Danielson was my commanding officer, but he was being pressured by the Pentagon. Still, I believed you were mentally fit. You were a damn good pilot once. But let's just make sure that the reason you're making this dive with D.J.

is to assist him and not to go off looking for some tooth."

Jonas opened the door, then turned to face Heller. "I know my responsibilities, Frank. I hope you remember yours."

Twenty minutes later, having showered and changed, Jonas entered the galley, where a dozen crewmen were noisily feasting on fried chicken and potatoes. He saw Terry seated next to D.J., the only vacant chair to her left.

"This seat taken?"

"Sit," she ordered.

He sat down, listening to D.J., who was involved in a heated debate with DeMarco and Captain Barre. Heller's absence was conspicuous.

"Doc!" D.J. sprayed half his mouthful of chicken out with the word. "You're just in time. You know that practice dive we had scheduled for tomorrow? Well, forget about it."

Jonas felt butterflies in his stomach. "What are you saying?"

Captain Barre turned to Jonas, swallowing a mouthful of food. "Storm front moving in from the east. No time for practice dives. If you're gonna descend this week, it's gonna be tomorrow, first light."

"Jonas, if you're not ready yet, I think you should be man enough to admit it and let me step in," interjected Terry.

"Nah, he'll be fine. Right, Doc?" said D.J., winking. "After all, you've been down to the Mariana Trench before."

"According to who?" Jonas felt the room go quiet, all eyes on him.

"Come on, Doc. It's all over the ship. Some reporter in Guam interviewed half the crew by radio an hour after you boarded."

"What? What reporter? How the hell—?" Jonas no longer felt hungry.

Terry nodded. "Same guy who was questioning you at the lecture. He claims two people died on the sub you were piloting. Told us you panicked because you hallucinated, claiming to have seen one of those Megalodons."

D.J. looked him squarely in the eye. "So, Doc, any of this true?"

The room was dead silent. Jonas pushed his tray away from him. "It's true. Only what this reporter left out is that I was exhausted at the time, having already completed two deep trench dives during the same week. I was pushed into service, okayed by the medical officer—your pal, Heller. To this day I'm not sure if what I saw was real or if I imagined it. But as far as tomorrow's dive's concerned, I made a commitment to your father to complete the mission and I intend to keep that commitment. I've piloted subs on more deep-sea missions than you've had birthdays, D.J., so if you have a problem with me escorting you down, then let's get it out on the table right now."

D.J. smiled nervously. "Hey, I've got no problem with you, so chill. Actually, Al and I were just talking about this giant prehistoric shark of yours. Al says that it would be impossible for a creature that size to exist in water pressures as great as those in the trench.

Now, me, I'm on your side. I say it's possible. Not that I believe your theory, 'cause I don't. But I've seen dozens of different species of fish down there. Now, if those little fish can withstand the water pressures, why couldn't this mega-shark, or whatever the hell you call it?" D.J. was grinning from ear to ear. Several crew members began snickering.

Jonas stood up to leave. "You'll excuse me. I think I've lost my appetite."

D.J. grabbed his arm. "No, wait, Doc, come on now. Tell me about this shark. I really want to know. After all, how will I recognize it if I see it tomorrow?"

"It'll be the big shark with the missing tooth!" blurted out Terry.

Laughter cascaded around them.

Jonas sat back down. "Okay, kid, you really want to know about these monsters, I'll tell you. The first thing you have to realize about sharks is that they've been around a lot longer than us, about four hundred million years. Compare that with humans, whose ancestors fell from the trees only about two million years ago. And of all the species of shark ever to have evolved, old Megalodon was the undisputed king. What little we know about these monsters is that nature endowed the creatures not just to survive but to dominate every ocean and marine species. So we're not just talking about a shark here, we're talking about a formidable killing machine, the apex predator of all time. Forget for a moment this species was a sixty-foot version of a great white shark. The Meg was a supreme

hunter, endowed with size and senses that would put a nuclear submarine to shame. The creature possessed eight highly efficient sensory organs that could track you down from miles away. It could smell and taste you, sense the beating of your heart or the electrical impulses generated by your moving muscles. Piss or bleed in the water, and you might as well have lit up a flare. And if it ever got close enough to see you, then you were already dead."

Leon Barre chuckled. "Hey, how do you know all this shit about some dead fish nobody's ever seen?"

The room quieted once more, awaiting Jonas's response.

"For one thing, we have their fossilized teeth, which not only tells us about their enormous size but reveals certain things about their predatory tendencies. We also have fossilized evidence from the species they fed on."

"Go on about their senses," said D.J., now truly curious.

Jonas gathered his thoughts, noting that other members of the crew had grown silent, listening as well. "The Megalodon, just like its modern-day cousin the great white, possessed eight sensory organs that allowed it to search, detect, identify, and stalk its prey. Let's start with its most amazing sensory organ, called the ampullae of Lorenzini. Along the top and underside of the Meg's snout were tiny, jelly-filled capsules beneath the skin that could detect electrical discharges in the water. Let me put that in layman's

terms. The Megalodon could detect the faint electrical field of its prey's beating heart or moving muscles miles away. That means if the Megalodon was circling our ship, it could still detect a whale calf in distress off the shoreline of Guam."

The room was silent now, all eyes focused on Jonas.

"Almost as amazing as the ampullae of Lorenzini was the Megalodon's sense of smell. Unlike man, the creature possessed directional nostrils, which could not only detect one part of blood or sweat or urine in a billion parts of water, but could also determine the exact location of the scent. That's why you see great whites swimming with a side-to-side motion of their heads. They're actually smelling the water in different directions. And a full-grown adult Megalodon's nostrils . . . they were probably the size of a grapefruit.

"Now we come to the monster's skin, a sensory organ and weapon combined in one. Running along either side of the Meg's flank was an organ we call the lateral line. Actually, the line is more of a canal that contains sensory cells called neuromasts. These neuromasts were able to detect the slightest vibrations in water, even the flutter of another fish's heartbeat. The skin itself was made up of denticles, which were essentially layered scales, sharp as scalpels. Rub your hand against the grain and your flesh would be sliced to ribbons."

Al DeMarco stood up. "You'll have to excuse me. I've got work to do."

"Ah, come on, Al," said D.J. lightheartedly. "There's no school tomorrow. We'll let you stay up late."

DeMarco gave D.J. a stern look. "Tomorrow happens to be a big day for all of us. I suggest we all get some rest."

"Al's right, D.J." agreed Jonas. "I've already mentioned the best parts anyway. But I'll answer your first question, about the shark's ability to deal with water pressure. Megalodon possessed an enormous liver that probably constituted one-fourth of its entire weight. Besides serving the creature's normal hepatic functions and storing fatty energy reserves, the liver would have allowed the Megalodon to adjust to any changes in water pressure, even at depths as great as those in the Challenger Deep."

"All right, Professor," said DeMarco, feeling baited, "let's assume, just for shits and giggles, that these Megalodon sharks do exist in the trench. Why haven't they surfaced? There's got to be a lot more food up here than down there."

"Conditioning. Above the warm bottom layer is six miles of freezing-cold water. Any Megalodon surviving in the trench did so because they were able to escape the colder waters above. The creatures would be conditioned over eons to remain in the depths. And there'd be no impetus to surface."

"Food's an impetus," said DeMarco, the cynicism rising in his voice. "What food source would be available in the Mariana Trench that could sustain a colony of predators the size of a sixty-foot great white?"

Jonas hesitated. "To be honest, I don't know. My assumption's always been that the Megalodon's food source would also have migrated to inhabit the deeper, warmer currents. Maybe that's what led them down there in the first place. Nature has a tendency to allow a species to adapt to certain limitations over millions of years. I think the trench waters, which maintain a much lower oxygen content than our surface waters, would effectively slow the creatures' metabolism down, greatly decreasing their appetites. Megalodons, being territorial predators, would probably thin out their numbers by devouring any weaker members of their own species. Every habitat has its food chain; the Challenger Deep is no exception."

"What nonsense," scoffed DeMarco. "We both know there's nothing inhabiting the Mariana Trench large enough to sustain even one Megalodon."

"How do you know?" Jonas retorted. "See, that closed-minded attitude is so typical. The very notion of a species existing in an unexplored environment like the Challenger Deep is impossible for you to comprehend simply because you haven't seen the species with your own eyes. It's far easier to criticize my theories than to consider the possibilities of existence. If you remember, it was only a short time ago that man refused to accept the notion that life could exist without photosynthesis, but it does. Who really knows what life forms inhabit the unexplored Challenger Deep? For your information, the unmanned submersible, *Kaiko*, recently recorded schools of unidentified fish inhabiting the deep waters

of the Mariana Trench. We also know giant squids, measuring sixty feet and weighing a good ton, prefer the abyss. Surely these creatures would be adequate dining for a limited number of Megs. And what if other prehistoric species also managed to survive without our knowledge or blessings?"

DeMarco shook his head in disbelief. "Your theories are based on nothing but conjecture, fueled by your own vivid imagination, motivated by your guilt. I've had enough of this nonsense for one night." DeMarco headed out the door.

D.J. whistled. "Well Doc, personally I'm glad you just hallucinated these things," he said, winking at his sister. "Now all of us can sleep real good. G' night, Terry." D.J. kissed his sister and followed DeMarco out of the galley. Seconds later, their laughter could be heard down the corridor.

Jonas felt humiliated. He stood up, leaving his dinner plate on the table, and headed out on deck.

*   *   *

It was a calm sea, but clouds could be seen moving in from the east. Jonas watched the half-moon dance along the black surface of the Pacific. He thought about Maggie. Did he still love her? Did it really matter anymore? He gazed at the black water and felt the butterflies return, unaware that, one deck up, Frank Heller was watching.

*   *   *

Jonas awoke sometime before dawn. His cabin was pitch black, and for a moment he didn't know where

he was. When he remembered, a shiver of fear flared in his gut. In a few hours he'd be in similar darkness with seven miles of frigid water over his head. He closed his eyes and tried to go back to sleep. He couldn't.

An hour later D.J. knocked on his door to wake him. It was time.

DESCENT

The dawn sky was a fierce tapestry of gray, gusting with thunderclouds that blew whitecaps across the roiling sea. Wind assaulted Jonas as he stepped out onto the main deck in his wetsuit. He had forced down a light breakfast of scrambled eggs and toast, needing to put something in his stomach before popping two of his yellow pills for the descent. In his left shoulder pouch were four more tablets. Despite the medication, he still felt anxious.

The *Kiku*'s crew were busy, half of them seeing to cables attached to the twin *Abyss Gliders*, others, in scuba gear, awaiting the release of the first submersible.

D.J.'s sub would be the first to go, its cocky young pilot giving last minute instructions to his older sister, who was wearing a matching wetsuit. Terry watched Jonas approach, never bothering to hide her disappointment. "So you decided to show."

"Give it a rest."

"I want to speak with you in private." She pulled him away from D.J. "Why are you doing this? Is it ego?"

"No. It's something I just have to do. A piece of me died down there, maybe this is the only way to make myself whole again."

"What if I paid you to sit this one out?"

Jonas shook his head, incredulous. "You want to bribe me to allow you to take my place?"

She nodded. "D.J. will go for it. No one else has to know."

"This is ridiculous. I'm going, that's all there is to it."

"Pack your little yellow pills, Dr. Feel Good?"

She grabbed his arm as he tried to walk away.

"D.J.'s my brother, Jonas. When our mother died, I practically raised him. So if you screw up down there . . . if anything happens to him, don't bother surfacing."

Without waiting for a reply, she turned her back, hugged D.J., then walked away.

Jonas shook his head. *J.T., you do have a way with women . . .*

D.J. waited until crewmen had attached the steel cable to his sub's claw. He waved to Jonas, then crawled through the rear hatch of his glider. Moments later, the big A-frame powered up, lifting the torpedo-shaped vessel off the deck, over the stern rail, and into the sea.

Alphonse DeMarco's booming voice faltered in the wind. "Let's go, Taylor, we're burning daylight."

As if we'll need it where we're going. Ducking down on all fours, Jonas climbed through the rear hatch of his submersible, straining his back as he sealed the Lexan pod behind him.

The interior of the pod was tight, the padding and shoulder harnesses smelling of new leather. Jonas realized the sub *was* new, and the sudden thought of taking an untested vessel seven miles below the surface only added to his angst.

He crawled forward, securing himself in the shoulder and waist harnesses. Mounted by his right shin was

the sub's battery, and on the opposite side was the life-support system. Two joysticks attached to padded elbow rests were situated in front of his chest, the portside control operating thrust, the starboard control on his right designed to steer. Magnetic couplings were situated along the inside of the glass, securing the sub's wings and tail to the interior pod, allowing him the option of jettisoning the heavy exterior assemblies in an emergency. Below his belly was a storage area, holding flashlights, a pony bottle of air, a medical kit, a diving knife, and a diving mask.

Small LCD computer screens mounted on a low forward rise provided him with sonar, radio, and life-support readouts. As he ran through a quick check of his vitals, the sub suddenly lifted away from the deck, sending his equilibrium spinning.

Jonas's heart raced as the big winch hoisted the *Abyss Glider* beyond the *Kiku*'s rail, offering him a frightening view of the harsh Pacific. The A-frame lowered him to a team of divers, who were waiting in the fifteen-foot swells. For several harrowing minutes he held on, feeling seasick, as the incoming storm's fury lifted and dropped the buoyant submersible relentlessly. Outside the capsule, teams of frogmen were detaching harnesses and checking the wing assemblies. Finally, one of the divers knocked on the Lexan nose cone, giving the all-clear sign.

Jonas started the engine, pressed forward on the throttle, then adjusted the midwings, aiming his vessel underwater.

The glider responded at once, nose diving beneath the waves. The sensation of nausea immediately subsided, yielding to smooth sailing. Jonas noticed the sub felt much heavier, perhaps even sluggish compared with the lightweight AG I he had test-piloted years ago. Still, no other submersible could compare with the *Abyss Glider*'s sleek design.

Jonas followed the thick steel cable down another thirty feet before seeing D.J.'s sub. The radio crackled, the young pilot's voice filtering through.

"Age before beauty, Professor. You take the lead, I'm right behind you."

Walk in the park . . . Jonas moved the starboard joystick forward, sending his ten-foot glider into a steep forty-five-degree descent.

D.J. followed him down, the steel recovery cable in tow, the two subs looping downward in a slow spiraling pattern.

Within minutes the curtains of gray light faded to a deep shade of purple, followed by pitch blackness. Jonas checked his depth gauge: a mere 1,250 feet. He searched a pad of toggle switches on his right, located the exterior lights, and flicked them on.

A column of light illuminated a patch of sea below, scattering a school of fish. Descending into nothingness was disorienting, and Jonas wondered if he'd be better off just focusing on his LCD readout. He checked his depth gauge again: 2,352 feet. "Relax and breathe," he whispered to himself. "This is a marathon, not a sprint, J.T. You've got a long way to go."

"Everything all right, Taylor?" Dr. Heller's voice crackled over the radio with an air of insinuation. Jonas realized Frank was assigned to monitor the two pilots' vital signs. He must have noticed Jonas's heart rate increase on the console's cardiac monitor, his pulse recorded over a metallic band located on each of the joysticks' hand grips.

"Yeah . . . I'm fine."

"Good. Now you can switch off your exterior light, you're wasting battery power. Nothing to see down there anyway."

Jonas gritted his teeth, then flipped back the toggle switch, casting his existence into darkness, save for the soft orange glow from his forward console. He took a deep breath, trying to focus on the nothingness before him.

In the distance he saw a flash of light, followed by a dozen more. Soon the underworld was twinkling with ten thousand points of light. He had entered the twilight zone, the ocean's vast midwater region, the most inhabited domain on the planet.

The deeper he descended, the more curious the fish became. Schools of hatchet fish flew past his nose cone, staring at him with bulbous eyes, their narrow bodies blinking blue by means of light-producing photophores. The glider propelled past harvests of bioluminescent jellyfish, their transparent bodies filtering red in his sub's emergency keel light.

"Abyssopelagic animals," Jonas whispered to himself, reciting the technical name for these unique groups

of fish, squid, and prawns. He watched as a four-foot gulper eel hovered in front of him, surfing on the nose cone's wake. Deciding to attack the larger sub, the eel spun around and opened its mouth, hyperextending and unhinging its jaws, revealing vicious rows of needle-sharp teeth. Jonas tapped the acrylic and the eel darted away.

To his left, a deep-sea anglerfish circled, an eerie light appearing over its mouth. The species possessed a rod fin that lit up like a lightning bug's tail. Small fish would mistake the light for food and swim straight toward it, right into the angler's wide-open mouth.

Even in the cold, perpetual darkness of the sea, nature had found a way to adapt.

Jonas hadn't noticed the cold creeping up on him. He glanced at his temperature gauge. Forty-two degrees outside. He adjusted the thermostat to heat the interior capsule.

The wave of panic happened without warning, jerking Jonas right off his stomach, causing him to slam his head against the ceiling of the pod. It was a desperate feeling, comparable to being buried alive in a coffin, unable to see, unable to escape. Sweat poured from his body, his breathing became erratic, and he found himself hyperventilating. He reached for two more pills, then, fearing an overdose, flicked on the exterior lights of the sub.

The beam revealed nothing but more blackness, but it served its purpose—to reorientate its pilot. Jonas

took a breath, then wiped the sweat from his eyes. He turned down the heat, the cooler air helping.

D.J. was calling him over the radio. "What's with the light, Doc? We have strict orders."

"Just, uh . . . testing to make sure they still work. How're you doing back there?"

"Okay, I guess. This damn cable's all tangled around the mechanical arm. Kind of like my telephone cord gets."

"D.J., if it's a problem, we should head back—"

"I've got it under control. When we get to the bottom, I'll flip around a few dozen times and unwind." D.J. laughed at his own joke, but Jonas could hear the tension in the younger pilot's voice.

Jonas called up to DeMarco. "D.J. says his cable's twisting around the mechanical arm. Can you do anything topside to relieve some of the pressure?"

"Negative. D.J.'s got the problem under control. We'll monitor him. You concentrate on what you're doing, and turn off that damn light. DeMarco out."

Jonas hit the toggle switch again, then checked his depth gauge: 17,266 feet. They had been descending now for forty minutes, and were still only halfway to the bottom. He rubbed his eyes, then attempted to stretch his lower back within the tight leather harness.

The cramped capsule reminded Jonas of the time he had to submit to ninety minutes' worth of MRIs. The massive machine had been situated only inches above his head, the sword of Damocles waiting to crush his

skull. Only the soft glow from the *Abyss Glider*'s control panel gave him a sense of direction, keeping him sane.

The Lexan pod creaked. The water pressure surrounding him was 8,000 pounds per square inch and rising. Jonas felt the telltale signs of claustrophobia creeping in again, his skin tingling, his face flushing. This time he fought the urge to flick on the 7,500-watt searchlight, focusing on his breathing. His eyes moved over the Lexan interior of the capsule, damp with condensation.

Why am I here?

Long minutes passed. The depth gauge numbers continued to mount: 23,850 . . . 28,400 . . . 30,560 . . . 31,200 . . . He stared out into the blackness, his hands trembling from nerves and fatigue. 33,120 . . . 34,000! He was now deeper than he'd ever gone before.

Jonas felt a slight trace of vertigo, which he hoped had more to do with the rich oxygen mixture in the submersible than with his medicine. His eyes moved from the inky water to the control panel readouts. The outside ocean temperature was thirty-six degrees . . . and rising!

D.J.'s voice shattered his thoughts. "Okay, Doc, turn on your exterior light, you should be able to see the hydrothermal ceiling."

Jonas complied, the light cannon piercing the darkness, illuminating a steaming, swirling, muddy layer of soot.

"Hang on, Doc, here's where it gets a bit rough."

The glider shook, jump-starting Jonas's heart. Lexan creaked, then the nose cone penetrated the mineral ceiling, the sweeping current slamming him sideways in his harness.

He began hyperventilating, the fear washing over him like a tsunami, his mind praying to his maker, begging for the ship's hull to maintain its integrity beneath the weight of the ocean's depths. *Please, Lord, don't let me die down here! Anywhere but here!*

And then he was through, piercing the crystal clear bottom waters as if entering the eye of a hurricane. Jonas opened his eyes wide, awestruck by the view. Below was a petrified forest of black smokers— towering chimneys of hardened mineral deposits, their open vents spewing thick brownish black clouds of superheated mineralized water into the abyss. Spread out along the sea floor surrounding these tall, skinny volcanoes were uncountable rows of giant albino clams, their white shells glowing as his heavenly light passed over them. Each was more than a foot in diameter, and there were thousands of them, lying in formation around the vents as if worshipping a god. The searchlight picked up movement along the bottom, and Jonas caught sight of vent crustaceans, albino lobsters, and albino crabs, all glowing in the darkness of the abyss, all completely blind.

D.J. was right. He had entered a different world.

THE BOTTOM

D.J.'s voice snapped him back to the reality of their mission. "Okay, Doc, I'm through. My glider has a tracking device that'll guide me to the UNIS, so follow me. It's gonna get very hot as we pass above those black smokers, so be careful. You catch a geyser of superheated water full on and it could melt the ceramic seals on your sub."

"Thanks for the warning." Jonas checked his digital temperature readout: 77 degrees Fahrenheit and still climbing as they descended toward the bottom. *How hot could it go? How much could the* Abyss Glider *handle?*

He followed D.J.'s submersible as it wove its way through the blackness, the trailing steel cable occasionally slapping against his nose cone. Water billowed up at them from below, heavy in sulfur, copper, iron, and other minerals that seeped out of the seabed's cracks.

Jonas maneuvered his sub between two of the smoking towers, his visibility virtually eliminated as he passed through the murk. His temperature gauge momentarily rocketed past 230 degrees, causing him to turn hard to port, grazing his left wing against the side of another black smoker.

As he descended beyond 35,000 feet, bizarre albino life forms came into view. Jonas knew that many species of fish living in the dark sea depths made their own light by means of chemicals called luciferins—a luminous bacteria that lived in their bodies. Nature had

endowed the species with white skin and a luminescent glow to attract prey and locate each other.

Life. The amount and variety within the trenches had shocked scientists, who had incorrectly theorized that no life form could exist on the planet without sunlight. Jonas felt awed at being in the Challenger Deep. In the most desolate location on the planet, nature had found a way to allow life to not only exist, but to thrive.

A wave of trepidation washed over him with the thought.

What else is down here?

Jonas was overwhelmed by a sudden urge to locate the damaged UNIS, help secure the tow line, and get the hell out of Dodge.

The glider passed over massive clusters of tubeworms, flowing like clumps of spaghetti in the warm currents. Pure white and fluorescent, except for the tips, which were blood red. Twelve feet long, five inches thick, in groups too numerous to even approximate. The tubeworms fed on the bacteria in the water. In turn, eelpouts and other small fish fed off the tubeworms.

D.J.'s sub slowed up ahead. Jonas backed off, careful to maintain a safe distance. The two aquanauts wanted to remain within sight of one another, but didn't want Jonas to get caught in D.J.'s trailing cable.

D.J.'s voice crackled over the radio. "It's up ahead, steady on course one-five-zero."

Jonas followed D.J.'s sub along the 200-million-year-old sea floor, maneuvering just above a winding highway-sized gulley.

"Doc, I'm getting hit by strong currents, better hold on." As if on cue, Jonas felt his tail section begin wagging like a dog's tail. The submersible pitched, its engine fighting to maintain course and speed.

"There it is!" D.J. announced.

The shell of the destroyed UNIS looked like a piece of scrap metal buried beneath a ton of debris. D.J. positioned his sub well above the remains, shining his spotlight over it like a streetlamp. "It's all yours, Doc. Go ahead and survey the damage."

Jonas moved closer to the UNIS, floating into the light of D.J.'s sub. He aimed his own spotlight at the shattered hull and drifted past it to the other side. *Something's different*, he thought, looking at the debris around the base. *It's moved.*

"What do you think?" D.J. asked over the radio. "Another landslide?"

"Maybe, but that's not what destroyed this UNIS. There are no boulders large enough to leave these kind of indentations." Remembering the tooth, Jonas strained his eyes for a glimpse of something white. He inched the glider closer, aiming its light between rocks.

And there it was!

"D.J., I can't believe it! I think I've located that tooth!" Jonas could barely contain his excitement. He extended his sub's mechanical arm, aiming the claw above the eight-inch white triangular object. He felt contact! Carefully, he lifted the object out of the crevice.

D.J. was laughing hysterically over the radio. So were Terry and DeMarco.

Jonas looked at the object he had traveled seven miles down to obtain.

It was the remains of a dead albino starfish.

THE MALE

Terry, Frank Heller, and Alphonse DeMarco nearly fell out of their chairs in uncontrollable fits of laughter. Jonas could hear them over the radio, could feel his blood pressure rising. For a long moment, he seriously considered ramming his submersible into the canyon wall.

"I'm sorry for laughing, man," said D.J., "but you gotta admit, that was pretty funny. The thought of a killer starfish crushing the UNIS—"

"Enough already!"

"Okay, okay. Hey, wanna laugh at my stupidity? Take a look at my sub's mechanical arm."

Jonas looked up. The steel cable had wound in a dozen chaotic loops around the six-foot mechanical limb of D.J.'s sub, so much so that the arm was barely visible. "D.J., that's not funny. You've got a lot of untangling to do before you can free yourself to attach the line."

"I can handle it. You work on clearing that debris."

Jonas lowered the mechanical arm, trying to focus on the task at hand. He felt his blood boiling, beads of sweat dripping down his sides. Within minutes, he had managed to clear a third of the debris from the UNIS, exposing several intact eyebolts.

"Nice job, Doc." D.J. was slowly revolving the mechanical arm in tight counterclockwise circles. Gradually, the steel cable began freeing itself from around the extended appendage.

"You need some help?" asked Jonas.

"No, I'm fine. Stand by."

Jonas hovered the *Abyss Glider* twenty feet off the bottom. Masao had been right, all of them had. He had hallucinated, allowed his imagination to wander, violating a major rule of deep-sea exploration. One mistake, one simple loss of focus, had cost the lives of his crew and his reputation as a submersible pilot.

What was left for him now? Jonas thought about Maggie. She'll want a divorce, no doubt. Jonas was an embarrassment. She had turned to Bud Harris, his own friend, for love and support while Jonas had built his new career on a lie. His triumphant return to the Challenger Deep had merely served as a wake-up call. He had wasted seven years of his life, destroying his marriage in the process.

A starfish, for Christ's sake . . .

Blip.

The sound caught him off-guard. Jonas located his sonar. A red dot had appeared on the abyssal terrain, the source of the disturbance approaching fast.

Blip.

Blip, blip, blip . . .

Jonas felt his heart racing. Whatever it was, it was big!

"D.J., check your sonar!"

"My sonar? Whoa . . . what the hell is that?"

"DeMarco?"

Alphonse DeMarco had stopped laughing. "We see it too. Has D.J. attached the cable yet?"

Jonas looked up, where the sub's mechanical arm was twisting wildly, attempting to free the last loops. "Not yet. How big would you estimate this object to be?"

"Jonas, relax," shot back Terry. "We know what you're thinking. Heller says sonar's merely detecting a school of fish."

"Heller's a doctor, and not a very good one! Whatever this is, it's homing in on our location!"

Jonas took several deep breaths, forcing himself to think. *Homing in . . . it is homing in! Homing in on our vibrations!* "D.J., stop twisting!" commanded Jonas.

"Jonas, I'm nearly—"

"Shut down everything, all systems. Do it now!" Jonas shut off his sub's power, the 7,500-watt searchlight going dark. "D.J., if this object is a Megalodon, it's homing in on the vibrations and electrical impulses from our subs. Kill your power! Now, goddammit!"

D.J.'s heart raced. He stopped twisting the mechanical arm. "Al, what should I do?"

"Taylor's crazy. Attach the cable and get the hell out of there."

"D.J. . . ." Jonas stopped speaking, his eye catching a massive object circling less than five hundred yards away.

It was glowing.

D.J.'s searchlight flickered off, dropping a cloak of darkness around the two submersibles. Without the glow from his LCD monitor, Jonas couldn't even see his own hand in front of his face, but he could feel it

shaking. He kept it close to the power switch for his own light.

Slowly, the circling object came into view, a vague, pale glow gliding back and forth through the overwhelming blackness. It was sizing them up, evaluating, as it moved silently a football-field length from their subs.

Jonas felt his throat constrict.

There was no doubt. He could see the conical snout, the thick triangular head, the crescent-moon tail. He estimated the Megalodon to be a good forty-five feet long and 40,000 pounds. Pure white, an albino ghost, just like the giant clams, just like the tubeworms.

The beast turned again, revealing a pair of claspers. . .

A male.

D.J.'s voice whispered across the radio. "Okay, Doc, I swear to you, I'm a believer. So what's your plan?"

"Stay calm. It's sizing us up. It's not sure we're edible. No movements, we have to be careful not to trigger a response."

"Taylor, report!" Heller's voice ripped through the capsule.

"Frank, shut up," whispered Jonas. "We're being watched."

"D.J.," Terry's voice whispered over the radio.

D.J. didn't respond. He was mesmerized by the frightening creature before him, paralyzed with fear.

Jonas knew they had only one chance; somehow they had to make it past the hydrothermal plume and

back into the frigid open waters. The Meg wouldn't follow, at least he prayed it wouldn't.

It was getting warm. The powerless subs were drifting, the bottom currents pushing them toward a patch of vents. Dripping with sweat, Jonas watched as the glow of the male's hide grew larger. He caught a glimpse of a bluish-gray eye.

The monster turned. It was coming straight for them!

The massive creature loomed ghostlike in the pitch black.

Mouth agape—

Rows of jagged teeth!

Jonas ignited his sub's exterior light, blasting 7,500 watts into the creature's sensitive nocturnal eyes. The male whipped its head sideways, disappearing with a flicker of its tail into the darkness.

D.J. screamed over the radio. "Holy shit, Doc—"

The concussion wave hit them seconds later. D.J.'s glider twisted and spun, the steel cable going taut, preventing it from drifting farther. Untethered, Jonas's ship swept into the side of a black smoker, striking it tail-first, the impact crushing the sub's propeller shaft.

The Megalodon instinctively followed the movement, diving toward Jonas's crippled glider, now lying upside down and powerless against the base of the black smoker. Jonas opened his eyes as the approaching glow filled the capsule. The monster's thick white snout lifted, the upper jaw pushing forward—

—the triangular head darting away, avoiding his sub's beacon of light.

Jonas closed his eyes, fighting to catch a breath. For a millisecond he felt gratitude that his death would be delivered by the pressure change and not by the hideous teeth of the creature that now stalked him.

The male rushed him again, then broke once more from its frontal assault, whipping its girth in a tight circle that sent a current of water rushing at the downed *Abyss Glider.* The impact wave tossed the powerless submersible over and over again, sending it tumbling deeper into the ravine.

Jonas felt warm liquid ooze down his forehead seconds before he slipped into unconsciousness.

THE KILL

D.J. Tanaka accelerated his *Abyss Glider* into a steep seventy-degree climb. He ignored the constant barrage begging him to respond, choosing instead to focus on the race at hand. Blood pounded in his ears, but his hands were steady. He knew the stakes were high—life and death. The adrenaline junkie grinned.

He stole a quick glance over his left shoulder. The albino monster had banked sharply away from the sea floor and was now pursuing him like a guided missile. D.J. estimated he had a twelve-hundred-foot lead, the frigid waters still a good two to three thousand feet away.

It was going to be close.

His sonar beeped louder—

The depth gauge rose—

Sweat poured from his angular face—

"Come on, baby! Climb!"

The small glider burst through the thick ceiling of mineral and debris, whipped sideways as if caught by a tornado, then burst free into the frigid open waters.

D.J. looked back over his shoulder. The Megalodon was nowhere in sight. He checked his exterior temperature gauge. Fifty-two degrees and falling.

Made it . . .

The glow of the albino's hide registered in D.J.'s vision a split second before the gargantuan mouth exploded sideways into the submersible. Spinning upside down, D.J. tried to scream, the sickening crunch

of ceramic and Lexan deafening his ears as his skull imploded, splattering his brains across the shattering cockpit glass.

*   *   *

The Megalodon snorted the warm blood into its nostrils, its entire sensory system quivering in delight. It rammed its snout farther into the tight chamber, unable to reach the remains of D.J. Tanaka's upper torso.

Clutching its crippled prey within its jaws, the male descended back into the warm currents, guarding its kill.

*   *   *

Jonas opened his eyes, though his sight refused to register in the pitch darkness. The submersible was bobbing, but he had no idea as to its orientation. A sharp pain shot up his leg. His foot was caught on something. He worked it loose and turned his body. A warm liquid drained into his eye. He wiped it away. Blood, he realized, though he could still not see his hand in front of his face.

How long had he been out?

The power had shut down, but the compartment was steaming hot. *I must be lying on the bottom, in that ravine,* Jonas thought. He reached out blindly, feeling for the controls, only to find he had slipped out of the pilot's harness and fallen to the other end of the capsule. He felt his way back into the cockpit and groped for the controls on the panel. He flipped the power switch, but nothing happened.

The AG II was dead, resting beneath 35,000 feet of water.

Above and outside the sub he saw something—a fraction of bioluminescent light refracted in the Plexiglas. Jonas pushed forward into the Lexan bubble, craning his neck upward.

In the distance he caught a fleeting glimpse of the male, swimming slowly toward the sea floor, a dark object dangling between its upper jaw and snout.

"D.J. . . ." The crippled submersible dangled from the predator's jaws, the steel cable still attached, the slack now looping and winding itself around the Megalodon's torso.

*   *   *

Frank Heller sat frozen in his chair. "We need to know what's going on down there," he said, pointing at the blank monitors.

Terry continued in vain to make radio contact. "D.J., can you hear me? D.J.!"

DeMarco was speaking rapidly with Captain Barre over an internal phone line. He and his crew were stationed in the stern, manning the A-frame's massive winch.

"Frank, Leon says there's movement registering on the steel cable. D.J.'s sub is still attached."

Heller jumped to his feet, moving to the TV monitor showing the winch on the stern deck. "Haul him up before he dies down there! If he's lost power, we're his only hope."

"What about Jonas?" Terry asked.

"We have no way of reaching him," DeMarco answered, "but we might be able to save your brother."

Heller leaned forward in his console and spoke into the mike. "Leon, you there?"

Leon Barre's voice boomed over the speaker. "Standing by!"

"Do it. Retract the cable!"

*   *   *

Jonas watched as the male passed directly overhead, its belly quivering as its jaws opened and closed. The ravenous predator continued to prod its snout into the remains of the submersible, but could not gain enough leverage to access the gushing meat wedged inside.

Jonas held his breath, praying the creature could not detect his presence, hoping beyond hope that it would not equate its last meal with his own powerless sub.

But the male was preoccupied, its attention fully focused on D.J.'s bloated remains, unaware that the steel cable looped around its torso was going taut, the slack being rapidly taken in from above.

Seconds later, the steel line bit into the monster's white hide, tearing into the shark's tender pectoral fins.

The cable's crushing embrace sent the male Megalodon into spasms. It spun its torso in a fit of rage, whipping its caudal fin to and fro in a futile attempt to free itself. The more it fought, the more entangled it became.

Jonas stared in helpless fascination as the Meg fought in vain, unable to release itself from the steel bonds. With its pectoral fins pinned to its side, it couldn't

stabilize itself. Shaking its monstrous head from side to side, it released powerful concussion waves that rocked Jonas's sub.

After several minutes, the predator stopped thrashing, exhausted. Within the entanglement of steel cable, the only sign of life came from the occasional flutter of its gills. Slowly, the *Kiku*'s winch began hauling the entrapped creature toward the frigid waters above.

The dying male thrashed again, its movements sending telltale signals of distress throughout the Challenger Deep.

Miles away, a much larger predator moved through the abyss, homing in on the vibrations.

THE FEMALE

It appeared out of nowhere, sweeping directly over Jonas, its deathly glow illuminating the black landscape like an enormous moon. Its sheer mass took several seconds to pass overhead. Until he caught sight of its towering tail fin, Jonas thought it might be some kind of submarine.

From the emergency light's glow along the bottom of his glider Jonas could see the underside of a triangular snout, followed by a hideous lower jaw. A collection of luminescent deep-sea remora that looked to be from another planet followed in tow. All had bioluminescent lures and needle-like teeth that jutted out from all conceivable angles. Some were squat with cactus-like protrusions, others long and eel-like, with crimson dorsal fins. A nasty half-moon-shaped bite scar ringed the underside of the Megalodon's left pectoral fin, followed by a protruding stomach that was clearly swollen pregnant. A pelvic fin passed, then the female's cloaca, its rim lacerated and scarred, confirming the identity of the monster as a very large female.

The female Megalodon was at least fifteen feet longer than its mate, weighing well over thirty tons. A casual slap of her caudal fin sent a concussion wave exploding against the damaged sub, lifting and pushing it farther down the gully. Jonas braced himself as the AG II skidded across the crevice and flipped twice before settling in another cloud of silt. He pressed his face to the nose cone and, as the muck settled, saw the

female rise toward the male, which was still struggling to free itself from the steel cable.

The female circled warily, her nostrils inhaling the remnants of D.J.'s blood. Suddenly she turned, driving her hyperextended jaws around the soft underbelly of her former mate, the colossal impact driving the smaller Megalodon fifty feet upward. Rows of seven-inch serrated teeth ripped open the male's white hide, the female whipping its monstrous head left, then right, left then right . . . until it tore away a ten-ton mouthful of flesh, exposing the mortally wounded male's stomach and intestines.

The *Kiku*'s winch bit into the slack, gaining momentum, pulling the cable upward even as the female chewed and swallowed.

Jonas panted as he watched the spectacle. The male's glow was diminishing as it rose, the female refusing to abandon her kill, circling after her suddenly animated prey. As if jolted by electricity she struck again, burying her snout deep within the gushing wound, her swollen white belly quivering in spasms as she gorged herself on huge chunks of flesh and entrails.

The male's body spasmed as it rose beyond the hydrothermal layer and into the cold. The female escorted it up, the hot blood of her mate bathing her in a soothing thick river of warmth as she rose out of the depths. She continued to feed, her murderous jaws entrenched deep within the wound, her teeth shredding the spleen and duodenum as hundreds of

gallons of warm blood rushed into her open mouth and over her torso, protecting her from the cold.

Trapped in his sub, Jonas watched the thrashing white glow disappear overhead. Seconds later, the batteries supplying the emergency lights petered out, leaving the blackness of the canyon to close in around him.

* * *

Terry, DeMarco, and Heller ran out on deck, where the ship's medical team and at least a dozen other crew members peered over the railing, waiting for their missing comrade to surface.

Captain Barre stared at the iron O-ring that suspended the pulley from the steel frame of the winch. It was straining under the weight of its load, threatening to snap apart at any moment.

He pulled DeMarco aside. "Don't know what's on the other end of this," he said gravely, "but it sure as shit ain't just D.J.'s sub."

ESCAPE

Jonas huddled in the suffocating darkness. The downed submersible refused to settle in the current, and he registered every bump, every creak, every ambient sound of the Challenger Deep. He was beyond frightened, yet he knew he'd suffocate if he didn't act quickly. The wings of his sub had been mangled in the crash, and the engine was out of commission. It would be impossible to ascend with the dead weight of the mechanical end of the craft. He had to find the emergency lever and jettison the Lexan escape pod.

But if he jettisoned free and floated toward the surface, the movement could attract the female!

Where was she? Had she risen out of the abyss and into the midwaters? Or had she circled back, waiting for him even now?

Jonas was drenched in sweat, beginning to feel dizzy again. He couldn't be sure if it was from loss of blood or the steadily diminishing supply of air. Waves of panic, accelerated by the claustrophobia, rattled his nerves. Seven miles of ocean sat on top of him! Seven miles!

Gotta breathe . . . Gotta get outta here . . .

Enveloped in darkness, his fingers groped along the floor beneath his stomach, locating the small storage compartment. Jonas leaned backward, pulling open the hatch, straining to reach the spare tank of air. He unscrewed a valve and released a steady stream into the pod.

Choose:

Stay here and die in peace, or take a chance and try to make it out of the trench alive by activating the escape pod, floating free . . . except you'll be exposing yourself to the monster that might be circling out there, waiting to eat you!

He chose.

Rolling over, Jonas strapped himself back into the shoulder harness. Suspended upside down, he felt along his right side until he found the metal latch box.

Opened it. Gripped the emergency lever. Readied himself.

Jonas yanked back hard on the handle. A bright flash seared the darkness behind him, jolting him against the pilot's harness as the capsule exploded through the water and across the canyon floor. The noise and burst of light terrified him—it was an announcement to the denizens of the deep—a dinner bell to feed!

He held his breath, waiting to see the albino killer.

The escape pod leveled out, then floated topside, gathering speed as it rose.

Within minutes he had reached the silt-covered ceiling. The rapid current grabbed the pod and whipped it around on its perpetual merry-go-round of gravel and soot and sulfuric gases, refusing to let go, until Jonas thrust his back over and over again against the pod's ceiling, helping release the submersible from the torrent's death grip.

The Lexan pod floated free.

The internal temperature dropped quickly, plunging into the forties. It would be several hours before he reached the surface, and Jonas knew he had to concentrate on keeping warm. His clothes were soaked with perspiration. His teeth began to chatter.

Pulling himself into a fetal position, he closed his eyes and tried to remain calm.

*   *   *

The *Kiku*'s crew stood by the guardrail in the stern, watching the steel cable emerge yard by yard from the heavy sea, waiting and hoping for D.J.'s submersible to peek out from under, dragged upward by its mechanical arm.

Terry pressed her forehead to the cold rail and prayed.

Shouts caught her attention. She opened her eyes, crewmen pointing to the green surface waters as they began to bubble . . . gurgling with a bright pink froth. Seconds later, the enormous white head of the male Megalodon broke the surface, the crushed ceramic and Lexan pod of the mangled *Abyss Glider* wedged between its horrible open jaws.

Crewmen screamed! Terry felt herself swooning.

The creature kept rising, revealing its own ravaged remains. Wound steel cable held together hunks of partially eaten flesh, muscle, and internal organs. A long spinal column and rib cage was exposed, clear back to the intact crescent-shaped caudal fin, which dangled in the churning sea beneath it.

The shocked crew could only stare as the remains of the partially devoured pigmentless monster were hauled out of the water and dragged over the rail and across the broad deck of the ship. As the monster's head struck the deck, the bloated, nearly unrecognizable remains of D.J. Tanaka poured out over the planks.

Terry collapsed to her knees and fainted.

*   *   *

The escaped pod had been rising steadily in the darkness for hours. Loss of blood and the bitter cold were pushing Jonas deeper into a state of shock. His shivering had ceased, yielding to a loss of feeling in his toes and fingers, and still he could see nothing but pitch-black water above his head.

Hang on, J.T. It's just a walk in the park . . .

*   *   *

Frank Heller lowered his binoculars and scanned the seascape with his naked eye from the bridge of the *Kiku*. The two Zodiac motorized rafts continued expanding their perimeter search, the high seas and blistering rain from the arriving storm making it near-impossible to see, let alone spot a three-foot red flag.

"Storm's getting worse. Taylor's probably dead. We're wasting time and risking a dozen lives in these seas looking for a corpse."

DeMarco stood beside him at the rail. "Masao insists we continue the search. Those coast-guard choppers had better get here soon."

"Al, we can't wait any longer. Assuming Taylor wasn't killed by the Megalodon, then he's certainly died from exposure to the cold."

DeMarco turned to look for the hundredth time at the ravaged torso of the albino monster lying on the main deck. The science team was examining the carcass, taking measurements, shooting photos and video. "How many more of those things could be down there?"

Heller shrugged. "I don't know. What's important is that they're down there, and not up here."

*   *   *

Terry Tanaka stood at the bow of the yellow Zodiac as it bounded along the swells, desperately searching the valley of waves ahead of her for any sign of the missing *Abyss Glider*. Until she found it, there would be no time for grieving, no time for the pain gripping her heart. She had to locate Jonas while any chance still remained.

There were two divers in her boat, plus Leon Barre, who was steering from the rear of the Zodiac. "Terry, that's it! DeMarco's called the search."

"DeMarco's not in charge, I am. Circle back again!"

He shook his head, but complied.

"Wait!" Terry saw something disappear behind a swell . . . a flicker of color. She pointed off the starboard bow. "There! Head over there."

The red vinyl flag was just visible over the crest of an incoming wave. Leon guided them to the capsule, which floated in the water. They could barely see

Jonas's body through the fogged surface of the Lexan escape pod.

"Is he alive?" Terry asked, as her divers readied their masks and flipped overboard.

She leaned over, waiting for an answer.

The pod was too heavy to lift from the water. Divers opened the rear hatch and reached in, grabbing Jonas by his legs. They hauled him out of the craft as it quickly filled with water and sank, disappearing beneath the waves.

One of the divers turned, signaling a thumbs-up. "Unconscious, but he's breathing!"

Terry lay back in the raft, tears of grief for her brother welling in her eyes.

HARBOR

Frank Heller couldn't figure out how the news had spread so quickly. It had taken less than three hours for the *Kiku* to reach the Aura Harbor naval base in Guam. Despite heavy winds and rain, two Japanese television crews and members of a local station were waiting for them on the dock, along with press reporters and photographers from the navy, the *Manila Times*, and the local *Guam Sentinel*. They surrounded Heller the moment he disembarked, bombarding him with questions about the giant shark, the dead pilot, and the surviving scientist who'd been airlifted ahead for medical treatment.

"Professor Taylor suffered a concussion and is being treated for hypothermia," Heller told them.

The cameramen trained their lenses on the ship's physician, but when the carcass of the Megalodon was hoisted off the *Kiku*'s main deck by crane, they scrambled for a shot.

An insistent young Japanese woman pressed her microphone at Heller. "Where will you take the shark?"

"It'll be stored in a refrigerated warehouse. The remains will eventually be taken to the Tanaka Oceanographic Institute."

"What happened to the creature? What killed it?"

"We're not certain at this point. The shark might have been ripped apart by the cable that entangled it, and drowned."

"It looks like it's been eaten," said a balding American with bushy eyebrows. "Is it possible another shark attacked this one?"

"It's possible, but—"

"Are you saying there are more of these monsters out there?"

"Did anyone see—?"

"Do you think—?"

Heller raised his hands. "One at a time." He nodded to a heavyset man from the Guam paper with his pen raised in the air.

"Our readers will want to know if it's safe to go boating?"

Heller spoke confidently. "Let me put your fears to rest. If there are any more of these sharks in the Mariana Trench, six miles of near-freezing water stands between them and us. Apparently, it's kept them trapped down there for at least two million years. It'll probably keep 'em down there a few million more."

"Dr. Heller?"

Heller turned. David Adashek stood before him. "Isn't Professor Taylor a marine paleobiologist?"

Heller glanced furtively at the crowd. "Yes. He has done some work—"

"More than some work. I understand he has a theory about these . . . dinosaur sharks. I believe they're called Megalodons?"

"Yes, well, I think I'll leave it to Dr. Taylor to explain his theories to you. Now if you don't mind, we've just lost a loved one, try to understand." Heller pushed

through the crowd, ignoring the flurry of questions that followed him.

"Gangway!" came a thundering voice from behind. Leon Barre was supervising the transfer of the Megalodon carcass onto the dock, a massive boom raising it by its crescent-moon-shaped tail.

A photographer pushed to the front and shouted, "Captain, could we get your picture with the monster?"

Barre waved his arm at the crane operator, who stopped the boom. Momentum sent the Megalodon's head swaying to and fro, drenching the crowd with bloody seawater. Cameramen scrambled for an angle, but the carcass was so long it would not fit into the frame. Barre stood beside the giant head, but was clearly unnerved to be so close to the mouth. He gazed inside the lower jaw line at the teeth, the front row standing upright, another five to six rows of replacement teeth folded neatly behind them, back into the gum line. Feeling his knees go weak, the burly sea captain backed away.

"Smile, Captain," someone shouted.

Barre turned, staring grimly ahead. "Just take the damn picture and let me be."

THE *MAGNATE*

It was another gorgeous day in San Diego, the sky near cloudless, the temperature a balmy 78 degrees. San Diego's harbor was teeming with boaters, the catamarans racing beneath the Coronado Bay Bridge, the whale watchers moving farther out to sea, hoping to catch a close-up view of California's Gray Whales, twenty-five thousand of which were passing through San Diego's waters on their annual 7,000-mile migration from the Bering Sea to Baja California.

The 97-foot Abeking & Rasmusen super-yacht, *Magnate*, moved at a leisurely three knots, its course paralleling the San Diego skyline. A sleek fortress of fiberglass and steel, she was white with pine-green trim, possessing a 25-foot beam and 9.5-foot draft. Her twin 1200 horsepower engines could drive her through choppy seas at an easy twenty knots, her lush interior making the ride a pleasure in any weather.

Bud Harris had purchased the yacht from the owner of a struggling Arena League football franchise. He had gutted the insides, redoing everything in polished teak and mahogany, the walls and cabinets in a deep cherry wood. The floors were blue sapphire marble, the bay windows tinted, running floor to ceiling in the master suite, which was complete with a small gymnasium, home entertainment center, and a Jacuzzi.

Maggie Taylor was lying topless on the teakwood deck of the master suite's private sundeck, her oiled body glistening under the noon-day sun.

Bud watched her from his Jacuzzi, reading the *Los Angeles Times*. "You always said a tan looks good on camera."

Maggie shielded her eyes, squinting up at him. "This is for you, baby," she said with a smile. She rolled over on her stomach and watched a tiny television. "How about another drink? This is hard work."

"You got it." He climbed out of the tub, wrapped himself in a towel, and headed back inside the air-conditioned stateroom.

Moments later, Maggie screamed his name. He ran out on deck to find her sitting up, clutching a towel to her breasts, staring openmouthed at the TV. "I don't believe it!"

"What!?!" Bud hurried over, gazing at the TV. "Jesus . . . is that thing real?"

The Megalodon's head and fang-filled jaws filled the screen, its body dangling from the crane of the *Kiku*.

Bud leaned over and turned up the sound:

". . . experts believe could be the giant prehistoric shark, *Carcharodon megalodon*, ancestor of the modern-day great white. No one seems to know how the shark could have survived, but Dr. Taylor, who was injured in the capture, may be able to provide some answers. Taylor is recovering at the naval hospital in Guam.

"In China today, negotiations for a trade . . ."

"Dr. Taylor? Maggie, you think they mean Jonas?"

"Who the hell else could they mean?" She rushed into the master suite, Bud shouting after her, "Hey? Where're you going?"

"I need to call my office." She grabbed the phone, dialing frantically. Her assistant answered. "It's Maggie. Any messages?"

"Mr. Henderson called twice, and I've got a dozen messages from media outlets looking for a quote. Something about your husband. Oh, and a David Adashek's been trying to reach you all morning."

"The rest can wait, give me Adashek's number."

Maggie hung up, then dialed the overseas operator to connect her to Guam. Several minutes later, the line was ringing.

"Adashek."

"David, what the hell is happening?"

"Maggie? I've been trying to reach you all morning. Where are you?"

"Never mind that. I just saw the news report. Where did that shark come from? Where's Jonas? Has anyone spoken with him yet?"

"Slow down. Jonas is recovering in the Guam naval hospital. He's okay, but there's a guard posted at his door so no one can speak with him. The Megalodon's for real. Looks like you were wrong about your husband."

Maggie felt ill.

"Maggie, you still there?"

"Shut up, I'm trying to think."

"Maggie, this could be the story of the decade. Jonas is a major player, you could still get to him before anyone else."

"That's true."

"Be sure to ask him about the other shark."

Maggie's heart skipped a beat. "What other shark?"

"The one that ate the one that killed the Tanaka kid. Everybody's talking about it, but the Tanaka Institute's people are refusing to comment. Jonas is the only one who knows what happened down there. Maybe he'd talk to you?"

Maggie's mind raced. "Okay, okay, I'm coming to Guam. Now listen carefully: I want you to stay on the story. Try to find out what the authorities are going to do to locate this other shark."

"Maggie, they don't even know if it surfaced. The crew of the *Kiku* are swearing it never left the trench, they're claiming the thing's still trapped down there."

"Just stay on it, someone will talk. There's an extra grand in it for you if you can get me some inside dope about this second shark. I'll call you as soon as I land in Guam."

"You're the boss."

Maggie hung up. Bud was standing next to her. "So?"

"Bud, I need your help. Who do you know in Guam?"

RECOVERY

The navy MP on duty outside Jonas's room at the Aura naval hospital rose to attention as Terry approached the door.

"Sorry, ma'am. No press allowed."

"I'm not with the press. My name's Terry Tanaka. I was with—"

"Oh . . . excuse me." The MP stepped aside. "My apologies, ma'am. And . . . my condolences." He averted his eyes.

"Thank you," she said softly, entering Jonas's room.

Jonas lay in bed, facing the window. A gauze bandage was wrapped around his forehead, an IV dripping into his left arm. He turned toward Terry as she entered, his face pale.

"Terry? I'm sorry . . ." he rasped.

Terry nodded. "Are you all right?"

"I will be. Have you talked to your father?"

"He'll be here in the morning."

Jonas turned toward the window, unsure of what to say. "This is my fault, I should have never—"

"You tried to warn us. We just ridiculed you."

"I shouldn't have let D.J. go. I should have—"

"Stop it, Jonas," Terry snapped. "I can't deal with my own guilt, let alone yours. D.J. was an adult, and he certainly wasn't about to listen to you. He wanted to go, and so did I, despite your warnings. We're all devastated . . . in shock. I don't know what's going

to happen next. I can't think that far ahead—" Tears flowed from her almond eyes.

"Take it easy." She sat down next to him on his bed, hugging him while she cried on his chest. Jonas smoothed her hair, trying to comfort her.

After a few minutes, she sat up and turned away from Jonas to wipe her eyes. "You're seeing me in rare form. I never cry."

"You don't always have to be so tough."

She smiled. "Yeah, I do. I told you, my mom died when I was very young. I've had to take care of Dad and D.J. all these years by myself."

"How's your dad doing?"

"He's a wreck. I need to get him through this. I don't even know what to do . . . Do you have a funeral? Should we cremate his remains?" The tears clouded in her eyes.

"Speak to DeMarco. Have him arrange a service."

"I just want this to be over. I want to get back to California."

Jonas looked at her a moment. "Terry, you need to know something. There were two Megs in the trench. The one that the *Kiku* hauled up, it was attacked by a larger female. She was rising with the carcass . . ."

"No, it's okay. Everyone on board was watching. Nothing else surfaced. Heller says the other creature, this female, couldn't survive the journey through the icy waters. You told us that yourself."

"Terry, listen to me." He tried to sit up, but the pain forced him down again. "The male's carcass . . . there was a lot of blood in the water. Megalodons are like

great whites. They're not warm-blooded like mammals, but they are warm-bodied."

"What's your point?"

"When the *Kiku* began hauling up D.J.'s sub, the male became caught in the steel cable. I saw the larger Meg, the female . . . she was rising with the carcass, remaining within the warm-blood stream. I watched her disappear into the colder waters. I think the male's blood trail was keeping her warm."

"How do you know she didn't return to the trench?"

"I don't. But she wouldn't be so quick to abandon her kill. If the female remained within her dead mate's blood stream, she could have made it to the thermocline. She's much bigger than the male, sixty feet or more. A shark that size could probably cover the distance from the trench to the warmer surface waters in less than an hour."

"Jonas, the second shark never surfaced, just the remains of the first . . . and D.J."

She wiped back tears. "I have to go. Try to get some rest."

She squeezed his hand, then left the room.

NIGHT

Jonas awoke with a start. He was in the *Abyss Glider* capsule, bobbing along the surface of the western Pacific. Sunlight glared through the Plexiglas sphere, waves washing over the escape pod's acrylic dome.

The *Kiku* was gone.

I've been dreaming, he thought. *The hospital . . . Terry . . . all a dream.*

He stared at his hands, covered in dried blood. He felt the lump on his scalp.

How long have I been out? Hours? Days?

The water beneath him rippled with curtains of sunlight. He stared down into the deep blue sea, watching . . . waiting for the Megalodon to appear.

He knew she was down there.

He knew she was coming.

The glow appeared first, then the snout, and that smile, the demonic grin. The albino predator rose majestically beneath him, her sinister mouth widening, her jaws opening, revealing her upper gum receding as her jawline and front row of serrated teeth jutted forward, hyperextending . . . her widening mouth a black abyss—

"Ahhhh!"

Jonas awoke with a start. He was in bed, his pajamas bathed in sweat. He was alone in his hospital room. The digital clock read 12:06 a.m.

A dream. A nightmare.

He fell back on the damp sheets and stared at the moonlit ceiling, then forced a deep breath, exhaling slowly.

The fear was gone. Suddenly, he realized he felt better. The fever, the drugs . . . maybe it was the vindication. *I'm hungry*, he thought.

He got out of bed, put on a robe, and walked into the corridor. Empty. He heard the sound of a TV down the hall.

At the nursing station he found the MP sitting alone, his feet on a desk, his shirt open, downing a submarine sandwich while he watched the late news. The young man jumped when he sensed Jonas standing behind him.

"Mr. Taylor . . . you're up."

Jonas looked around. "Where's the nurse?"

"She stepped out for a minute, sir. I told her I'd . . . I'd cover for her." He stared at the bandage on Jonas's head. "You sure you ought to be out of bed, sir?"

"Where can I find something to eat?"

"Cafeteria's closed till six."

Jonas looked desperate.

"You can have some of this." He picked up another half of the bulging sandwich, and held it out for Jonas.

Jonas stared at it. "No, that's all right—"

"Go ahead. It's good stuff."

"All right, sure, thanks." Jonas took the sandwich and began to eat. He felt like he hadn't tasted food in days. "This is great," he said between bites.

"Italian subs are hard to come by out here," the young man said. "Only place I know is halfway around the island. Me and my buddies, we make the trip once a week, just to kind of remind us of home. I don't know why they don't open something closer to the base. Seems to me . . ."

The kid continued talking, but Jonas wasn't listening. Something had caught his eye on the television. "Excuse me," Jonas said. "Can you turn that up?"

The MP stopped talking. "Sure." He raised the volume.

". . . over forty pilot whales and two dozen dolphins beached themselves along Saipan's northern shore. Unfortunately, most of the mammals died before rescuers could push them back out to sea. In other news . . ."

Jonas turned off the volume on the TV. "Saipan. That's in the middle of the northern Marianas, isn't it?"

"That's right, sir. Third island up the chain."

Jonas looked away, thinking.

"What is it, sir?" the MP asked.

Jonas looked at him. "Nothing. Thanks for the sandwich." He turned and headed back down the hall.

The MP watched Jonas hurry back to his room. "Sir," he called after him, "you sure you're all right?"

SURFACE

The 455-foot cargo ship, RMS *St. Columba*, pushed through the dark waters of the western Pacific, her mass displacing 7800 tons. The vessel had set sail from the United Kingdom two months earlier, making her way to South Africa, the Ascensions, and the Canary and St. Helena Islands before continuing her voyage along the Asian coast. While most of her gross tonnage was devoted to cargo, she also carried seventy-nine passengers, the majority of them boarding in Japan, bound for the Hawaiian Islands.

Twenty-year-old Tehdi Badaut stood on the bow of the main deck, watching the last remnants of day bleed into the western horizon. The French-Portuguese first officer had been assigned to oversee the transportation of six Arabian stallions, caged in pairs in specially built stalls that were mounted in the forward deck. Two of the horses were studs, worth a small fortune, the others all national and legion of honor winners.

Tehdi approached the first stall, offering a carrot to a three-year-old black mare. He enjoyed caring for the animals, and the truth was, there were worse duties on board. "How's my lady tonight? Bet you wish you could run around this ship, huh? I'd love to take you out of that cage, but I can't."

The mare shook its head, agitated.

"What? Suddenly you don't like my carrots?"

The other horses started bucking, too, prancing in tight circles, rising up on their hindquarters. Within

minutes they were all snorting and bucking, bashing their frames against their wooden stalls.

The first officer pulled the radio from his back pocket. "It's Badaut, on the main deck, forward. Better send that horse trainer, something's wrong with the stallions."

* * *

The female moved effortlessly through the thermocline, its torpedo-shaped body gliding with slow, snake-like movements. The distinct rhythm of her movements was perpetrated by the creature's powerful swimming muscles, which attached internally to her cartilaginous vertebral column and externally to her thick skin. As her flank muscles contracted, the Megalodon's crescent-moon-shaped tail fin pulled in a rhythmic, undulating motion, propelling the monster forward. The immense tail, or caudal fin, gave the shark maximum thrust with minimal drag while maintaining a streamlined flow through the sea.

Stabilizing the 60-foot Megalodon's forward thrust were her fins: the enormous dorsal, situated atop her back like a seven-foot sail, and her pair of broad pectoral fins, which provided lift and balance, like the wings of a passenger airliner. A smaller pair of pelvic fins, a second dorsal, and a tiny anal fin rounded out the complement.

She was one of the last of her kind, and the first in more than 80,000 years to venture from the abyss. Hunger had driven her from her warm-water purgatory, and she had guarded her kill nearly to the surface, until

the gray curtains of daylight had burned into her sensitive nocturnal eyes, forcing her retreat into the depths. She had remained there for several hours, circling in two thousand feet of water, her ampullae of Lorenzini teased by the electrical impulses emanating from the *Kiku's* keel, which she perceived to be a larger challenger. When the *Kiku* had finally left (taking her kill with it) the female had followed it toward Guam, her primordial senses gradually becoming attuned to the magnetic variations in her new geography.

Although the Megalodon had no external ears, the female could "hear" sound waves as they struck sensory hair cells located in her inner ear. Carried by the auditory nerve, these signals not only alerted the predator to variations within her environment, but allowed her to track the precise direction the disturbances were originating from.

Unlike the trench, there were disturbances everywhere. The female could feel deep, tantalizing heartbeats coming from distant pods of whales, and she could sense a cacophony of sounds created by the splashing of dozens of breaching dolphins. More alien acoustics and electrical fields teased her senses . . . but she remained in the midwater realm, waiting until the painful ultraviolet rays had diminished before rising once more.

Hitching a ride on an upwelling of cold, nutrient-rich water, the gargantuan female ascended, the oxygen-rich surface waters continuing to stimulate her hunger.

*   *   *

The horse trainer, an attractive Floridian woman named Dawn Salone, watched helplessly as a half-Arabian pinto filly bashed its head against the wooden gate of its stable, the other horses following suit. "What the hell's spooking them? I've never seen anything like this."

"They're getting worse," said Tehdi. "Perhaps you should tranquilize them before they injure themselves. And those wooden gates . . . they won't hold up too much longer."

The moon peeked out from behind a cloud formation, casting its glow upon the Pacific—

—illuminating a seven-foot dorsal fin that had surfaced ten yards off the starboard beam.

The horses went into a frenzy, neighing and bucking, their coats lathered in sweat. A few of the taller stallions smashed their skulls against the fifteen-foot stable roofs.

Dawn had seen enough. "I'll get the tranquilizer gun, you stay with them." She headed aft, jogging along the starboard rail as she headed for the cargo ship's infrastructure—

—never noticing the 62,000-pound albino creature now gliding through a stream of surface refuse and human waste along the side of the steel vessel.

SAIPAN

Moonlight retreated behind a canopy of cirrus clouds. Small waves lapped along Saipan's deserted beaches. Somewhere at sea, a humpback moaned a distress call, the haunting siren blotted out by the thundering of steel propellers.

The landing struts of the two-passenger Guimbal G2 Cabri helicopter bounced twice upon the dirt runway before settling down. The pilot, retired navy captain James "Mac" Mackreides glanced over at his lone passenger, who looked a bit shaken after the forty-five-minute flight.

"You okay, J.T.?"

"Fine." Jonas took a deep breath as the chopper's rotary blades gradually slowed to a stop. They had landed on the perimeter of a makeshift airfield. A faded wooden sign read, "Welcome to Saipan."

"Yeah, well, you look like hell."

"Maybe it's because your flying hasn't improved since the navy discharged you."

"Hey, pal, I'm the only game in town, especially at three in the goddamn morning. What's so damn important anyway that you needed to fly out to this godforsaken island now?"

"You mentioned that fisherman friend of yours might know the location of a recent whale kill. I need to examine that carcass."

"Because of this mega-shark?"

"Megalodon, and yes."

"At this time of night? We really need to get you laid."

"Mac, this is important. Where's your friend?"

"First, he's not my friend, he's a business associate. Second, this is gonna cost me, which means it'll cost you double." Mac climbed down from his chopper.

Jonas followed suit. "So where is he? I thought he was supposed to meet us here?"

"He's a fisherman, shit for brains. They usually keep the fish near the water."

Jonas followed Mac down a path leading to the beach, the sounds of the crashing shoreline in the distance.

*   *   *

Jonas Taylor had met James Mackreides seven years earlier at a naval mental facility. Jonas had been ordered to spend ninety days in the psychiatric ward following the incident aboard the *Seacliff*. After two months of "help," the dishonorably discharged submersible pilot found himself in a state of deep depression, separated from Maggie, his career in ruins. Unable to leave the mental ward, he felt alone and betrayed.

Until he had met Mac.

James Mackreides lived to buck authority. Drafted and sent to fight in Vietnam when he was only eighteen, he was assigned to the 155th Assault Helicopter Corps, and was stationed in Cambodia, long before any U.S. armed forces were supposed to be in there. Mac was eventually forced to take over the team after six of their commanding officers were ambushed in a daring day raid. Trained by the navy to

fly Cobras, Mac survived the insanity of Vietnam from that point on by deciding himself when, where, and if it was time for his team to wage war. If an assignment seemed ridiculous, he never questioned his orders, he just did something else. When ordered to bomb the Ho Chi Minh Trail, Mac would organize his troops for battle, then lead his squadron of choppers to a U.S. hospital, pick up a group of nurses, and spend the day on the beaches of Con Son Island. Later that night, he'd submit his report on the outstanding job his men did in "banging" the enemy. The navy never knew any better. On one such adventure, Mac's team landed one of their two-million-dollar helicopters in a delta, shot it to pieces, then blew it up with a claymore mine. Mac reported to his superiors that his squadron had been under heavy fire, but his men had heroically managed to hold their own against superior forces. For their bravery, the young captain and his men received Bronze Stars.

This was not to say that Mackreides's team didn't see their fair share of combat. Mac simply refused to risk the lives of his men if he determined certain actions to be senseless. Of course, to Mac, the entire Vietnam conflict was senseless.

After the war, Mackreides continued flying for the navy, if only because it opened up other avenues of free enterprise. With airships at his disposal, he could supply small-time operators from Guam to Hawaii with everything under the sun. This went on for two years, until another commanding officer finally got

wise when he caught his enlisted men lining up for a Hawaiian "Lay" tour. Mac was charging two hundred dollars for thirty minutes in the back of his chopper with two Hawaiian prostitutes and a six-pack of beer.

The "flying bordello" incident earned Mackreides his discharge, a mandatory psychiatric evaluation, and an extended stay at the navy's mental institution. It was either that or military prison. Confined against his will, the rebel without a cause found himself suffocating, with no outlet to express his disdain for authority.

Then he met Jonas Taylor.

In Mac's professional opinion, Jonas was yet another victim of the military's blame game, the refusal of higher-ups to take responsibility for their actions. This made Taylor a kindred spirit of sorts, and Mackreides felt a moral obligation to help his new comrade-in-arms.

Mac decided the best remedy for his newfound buddy's depression was a road trip. Stealing the coast-guard's helicopter had been easy, landing it in the parking lot of Candlestick Park slightly more challenging. Getting into the 49ers-Cowboys game proved to be the toughest part. After watching the game in a skybox and partying till dawn, the two "madhouse cowboys" returned to the hospital the next evening by cab, drunk, stupid, and happy. The coast guard located the chopper two days later, parked at a body shop, a 49ers logo painted on either side of the cabin.

The two had remained close friends ever since.

*   *   *

The last boat anchored in the shallow water along the beach hardly looked seaworthy. Eighteen feet long, carrying a deep draft that left less than two feet of free board, the wooden vessel lay low in the water, its worn gray planks showing specks of red paint that dated back to the Korean war. Only one person was on board, a Filipino man in his late sixties, wearing a sweatshirt and jeans. He was busy repairing a crab trap hijacked from another islander.

Mac waved. "Felipe!"

The old man ignored him.

"Hey, Felipe, what's wrong?"

"What's wrong? You owe me money, that's what's wrong. You ask me for three girls, I get you three girls."

"Girls, Felipe. You sent me livestock. The fat broad weighed more than me, and the older one had no teeth."

"Ahh." The old man waved his hand at Mac. "This your friend?"

"Jonas Taylor." Jonas extended his hand.

Felipe ignored it. "Dead humpback floating two miles out. Cost you one hundred American. Cash up front."

Mac shook his head. "Fifty, which is worth more than your whole damn boat."

"Eighty. You take it or leave it."

"Fine." Jonas turned to his friend. "Mac, pay the man."

"What? You don't have any money?"

"You owe me twice that. Bail money? Mexico?"

"You remember that, huh?" Mac dug into his wallet, then tossed Felipe two twenty-dollar bills. "You'll get the rest if and when we make it back to the dock in one piece."

"Ahh."

Jonas and Mac climbed aboard.

*   *   *

Jonas knew he needed some kind of evidence to prove the female had surfaced. The numerous whale and dolphin beachings weren't enough, but if Felipe had seen a dead humpback and the female had killed it, then the oversized bite radius would be all the proof he needed.

It took twenty minutes to locate the dead whale.

"There she is," announced Felipe. "Now give me my money."

The bleeding whale carcass bobbed along the calm surface, its stench overpowering. There were no wounds appearing along its dorsal side, so Jonas grabbed an oar, using it to manipulate the bloated carcass, bobbing it up and down in an attempt to flip it over.

"Lose that oar, it cost you another twenty dollar!"

Mac rolled his eyes. "Okay, Jonas, now what?"

"I need to see the underside of this whale."

"Yeah? You planning on getting in?" Mac shined his light on the carcass. "Lots of blood in the water, you'd think there'd be sharks?"

Jonas stopped to think about that when something was illuminated in Mac's flashlight beam. "Mac,

shine your light near that bleeding wound, that's it, right there."

The beacon settled on a triangular white object jammed into an exposed section of the whale's ribcage just below the waterline.

"Christ," said Jonas, "I think that's a tooth!"

"A tooth? How big did you say this megala thingy was?"

"Sixty feet." Jonas looked around the boat. "Mac, I need something to pry it out with."

"What am I? Mr. Goodwrench?" Mac opened a toolbox. Removed a hammer and handed it to Jonas. "And don't drop it, or Happy Harry here will charge me another twenty dollars."

Jonas leaned over the side, attempting to pry the tooth from the whale's rib using the back end of the hammer.

Mac grabbed the oar, assisting him.

The tooth flipped high into the air, Jonas leaning out and catching it—

—as an ivory-white jaw, as large as a double garage, gracefully broke the surface along either side of the whale's remains. Massive teeth, the uppers as wide as dinner plates, clamped down upon the dead humpback . . . and submerged, taking the entire bloated carcass with it.

Mac and Jonas stared at the surface, pie-eyed. Felipe crossed himself.

Seconds later, the whale carcass burst to the surface again, bobbing free.

"Okeydokey," Mac said. "That's all the proof I'll be needing."

Felipe backed toward the motor and gunned the engine. It flooded, coughing blue smoke, then died. Grabbing the hammer from Jonas, the Filipino tore off the engine's hood and proceeded to whack the motor with the hammer, the blows reverberating across the deck.

Jonas yelled, "Felipe . . . no!"

"Too late." Mac pointed to starboard where a stark-white dorsal fin was rising as the Meg surfaced, slowly circling the boat.

Jonas felt his throat constrict. "Leaving now would be a really good thing."

Mac moved toward the engine, pushing Felipe aside as he hurriedly checked the spark plugs. He tried the engine again. It spewed more smoke and died.

The dorsal fin changed course, moving slowly toward the boat. Underwater, the Meg's albino snout grazed the boat's keel, tasting it—

—jolting it with enough force to knock Jonas and Mac off their feet.

Felipe tripped over his crab trap and fell into the water.

Jonas grabbed the oar. Searched for Felipe—

—whose scream was suddenly cut off by an enormous splash.

For a long moment, Mac and Jonas just stared at the surface, waiting. Then Mac hurried back to the engine,

grabbed Felipe's hammer, and started smashing it against the motor as he tried to turn it over—

Miraculously, it started!

Grabbing the wheel, he gunned the engine, veering them away from the carcass, steering them toward land.

The shoreline beckoned two miles away.

Mac looked at Jonas, visibly shaken. "Christ, that poor bastard—"

"Uh, Mac?" Jonas pointed behind them.

A twenty-foot-high wake was racing after the boat, an unseen luminous mass pushing it.

Mac zigged and zagged, but the wave continued closing the distance. "Okay, professor, I'm open to suggestions!"

"She's homing in on our engine."

"No shit? You went to college for that, did you?"

As they watched, the wake disappeared, the monster going deep.

"Thank God," said Mac.

Jonas looked around. "No, Mac . . . this isn't good. She'll come up from below."

"How do you know that?"

"Don't you ever watch *National Geographic*? It's what they do!"

They sideswiped a marker buoy, causing its bell to toll.

"Okay, Mac . . . radical idea time!"

*   *   *

The female circled in 350 feet of water, the annoying whine of the engine reverberating in her head. Sensing the challenge, refusing to share her kill, the agitated predator pumped its tail harder and charged the surface. Soulless gray-blue eyes rolled back an instant before—

Wa-boosh! The sea erupted as the Meg smashed straight up through the keel of Felipe's boat, splintering it into kindling.

The female flopped sideways back into the sea, debris raining everywhere. An eerie silence followed, save for the dull *gong* of the marker buoy's bell.

It tolled once more, then ceased midgong.

Having watched the demolition from a safe distance, Jonas and Mac, dripping wet and hugging the buoy, balanced on its steel frame. Jonas's right hand gripped the bell, silencing it.

Thirty feet below, the white glow passed beneath them, heading back out to sea.

THE MEETING

Terry Tanaka entered the Aura naval hospital and glanced at her watch—8:40 a.m. That gave her exactly twenty minutes to get Jonas to Commander McGovern's office, assuming he was in any condition to travel. She walked down the empty hallway, the navy MP no longer on duty. Jonas's door was ajar.

Inside, a woman with platinum blond hair was ransacking a chest of drawers. The bed was empty. Jonas was gone.

"Can I help you?" Terry asked.

Maggie jumped. "I'm . . . I'm looking for my husband."

"You won't find him in a drawer. Wait . . . you're Maggie?"

Maggie's eyes narrowed. "That's right, I'm *Mrs.* Taylor. Who the hell are you?"

"Terry Tanaka."

Maggie eyed her up and down. "Well, well . . ."

"I'm a friend. My brother . . . he was the one who was killed. I stopped by to drive Dr. Taylor to the naval base."

Maggie's disposition changed. "Sorry . . . about your brother. Did you say naval base? What does the navy want with Jonas?"

"There's a hearing . . . exactly what are you doing here?"

"My husband was nearly killed. Where else would I be but by his side?"

Terry frowned. "Not that it's any of my business, but—"

"—but you're right," said Maggie, "it's not your business. Anyway, since Jonas obviously isn't here, he must already be at the meeting, so maybe you can take me?"

*   *   *

The hearing at Guam's naval base took place in a refrigerated warehouse that had once been used to "hold" the bodies of deceased soldiers awaiting transport back to the States. Under three sets of mobile surgical lights lay the remains of the male Megalodon. Two Japanese men, scientists from JAMSTEC, were busy examining the enormous jaws of the ancient predator.

An MP handed Terry and Maggie each a lined coat as they entered the cooler.

A conference table and chairs had been set on the far side of the room. Frank Heller and Al DeMarco were consoling Masao, who wore dark sunglasses to obscure his red-rimmed eyes. Terry embraced her father, then introduced Maggie.

Commander Bryce McGovern, a silver-haired veteran of two wars, entered the warehouse, followed by an aide and a Frenchman in his late forties. "I'm Commander McGovern. This is Andre Dupont of the Cousteau Society."

"I'm Tanaka," Masao said. "My daughter, Terry."

The commander shook her hand. "We're all sorry about what happened to your brother. Mr. Tanaka, is everyone present?"

"Dr. Tsukamoto and Dr. Simidu have just arrived from the Japan Marine Science and Technology Center. But Jonas Taylor is not here. Apparently, he left the hospital late last night."

McGovern grimaced. "Our only real witness. Anyone know where the hell this guy went?"

Terry pointed to Maggie. "There's his wife. Ask her."

Maggie flashed a smile. "I'm sure Jonas will show up eventually. Studying these creatures was such a big part of our lives."

Terry rolled her eyes.

"Let's get started," said McGovern, taking his place at the head of the table. "If everyone can find seats . . . including the two gentlemen by the shark." The commander waited. "The Mariana Trench is under United States jurisdiction. As such, the United States Navy has assigned me to investigate the incident that occurred in the Challenger Deep. With all due respect to the bereaved, my rules are simple: I'm going to ask the questions and you people are going to give me the answers. First question," he pointed toward the Megalodon carcass, "would somebody please tell me what that thing is over there?"

Dr. Simidu, the younger of the two Japanese, was the first to speak. "Commander, JAMSTEC has examined the teeth of the creature and compared it with those

of *Carcharodon carcharius*, the great white shark, and its extinct predecessor, *Carcharodon megalodon*." Simidu unfolded a towel, revealing one of the male Megalodon's teeth. "This is an upper tooth. As you can see, the tooth has a chevron, or scar, above the root, identifying it as a Megalodon. Its existence in the Mariana Trench is shocking, to say the least."

"Not to us, Dr. Simidu," replied Andre Dupont. "The disappearance of the Megalodon has always been a mystery, but the HMS *Challenger*'s discovery in 1873 of several ten-thousand-year-old fossilized teeth dredged from the floor of the Mariana Trench made it clear that some members of the species may have survived."

McGovern paused, allowing his aide, a stenographer, to catch up. "Next question: How many more of these creatures are down there, and is there a danger to the local island population?"

"There's no danger." All heads turned to Frank Heller. "Commander, the shark you see here attacked and killed the pilot of one of our deep-sea submersibles, then apparently got itself entangled in our cable and was attacked by another one of its kind. These creatures have been trapped in a tropical layer at the bottom of the Mariana Trench for God knows how many millions of years. The only reason you even see this specimen before you is because we accidentally hauled it up to the surface."

"So you're telling me at least one more of these . . . these Megalodons exists, but it's trapped at the bottom of the trench."

"That's correct."

"You're wrong, Frank." Jonas entered from the rear door, followed by Mac, their clothing still damp. Jonas stopped as he laid eyes on his wife. "Maggie? What are you doing here?"

She looked up innocently. "I came as soon as I heard."

"Yeah, I'll bet you did."

"Dr. Taylor, I presume?" McGovern was losing patience.

"Yes, sir. And this is James Mackreides, a friend of mine."

McGovern's eyes blazed. "Yes, the captain and I know one another." He signaled to the MP. "Get these men some coats."

"There was a second shark, Commander, a female, much larger. She followed the male's blood trail out of the abyss. She's hunting in our surface waters as we speak."

Masao looked incredulous.

"It's true, Commander," said Mac, "and I've got the stained skivvies to prove it. Jonas, show him the tooth."

Jonas passed McGovern the tooth he had taken from the humpback whale's carcass. The commander compared it to the tooth Dr. Simidu had handed him. The female's dwarfed the male's!

Masao shook his head. "My God . . ."

"A predator that size in these coastal waters," McGovern said, "it'll be a human smorgasbord."

Dr. Simidu objected, "Megalodon hunted whales, Commander, not humans."

Mac mumbled to Jonas, "And the occasional fisherman."

McGovern massaged his brow, clearly out of his element. "Dr. Taylor, since you seem to be the closest thing to an expert on these creatures and you were present in the trench, perhaps you can tell me how this monster managed to surface. Dr. Heller seems convinced these creatures were trapped below six miles of frigid water."

"They were. But the first Meg, the male, was bleeding badly. The second, this female, was ascending within its dense blood stream. As I tried to explain yesterday to Terry, if the Megalodons are like their cousins, the great whites, their blood temperatures will be about twelve degrees higher than the surrounding ocean water, or, as in the case of the hydrothermal layer of the trench, about ninety-two degrees. The *Kiku* hauled the first Meg topside and the female followed her kill straight up to our warmer surface waters, protected by a river of hot blood streaming out of its mate."

"You keep referring to this second shark as a female," Andre Dupont interrupted. "How do you know for sure?"

"Because I saw her. She passed over my sub when I was in the trench. She's much larger than this first shark . . . and she's pregnant."

Conversations broke out across the conference table.

Mac looked at Jonas. "Good God, how the hell do you know she's pregnant? You do a gynecological exam down there?"

McGovern banged his palm on the table for quiet. "What else do we need to know about this . . . female?"

"Like its mate, it's totally white, actually bioluminescent when the light hits its hide. This is a common genetic adaptation to its deep-water environment, where no light exists. Its eyes will be extremely sensitive to light. Consequently, it won't surface during the day." He turned to Terry. "That's why no one on board the *Kiku* saw her rise. She would have stayed deep enough to avoid the light. And now that the shark has adapted to our surface waters, I think she's going to be very aggressive."

"Why do you say that?" Dr. Tsukamoto spoke for the first time.

"The deep waters of the Mariana Trench are poorly oxygenated compared to our surface waters. The higher the oxygen content, the more efficiently the Megalodon's system will function. In its new, highly oxygenated environment, the creature will be able to process and generate greater outputs of energy. In order to accommodate these increases in energy, the Meg will have to consume greater quantities of food. And, I don't need to tell you, sufficient food sources are readily available."

McGovern's face darkened. "Our coastal populations could be attacked."

"No, Commander, these creatures are too large to venture into shallow water. So far, the female has only attacked whales—"

"And D.J.!" Heller reminded him.

"That was an accident," Jonas retorted. "We shouldn't have been down there."

"And if this female eats a group of divers? Will you make the same excuse then?"

"There's another concern," said Masao. The room quieted. "This female's presence could potentially affect one of the whale migrations."

"Whale migrations?" McGovern looked perplexed.

"Hai. Whale migration patterns began millions of years ago. Some scientists theorize the mammals first migrated into colder polar waters not just to follow the food, but to escape Megalodon attacks. I'm not saying one creature could change the annual southern migrations now occurring along the coastlines, but even a slight change could create an ecological disaster. For instance, if the whale populations that currently inhabit the coastal waters off Hawaii were to suddenly flee to Japan's coastal waters in an attempt to avoid the Megalodon, the area's entire marine food chain would be affected. The additional presence of several thousand whales would cause an imbalance among those species that share the same diets as these mammals. The competition among marine life for plankton, krill, and shrimp could drastically reduce the populations among other species of fish. The inadequate food supply would

change breeding patterns, severely affecting the fishing industry in that locale for years to come."

Dr. Simidu and Dr. Tsukamoto whispered to each other in Japanese.

McGovern stood up, thinking on his feet. "Let me be sure I'm understanding this situation correctly. Essentially, we have an aggressive sixty-foot version of a great white shark on the loose, a pregnant female, no less, whose mere presence could indirectly affect the fishing industry of some coastal nation. Does that about sum it up?"

Jonas nodded. "Yes, sir."

"So how do we deal with the situation?"

"Commander, why must you do anything?" Andre Dupont asked. "Since when does the United States Navy concern itself with the behavioral patterns of a fish?"

"And what if this 'fish' starts devouring small boats or scuba divers? What then, Mr. Dupont?"

"Dr. Taylor," said Dr. Tsukamoto, "if this creature's presence alters the migration patterns of whales around Japan, our entire fishing industry could suffer a major setback. Theoretically, JAMSTEC and the Tanaka Institute could be held legally responsible. The UNIS program has already been suspended, and we can't afford any more financial setbacks. JAMSTEC therefore officially recommends that this creature be found and destroyed."

McGovern nodded. "I happen to agree. I don't think nature intended to release these monsters from the

abyss. That was your doing. Despite your assurances, I can't take the chance that this . . . female might venture into populated waters. And what if she has her pups along our coasts? Christ, we could be looking at dozens of these monsters in the next decade. What then?"

"There's no precedent for this," Dupont retorted. "At the very least, we're dealing with an endangered species, on the brink of extinction, at the most, the scientific find of the century. You declare war on this shark, and everyone from PETA to the Cousteau Society will be picketing your naval base starting tomorrow."

"Jonas," Masao was a voice of reason, "in your opinion, in which direction will this Megalodon head?"

"Difficult to predict. She'll follow the food, that's for sure. Problem is, there are four distinct whale migration patterns occurring at this time of year in this hemisphere. West toward the coast of Japan, east and west of the Hawaiian Islands, and farther east, along the coast of California. At this juncture, it appears the female's heading east, toward Hawaii. I'm guessing she'll continue east, eventually ending up in California waters . . . Wait a minute!"

"What is it, Taylor?" McGovern asked.

"Maybe there's another option. Masao, how close to completion is the Tanaka Lagoon?"

"Two weeks, but JAMSTEC cut off our funding. Jonas, you're not thinking of capturing this creature?"

"Why not? If the lagoon was designed to study whales in a natural environment, why couldn't we

use it to capture the Meg?" Jonas turned to face the JAMSTEC directors. "Gentlemen, consider the opportunity we'd have to study this predator!"

"Tanaka-san," Dr. Simidu asked, "is this option feasible?"

"Simidu-san, hai, it is possible, assuming we can locate the female."

"Capture it?" Terry stood, furious. "Dad, what are you thinking? One of these monsters ate D.J. We're responsible for allowing this female to surface. We need to kill it before it hurts anyone else, or starts laying eggs, or having babies . . . or whatever the hell these things do to breed!"

Masao turned to his daughter, removing his sunglasses. "Kill? Is that what I've taught you? Do you know what this creature is, Terry? It is not a monster, it is a work of nature, the culmination of a billion years of evolution. Killing this majestic animal is out of the question. Its capture, however, would bring great honor, great meaning to D.J.'s death. It's what your brother would want."

"It's not what I want!" Terry stomped toward the exit and left, slamming the warehouse door behind her.

Maggie smiled. "Temperamental little thing, isn't she?"

The two representatives from JAMSTEC were talking rapidly in Japanese. Dr. Simidu turned to Masao, "Tanaka-san, I have the authority to release funding to your Institute, and would do so, if you really believe you can capture this female."

Masao looked to Jonas. "Taylor-san?"

"The lagoon would have to be finished quickly, the *Kiku* refitted. If we could locate the creature, perhaps we could tranquilize it, then drag it in using nets and inflatable buoys."

"Inflatable buoys . . ." Maggie was scribbling notes. "And why do you need them exactly?"

Jonas turned to his wife. "Unlike whales, sharks don't float. Being inherently heavier than seawater, if they stop swimming they'll sink. Once we tranquilize the female, she'll sink and drown unless we can keep water pumping through her gills."

Mac snickered. "Oh, is that all."

"Tanaka-san," said Dr. Tsukamoto, "you have lost a son to these creatures. With respect, if you so desire to capture this female, we will agree to underwrite the project and allow you to complete the lagoon. Of course, assuming you are successful, JAMSTEC will expect full access to the captured Megalodon, as well as our agreed-upon financial share of the lagoon's tourism trade."

Masao paused, tears welling in his eyes. "I think D.J. would have wanted this. My son dedicated his life to the advancement of science. The last thing he'd want would be for us to destroy this unique species. Jonas, will you help us capture the Megalodon?"

"Of course he will," said Maggie, jumping in.

"Hold it gentlemen . . . and lady," said McGovern, rejoining the conversation. "Mr. Tanaka, just so we understand each other, the navy cannot support any of

these efforts. My recommendation to my commanding officer will be to use gunboats to patrol the island shorelines. Now, should you manage to capture the shark first, so be it. Personally, I hope you're successful. Officially, however, the navy cannot recognize this course of action as being a viable option." McGovern stood up again, signaling an end to the meeting.

"By the way, Dr. Taylor," the commander turned to face Jonas, "what makes you so sure this female will travel all the way to California's waters?"

"Because, Commander, as we speak, more than twenty thousand whales are migrating from the Bering Sea south toward the peninsula of Baja, Mexico, and the Megalodon can hear their beating hearts."

STRATEGY

The officer's galley onboard the *Kiku* had been converted into a war room. On one wall Jonas had attached a large map illustrating the migration patterns of the whales. Red pins indicated the locations where whale carcasses had recently been spotted by coast-guard helicopters. A pattern was becoming apparent: the female was heading away from Japan to the northeast, possibly toward the Hawaiian Islands.

Next to the whale map hung a large diagram illustrating the internal anatomy of the great white shark.

Jonas had convinced Masao to add Mac to the payroll, needing his skills as a helicopter pilot for night patrols. Then there was Maggie.

Maggie had pitched her TV station on filming the expedition, using their funding as a means to buy her way aboard. Jonas had mixed feelings about this, but tucked them away for the time being. He knew Masao needed the money to finance the Meg's capture. He also knew, at some point, he'd confront his wife about their marriage.

Terry and Masao filed into the galley, taking seats opposite DeMarco and Mac. Maggie and her cameraman, Fred Barch, sat in the back of the room. Frank Heller was the last to arrive.

Masao addressed the group, with Maggie's cameraman filming. "As you know, I've appointed Jonas to head this expedition. If there's anyone in the

room who has a problem with that, speak now." He glanced at his daughter and Frank, neither of whom made eye contact. "Jonas?"

Jonas stood. "Before I review my plan to capture the female, it's important everyone knows exactly what we're dealing with." He pointed to the anatomical chart. "Megalodon's no ordinary predator. It's intelligent, it can sense vibrations in the water miles away, and it can detect the electrical impulses of its preys' beating hearts. Its nostrils are directional, allowing it to target one particle of blood or urine in billions of particles of seawater—"

"Yes, we know all this," Terry said. "We'll all make sure we use the bathroom before we hunt her down."

Jonas shot her a look, then walked to the back of the room to a pneumatic drill. Loosening its vise, he attached the female's tooth to the hammer end, then held up a square piece of 3-inch titanium from a UNIS robot. "Megalodon teeth are among the hardest substances ever created by nature. Each tooth is serrated, like a steak knife, designed to puncture whale bone."

Jonas positioned the titanium plate beneath the tooth, then flipped on the drill's power switch. When the air pressure indicator pointed to green, he hit the ON switch—

—the tooth instantly blasting through the titanium plate, its tip protruding from the other side. He powered off the machine and returned to his seat.

"That was 10,000 pounds per square inch of pressure. The female's jaw probably exerts twice that force. Now imagine a mouth the size of a small bus filled with hundreds of these teeth—a jaw big enough to swallow our mini-sub whole."

In the back of the room, Maggie's eyes widened as an idea came to her. "Jonas, let's say we wanted to film her capture underwater."

Terry scoffed. "Are you suicidal or just stupid?"

"I'm talking to my husband, sweetheart." She turned to Jonas. "How large would a shark cage have to be in order to prevent the Meg from swallowing it?"

Fred Barch stopped filming. "Hey, I'm not getting in any cage."

"A shark cage would be crushed," Jonas replied. "However a Lexan tube, say twelve feet in diameter and cylindrical, would be too large and slippery for the female to expand its jaws around."

"I'm still not getting in any tube," said the cameraman.

"I don't care about filming it," spat Terry, "I just want this monster captured before anyone else gets hurt."

Maggie ignored her, jotting down notes.

"And I want to know how you're going to find one fish in all that ocean," stated DeMarco.

Jonas pointed to the map. "These are the locations of the winter breeding grounds of whales currently migrating south from the Bering Sea. The Megalodon can detect the massive vibrations produced by whale populations to the east and west of Guam. Based on

recent kills, she seems to be heading east, toward the pods moving along the coastal waters off Hawaii."

Jonas looked at Masao. "It's not going to be easy to locate her, but we know that her eyes are too sensitive to surface during the day. That means she'll do the majority of her hunting at night, attacking whales, forcing her close to the surface. Mac's helicopter has been equipped with a thermal imager and monitor, which will assist us in spotting both the Megalodon and the whale pods in the dark. I'll be riding shotgun, using a pair of night-vision binoculars. The Meg's hide is white, making her easier to locate, so that helps."

Jonas held up a homing dart the size of a cardboard paper towel roll. It was attached to an electronic device roughly the size of a pocket flashlight. "This transmitter dart fits into the barrel of a high powered rifle. If we can inject the homing dart close to the Megalodon's heart, we'll not only be able to track her, we should also be able to monitor her pulse rate."

"What good will that do?" asked DeMarco.

"Once we tranquilize the Meg, knowing her heart rate could be vital to our own safety, as well as to the female's survival. The harpoons will contain a mixture of pentobarbital and ketamine. The pentobarbital will depress the Meg's cerebral oxygen consumption, which concerns me a bit. The ketamine is more of a nonbarbiturate general anesthetic. The Meg's heart should slow significantly once the combination of drugs take effect. I've estimated the dosages based on the female's size."

Heller looked up. "Those are some nasty drugs. Have you even considered the side effects?"

Jonas nodded. "The pentobarbital could cause some initial excitement in the Meg."

"What the hell does that mean?" asked DeMarco.

Mac slapped both palms on the table. "It means she's gonna be one mighty pissed off fish just before she goes into la-la land."

Masao looked at Jonas. "Once we tranquilize the creature, how will you drag it to the lagoon?"

"That's the tricky part. The harpoon gun will be positioned at the *Kiku*'s stern. We'll use the steel cable that's wrapped around the big winch as its line. The harpoon won't remain fastened very long in the Meg's hide, so it's important that we get the harness around her as quickly as possible. The harness itself is basically a thick two-hundred-foot fishing net with flotation buoys attached every twenty feet along its perimeter. The net should level her out and allow seawater to enter her mouth, forcing her gills to breathe. Once she's secured, it's just a matter of getting her into the lagoon."

Terry looked skeptical. "And how do you propose we secure the net around a thirty-ton sleeping shark?"

"Once she's asleep, I'll enter the water in the *Abyss Glider* and use the sub to align the net into position."

Terry looked at Jonas, incredulous. "You're going back in the water with that monster?

"We'll be monitoring the Megalodon's heart rate, and I'll be in constant communication with the *Kiku*.

If the Meg begins to wake, her pulse rate will increase rapidly as a warning. The AG I's a fast sub, I'll have no problems getting out of harm's way. Believe me, I have no desire to play hero. The Meg will be knocked out long before I enter the water in the glider."

Jonas looked over his team. "The female hasn't fed for seventy-two hours, so tonight could be the night. There's a sense of urgency here. First, the longer we take, the wider the search perimeter, the more ocean we're dealing with. Second, she's pregnant. We need to capture her before she births those pups.

"Better get some rest, it could be a long night."

*   *   *

The *Kiku* plowed east through the Pacific, the setting sun kissing the western horizon, painting the sky a golden hue.

Maggie stood at the stern rail, speaking on her cell phone with Bud. "Darling, did you get the equipment list I e-mailed you?"

"I got it," Bud said. "I also have an estimate of the bill. Do you have any idea how much this scheme of yours will cost?"

"The station will cover most of it, and you'll be co-producer of the number one newscast in all of California."

"Maggie, I don't know about this, is it really worth the risk?"

She saw Jonas approaching. "For the evening news anchor, you bet your ass. Order the equipment, I'll check back later. Gotta run."

Maggie hung up, then turned to Jonas, pouring on the charm. "So? How's it feel to be vindicated after all these years?"

"It doesn't change anything."

"Of course it does. It changes public perception. Trust me, perception's everything."

"Tell that to the families of those men who died."

"It was an accident, Jonas. Life goes on. Take my advice. Let yourself off the hook."

She gazed at the sunset. "So beautiful, isn't it? Reminds me a little of our honeymoon."

Jonas stared at her profile. "What happened to us, Maggie?"

"Jonas, we're so beyond this—"

"Just answer the question."

She turned to face him. "Okay, if you really need to know. The man I fell in love with was a cocky navy commander with an ambition that matched my own stride for stride. You knew you were the best, and that turned me on."

"And after the accident?"

"The Jonas Taylor who surfaced from the Mariana Trench just wasn't the same man I fell in love with."

"Shit happens, Maggie. People change."

She touched his cheek, her eyes all business. "I don't."

ATTACK

The full moon reflected off the windshield of the helicopter, illuminating the interior of the small compartment. Jonas was up front in the passenger seat, using the night vision binoculars. Seated in back directly behind him was Terry, who was holding the high-powered rifle and a backpack full of transmitter darts. If they could locate the Megalodon, it would be Terry's job to tag it, allowing the *Kiku* to track it and move closer.

Maggie was seated next to Terry, holding the heavy video camera mounted on a steady-cam. The chopper only held four passengers, and she was not about to allow Fred Barch to hog her glory.

Situated between Jonas and Mac was a monitor wired by cable to an Agema Thermovision 1000 infrared imager. Mounted below the helicopter was a small gyrostabilized platform that held the thermal imager pod in place. The thermal imager was designed to detect objects in the water by the electromagnetic radiation the object emitted. The internal temperature of a warm body would appear on the monitor as a hot spot against the image of the cold sea. The warm-blooded whales were easily detected; the Megalodon's internal temperature would be slightly cooler.

For nearly seven hours, Mac had flown his chopper along a thirty-mile perimeter of ocean, hovering two hundred feet above the black Pacific. They had located nearly a dozen pods of whales without seeing a trace of

the Megalodon, and the initial excitement Jonas had felt was quickly fading into boredom as he realized just how difficult their task was going to be.

"This is crazy, Jonas," Mac shouted over his headphone's mouthpiece. "It's worse than looking for a needle in a haystack."

"How are we set for fuel?"

"Another fifteen minutes and we'll have to turn back."

Jonas refocused his ITT Night Mariner Gen III binoculars on the Pacific. The bifocal night glasses penetrated the dark, improving light amplification by using a coating of gallium arsenide on the photocathode of the intensifier, turning the black sea a pale shade of gray.

In the back seat, Maggie had drifted off to sleep. Terry watched her, then quietly opened her backpack on the floor and removed a 20 mm explosive . . . swapping it for the tracking device.

Jonas spotted another pod of whales. "Mac, eleven o'clock. Looks like humpbacks. Let's follow them a while, then we'll turn back."

"You're the boss." Mac changed course to intercept the pod.

Jonas was growing worried. With each hour that passed, the search perimeter extended an additional ten miles. Soon there would simply be too much ocean to cover, even with their sophisticated tracking equipment.

Exhausted, Jonas felt himself becoming mesmerized by the moonlight dancing across the ocean, barely

noticing the white blur streak across his peripheral vision. The moon had illuminated something below the surface. For a moment it had seemed to glow.

"See something, J.T.?"

"Not sure." He focused on the whale pod, locating three spouts. "I can make out two bulls, a cow and her calf . . . no, make that two cows, five whales total. Get us on top of them, Mac."

The helicopter hovered above the pod, keeping pace as the whales changed direction, turning north.

Jonas searched the sea to the left and right of the pod. His heart jumped in his chest, "There!"

Behind the pod, a white glow appeared, streaking beneath the surface like a giant luminescent torpedo.

Maggie stirred. Terry leaned forward, staring at the monitor. "What is it? Is it the shark?"

"Affirmative."

"What's she doing?" Maggie asked, fixing the camera to her shoulder.

Jonas looked at Mac. "I think she's stalking the calf."

*　　　*　　　*

One hundred feet below the black Pacific, a deadly game of cat and mouse was taking place. The humpbacks had detected the hunter's presence miles back, the mammals altering their course repeatedly to avoid a confrontation. As the albino predator closed to intercept, the two cows moved to surround the calf, the larger bulls taking positions at the front and rear of the pod.

The Megalodon slowed, circling to the right of her quarry, sizing up her prey, marking the position of the calf. Faster than the whales, the female darted in and out, testing the reaction time of the two bulls.

As the shark crossed in front of the lead male, the forty-ton bull broke from the group and made a run at her. Although the humpback whale possessed baleen instead of teeth, it was still quite dangerous, able to ram the female with its enormous head. The male humpback's charge was sudden, but the Meg was far too quick, accelerating away from the bull, then returning in a wide arc.

* * *

"What do you see?"

Jonas was peering through the night glasses. "Looks like the lead bull is chasing the Megalodon away from the pod."

"Wait a minute, did you say the whale's chasing the Meg?" Maggie chuckled. "I thought this Megalodon of yours was supposed to be fearsome?"

"Sure, you can say that now," said Mac. "Try hanging from a buoy, you'll change your tune real fast."

Jonas turned to Terry. "You ready with that tracking dart?"

She nodded.

* * *

Once more the pod altered its course, this time heading southeast to lose the hunter. The Megalodon compensated, selecting an alternative course, targeting the massive bull guarding the rear. This angle presented

a different problem for the shark, which instinctively feared the humpback's powerful fluke.

The Megalodon remained parallel with the bull, darting closer, pulling away, trying to entice it to leave the pod and attack. She grew bolder with each foray, snapping at the humpback, once even biting at its enormous right pectoral fin.

The bull finally turned upon the Meg, chasing it from the rest of the pod. Only this time the female retreated to the rear, distancing the bull from the safety of the pack.

As the male humpback turned to rejoin the others, the albino hunter circled back with a frightening burst of speed and launched her 62,000 pounds at the retreating humpback's exposed flank. Her open mouth latched onto the whale, her teeth puncturing blubber and muscle, her powerful jaws holding on.

The bull spasmed and writhed in agony, its wild contortions only serving to aid the Megalodon's serrated teeth, which sliced cleanly through the humpback's gushing grooves. An agonizing, high-pitched moan reverberated from the bleeding rorqual as the albino predator shook itself loose, choking down a 12,000-pound mouthful of blubber.

*   *   *

"What the hell was that?" yelled Mac

"I can't be sure," said Jonas, the night glasses pressed against his eyes, "but I think the Meg just attacked one of the bulls."

"The pod's moving off."

"Forget the pod, Mac. Stay with the wounded bull."

*   *   *

A river of hot blood gushed from the gaping wound as the crippled humpback feebly attempted to propel itself forward with its massive lateral flippers.

The Megalodon circled below its wounded prey, allowing it to settle before launching its second attack—this one even more devastating than the first.

Seizing the baleen-fringed edges of the dying creature's mouth within its seven-and-a-half inch fangs, the Meg ripped and tore apart an entire section of the humpback's throat, whipping its enormous head to and fro until a long strip of grooved hide and blubber peeled away from the mammal's body like husk from a ripe ear of corn.

Helpless and in agony, the tortured humpback slapped its fluke repeatedly along the bloody surface as it wailed a death song of warning to its fleeing pod.

The Megalodon circled deep again, waiting for its wounded prey to die. That's when the female's lateral line detected the heavy vibrations coming from the surface above.

*   *   *

Maggie aimed her camera out her portside window. "Jonas, can you describe what's happening down there for my viewers?"

"Hard to tell, there's so much blood in the water. What's your thermal imager picking up, Mac?"

"I can't see shit from shine-ola. The blood's spreading out over the surface so fast, it's camouflaging everything."

"Bring us closer," Maggie yelled.

Mac descended to fifty feet. "How's that?"

Maggie focused through her viewfinder. "I still don't see the Meg, just that damn whale."

Terry aimed the barrel of her rifle out the open section on the starboard side of the cockpit. She stood in her seat, looking down through the night scope. She could just make out the Megalodon's white hide, circling below the dying whale. Her finger slipped around the trigger. She took a breath . . . *this is for you, D.J.*—

—as the blur suddenly disappeared. "Damn fish . . . it just went deep again. Mac, we need to be lower."

Mac adjusted the airship's altitude, dropping another twenty feet.

Jonas's heart raced. "Something's not right. She wouldn't just go deep, not with her kill so close."

"Probably scared her off," said Maggie, shifting her angle to aim over Terry's shoulder. "Oh yeah, that's much better. God, look at that whale bleed. Now if only the guest of honor wasn't such a wimp."

Jonas felt sweat pouring down his face. "She has to sense the chopper's vibrations, I wonder if she perceives us as a threat? Mac, I've got a bad feeling about this. Take us higher."

"Higher? But I—"

"Goddamnit, Mac, higher—now!"

The sea exploded in a bloody froth as the Megalodon launched its girth out of the water at its challenger. The conical snout struck the thermal imager, shattering it on impact, the midair collision sending the chopper caroming sideways—

—swinging Jonas's cockpit door open, his right foot losing its grip on the floorboard as the G-force of the copter's roll pushed him out, only the seat belt keeping his body from falling into the night and down into the gaping mouth and exposed teeth—

—as Maggie and Terry wrestled for position, Terry's finger inadvertently pulling the rifle's trigger—

—the 20 mm shell rocketing past the Meg's left pectoral fin, exploding as it struck the surface below—

—the cabin spinning, Mac screaming, "Come on!" as he clutched his control stick with both hands, the ocean racing at him in his peripheral vision as he fought a thirty-degree down angle, until . . .

—the rotors finally caught air.

Mac pulled the chopper out of its nosedive, leveling off just above the waves. The veteran pilot groaned with relief as his airship soared above the Pacific and climbed, making its getaway.

"Gawd-damn, Jonas, I think I just shit my pants!"

Jonas fought to catch his breath. His limbs quivered, his voice abandoning him. After a good minute, he forced the words out of his parched throat. "She's . . . she's a lot bigger than I thought."

Terry gritted her teeth, saying nothing.

Maggie stared at her. "What was that explosion?"

"I wouldn't know."

"Bullshit!"

Jonas reached back and grabbed her backpack. Found two more 20mm shells. "Nice."

Mac shook his head. "We're low on fuel. I'll radio the *Kiku* to rendezvous. Hopefully we won't have to ditch."

The three passengers looked at him, the blood rushing from their faces.

Mac smiled to himself, not bothering to mention his reserve tank.

PEARL HARBOR

The *Kiku* was berthed next to the USS *John Hancock*, the 563-foot Spruance class destroyer that had arrived in port earlier that morning. Under pressure from animal rights activists, Commander McGovern had personally arranged the docking space for Masao Tanaka's vessel, while he secretly recruited a makeshift crew to report to Pearl Harbor for a "special assignment."

Captain Barre stood on the *Kiku*'s stern deck, overseeing the installation of a harpoon gun behind the ship's massive A-frame. Jonas and Mac were with Alphonse DeMarco, watching the engineer check and recheck the battery system on the *Abyss Glider I*. The AG I was a smaller, sleeker version of the deep-sea sub Jonas had piloted in the Mariana Trench. Designed for speed, the one-man vessel was smaller in length and weighed a mere 462 pounds, with the majority of that weight located in the instrument panels in the Lexan nose cone.

"Looks like a miniature jet fighter," said Mac.

"Handles like one too," DeMarco grunted.

"Is this the same model the Tanaka kid was attacked in?"

"No," said Jonas, "the AG II was bigger, the hull thicker and much heavier."

"The AG I was its prototype," said DeMarco. "It was only designed for depths up to two thousand meters. This hull's made of pure aluminum oxide, extremely

sturdy, but positively buoyant. My baby can move fast, turn on a dime, even leap straight out of the water."

"Yeah? Can it out-leap the monster we saw last night?" Mac asked.

Jonas looked at his friend. "It would take a rocket to out-jump that fish."

"A rocket? You've got one." DeMarco climbed through the rear hatch, then pointed to a lockbox on the left side of the pilot's control console. "See this lever? Turn it a half click counterclockwise, then pull it toward you, and it'll ignite a small tank of hydrogen installed in the tail. Never used it to launch the AG straight out of the water, but it would free up the sub in case you ever got stuck in the muck at the bottom."

"How long a burn?"

"Hell, I don't know . . . fifteen, maybe twenty seconds tops. Once the sub's freed, she'll float topside anyway, assuming you've lost power." DeMarco inched his way out of the sub. "Course, you already knew that."

"Hey, Jonas!" Mac was at the portside rail, pointing at two tugboats that were busy pushing an antiquated nuclear submarine into an empty berth. The black vessel looked familiar. A dozen crewmen stood on deck, proudly standing by with ropes to tie the ship off.

Jonas stared at the insignia SSN-571 as if seeing a ghost. "Son of a bitch, that's the *Nautilus*. I thought they put her out to pasture in Groton?"

Mac nodded. "It's McGovern. He's in way over his head, fighting a losing publicity battle with the animal

rights lovers. Bottom line: If you're ordered to kill a fish, kill it with a legend. Navy vets love the *Nautilus*. So McGovern ordered her refit for one last sail into the sunset."

"Christ."

*   *   *

It was back on September 30, 1954, that the *Nautilus* became the U.S. Navy's first commissioned nuclear powered ship. The submarine would shatter all submerged speed and distance records and become the first vessel to travel beneath the ice floe to reach the geographic North Pole. After serving the navy for twenty-five years, the famous submarine was eventually decommissioned, but only after having logged nearly a half million miles at sea.

As Jonas watched, two officers showed themselves in the sub's conning tower. "Holy shit. It's Danielson. Can you believe this?"

"Your former CO? Yeah, I already knew. A friend stationed on Guam told me Danielson volunteered when he heard you were involved. In fact, it was his suggestion to McGovern to use that old tin can to go after the shark."

As the *Nautilus* passed the *Kiku*, United States Navy Captain (Ret.) Richard Danielson squinted in the sunlight, stealing a glance at his former deep-sea pilot.

"Hi, Dick, how's it hanging?" muttered Mac, a smile plastered on his face.

"He probably heard you."

"Hey, Danielson can kiss my big hairy ass. This guy destroyed your career, not that I give a shit about the navy, mind you. How many months did he stow you away in that loony bin before your ol' buddy Mac here saved your sorry butt? Two months?"

"Three. Probably would have been easier if I had just told those doctors I imagined the Meg. You know, psychosis of the deep, temporary insanity brought on by fatigue."

"Would have been a lie, pal."

"Yeah, well somehow I don't think Danielson volunteered so he could apologize to me in person. Megalodon or not, the guy blames me for killing two of his men."

"Hey, J.T., no living person on this planet would have done any different than you if they had seen what we saw coming at us last night. And I told that to Heller."

"What'd he say?"

"Heller's an asshole. If he'd have been with me in 'Nam, he'd have been a casualty of friendly fire." Mac looked toward the stern. "When's that big net of yours due to arrive?"

"This afternoon."

"Good. Hey, you should've heard the old man ripping Terry a new one. Man, was he pissed. Meanwhile, what the hell's going on with you and the old lady?"

"I don't know. I know she's screwing Bud, but . . . I guess a part of me still loves her."

Mac turned to his friend, looking like he just swallowed turpentine. "Jonas . . . Jonas, you hopeless sack of shit. What were the three rules I taught you about women?"

"I don't remember."

"Come on!"

"No glove, no love. Use lemon juice to check for open wounds—"

"And never marry a woman who can't name at least two of the five Marx Brothers. Maggie was no good from the get-go and I told you that when you married her! Women like Maggie, they play by a different set of rules. Let her go, move on. Let this prick Harris deal with her. Trust me, he'll be bankrupt within a year."

Jonas stared at the horizon, a line of storm clouds building in the distance.

"So between me and thee, you really think this shark of yours will end up in California waters? I mean, no pressure, J.T., but I could really use that bonus Tanaka's offering."

"I don't know. Maybe. The truth is, our window of opportunity's closing quickly. Tracking the Megalodon in coastal waters is one thing, locating her in open ocean . . . probably impossible."

"What about California?"

"If it happens, it could take weeks, maybe years. No one can predict what a predator like this will do." Jonas paused, pointing to the horizon. "Looks bad. What do you think?"

Mac looked to the west, where dark storm clouds had gathered. "No hunting by chopper tonight, I'd say."

Jonas nodded. "Hope the Meg agrees with you."

*　　　*　　　*

Frank Heller stood on the pier, watching two crewmen secure the submarine's thick white bow lines, carefully lining the slack up along the deck of the *Nautilus*. Moments later, Captain Richard Danielson emerged from the forward section of the hull. He smiled at Heller, slapping the "571" painted in white along the black conning tower.

"So, Frank, what do you think of my new command?"

Heller shook his head. "I'm just amazed this old barge still floats. Why the hell would McGovern assign a decommissioned sub to hunt down this shark?"

Danielson strode across the open gangway. "My idea. McGovern's in a tough position. The publicity's killing him. But the *Nautilus*, she's a different story. The public loves this old boat. She's like an aging war hero, going out with one last victory. McGovern went crazy for the idea—"

"I don't like it. You have no concept of what you're dealing with, skipper."

"I read the reports. Don't forget, I tracked Russian Alphas for five years. This mission's nothing. One tube in the water and this overgrown shark is fish food."

Frank was about to respond when he saw a tall officer exit the sub, a big smile planted on his face.

"Denny?"

"Hey, big brother!" Chief Engineer Dennis Heller came bounding down the ramp and bear-hugged Frank.

"Denny, what in the hell are you doing aboard this rusty tin can?"

Dennis glanced at Danielson. "I'm due to retire this year. Turns out I'm thirty hours shy on active duty. I figured, why not serve them aboard the *Nautilus* with my first CO. Besides, shore leave in Honolulu beats the hell out of Bayonne, New Jersey."

"Sorry to disappoint you, Chief," interrupted Danielson, "but all shore leaves are cancelled until we fry this Megala . . . whatever Taylor calls it. By the way, Frank, I saw him on board your boat this afternoon. Honestly, I can't stomach the man."

"Turns out he was right. Why not just leave it alone—"

"So he was right. His actions still killed two of my crew, or did you forget?"

"It's our fault too." Heller lowered his voice to his former commanding officer. "I should have never allowed you to talk me into pushing him on that last dive."

"He was fine—"

"He was fried! Taylor was one of the best deep-sea pilots in the business. And that mission had nothing to do with the navy, it was those neo-cons working the Pentagon who were pushing that whole energy agenda!"

"You're out of line, Doctor." Danielson's neck was turning red.

"Whoa, Frank, Captain, take it easy." Dennis moved between them. "Come on, Frank, I'll take you out for a quick bite. Skip, I'll be back at sixteen-thirty hours."

Danielson stood in silence as the two men headed into town, the first drops of rain echoing against the outer steel casing of the *Nautilus*.

JAWS, MAUI

The towering swells, driven by the impending storm, rolled onto the rocky beach, carrying large chunks of whale blubber and debris. The two-hundred-odd tourists didn't seem to mind. They'd been gathering all day to watch local surfers brave some of the most dangerous waves on the planet.

It takes a variety of conditions to form big waves, the two most important being the distance a wave travels over deep ocean, and the effect created when the wave hits shallow water. Monster waves at the Maui site known to surfers and wind surfers as "JAWS" occur about a dozen times a year, a result of the unique shape of the geography's underwater ridge and a dramatic depth change from 120 feet to just 30 feet as waves strike the shallows. When storm swells longer than 1,000 feet meet the underwater ridge, waves can rise as high as 70 feet, a condition that sends hard-core surfers flocking to Maui. Because the waves are moving so fast, Wave Runners must tow the surfers into the path of these giant swells, with rides lasting as long as thirty seconds . . . and wipeouts sometimes fatal.

The big name surfers had been at it all day, Laird Hamilton, Pete Cabrinha, Dave Kalama. Now, as the sun began to set, the youngsters moved in to try their luck. Eighteen-year-old Zach Richards had been cutting waves on Oahu's North Shore since he was twelve. His younger brother, Jim, had only recently begun training on the big waves, but he was more than

game, especially with an audience of spectators and cameras.

Jim pulled on his black wet suit while Zach and his surfer buddies, Scott and Ryan, decided who would man the two Jet Skis. As he headed for the beach, he circled around a group of girls he knew from high school. His target, Maria McGuire, a knockout brunette, caught his eye and gave him a quick wave, jump-starting his heart—

—until he saw Michael Barnes, a twenty-two-year-old with a tattoo on every muscle, join his brother's group.

Surfing is a spiritual release, with everyone watching out for one another, especially when it comes to riding the big waves. Barnes was driven strictly by ego, which was why none of the big surfers on the island allowed him to join their group.

Jim watched Scott tow his brother out to the breakpoint, Ryan readying the second Wave Runner as Barnes approached. "She's out of your league, faggot."

"Huh?"

"Maria. Don't even bother." Barnes pushed him aside with his board, then jumped into the surf and paddled out to hitch a ride on Ryan's tow rig.

"Asshole . . ." For a moment Jim debated whether to go out. But Scott was on his way in with a tow, and Maria was watching, rooting him on.

There was no turning back. Bellying up on his board, he dove into the surf.

Ten minutes later, the three surfers and two Jet Skiers were waiting beyond the breakpoint for the next incoming set. They were a good half-mile out, in water more than 120-feet deep.

* * *

The female moved lazily along the sea floor, digesting the remains of her last meal. Nestled within her swollen oviduct were live young, each seven to twelve feet long, weighing upwards of a ton.

Almost two years had passed since the violent act of copulation that had impregnated the female. As embryos, her unborn pups had been sheathed in a protective, transparent capsule, nourished by an external placenta-like yolk sac attached to their gut. Over time these capsules had ruptured, exposing the developing Megalodon sharks to a womb whose liquified world was far different from the chemistry of the ocean. As the day of their birth rapidly approached, their mother's uterus steadily regulated its ion-water balance, preparing the unborn young for their emergence into the sea.

For all its life-giving chemicals, the depths of the Challenger Deep were not equipped to sustain a large colony of apex predators, so it was left to nature to balance the scales and thin the herd. Undernourished, the unborn Megs at first subsisted on ovulated, unfertilized eggs. But as they grew larger, the pups instinctively turned to cannibalism, the larger infants feeding upon their smaller, less fortunate siblings.

What had begun as a brood of seventeen was down to three.

For the big female, inhabiting the abyss meant longer gestation periods than her surface-breeding ancestors had to endure, her internal anatomy delaying contractions until her pups could achieve greater size. This evolutionary feature, designed to increase the pups' rate of survival in the wild, was taking a toll on their mother, forcing the female to expend greater amounts of energy during these final weeks of pregnancy.

Expending more energy meant an increase in feeding.

Since leaving her abyssal habitat, the female had attacked more than a dozen different whale pods. Most of these earlier assaults had failed, but the Meg was learning, having succeeded in her last three tries.

Failure or not, the whale pods around Hawaii were spooked by the hunter's presence. Haunting calls from the humpback and gray whales reverberated through miles of ocean. Almost as one, the pods began altering their migratory course, skirting west, away from the suddenly dangerous coastal waters of Hawaii. By morning of the third day, few whales could be found off the island chain.

The Megalodon sensed the departure of its prey, but did not give chase. Gliding effortlessly through the thermocline, the boundary between sun-warmed waters and the ocean depths, it headed toward the shallows, its senses enticed by a strange new stimulus.

*   *   *

Zach and Barnes lay prone on the Wave Runner's tow rigs, waiting impatiently for their first set of waves to arrive. The sun was going down, the air had turned chilly, and Barnes was losing his audience as the beachgoers, sensing the best action had passed, began heading in.

Scott was the first to register the arriving swells. "Here we go!"

The two Wave Runners took off with their surfers, leaving Zach behind.

The first wave struck the underwater ridge, rising majestically like a deep blue mountain. Zach was on the inside as the 28-footer broke from left to right. He was in a zone, a mind space where his only focus remained at the front of his board and a hundred feet down the line. Rooted within this tunnel vision, he never saw what was happening behind him.

Fifty feet to Zach's left, Barnes had just made his turn, pulling into the wave's tube, enjoying the beginning of what he knew would be an "insane" ride. For a quick second, he stole a glance toward the beach, hoping to see the brunette chick, his peripheral vision catching a bizarre wall of white water emerging on his right.

Barnes turned, never seeing the creature break through the wave—

—and surfed right into the open mouth of the Megalodon!

Momentum slingshot Barnes into darkness, sending him smashing headfirst into an arching wall of cartilage. He bounced across an undulating tongue as rows of

serrated white teeth gnashed his surfboard and tossed him about, spraying him with splinters. Disoriented, unable to catch a second to reason, Barnes's mind was convinced he was underwater, being pummeled by the wave's fury, the lacerations now flailing at his wet suit and skin caused by the sharp ridges of coral along the bottom, and not serrated white teeth. Dark sky became incoming sea and now he really was underwater, holding on, the mouth he believed to be the underbelly of the wave opening and closing, searching for his flesh, a hideous tongue pushing him towards chomping rows of teeth . . . and suddenly, he knew!

Michael Barnes heard himself scream—

—as his existence was crushed into scarlet oblivion.

* * *

Ryan circled on his Wave Runner, searching for Barnes. As the roar of the breaking wave passed, he suddenly heard noise coming from the beach—high-pitched screams of terror! He looked back, shocked to see dozens of onlookers waving frantically at him.

And then he saw the circling dorsal fin—as tall as a small sailboat—and he gunned the engine, racing toward shore.

* * *

Her appetite primed, the female circled the kill zone, gnashing her teeth as she swam, searching the area for vibrations. Beneath her thick skin, along her lateral line, a canal extended the entire length of her body. The upper section of this canal held sensory

cells called neuromasts. Mucus contained in the lower half of the canals transmitted vibrations from the seawater to these sensation cells, giving the predator a spectacular "vision" of her surroundings through echolocation. Somewhere close was more prey, and her senses were isolating it.

*   *   *

Jim Richards shivered from the cold, waiting for one of the Wave Runners to come back out and get him. The swells were pushing him closer to the breakpoint, but were still moving too fast to catch.

What the hell's taking them so long?

Something struck his leg, causing him to look down.

"Jesus." Small bits of bloody flesh clung to his surfboard. He felt vomit rising in his throat and swallowed hard to keep it down.

Then he spotted the dorsal fin. It was impossibly tall, growing taller . . . gliding straight for him! Jim pulled his legs onto his surfboard and froze, willing his muscles and nerves to be still, but looking down, he saw his board was quivering in the water.

The Megalodon rose to the surface, the sheer mass of its moving girth creating a current that towed the surfboard and its passenger sideways and out to sea. Beyond the dorsal, the upper section of a half-moon-shaped tail slashed back and forth along the surface. Stretching higher than Jim's head, it swatted past his face, missing him by mere inches.

Jim felt something lifting him. His heart fluttered, anticipating the bloody mouth and rows of fangs. But the shark was still swimming away from him; the pressure had been caused by a swell. The next waves were coming in, fast and furious, and he needed to catch one.

He turned around, the monster already a good sixty feet behind him.

Go!

Jim rolled onto his stomach and paddled, stroking as fast as he could, his pounding heart threatening to explode from his chest.

The Megalodon turned, zeroing in on these new vibrations. The female's peppered white snout broke the surface thirty feet behind him, snorting sea like a Brahma bull.

Jim slammed his face against the board, simultaneously gripping the outer edges with his ankles as he plunged his arms into the water, double-stroking furiously. He screamed as he registered the monster's breath along the soles of his bare feet, and then he fell over the edge of a cliff and screamed.

Jim plunged down the rolling mountain of water, popping up at the last moment on his exhausted legs, feet wide, crouching low. He reached back with his right hand, the 36-foot wave roaring at him like a tornado, its whitewater crest, twenty feet above his head, threatening to bury him in the sea floor.

Jim cut hard to his right as the Megalodon burst through the wave, missing him by two board lengths,

its forward inertia sending it momentarily airborne. The surfer stole a quick glance, then dug in, refusing to be tossed, riding the wave out 50 yards . . . 100 . . . until he felt it dying, his hope dying with it.

The ride over, Jim sank onto his board, the shoreline a good seventy yards away.

The dorsal fin turned, racing for him!

He heard the outboard. Turned to see his brother on the Jet-Ski, waving frantically.

Jim dove into the water, swimming toward him.

Zach never slowed. With the monstrous shark less then twenty feet behind Jim, he cut across its path, racing by his brother, who leaped onto the Wave Runner's tow rig and held on.

The Wave Runner shot through the shallows and straight onto the beach, the delirious crowd chanting, "Jim, Jim, Jim . . ."

Zach leaped off the Wave Runner and hugged his brother, slapping him on the back, telling him what a great job he'd done. Jim was exhausted, shaking with fear, the burst of adrenaline nearly forcing him to puke. He caught himself as Maria appeared, a huge smile stretched across her face, tears in her brown eyes as she hugged him.

"Are you okay?" she asked. "You scared the shit out of me!"

Jim cleared his throat and took a breath. "Yeah . . . no problem." Then, seeing his opening, he gave Maria a crooked smile and said, "So, you doing anything tonight?"

BATTLE AT SEA

Moments after Jim Richards had been pulled from the surf, the coast-guard air rescue arrived, hovering two hundred feet above the breaking swells. Spotting the predator's glow, the chopper followed the female as she headed out to sea, radioing her position to the naval base at Pearl Harbor. Within minutes, both the *Nautilus* and the *Kiku* had put to sea, racing north past Mamala Bay. By the time the *Kiku* reached Kaena Point, the incoming storm had reached gale-force proportions, the raging night fully upon them.

Jonas and Terry were in the pilothouse as the door leading to the deck tore open against the howling wind. Mac slipped into the dry compartment, slamming the hatch closed behind him, his yellow slicker dripping all over the floor.

"Copter's secured. So's the net and harpoon gun. Captain says we're in for a rough one."

"This may be our only chance. If we don't at least tag the female before she heads into open water, we may lose her for good."

The three entered the CIC, where Masao was standing over a crewman seated at the sonar console. He looked grim. "The coast guard broke off its pursuit because of the weather." Masao turned to the crewman. "Anything on sonar yet, Pasquale?"

Without looking up, the technician shook his head. "Just the *Nautilus*." Everyone grabbed a console as a

twenty-foot swell lifted and tossed the research vessel from one side to the other.

Captain Barre stood at the helm, his sea legs giving naturally with the roll of his vessel. "Hope nobody had a big dinner. This storm's gonna be a bitch."

*   *   *

Life on board the world's first nuclear-powered submarine was relatively calm as the ship entered Waimea Bay one hundred feet below the raging storm. Though refitted several times during its life span, the sub still possessed a single nuclear reactor that created the superheated steam necessary to power its twin turbines and two shafts. It was an antiquated system, far from battle-ready.

Commander Danielson, too, felt far from battle-ready, but the retired naval man was more than game. "Anything on the sonar, Ensign Raby?"

The sonar man was listening with his headphones while watching his console screen. The screen was designed to give a visual representation of the difference between the background noise and a particular bearing. Any object within range would appear as a light line against the green background. Because they were searching for a biologic, sonar was actively pinging the area every three minutes, Raby looking for return signals. "Lots of surface interference from the storm. Nothing else yet, sir."

"Very well, keep me informed. Chief of the Watch, what's our weapons status?"

Chief Engineer Dennis Heller, six years younger than his brother Frank, yet still one of the oldest members of the sub's makeshift crew, looked up from his console. "Two Mark 48 AD-CAP torpedoes ready to fire on your command, sir. Torpedoes set for close range, as per your orders. A bit tight, if you don't mind my saying, sir."

"Has to be, Chief. When sonar locates this monster, we'll need to be as close as possible to ensure an accurate solution."

"Captain Danielson!" The radioman leaned back from his console. "Sir, I'm receiving a distress call from a Japanese whaler. Hard to make out, but it sounds as if they're being attacked."

"Navigator, plot an intercept course, ten degrees up on the fair-weather planes. If this is our friend, I want to kill it and be back at Pearl in time for last call at Grady's."

*　　　*　　　*

The Japanese whaler rolled with the massive swells, rain and wind pelting her crew mercilessly. The vessel's hold was dangerously overloaded with its illegal catch: the carcasses of eight gray whales. Two more had been lashed to the port side of the ship with a cargo net.

A pair of lookouts held on to the main mast, disoriented by weather and darkness. The two sailors had been assigned the hazardous duty of making sure the valuable whale blubber remained firmly secured during the storm. Unfortunately for the exhausted men, their searchlight hardly penetrated the maelstrom. Sporadic flashes of lightning afforded them their only real vision of their precious cargo.

Flash. The ocean dropped from view as the ship rolled to starboard, the cargo net groaning with its keep. The sailors hung on as the poorly ballasted vessel rolled back to port.

Flash. The sea threatened to suck them under, the net actually disappearing momentarily beneath the waves.

Flash. The vessel rolled again to starboard, the net reappearing. The men gasped — a massive white triangular head had risen from the sea with the cargo!

Darkness. The whaler rolled, its lookouts blind in the storm. Silent seconds passed. Then, *flash*, a fork of lightning lit the sky and the horrible head reappeared, its mouth bristling razor-sharp teeth.

The crewmen screamed, but the storm muted the sound. The senior mate signaled to the other that he would find the captain.

Flash. The unimaginably large jaws were tearing at the carcass now, the head leaning sideways against the rolling vessel, its teeth gnashing at the whale blubber.

The ship rolled to starboard once more. The senior mate struggled to make it belowdecks, squeezing his eyes shut against the gale and holding tight to the rope ladder. He could lower himself only a rung at a time as the ship listed to port . . . and kept rolling! He opened his eyes, felt his stomach churn.

Flash. The sea kept coming, the triangular head gone. But something was pulling the ship onto its side and into the water.

*   *   *

"Captain, the whaler is two hundred yards ahead."

"Thank you, Chief. Take us to periscope depth."

"Periscope depth, aye, sir."

The sub rose as Danielson pressed his face against the rubber housing of the periscope and stared into darkness. The scope turned night into shades of green, but the storm and rolling waves severely reduced visibility.

Flash. The raging Pacific was illuminated, and for an instant Danielson caught the silhouette of the whaler lying on its side. "The whaler's sinking, contact the coast guard," he ordered. "Where's the nearest cutter?"

"Sir," responded the radioman, "the only surface ship within twenty miles is the *Kiku*."

"Skipper, there's something else out there, circling the whaler!"

* * *

Pasquale held the headset tightly against his ears, verifying the message once more. "Captain, we're receiving an emergency call from the *Nautilus*." All heads in the control room turned. "A Japanese whaler's down, twelve nautical miles to the east. They say there may be survivors in the water, but no other surface ships are in the area. They're requesting immediate assistance."

Masao looked at Jonas. "The Meg?"

"If it is, we don't have much time."

"Get us there quickly, Captain," ordered Masao.

* * *

The Japanese whaler lay on her port side, refusing to sink, instead rising and falling with the twenty-foot swells. Within the bowels of the vessel, eleven men struggled in darkness to escape a chamber of death in which they could not tell which way was up. The cold ocean hissed from all directions, battering the keel, searching for a way inside the battened-down ship.

Below the waves the Megalodon tore at the remains of the whale meat lashed to the cargo net. It was her physical presence, in great part, that supported the vessel from below, keeping the dying ship afloat.

The senior lookout had been thrown overboard when the ship had toppled. Somehow he had managed to climb back on board, and now he struggled to hold on. From within, he heard the screams of his shipmates. Kicking open one of the battened-down hatches, he shone his flashlight inside. Four crewmen crawled out from below, joining him on the tilting main deck.

*   *   *

"Skipper, I can hear shouts," said the sonar man. "There are men in the water."

"How far away is the *Kiku*?"

"Six minutes," Chief Heller called out.

Danielson tried to think. What could he do to distract the Megalodon, keep the monster from the survivors? "Chief, continuous pinging, loud as you can. Sonar, watch the creature, tell me what happens."

"Continuous ping, aye, sir."

Ping . . . ping . . . ping. The metallic gongs rattled through the hull of the *Nautilus*, the deep throb of

the reverberations radiating acoustically through the seawater.

* * *

The deafening pings reached the female's lateral line in seconds. The dense sound waves overloaded her senses, sending her into a rage. An unknown creature was challenging the female for her kill. Abandoning the last scraps of whale meat entangled within the cargo net, the Megalodon circled below the sinking whaler, shook her throbbing head twice, then homed in on the source of the annoying sounds.

* * *

"Skipper, I've got a bearing on the biologic. Sixty meters and closing. You've definitely got its attention!"

"Forty meters and closing."

"Chief?"

"I've got a temporary solution, sir, but the explosion could harm the crew of that whaler."

"Twenty meters, sir!"

"Helm, change course to zero-two-five, twenty degrees down-angle on the planes, take us to eight hundred feet, make your speed fifteen knots. Let's see if she'll chase us, then put some ocean between this fish and that whaler."

The sub accelerated in a shallow descent, the Megalodon in pursuit. The female measured less than half the *Nautilus*'s length, and the submarine, at 3,000 tons, easily outweighed her. But the female was faster and could outmaneuver its adversary; moreover, no

adult Mcgalodon would allow a challenge within its domain to go unanswered.

The female accelerated at the sub's steel hull like a berserk sixty-foot locomotive.

"Ten meters . . . brace for impact!" The sonar man ripped off his headset.

BOOM!

The *Nautilus* rolled sideways, several crewmen hurtling from their posts. The power died, darkness enveloping the crew, as steel plates groaned all around them. Red emergency lights flickered on, but the engines had stopped, and the sub now drifted, listing at a forty-five-degree angle.

The Megalodon circled, carefully measuring her challenge. The collision had caused a painful throbbing in her snout. The female shook her head, several broken teeth falling out. In time they would be replaced by those lying beneath them in reserve.

Captain Danielson felt warmth seep into his right eye. "All stations report!" he yelled, wiping the blood from his forehead.

Chief Heller was the first to call out. "Engine room reports flooding in three compartments, sir. Reactor is off-line."

"Radiation?"

"No leaks found."

"Batteries?"

"Batteries appear functional and are on-line, Captain, but the stern planes are not responding. We got hit just above the keel."

"Son of a bitch." Danielson was fuming . . . how could he have allowed a fish to cripple his boat! "Where's the creature now?"

"Circling, sir. Very close," reported sonar.

"Captain," said the chief. "Damage control says one screw is out, the other should be on-line within ten minutes. Emergency batteries only, sir."

"Torpedoes?"

"Still ready, sir."

"Flood torpedo tubes one and two sonar, I want a firing solution."

The hull plates groaned . . . followed by a bizarre scratching sound.

Danielson looked around, baffled. "Raby, what the hell is that noise?"

"Sir?" the sonar man looked pale. "I think the Megalodon's attempting to bite through our hull."

*   *   *

The *Kiku* arrived at the last known coordinates of the whaler, but without the support of the Meg, pushing from below, the ship had gone under without a fight.

Jonas and Heller, dressed in life jackets and secured to the ship by lines around their waists, stood at the bow. Heller guided the searchlight. Jonas held the rifle loaded with the tracking dart in one hand, a life ring in his other. The *Kiku* rose wildly and fell. Swells crashed over her bow, threatening to send both men into the sea.

"There!" Jonas pointed to starboard. Two men clung to what was left of the whaler's mast.

Heller aimed the light, then called Barre on his walkie-talkie. The bow swung hard to starboard.

Jonas handed the rifle to Heller, held on to the rail, and threw the life ring toward the men. With the sea breaking in peaks and valleys and the *Kiku* bucking Jonas like a wild bronco, he could not tell whether the men could even see the flotation device, let alone reach it.

"Forget it, Taylor!" Heller yelled. "You'll never reach them!"

Jonas continued scanning the water as the bow dropped thirty feet, another swell rising ten yards away. They rose again and Jonas saw the light flash on the men. One was waving.

"Tie me off!" Jonas screamed.

"What?"

As the bow dropped, Jonas placed one foot onto the rail. When it rose again, he leaped into the maelstrom with all his might. Propelled by the rising deck, he launched into the air, falling beyond the next incoming swell.

Cold water shocked his body, driving the breath from his chest, sapping his strength. He rose with the next wave but was unable to see anything, then swam as hard as he could in the direction he prayed was correct.

Without warning, Jonas found himself falling into a valley between two swells. Swimming was not an option: he was being hurled up and down mountains of water. And then his head smashed into a hard object, blacking his vision.

*   *   *

The Meg couldn't tell if the creature was alive, its piercing vibrations having ceased. Her taste buds in her rostrum told her the strange fish was inedible. Still, she circled again, occasionally attempting to bite down upon the object, but the creature was simply too large.

And then the Meg detected familiar vibrations along the surface. *Prey* . . .

*   *   *

"It's moving off, skipper! She's heading back to the surface."

"Engines back on-line, Captain," reported Chief Heller. As if in response, the *Nautilus* leveled out.

"That's my girl. Helm, bring us around, make your course zero-five-zero, up ten degrees on the planes, take us to four hundred feet. Chief, I want a firing solution on that monster. On my command, start pinging again. When she descends to attack, we'll hit her with both torpedoes!"

Heller looked worried. "Sir, engineering warns the ship can't withstand another collision. I strongly suggest we return to Pearl and—"

"Negative, Mr. Heller. We end this now."

*   *   *

A hand grabbed Jonas by his collar and hung on. The senior lookout pulled Jonas onto the fallen mast and sputtered something in Japanese, obviously grateful. Jonas tried to look around. The second sailor was gone. He felt a strong tug on his waist—Heller and his men were pulling him back.

"Hold on!" Taylor grabbed the sailor from around his waist, and the two were dragged backward along the surface toward the *Kiku*.

*   *   *

The Meg locked in on the vibrations and circled its prey—

—as the pinging began anew. The female could smell blood, but the aggressive challenge of the vibrations overwhelmed her hunger. She wheeled around in a fluid motion, a white blur on course with its challenger.

*   *   *

"Six hundred meters and closing quickly, Captain," called out the sonar operator.

"Chief Heller, do we have a firing solution?"

"Aye, sir!"

"On my command . . ."

"Three hundred meters . . ."

"Steady, gentlemen."

"One hundred and fifty meters!"

"Let her come . . ."

"Skipper, course change!" Sonar looked up, frantic. "Sir, I lost her!"

Danielson ran to the console, sweat and blood dripping down his face. "What happened?"

Sonar was bent over, cupping his ears, trying to hear. "Sir, she went deep. I can barely hear her. . . . Wait . . . Oh shit, she's below us!"

"Full speed ahead!" ordered Danielson.

The crippled submarine lurched forward, struggling to reach a speed above ten knots. The Megalodon rose from below, homing again on what it perceived to be the creature's tail. Her snout impacted the steel plates at thirty knots, puncturing the already buckling hull. This time the casing gave, spreading a gap between the steel plates, venting the engine room to the sea.

The collision ruptured the submarine's aft ballast tanks. As the keel of the *Nautilus* filled with seawater, the crew's environment shifted to a forty-five-degree tilt. The engine room was hardest hit. Assistant Engineer David Freeman tumbled backward in the dark. His head slammed hard against a control panel, knocking him unconscious. Lieutenant Artie Krawitz found himself pinned under a collapsed bulkhead, his left ankle shattered. As the engine room filled with water, he managed to free himself and crawl upward into the next compartment, sealing the watertight door seconds before the sea could rush in.

"Damage report!" commanded Danielson.

"Engine room's flooded," Heller reported. "Sir, I can't raise—"

A loud wail, followed by flashing red sirens cut the chief engineer off.

"Core breach!" he yelled. "Someone's got to shut it down!"

"Helm, high-pressure air into the ballast tanks, put us on the ceiling. Heller, get down to the reactor room—"

"On my way!"

The *Nautilus* rose, still listing to starboard as she climbed toward the surface.

Heller ran through a maze of chaos. In every compartment, crew members attempted to staunch the flow of seawater spraying from a thousand leaks. At least half of the electrical consoles looked down.

Outside the engine room, Lieutenant Krawitz was frantically throwing switches, shutting down the nuclear reactor.

Heller joined him, shutting off the alarm. "Report, Lieutenant."

"Four dead in here, a whole section of pipe collapsed on impact. Everyone and everything aft of the engine room is underwater."

"Radiation?"

The officer looked at his friend of ten years. "Denny, this ship's over forty years old. We've lost the integrity of the hull, the steel plates are falling off like shingles. We'll drown before any radiation kills us."

*   *   *

Jonas was hauled onto the *Kiku*'s main deck and then dragged into the pilothouse. A moment later, Frank Heller and his men returned with the Japanese seaman.

"Taylor, are you insane?" screamed Heller.

"Frank, quiet," said DeMarco. "We're receiving a distress call from the *Nautilus*."

Heller strode into the command center. "A distress call?"

Bob Pasquale cupped his ears, trying to hear. "They're surfacing. No power. They need our assistance immediately!"

Captain Barre barked orders to change course. The *Kiku* turned, fighting against the relentless swells.

*   *   *

David Freeman had regained consciousness, his face pressed hard against the watertight door where a small pocket of air remained. The chamber was bathed in red emergency lighting. Blood gushed from his forehead.

As the *Nautilus* rose, debris began seeping out of the gap in the hull and into the Pacific. The Megalodon rose with the sub, snapping its jaws at anything that moved. The predator smelled Freeman's blood.

Driving her enormous head into the opening, the Meg separated the already loose steel plates, enlarging the gap in the hull significantly. Her white glow illuminated the flooded compartment, catching the engineer's attention. Holding his breath, he ducked underwater, looked down . . . and gulped a mouthful of seawater! The monster's ten-foot-wide jaws opened and closed below him, the upper jaw pushing forward and away from the creature's head like something out of a 3-D horror film.

The hideous triangular teeth were now less than five feet away. Freeman felt his body being sucked into the vortex. He surfaced. Tore at the door, his screams muffled by the rising sea. Unable to escape, he chose an alternative death, ducking his head underwater, inhaling the salt water deep into his lungs, struggling

to kill himself before the mouthful of teeth could reach him.

The female inhaled the heaving body into her mouth, crushing and swallowing it in one gulp. The warm blood sent her into a renewed frenzy. She shook her head, freeing herself from the opening, then circled the *Nautilus* again as it burst through the surface.

*   *   *

"Abandon ship! All hands, abandon ship!" Captain Danielson barked his orders as the *Nautilus* tossed hard to starboard against the incoming swells.

Three hatches exploded open, water pouring into the hull, pink phosphorescent flares piercing the blackness. Three yellow rafts inflated instantaneously and were lashed to the side of the boat. Survivors rushed to board, struggling to maintain their balance against the raging sea. The *Kiku* was close, her spotlight now guiding the rafts.

Danielson was in the last life raft. Bolts of lightning lit the seascape as he looked back at the *Nautilus*. Within seconds, the submarine was overcome by the sea. Her once-mighty bow rose out of the ocean, then another swell drove the ship toward her final resting place at the bottom of the Pacific.

Flash. The first raft reached the *Kiku*. Fifteen men scrambled up a cargo net draped along her starboard side. A swell slammed against the ship, lifting it, then dropping it thirty feet.

Flash. The force of the wave had tossed some of Danielson's crew back into the sea. Like insects they scrambled to reach the net, climbing once again.

Jonas aimed the spotlight into the swell, locating a seaman. It was Dennis Heller. Frank saw his younger brother struggling to stay afloat less than fifteen feet from the *Kiku's* cargo net.

Frank tossed a ring buoy to his brother as the second raft closed in from behind. Dennis grabbed at the life preserver and held on as his brother pulled him toward the *Kiku.* The crew from the second raft were already scaling the cargo net, the last group now within ten feet of the ship.

Dennis reached the net and began climbing. He was halfway up when his shipmates from the third raft joined him.

Frank Heller lay prone on deck beneath the starboard rail, one hand holding the metal pipe, the other extending toward his brother, now only two body-lengths away. "Denny, give me your hand!" They touched momentarily—

—as a rogue wave rolled over the starboard deck, battering the ship.

Flash. The white monster appeared from out of the swell, grasping Dennis Heller in its jaws. Frank froze in place, unable to react as the tip of the snout passed less than a foot from his face. The Meg seemed to hang in midair, suspended in time. And then the creature slid back into the sea, dragging Dennis Heller backward with her.

"No, no, noooo!" Frank screeched at empty sea, waiting for the creature to return with his brother.

Danielson and the others were still holding onto the net, having witnessed the scene. Petrified, they climbed for their lives with reckless abandon.

The Meg rose again, the bloody remains of Dennis Heller still shredded within its front row of teeth. Danielson turned and screamed, flattening himself against the cargo net.

Jonas spun the searchlight's beam toward the Meg with his left hand as he raised the rifle with his right. He was close, a mere thirty feet. Without aiming, he pulled the trigger.

The homing dart exploded out of the barrel, burying itself within the creature's thick white hide as the barbed device attached itself firmly behind the female's right pectoral fin.

The searchlight's powerful beam blazed into the right eye of the nocturnal predator, burning the sensitive ocular tissue like a laser. The pain sent the monster reeling backward into the sea, repelling her attack only feet from Danielson.

The skipper and his men collapsed onto the deck and were pulled, one by one, inside the shelter of the pilothouse. Jonas grabbed Frank, tugging him backward, but he refused to let go of the rail.

"You're dead, monster, you hear me!?!" Heller screamed into the night, his words deadened by the wind. "You're fucking dead!"

OPENING DAY

The crowd of nearly six hundred invited guests milled about the southern end of the arena, waiting for the ceremony to begin. Two weeks had passed since the disaster at sea. Nine members of the *Nautilus*'s crew had perished, as had fourteen from the Japanese whaler. A ceremony honoring the dead had taken place at Pearl Harbor. Two days later, Captain Richard Danielson retired from the navy.

Commander Bryce McGovern was on the hot seat. Who had authorized the United States Navy to hunt the Megalodon? Why had McGovern selected the *Nautilus* to complete the mission, knowing the decommissioned submarine was far from battle-worthy? The families of the deceased were outraged, and an internal investigation was ordered. Many believed Commander McGovern would be the next naval officer to be "retired."

Frank Heller was a raging bull. His brother Dennis had been his only family, and Heller's hatred for the Megalodon was all-consuming. He informed Masao he was through, stating that he had his own plans for the "white devil." After the ceremony in Oahu, he flew home to California, and no one had heard from him since.

Maggie broke the story about the Tanaka Institute's plans to capture the Megalodon. From that moment on, the hunt for the Megalodon had turned into a media circus. JAMSTEC was secretly delighted

at the publicity, as it stood to share in the proceeds from Tanaka Lagoon. Construction crews had worked around the clock to complete the facility.

Now everyone wanted to know one thing: when would the guest of honor arrive?

The *Nautilus* controversy kept the governor of California, as well as other politicians, away from the lagoon's opening ceremony. The networks had no such fear, and were there en masse. CNN's Rudi Bakhtiar interviewed Masao, while Maggie waited in the wings, growling about "sloppy seconds."

"Mr. Tanaka, it's been weeks since the Megalodon was last seen, with many experts believing the creature has returned to deep water. What are the Institute's plans?"

"We still believe she'll migrate east. As long as we're funded, we'll continue the search."

"And the homing device?"

"Unfortunately, it may have failed. Either that, or the creature managed to tear it loose."

"A lot of people have died, including your own son, who you'll be honoring in a few minutes. If you could turn back time, what would you have done differently?"

"You cannot control karma, it is either good or bad. Our mission in the trench was honorable, our karma bad. Perhaps it will change, I don't know."

The news reporter turned to face the camera. "And so the Tanaka Lagoon opens. The real question

now—where is its 62,000-pound guest of honor? In Monterey, Rudi Bakhtiar, CNN Headline News."

Masao stepped to the podium. Above his head, a banner read: D.J. TANAKA LAGOON.

"Colleagues and guests, on behalf of the people of California, I dedicate this research facility to my son, D.J. Tanaka."

At the far end of the access canal, a pair of King Kong–size, steel doors cracked open and the Pacific rushed in, filling the world's largest swimming pool.

Jonas stood next to Mac on the lower observation deck, watching the water level rise three feet a minute. *Fourteen days, and still no sign of the female.* For six consecutive nights following the attack on the *Nautilus,* he and Mac had flown over Hawaii's coastal waters in search of the Meg. The homing device had worked, allowing the copter to track the predator as it headed east, the *Kiku* always trailing close behind. But the female, perhaps still in pain, refused to surface, remaining deep. And then, on the seventh day, the signal had simply disappeared.

The *Kiku* and its helicopter circled the area over the next forty-eight hours, unable to relocate the signal. Frustrated, Jonas finally recommended to Masao that the *Kiku* should return to Monterey, hoping the Megalodon might head for the California coastline and the thousands of migrating whales. Now, almost a week later, there was still no sign of the female.

Where had she gone?

NETWORK

Maggie felt her blood pressure rising as she waited impatiently for Fred Henderson to get off his phone. Finally, she stood over her producer's desk and snatched the receiver out of his hand. "He'll have to call you back," she said into the mouthpiece, and hung up.

"Maggie, what the hell do you think you're doing? That was an important call—"

"Important my ass, you were talking to your accountant."

"All right, you have my undivided attention. Speak."

"You cancelled my expense account, and my cameraman. Why?"

"Why?" The station manager put his feet up on his desk. "Why do you think? You've been at this a month. So far, I've seen footage of bleeding whales, dying whales, dead whales, and your husband—or ex-husband, whatever he is—lecturing about how mean this shark is. This morning you gave us footage of an empty aquarium. What I don't have is footage of the goddamn shark."

"What if I got you underwater footage of the Meg, I mean the real McCoy, scary as hell."

"I'm listening."

"At some point, the female's bound to show up where Jonas predicted. What if I was there, waiting for it . . . in a shark cage."

"You're nuts."

"Just listen to what I have to say." For the next thirty minutes, she briefed her station manager about her plan to film the Megalodon.

Henderson leaned back in his leather chair. "You've got balls, lady, I'll say that for you. But how can we be sure that your husband really knows where this monster's headed?"

"Listen, Fred, if there's one subject my soon-to-be ex knows about, it's these damn sharks. Christ, he's spent more time studying them over the last seven years than he has with me. This is the biggest story to hit this century, and I'll give you footage that will rocket this station to the top. This is Pulitzer stuff."

Henderson was sold. "Tell me what you need."

*   *   *

Bud was reading the paper when Maggie rapped on the back window of the limousine an hour later. When he unlocked the door, she ripped it open, climbed onto his lap, and planted a huge kiss on his lips.

"We got it, Bud! He loves it! The network agreed to back me on everything!" She kissed him again, pushing her tongue into his mouth, then came up for air and leaned her forehead against his.

"Bud," she whispered, "this is really the one, the story that makes me an international star. And you'll be there with me. Bud Harris, executive producer. Right now, though, I really need your help."

Bud smiled, enjoying the con. "Okay, darling, just tell me what you need."

"For starters, we'll need the *Magnate*. And a skeleton crew. I've already spoken with three cameramen and a sound guy who have underwater experience. We'll all be meeting on board the *Magnate* in the morning. When will my equipment arrive?"

"Tomorrow. We'll pick it up on our way back to San Diego."

"Not San Diego, Bud. Our target's the Red Triangle."

THE CANYON

Situated less than two hundred yards offshore from the Tanaka Lagoon's western wall lay the deep waters of the Monterey Bay Canyon, an anomaly of underwater geology, its dynamic incision along the California coastline rivaling the size and shape of the Grand Canyon.

Created by the subduction of the North American plate over millions of years, the massive underwater gorge traverses over sixty miles of sea floor, plunging more than a mile below the ocean's surface. There, the canyon meets the ocean bottom, eventually dropping another 12,000 feet in depth. Originally located in the vicinity of Santa Barbara, the entire Monterey Bay region was pushed ninety miles northward over millions of years, carried along the San Andreas fault zone on a section of granite rock known as the Salinian Block. The canyon itself is a confluence of varying formations; steep and narrow in some places, as wide as a Himalayan valley in others. Sheer vertical walls can drop two miles to a sediment-buried sea floor that dates back to the Pleistocene. Closer to shore, twisting chasms, some as deep as 6,000 feet, reach out from the main artery of the crevice like fingers of a groping hand.

*   *   *

The female moved through the pitch-black mid-waters of the Monterey Bay Canyon, following the steep walls of the C-shaped crevasse. Millions of

years ago, this same California coastline had been a favorite habitat of the Megalodon's ancestors . . . until the tropical seas had turned cold and the whales had altered their migration pattern. Having lost the staple of their diet, the apex predators eventually disappeared, "starved into extinction," according to the so-called experts.

Having been blinded in her left eye, the Megalodon had fled the waters off the Hawaiian Islands and come upon a warm undercurrent flowing southeast along the equator.

Riding the river of water just as a Boeing 747 rides an airstream, the female had traveled across the Pacific Ocean, arriving in the tropical waters off the Galapagos Islands. From there, she had migrated north along the coast of Central America, hunting gray whales and their newborn calves.

And then, as she approached the waters off Baja, her senses had become overwhelmed by the pounding of tens of thousands of beating hearts and moving muscles. The female changed course, following the coastline north, eventually ending up in the Monterey Bay Canyon.

Something seemed familiar. Perhaps it was the hydrothermal vents or the steep canyon walls. Territorial by nature, the sixty-foot female claimed the area as her own, an expanse of ocean awarded by her mere presence as its supreme hunter. Her senses indicated there were no other adult Megalodons in

the area to challenge her rule. The territory therefore became hers to defend.

The female had not eaten in days, preparing for the labor of birthing her pups. Driven by hunger, her senses quickly targeted the closest available prey. For three hours, the predator had been stalking the blue whale and its calf, moving 2,300 feet directly beneath them, shadowing them in the darkness. The female waited to attack, refusing to venture into the daylight.

Nightfall was coming . . .

RED TRIANGLE

The Ana Nuevo and Farallon Islands are a series of windswept rocks situated twenty-six miles west of San Francisco's Golden Gate Bridge. These are jagged landscapes, uninhabited by people, dominated by one mammal—the northern elephant seal.

Reaching lengths of more than fifteen feet and weighing 6,000 pounds, the northern elephant seal is the largest pinniped in the world and the most sexually dimorphic, with an alpha male bull mating with as many as four dozen females. Pelagic, they spend most of their time underwater and can hold their breath on a single dive for well over an hour. Winter months are spent onshore at rookeries where they mate, birth, and fight for dominance. But each spring and summer, they return to the Farallons where they lay about the rocky beaches, playing, sleeping, and molting.

The presence of these massive creatures entice another species to visit the remote island chain: *Carcharodon carcharius*, the great white shark. The seals are the predator's favorite delicacy, and the sharks circle these islands en masse, giving this expanse of deadly sea the nickname the Red Triangle.

*   *   *

Anchored in six hundred feet of water, the super yacht, *Magnate*, reflected the last golden flecks of sunlight. On her main deck, a weary crew of cameramen and technicians watched as thousands of California seals and sea lions stretched out upon the

rocky, uninhabited landmass, barking and flopping against one another.

Of all the documented attacks by great whites worldwide, more than half occurred in the Red Triangle. If Jonas's prediction proved accurate, Maggie reasoned that the Megalodon, like its modern-day cousin, would be drawn to the area to feast on elephant seals. For days her film crew had waited impatiently for the creature to show. Underwater video cameras, audio equipment, and special underwater lights littered the ship's deck, along with cigarette butts and candy wrappers. A community laundry line had been hung along the upper deck, dangling sweatshirts and towels.

Now the long hours of boredom, sun, and the occasional nausea associated with seasickness had finally gotten to the crew. And yet even these conditions would have been tolerable had it not been for the overwhelming stench that hung thick in the chilly Northern California air.

Trailing the yacht on a thirty-foot steel cable floated the rotting carcass of a male humpback whale. The pungent smell seemed to hover over the *Magnate* as if to mark the crime, for killing a whale in the Monterey Bay National Marine Sanctuary was indeed a criminal act. No matter: with his financial influence, Bud had made a deal with two local fishermen to locate and deliver a whale carcass to their location, no questions asked. But now, after nearly thirty-eight hours of the wicked stench, the *Magnate*'s crew were ready to mutiny.

"Maggs, listen to me," begged her director, Perry Meth, "give us a break here. Twelve hours of shore leave, that's all I'm asking. It could be weeks, months before this Megalodon even ventures into these waters. All of us need a break, even a fresh shower would be heaven. Just get us off this smelly barge."

"Perry, listen to me. This is the story of the decade, and I'm not about to blow it because you and your cronies feel the need to get drunk in some sleazy hotel bar."

"That's not fair—"

"No, what's not fair is that it's my ass on the line. Do you have any idea how difficult it was to organize all this? The cameras? The shark tube? Not to mention that hunk of whale blubber floating behind us?"

"Speaking of that, whatever happened to your campaign for protecting the whales? I would have sworn that was you I saw onstage accepting a Golden Eagle on behalf of the Save the Whales Foundation."

"Grow up, Perry, I didn't kill the damn thing, I'm just using it as bait. I mean, cut me some slack. There are thousands of them migrating along the coast." She tossed her blonde hair, causing strands of it to stick to her oiled bare shoulders.

Perry lowered his voice. "The crew's not happy about all this; they feel you're grasping at straws. Honestly, what're the chances of the Megalodon actually showing up in the Red Triangle? No one's even reported seeing the fish in weeks."

"The Meg will show, believe me, and we'll be the ones to get the footage."

"In what, that hunk of plastic?" He pointed to the ten-foot-high Lexan shark tube, which stood upright on the main deck, rigged to a winch. "Christ, Maggie, you'd have to be suicidal—"

"That hunk of plastic is three-inch-thick bullet-proof Plexiglas. Its diameter is too wide for the Meg to get its mouth around it." Maggie laughed. "I'll probably be safer in there than you guys will be on the *Magnate*."

"There's a comforting thought."

Maggie ran her fingers across her director's sweaty chest. She knew Bud was still in bed, sleeping off another hangover. "Perry, you and I have worked very hard together on these projects. Hell, look how much good our whale documentary did for those beasts."

He smirked. "Tell that to your dead humpback."

"Forget that already. Think big! I thought you wanted to direct movies?"

"I do."

"Then see this project for what it is, a door-opener into Hollywood, the story that puts us both on top. How does executive producer sound to you?"

Perry thought for a moment, then smiled. "It's a start."

"It's yours. Now, can we forget about the dead whale for a moment?"

"I guess so. But listen, as your executive producer I highly recommend we do something to create a little diversion, because your film crew's losing patience."

"I agree, and I've got an idea. I've been wanting to do a test run on the shark tube. What do you say we get it into the water and I'll shoot some footage this evening."

"Hmmm, now that's not a bad idea. That'll give me a chance to position the underwater lights." He smiled. "Maybe you'll be able to get some nice footage of a great white. That alone might be worth a few minutes on the weekend wrap-up."

Maggie shook her head. "See, that's your problem— you think way too small."

Bending over to pick up her wet suit, her sweatshirt rolled up, rewarding Perry with a glimpse of her tanned, thonged behind. "One last thing. Do me a favor and don't mention anything to Bud about being my executive producer." She smiled sweetly. "He gets jealous."

LIFE AND DEATH

The ghostly mass of the albino predator ascended effortlessly toward the surface. Darkness had fallen, it was time to feed.

The hunter quickly closed the distance to the calf. The mother blue stopped feeding, detecting the danger approaching rapidly from behind. She rose to the surface and forcefully nudged her young to remain in tight formation. Mother and offspring propelled their bodies faster, the Megalodon circling below, waiting for an opportunity to seize the calf.

The female darted closer, snapping at the blue whale's small pectoral fins, each feint designed to force the adult away from its offspring.

The mother whale charged, momentarily abandoning her calf.

The Meg circled back quickly, its jaws opening to seize the calf—

—when suddenly she was seized by muscle cramps that sent her arching in an uncontrollable spasm.

The female abandoned her prey, descending rapidly to the canyon floor. Her muscular body quivered with contortions, forcing her to swim in tight circles. Finally, with a mighty shudder that shook her entire girth, a fully developed Megalodon pup emerged from its mother's left oviduct.

It was a female, pure white and eleven feet long, already weighing 1,900 pounds. The teeth were smaller but sharper than its mother's. With its senses fully

developed, the newborn was fully capable of hunting and surviving on its own. It hovered momentarily, icy-blue eyes focused on the adult, instinct warning the pup of imminent danger. With a burst of speed, it glided south along the canyon floor.

Still circling in convulsions, the female shuddered again, expelling a second pup, tail-first, out of its womb. This time a male, slightly smaller than its sibling by three feet. The pup shot past its mother, barely avoiding a mortal, reflexive bite from the jaws of its cold, uncaring parent.

Minutes passed. Then, with one last convulsion, the Meg birthed her final pup in a cloud of blood and embryonic fluid. The runt of the litter, a seven-and-a-half-foot male, twisted out of its mother's orifice and twirled toward the bottom, righted itself, then shook its head to clear its vision.

With a flick of her powerful caudal fin, the Meg pounced upon the runt from behind, severing its entire caudal fin and genitals as she snapped her jaws shut around its lower torso. Convulsing wildly, trailing a stream of blood, the dying pup writhed to the bottom.

Giving chase, mom finished off her newborn in one last bite.

The Megalodon hovered near the bottom, exhausted from the efforts of labor. Opening her mouth, she allowed the canyon's current to circulate through her mouth, causing her gill slits to flutter as she breathed. Water passed in and out of her nostril passages, feeding

information to her brain. It moved along the underside of her snout, plugging her in to the faint electrical fields generated by the swimming muscles and beating hearts of her quarry. It ran along her lateral line, stimulating her neuromast cells, allowing her to "feel" the ocean's currents and the presence of solid objects within her environment.

The female heard every sound, registered every movement, tasted every trail, and saw every sight, for *Carcharodon megalodon* did not just move through the sea, the sea moved through the Megalodon.

Slowly, the creature's head rotated from side to side, her nostrils flaring, channeling water. The predator was homing in on an intoxicating scent.

Needing to feed, she swung her caudal fin back and forth, regaining her momentum, gliding over the canyon floor, heading north—

—passing within thirty feet of the concrete canal entrance that connected the Tanaka Lagoon with the Pacific Ocean.

VISITORS

They came without warning, their presence energizing the yacht's disgruntled crew. Captain Talbott spotted the lead-gray dorsal fin first, slicing through the dark waters of the Pacific twenty feet off the *Magnate*'s starboard bow. Within minutes, two more fins appeared, cutting back and forth through the slick of blood seeping out of the dead whale.

Perry Meth found Maggie already dressed in her white wet suit, ready for the night's dive.

"Okay, Maggie, you wanted some action. How about a test dive with three great whites?"

Maggie felt her heart race. "Sure, sounds like fun. Is everyone ready?"

"Both remotes are in the water, underwater lights are on, and the plastic tube's all set."

"Where's Bud?"

"Still asleep."

"Good. He's been on the rag about this whole trip. Now remember, when you start filming, I want it to look like I'm all alone in the water with the sharks. How much cable's attached to my tube?"

Perry thought. "Maybe two hundred feet. We'll keep you within seventy to maintain the light."

"Then I'm ready," she announced. "Grab my camera, I want to be in the water before Bud wakes up."

She followed him to the main deck. The crew had already lowered the Lexan shark cylinder over the side. The container had been custom-made for Maggie

from a design originally developed in Australia. Unlike a steel-mesh shark cage, the shark tube could not be bitten or bent, save for its buoyancy tanks, attached to its top hatch. It would maintain positive buoyancy forty feet below the surface, affording its diver an unobstructed view of the underwater domain. A steel cable served as a leash, running from the top of the cylinder to a winch on board the *Magnate*.

Secured to the yacht's keel were two remote-operated underwater cameras attached to monitors on deck. While Maggie was in the tube filming, the crew would be filming Maggie. If the lighting worked properly, the shark tube would remain invisible in the water, giving the terrifying appearance of seeing the diver exposed and alone in the water among the circling sharks.

Maggie positioned her face mask, checking to make sure she was receiving an adequate supply of air. She had been diving for ten years now, though rarely at night. The practice would do her good.

Two crewmen helped her down the ladder. The *Magnate* had eight feet of freeboard and she climbed down carefully, balancing on the bobbing cylinder's buoyancy tanks. Perry handed her a flipper, then the other, then climbed halfway down the ladder to hand her the thirty-seven–pound underwater camera. He waited while she fixed her dive mask to her face. It was a bulky contraption that wrapped around her chin, allowing her to breath through her nose and mouth at once, and communicate via a speaker and headphone embedded in the mask.

"You ready?"

She nodded and took a quick glance around to confirm the location of her subjects. Satisfied she was not about to be attacked, Maggie squatted on the edge of the tube, lowered herself into the water and into the tube, pulling the hatch door closed above her.

She sank into the center of the plastic tube, treading water. The current was moving away from the yacht. Perry instructed his team to release steel cable, the underwater cameras focusing on the tube as it sank beneath the keel and drifted out to sea.

"Stu, how're your remotes functioning?"

Chief technician Stuart Schwartz looked up from his dual monitors. "Remote A's a little sluggish, but we'll get by. Remote B's perfect. I can zoom right up on her. Too bad she didn't wear her thong."

The sound woman, Stuart's wife, Abby, slapped him from behind. "Focus on your job."

*   *   *

Maggie shivered from the potent combination of adrenaline and fifty-eight-degree water. Her world was now shades of grays and blacks, visibility poor. She could see the *Magnate*'s keel in the distance and wondered how she looked.

"Hello? Can you guys hear me?"

"Loud and clear," reported Abby, her voice filtered.

Maggie looked around. Moments later, the first predator entered her arena.

It was a male, seventeen feet from snout to tail, weighing a full ton. Its head and dorsal surface

were lead gray, blending perfectly with the water. It circled the plastic tube warily, and Maggie rotated to compensate.

Her eyes detected movement from below as a fifteen-foot female rose out of the shadows, catching the newswoman totally off guard. Forgetting she was in a protective tube, she panicked, frantically kicking her fins in an effort to get away. The shark's snout banged into the bottom of the tube just as Maggie's head collided with the sealed hatch above. She smiled in relief and embarrassment at her own stupidity.

Stuart Schwartz was also smiling. The footage looked incredible, and scary as hell. Maggie appeared totally alone in the water with the three killers. The *Magnate*'s artificial lights were just bright enough to highlight Maggie's white dive suit. The effect was perfect. Viewers would not be able to detect the protective tube.

"Perry, this is great stuff," he announced. "Our audience'll be squirming in their seats. I gotta admit it, Maggie really has a knack for the work."

Perry stood behind Stuart, watching the monitor focused on the humpback carcass. One of the sharks had bitten onto the waterlogged remains and was tearing away a mouthful.

"Film everything, Stu. Maybe we'll be able to convince her to quit before this Megalodon actually shows up."

But Perry had a hard time believing that himself.

* * *

The helicopter soared over the breathtaking California coastline, the Pacific crashing into the cliffs below.

Jonas held the night binoculars with two hands, steadying them against the herky-jerky motion of the helicopter. A new thermal imager had been purchased to replace the damaged unit, but after three weeks without a Megalodon sighting, it was the last money JAMSTEC would be laying out for the expedition.

Mac followed the coastline south, hovering at an altitude of two hundred feet. Terry was in back, the rifle balanced upright between her legs. Her presence on the chopper had been at the insistence of her father. But Masao had no control over her attitude, "So, Jonas, where's the bitch now?"

"My opinion? I think she's in California waters."

"I meant your wife."

Mac snickered.

"Is there a problem between you two?"

"Terry doesn't trust her."

"Shut up, Mac."

Mac continued, "It's a female thing. Women sense deception like a Meg smells blood. That's why they're so good at it."

"It wasn't Maggie who snuck that live round on-board the chopper," Jonas said, accusingly.

"So I want that monster dead. Sue me!"

"That's not what your father wants."

"My father's head's in the clouds. As for your ex, I know women like her. She'll lie, cheat, and steal to get

what she wants. But don't worry, because it's obvious she doesn't want you!"

Mac whistled.

Jonas and Terry turned simultaneously and said, "Shut up, Mac."

They rode for several minutes in silence. On the thermal imager's monitor, pods of whales continued their migration south along the coastline.

"Mac, I can't recall ever seeing so many whales in one place," said Jonas, attempting to make conversation.

"Who cares?" Mac stared at Jonas with a burnt-out look. "We're wasting our time. That fish of yours could be a million miles from here."

Jonas turned back to face the ocean. He knew Mac was thinking about calling it quits, and would have days ago if it hadn't been for their friendship. He couldn't blame him. Money was tight and paychecks were being held. If the female had been feeding in these waters, there would've been traces of whale carcasses washing ashore. None had been reported.

Mac's right, Jonas thought to himself, and for the first time in years, he felt truly alone. *How many years of my life have I wasted chasing this monster? What do I have to show for it? A marriage that fell apart years ago, a struggle to make ends meet . . .*

"Hey!" Terry pointed to the yellow-red blurs of heat—whales—on the monitor.

"Whales. So?"

"Follow the line," she said, pointing to a section of pods that were breaking formation. "See? They're

changing course. Don't you get it? They were all heading south, but these pods here, they're veering sharply to the west."

Jonas turned Mac. "She's right. They're changing course to avoid something."

Mac shook his head. "You two are grasping at straws. I say we land in San Francisco, then hit Chinatown for some dim sum . . . your treat."

"Mac . . . please?"

Mac looked down again at the thermal imager. If the Meg was heading north along the coast, it would be logical for the pods to avoid her.

"Okay, J.T., one last time." The helicopter banked sharply to starboard, changing course.

*　　　*　　　*

Maggie checked her camera. She had plenty of film left but only another twenty minutes of air. The shark tube had drifted beneath the humpback carcass, allowing for a spectacular view. But Maggie knew footage of great whites feeding had become commonplace. She was after much more.

I'm wasting film, she thought. She turned to signal the *Magnate* to pull her in, then noticed something very troublesome.

The three great whites had all vanished.

*　　　*　　　*

Bud Harris kicked the silk sheets off his naked body and reached for the bottle of Jack Daniel's. Empty.

"Damnit!" He sat up, his head pounding. It had been two days and still he couldn't get rid of the nagging

sinus headache. "It's that damn whale," he said aloud. "The smell's killing me."

Bud staggered to the bathroom, picked up the bottle of aspirin, struggling to get the childproof cap lined up correctly. "Screw it," he yelled, tossing the bottle into the empty toilet. He looked at himself in the mirror. "You're miserable, Bud Harris," he said to his reflection. "You're too rich to be miserable. Why do you let her talk you into these things? Well, enough's enough!" He slipped on a crushed velvet sweat suit and docksiders, then left his master suite and headed down the circular stairwell to the main deck.

"Where's Maggie?" he demanded.

Abby Schwartz sat on deck, monitoring the audio track. "She's in the tube. We're getting some great footage."

"Where's that director guy?"

Perry looked up. "Right here, Bud. What do you need? I'm kind of busy."

"Pack up, we're leaving!"

Perry and Abby looked at one another. "Maybe you ought to speak with Maggie—"

"Maggie doesn't own this yacht, I do." He grabbed the makeshift laundry line and tore it down. "This isn't the USS *Minnow*! Now where's Maggie?"

"Take a look." Perry pointed to the row of monitors.

"Christ . . ." A smile broke on Bud's face. "That looks pretty cool."

"Hey!" Stu Schwartz held up his hand. "Something's happening out there. My light meter just jumped. It's getting brighter."

* * *

Maggie saw the glow first, illuminating what remained of the humpback carcass. Then the head appeared, as big as her mother's mobile home and totally white. She felt her heart pounding in her ears, unable to comprehend the size of the creature that was casually approaching the bait. The snout rubbed against the offering first, tasting it. Then the jaws opened. The first bite was a nibble, the second took her breath away—as the jaws opened into a tunnel, slamming down on a three-ton chunk of blubber.

The mammoth head shook itself loose from its meal, sending a flurry of blubber shards swirling in all directions. As the monster chewed, the movement of its powerful jaws sent quivers down its six gill slits, reverberating the loose flesh along its stomach.

Maggie felt herself drifting to the bottom of the shark tube, unable to move. She was in awe of this magnificent creature, its power, its nobility and grace. She raised her camera slowly, afraid she might alert the creature.

* * *

"Christ, pull her back in!" Bud ordered.

"Are you crazy? This is what we came here for!" Perry was excited. The whole crew was excited . . . or scared. "What a monster! Goddamn, this is amazing footage!"

"Pull her back in now, Meth," Bud warned, "or you'll be joining her."

Bud's crew closed ranks around him. The boss meant business.

"Okay, okay, but she's gonna be mighty pissed off." The director signaled to his assistant, who activated the winch.

The steel cable snapped to attention as it began dragging the shark cylinder through the water.

*   *   *

The Meg stopped feeding, her senses alerted to the sudden movement. Being plastic, the shark tube had not given off any electronic vibrations, and so the predator had ignored it. Now the big female abandoned the carcass, sculling forward to examine this new stimuli.

Maggie's heart fluttered as the tube jerked backward through the water, the Megalodon keeping pace. "Hey? What the hell are you assholes doing?"

Bud's voice came over her headpiece, filtered. "Maggie, you okay?"

"Bud Harris, if you have any desire to touch my naked body again, you'd better stop what you're doing. Now!"

The Meg rubbed its snout along the curvature of the shark tube, confused. It's head swayed, allowing it to focus on her with its good eye.

Christ, it sees me . . .

The tube stopped moving.

The Meg's enormous mouth opened and closed, almost as if it was speaking to her. Then its jaws opened wider, exposing its frightening front rows of teeth, which attempted to bite down upon the cylinder.

The smooth plastic surface slid harmlessly away.

Maggie smiled. "What's wrong, gorgeous? Too big for ya?" Regaining her swagger, she repositioned the camera, filming down the shark's cavernous gullet. "Can you say Academy Award?"

Applause filtered through her headpiece.

Maggie held up her hand, acknowledging the crew's appreciation.

The Megalodon turned and disappeared into the darkness. Maggie caught a flicker of its caudal fin on film before it vanished into the lead-gray periphery. She took a breath, all smiles.

*　　　*　　　*

"It moved off," confirmed Perry.

"Thank Christ," said Bud. "Okay, get her out of there before it comes back."

"Ohhhh shit!" yelled Stu, who impulsively backed away from the monitors.

The Meg had circled. It was accelerating at the tube.

*　　　*　　　*

Maggie screamed, her air tank banging against the back of the tube as the 62,000-pound monster bull-rushed the cylinder, rotating its hyperextended jaws. The impact sent Maggie's face mask smashing into the interior forward wall of the tube, her head spinning

from a concussion wave that would have shattered her skull had she not been underwater.

The cylinder was driven backwards. It smashed against the *Magnate*'s keel, shattering cameras and lights, giving the enraged Megalodon enough leverage to wrap its mouth around its elusive prey, the tips of a few of its teeth catching onto the cylinder's drainage holes.

The Meg had established a grip, although, try as it might, the creature could not generate enough leverage with its jaws to crush the maddeningly wide tube.

Frustrated, the beast drove its kill to the surface, the plastic cylinder still locked sideways in its bite. Swimming away from the *Magnate*, which it perceived as another challenger, it plowed the tube ahead of its open mouth, creating a twenty-foot wake along the surface.

The spool of steel cable unwound ten feet a second, then the entire assembly was wrenched away from the decking. It smashed through the mahogany guard rail and splashed into the sea.

The Megalodon's upper torso rose vertically out of the Pacific, then, in an unfathomable display of brute strength, it lifted the Lexan tube above the waves and, as if in slow motion, shook it back and forth, left, then right, water streaming out of the tube's vent holes.

Maggie couldn't hold on, flopping one way, then the next, her air tank denting, the cylinder gathering speed as its weight grew lighter, its contents draining, each collision bringing her closer to unconsciousness.

The effort of supporting the shark tube and its passenger quickly wore down the Megalodon. The female released her death grip on the cylinder, circling it as it sank slowly beneath the waves.

CAT AND MOUSE

The helicopter roared over the Farallon Islands, approaching the luxury yacht anchored just off the jagged southern coastline.

Jonas looked through the night binoculars, zooming in on the deck of the ship. "Wait a minute . . . I know that yacht. That's the *Magnate*! Bud Harris's ship!"

"The guy banging your wife?" Mac circled the yacht. "Let's see if we can take out his satellite dish with my tool chest."

Jonas pulled the glasses away from his face. "Something's going on down there, the crew's in a panic."

*   *   *

Chaos reigned on board the *Magnate*. Captain Talbott had started the engines, then shut them down, afraid the noise would attract the Meg. Perry was excited, yelling orders to cameramen to climb to the highest point of the yacht to film. Bud was in a state of shock, watching by the starboard rail, helpless, as Stuart and Abby continued to try to communicate by radio with Maggie.

When the helicopter appeared, Bud had panicked, thinking it was the coast guard, afraid the authorities had come to arrest him because of the humpback carcass.

"Bud!" Captain Talbott yelled from the pilothouse, "some guy in that helicopter wants to speak with you. Says his name is Jonas."

"Jonas?" Bud ran to into the control room and snatched the radio. "Jonas, it's not my fault. You know Maggie, she does whatever she wants!"

"Bud, calm down," commanded Jonas. "What're you talking about?"

"The Meg. It took her. She's trapped in that damn shark tube. It wasn't my fault!"

* * *

Mac circled overhead. Terry spotted the Megalodon. She was circling in fifty feet of water, three hundred yards off the *Magnate*'s bow.

Jonas focused with the night glasses. He could just make out Maggie's white wet suit. "I think I see her. Bud, how much air's left in her tank?"

Perry Meth's voice filtered over the radio. "No more than five minutes. If you guys can distract the Meg, we could get her out of there!"

Jonas tried to think. What would draw the monster's attention away from Maggie? The copter? Then Jonas noticed the yellow Zodiac on the *Magnate*'s deck.

"Bud, the Zodiac, get it ready to launch," ordered Jonas. "I'm coming aboard."

* * *

Maggie fought to stay awake. Everything hurt, but the pain was good, it kept her conscious. Her face mask had a hairline crack and was leaking seawater into her eyes. The earpiece was buzzing with static. Her ears were ringing, and it hurt to breathe. The Megalodon continued circling counterclockwise, watching her with its one functional basketball-size gray eye. The

glow from its hide cast an eerie light, illuminating Maggie's wet suit. She checked her air supply again: down to three minutes.

I've gotta make a break for it, she told herself, but refused to uncurl from her ball.

*   *   *

Jonas hung on a cable from the chopper's winch, a radio transmitter and receiver around his neck. "Remember, Mac," he yelled, "wait until I say before you hit her with the beam. Once I'm in the boat, I'll need you to tell me where the Meg is."

Terry squeezed out his door next to him. "I'm coming, too!"

"Forget it," Jonas yelled, "it's too dangerous."

"You want to rescue Maggie, fine, but I'm still after that shark!" Terry pointed the transmitter rifle at his face. "It's a female thing. Slide over!"

Jonas allowed her to share the harness.

Mac's voice called out, "For the record, are you guys doing this outta love, greed, or because you two can't resist being morons?"

"Does it matter?"

"Just wanted to know what to say at the funeral."

Mac activated the winch, lowering them to the *Magnate*.

Stu and Perry secured them by the waist as they dropped to the main deck. Bud pointed to the starboard rail. "Zodiac's in the water. What do you want us to do?"

"We'll distract the Meg. Once she follows, get your yacht over to Maggie's location and get her the hell out of there, fast."

Jonas and Terry climbed over the rail, lowering themselves by aluminum ladder to the awaiting yellow motorized raft. Jonas started the engine, looking up at Bud.

"Wait for Mac to signal you that the Meg has moved off. Then get Maggie, okay?"

Bud nodded in agreement.

Abby appeared at the rail. She tossed Jonas a headset. "We've reestablished contact with Maggie."

Jonas gunned the engine. The rubber raft skimmed across the surface, its engine a high-pitched whine. He shouted over the headset, "Maggie, can you hear me?"

"Jonas? Is that you?"

"Hang in there, baby, we'll lead the Meg away. How deep are you?"

"I don't know, maybe ninety feet! Jonas, hurry, my mask cracked, the pressure's unbearable, and I'm almost out of air.

Terry tried her headset. "Mac, can you hear me?"

The helicopter was hovering a hundred feet above the Zodiac. "Barely. The Meg hears your engine! She stopped circling . . . she's rising! Hard to starboard!"

Terry yelled at Jonas, "Hard to starboard!"

Jonas veered hard to his right as the Meg surfaced, its jaws snapping, just missing the boat. He headed for the nearest Farallon island, the albino dorsal fin

right behind them its presence sending elephant seals leaping out of the water onto the rocks.

* * *

The *Magnate* sprang to life, her twin engines growling as they pushed the yacht ahead. Maggie was already out of the cylinder. She released her weight belt, grabbed the underwater camera, and allowed her buoyant tanks to carry her to the surface, careful to exhale slowly.

* * *

"Jonas, move! Zigzag or something!" Terry yelled, as the creature's snout collided with the back of the Zodiac.

"Hold on!"

Jonas zigzagged, then circled around a rock formation, nearly shredding the raft's skin on its jagged surface.

Terry looked around. The fin was gone. "Mac, where is she?"

"She went deep! I lost her!"

* * *

Maggie's heart pounded in her ears as she rose through the dark sea. Her head broke the surface and she exhaled, then gasped a few quick breaths. The *Magnate* was bearing down on her and she waved. The ship slowed. She leaped for an aluminum ladder, grabbed hold of a rung, but it was too slick and she fell away.

The yacht stopped. She swam to it, smiling to cheers from her production crew.

"Way to go, champ," yelled Perry.

"Maggie, get in the goddamn boat!" screamed Bud.

Exhausted, she released the heavy air tanks, allowing them to fall off her shoulders, then climbed the aluminum ladder, a rung at a time, her left hand still holding the heavy underwater camera.

Bud was hanging over the side, reaching down. "Damnit, Maggie, come on!"

Maggie felt a wave of dizziness. "If you want to help, take the goddamn camera!" She swung it toward him with her last bit of energy.

Bud grabbed the dripping case, hefting it over the rail to Abby, who caught it in both hands . . . then screamed!

Maggie was rising—but from within the creature's mouth! The Megalodon's upper torso continued moving higher, past the starboard rail, the crewmen screaming, backing away—

—as Maggie, barely conscious, imagined a warm scarlet blanket was being wrapped around her waist, protecting her against the painful cold.

The albino monster slipped back into the sea, tightening its grip around her torso, its teeth puncturing her white wet suit, turning it crimson, while crushing her ribcage, collapsing a lung.

She managed a final rasp before her head submerged.

Bud was hyperventilating, his limbs no longer his to control. The keel's underwater lights were on, illuminating the monster's head. Looking down, he couldn't move, staring at the face of a devil that

stared back at him, hovering ten feet underwater. The creature appeared to be smiling, while Maggie, wedged in its mouth, thrashed about, screaming in silence as she drowned in its grasp. The ungodly beast seemed to be toying with her. Blood poured from his lover's open mouth and she convulsed one last time—

—as the shark turned an eye on Bud. The hideous mouth opened wide, creating a vacuum that sucked Maggie into its black vortex and out of sight, expelling a car-size burp of air and blood.

Bud shook. Unable to move, he closed his eyes and waited to die.

The monster rose again for its next meal, its jaws open.

The bolt of light from the helicopter smashed through the darkness as if guided by the hand of God. It burned into the Meg's one good eye, blinding the creature, sending a white-hot wave of stabbing pain into the optic lobe. Its massive head whipped sideways, bashing against the *Magnate*—

—as Terry fired the transmitter dart from the Zodiac's bow at point-blank range.

The dart pierced the creature's right flank as it slammed back into the water, the tremendous wake flipping the Zodiac, tossing Jonas and Terry overboard. They surfaced, climbing quickly up the aluminum ladder and over the crushed mahogany rail.

His world spinning out of control, Jonas Taylor collapsed to the deck and vomited.

MORNING, MOURNING

There was no moon, no stars. Not a wave stirred. Bud stood at the rail and waited, the underwater lights of the *Magnate* illuminating the yacht's hull and surrounding sea. And then the whispers came, tickling his ear.

"Bud? . . . Baby, where are you?"

"Maggie? Maggie, is that you?" Bud leaned over the rail, searching the black sea.

"Bud, my love, please help me," the whispers cooed into his ear.

"Oh God, Maggie, where are you?" Hot tears rolled down his cheeks. He watched a droplet fall into the ocean.

Bud waited until he felt its aura rising. Then he saw the glow, followed by the snout, still hovering below the surface. The jaws yawned opened, revealing icy cold blackness. The words came again, tearing at his heart . . . "Bud, please, I don't want to die."

"Maggie!"

Bud shot up in bed, tearing loose his IV. The nurse ran in, followed by an orderly, who grabbed his arm. "It's okay, Mr. Harris," she soothed. "It's okay." The orderly strapped him down, bound his wrists and ankles, as the nurse shot a syringe of sedative into his IV drip.

Bud fell backward in slow motion onto the *Magnate*'s deck. He watched the sky, helpless, as the gray haze of dawn approached.

*   *   *

Jonas awoke in the *Abyss Glider*. The sky was blue, the sea below the Lexan pod a mouse gray. Three-foot swells bobbed the AG I up and down along the surface.

He saw the swimmer approach. Recognized the black hair, almond eyes. It was D.J.

The powerless sub's heavy nose cone dropped, inverting him, forcing him to stare into the depths. Jonas hung suspended upside down, waiting for D.J. to pull him out. He looked below into the mist and waited.

The surreal glow appeared.

"D.J., you'd better hurry."

The sinister mouth widened, revealing rows of teeth. The half-moon tail wagged faster, propelling the shark closer.

"C'mon, kid." Jonas turned. But it wasn't D.J.—D.J. was dead. It was Terry!

"Terry, get away!"

She smiled, waving at Jonas, swimming closer.

The monster's mouth opened wider, revealing hideous pink gums . . .

"No!"

*   *   *

The heavy pounding on his front door woke him. "Terry?"

Three more knocks.

Jonas rolled off the sofa, spilling the remains of the half-empty bottle of Jack Daniel's on the carpet.

Staggering, he opened the door, daylight burning into his eyes.

"Masao?"

"Taylor-san, let me in."

Jonas stood aside.

"I have been trying to reach you all morning. You have coffee?" Masao went into the kitchen.

"Upper shelf, I think. What time is it?"

"Three-twenty. No more alcohol, okay? It'll rot your liver." Masao made coffee, handed a cup to Jonas. "I am truly sorry about your wife. She died a noble death, doing what she believed in."

"Death is death." Jonas shook his head, taking a seat at the kitchen table. "I'm sorry, Masao, I can't do this anymore."

"Can't? What can't you do?"

"There's been too much death. Let the authorities handle the Meg."

Masao sat down. "Authorities? I thought you were the authority? Jonas, we have a responsibility. I feel it. I know you do as well." Tanaka looked into Jonas's eyes, bloodshot and exhausted. "A tired mind should not make decisions, but we are running out of time."

"I already made my decision. I'm through."

"Hmm. Taylor-san, you are familiar with Sun Tzu?"

"No."

"Sun Tzu was a great warrior, he wrote *The Art of War* more than twenty-five hundred years ago. He said, 'If you know neither the enemy nor yourself, you will succumb in every battle. If you know yourself but

not the enemy, for every victory gained you will also suffer a defeat. But if you know the enemy and know yourself, you need not fear the result of a hundred battles.' Do you understand?"

"I don't know, Masao. I can't think right now."

Masao placed his hand on Jonas's shoulder. "Jonas, who knows this creature better than you?"

"This is different."

Masao shook his head. "The enemy is the enemy." He stood. "But, if you will not face our foe, then I suppose my daughter will." He headed for the front door.

"Terry?" Jonas stood. "Masao, wait—"

"Terry can pilot the AG I. My daughter knows her responsibility. She is not afraid."

"Forget it then, I'm going!"

"No, my friend. As you say, this is different. D.J.'s death must not be a meaningless one. The Tanaka clan will finish this business ourselves."

"Five minutes . . . give me five minutes to get dressed." Jonas ran into the bedroom.

Masao smiled to himself and turned on the television.

Channel 9 Action News was showing Maggie's underwater footage taken from the Lexan cylinder.

". . . and shot this amazing film moments before she died in the creature's jaws. Maggie Taylor gave her life to her profession, leaving these incredible scenes as her lasting legacy. A public service will be held on Thursday,

and Channel 9 will be presenting a two-hour special tonight at eight honoring Mrs. Taylor.

"In a related story, a federal judge ruled today that the Megalodon has officially been listed as a protected species of the Monterey Bay National Marine Sanctuary. We bring you live to the steps of the Federal Court Building."

Masao turned up the volume.

"Here he comes . . . Mr. Dupont, Mr. Dupont, were you surprised today how quickly the judge ruled in favor of protecting the Megalodon, especially in light of the recent attacks?"

Andre Dupont of the Cousteau Society stood next to his attorney, several microphones pressed to his face. "No, we weren't surprised. The Monterey Sanctuary is a federally protected marine park designed to protect all species, from the smallest otter to the largest whale. There are other marine predators in the park—orcas, great whites. Each year, we see isolated attacks by great white sharks on divers or surfers, but these are isolated attacks only. Studies have shown that the great white sometimes mistakes a surfer for a seal. Humans are not the staple of the great white's diet, and we certainly are not the preferred food source of the sixty-foot Megalodon. Of greater importance will be our effort to immediately place *Carcharodon megalodon* on the endangered species list so it is protected in international waters as well."

"Mr. Dupont, what is the Cousteau Society's opinion of the Tanaka Institute's plan to capture the Megalodon?"

"We believe all creatures have a right to exist in their natural habitat. However, in this case, we are dealing with a species that nature may have never intended to interact with man. The Tanaka Lagoon is certainly large enough to accommodate a creature of this size, therefore we agree it might be best if the Megalodon was captured."

The Channel 9 anchor reappeared.

"We had our field reporter, David Adashek, conduct an unofficial street poll to see what the public's opinion is. David?"

"Trudy, opinions seem to favor capturing the monster that destroyed the lives of so many, including my close friend Maggie Taylor. Personally, I feel the creature is a menace, and I've spoken to several biologists who concur it's not unfeasible the shark may have acquired a taste for humans. If true, we can expect more gruesome deaths, especially in light of today's federal court ruling. This is David Adashek reporting, Channel 9 News."

*   *   *

Jonas was watching the same report from the television in his master bedroom. He stared at David Adashek, his heart racing as he realized Maggie had set him up that night at Scripps. "God, Maggie, what did I ever do to make you so bitter?"

But Jonas knew in his heart: the long hours, the traveling, the nights spent alone in his study, writing his books. Tears rolled down his cheeks. "I really am sorry, Maggie, so sorry." At that moment, Jonas felt more love for his wife than he had in the last two years.

He washed his face, then grabbed his duffel bag and shoved a few days' worth of clothing inside. He pulled out his workout bag, already loaded with his wet suit. Jonas looked inside, verifying that his good-luck charm was packed. He took a moment to examine the blackened seven-inch fossil, as wide and as large as the palm of his hand. He felt its sharp serrated edges as he ran the tooth across his fingers.

He replaced the tooth in its leather pouch, dropped it in the gym bag, then slung the duffle over his shoulder.

He looked in the mirror. "Okay, J.T., time to get on with your life."

When he walked out the front door, Masao Tanaka was waiting.

WHALE WATCHERS

For two long days and nights, the *Kiku*, her helicopter, and three coast-guard cutters cruised the Monterey Bay National Marine Sanctuary, attempting to locate the homing signal of the transmitter. The device implanted in the hide of the Megalodon possessed a range of up to twelve miles, gaining strength as the receiver got closer. But after searching four hundred nautical miles of ocean, no signal could be detected.

Hundreds of whales continued migrating south through the sanctuary without any noticeable changes in activity among the pods. On the third day, the coast guard gave up the search, theorizing that either the Megalodon had left California waters or the transmitter had malfunctioned.

Two more days passed, and even the crew of the *Kiku* began to lose hope.

*   *   *

Rick and Naomi Morton were celebrating their tenth anniversary in San Francisco, glad to have escaped the cold weather of Pittsburgh and their three children. They had never actually seen a real whale, so the idea of spending the day whale watching seemed exciting. Wearing only a lightweight windbreaker ("It's California, how cold can it be?") and loaded with camcorder, binoculars, and his trusty 35 mm, Rick followed his wife on board *Captain Jack's Whale Watcher*, a forty-two-foot sightseeing boat docked at the Monterey Bay wharf. The couple found an empty

spot on a bench along the stern, then huddled, freezing, with the twenty-seven other passengers. The boat chugged ahead, its exhaust choking those passengers seated behind the pilothouse.

The presence of the Megalodon had initially hurt business among Monterey's whale-watching boats. But the tourists gradually returned, mostly because the predator had not been seen in almost a week, and surfaced only at night. For their part, tour-boat operators cancelled all sunset excursions rather than risk a confrontation with the creature.

Twenty minutes and two cups of hot chocolate later, a deckhand announced over a crackling speaker, "Welcome aboard *Captain Jack's Whale Watcher*. You folks are in for a real treat today. The humpbacks have been putting on a great show all morning, so get those camcorders ready."

Moments later, "Folks, this is really exciting! On our port, or left side, is an unusually large pod of orca." Everyone moved to the port side, cameras poised. "Orca, also known as killer whales, are extremely intelligent hunters, able to kill whales many times larger than themselves. Looks like we're catching this pod in the middle of a hunt."

Rick focused his binoculars on the pack of towering black dorsal fins moving parallel to the boat, now less than two hundred yards away. There were at least thirty orca, a dozen converging on a smaller object, the rest racing along the perimeter for their turn at the prey. Rick watched, fascinated by the battle tactics.

And then he saw what looked like an albino shark, its three-foot dorsal fin half bitten and bleeding as the wolf pack tore at its hide.

*   *   *

The male Megalodon pup raced along the surface, prevented from submerging by the much larger predators below. The pod of orca had tracked the male as it hunted along the Farallon Islands. Being rogue hunters, Megalodon had only one natural enemy beside their own kind—orca. The whales, swarming pack hunters, could take an adult Megalodon down, if they could keep the shark from going deep. In ancient seas, a confrontation between a pod of orca and an adult Megalodon was a rarity, the two formidable species usually avoiding one another . . . but the rules of engagement changed when it came to Megalodon young.

With frightening speed and power, the orca males, each as least twice as large as their battered adversary, snapped at the pup, preferring to ride it to exhaustion than kill it outright. Eventually they'd take turns flipping its broken carcass high into the air, making a sport of the demise of the would-be future king of Monterey Bay.

*   *   *

Bud Harris gathered his belongings and stuffed them into a brown paper bag provided by the orderly. Unshaven, badly in need of a shower, the once-proud entrepreneur had been reduced to a feeble shell of his former self. Deeply depressed after having witnessed his

lover's death, Bud was also suffering from exhaustion brought on by a lack of REM sleep. Memories of his awful experience were now manifesting themselves in his subconscious mind in the form of night terrors. More frightening than the worst nightmare, the night terrors were violent, surreal dreams of death. For the last five nights, Bud had let out bloodcurdling cries that rocked the west wing of the hospital's fourth floor. Even after the frantic nurses had managed to wake him, he would still be screaming, blindly flinging his fists into the air. After the second episode, orderlies had to strap his wrists and ankles to the bed while he slept.

Bud Harris no longer cared whether he lived or died. He felt alone and in pain, uninterested in eating and afraid to sleep. Extremely worried, his doctors wanted to bring in a psychiatrist. Bud wasn't interested.

The nurse arrived to escort her patient out of the hospital with the traditional wheelchair ride. "Mr. Harris, is anyone meeting you downstairs?"

"No."

Two men strode up to the nurse.

"We're here to meet Mr. Harris."

Bud looked up at them. "Who the hell are you?"

"Frank Heller. This is my associate, Richard Danielson." Heller held out his hand.

Bud ignored it. "Danielson? You're the asshole who got all those navy guys killed going after the shark. Should have killed it when you had the chance." Bud

stood, walking away from the wheelchair and the two men. "I'll find my own way out."

"That's why we're here," Heller said, following him down the corridor. "My brother, Dennis, was butchered by the same monster that killed Maggie Taylor."

"Yeah? Well, I'm sorry for your loss, now if you'll excuse me . . ."

"Hold it," said Danielson. "This thing has killed a lot of people. We thought you'd want to be involved in a little payback." Danielson looked at Heller. "Maybe we were wrong."

The thought of killing the Megalodon seemed to set off a spark in Bud. He focused his eyes on Danielson for the first time. "Okay, I'm in. What is it you need? Money? Weapons?"

"Your boat."

"My boat." Bud shook his head. "That's how I got into this mess in the first place."

* * *

The gray whale's head remained out of the water, allowing passengers to reach over the rail and touch it.

"Wow! Rick, did you get that one on tape?" asked Naomi. "I touched its barnacle . . . eww."

"Got it."

"Get some more still shots, okay?"

"Naomi, I've got two full rolls already. Give it a rest."

The whale submerged. The passengers reloaded their cameras and waited.

The patch of sea began swirling, then pooled a dark red.

"Hey . . . is that blood?"

A member of the crew leaned over to get a better look. "Hell if it ain't."

Naomi turned to Rick, "Does that mean yes or no?"

"It's rising again, get your cameras ready!" Twenty camcorders rose in unison.

The gray whale surfaced, then rolled over on its side. A few tourists reached overboard to touch it—

—when the torso rotated again, revealing a gushing wound the size of a sand trap.

The passengers stared, mesmerized . . . until a monstrous set of jaws broke the surface along either side of the dead whale, giving it a vicious shake before dragging it underwater.

Passengers screamed and backed away. The crewman ran into the pilothouse. Seconds later, the engines caught, the boat veering away.

Fifty feet below, the predator registered the sudden electrical discharge.

* * *

The *Kiku* was eight miles due west of the Tanaka Institute, most of her crew still asleep from the previous night's patrol. Terry Tanaka, wearing a sweatshirt, shorts, and sunglasses, lay on a lounge chair on the uppermost open deck, facing the sun.

Jonas joined her. "Aren't you cold?"

She smiled. "It's warm in the sun. You should try it. You'd look good with a tan."

"Yeah. I think when this is all over, I'll take a vacation, get away somewhere. Maybe a tropical island."

"Take me with you."

Jonas wasn't sure if she was being serious or sarcastic. "Where would you want to go?"

"Tahiti. Bora Bora. At this point, I'd settle for the Jersey Shore."

"Not me. No more settling in my life. Bora Bora it is."

"It's expensive," she said. "We'd have to share a room."

"They have waterfront bungalows, some actually on stilts in the middle of the bay. On second thought, I think we should stick to the beach."

"Agreed."

"Jonas Taylor, report to the CIC immediately." Masao's voice squawked over the metal speaker, sounding urgent.

They hurried down the stairwell together, entering the command information center.

Masao was waiting. "Coast guard just picked up a distress call from a whale-watching boat not far from here."

"The female? In broad daylight? How—" The answer popped into Jonas's head almost as quickly as he said it. "She's blind, we must've permanently blinded her! Christ, how could I have been so stupid?"

"The monster's blind?" asked Terry. "That's a good thing, right?"

"Not if she's surfacing in the day. A Megalodon losing its sight's a lot different than you or me going blind. She has other sensory organs that are used to guide her in the darkness. No, I'd say things just got worse."

"Masao, I've got her tracking device on sonar," announced Pasquale. "Faint, but it's her. She's four miles due north, steady on course zero-three-zero."

Captain Barre adjusted their course and speed.

Terry turned to Jonas, "Here comes your flyboy."

Mac came stumbling in, still half asleep.

"Mac, we've located the Meg. You ready to go?" asked Jonas.

Mac rubbed his eyes. "Sure, just give me thirty seconds to pour some coffee into my eyes."

"Jonas, Alphonse, get to your stations," ordered Masao. "Mac—"

"I'm leaving, I'm leaving." Mac headed out through the pilothouse. Moments later, the helicopter lifted off the deck of the *Kiku*.

*   *   *

For the whale watchers, the safety of land was still a good two miles away. With no sign of the Megalodon, talk had shifted from the terrifying experience to whether they would be receiving a refund.

WHUMPPP!

The collision knocked Naomi off her bench. Passengers screamed. Naomi grabbed Rick's arm and held on, her nails digging into his flesh.

The female had tasted her prey, pushing her snout hard against the keel of the moving boat. Her senses told her this was not food. Satisfied, the Meg circled back to guard the remains of her kill.

Having seen the footage of the Megalodon on television, realizing this same creature was now attacking his boat, the captain of the whaler grabbed the wheel and began zigzagging. The boat's bow slammed back and forth against the sea's three-foot swells.

The Megalodon slowed. These new vibrations were different, the creature wounded. Instinct took over, and the female banked sharply, rising to the surface as she homed in once more.

*   *   *

"Jonas, you read me?"

"Go ahead, Mac," yelled Jonas into the walkie-talkie. He and DeMarco were positioned at the *Kiku*'s stern, ready at the deck-mounted harpoon gun.

"I'm about two hundred feet above the whale-watching boat. Hard to see anything because of the reflection. Stand by, I'm coming around." Mac turned the airship, facing south. "And thar she blows!"

"Where?"

"Right behind the whale watcher's keel. Christ, she's gotta be twice the size of that boat, and she's coming in fast! Damn tourists, don't they know not to feed the animals?"

The *Kiku* was bearing down on the tour boat's wake, coming up along its portside beam, attempting to

bring its stern and harpoon gun ahead of the transom to give Jonas a clear shot.

Jonas spun the harpoon gun counterclockwise on its base and focused through its sight. The *Kiku*'s main deck towered twenty-five feet higher than the smaller boat. He released the safety just as the whale watcher began zigzagging again.

"Mac, where is she, I still can't see her?"

"Starboard side of the whaler's transom and she's coming up fast! Wait, you'll see her fin!"

*   *   *

The tourists were standing, dumbfounded by the sudden appearance of a navy frigate, more stunned by its close maneuvers. The *Kiku*'s bow wake was pummeling the tour boat as it attempted to position itself alongside the smaller boat.

Rick Morton stood by the transom, fighting with his wife to release his arm so he could film the passing ship. "Naomi, let go!" She released his arm as the boat zigzagged again.

As he lifted the camcorder, a different object appeared in his eyepiece.

Naomi screamed. The whale-watching boat shuddered, its rear end dropping down into the water, sending waves over the deck.

The Megalodon's head was resting on its side, its sheer weight sinking the stern as its jaws gnawed the wooden transom.

Rick slid down the sudden slope, his forehead colliding with the tip of the predator's snout. Naomi

grabbed her husband and dragged him away. Rick hugged her tightly, closing his eyes.

Jonas fired.

The harpoon exploded out of the cannon, trailing smoke and steel cable. The projectile struck home, burying itself four feet deep into the Megalodon's thick hide, inches from the dorsal fin.

The monster spasmed. Arching its back, it whipped its head sideways and submerged, jerking the steel line faster than its spool could unravel slack.

The *Kiku* lurched hard to starboard, smashing into the whale-watcher. DeMarco flipped backward over the guardrail, Jonas lunging after him, catching his right ankle with both hands just before he disappeared over the side. He held on, feeling his own feet slide out from beneath him before two crewmen helped haul DeMarco back on deck.

The engineer's face was flushed purple, his eyes bugged out. "Goddamn." He coughed. "I owe you."

WHOMP!

The Meg rammed the *Kiku*'s keel, the force of the blow bending steel plates, sending Jonas, DeMarco, and the two crewmen flopping to the deck.

*   *   *

"Hard to port," growled Captain Barre, picking himself up off the control-room floor. "Masao, when the hell's this shark gonna fall asleep?"

"Just lead it away from that tour boat!"

*   *   *

Hovering two hundred feet above the Pacific, Mac watched the *Kiku* change course and race to open waters. The enraged Megalodon submerged, running deep before circling back to ram the ship again.

As Mac watched, the ship shuddered behind another devastating blow. "Je-sus. Jonas, you guys okay down there?"

"We're taking a beating. What's it look like to you?"

"Looks like I'm flying home alone. What happened to those drugs of yours?"

"My guess would be a bad reaction. Stand by!"

Jonas ran into the control room.

Terry was watching the cardiac monitor. "I think she's OD'-ing! Her pulse just rocketed from seventy-seven to two hundred and twelve beats per minute."

"Hold on," yelled Pasquale, "she's breaching again!"

Wa-BOOM!! The *Kiku* shuddered, the impact sending books and charts flying.

"She's gonna tear my ship apart!" yelled Barre, grabbing his ringing phone. "Captain here!"

"Engine room! Captain, another blow like that last one and we'll be swimming home."

"If it's leaking plug it, if it don't work fix it!" Barre slammed the receiver down, then turned to Jonas. "Well Mr. Scientist?"

*   *   *

The Megalodon's brain was on fire, her blood boiling, her heart racing out of control. The predator's sensory system was overloaded by the madness brought on by

the overdose of pentobarbital. Unable to reason, the female simply followed her instinct: attack her enemy.

Plunging to a depth of fifteen hundred feet, the Meg spun around and raced to the surface. The crescent tail whipped back and forth, the monster a white blur streaking upward. Homing in on the vibrations of the *Kiku*'s propellers echoing in her brain, the Megalodon rammed the source again, smashing the forward compartment of the ship's keel.

This time, the force of the blow knocked the giant predator senseless, stymieing her heart rate long enough for the pentobarbital and ketamine to take hold, shutting down the creature's central nervous system.

*   *   *

"Heart rate's plummeting!" yelled Terry. "One-fifty . . . one hundred . . . stabilizing at eighty-three beats per minute."

"We don't have much time." Jonas picked up the receiver of the internal phone.

"Al, take up the slack and release the net. I'm on my way!"

Terry grabbed his arm. "How can you be sure?"

He looked her in the eye. "I'll be fine. But I need your help."

She followed him out onto the deck.

*   *   *

The female was losing feeling in her tail. She slowed, barely moving, hovering almost twelve hundred feet beneath the *Kiku*.

DeMarco and his assistant, Wade Maller, stood at the stern, watching the *Kiku*'s winch gather in steel cable.

"Wade, half-speed when you reach a thousand feet," instructed DeMarco. "Once we feel resistance on the line, secure the winch at five hundred feet and we'll tow this bitch in." He turned to see Jonas in his wet suit, preparing to crawl in the rear hatch of the *Abyss Glider*, the sub already secured in its saddle.

"Jonas, wait!" Terry moved close, pulling him toward her, whispering in his ear. "Don't forget about Bora Bora."

Jonas smiled as the butterflies in his stomach teased at his groin. "Just get the suntan oil ready." He crawled into the submersible, lying prone in its one-man chamber, inching forward until he could strap himself into the shoulder rig.

In one steady motion, the sub was lifted away from the deck, swung over the starboard rail, and lowered into the Pacific.

He allowed the glider to sink, clearing the saddle before starting the engine. The sub leaped forward, into the vast blue world.

"Taylor-san, can you hear me?" Masao's voice filtered over his radio.

"Yes, Masao, loud and clear. I'm at five hundred feet. Visibility's good."

"Can you see the Meg?"

Jonas's eyes followed the cable down, straining to see. Something was below. He could see a slight

glow, but not as big as he expected. "Stand by." Jonas accelerated the submersible, descending at a forty-five-degree angle. He felt the interior temperature drop and checked the depth gauge again. Eight hundred sixty feet.

Then he saw the Meg.

She was suspended face-up, her tail dropping out of sight below her unmoving girth. With no water able to enter her mouth, her gills could not function.

She was drowning.

"Masao, the Meg's out cold, she's not breathing. You've got to tow her immediately. Do you copy?"

"Hai. Stand by." The *Kiku*'s engines restarted with a metallic, grinding sound. The line grew taut, and the Megalodon jerked upward at the sub, the sudden movement nearly stopping Jonas's heart. He circled the glider around her quickly, watching as she leveled off.

Moving closer, he drew the submersible parallel with the Megalodon's gills, focusing his attention on the six 15-foot long vertical slits. They were closed, inactive.

Christ, how do you resuscitate a shark?

Open her mouth!

He raced ahead to her lower jaw, which was clamped shut.

J.T., you are one insane asshole . . .

Aiming the Lexan nose cone at the powerful muscle surrounding the shark's mandible, he accelerated, ramming the impinged joint.

The lower jaw dropped. Seawater rushed in.

Seconds later, the gills began to flutter.

He beamed proudly. "Now don't make me do CPR."

"Good job, Taylor-san!"

"Thanks. Masao, have DeMarco take in another three hundred feet of cable so I can secure her in the netting."

Moments passed, the Meg rising slowly, pulled from above by the winch. Jonas followed her up, marveling at the size of the creature, her beauty, her savage grace. The paleobiologist found himself appreciating the Megalodon for what it was, a product of evolution, perfected by nature over hundreds of millions of years. She was the true master of the ocean, perhaps the last of her kind, and Jonas felt glad they were saving rather than destroying her.

The Meg stopped rising at two hundred and thirty feet. Jonas continued to the surface, circling until he had located the marker buoy signifying the towing end of the net. Extending the glider's retractable arm, he snatched the marker with the claw on the first try, then submerged, dragging the heavy netting straight down on a ninety-degree descent, stretching out the rolled-up slack.

The harness was a weighted cargo net, designed to sink uniformly in order to haul in tuna. Jonas had ordered flotation buoys attached along its perimeter. The inflatable devices were designed to be operated from the *Kiku*. In this way, the Megalodon could be released safely once secured inside the lagoon, with

the net simply dropping away as the devices were deflated.

Jonas brought the AG I to eight hundred feet, moving well below the dormant monster. Satisfied, he raced beyond the Meg's lifeless caudal fin. "Masao, I'm in position. Inflate the harness."

"Stand by." Slowly, the net's perimeter buoys sprang to life, conforming the suddenly buoyant net to the contours of the Megalodon. The 62,000-pound monster rose, tension releasing from the harpoon.

"That's good, that's enough," yelled Jonas. "I think we're home!" He descended past the half-moon tail, feeling cocky. Moved past the belly—

"Whoa!"

Jonas circled back and hovered. Something was different. "Oh, shit. Masao, we've got a problem. The female gave birth!"

"Taylor-san, are you certain?"

"Unless she went on a crash diet, yeah. Stand by with the glider's saddle, I'm coming aboard."

"Taylor-san, before you surface, Captain Barre requests that you check the damage to the ship's keel."

"On my way." Jonas accelerated past the captive female, moving the clanging hull of the *Kiku*.

"Oh . . . Christ."

DUSK

"I counted seven bent plates, at least three of which were taking on water," Jonas explained. "They're right on the seam, no way you can seal them. The starboard shaft's completely bent, it won't turn at all. The portside shaft's turning, but it's also damaged, making a helluva noise. Rev her any faster than six to seven knots and she'll tear loose."

"Will we sink?" Masao asked Captain Barre. The ship had taken on a tremendous amount of water, her draft had increased thirty percent, her decks now listing at a fifteen-degree angle to starboard.

"Sink? Yes. Maybe not tonight, who knows, maybe not tomorrow. We sealed off the forward compartment, but she's still takin' on water from other areas."

"How long until we arrive at the lagoon?" asked DeMarco.

"Pulling that monster out there, that's a lot of drag, lots of work for one screw. It's just after seven. I say we make it back tomorrow morning, just after dawn."

DeMarco looked at Barre, then back at Jonas. "Christ, Jonas, will the Meg stay unconscious that long?"

"I hate to add to all the uncertainty, but honestly, I don't know. There's no way of telling. I gave her what I thought was a sufficient dosage to keep her under twelve to sixteen hours."

"Taylor-san, can we inject her again?" asked Masao. "Maybe wait until dawn?"

"She'll die," said Jonas matter-of-factly. "You can't keep an animal this size under for so long without permanent damage to her nervous system. She'll need to come around and breathe on her own or she'll never regain consciousness."

Masao scratched his head, unsure. "Not many options. Captain, how many crew members do you need to run the ship? Maybe we evacuate some of the men now—"

"No. With the damage to the screw and the sea knocking on the door, I need every hand I've got, plus some. We leave this ship, we're all gonna leave together."

"Masao, let me make a suggestion," offered Jonas. "The cardiac monitor should warn us if the Meg's coming around. But just in case, let me go back down in the AG I before dawn and keep vigil. If she appears to be waking up, we'll release the line and get out of here. If we're not already in the lagoon, we'll be damn close. Without the additional weight of the Meg, we should be able to make it in fairly quickly."

"What happens when the Megalodon wakes up?" asked Masao.

"She'll have a bad hangover, probably be a little irritable. I wouldn't be surprised if she followed us right into the lagoon."

"More like chased us in," added DeMarco.

Masao thought it over. "Okay, Taylor-san, you take the glider out in the early morning and keep an eye on our fish. DeMarco, you have first watch on the cardiac

monitor. I'll relieve you at midnight. Any changes, we call Jonas right away." Masao stopped, listening to the thunder rumbling in the distance. "That a storm moving in?"

Mac entered the CIC, having just refueled his chopper. "Not thunder, Masao. That's the sound of helicopters. News choppers, five of 'em to be exact, and there's more coming. I'd say it's gonna be mighty crowded around here by dawn."

*   *   *

Frank Heller paused from his work, looking up at the television screen for the fourth time in the last hour to watch the latest news update:

". . . two hundred feet below us, lying in a comatose state is the sixty-foot prehistoric Megalodon, a monster responsible for at least a dozen deaths over the last thirty days. From our view, you can clearly see the creature's snowy-white hide, its skin glowing under the reflection of the full moon.

"At her present course and speed, the heavily damaged *Kiku* is expected to reach the entrance of the Tanaka Lagoon sometime before dawn. Channel 9 News will be keeping a vigil all night, bringing you the latest on this breaking story. This is Michelle Prystas, Action News, reporting live from the . . ."

"Turn it off already, Frank," yelled Danielson. They were aboard the *Magnate*, assembling a homemade depth charge in the yacht's exercise room. Danielson was hard at work, installing the fuse to the four-by-

two-foot steel barrel. "Haven't you had enough? You've been watching the same story all night."

"You asked me to find out how deep the Meg is," Heller said in his defense. "Did you expect me to swim out with a tape measure? From the camera angle, I'd guess she's about one hundred and fifty to two hundred feet down. What kind of kill zone you rigging that charge with?"

"Enough to fry that fish and the rest of her kind. I've added extra amatol, which is rather primitive but highly explosive. The challenge will be getting close enough to make an accurate drop. We'll have to rely on Harris for that. Where the hell is he anyway?"

"Up on deck. Did you hear the guy screaming in his sleep?"

"Half of San Francisco heard him. I'll tell you something, Frank, I haven't been sleeping well myself."

"Relax, skipper, after tomorrow, you'll be sleeping like a baby."

*   *   *

Bud Harris was at the starboard rail, staring at the reflection of moon on the black sea. The *Magnate* was anchored three hundred yards south of the Tanaka Lagoon, and in the lunar light, Bud could just make out the white concrete wall of the huge canal entrance.

"Maggie . . ." Bud drained his beer as he watched small wakes lap at the hull. "Look what you've got me into. Hanging out with a bunch of navy bozos, playing war against some freakin' fish."

Bud tossed the empty can in the water. Opened another. "Ahh, Maggs. Why couldn't you have just dropped the stupid camera?" Hot tears rolled down his cheeks. "Well, don't worry, your man's gonna kill that monster and cut out its eyes." He turned, staggering past the grand spiral staircase to one of the guestrooms. Bud found he could no longer sleep in the yacht's master suite. Maggie's perfume still lingered, her presence too vivid. When the mission was over, he planned to sell the yacht and move back East.

Collapsing onto the queen-size bed, he passed out.

* * *

The three-foot albino-white dorsal fin cut the surface, circling the discarded aluminum can as it sank into the black waters of the sanctuary.

DECISIONS

The *Kiku* crawled across the Pacific, escorted by the circling helicopters. Terry stood by the stern rail, staring at the soft white glow reflecting in the moonlight. Her hand caressed the switch controlling the air pressure feeding the net's inflatable buoys.

"Be easy to do, wouldn't it?"

Terry turned, surprised to find Jonas watching her.

"Release the net and she drowns. Been thinking about it myself. But it's not what he'd want."

"Maybe it's what I want."

"Then do it."

Terry fingered the controls. Her hand quivered.

Jonas placed his hand over hers. "It won't bring him back."

"And Maggie? What about her? We could do it for both of them."

"D.J. made his own decisions, so did Maggie. Sometimes decisions involve risk. Seven years ago, I allowed fear and guilt to rule my life. That was a mistake, one of many I've made. Your father made a mistake, too, but he's a good man. Give up now, and it'll destroy him."

Her eyes teared up. "My mother's death forced him to give up his dreams. I finally realized completing that stupid whale lagoon was the only thing keeping him going."

She turned to face him and wept. Jonas hugged her to his chest.

*   *   *

Jonas opened his eyes, his internal alarm clock going off moments before his watch. It was still dark, and he was in the lounge chair with Terry snuggled against his chest under the wool blanket, keeping him warm. Gently, he stroked her soft hair with his callused fingertips.

She stirred. "Go back to sleep," she mumbled.

"I can't. It's time."

She opened her eyes, twisting around to face him. She stretched, her arm reaching around his neck, hugging him. "I'm too cozy to move, Jonas. Let's sleep another five minutes."

"I can't. Sorry."

"Am I rushing things? I am . . . I'm sorry. I just thought—"

"It's not that. My relationship with Maggie ended years ago, I was just too preoccupied to notice." He smiled, thinking of Mac.

"What?" She teased at his hair. "Come on!"

"Can you name any of the Marx Brothers? Three would be great. Even two—"

"Marx Brothers? I don't know? Karl?"

"No, Karl was—"

She buried her mouth against his, stifling the retort.

*   *   *

DeMarco paced around the *Abyss Glider*, checking his watch again. *Where was the man?* The eastern sky was already turning gray, the media helicopters still buzzing overhead.

"Damn press," he muttered.

Terry walked by, smiling. "Morning, Al."

"Where the hell is Jonas?"

"He's coming."

Jonas hustled out of the *Kiku*'s infrastructure, zipping up his wet suit. "Sorry. Forgot my good luck charm." He held up the fossilized Meg tooth, black with age, but still extremely sharp, at least seven inches long.

DeMarco shook his head. "Ever hear of a rabbit's foot?"

Jonas winked at Terry, fighting to take his eyes off her. For the first time in as long as he could remember, he felt happy. He crawled inside the glider, allowing DeMarco to seal the hatch closed.

Five minutes later, the *Abyss Glider* slipped out of its saddle and descended into the gray sea.

Jonas flicked on the exterior light, descending below the *Kiku*'s keel, circling for a quick inspection. It looked worse, the ship sitting lower in the water, listing hard to one side. He accelerated past the slowly churning screw, then dropped to three hundred feet, approaching the dormant creature from its left flank.

The Megalodon's glow illuminated the dark sea for fifty yards in all directions. Schools of fish darted back and forth along her hide, jellyfish caught within the netting. Jonas turned his exterior light off. Banking in a tight circle, he maneuvered the AG I next to the creature's head, the cranium measuring nearly three times the length of the sub.

The mouth was agape, water passing through. Jonas hovered close to the Meg's right eye, the pupil involuntarily rolled backward in the monster's head. It was a natural response, the Meg's brain automatically repositioning the now-useless organ for its own protection.

"Jonas!"

His heart jumped from his chest, his harness pulling hard against his shoulders.

"Damnit, Terry, you scared the hell out of me."

He could hear her laughing through the radio. "Sorry. Hey, we're still steady at eighty-five beats per minute. How's the Meg?"

"Sleeping like a baby. How close are we to the lagoon?"

"Less than four miles. Barre says another two hours, tops. Hey, you're about to miss a gorgeous sunrise."

Jonas smiled. "Sounds like the beginning of a great day."

DAWN

They had been waiting all night, anchored close to shore, a pilgrimage gathered as if summoned by the creature itself. Some were scientists, but most were tourists and thrill seekers, apprehensive yet prepared to face the risks in order to be part of history. Their transports varied in size, from Wave Runners to yachts, from small outboards to larger fishing trawlers. Every whale-watching company within a fifty-mile radius was represented, their rates sufficiently inflated for the event. More than three hundred camcorders, batteries charged and cassettes loaded, stood ready.

Andre Dupont leaned against the rail of the forty-eight-foot fishing trawler, watching through binoculars as the gray haze of the winter sky grew lighter across the horizon. He could just make out the bow of the *Kiku*, still a good two miles northwest of the canal entrance. He walked back toward the cabin.

"Etienne, she's close now," Dupont whispered to his assistant. "How far out will our captain bring us?"

His assistant, Etienne, shook his head. "Sorry, Andre. He refuses to leave the shallows with the monster so close. He won't risk the boat. Family business, n'est-ce pas?"

"Oui. I do not blame the man." Dupont looked around in all directions, the morning light revealing several hundred boats. The Frenchman shook his head. "I fear that our other friends will probably not be as cautious."

* * *

Frank Heller sat in the *Magnate*'s bridge, watching the *Kiku* crawl at its agonizingly slow pace through a pair of high-powered binoculars. He shared none of Andre Dupont's exhilaration, only rage. In his shirt pocket was a photo of his brother and his brother's family. The side of his neck felt tight, throbbing with his rising anger. He imagined himself sitting down with his two nephews one day in the near-future, describing how he had killed the monster that took their daddy. The thought strengthened his resolve.

"It's time, Mr. Harris," he said, not looking away from the horizon.

Bud engaged the throttle. The *Magnate*'s twin engines jumped to life, pushing the yacht toward their destiny.

* * *

Dawn's first light filtered curtains of gray down through the depths. Jonas watched as the creature's entire torso became visible, a lethal dirigible being led toward its new hangar. He brought the AG I's Lexan nose cone within five feet of the female's right eye, the blue-gray pupil still rolled back in its head, the light exposing a bloodshot white-yellow membrane.

"Jonas?" Terry's voice crackled over the radio. "I think something's happening with the Meg. Her pulse has been climbing steadily. It's at eighty-seven, flirting with ninety. I think she's rousing herself, trying to come out of it."

"Jonas, DeMarco here. I've reloaded the harpoon gun as per Masao's latest orders. If your monster wakes up before we enter the lagoon, I'm injecting it again, whether you like it or not. Consider yourself warned."

Jonas thought about arguing, but changed his mind. DeMarco was right. If the Meg regained consciousness before the *Kiku* could get her safely in the lagoon, the ship and its entire crew would be in danger. He stared at the creature's open jaws. Coursing through its DNA was four hundred million years of instinct. The predator would not think or choose; she would only react, each cell attuned to her environment, every response preconditioned. Nature itself had decided that the species would dominate the oceans, commanding it to perpetually hunt and make babies in order to survive.

Jonas whispered, "We should have left you alone."

"Jonas!" Terry's voice pierced his thought. "Didn't you hear me?"

"Sorry, I—"

"Your friend's yacht's bearing down on us! Five hundred yards and closing fast!"

"The *Magnate*? What's Bud doing?"

* * *

DeMarco focused his binoculars on the yacht, his line of sight finally drifting back toward the activity in the stern. Two men, supporting a steel drum, were balancing their cargo on the transom.

"What the hell?" swore the engineer.

Three hundred yards. Two hundred . . . and then DeMarco caught a face . . . Heller! He refocused on the steel drum and realized—

"Jonas!" DeMarco snatched the mike out of Terry's hand. "It's a depth charge, they're coming right at you! Get deep!"

*   *   *

Jonas leaned hard on the joystick, circled right, then rolled the sub beneath the Megalodon's massive pectoral fin and dived.

*   *   *

Mac pulled back on the joystick, the helicopter leaping off the *Kiku*'s listing deck. Circling the airship hard to his left, he raced to intercept the incoming yacht as if leading an air assault on a North Vietnamese patrol boat.

Bud looked up as the helicopter appeared out of nowhere, bearing down on his bridge on a head-on collision course. The millionaire screamed, yanking the wheel hard to port seconds before the platform supporting the chopper's thermal imager smashed into the *Magnate*'s radar antenna, ripping it off of its aluminum base.

Debris exploded across the deck, the air raining shrapnel. Reacting as if a grenade had just gone off above their heads, Danielson and Heller dove for cover, abandoning the depth charge. The maneuver left the five-hundred-pound explosive teetering precariously on the transom. As the yacht veered hard to port, the steel drum rolled over the transom and plunged into

the ocean. Seawater rushed into the canister's six holes, filling the pistol chamber, sinking the bomb.

Cursing, Heller sat up, looking back in time to see the helicopter bank sharply, nose-dive toward the ocean, then level out. This time, it would make its run from the stern.

"Lunatic!"

"The charge!" screamed Danielson, "Get down!"

*   *   *

Mac pushed down on the joystick, yelling into the wind, "Mac attack!" a smile fixed on his face.

Wa-BOOM!!

The underwater blast sent a geyser of sea rocketing skyward, catching the pilot off-guard. He yanked desperately on the joystick as the tail of his copter swung out from behind him, his landing gear smashing into the upper deck of the *Magnate*, tearing the roof off the luxurious stateroom, shearing the bottom off his helicopter.

The airship spun out of control, the blades unable to regain draft.

Before Mac could react, the copter slammed sideways into the ocean.

*   *   *

At three hundred and twelve feet, the depth charge's spring had released, thrusting the percussion detonator against the primer. The crude weapon had imploded, then exploded with a flash and subsonic boom. Although the lethal radius of the bomb measured

only twenty-five feet, the resulting shock wave was devastating.

The invisible force of current caught the *Abyss Glider* broadside, rolling the winged craft over and over again. Jonas pitched hard against the Lexan cone, cracking his head against the curved windshield, nearly knocking himself out.

*   *   *

Aboard the *Kiku*, lights shattered and bodies flew as the ship's fittings loosened with the blast. Captain Barre yelled at his exhausted crew to seal off the engine room, but the roar of the media helicopters drowned out his voice.

Terry Tanaka knelt on deck, her first thoughts of Jonas. She located the radio transmitter and yelled, "Jonas! Jonas, come in, please!"

Static.

"Al, I'm not getting a signal."

"Terry . . ." Masao stumbled toward them, his head soaked in blood. He collapsed before she could reach him.

"Call the doctor!" she screamed, pressing her palm to his fractured skull.

*   *   *

The chilly Pacific snapped Mac to attention. He opened his eyes, startled to find himself submerged upside down and underwater, sinking fast. Forcing himself to remain calm, he located the shoulder harness release and ducked out of the cockpit's open side door, kicking toward the surface.

*   *   *

Jonas waited until the aftereffects of the shock wave subsided, then attempted to roll the submersible right-side up. The power was dead. He swore to himself, then began rolling hard against the interior, gradually gaining enough momentum to rotate the sub right-side up. As he completed the maneuver, he could feel the natural buoyancy of the sub taking over as it gradually began to rise, tail-first, the heavier nose cone dropping.

"Terry, come in." The radio, like everything else on the sub, was dead.

A glow loomed on his right, lighting up the interior. Jonas turned to find himself hovering within three feet of the female's basketball-size pupil.

The blue-gray eye was open. Though blind, it stared directly at Jonas.

The Megalodon was awake.

CHAOS

Bud Harris dragged himself off the polished marble floor, unsure of what had just taken place. The *Magnate* was drifting, her twin engines down. He glanced out the tinted glass in time to see the helicopter's blades slip beneath the waves.

"Hope you die," he muttered, then pressed the "on" switch, attempting to restart the engines.

Nothing happened.

"Danielson, Heller! Where the hell are you morons?" Bud headed out on deck, locating the two men standing by the transom.

"Well? Is the monster dead?"

Danielson and Heller looked at one another. "Yeah, it's gotta be," said Danielson, not sounding very sure of himself.

"You don't seem certain."

"We had to release the charge a little early when that chopper attacked," answered Heller. "We should really get out of here."

"Well, boys, that's gonna be a bit of a problem," said Bud. "The engines are dead. Your damn explosive apparently loosened something, and I'm not exactly a licensed mechanic."

"Christ, we're stuck out here with that monster?" Heller shook his head, his jaws locked tight.

"Frank, it's dead. Trust me," said Danielson. "We'll be watching it float belly-up any second now."

Heller looked at his former CO. "Dick, it's a shark. It's not going to float. If it's really dead, it'll sink to the bottom."

They turned in unison, a splashing sound to their left. A hand appeared at the ladder, followed by Mac, who dragged himself, dripping wet, on board the *Magnate*.

"Beautiful morning, isn't it, assholes?" he said, collapsing on a deck chair.

*   *   *

Jonas lay on his stomach, head down, his claustrophobia causing shortness of breath. The lifeless *Abyss Glider*'s left midwing had caught on the cargo net, keeping the sub eye level with the Megalodon. Jonas watched in fascination and horror as the female's blue-gray eye continued focusing involuntarily on the tiny submersible.

She's blind, but she still knows I'm here. Don't move. Don't even breathe.

The caudal fin animated, swishing in labored, side-to-side movements, propelling the predator slowly forward. The gill slits towered into view, passing quickly. And then the prominent snout suddenly whipped back and forth, freeing the AG I's wing from the net as the most frightening animal on the planet became cognizant of its surroundings.

The submersible continued to rise tail-first. Jonas looked down, watching the Megalodon lurch forward, but the cargo net ensnarled her pectoral fins, the harpoon restricting her movement. Enraged, she rolled

once, then twice, twisting and tangling herself tighter in the trap.

The AG I tossed backward in the Meg's wake. With no means of control, Jonas spun away, losing sight of the creature. Then, as the sub's nose cone drifted downward, he caught a glimpse of the furious creature, completely entwined from her gill slits to her pelvic fin in the cargo net.

"Good . . . she's going to drown," he whispered to himself.

* * *

The myriad boaters anchored outside the Tanaka Lagoon had witnessed the super-yacht break from the group to rendezvous with the incoming guest of honor. They had seen the helicopter loop downward to intercept the vessel, only to end up crashing into the sea as the depth charge had detonated. Now, the onlookers grew anxious, wondering if the explosion had killed the creature they had paid good money to see. Almost as one, several dozen of the larger fishing boats and tours grew daring, gradually moving toward the listless *Kiku*, intent on filming the creature, dead or alive.

Nine media helicopters were hovering, continually shifting positions in their attempt to gain better camera angles. The underwater explosion created a new twist on the story. The networks ordered their helicopter crews to lower altitudes in order to assess whether the Megalodon had survived.

David Adashek was in the back of the Channel 9 Action News copter, straining to see over his cameraman's shoulder. The creature's white hide was visible, but whether the shark was dead or alive was impossible to ascertain. The pilot tapped his arm, motioning him to look down.

Racing toward the Megalodon was a flotilla of pleasure boats.

* * *

From the tip of her snout to the edge of her caudal fin, the Megalodon's skin contained fine, toothlike prickles called dermal denticles, literally "skin teeth." Sharp and sandpaper-like in texture, the denticles were another in the predator's arsenal of natural weapons. As the female twisted insanely within the cargo net, the dermal denticles sawed through the rope, slicing it to ribbons.

Jonas watched the female shake free from her bonds. His pulse pounded in his throat as she turned in his direction, jaws slack, triangular teeth splayed. Desperate, Jonas tried the power switch again—still dead—as the monster propelled itself past him and toward the surface.

* * *

Bud and Mac had gone below to the engine room, leaving Danielson and Heller on deck. Frank was leaning across the transom, staring into the green water, when the white mass materialized below.

"Oh, Christ . . ."

WHOMP! The stern exploded beneath his feet, fiberglass splintering in a thousand directions as Danielson and Heller fell backward onto the tilting deck.

* * *

DeMarco manned the harpoon gun, training the barrel on his target. He released the safety as the Meg surfaced. He watched as she swam upside down below the waterline, a river of sea passing into her mouth as she exposed her glistening white belly to the world.

It was too good a target to pass up.

DeMarco aimed, pulled the trigger . . .

Click.

"Goddamnit!" The explosion had jammed the gun's inner chamber.

The entire crew was on deck, frantically donning orange life vests.

In the control room, the ship's physician tended to Masao, still unconscious. Terry and Pasquale stood over them.

"He's fractured his skull," said the doctor. "We need to get him to a hospital as soon as possible."

She could hear the swarm of media copters hovering above. "Pasquale, get on the radio, try to get one of those news choppers to land on the *Kiku*. Tell 'em we have a serious injury. Doc, stay with my father. I'll be right back."

She ran out of the CIC, making her way to the hangar deck.

* * *

David Adashek saw her waving emphatically on the helo-deck. "Hey, I know that girl, that's Tanaka's daughter. Look's like an emergency. Captain, can you land this bird on the *Kiku*'s deck?"

"What for?"

"Stand by!" the cameraman yelled. "My producer's screaming at me to get close-ups of the Meg. He'll have my balls for breakfast if you land on that ship."

"Are you crazy?" David said, "The Meg's attacking the ship."

"All the more reason why we're not landing."

"Hey," said the pilot, "I'm getting a distress call from the *Kiku*. They're requesting we transport an injured man to shore. Radioman says it's Masao Tanaka. Looks serious."

"Land the copter," ordered Adashek.

The cameraman looked at him with a scowl. "Blow me."

Adashek ripped the camera from the man's grip, holding it out his open door. "Choose now. We land or I feed this to the Meg."

Moments later, the helicopter touched down on the *Kiku*'s tilting deck.

*   *   *

The Megalodon circled beneath the *Kiku*. The ship's exposed metal hull, immersed in seawater, generated galvanic currents—electrical impulses that stimulated the female's ampullae of Lorenzini like fingernails on a chalkboard, driving her to attack.

Sweating profusely, Jonas could feel his claustrophobia building as he strained to reach the battery connections at the rear of his sub. Blindly, he groped at the terminals inside the rear panels, searching in vain for a loose connection.

A sudden current twisted the AG I around and upward, giving Jonas an unobstructed view of a scene that sent pangs of fear through his heart: the Megalodon was pushing her snout inside the venting keel of the *Kiku*!

* * *

The *Kiku*'s crew gathered around the news chopper, each man hoping for a ride.

Leon Barre pushed his way through the crowd. "Get Masao aboard that chopper. We don't need his blood in the water!"

The pilot of the news copter looked at Adashek and the cameraman. "Okay, boys, someone has to give up his seat for the old man. Which one of you is going to play the hero?"

The cameraman looked at Adashek with an evil grin. "Hope you can swim, tough guy."

David felt butterflies in his stomach as he exited the safety of the chopper, allowing the doctor and Terry Tanaka to load Masao on board. Moments later, he stood on the lopsided deck, his heart in his mouth as the helicopter flew off toward the mainland.

Nice job, dickhead. You're supposed to be reporting the news, not making it.

* * *

Crumpled against the mahogany rail, Richard Danielson stood painfully, grabbed Heller beneath his armpits, and hoisted him to his feet. "Frank, we're sinking!"

"No shit." Heller looked around. "Where are Harris and Mac?"

"Probably dead. If so, they're lucky."

"The Zodiac!" Heller pointed at the motorized raft. "Give me a hand."

The two men released the catches to the pulleys supporting the bulky raft. It dropped to the surface with a *splat*.

"You first, Frank."

Heller hesitated, then swung his leg over the rail. Danielson followed him in.

The outboard whined to life. Heller gunned the throttle, sending the raft's lightweight bow lifting away from the sea as the Zodiac skimmed over the waves, accelerating toward land and the pack of oncoming boats.

"Frank, watch out!"

With little room to maneuver, Heller was forced to veer around the first wave of boats.

The second wave's wake flipped the off-balanced Zodiac upside down.

Danielson and Heller were thrown headfirst into the Pacific, surfacing in the path of still more pleasure craft.

One hundred yards to the west, the Megalodon rose straight out of the Pacific, attempting to snatch one of the low-flying helicopters. The monster's heart-stopping appearance started a chain reaction. Two of the incoming fishing boats veered sharply into adjacent vessels, creating two separate pile-ups. Chaos reigned among the other craft as the rules of boating were tossed aside for self-preservation. Screams rent the air as weekend captains frantically tried to turn back, only to crash into the unwitting boaters behind them.

Circling in a tight formation forty feet above the melee, the pilots of the eight news copters panicked, realizing for the first time how massive the Megalodon actually was. Their first reaction was to achieve a safer altitude. Eight joysticks were simultaneously yanked backward, eight sets of rotors climbing toward the same airspace.

The pilots were so frightened of the monster below they completely ignored the danger above. Two copters rose at intersecting angles, their rotors slashing into one another, igniting a cataclysm. Flying shrapnel ricocheted into the paths of the other helicopter blades. In a matter of seconds, all eight choppers either had careened sideways against another airship or had been hit with shrapnel, causing their rotors to shatter. Matching fireballs exploded upward two at a time, raining metal, gasoline, and human body parts across the crowded sea.

Swimming fifty feet below the carnage, the predator circled slowly, snapping at the sinking debris, attempting to isolate food with her powerful senses.

Danielson swam toward the nearest pleasure craft, a thirty-two-foot speedboat overloaded with seven passengers and a golden retriever. The sleek boat had stalled, blocking traffic. He tried pulling himself aboard, but couldn't reach high enough. The preoccupied passengers didn't see him, nor could they hear his pleas for help over the fireballs and thunder of the choppers. Then he saw the ladder behind the transom and kicked toward it.

The attack came without warning, dragging Danielson underwater by his legs. He struggled in time to catch the ladder in a death grip, registering the feel of the sun-warmed aluminum, refusing to let go. The Megalodon's teeth severed both legs at the knees and Danielson slipped out of the monster's mouth, blood pouring from both open wounds.

Danielson screamed, still dangling from the ladder. Now the passengers in the stern heard him, several reaching for him, pulling him up by his wrists—

—as the Meg's head appeared behind the boat.

Terrified, the passengers released Danielson—

—the Meg snatching him as he slipped overboard. Tossing his mangled body into the air above her open mouth, the shark snatched its prey as a dog might catch a biscuit.

The monster slipped back beneath the waves before the first screams from the petrified witnesses could be uttered.

FEEDING FRENZY

The once-mighty United States Navy frigate dipped sideways, the *Kiku*'s waterlogged hull finally pulling her beneath the waves. The twenty-three crew members, packed into two lifeboats, rowed desperately to escape the swirling currents of the sinking vessel that seemed to reach for them from below. The outboard motors were not used—in fear that they might alert the monster.

Leon Barre, tears in his eyes, watched as the bow of his command slid silently into the Pacific. Terry Tanaka scanned the surf for any sign of Jonas or his *Abyss Glider*. David Adashek was visibly shaking, praying quietly, as were many of the crew. Next to him, crouched at the ready, DeMarco waited for the albino monster to reappear, a loaded Colt .45 shaking in his hand.

Captain Barre stood above the rowers, scanning the tangle of boats and helicopter wreckage a half mile away. "Son of a bitch," he swore aloud. "Do we start the motors or wait?" He looked into the eyes of his men, seeing their fear. "DeMarco?"

"After seeing that carnage, I have to believe those ships have the Meg's attention."

"How fast can these boats move?"

"Overloaded like we are, maybe it'd take us fifteen, twenty minutes to make land." The men looked up at him, nodding their heads.

"Wait." Terry looked to each man as she spoke, "Jonas said this creature can feel the vibrations of the engines. I think we should wait, let the Megalodon clear the area."

"And what if she doesn't?" asked Wade Maller. "I've got a wife and kids who'd like to see me again!"

Another crewmen spoke out. "You expect us to just sit here and wait to get eaten alive?"

DeMarco held up his hands. He looked at Terry. "Jonas is dead, and the rest of us might wind up the same way if we do nothing."

Murmurs of agreement. In the distance they could hear an occasional scream.

Terry felt a lump in her throat. She tried to swallow, holding back tears.

Jonas was either injured or dead, and they were going to leave him. She stared ahead, watching as a cigarette speedboat rose from the water and flipped. More screams tore the air. Terry realized they had no choice.

Both engines jumped to life, Leon Barre's boat taking the lead, heading south to skirt around the chaos ahead.

*   *   *

Frank Heller had managed to swim to one of the boats. Exhausted and frightened beyond reason, he remained in the water, clinging to the side of a fishing trawler's tuna net, eyes closed, waiting for death.

Minutes passed.

"Hey!"

Frank opened his eyes. A muscular black man was leaning overboard. "This ain't no time to be taking a dip, old man. Get your ass in the boat." A large hand grabbed a hold of Heller's life vest and dragged him out of the water.

* * *

Bud Harris slogged chest-deep in seawater in the flooding engine room of his yacht. The chopper pilot who had caused this mess was trying to get the engine to start.

"No good, she's dead."

"Then so are you."

Bud trudged up the stairs to the next deck.

Mac searched for the pumps. Flipped the toggle switch. The motors churned, vibrating the entire vessel as seawater was expelled overboard. He clicked the pumps off. "Way too noisy."

He left the engine room, finding his way to the pilothouse. Activating the radio, he sent a mayday call to the coast guard.

Bud entered the chamber. In one hand was an unopened bottle of Jack Daniel's, in the other, a .44 Magnum.

Mac saw the gun and chuckled. "Hey, Dirty Harry, you gonna kill the shark with that?"

Bud pointed the gun at Mac's head. "No, flyboy, but I may just kill you."

* * *

The powerless *Abyss Glider* bobbed four feet below the surface, the heavier nose cone pointing straight

down at the ocean floor. Jonas was standing upright, his knees balancing on the shoulder harness, working on the battery in the rear of the sub. He was drenched in sweat, his breathing becoming increasingly difficult as his air supply diminished. Having located the disconnected electrical cables, he reattached them, bearing down with all his strength on the rusty wing nut in an attempt to tighten the connection with nothing but his fingers. The wing nut turned one revolution and stopped.

"That'll have to do," he grunted, twisting his body upside down, sliding back into the pilot's prone position. He felt the blood rush to his head. "Okay, baby, give daddy some juice."

The AG I flickered to life, blowing cool air on his face from its ventilation system. He pushed forward on the joystick, leveling out the sub, hovering it along the surface.

He looked around.

The *Kiku* was gone. To his right he saw the *Magnate*, listing but still afloat.

And then he spotted the flotilla.

* * *

Having remained in the waters adjacent to the Tanaka Lagoon, Andre Dupont and several dozen other boaters had looked on in horror as the Megalodon rose from the sea to wreak havoc among their unfortunate comrades. Even at a distance of a half-mile, the size and ferocity of the monster shocked the camera buffs.

The nature of the event had changed: This was no longer a game, people were dying!

A common thought passed through the group: Remaining in the water meant they too could be eaten! Forgetting about their ports of origin, the boaters swung their craft around and raced to the closest beach, a stretch of sand separating the lagoon's arena wall and the ocean.

The exodus left the fishing trawler as the only remaining boat near the lagoon. Etienne walked over to the rail and nudged Dupont. "Andre, the captain agreed to keep us in the shallows."

Dupont continued to look through his binoculars. "He's not going to beach the boat, like the others?"

Etienne smiled. "Captain says he just painted the keel, doesn't want to scratch it up. Still, how long should we remain? It's not safe."

Dupont looked at his assistant. "Those people out there, they are all going to die. I think we should do something."

"Captain says the coast guard is on the way."

"Etienne!" Dupont pointed to the south where the *Kiku*'s two lifeboats were making a run for the beach.

* * *

Jonas accelerated to thirty knots, holding his depth steady at twenty feet. Moments later, he came within view of the massacre.

Three smaller speedboats were in the process of descending to their final resting places, their fiberglass

hulls torn apart. Jonas surfaced, afraid of what he was about to see.

The flotilla, once twenty strong, now consisted of a maze of floating fiberglass and the remains of cabins, decks, and broken hulls. Jonas counted eight fishing boats that appeared intact, their decks overloaded with panicked civilians. A coast guard rescue chopper hovered overhead, raising a hysterical woman in a harness. Those remaining on board seemed to be yelling, pushing each other in an attempt to be next.

Where was the Megalodon?

Jonas descended to thirty feet, circling the area. Visibility was poor, debris everywhere. He felt his heart pounding, his head moving rapidly in every possible direction.

Then he spotted the caudal fin.

The female was moving quickly away from Jonas, her tail disappearing into the gray mist. He verified her course on his instrument panel.

She was heading toward land.

*   *   *

The two lifeboats were less than a half-mile from the shoreline when the alabaster dorsal fin sliced in front of the lead boat and submerged, sending waves of panic among the *Kiku*'s crew.

Barre signaled to the other boat's helmsman to separate.

*   *   *

One hundred and eighty feet below the boats, the female circled, confused. Her senses had registered

one prey, now there were two. She rose to attack the closest outboard.

Terry and DeMarco never saw the shark rise, only an explosion of bright blue sky, followed by bodies, then icy-cold water as their world spun like a gyroscope and then submerged, their lifeboat flipping on top of them.

Twelve heads broke the surface. Twelve pairs of hands reached for the capsized hull, its fragmented wooden hull glistening in the fading sun.

Twelve beating hearts . . . twelve dinner bells.

The albino dorsal fin circled slowly, its owner sizing up her next meal. The female rolled on her side, moving lazily just below the surface. The creature's sheer mass pulled the capsized lifeboat and its crew, its caudal fin slapping the surface, the crew's hearts jumping with each echoing clap. Water streamed into her open mouth, creating a gully as she moved nearer.

One of the men panicked and swam away.

The monster altered course, her streamlined body moving in quickly behind him.

Terry gasped, too petrified to scream as she watched the man struggle in the Megalodon's riptide. He kicked against the current, stroking with all his might, screaming as he glanced over his shoulder and saw the open mouth—

—just before he slid backwards down its gullet.

"Oh, God. . . oh my God," cried Adashek.

Like drowning rats, the surviving eleven tried to claw their way higher onto the capsized lifeboat.

Adashek grabbed onto the invested outboard engine, pulling himself higher. DeMarco's fingers were raw and bleeding, gripping the wooden hull. He knew he couldn't hang on, knew it didn't matter if he could. The hunter circled slowly, her undertow tugging them once more. This time DeMarco didn't fight it. He thought of his wife—she'd be waiting in the parking lot for him. He had promised her this would be his last voyage. She hadn't believed him.

Terry saw DeMarco drift away. "Al! Al, swim!" She pushed away from the boat, paddling lightly in his direction. Reaching him, she grabbed his arm from behind, pulling him toward her.

"No! Leave me! I can't take it anymore!"

The Meg moved toward them, again on its flank, content to consume her meal one at a time.

Terry fought to catch a breath. Twenty feet from the monster's snout, she could see the peppered-black ampullae of Lorenzini . . . the rows of teeth . . . the human flesh still caught between several fangs.

Terry and DeMarco kicked wildly as the jaws opened wider to accommodate its prey, pink gums exposed, serrated teeth reaching for them—

Six hundred and fifty pounds of submersible and pilot leapt out of the sea, the AG I momentarily blotting out the sun before smashing down hard upon the exposed upper jaw of the Megalodon. The triangular head lifted straight out of the water, blood oozing from its grapefruit-sized left nostril.

The AG I circled past the snapping jaws and dove.

Like a mad bull, the Megalodon plunged below the waves to give chase.

Jonas stole a quick glance over his shoulder, confirmed he was being chased, and pushed down on the joystick, whipping the *Abyss Glider* hard to port.

Despite his top speed the Meg was still gaining. *Where to go? Lead her away from Terry, away from the others.* He felt a bump from behind as the Meg rammed his tail fin. He plunged the ship deep, then banked a hard starboard roll and shot to the surface.

The AG I flew out of the water like a flying fish—

—the leaping Megalodon right behind it, its jaws snapping empty air.

Jonas's starboard midwing sliced through the surf, the sub righting itself underwater, heading deep.

The predator flopped back into the ocean, its thunderous splash rivaling that of the largest humpback whale.

Jonas pushed down on the joystick—

Nothing! *The landing must have jarred the battery cable loose again.*

Desperate, he twisted his upper body around, feeling for the loose connection, and quickly slammed it home.

The power engaged, but Jonas had no time. Extending his legs, he kicked his bare left foot against one joystick, pressing his right down against the other.

The submersible jumped, milliseconds ahead of the ten-foot snapping jaws, the passing caudal fin slapping hard against the Lexan nose cone, nearly shattering it.

In one motion he twisted back around in the tight capsule, praying the battery connection would hold.

The Megalodon was upon him again, snapping at his tail assembly. Jonas whipped the sub to port—

—as a red flicker beckoned from his control panel. The batteries were dying!

Jonas spun the submersible around in a tight circle . . . *where was the Meg?* Unable to locate the shark he slowed, registering the rumble of a heavy engine approaching in the distance.

*   *   *

It took Andre Dupont ten minutes to convince the captain of the fishing trawler that his institute would pay for any damages to his vessel. A wad of cash from Etienne sealed the deal, sending the boat racing to rescue the lifeboat's eleven survivors.

Terry Tanaka was pulled on board. She tried to stand, then simply collapsed on deck. Adashek vomited from the stress. DeMarco and several other shipmates fell to their knees, all thanking their maker for sparing their lives.

Twenty-five feet away, the Megalodon grasped the capsized lifeboat in its hyperextended jaws and shook the wooden hull into kindling.

On the opposite side of trawler, the tail assembly of Jonas's powerless submersible bobbed to the surface like a cork.

Jonas kicked at the batteries, but he knew it was hopeless. The voltmeter read zero. The heavier Lexan nose cone settled deeper in the water, Jonas hanging head down in the pilot's harness, reliving a nightmarish déjà vu.

It was eerily quiet, save for the sound of water lapping at the sub. Jonas peered into the gray mist beneath him, the blood pounding in his temples, his hands trembling.

"Get out . . . get out of the sub, J.T.! Do it! Move!" But he couldn't move . . . too afraid, all he could do was stare at the flickering beams of sunlight filtering below.

The female was wary. She had been circling below, sensing her challenger was wounded, waiting for it to die. Now it was time to feed.

She ascended slowly, rising through the gray curtains of light that could no longer harm her, her great caudal fin beating harder as she rose, her jaws agape, opening and closing, nostrils flaring, searching for a scent.

At four hundred feet Jonas saw her. The white face, the satanic grin. It was seven years ago and he was back on the *Seacliff* . . . only this was different, this time there was no retreat, no escape. *I'm going to die*, he thought.

Strangely, he felt no fear.

And then Masao's words came back to him. "If you know the enemy and know yourself, you need not fear the result of a hundred battles."

"I know my enemy," he said aloud, the monster whipping itself into a frenzy as it drove harder toward the surface.

Seventy feet . . .

Jonas reached forward with his right hand, grasped the lever, turning it counterclockwise.

Forty feet.

The mouth opened.

Jonas forced deep breaths.

Twenty feet! The jaws were now fully hyperextended!

Jonas screamed involuntarily, pulling the lever toward him. Hydrogen fuel ignited, transforming the AG I into a rocket, blasting it straight down through the open jaws of the Megalodon.

The black opening jumped at Jonas, the glider shuddering as its wings shredded, the pod shooting on through the open gullet, past cartilaginous ribs before slamming into gelid blackness.

Jonas lay unconscious, suspended from his shoulder harness.

He had entered the gates of hell.

HELL

The Megalodon exploded from the Pacific, its caudal fin nearly clearing the water. For a frozen moment, the thirty-ton monster hung in space like a marlin, then plunged back into its liquid realm, mouth open, dying to quench the fire that burned within.

The Meg's digestive system was relatively short. After food entered its stomach, it traveled through the duodenum, the beginning of the small intestine. Located inside the duodenum was a series of folds—the spiral valve. Similar in shape to a corkscrew, the spiral valve rotated within the Meg's small intestine like a Slinky, providing additional absorption area for the shark to maximize the nutrients of its meal. But the shape of the organ also served another purpose, providing the creature with a means of regurgitating items that could not be properly digested. It is a violent act, so powerful it actually turns the stomach inside out so that it protrudes from the shark's mouth like a pinkish balloon.

The capsulelike remains of the *Abyss Glider* were wreaking havoc within the female's stomach. Circling rapidly in 600 feet of water, the Meg's jaws heaved open in a sudden spasm, its insides attempting to vomit the eight-foot capsule from its gullet.

*   *   *

Jonas was slammed back into consciousness, the escape pod heaving in darkness, flipping over again and again as the Megalodon's involuntary muscles

attempted to regurgitate the capsule back out through its mouth. But the opening was too narrow, the glider's remains unable to align correctly with the orifice. After a dozen attempts, the spasming spiral valve resettled, and the escape pod settled within its alien, pitch black confines.

Jonas hyperventilated. His hands felt for the toggle switch activating the sub's small backup generator, powering the life-support system and emergency lights. He flipped every switch until—

—an exterior light activated, revealing blistering pink insides and swirling brownish objects. Thick, hot, fist-sized chunks of mutilated whale blubber slapped across the acrylic cone. Jonas felt queasy, but couldn't stop himself from looking. He could discern the remains of a porpoise's head, a sneaker, several pieces of wood, and then something that made him gag.

It was a human head, the face—badly burned from stomach acid but still recognizable . . . Danielson!

Jonas gurgled, his scream cut off by the rising vomit. The walls closed in upon him, and he convulsed in fear. The sub shifted hard to one side, rolling with the gaping stomach, sloshing the remains of Taylor's former commanding officer out of sight as the host hurled itself in and out of the ocean, thrashing in agony.

*   *   *

Andre Dupont sat on deck, catching his breath, watching in amazement and fear as the greatest creature ever to inhabit the oceans spasmed out of control. Terry stood, her legs quivering, tears streaming

down her cheeks. She had seen the fuel ignite, knew what Jonas had done. At that moment, she realized how deep her feelings were for him.

Leon Barre was arguing with the fishing trawler's owner, warning him that the boat's engines would attract the monster. The older man swore at Barre, swore at Dupont, but decided it might be best to cut the motor.

* * *

Jonas shook uncontrollably, unable to catch a breath, his nerves trembling amid horrific carnage the likes of which could not be imagined. This was claustrophobia, this was hell.

"Stop it! You're alive! Find a way out!"

He forced his mind to reason. *There are two ways out, the way you came in, and . . . and—*

"I can kill it."

It was a statement of fact, a rational thought declared in an irrational setting. "I can kill it." He said it over and over again, convincing himself, building courage, allowing the plan to germinate.

Then he felt it, the reverberation of a pulse, the beating of the monster's heart.

"It's close! It has to be close! Find a way! Tear it out!"

A calm resolve began to settle over Jonas. He had a plan—a ray of hope . . . one shot at escaping, one Lotto chance at surviving an impossible circumstance, but it was there, and it was more than Maggie had, more than Danielson.

Rolling onto his side, he located the small storage compartment below his seat cushion and removed the flashlight, dive mask, and the small pony bottle of air. He made sure the oxygen flowed. Satisfied, he searched for the underwater knife.

It was gone. Now what? How could he possibly cut through the thick muscular tissue of the Meg's stomach lining? Desperate, he felt around the capsule, his fingers settling on the fossilized Meg tooth.

The irony was not lost on him. He smiled. *An eye for an eye . . .*

Jonas secured the small cylinder of air around his head with Velcro straps and fixed the mask to his face, breathing through the regulator.

He was ready.

Flipping around, he unscrewed the escape hatch in the sub's tail. The rubber housing lost its suction with a hiss as he pushed the circular door open. A thick liquid, hot to the touch, oozed into the sub. He poked his head out of the open hatch, shining the flashlight into the darkness.

The mini-sub was wedged tightly in a confined chamber of muscle, its walls constantly moving, churning debris in a caustic atmosphere of humidity, burning excretions, and seawater. The digestive organ protested his presence, high-pitched gurgling noises alternating with a series of low, resonating growls. Beneath it all, the constant thumpa-thumpa of the Megalodon's heart vibrated through Jonas's body.

With no discernible top or bottom, the stomach simply appeared to be a pocket of continually collapsing and expanding muscle. Jonas crawled out of the glider, feeling the submersible shift position as he did so. His right foot touched the stomach lining, giving him the sensation of stepping on a surface of molten putty. A thick liquid oozed from pores in the stomach muscle, squishing between his toes and scalding his feet.

Without warning, the stomach bulged beneath him, the entire compartment rolling 270 degrees. Both his feet slipped out from under him, tossing him blindly onto his back. He could feel the heat of the mucus lining attacking his wet suit. Gagging, he rolled over on all fours and crawled on his hands and knees on the uneven, thickly muscled surface.

His exposed flesh began to burn, and the change in temperature started fogging his mask. Holding his breath, he rose to his knees, removed the mask, and spit inside, rubbing the glass clear. He gagged at the acidic smell, which began to burn his eyes.

Jonas sucked hard on the regulator, returning the mask to his face. Yes, that was better. *Stay calm, breathe slowly*, he coached himself. *Find the cardiac chamber. Feel and listen!*

The stomach shifted again, the *Abyss Glider* rolling at him, driving him down as the Megalodon surfaced. He slid on his belly, his legs suctioned down a two-foot gap leading into the intestines, his upper body following fast!

His head disappeared!

An arm lunged out of the hole, his hand gripping the fossilized tooth, plunging it into the stomach lining like a pickax.

Jonas pulled himself from the hole as the stomach rolled again, a wave of hot refuse washing over him. The mini-sub pinned him to the stomach lining. He held on for dear life as the Meg rose again.

On all fours he registered the sensation of his knees reverberating. Holding the tooth in one hand, the precious flashlight in the other, he drove the serrated edge into the stomach lining, using it like a saw. The thick fibrous tissue began splitting and bleeding, but it was slow work, like cutting through raw meat with a butter knife. Jonas pressed his weight behind each cut, tracing a four-foot-long incision into the thick tissue, rubbing the edges of the blade against the resilient muscle.

*   *   *

With his left hand, Bud Harris flipped the toggle switch, restarting the *Magnate*'s pumps. In his right hand was the gun, cocked and pointed at Mac's head.

"You're activating the pumps?" asked Mac. "You'll attract the Meg."

"I want to attract the Meg. Now move!" Bud pushed the barrel of the gun to the back of Mac's neck, forcing him up the steps and back out to the main deck.

The late afternoon sun beat down on the rapidly sinking yacht.

"That monster destroyed my life, took the one person I truly cared for," said Bud. "It continues to

haunt me, preventing me from sleeping, preventing me from living. And you?" Bud pushed his face next to Mac's. "You had to interfere, had to play the hero."

Bud stepped back, motioning for Mac to walk toward the starboard rail. "Go ahead."

"Go ahead and what?" Mac listened for the coast-guard copter, trying to stall.

Bud fired the Magnum, blowing a three-inch hole in the deck. "You wanted to save this monster, now you can feed him." He fired again, this time nicking Mac in his right calf muscle. Mac collapsed onto one leg, blood oozing from the wound.

"The next shot will be at your stomach, so I suggest you jump now."

Mac moved to the rail, climbing over. "This is called murder. You know what they do with murderers?" Mac eased himself into the ocean.

Bud watched him tread water, moving away from the *Magnate*. "This is California. Murder and getting convicted of murder are two different things."

* * *

The female's inflamed stomach was convulsing in involuntary spasmodic contractions along her belly. Agitated, she attacked every motion that attracted her senses, a passing school of fish, sand from the driving current—

The vibrations sent ripples coursing across her lateral line. Accelerating within the thermocline, the female homed in on the hull of the *Magnate* and rammed it, opening a massive fourteen-foot gash along the stern.

Within seconds the yacht began spinning as the flood waters pulled it into the deep.

Bud stood in the bow, holding onto the mahogany rail with one hand, using Mac as target practice with the other. He laughed, amused until the yacht heaved beneath him and the deck started spinning.

The dorsal fin circled, the shark's senses more attuned to the dying *Magnate* than Mac.

Bud aimed at the towering fin and fired, blasting two bloody holes into the albino hide.

The last shot he saved for himself.

As Mac watched, Bud shoved the gun into his mouth and pulled the trigger, blasting the back of his head open like a watermelon.

*   *   *

Through Dupont's binoculars, Leon Barre watched the dorsal fin circle the *Magnate*, three hundred yards away. "Now, Captain, we should go now!"

The trawler's twin engines growled to life, the race on.

The female whipped her head around, her instincts gone mad. She accelerated in pursuit.

*   *   *

Jonas was exhausted, frightened, and running low on air. Whale blubber and other debris were piling up all around him, making him queasy. He refused to look, afraid to see what, or who, it might be.

The tooth finally sliced through the six-inch-thick lining, and Jonas pushed his head and arms through

the slit. Having exited the stomach, he found himself in a totally different environment.

The cardiac chamber was a fleshy crawl space no more than a foot wide. Jonas squeezed his body prone into the space, wedging his back against a layer of striated muscle. It gave. Feeling the steady vibrations, he inched his way toward the source, one hand holding the flashlight, the other gripping the tooth.

The bass drum pounded in his brain, its reverberations seeping into his being. He felt the massive organ before he saw it—a throbbing five-foot rounded mass of muscle, enveloped by thick cords of blood vessels.

* * *

The fishing trawler was within two hundred yards of the beach when the Megalodon rammed its keel from below, the impact crushing the twin engines' drive shafts and nearly flipping the boat on its side.

The deck tilted wildly, the force of the collision tossing DeMarco, Terry, and four crewmen over the side into the sea.

The Megalodon went deep, circling below its wounded prey, the icy depths flowing through her open mouth, soothing the burning sensation within her gullet as she prepared to attack once more.

* * *

Jonas wrapped his body around the throbbing heart, his left hand gripping a thick root of blood vessels feeding the four-chambered muscle. His right hand stabbed and sliced blindly in the dark confines, hot liquid gushing everywhere.

*   *   *

Terry surfaced, shocked to see the trawler drifting away from her. Exhausted, it was all she could do just to stay afloat.

The crew yelled at her to swim.

*   *   *

Circling in fifteen hundred feet of water, the female sensed her prey struggling along the surface. She rose once more to feed.

*   *   *

Jonas hacked at the aorta in the pitch black, no longer caring if he lived or died, intent only on sending his monster back into extinction.

A sudden jolt of terror overcame Terry and she swam.

The Meg passed through curtains of warm light, following them up

DeMarco pleaded for Terry to swim faster!

The Meg opened its jaws, then hyperextended them wider—

Two hundred feet.

Andre Dupont saw the luminescent glow. "Oh dear God—"

One hundred feet.

The female's upper jaw, teeth, gums, and connective tissue emerged from under the snout, projecting forward and away from the skull. The eyes, blind, rolled protectively back in the creature's head. The Meg would consume its prey in one gargantuan bite.

Fifty feet.

Terry reached the boat! Strained to grab DeMarco's hand—

—unable to reach it!

* * *

Jonas Taylor could not maintain a grip on the slippery cords. From the shifting angle of the cardiac chamber, he knew the Meg was rising to attack. He thought of Terry.

Anger and adrenaline coursed through his muscles. Wrapping the crook of his left arm around the bundle of cords, he braced his bare feet against the soft tissues of the inner chamber walls and pulled the beating heart downward with all his might. With one powerful slash, he cut deep into the exposed cords with the tooth, severing the organ from its blood supply!

* * *

Twelve feet from the surface, its upper jaw locked in hyperextension, the Megalodon slowed. Its nocturnal eyes bulged, its muscles frozen. The only movement came from the powerless caudal fin, which twitched involuntarily.

In total darkness, Jonas lay on his back, covered in hot blood that continued drenching him in buckets. Against his heaving chest lay the detached heart of the 62,000-pound Megalodon. He struggled to breathe from the regulator, hyperventilating from his effort. The drums had stopped, but the claustrophobic chamber was flooding with blood.

Jonas wriggled out from beneath the massive organ, and slid back down the tight walls of the cardiac

chamber. His fingers felt something hard, yes, the light. He wiped the lens but the beam was barely perceptible. Feeling around in the near-darkness, he groped blindly for the incision he had made in the stomach.

* * *

Terry Tanaka had expected to die. When death did not come, she opened her eyes. The Megalodon's mouth hung open below her . . . the shark sinking! Blood surfaced in gouts, pooling around Terry's lower body.

"Terry, grab the rope," said DeMarco.

"Al, I'm okay. Throw me a mask!"

"Terry!"

"Just do it!"

Dupont grabbed a snorkel and mask and tossed them to her. She pulled the mask over her head, positioned the mouthpiece, and peered below. Through the scarlet-tinted brine, Terry saw a river of blood pouring out of the Megalodon's mouth as it continued to sink. The caudal fin had stopped moving.

* * *

Waves of panic rushed over Jonas as he lost all orientation in the darkness. Frustrated, he screamed into the dying pony bottle's regulator—

—his right leg pushing through the stomach incision. He pushed his head inside, flopping forward. *Where was the AG I?*

The Megalodon was angled upright, the lining of its internal anatomy too slippery to climb. Jonas lost his balance and fell into a mass of debris piled at the

lower end of the stomach. His head struck something solid—the tail section of the *Glider*.

The exterior light from the AG I cast an eerie luminescent glow in the stomach, revealing the effects of its dying host. The muscular lining no longer convulsed. The undigested contents of the intestines were backing up into the stomach and seeping into a pool, actually raising the nose cone of the submersible. Jonas looked up. Sixteen feet above the stomach entrance, seawater poured into the esophagus, the only possible way out.

Jonas relocated the tail section, now sinking beneath three feet of deformed, half-digested whale blubber. He dug with his arms, scooping a hole in the refuse. His hands found the outer hatch and yanked it open. Slick with the Meg's blood, he slid through the opening, then reached back and secured the hatch.

Standing upright in the eight-foot-long capsule, he felt for the controls that would ignite the hydrogen fuel, praying there was enough left to free himself from his purgatory.

Turning the handle counterclockwise, he pulled.

The remains of the hydrogen ignited, propelling the pod upward along the stomach lining like a rocket scaling a wall. Jonas gripped the joystick as the nose of the AG I shot through the water-filled esophagus, revealing open jaws and a beautiful blue exit into the Pacific!

WHUMMMMP!

The AG I slammed to a halt, the pod wedged upright, caught along the sharp points of the Megalodon's upper and lower rows of teeth.

The carcass continued to sink, taking Jonas with it.

"No! No way!" Jonas launched his frame against the interior of the sub, inching the vessel out of the death-grip—

—each jolt driving the points of the shark's teeth deeper into the Lexan surface.

He hit it again and again, beads of water striking his forehead, as water pressure building in his ears as the pod inched its way toward—

Freedom!

With a last terrible scrape of dental bone on bulletproof plastic, the escape pod popped free from the death grip of the Megalodon and rose like a helium balloon toward the surface.

Jonas breathed. He laughed. He prayed Terry was still alive.

Then he saw the spreading cracks, seawater seeping through the damaged shell of the escape pod.

*   *   *

Mac could swim no farther. Unable to catch his breath, his legs numb, he sensed the creature circling, felt the current generated by its mass before actually spotting the three-foot triangular dorsal fin.

"A great white? Get lost you midget." The caudal fin of the thirteen-foot predator slashed back and forth along the surface, circling him, the shark's nostrils guided to Mac's bleeding leg.

"All right God, here's the deal. You let me escape the Grim Reaper this time, and I promise not to violate most of the commandments."

The shark went deep.

"Okay, all of them, all of them!"

Mac jumped as the harness fell next to him. He looked up, shocked to see the coast-guard rescue chopper.

He slipped one arm into the harness and frantically signaled to the crew to pull him out of the water. The conical head of the shark rose out of the sea just as he was yanked upward.

Mac looked up at the silhouette of the rescue chopper, a smile on his face, tears welling in his eyes. "Well, what do you know . . . rescued by the good ol' U.S. Navy. Saving my sorry ass after all these years." He shook his head. "Lord, you do have a sense of humor after all."

* * *

The Lexan cylinder slowed as it took on water, the integrity of the escape pod in serious jeopardy. At five hundred feet, what had been a tiny crack suddenly spider-webbed above Jonas's head. Physically and mentally drained, he could only watch as the cracks began circling the circumference of the cylinder.

Below, the satanic face of the Megalodon continued sinking into the canyon, trailing a river of blood. Jonas watched until the glow diminished, then disappeared entirely into darkness. He had escaped certain death

twice, but to survive this day, he needed one more miracle.

Pressure. Air. Pressure and air. The all-consuming mantra entered his mind. Jonas knew nitrogen bubbles were beginning to form in his blood stream.

Four hundred feet. A fine spray of water soaked the interior of the pod. When the crack completed the circumference, the integrity of the structure would collapse under the tremendous pressures.

He tried to prepare himself.

At three hundred feet, the torpedo-shaped pod began vibrating.

I'm too deep . . .

*   *   *

"Terry, get out of the damn water now!" screamed DeMarco.

Terry ignored him, her face down in the water, breathing through the snorkel. The Megalodon was dead, that she knew. But her heart told her that Jonas had survived. She watched as the white glow disappeared.

Andre Dupont sat on the transom as Leon Barre and the trawler's captain disassembled one of the engines. Andre felt dazed and depressed. All his efforts to save the creature—the lobbying, the expense—all for naught. The greatest predator of all time . . . lost.

"I could have died today," he whispered to himself. "For what? To save my killer? What would the society tell my wife and children? 'Ah, Marie, you should be a

proud widow. Andre died in the most noble of fashions, giving his life to feed an endangered species.'"

Dupont stood, stretching his sore back. The setting sun still shone strong enough to warm his skin. He watched the golden-yellow beam blaze a path from the horizon across the dark Pacific to the trawler. That was when he sighted the fin.

"Hey! Quickly . . . get the girl out of the water!"

The bone-chilling Pacific poured onto Jonas's head, washing away the Meg's blood. The additional weight had slowed his ascent to a crawl. Jonas shivered in his wet suit. He was afraid to move. He glanced at the depth gauge: two hundred feet.

The pod stopped moving. It began to sink.

Wedging his back against the leather pad, Jonas kicked at the glass.

The pod cracked open, releasing him to the sea.

* * *

The three-foot fin circled the fishing trawler. Eleven men as one screamed for Terry to get out of the water.

"That's a great white," yelled Wade Maller. "Terry, it's homing in on the blood!"

The trawler's captain went below and returned with a shotgun. The dorsal fin circled the girl. The captain took aim.

Terry disappeared below the waves.

The shark followed.

* * *

Jonas's muscles felt like lead in the freezing seawater, his ears ringing, crushed behind more than four atmospheres of pressure. His nose began bleeding, his legs aching as he scissor-kicked, toward a surface too far away.

One hundred feet.

So deep . . .

Eighty feet.

It wasn't his body anymore.

Don't . . . stop . . .

At fifty-eight feet Jonas saw a heavenly light, the periphery of his vision clouded by darkness.

At thirty-three feet, he blacked out.

Jonas felt nothing. He was flying, moving toward the light without his body, no more pain, no more fear.

I'm in heaven.

*   *   *

Terry grabbed Jonas's wrist as his body began slipping back into the abyss. She kicked hard, pulling water with her left hand. She felt the shark circling. She swam harder.

As her face broke the surface, Terry pulled Jonas's head free of the ocean. He was blue, no sign of breathing. She saw the dorsal fin surface eight feet away, accelerating toward her as the triangular snout broke the water.

The fishing net arced through the air, its lead weights dropping it around and beneath the predator. The creature twisted, attempting to escape, but the captain of the trawler had pulled the net taut. The shark was trapped.

Terry pulled Jonas to the boat. A dozen hands dragged them on board. DeMarco wrapped him in blankets, then verified a weak pulse.

Terry pushed DeMarco aside and began mouth-to-mouth.

A minute passed.

She pressed both palms to Jonas's belly, expelling water from his mouth, and began again.

Another minute passed.

Jonas coughed up a mouthful of water. Terry and DeMarco rolled him onto his side, allowing him to expel the seawater and vomit. She massaged his neck. "My God . . . Are you okay?"

"Just . . . a bad case of indigestion."

She laughed and leaned in closer. "Groucho, Chico, Zeppo, and Gummo, but Harpo was always my favorite."

Jonas smiled. "Bora Bora, huh? Do they have nice hospital facilities?"

"Some of the best." She rubbed his back.

Exhausted, Jonas squinted against the golden dusk.

"Try not to move," she said, stroking his hair. "The coast guard's on its way. They're going to tow us into the lagoon. We have a recompression chamber on site at the Institute." She smiled at him, tears in her eyes.

Jonas looked at her beautiful face, grinning through the pain. *I am in heaven.*

*   *   *

The shark thrashed back and forth within the fishing net, five feet below the surface, unable to free

itself. Andre Dupont followed the captain throughout the boat, attempting to reason with him.

"Captain, you can't kill it," yelled Dupont. "It's a protected species!"

"Look at my boat. She's busted up. I'll kill this fish, stuff it, and sell it to some tourist from New York for twenty thousand. You gonna give me that much, Frenchy?"

Dupont rolled his eyes. "Harm that shark, and you're going to prison!"

The captain's response was interrupted by the blare of the coast guard's horn.

*　　　*　　　*

A crewman aboard the coast guard cutter tossed a towline to the disabled fishing trawler. Leon Barre attached it to the ship's bow. Within seconds, the line went taut, and the trawler was dragged into the Tanaka Lagoon.

Behind the trawler's transom, the two-thousand-pound predator continued thrashing within the net.

The massive doors separating the Monterey Bay Sanctuary from the lagoon had been left open for the *Kiku*. The cutter entered the canal.

*　　　*　　　*

Jonas was leaning against the transom when the sharp pains struck his elbows. Within seconds, every joint was on fire, stabbing pains running throughout his body.

Terry grabbed him. "What is it?"

"Bends. How much farther?"

They swung south into the main tank of the lagoon, the coast guard towing the fishing trawler toward the eastern bleachers where a physician and nurse were waiting.

"Almost there. Lean against the transom. Try to hold on."

The pain increased; he was dizzy, nauseated. His joints felt as if the Megalodon's teeth were biting down. Opening his eyes, he focused on the great white being towed along the port side of the stern.

Masao Tanaka was waiting by the bleachers, his head heavily bandaged. Mac was there, too, a female paramedic tending to his leg while he flirted.

Terry saw her father and ran to the bow. She waved.

Tears of joy flowed down Masao's cheeks as he waved back.

* * *

Jonas doubled over in pain, he could feel himself losing consciousness. He tried to focus on the predator in the water. She was struggling fiercely, twisting within the confines of the fishing net. Her albino hide cast a soft glow in the growing dusk.

For a brief moment, man and beast made eye contact. The creature's eyes were blue-gray. Jonas stared incredulously at the baby Megalodon. He closed his eyes and smiled.

And then the pain became overwhelming and the submersible pilot lost consciousness as the physician and two paramedics loaded him onto the gurney.

The MEG
series continues in
THE TRENCH (part 2)
and
MEG: PRIMAL WATERS
(part 3).

To contact the author, receive free monthly updates,
or to enter contests to become characters in his
novels, go to
www.SteveAlten.com

ATTENTION SECONDARY SCHOOL TEACHERS

MEG is part of *Adopt-An-Author*, an innovative nationwide non-profit program gaining attention among educators for its success in motivating tens of thousands of reluctant secondary school students to read. The program combines fast-paced thrillers with an interactive website AND direct contact with the author. All teachers receive curriculum materials and posters for their classrooms. The program is FREE to all secondary school teachers and librarians.

Volume discounts are available to participating schools through Apelles Publishing.

For more information and to register for Adopt-An-Author, go to www.AdoptAnAuthor.com

Coming Halloween 2008 in
mass-market paperback:

*a 1500 year old legend . . .
One man's nightmare.*

The LOCH

by
Steve Alten
from Apelles Publishing

Special Sneak Peek

PROLOGUE

Moray Firth
Scottish Highlands
25 September 1330

THE DEEP BLUE WATERS of the Moray Firth crashed violently against the jagged shoreline below. William Calder, second Thane of Cawdor, stood on an outcropping of rock just beyond the point where the boiling North Sea met the mouth of the River Ness. Looking to the south, he could just make out the single-sheeted Spanish galley. The tall ship had been in port since dawn, its crew exchanging silver pieces for wool and cod.

Calder's daughter, Helen, joined him on the lookout. "Ye're needed. A wounded man's come ashore, a soldier. He's demandin' tae see a Templar."

*   *   *

The young man had been left on a grassy knoll. His face was pale and unshaven, his blue-gray eyes glassy with fever. His battle dress, composed of chain mail, was stained crimson along the left quadrant of his stomach. A long sword lay by his side, its blade smeared in blood.

A silver casket, the size of a small melon, hung from his unshaven neck by a gold chain.

William Calder stood over the soldier, joined by two more of his clan. "Who are ye, laddie?"

"I need tae speak wi' a Templar."

"Ye'll speak tae no one 'til ye've dealt wi' me. In whit battle did ye receive yer wounds?"

"Tebas de Ardales."

"An' who did ye fight under?"

"Sir James the Good."

"The Black Douglas?" Calder turned to his men. "Fetch a physician and be quick. Tell him we may need a chirurgeon as well."

"Yes, m'lord." The two men hurried off.

"Why dae ye seek the Templar, laddie?"

The soldier forced his eyes open against the fever. "Only the Templar can be trusted tae guard my keep."

"Is that so?" Calder bent to remove the prized object resting upon the man's chest piece—the soldier's sword raising quickly to kiss Calder's throat. "I'm sorry, m'lord, but I wis instructed tae relinquish this only tae a Templar."

*   *   *

The sun was late in the summer sky by the time Thomas MacDonald arrived at William Calder's home. More Viking than Celt, the burly elder possessed thick auburn-red hair and a matted matching beard. Draped across his broad shoulders was a white tunic, emblazoned with four scarlet equilateral triangles, their points meeting in the center to form a cross.

MacDonald entered without knocking. "A'right, William Calder, why have ye summoned me frae Morayshire?"

Calder pointed to the young soldier, whose wounded left side was being bandaged by a physician. "The laddie

claims tae have fought under the Black Douglas. Says he traveled frae Spain tae seek the Templar."

MacDonald approached. "I'm o' the Order, laddie. Who are ye?"

"Adam Wallace. My faither wis Sir Richard Wallace o' Riccarton."

Both men's eyebrows raised. "Ye're kin tae Sir William?"

"He wis my first cousin, my faither his uncle. I still carry William's sword in battle."

Calder examined the offered blade, sixty-six inches from point to pommel. "I dinnae see any markings on the hilt that designate this tae be Sir William's."

MacDonald nodded. "William aye kept it clean. A fine sword it is, fit for an Archangel tae wield, yet light in his terrible hand. " He pointed to the silver casket. "Tell me how ye came by this?"

"I served under Sir William Keith for jist under a year, ever since the Bruce fell tae leprosy. Oor king had aye wished tae take part in the crusades against the Saracens, but kent he wis dyin'. He asked for the contents o' this casket tae be buried in the Church o' the Holy Sepulchre in Jerusalem. The Black Douglas wis tae lead the mission, joined by Sir William Sinclair, Sir Keith, an' mysel'."

"Go on."

"When we arrived in Spain, Alfonso XI of Castile and Leon . . . he convinced Sir James tae join his vanguard against Osmyn, the Moorish governor of Grenada. The Black Douglas agreed, an' we set off on the twenty-fifth

of March, that is, all but Sir William Keith, who had
injured his arm frae a fa' an' couldnae fight."

"Whit happened?"

"The battle went badly. The Black Douglas wis
deceived by a feint, an' the Moors' cavalry broke
through oor ranks. It happened so fast, bodies an'
blood everywhere, that I could scarcely react. I saw
Sir William Sinclair fa' doon, followed by the Black
Douglas. An' then a sword caught my flank, an' I fell.

"When next I awoke, it wis dark. My nostrils were
fu' o' blood, an' my left side burned. It wis a' I could
dae tae regain my feet beneath the bodies. I wanted tae
flee, but first I had tae find the Black Douglas. By the
half-moon's light, I searched one corpse tae the next
'till I located his body, guardin' the Bruce's casket even
in death. By then, the dawn had arrived an' Sir Keith
wi' it. He dressed my wounds, but fearful o' another
Islamic attack, suggested we separate. I wis tae return
tae Scotland, then make my way to Threave Castle,
stronghold o' Archibald the Grim, Sir James's son.
Sir Keith wis tae return tae the Lowlands an' Melrose
Abbey wi' the casket."

"But yer plans changed, I see."

"Aye. On the eve o' oor sail, Sir Keith took sick wi'
dropsy. Fearful o' his condition, I decided it best if the
casket remained wi' me and too' it frae him."

Calder pulled MacDonald aside. "Do ye believe
him?"

"Aye."

"But why does he seek a Templar?"

"Bruce wis a Mason, born intae the Order. The contents o' the casket belong tae Scotland. It represents nothin' less than oor freedom."

MacDonald turned back toward Adam. "Ye were right tae come here, laddie. Whit lies within that silver container's far ower important tae leave in any abbey. There's a cave, a day's walk frae here, known only tae the Templar. If Cooncil agrees, then I'll take the casket there and—"

"No ye willnae!" Adam interrupted. "The coven's between the Bruce an' the Wallace Clan. Direct me, an' I shall take it there mysel'."

"Dinnae be a fool, ye dinnae ken whit ye're sayin'. The cave I've in mind leads tae Hell, guarded by the De'il's ain minions."

"I'm no' feart."

"Aye, but ye will be, Adam Wallace. An' it's a fear ye'll carry wi' ye 'til the end o' yer days."

CHAPTER 1

Sargasso Sea, Atlantic Ocean
887 miles due east of Miami Beach

THE SARGASSO SEA is a two-million-square-mile expanse of warm water, adrift in the middle of the Atlantic Ocean. An oasis of calm that borders no coastline, the sea is littered with sargassum, a thick seaweed that once fooled Christopher Columbus into believing he was close to land.

The Sargasso is constantly moving, its location determined by the North Equatorial and Gulf Stream currents, as well as those of the Antilles, Canary, and Caribbean. These interlocking forces stabilize the sea like the eye of a great hurricane, while causing its waters to rotate clockwise. As a result, things that enter the Sargasso are gradually drawn toward its center like a giant shower drain, where they eventually sink to the bottom, or, in the case of oil, form thick tar balls and float. There is a great deal of oil in the Sargasso, and with each new spill the problem grows worse, affecting all the sea creatures that inhabit the region.

The Sargasso marks the beginning of my tale and its end, and perhaps that is fitting, for all things birthed in this mysterious body of water eventually return here to die, or so I have learned.

If each of us has his or her own Sargasso, then mine was the Highlands of Scotland. I was born in the village of Drumnadrochit, seven months and twenty-five years ago, give or take a few days. My mother, Andrea,

was American, a quiet soul who came to the United Kingdom on holiday and stayed nine years in a bad marriage. My father, Angus Wallace, the cause of its termination, was a brute of a man, possessing jet-black hair and the piercing blue eyes of the Gael, the wile of a Scot, and the temperament of a Viking. An only child, I took my father's looks and, thankfully, my mother's disposition.

Angus's claim to fame was that his paternal ancestors were descendants of the great William Wallace himself, a name I doubt most non-Britons would have recognized until Mel Gibson portrayed him in the movie, Braveheart. As a child, I often asked Angus to prove we were kin of the great Sir William Wallace, but he'd merely tap his chest and say, "Listen, runt, some things ye jist feel. When ye become a real man, ye'll ken whit I mean."

I grew to calling my father Angus and he called me his "runt" and neither was meant as an endearing term. Born with a mild case of hypotonia, my muscles were too weak to allow for normal development, and it would be two years (to my father's embarrassment) before I had the strength to walk. By the time I was five I could run like a deer, but being smaller than my burly, big-boned Highland peers, I was always picked on. Weekly contests between hamlets on the football pitch (rugby field) were nightmares. Being fleet of foot meant I had to carry the ball, and I'd often find myself in a scrum beneath boys twice my size. While I lay bleeding and broken on the battlefield, my inebriated

father would prance about the sidelines, howling with the rest of his drunken cronies, wondering why the gods had cursed him with such a runt for a son.

According to the child-rearing philosophy of Angus Wallace, tough love was always best in raising a boy. Life was hard, and so childhood had to be hard, or the seedling would rot before it grew. It was the way Angus's father had raised him, and his father's father before that. And if the seedling was a runt, then the soil had to be tilled twice as hard.

But the line between tough love and abuse is often blurred by alcohol, and it was when Angus was inebriated that I feared him most.

His final lesson of my childhood left a lasting impression.

It happened a week before my ninth birthday. Angus, sporting a whisky buzz, led me to the banks of Aldourie Castle, a three-century-old chateau that loomed over the misty black waters of Loch Ness. "Now pay attention, runt, for it's time I telt ye o' the Wallace curse. My faither, yer grandfaither, Logan Wallace, he died in these very waters when I wis aboot yer age. An awfy gale hit the Glen, an' his boat flipped. Everyone says he drooned, but I ken better, see. 'Twis the monster that got him, an' ye best be warned, for—"

"Monster? Are ye talkin' aboot Nessie?" I asked, pie-eyed.

"Nessie? Nessie's folklore. I'm speakin' o' a curse wrought by nature, a curse that's haunted the Wallace men since the passin' o' Robert the Bruce."

"I dinnae understand."

Growing angry, he dragged me awkwardly to the edge of Aldourie Pier. "Look doon, laddie. Look doon intae the Loch an' tell me whit ye see?"

I leaned out carefully over the edge, my heart pattering in my bony chest. "I dinnae see anythin', the water's too black."

"Aye, but if yer eyes could penetrate the depths, ye'd see intae the dragon's lair. The de'il lurks doon there, but it can sense oor presence, it can smell the fear in oor blood. By day the Loch's ours, for the beast prefers the depths, but God help ye at night when she rises tae feed."

"If the monster's real, then I'll rig a lure an' bring her up."

"Is that so? An' who be ye? Wiser men have tried an' failed, an' looked foolish in their efforts, whilst a bigger price wis paid by those drowned who ventured out oot night."

"Ye're jist tryin' tae scare me. I'm no' feart o' a myth."

"Tough words. Very well, runt, show me how brave ye are. Dive in. Go on, laddie, go for a swim and let her get a good whiff o' ye."

He pushed me toward the edge and I gagged at his breath, but held tight to his belt buckle.

"Jist as I thought."

Frightened, I pried myself loose and ran from the pier, the tears streaming down my cheeks.

"Ye think I'm hard on ye, laddie? Well, life's hard, an' I'm nothin' compared tae that monster. Ye best pay attention, for the curse skips every other generation, which means ye're marked. That dragon lurks in the shadow o' yer soul, and one day ye'll cross paths. Then what will ye dae? Will ye stand and fight like a warrior, like brave Sir William an' his kin, or will ye cower an' run, lettin' the dragon haunt ye for the rest o' yer days?"

*　　*　　*

Leaning out over the starboard rail, I searched for my reflection in the Sargasso's glassy surface.

Seventeen years had passed since my father's "dragon" lecture, seventeen long years since my mother had divorced him and moved us to New York. In that time I had lost my accent and learned that my father was right, that I was indeed haunted by a dragon, only his name was Angus Wallace.

Arriving in a foreign land is never easy for a boy, and the physical and psychological baggage I carried from my childhood left me fodder for the bullies of my new school. At least in Drumnadrochit I had allies like my pal, True MacDonald, but here I was all alone, a fish out of water, and there were many a dark day that I seriously considered ending my life.

And then I met Mr. Tkalec.

Joe Tkalec was our middle school's science teacher, a kind Croatian man with rectangular glasses,

a quick wit, and a love for poetry. Seeing that the "Scottish weirdo" was being picked on unmercifully, Mr. Tkalec took me under his wing, allowing me special classroom privileges like caring for his lab animals, small deeds that helped nurture my self-image. After school, I'd ride my bike over to Mr. Tkalec's home, which contained a vast collection of books.

"Zachary, the human mind is the instrument that determines how far we'll go in life. There's only one way to develop the mind and that's to read. My library's yours, select any book and take it home, but return only after you've finished it."

The first volume I chose was the oldest book in his collection, *The Origins of an Evolutionist*, my eyes drawn by the author's name, Alfred Russel Wallace.

Born in 1823, Alfred Wallace was a brilliant British evolutionist, geographer, anthropologist, and theorist, often referred to as Charles Darwin's right-hand man, though their ideas were not always in step. In his biography, Alfred mentioned that he too was a direct descendant of William Wallace, making us kin, and that he also suffered childhood scars brought about by an overbearing father.

The thought of being related to Alfred Wallace instantly changed the way I perceived myself, and his words regarding adaptation and survival put wind in my fallen sails.

"... *we have here an acting cause to account for that balance so often observed in Nature—a deficiency in one*

*set of organs always being compensated by an increased
development of some others . . ."*

My own obstinate father, a man who had never
finished grammar school, had labeled me weak,
his incessant badgering (I need tae make ye a man,
Zachary) fostering a negative self-image. Yet here was
my great-uncle Alfred, a brilliant man of science, telling me that if my physique made me vulnerable, then
another attribute could be trained to compensate.

That attribute would be my intellect.

My appetite for academics and the sciences
became voracious. Within months I established myself
as the top student in my class, by the end of the school
year, I was offered the chance to skip the next grade.
Mr. Tkalec continued feeding me information, while
his roommate, a retired semipro football player named
Troy, taught me to hone my body into something
more formidable to my growing list of oppressors.

For the first time in my life, I felt a sense of pride.
At Troy's urging, I tried out for freshman football.
Aided by my tutor's coaching and a talent for alluding
defenders (acquired, no doubt, on the pitch back in
Drumnadrochit) I rose quickly through the ranks, and
by the end of my sophomore year, I found myself the
starting tailback for our varsity football team.

Born under the shadow of a Neanderthal, I had
evolved into *Homo sapiens*, and I refused to look back.

Mr. Tkalec remained my mentor until I gradu-
ated, helping me secure an academic scholarship at

Princeton. Respecting my privacy, he seldom broached subjects concerning my father, though he once told me that Angus's dragon story was simply a metaphor for the challenges that each of us must face in life. "Let your anger go, Zack, you're not hurting anyone but yourself."

Gradually I did release my contempt for Angus, but unbeknownst to both Mr. Tkalec and myself, there was still a part of my childhood that remained buried in the shadows of my soul, something my subconscious mind refused to acknowledge.

Angus had labeled it a dragon.

If so, the Sargasso was about to set it free.

*   *   *

The afternoon haze seemed endless, the air lifeless, the Sargasso as calm as the Dead Sea. It was my third day aboard the *Manhattanville*, a 162-foot research vessel designed for deep-sea diving operations. The forward half of the boat, four decks high, held working laboratories and accommodations for a dozen crew members, six technicians, and twenty-four scientists. The aft deck, flat and open, was equipped with a twenty-one-ton A-frame PVS crane system, capable of launching and retrieving the boat's small fleet of remotely operated vehicles (ROVs) and its primary piece of exploration equipment, the *Massett-6*, a vessel designed specifically for bathymetric and bottom profiling.

It was aboard the *Massett-6* in this dreadful sea that I hoped to set my own reputation beside that of my great Uncle Alfred.

Our three-day voyage had delivered us to the approximate center of the Sargasso. Clumps of golden brown seaweed mixed with black tar balls washed gently against our boat, staining its gleaming white hull a chewing tobacco brown as we waited for sunset, our first scheduled dive.

Were there dragons waiting for me in the depths? Ancient mariners once swore as much. The Sargasso was considered treacherous, filled with sea serpents and killer weeds that could entwine a ship's keel and drag it under. Superstition? No doubt, but as in all legend, there runs a vein of truth. Embellishments of eye-witnessed accounts become lore over time, and the myth surrounding the Sargasso was no different.

The real danger lies in the sea's unusual weather. The area is almost devoid of wind, and many a sailor who once entered these waters in tall sailing ships never found their way out.

As our vessel was steel, powered by twin diesel engines and a 465-horsepower bow thruster, I had little reason to worry.

Ah, how the seeds of cockiness blossom when soiled in ignorance.

While fate's clouds gathered ominously on my horizon, all my metallic-blue eyes perceived were fair skies. Still young at twenty-five, I had already earned a bachelor's and master's degree from Princeton and a doctorate from the University of California at San Deigo, and three of my papers on cetacean communication had recently been published in *Nature*

and *Science*. I had been invited to sit on the boards of several prominent oceanographic councils, and, while teaching at Florida Atlantic University, I had invented an underwater acoustics device—a device responsible for this very voyage of discovery, accompanied by a film crew shooting a documentary sponsored by none other than *National Geographic Explorer*.

By society's definition, I was a success, always planning my work, working my plan, my career the only life I ever wanted. Was I happy? Admittedly, my emotional barometer may have been a bit off-kilter. I was pursuing my dreams, and that made me happy, yet it always seemed like there was a dark cloud hanging over head. My fiancée, Lisa, a "sunny" undergrad at FAU, claimed I had a "restless soul," attributing my demeanor to being too tightly wound.

"Loosen up, Zack. You think way too much, it's why you get so many migraines. Cut loose once in a while, get high on life instead of always analyzing it. All this left-brain thinking is a turnoff."

I tried "turning off," but found myself too much of a control freak to let myself go.

One person whose left brain had stopped functioning long ago was David James Caldwell II. As I quickly learned, the head of FAU's oceanography department was a self-promoting hack who had maneuvered his way into a position of tenure based solely on his ability to market the achievements of his staff. Six years my superior, with four years less schooling, David nevertheless presented himself to our sponsors as if he were

my mentor, me, *his* protégé. "Gentlemen, members of the board, with my help, Zachary Wallace could become this generation's Jacques Cousteau."

David had arranged our journey, but it was my invention that made it all possible—a cephalopod lure, designed to attract the ocean's most elusive predator, *Architeuthis dux,* the giant squid.

Our first dive was scheduled for nine o'clock that night, still a good three hours away. The sun was just beginning to set as I stood alone in the bow, staring at endless sea, when my solitude was shattered by David, Cody Saults, our documentary's director, his cameraman and wife, and the team's sound person.

"There's my boy," David announced. "Hey, Zack, we've been looking all over the ship for you. Since we still have light, Cody and I thought we'd get some of the background stuff out of the way. Okay by you?"

Cody and I? Now he was executive producer?

"Whatever you'd like, Mr. Saults."

The cameraman, a good-natured soul named Hank Griffeth, set up his tripod while his wife, Cindy, miked me for sound. Cindy wore a leopard bikini that accentuated her cleavage, and it was all I could do to keep from sneaking a peek.

Just using the right side of my brain, Lisa . . .

Cody chirped on endlessly, forcing me to refocus. ". . . anyway, I'll ask you and David a few questions off-camera. Back in the studio, our editors will dub in Patrick Stewart's voice over mine. Got it?"

"I like Patrick Stewart. Will I get to meet him?"

"No, now pay attention. Viewers want to know what makes young Einsteins like you and David tick. So when I ask you about—"

"Please don't call me that."

Cody smiled his Hollywood grin. "Listen kid, humble's great, but you and Dr. Caldwell are the reason we're floating in this festering, godforsaken swamp. So if I tell you you're a young Einstein, you're a young Einstein, got it?"

David, a man sporting an IQ seventy points lower than the deceased Princeton professor, slapped me playfully across the shoulder blades. "Just roll with it, kid."

"We're ready here," Hank announced, looking through his rubber eyepiece. "You've got about fifteen minutes of good light left."

"Okay boys, keep looking out to sea, nice and casual . . . and we're rolling. So Zack, let's start with you. Tell us what led you to invent this acoustic thingama-jiggy."

I focused on the horizon as instructed, the sun splashing gold on my tanned complexion. "Well, I've spent most of the last two years studying cetacean echolocation. Echolocation is created by an acoustic organ, unique in dolphins and whales, that provides them with an ultrasonic vision of their environment. For example, when a sperm whale clicks, or echolocates, the sound waves bounce off objects, sending back audio frequency pictures of the mammal's surroundings."

"Like sonar?"

"Yes, only far more advanced. For instance, when a dolphin echolocates a shark, it not only sees its environment, but it can actually peer into the shark's belly to determine if it's hungry. Sort of like having a built-in ultrasound. These clicks also function as a form of communication among other members of the cetacean species, who can tap into the audio transmission spectrum, using it as a form of language.

"Using underwater microphones, I've been able to create a library of echolocation clicks. By chance, I discovered that certain sperm whale recordings, taken during deep hunting dives, stimulated our resident squid population to feed."

"That's right," David blurted out, interrupting me. "Squid, intelligent creatures in their own right, often feed on the scraps left behind by sperm whales. By using the sperm whales' feeding frequency, we were able to entice squid to the microphone, creating, in essence, a cephalopod lure."

"Amazing," Cody replied. "But fellows, gaining the attention of a four-foot squid is one thing, how do you think this device will work in attracting a giant squid? I mean, you're talking about a deep-sea creature, sixty feet in length, that's never been seen alive."

"They're still cephalopods," David answered, intent on taking over the interview. "While it's true we've never seen a living specimen, we know from carcasses that have washed ashore and by remains found in the

bellies of sperm whales that the animals' anatomies are similar to those of their smaller cousins."

"Fantastic. David, why don't you give us a quick rundown of this first dive."

I held my tongue, my wounded ego seething.

"Our cephalopod lure's been attached to the retractable arm of the submersible. Our goal is to descend to thirty-three hundred feet, entice a giant squid up from the abyss, then capture it on film. Because *Architeuthis* prefers the very deep waters, deeper than our submersible can go, we're waiting until dark to begin our expedition, hoping the creatures will ascend with nightfall, following the food chain's nocturnal migration into the shallows."

"Explain that last bit. What do you mean by nocturnal migration?"

"Why don't I let Dr. Wallace take over," David offered, bailing out before he had to tax his left brain.

I inhaled a few temper-reducing breaths. "Giant squids inhabit an area known as the mid-water realm, by definition, the largest continuous living space on Earth. While photosynthesis initiates food chains among the surface layers of the ocean, in the midwater realm, the primary source of nutrients come from phytoplankton, microscopic plants. Mid-water creatures live in absolute darkness, but once the sun sets, they rise en masse to graze on the phytoplankton, a nightly event that's been described as the largest single migration of living organisms on the planet."

"Great stuff, great stuff. Hank, how's the light?"

"Fifteen minutes, give or take."

"Let's keep moving, getting more into the personal. Zack, tell us about yourself. Dr. Caldwell tells me you're an American citizen, originally from Scotland."

"Yes. I grew up in the Scottish Highlands, in a small village called Drumnadrochit."

"That's at the head of Urquhart Bay, on Loch Ness," David chimed in.

"Really?"

"My mother's American," I said, the red flags waving in my brain. "My parents met while she was on holiday. We moved to New York when I was nine."

With a brazen leer, David leaned forward, mimicking a Scots accent, "Dr. Wallace is neglecting the time he spent as a wee laddie, hangin' oot wi' visitin' teams o' Nessie hunters, aren't ye, Dr. Wallace?"

I shot David a look that would boil flesh.

The director naturally jumped on his lead. "So it was actually the legend of the Loch Ness Monster that stoked your love of science. Fascinating."

And there it was, the dreaded "M" word. Loch Ness was synonymous with Monster, and Monster meant Nessie, a cryptozoologist's dream, a marine biologist's nightmare. Nessie was "fringe" science, an industry of folklore, created by tourism and fast-talkers like my father.

Being associated with Nessie had destroyed many a scientist's career, most notably Dr. Denys Tucker, of the British Museum of Natural History. Dr. Tucker

had held his post for eleven years, and, at one time, had been considered the foremost authority on eels . . . until he hinted to the press that he was interested in launching an investigation into the Loch Ness Monster.

A short time later he was dismissed, his career as a scientist all but over.

Being linked to Loch Ness on a *National Geographic* special could destroy my reputation as a serious scientist, but it was already too late. David had led me to the dogshit, and, as my mother would say, I had "stepped in it." Now the goal was to keep from dragging it all over the carpet.

"Let me be clear here," I proclaimed, my booming voice threatening Hank's wife's microphone, "I was never actually one of those 'Nessie' hunters."

"Ah, but you've always had an interest in Loch Ness, haven't you?" David crowed, still pushing the angle.

He was like a horny high school boy, refusing to give up after his date said she wasn't in the mood. I turned to face him, catching the full rays of the setting sun square in my eyes—a fatal mistake for a migraine sufferer.

"Loch Ness is a unique place, Dr. Caldwell," I retorted, "but not everyone who visits comes looking for monsters. As a boy, I met many serious environmentalists who were there strictly to investigate the Loch's algae content, or its peat, or its incredible depths. They were naturalists, like my great ancestor, Alfred Russel Wallace. You see, despite all this non-

sense about legendary water beasts, the Loch remains a magnificent body of water, unique in its—"

"But most of these teams came searching for Nessie, am I right?"

I glanced in the direction of David's boyish face, with its bleached-blond mustache and matching Moe Howard bangs, but all I could see were spots, purple demons that blinded my vision.

Migraine ...

My skin tingled at the thought. I knew I needed to pop a *Zomig* before the brain storm moved into its more painful stages, yet on I babbled, trying desperately to salvage the interview and possibly, my career.

"Well, David, it's not like you can escape it. They've turned Nessie into an industry over there, haven't they?"

"And have you ever spotted the monster?"

I wanted to choke him right on-camera. I wanted to rip the shell necklace from his paisley Hawaiian shirt and crush his puny neck in my bare hands, but my left brain, stubborn as always, refused to relinquish control. "Excuse me, Dr. Caldwell, I thought we were here to discuss giant squids?"

David pushed on. "Stay with me, kid, I'm going somewhere with this. Have you ever spotted the monster?"

I forced a laugh, my right eye beginning to throb. "Look, I don't know about you, *Dr. Caldwell*, but I'm a marine biologist. We're supposed to leave the myth chasing to the crypto guys."

"Ah, but you see, that's exactly my point. It wasn't long ago that these giant squids were considered more myth than science. The legend of the Scylla in the *Odyssey*, the monster in Tennyson's poem, 'The Kraken.' As a young boy growing up so close to Loch Ness, surely you must have been influenced by the greatest legend of them all?"

Cody Saults was loving it, while tropical storm David, located in the latitude of my right eye, was increasing into a hurricane.

". . . maybe hunting for Nessie as a child became the foundation for your research into locating the elusive giant squid. I'm not trying to put words in your mouth, but—"

"Butts are for crapping, Dr. Caldwell, and so's everything that follows! Nessie's crap, too. It's nothing but a nonsensical legend embellished to increase Highland tourism. I'm not a travel agent, I'm a scientist in search of a real sea creature, not some Scottish fabrication. Now if you two will excuse me, I need to use the head."

Without waiting, I pushed past David and the director and entered the ship's infrastructure, in desperate search of the nearest bathroom. The purple spots were gone, the eye pain already intensifying. The next phase would be vomiting—brain-rattling, vein-popping vomiting. This would be followed by weakness and pain and more vomiting, and eventually, if I didn't put a bullet through my skull, I'd mercifully pass out.

It was misery, which is why, like all migraine sufferers, I tried to avoid things that set me off: direct lighting, excessive caffeine, and the stress that, to me, revolved around the taboo subject of my childhood.

My stomach was already gurgling, the pain in my eye crippling as I hurried past lab doors and staterooms. Ducking inside the nearest bathroom, I locked the door, knelt by the toilet, shoved a sacrificial digit down my throat, and puked.

The intestinal tremor released my lunch, threatening to implode the blood vessels leading to my brain. It continued on, until my stomach was empty, my will to live sapped.

For several moments I remained there, my head balanced on the cool, bacteria-laced rim of the toilet.

Maybe Lisa was right. Maybe I did need to loosen up.

* * *

It was dark by the time I emerged on deck, my long brown hair matted to my forehead, my blue eyes glassy and bloodshot. The migraine had left me weak and shaky, and I'd have preferred to remain in bed, but it was nearly time to descend, and I knew David would grab my spot aboard the sub in a New York minute if I waited any longer.

A blood-red patch of light revealed all that was left of the western horizon, the sweltering heat of day yielding to the coolness of night. Inhaling several deep lungfuls of fresh air, I made my way aft to the stern, now a hub of activity. The ship's lights were on, creating a theater by which four technicians and

a half dozen scientists completed their final check on the *Massett-6*, the twenty-seven-foot-long submersible now suspended four feet off the deck like a giant alien insect.

Able to explore depths down to thirty-five hundred feet, the *Massett-6* was a three-man deep-sea sub that consisted of an acrylic glasslike observation bubble, mounted to a rectangular-shaped aluminum chamber, its walls five inches thick. Running beneath the submersible was an exterior platform and skid that supported flotation tanks, hoses, recording devices, gas cylinders containing oxygen and air, primary and secondary batteries, a series of collection baskets, arc lights, a hydraulic manipulator arm, and nine 100-pound thrusters.

I caught David leaning against the sub, hastily pulling on a blue and gold jumpsuit—*my* jumpsuit—when he saw me approach. "Zack? Where've you been? We, uh, we didn't think you were going to make it."

"Nice try. Now take off my jumpsuit, I'm fine."

"You look pale."

"I said I'm fine, no thanks to you. What was all that horseshit about Loch Ness? You trying to discredit me on national TV?"

"Of course not. We're a team, remember? I just thought it made for a great angle. *Discovery Channel* loves that mysterious stuff, we can pitch them next."

"Forget it. I've worked way too hard to destroy my reputation with this nonsense. Now, for the last time, get your scrawny butt outta my jumpsuit."

"We're ready here," announced Ace Futrell, our mission coordinator. "Mr. Wallace, if you'd care to grace us with your presence."

The cameras rolled. David, back to playing the dutiful mentor, animated a few last-minute instructions to me as I slid my feet into the jumpsuit. "Remember, kid, this is our big chance, it's our show. Work the audience. Relate to them. Get 'em on your side."

"Chill out, David. This isn't an infomercial."

The hatch of the *Massett-6* was located beneath the submersible's aft observation compartment behind the main battery assembly. Kneeling below the sub, I poked my head and shoulders into the opening and climbed up.

The vehicle's interior was a cross between a helicopter cockpit and an FBI surveillance van. The claustrophobic aluminum chamber was crammed with video monitors, life-support equipment, carbon dioxide scrubbers, and gas analyzers, along with myriad pipes and pressurized hoses. Conversely, the forward compartment was a two-seat acrylic bubble that offered panoramic views of the sub's surroundings.

Taking my assigned place up front in the copilot's seat, I tightened the shoulder harness, then inspected the controls of my sonic lure, which had been jury-rigged to the console on my right. Everything seemed stat. Looking above my head out of the bubble, I watched as a technician double-checked the lure's underwater speaker, now attached to the vessel's exterior tow hook.

Donald Lacombe, the sub's pilot, joined me in the cockpit, wasting little time in establishing who was boss. "All right, boy genius, here's the drill. Keep your keister in your seat and don't touch anything without being told. *Capische?*"

"Aye, aye, sir."

"And nobody likes a smart-ass. You're in my vessel now, blah blah blah blah blah." Tuning him out, I turned to watch Hank Griffeth as he climbed awkwardly into the aft compartment. A crewman handed him up his camera, then sealed the rear hatch.

The radio squawked. "Control to *Six*, prepare to launch."

Lacombe spoke into his headset, clearly in his element. "Roger that, Ace, prepare to launch."

Moments later, the A-frame's crane activated, and the submersible rose away from the deck, extending twenty feet beyond the stern. The *Manhattanville's* keel lights illuminated, creating an azure patch in the otherwise dark, glassy surface, and we were lowered into the sea.

For the next ten minutes, divers circled our sub, detaching its harness and rechecking hoses and equipment. Lacombe kept busy, completing his checklist with Ace Futrell aboard the research ship, while Donald showed me photos of his children.

"So when will you and this fiancée of yours start having kids? Nothing like a few rug rats running around to make a house a home."

No problem havin' children, runt. The Wallace curse skips every other generation.

"Zack?"

"Huh?" I shook my head, the lingering ache of the migraine scattering my estranged father's words. "Sorry. No kids, at least not for a while. Too much work to do."

I returned my attention to the control panel, forcing my thoughts back to to our voyage. Descending thousands of feet into the ocean depths was similar to flying. One is always aware of the danger, yet comforted in the knowledge that the majority of planes land safely, just as most subs return to the surface. I had been in a submersible twice before, but this voyage was different, meant to attract one of the most dangerous, if least understood, predators in the sea.

My heart pounded with excitement, the adrenaline escorting Angus's words from my thoughts.

Ace Futrell's commands filtered over the radio. "Control to *Six*, you are clear to submerge. Bon voyage, and good hunting."

"Roger that, Control. See you in the morning."

Lacombe activated the ballast controls, allowing seawater to enter the pressurized tanks beneath the sub. Weighed down, the neutrally buoyant *Massett-6* began to sink, trailing a stream of silvery air bubbles.

The pilot checked his instruments, activated his sonar, engaged his thrusters, then turned to me. "Hey, rookie, ever been in one of these submersibles?"

"Twice, but the missions were only two hours long. Nothing like this."

"Then we'll keep it simple. Batteries and air scrubbers'll allow us to stay below up to eighteen hours, but maneuverability's the pits. Top speed's one knot, best depth's thirty-five hundred feet. We drop too far below that, and the hull will crush like a soda can. Pressure will pop your head like a grape."

I acknowledged the pilot's attempt to put me in my place, countering with my own. "Know much about giant squids? This vessel's twenty-seven feet. The creature we're after is more than twice its size—forty to fifty feet—weighing in excess of a ton. Once we make contact with one of these monsters, be sure to follow my exact instructions."

It's okay to use the "M" word when attempting to intimidate.

Lacombe shrugged it off, but I could tell he was weighing my words. "Three hundred feet," he called out to Hank, who was already filming. "Activating exterior lights."

The twin beams lanced through the black sea, turning it a Mediterranean blue.

And what a spectacle it was, like being in a giant fishbowl in the middle of the greatest aquarium on Earth. I gawked for a full ten minutes before turning to face the camera, doing my best Carl Sagan impression.

"We're leaving the surface waters now, approaching what many biologists call the 'twilight zone.' As we move deeper, we'll be able to see how the creatures

that inhabit these mid-water zones have adapted to life in the constant darkness."

Lacombe pointed, refusing to be upstaged. "Looks like we've got our first visitor."

A bizarre jellylike giant with a pulsating bell-shaped head drifted past the cockpit, the creature's transparent forty-five-foot-long body set aglow in our artificial lights.

"That's a siphonophore," I stated, fully immersed in lecture mode. "Its body's made up of millions of stinger cells that trail through the sea like a net as it searches for food."

Next to arrive were a half dozen piranha-sized fish, with bulbous eyes and terrifying fangs. As they turned, their flat bodies reflected silvery-blue in the sub's beams.

"These are hatchet fish," I went on. "Their bodies contain light-producing photo-phores which countershade their silhouettes, allowing them to blend with the twilight sea. In these dark waters, it's essential to see but not be seen. As we move deeper, we'll find more creatures who rely on bioluminescence not only to camouflage themselves, but to attract prey."

Jellyfish of all sizes and shapes drifted silently past the cockpit, their transparent bodies glowing a deep red in the sub's lights. "Pilot, would you shut down the lights a moment?"

He shot me a perturbed look, then reluctantly powered off the beams.

We were surrounded by the silence of utter blackness.

"Watch," I whispered.

A sudden flash appeared in the distance, followed by a dozen more, and suddenly the sea was alive with a pyrotechnic display of bioluminescence as a thousand neon blue lightbulbs flashed randomly in the darkness.

"Amazing," Hank muttered, continuing to film. "It's like these fish are communicating."

"Communicating and hunting," I agreed. "Nature always finds a way to adapt, even in the harshest environments."

"Two thousand feet," the pilot announced.

An adult gulper eel slithered by, its mouth nearly unhinging as it engulfed an unsuspecting fish. All in all, I couldn't have asked for a better performance.

But the best was yet to come.

It was getting noticeably colder in the cabin, so I zipped up my jumpsuit, too full of pride to ask the pilot to raise the heat.

Hank repositioned his camera, then reviewed the list of prompts Cody Saults had given him. "Okay, Zack, tell us about the giant squid. I read where you think it might actually be a mutation?"

"It's just a theory."

"Sounds interesting, give us a rundown. Wait . . . give me a second to re-focus. Okay, go ahead."

"Mutations happen all the time in nature. They can be caused by radiation, or spontaneously, or sometimes

by the organism itself as a form of adaptation to changes within its environment. Most mutations are neutral, meaning they have no effect upon the organism. Some, however, can be very beneficial or very harmful, depending upon the environment and circumstance.

"Mutations that affect the future of a particular species are heritable changes in particular sequences of nucleotides. Without these mutations, evolution as we know it wouldn't be possible. For instance, the accidents, errors, and lucky circumstances that caused humans to evolve from lower primates were all mutations. Some mutations lead to dead ends, or extinction of the species. Neanderthal, for instance, was a dead-end mutation. Other mutations can alter the size of a particular genus, creating a new species altogether.

"In the case of *Architeuthis dux*, here we have a cephalopod, a member of the family *teuthid*, yet this particular offshoot has evolved into the largest invertebrate on the planet. Is it a mutation? Most certainly. The question is, why did it mutate in the first place? Perhaps as a defense mechanism against huge predators like the sperm whale. Was it a successful mutation or a dead end? Since we know so little about the creatures, it's impossible to say. Then again, who's to say *Homo sapiens* will be a success?"

The pilot rolled his eyes at my philosophical whims. "We just passed twenty-three hundred feet. Isn't it time you activated that device of yours?"

"Oh, yeah." Reaching to my right, I powered up the lure, sending a series of pulsating clicks chirping through the timeless sea.

I sat back, heart pounding with excitement, waiting for my "dragon" to appear.

* * *

"Yo, Jacques Cousteau Junior, it's been six hours. What happened to your giant octopus?"

I looked up at the pilot from behind my copy of *Popular Science*. "I don't know. There's no telling what kind of range the lure has, or whether a squid's even in the area."

The pilot returned to his game of solitaire. "Not exactly the answer *National Geographic*'ll want to hear."

"Hey, this is science," I snapped. "Nature works on her own schedule." I looked around at the black sea. "How deep are we anyway?"

"Twenty-seven hundred feet."

"Christ, we're not deep enough! I specifically asked for thirty-three hundred feet. Giant squids prefer the cold. We need to be deeper, below the thermocline, or we're just wasting our time."

Lacombe's expression soured, knowing I had him by the short and curlies. "*Six* to Control. Ace, the kid wants me to descend to thirty-three hundred feet."

"Stand by, *Six*." A long silence, followed by the expected answer.

"Permission granted."

* * *

A half mile to the south and eleven hundred fathoms below, the monster remained dead still in the silence and darkness. Fifty-nine feet of mantle and tentacles were condensed within a crevice of rock, its 1,900-pound body ready to uncoil like the spring on a mousetrap.

The carnivore scanned the depths with its two amber eyes, each as large as dinner plates. As intelligent as it was large, it could sense everything within its environment.

*   *   *

The female angler fish swam slowly past the outcropping of rock, dangling her own lure, a long spine tipped with a bioluminous bait. Attached to the underside of the female, wagging like a second tail were the remains of her smaller mate. In an unusual adaptation of sexual dimorphism, the male angler had ended its existence by biting into the body of the female, his mouth eventually fusing with her skin until the two bloodstreams had connected as one. Over time, the male would degenerate, losing his eyes and internal organs, becoming a permanent parasite, totally dependent upon the female for food.

Feeding for two, the female maneuvered her glowing lure closer to the outcropping of rock.

Whap!

Lashing through the darkness like a bungee cord, one of the squid's eighteen-foot feeder tentacles grasped the female angler within its leaf-shaped pad, piercing the stunned fish with an assortment of hooks

protruding from its deadly rows of suckers. Drawing its prey toward its mouth, the hunter's parrotlike beak quickly crushed the meat into digestible chunks, its tongue guiding the morsels down its throat, the meat actually passing through its brain on its way to its stomach.

Architeuthis dux pushed its twelve-foot torpedo-shaped head out of its craggy habitat, then swallowed the remains of the angler fish in one gulp.

The giant squid was still hungry, its appetite having been teased over the last eight hours by the sonic lure. Though tempted to rise and feed on what it perceived as the remains of a sperm whale kill, the immense cephalopod had remained below, refusing to venture into the warmer surface waters.

Now, as it finished off the remains of its snack, it detected the enticing presence moving closer, entering the cooler depths.

Hunger overruled caution. Drawing its eight arms free of the fissure, it pushed away from the rocky bottom and rose, its anvil-shaped tail fin propelling it through the darkness, its movements alerting *another* species in the Sargasso food chain to its presence.

*   *   *

Blip.

Blip . . . blip . . . blip . . .

Donald Lacombe stared at the sonar, playing up the drama for the camera. "It's a biologic, and it's big, headed right for us. Fifteen hundred feet and closing."

"Are we in any danger?" I asked, suddenly feeling vulnerable.

"I don't know, you're the marine biologist. Nine hundred feet. Stand by, it's slowing. Maybe it's checking us out?"

"It doesn't like the bright lights," I countered. "Switch to red lights only."

The pilot adjusted the outer beams, rotating the lenses to their less-brilliant red filters. "That did it, it's coming like a demon now. Three hundred feet. Two hundred. Better hold on!"

Seconds passed, and then the *Massett-6* shuddered, rolling hard to starboard as the unseen beast latched on to our main battery and sled.

My heart pounded, then I nearly jumped out of my shoes when the padded sucker, as wide as a catcher's mitt, snaked its way across the outside of our protective bubble.

Eight more tentacles joined in the dance, each appendage as thick as a fire hose, all moving independently from its still unseen owner.

Even the pilot was impressed. "Jeez—us, you actually did it! And will you look at the size of those tentacles? He must be a monster."

"She," I corrected. "Females grow much larger than males, and this monster's definitely a female."

Ah, the "M" word again. If only I had known . . .

The pilot flicked the toggle switch on his radio. "*Six* to Control, break out the bubbly, Ace, we've made contact."

We could hear clapping coming from the control room.

"We're getting the feed. Congratulations, partner," David broke in over the radio, "we did it."

"Yeah, *we*," I mumbled.

The sound of wrenching aluminum caused me to jump. "What was—"

"Stand by." Lacombe seemed genuinely concerned, and that worried me. At three thousand feet, water pressure is a hundred times greater than at the surface, meaning even the slightest breach in our hull would kill us in a matter of seconds.

What if she tears loose a plate? What if she breaks open a seal?

The thought of drowning sent waves of panic crawling through my belly.

"Hey!" Hank aimed his camera at one of the video monitors. The grainy gray picture revealed an impossibly large tubular body and the edge of one gruesome eye, as massive as an adult human's head. Several of the squid's tentacles were tugging at the sealed lid on one of the collection baskets.

"She's only after the fish," I declared, praying I was right. The creature tore the lid off the steel basket as if it were a child's toy, releasing 200 pounds of salmon to the sea.

As we watched, one of the two longer feeding tentacles deftly corralled a fish, while the others resealed the collection basket, preventing more fish from drifting away.

The pilot shook his head, amazed. "Now that's impressive."

"Yes," I agreed, trying to mask my concern. "Her brain's large and complex, with a highly developed nervous system."

"Control to *Six*." This time it was the surface ship's radioman who sounded urgent.

Lacombe and I looked at one another. "*Six* here, go ahead, Control."

"We've detected something new on sonar. Multiple contacts, definitely biologics, not a squid, and like nothing we've ever heard. Depth's seven thousand feet, range two miles. Whatever they are, they've just adjusted their course and are ascending, heading in your direction. Feeding the acoustics to you now. Dr. Caldwell seems to think it's just a school of fish, but we're officially recommending you surface immediately, do you concur?"

Lacombe turned the volume up on his sonar so Hank and I could listen.

Blee-bloop . . . Blee-bloop . . . Blee-bloop . . . Blee-bloop . . .

The pilot looked at me, waiting for a verdict.

"Way too loud to be a school of fish," I whispered, my mind racing to identify the vaguely familiar pattern. "Sounds almost like an amphibious air cavity."

"Must be a whale," offered Hank.

"At seven thousand feet? Not even a sperm whale can dive that deep." I plugged my own headset into the console to listen privately.

Blee-bloop . . . Blee-bloop . . . Blee-bloop . . .

It was a freakish sound, almost like a water jug expelling its contents.

And suddenly my brain kicked into gear. "I don't believe it," I whispered. "It's the *Bloop*."

"What the hell's a Bloop?"

"We don't know."

"What do you mean you don't know?" the pilot shot back. "You just called it a Bloop."

"That's the name the Navy assigned it. All we know is what they're not. They're not whales, because of the extreme depths, and they're not sharks or giant squids, because neither species possesses gas-filled sacs to make noises this loud."

"Are they dangerous?" Hank asked. "Will they attack?"

"I don't know, but I sure as hell don't want to find out this deep."

Lacombe got the message. "*Six* to Control, we're out of here." Grabbing his control stick, he activated the thrusters, adjusting the submersible's fairwater planes.

We began rising, crawling at a snail's pace.

"Look!" yelled Hank. The giant squid had abandoned the catch basket and was now scampering up the bubble, its tentacles wrapping around the cockpit glass, blocking much of our view. "She knows it's out there, too."

"What scares a giant squid?" I wondered aloud, then grabbed my arm rests as the submersible was jolted

beneath us and the sound of twisting metal echoed throughout the compartment.

Lacombe swore as he scanned his control panel. "It's your damn octopus. It's wedging itself beneath the manipulator arm."

"She's frightened."

"Yeah, well so am I. That sound you're hearing is our oxygen and air storage tanks being pried away from the sub's sled. We lose that and the *Massett-6* becomes an anchor." The pilot repositioned his headset as he dialed up more pressure into the ballast tanks. "*Six* to Control, we've got an emergency—"

Another jolt cut him off, followed by an explosion that rattled our bones and released an avalanche of bubbles. Thunder roared in our ears as the sea quaked around us. Red warning lights flashed across Lacombe's control panel like a Christmas display, and the once cocky pilot suddenly looked very pale. "*Six*, we just lost primary and secondary ballast tanks. Internal hydraulic system is off-line. Propulsion system's failing—"

And then, my lovelies, the *Massett-6* began falling.

It fell slowly, tail first, but it was worse than any thrill ride I'd ever been on. Metal groaned and plates shook, and my hair seemed to stand on end, rustling against the back of my chair.

The rest of me just felt numb.

The pilot glanced in my direction, his expression confirming our death sentence.

Ace Futrell's voice over the radio sent a glimmer of hope. "Control to *Six*, hang in there, guys, we're readying an ROV with a tow line. What's your depth?"

Lacombe's perspiring face glistened in the control panel's translucent light. "Three-three-six-four feet, dropping fifty feet a minute. Better get that ROV down here quick!"

I felt helpless, like a passenger aboard an airliner that had just lost its engines, accompanied by an inner voice that refused to shut up. *What are you doing here? God, don't let me die . . . not yet, please. Lisa was right, I should've lived a little. Lord, get me out of this mess, and I swear, I'll—*

The sub rolled and rattled, shattering my repentance, and I fell back in my seat, my sweaty palms gripping the armrests, my eyes watching the depth gauge as I tensed for our one final, skull-crushing implosion.

"Jesus, there's something else out there!" Hank cried, pointing between the squid's thrashing tentacles.

I leaned forward. Several long, dark figures were circling us, stalking the squid. I could see shadows of movement, but before I could focus, our bubble became enshrouded in clouds of ink.

The Bloops were launching their attack.

Through my headphones, I could hear them as they tore into the giant squid, their sickening high-pitched growls, like hungry fox terriers, gnawing upon their prey's succulent flesh.

My mind abandoned me then. Too terrified to reason, I squeezed my eyes shut—and was suddenly hit with a subliminal image from my childhood.

· *Underwater.*
Deathly cold.
The darkness—pierced by a funnel of heavenly light!
Get to the light . . . get to the light—

"The light!" Opening my eyes, I tossed aside my shoulder harness and twisted the knob on the control station panel, changing the arc lights from red back to normal.

The sea appeared again, and we could see the torn hydraulic hoses and the sub's mangled manipulator arm dangling from its ravaged perch, along with the severed remains of lifeless tentacles, all swirling in a pool of black soup.

"Control to *Six*. The ROV's in the water. Hang in there, Don, we're coming to get you."

"Huh?" Lacombe pulled himself away from the spectacle outside to check our depth. "Control, we just passed thirty-eight hundred feet. Put the pedal to the metal, Ace, we're living on borrowed time."

I was on my feet now, looking straight up through the bubble cockpit at a lone tentacle still wrapped around the sub's tow arm. The arm's death grip was preventing the rest of the dead squid's gushing mantle and head from releasing to the sea.

Lost in the moment, I stood and watched that lifeless appendage as it slowly unfurled. The remains of

the giant squid's torpedo-shaped body released, drifting up and away, away from our light.

They were upon it in seconds, long brown forms darting in and out of the shadows, each maybe twenty to thirty feet in length, ravaging the carcass like a pack of starving wolves.

They were dark and fast and were too far away for me to identify, but their size and sheer voracity intensified my fear. I was witnessing a gruesome display of Mother Nature—it was pure animal instinct—and for a brief moment I felt relieved I'd be dead long before their voracious jaws ever tore into my flesh.

Craaaaack . . .

Death danced before me once more as the hairline fracture worked its way slowly, inch by crooked inch, across the acrylic bubble. The fear in my gut seemed to suck me in like a black hole.

Lacombe grabbed desperately for his radio. "Ace, where's that goddamn ROV?!"

"She just passed twenty-two hundred feet."

"Not good enough, Control, we're in serious trouble down here!"

I fell back in my chair again, then I was up on my feet, unable to sit, unable to keep still, the pressure building inside the cabin, building inside my skull, as the crack in the acrylic bubble continued spiderwebbing outward, and the depth gauge crept below 4,230 feet.

I closed my eyes, my breathing shallow, insane last thoughts creeping into my mind. I imagined David

Caldwell reading my eulogy at a grave site. ". . . sure, we'll miss him, but as the Beatles said, oh blah dee, oh blah da, life goes on . . . bra—"

Just when I thought things couldn't get worse, the Grim Reaper proved me wrong. With a sizzling hiss, the sub's batteries short-circuited, casting the three of us in a sudden, suffocating, claustrophobic darkness.

Panic seized me, sitting on my chest like an elephant. I gasped for air, I couldn't breathe!

Neon blue emergency lights flashed on as the blessed backup generator took over.

I wheezed an acidic-tasting breath, then another, as I watched the blue lights begin to dim.

"Just hang on, just hang on, we'll be all right." Lacombe was hyperventilating, clearly not believing his own lie.

The aft compartment's five-inch aluminum walls buckled in retort.

All of us were losing it, waiting our turn to die, but poor Hank couldn't take any more. Limbs shaking, his eyes insane with fear, he announced, "I gotta get out of here—" then lunged for the escape hatch.

Paralyzed, I could only watch the drama unfold as Donald Lacombe leaped into the rear compartment and tackled the cameraman, pinning him to the deck. "Kid, get back here and help me! Kid?"

But I was gone, my muscles frozen, my mind mesmerized, for staring at me from beyond the cockpit's cracking acrylic windshield was a pair of round, sinister, opaque eyes . . . cold and soulless, unthinking eyes

of death . . . mythic and nightmarish, eyes that burn into a man's mind to haunt him the rest of his days . . . as final as a casket being lowered into the earth and as unfeeling as the maggots that reap upon the flesh.

It was death that stared at me, brain-splattering, final as final can be death—and I screamed like I've never screamed before, a bloodcurdling howl that halted Hank Griffeth in his delirium and sent Donald Lacombe scrambling back over his seat.

The dragon can sense yer fear, Zachary, he can smell it in yer blood.

"What? What did you see?"

I gasped, fighting for air to form the words, but the creature was gone, replaced by a blinking red light, now closing in the distance.

Lacombe pointed excitedly, "It's the ROV!"

The mini torpedo-shaped remotely operated vehicle homed in on the sonic distress beacon emanating from our tow hook. Within seconds, the end of the tow-cable was attached, the line instantly going taut.

Our submersible groaned and spun, then stopped sinking.

I closed my eyes and continued hyperventilating, still frightened beyond all reason.

"Control, we're attached, but the pressure's cracked the bubble. Take us up, Ace, fast and steady!"

"Roger that, Don. Stand by."

Tears of relief poured from my two companions' eyes as the crippled *Massett-6* rose. As for me, I could

only stare at the depth gauge as I trembled, counting off seconds and feet as we climbed.

4,200 feet . . . 4,150 . . . 4,100 . . .

To my horror, the cracks in the acrylic bubble continued radiating outward, racing to complete the fracture.

3,800 feet . . . 3,700 . . . 3,600 . . .

My mind switched into left-brain mode, instantly calculating our constant rate of ascent against the pattern of cracks and declining water pressure squeezing against the glass.

No good, the glass won't hold . . . we need to climb faster!

A pipe burst overhead, spewing icy water all over my back. Leaping from my seat, I attacked the shut-off valve like a madman.

"Faster, Control, she's breaking up!"

3,150 . . . 3,100 . . . 3,050 . . .

The pipe leak sealed, I curled in a ball, allowing Hank to replace me up front.

2,800 feet . . . 2,700 . . . 2,600 . . .

The first droplets of seawater appeared along the cracks in the bubble. "Come on, baby," Lacombe chanted, "hold on . . . just a little bit longer."

1,800 feet . . . 1,700 . . . 1,600 . . .

We seemed to be rising faster now, the ebony sea melding around us into shades of gray, dawn's curtains filtering into the depths.

The pilot and cameraman giggled and slapped one another on the back.

Hyperventilating, I exhaled and inhaled, preparing my lungs for the rush of sea I prayed would never come.

"Thank you, Jesus, thank you," Hank whispered, crossing himself with one hand, wiping sweat and tears from his beet-red face with the other. "Praise God, we're saved."

"Told you we'd make it," Donald said, his cockiness returning with the light.

"My kids . . . I can't wait to hug them again."

What were they talking about? Didn't they realize we were still too deep, still in danger?

"Hey, Zack, hand me my camera, we need to document our triumphant return."

Like a zombie, I reached to the deck and picked up the heavy piece of equipment, passing it forward, confused about why we were still alive.

See, you're not such a genius, you can be wrong. Now lighten up. As Lisa would say, enjoy the ride.

1,200 feet.

1,000 feet.

800 feet . . .

David's voice blared over the radio. "Dr. Wallace, you still with us?"

Hank swung his camera around, but I pushed the lens away.

"Dr. Wallace? Hello? Say something so we know you're alive."

"Fuck you."

600 feet . . . 520 feet . . . 440 feet . . .

The ocean melded from a deep purple into a royal blue as we passed the deepest depths a human had ever ventured on a single breath.

The second deepest point, only a few feet higher, had resulted in death.

365 feet . . .

Good . . . keep going, the water's weight subsiding every foot, the cracks slowing now.

310 feet.

I wiped away tears, my face breaking into a broad smile. Hank slapped me on the back and I giggled. *Maybe we were going to make it.*

"Control to *Six*, divers are in the water, standing by. Welcome back, team."

Lacombe winked at Hank. "Hey, Control, wait until you see what we've got on film."

Life is so fragile. One moment you're alive, the next, a semi-tractor trailer plows into you and it's all over, no warning, no final words or thoughts, everything gone.

At 233 feet, the bubble exploded inward, the Sargasso roaring through our sanctuary like a freight train, blinding us in its suffocating fury.

I saw the pilot's face explode like a ripe tomato as shards of acrylic glass riddled his harnessed body like machine gun fire. Hank appeared out of the corner of my eye, and then the Atlantic Ocean lifted me from my perch and bashed me sideways against the rear wall. Only the sudden change in pressure kept me conscious, squeezing my skull in its vise. Buried beneath this

howling avalanche, I lashed out blindly in the darkness, my muscles lead, my hands groping . . . my mind recognizing the rear hatch even as it ordered my spent arms to turn its wheel.

I felt the surface ship's support cable *snap* beneath the weight of the sea. My hands held on desperately to the hatch as the freed submersible tumbled backward, falling once more toward the abyss.

The sudden loss of pressure tore at my eardrums.

And then, miraculously, the hatch yawned open.

My kids . . . I can't wait to hug them again . . .

Hank!

The left side of my brain screamed at me to get out, my chances of making it to the surface already less than 10 percent, but it was my right brain that took command, suddenly endowing me with the courage of Sir William Wallace himself.

I groped for Hank. Grabbed him from behind his shirt collar, then pushed his inert 195-pound body out the hatch, into the Sargasso's warm embrace.

A laborious twenty-five seconds had passed, and I was struggling to haul an unconscious man topside through 245 feet of water.

Get to the light . . .

I kicked and paddled, forcing myself into a cadence so as not to excessively burn away those precious molecules of air.

You'll never make it, not with Hank. Let him go, or you'll both drown.

But I didn't let go, not because I wanted to be a hero, not because I actually believed we would make it, but because, at that moment, I knew in my heart that his life was more important than mine.

My lungs seemed on fire, my beating heart the only sound I could hear.

Was I even making progress? My legs were lead . . . were they even kicking?

Scenes from my adolescence flashed before my eyes. My inner voice took over the play-by-play: *This should be the last play, Princeton down by four. Here's the snap, the quarterback pitching to Wallace. He escapes one tackle, then another, and he's heading for daylight.*

The light . . . so precious. Get to the light.

He's across mid-field . . . he's at the forty . . .

Get . . . to . . . the . . . light . . .

Wallace's at the thirty . . . the twenty . . .

The liiiiii . . .

He's at the ten, with just one defender to beat . . .

Shadows closed in on my peripheral vision. I saw death's dark hand reach for me . . . reach for Hank.

Oh, no! Wallace's tackled at the goal line as time expires.

Out of air, out of strength, out of heartbeats, my willpower gone, I slipped out of my body, and drowned.

Again.

THE LOCH

On Sale Now